Tennessee Smith

Tennessee Smith

James E. Hitt

Thomas Congdon Books  E.P. DUTTON   New York

For information contact:
E.P. Dutton, 2 Park Avenue,
New York, N.Y. 10016

Library of Congress Cataloging in Publication Data

Hitt, James E.
    Tennessee Smith.

    I. Title.
PZ4.H6759Te   [PS3558.I84]   813'.5'4   78-20976

ISBN: 0-525-21546-8

Published simultaneously in Canada by Clarke, Irwin & Company Limited, Toronto and Vancouver

Designed by Mary Beth Bosco

10 9 8 7 6 5 4 3 2 1

First Edition

To Alex G. Campbell, Jr.

former pupil, long-time friend, and multifaceted
benefactor, who stands in the foot of a rainbow
and beckons the stragglers with handfuls of hope

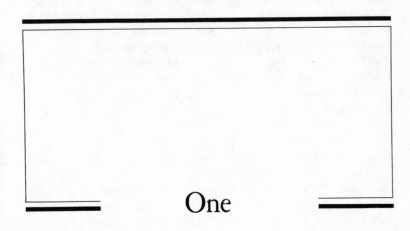

One

Forest paths are first mapped out by wild animals and afterward followed by men. So it was with a narrow trail that grew from dim tracks out of rough hollows and ran eastward for a quarter-mile along the foot of a great brush-studded escarpment of the Cumberland Mountains, then left the escarpment at a cabin-sized boulder and turned downslope under north-hillside trees, pointing a descent to Smoky Water Cove. It was used by men of late, though it was still primarily an animal's trail.

Coming along the path in late afternoon, a slender, red-haired woman in riding skirt and white shirtwaist halted uneasily at the huge boulder, head up and dark eyes questing like a suspicious doe's. She stood motionless for a long moment, a loose jacket slung over one arm, her fine-boned, freckled face turned back toward the way she had come, listening. Somewhere in that forest country of narrow ridges, deep hollows, and boulder-strewn ravines, she believed there was a human presence of some sort that lurked or followed her. Her skin had prickled and smoothed down and prickled again all the way from Long Hollow, where she had two blooded horses hidden out from the guerrillas and partisan rogues that still infested the Cumberlands, though the war should have ended over a month before with Lee's surrender to Grant at Appomattox Court House in Virginia.

Stella McEveride knew, of course, that she had no business being up in these woods alone—a woman, and the wife of a "damned Lincolnite" at that, unattended in the wilds of a mountain country ravaged by war, harassed by bushwhackers, and torn by divided sentiment. Certainly she'd heard enough tales of women outraged by marauders in remote mountain settlements during the war. Her anxiety, however, stemmed mostly from an old, nagging fear that her horses would be stolen, and only the danger of getting lost in darkness kept Stella from returning now to Long Hollow to assure herself that no rogue had followed her to them.

Until the morrow, though, there was nothing she could do about the horses that made sense; so she shrugged her concern to the back of her mind and looked down at Smoky Water Cove, which lay beyond dropping slopes of gently stirring treetops far below her. The view from here, high under the escarpment, was Stella's favorite, and it usually induced in her a mood of dreamy hope for the future of McEveride Plantation. The cove was a wide, mottled-green arrowhead of rolling grassland which seemed thrust into the mountain and embedded there. Down the cove, beyond long, reaching shadows of mountain cliffs, the gray-shingled roof of the McEverides' colonial farmhouse was visible through the pastel-green foliage of oaks, maples, and tulip poplars. The uniform green of grass and weeds in the unplowed fields and ungrazed pastures of the plantation and the absence of livestock everywhere were eloquent reminders of an attrition, sustained through four years of war, that had forced the South to make her last stands on her knees.

But Stella McEveride saw the plantation not as it was now but as it should be in the coming years. She saw fields of brown earth pushing green shoots of grain; fields of dark-green alfalfa working in the sun; Negro boys leading blanketed horses to and fro in the barnyard; mares with romping colts, Kentucky Thoroughbreds and Tennessee saddle stock, grazing in the pastures; stallions, full of fight and lust, whistling and stamping in the stud enclosures. Stella saw, too, of course, a white-columned mansion and vast horse farm that had shaped her growth, springing from distant ashes in Kentucky to a new birth in Tennessee. . . .

From her new home in Morrisburg, Kentucky, she had made a special trip out to see those ashes of the mansion and the elaborate stable complex that had stood there. To her they were as poignant a consideration as the remains of a cremation would have been. Nobody could be found who knew who was responsible for setting fire to the buildings. Raiders had come to Belmont Grange for horses, they said. The fire had occurred in October of '62, only days before the battle of Perryville, when a Confederate army under Bragg and Union forces commanded by Buell were maneuvering for position along the banks of the Kentucky River. The arsonists could have been from either army—or from neither. The burning of Belmont Grange, however, had given additional evidence of the sagacity of Stella's father. For in '59 Jock Cameron had come close to breaking his seventeen-year-old daughter's heart by selling the great combination horse-breeding farm and tobacco plantation at a peak price. He'd disposed of all the slaves at the same time, the field hands going to Bedford Forrest in Memphis and the hostlers to Bart Whitby's stables in Maryland. The house servants were freed and retained on a stipend-and-found basis.

When Stella had protested the sale, big, red-bearded Jock had explained, "There's a war coming, honey—don't let the fools tell you different—and the South will lose it. We don't have the right kind of resources or the right kind of temperament to win an all-out war against the North. Well, anyhow, irresponsible armies, North and South, will tramp through here, likely taking what they want and fouling up what they don't. Would you believe I said all this to the shortsighted fool I sold the plantation to? *He* knew better. So let *him* take the loss. Same, really, with the slaves. Slavery's doomed, whether war comes or not. It's uneconomical. Let somebody else own 'em, then, until they're freed. We can't sell the house slaves, of course. Too personal. They're freed in my will, anyhow. Might as well beat the government to it. . . . Only difference here, Stella, is that you can *see* the plantation and the niggers. I've liquidated every investment I had in the South. Now half our money is invested in English securities. The other half is divided between investments in the North that will soar sky-high when war does come and money drawing interest in Philadelphia and New York banks until I find a better use for it. I won't tell you how much it all comes to." His grin was a slash of white in the red forest of his beard. "Might spoil you to find out you're a rich girl."

"If war comes," she asked, "which side will you be on?"

"Hard to say," he replied. "I'm driven toward the South by abolitionist hypocrisy in the North, and I'm bound to the South by social ties. On the other hand, I'm drawn to the North by business interests, and I'm against secession. Guess I'm like most of Kentucky. I'll stay neutral if I can."

A thought, like summer lightning, flashed through Stella's mind. "Dad," she cried, "where will we live? Have you sold *my* horses, too?"

"Didn't I tell you? Well, I'm damned! I've bought you a house and a hundred and fifty acres of meadow and pasture land. Ideal place for your horses—until war starts and raiders run 'em off. You ought to sell those horses. Two things to remember in business, honey: Don't hang on too long and don't let sentiment cloud your judgment. If you do, you'll lose those horses."

"Where is this place?"

"On the outskirts of Morrisburg. Morrisburg because it's far enough back to be out of the path of armies and close enough to be in reach of all those young rascals who don't seem to mind red hair and freckles."

"Thought you didn't have any investments left in the South."

"Well, only this modest one."

The house Jock moved her to was one of the showplaces of Morrisburg. Knowing her father, Stella was not surprised. It was a two-storied red-brick edifice with six massive white columns and a short balcony with a black iron railing over the front doorway. A wide lawn stretched back under huge old trees to well-developed gardens, and all the beautiful grounds, as well as the sweep of pasture land, were enclosed by several miles of white fence. Stella was especially delighted with the red-painted barn and stables.

"This is some modest place, all right," she observed with a gamin grin. "I'll need ten servants jumping to run it."

"Well, you've got 'em," Jock told her. "Make 'em jump."

Having established her safely in her new home, Jock was off again by rail and boat in pursuit of his favorite phantom, which he referred to, for want of a better designation, as business. Three years before, on a visit to New Orleans, his wife had been swept away by yellow fever, along with Stella's maternal grandfather, grandmother, and maiden aunt. Since then Jock had been too restless to remain long in any one place. This time he was taking a sentimental journey down the Mississippi on the *Dolly Claybourne*, a steamboat bearing his wife's maiden name. Somewhere between Vicksburg and Natchez, in a torrential rainstorm at midnight, the *Dolly Claybourne* struck a waterlogged derelict barge that had been set adrift by high water upstream, and went down with her bottom ripped out, taking Jock Cameron, along with over a hundred others, to the bottom of the river. The sinking of this veritable floating palace, with all her extravagant and sumptuous appointments, marked another instance of Jock's sense of timing in matters of business—though some of his envious friends called it luck—because Jock had sold his interest in the steamboat at a very good price only a month before she went down . . . .

Standing high under the escarpment, Stella McEveride suddenly heard an alien sound that wrenched her from her memories. Holding her breath, she listened intently. She was almost certain she'd heard a horse heave down under the trees below her, possibly down a ravine that divided the slope to her right—heave the way a horse might if it were tied to a bush or tree and bored with waiting. Stella drew a small-sized pistol, a five-shot Remington .36, from one of the large side pockets of the jacket on her arm, examined the caps on its nipples, spun the cylinder, and returned the revolver to the pocket.

Stella McEveride with a pistol was not one to be panicked by the heave of a horse she might have heard. When she heard nothing further, she turned down the slope, moving with the surefooted freedom of a sun-blackened boy—though there was little beyond supple strength that was boyish about her slender woman's body, with its rounded, pronounced contours. She rejected stealth for the same reason that a boy makes noise on a lonely road at night, and boldly followed the path until it joined an overgrown woods road that led into the cove. Swinging down the old wagon trace, she even found herself stifling an impulse to whistle a strain of "The Yellow Rose of Texas," an often-heard song before the boys in gray had stopped singing in Tennessee. Suddenly, up ahead, a crow loafing westward through the trees changed its course and went flapping off at a right angle, cawing a raucous alarm.

Stella walked on now with her hand clutching the pistol butt in the jacket pocket. The crow might have seen an owl or a fox or even a house cat hunting far from its home. Usually, though, crows came snarling in at such enemies, calling the clan. Every fine hair on Stella's body was bristling now, warning her to expect a larger predator. She was not wholly surprised, therefore, when a man rose from a dense thicket of rhododendrons and sprang lightly to the roadway before her. But instinctive alarm almost stopped her breath when she saw what kind of man he was.

The man was a savage of some sort, possibly an Indian. Before his moccasined feet hit the roadway, Stella had thought he was a Negro, so striking was the whiteness of eyes and teeth in the darkness of his face. He was wearing, in a slovenly manner, some white man's dark business suit, glaze-splotched with grease and dirt, with two Navy pistols strapped outside the coat. Whatever he was, he was a magnificent specimen of it, physically—medium-tall, powerfully muscled, sleek-skinned. He was as handsome and as feral as a black-panther tom aprowl under a rutting moon—and as free from inhibitions.

When his right hand drifted naturally to the front of his trousers and started fumbling, Stella's heart almost died in her breast. He said something unintelligible in a voice guttural and soft. Then he took one step, like a stalking cat.

Stella backed up, struggling against a sense of unreality. Without drawing the pistol from her jacket, she thumbed the hammer back to full cock. "What—what do you want?" she asked uncertainly.

The man told her what he wanted, in words she had heard as a child through cracks in barn walls and around corners. "I don't kill no woman much," he added, his black eyes like wet marbles behind thick, narrowed lids. "Dead cunt no good."

Stella could feel the blood drain out of her face. She was so frightened that she felt no anger, no indignation at all; but she was no longer uncertain. She lifted the pistol, catching the man on the point of coming to her and stopping him with the sight of her gun. He hung there, watching her, grinning now like a waiting wolf. When the sights of the pistol lined up between his wet, slitted eyes, Stella pulled the trigger with a firm, purposeful finger. The gun roared, and the man jerked in a quarter-turn, clapping a hand to the side of his head. He fell to his knees, then leaped up, almost dancing, and shouted, "Goddamn!" at the top of his voice, and then, "White-eyes bitch!" Already blood covered the right side of his face and neck, spattering a shoulder and arm.

Stella fired again and missed, then again, and the man dived headlong into the thicket. She fired after him and heard the rhododendrons thresh and rattle behind his desperate progress. Whirling around, she started running down the old roadway. Though she had one load left in the Remington, her confidence in her ability to hit anything with it was gone.

The man was coming after her, keeping to the underbrush, she believed, but she was too smart a runner to look back. When an urgent voice from back up the old woods road began shouting her name, she kept her head; panic could make her overreach herself and go sprawling on the steep downslope, and already her heart was drumming the breath from her lungs. She raced on, blaming herself for not shooting at the man's middle with her first shot.

Finally, from somewhere behind her came the racket of a starting horse with its stammer of thudding hoofs and swishes of brush and, closely following, the ringing crack of a rifle that whipped through the forest and boomeranged from the crags of the escarpments.

"Stella McEveride!" the same voice shouted again. "You all right? Where are you?"

Stella lurched to a halt and faced about. "Here!" she quavered, and wondered at her trembling. "Down here!"

By straining her ears she was barely able to hear the man's approach—a padding of long-trotting feet that stopped behind a thicket just around the nearest bend in the road. "Hey, Mrs. McEveride!" the man called.

"I'm here," Stella answered, and thumbed back the hammer of the Remington.

She thought she heard a low chuckle. "Now, don't you take a shot at my topknot when you see a secesh Indian," the man said. "I'm John Redwing, ma'am. I used to live with the McEverides."

Stella kept the pistol cocked and leveled. "I've heard of you," she said. "Come on out."

A lithe, hawk-faced man stepped into view, wearing a Confederate uniform jacket and carrying a Spencer rifle. His large brown eyes were somberly amused as she slowly lowered her revolver. "I saw blood on the road," he informed her, "but I reckon you just scratched him, ma'am. The way he rode down the timber back there, I swore he was a scalded cougar."

"Did *you* shoot back there? At that man?"

"I shot at something. Mostly for luck. If you don't mind, I'll see you back to the plantation, ma'am."

They turned down the old road, walking in the wagon-wheel traces with weeds and occasional bushes between them. The shadows under the trees seemed to have lightened somewhat with John Redwing's coming. Stella had heard Judge McEveride tell a great many stories involving the Cherokee, who had spent much of his boyhood and youth at the McEveride plantation. His parents, ill with smallpox, had been dropped out of a migration of Cherokees from North Carolina to the Indian Nations of the West and had died at the McEveride place. They had left the boy John Redwing, whom Judge McEveride had cared for and schooled along with the judge's own sons, Paul and Tennessee. In later youth Redwing had divided his time between his people and the McEverides. When the war came on, he had served with a band of Cherokees in upper east Tennessee, tracking down conscription dodgers in the Smokies for the Confederate forces, until a Union army under Burnside had occupied Knoxville and brought the Confederacy's domination of east Tennessee to an end. Thereafter, according to a rumor the judge had heard in Overton, Redwing had enlisted for regular service somewhere with the Confederate army.

"How did you know my name, Mr. Redwing?" Stella suddenly thought to ask.

"Why, I touched here right after Paul lost his leg at Chickamauga. I saw Jubal, and he told me Paul was getting him a medical discharge from the Yankees and marrying a Miss Stella Cameron, whose folks had raked up mightnear all the loose money in Kentucky and stored it away by the tow sackfuls up North in Yankee banks." He watched Stella's eyes darken and then added, "That's close to what Jubal said— or could've said, except that his manners ain't as bad as John Redwing's, ma'am."

"So you don't like Paul," Stella observed coolly. "Why is that? Because he's Union and you're Confederate?"

"I won't admit I don't like him," Redwing answered carefully. "But we ain't close. Never was. Seems Paul was always off reading books or in a stew about honor and principles or taking stands and such, while me and Tennessee and Jubal were forever running the woods. At that, though, I was closer to him than Tennessee was. I used to hide out in the library myself. But that Tennessee never read anything he wasn't made to read—except a track in the woods, maybe."

They left the woods, crossing a rail fence into an upper pasture. Walking behind Redwing down an old cowpath, Stella said curiously, "I've heard very little about my brother-in-law. Paul's hardly mentioned Tennessee, and the judge goes into a shell when he's asked about."

"A sore subject," Redwing agreed. "The boys took opposite sides in the war, and the judge swears he's neutral. He ain't, but that's what he claims—and thinks, too, likely."

"He's a sort of wild one, isn't he? Tennessee, I mean."

"Wild one?" Redwing chuckled. "He ought to have my skin and me his. He could always beat me at things an Indian ought to do better'n a white man. Yeah, he's wild—like a wolf's wild when you think he's a dog just because he was raised like one."

They crossed the rolling pasture, and Redwing stopped under a giant scaly-bark hickory that stood beside a rail fence. "I'll wait here till you get home, ma'am." He gestured toward a two-storied white house visible across the fields in a grove of stately trees. "I don't reckon I'll show up down there yet awhile."

"Look, Mr. Redwing," Stella said, "was that some outlaw kin of yours back there?"

The Cherokee strained for her meaning, his dark hawk's face intent. Finally he said, "Why, ma'am, that feller was one of Parson Krull's guerrillas. I wasn't following *him*. I was trying to keep an eye on *you*. Mountains crawling with rogues and you traipsing up there alone. Poor judgment, ma'am."

"I know that now," Stella agreed. "I've heard of Parson Krull, of course." She thought of her horses. "Do you think he and his men are just passing through?"

"Well, they been crouched down in the mountains back up there about a week, waiting for something. Today I may of found out what. Your horses, for one thing. They been scouting down in ones and twos. . . . Ma'am, you tell the judge and Paul I said you-all ought to move into Overton till the soldiers clean these Krulls out. They both know what reason Parson Krull's got to cause McEverides grief. It's my opinion the parson aims to raid the McEverides, ma'am."

"What reason *does* he have?" Stella wanted to know. "I've never heard."

"Don't reckon there's any secret about it," Redwing said. "Happened maybe thirty years ago. Parson Krull was a sort of jackleg preacher. Claimed to be an abolitionist and was always trying to incite slaves to run away. They claim he'd help 'em run off, and then he'd sell 'em somewhere else. Sometimes, when he got real pressed, he'd murder 'em and sink 'em in a swamp—you know, get rid of the evidence. Some allowed the parson had a connection with the Seminoles for passing slaves to Florida, where the Indians would take 'em under wing. Well, anyhow, the judge went after the parson, caught him running off slaves, and convicted him in open court. They burned the letters *S T* for *slave thief* on him and run him out of the state. He missed hanging by a hair. Their mistake was they *didn't* string him up, because during the war he come back with a gang and turned into the worst murdering rogue in the South. Guerrillas and bushwhackers on both sides hate him like poison. They claim Tinker Dave Beatty and Champ Ferguson both swore during the war they'd kill him on sight if he ever come around here."

Freckles were crowding Stella's pale face. "But how could he know about my horses?" she said faintly.

"Somebody up there working with him," Redwing guessed. "He's too cagey to bust in here blind. But folks would mention you had the horses. Mountains are full of folks hate the McEverides. Secesh hate Paul, Lincolnites hate Tennessee; both likely resent the judge, who claims neutral. There'd been some bushwhacking here if mountain folks hadn't been watching each other so close." His black eyes roved back the way they had come and swept the edge of the forest. "And if folks wasn't in mortal dread of what Tennessee might do, he gets back. I couldn't swear he'd do anything, but if I was a bushwhacker, I wouldn't count on him failing to."

Stella steadied herself with a hand on the top rail of the fence. "It's clear, then, we're in danger," she said. "We ought to move into town tonight, but we have only the judge's buggy when he gets back from Overton. We'd have to leave the Negroes to face whatever danger threatens. We won't do that, so I'm going to send a message by pigeon to Betty Cravens in Overton. Betty and I correspond with homing pigeons. She can get word to Colonel Blackwell. Paul has a right to demand the protection of the Union soldiers stationed there."

"Arm the niggers till the soldiers come," Redwing advised. "They'll fight with Jubal leading 'em."

"But Jubal's gone," Stella told him. "He has his freedom now, you know." Then she added, not sounding the way she meant to, "Out enjoying the Jubilee."

"He'll be back, then," Redwing predicted. "He ain't free of his memory."

Leaving Redwing standing by the rail fence, Stella made her way to the nearest field and followed a path which ran along its west edge beside a gully, under trees festooned with great loops and swings of grapevine. She had to determine, before she reached the house, how much of her encounter with the savage she was going to tell Paul. Not much, she decided. In fact, now that she considered further, none of it. She would tell about meeting John Redwing and deliver the Cherokee's warning, stressing the presence in the mountains of Parson Krull's guerrillas and the imminent threat to the McEverides they undoubtedly posed. But she would not mention the savage's intention to rape her.

Paul had begged her more than once not to go alone to check on the horses in Long Hollow. She knew that his anxieties over her safety were alive in him constantly and that they went far beyond his fear that she might receive some bodily injury. He lived in horrible dread of not being physically able to play a man's role in his relations with her—of not being able to redress some insult to her; of not being able to go to her rescue if she became endangered; of not being able, in short, to defend her person and her honor, since a husband, if he is a man, is expected to protect his wife. Stella had had no idea of what a devastating trauma the loss of a leg could be to a proud, sensitive man. How carefully she had striven to restore his self-respect, his self-confidence, his desire to live, resorting to a dozen stratagems! She had scoffed at physical standards for measuring manhood; she blushed when she recalled what she had been willing to do on occasion to convince him of his own virility. And he *was*, she thanked God, far along the road back now.

Leaving the fields, Stella crossed the side road and entered the driveway, at the end of which she could see Paul, in his usual place on the columned veranda of the house, waiting, watching. . . . She knew for whom he waited and watched but no longer felt any impatience with his concern, since she recognized now that it was justified.

But Paul's mind had carried him in a different direction this time. "Stella," he burst out as she approached the steps, "I've been thinking. You have some business you want to settle in Philadelphia and New York, and I want to get fitted for a cork leg in New York. What say we go at once? We can turn the trip into the honeymoon we never had."

Stella stood for a moment at the foot of the steps. "I don't know, Paul." She moved up the steps. "Listen to what I found out—"

Paul's eyes were bright with some inward excitement. "We could have a lot of fun," he said rapidly. "And I want that cork leg. I want to stand on two feet before any man. I'm a good shot with a dueling pistol or Navy Colt. Oh, maybe not a wizard like Tennessee, but good enough to call the hand of any man who comes leering to touch you or wagging his dirty mouth."

Coming close, Stella leaned over him. "Maybe we *will* go, darling." She kissed him and straightened. "Listen, Paul. I ran into something alarming up there today." She told him about meeting John Redwing and gave him the Cherokee's warning about the presence of Parson Krull's guerrillas in the mountains, emphasizing what Redwing thought their presence meant. Paul surprised her by not scolding her this time for going alone to Long Hollow. Gravely he asked her several questions, then sat thinking.

Finally he said quietly, "Go send your pigeon to Betty Cravens. If Redwing thinks we're in danger, we probably are. Before you send the message, though, bring me my Navy Colt and tell Lula May to fix me a mint julep. I'll wait out here for Father. Be like him, though, to get in after dark."

It was nine o'clock, after Stella and Paul had both eaten supper, when Judge McEveride got home. She saw him briefly and gave him the information about the Krull gang and repeated Redwing's words of caution. Like Paul, the judge took the warning seriously, since it came from John Redwing, but seemed to doubt the immediacy of their danger. He wished that John had mentioned some of his evidence that there were guerrillas waiting around in the vicinity. Stella left him and Paul, hoping to draw Paul upstairs and then get back to inform the judge of the savage's attempt to rape her. She thought submission of that evidence would change the old jurist's mind about the imminence of the threat.

Paul swung up beside her before she reached the stairs. "Stella," he urged, "let's make that trip while the army's clearing the neighborhood of those Krulls. Let's go tomorrow. I wish we were gone tonight. I've got a feeling. . . .Well, I can't bear to think what could happen to you."

Stella reached a hand to smooth the ash-blond hair back from his forehead. Then, as the shy adoration in his eyes twisted her heart, she kissed him. "All right, darling," she promised, "we'll leave tomorrow."

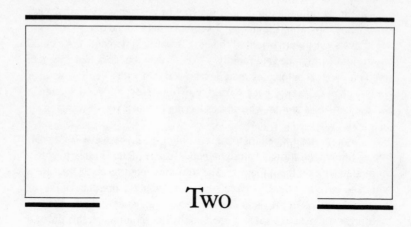

Two

Stella had met Paul McEveride at Belmont Grange when he came visiting with her cousin, Thornton Maybank. Paul and Thornton had been roommates at Episcopal Academy in Virginia, and Paul had spent one of the summer months with Thornton at the end of their first year together. On the morning they came calling, Stella had gone out in the pastures with a bridle to bring in Dan, her favorite hunter. Then, after the sleek, spirited claybank had come to her call, she'd mounted him from a stump and come flying back to the stables, riding astride in her divided skirt, thereby fracturing several rules of decorum for young ladies in the bluegrass country of 1857. Coming like the wind, the claybank took two fences in stride, with Stella riding bareback like a wild Indian, her hair flaming behind her and her freckled face alive with joy. As the hunter cleared a third fence and came pounding up to the stables, Stella caught a blurred glimpse of Thornton and another boy standing in the forefront of several grinning hostlers and stable hands who had left their tasks to watch a performance that evidently was not wholly unexpected. Bringing the horse to a plunging halt, Stella slid off and stood before the boys, well pleased with the stranger's wide-eyed look of shock and admiration.

"All right for you, missy!" old Tobe yelled from the back porch of the big house. "You wait till I tell Marse Jock. You know what he done told you about trying to break yo' neck on that hoss. You, missy—why can't you ride like a lady supposed to?"

Stella tossed her head, the distance allowing her to ignore him, and occupied herself with Thornton's introduction of Paul McEveride. Then she called, "William, come get this horse. Turn him back in the pasture. I've changed my mind about riding him."

She had been attracted to slim, fair Paul McEveride at first sight. She thought his thin face, with its sensitive, almost ascetic features, looked intrepid and handsome; and with a leap of imagination she thought of Saint George and the dragon. They were both fifteen, she three months the younger, but she knew she was growing up when she would not permit one of her girl friends to tell him that she, Stella, "liked" him. And she never did think that he was too young for her. During that month of June they rode together, went fishing, picnicked, played croquet, and went to parties. Sometimes, though not often, Thornton accompanied them.

It was on one of their picnics that Paul revealed to both Stella and Thornton his possession of a special kind of courage, causing such wonder in them that after that day neither of the cousins could ever again be casual about anything concerning Paul McEveride. The three had eaten from a spread cloth near a spring in a grove of trees and were strolling along the top of Hindman's Bluff for the view. Pom Pom, a Prussian toy dog that Stella had taken over when her mother died, was flying about the grassy open like a windblown fluff of cotton, yipping shrilly at the butterflies. Thornton, who had noticed that his friend was giving the edge of the bluff a wide berth, was taking delight in mincing along the very lip of the precipice, looking almost straight down to the white-water rapids of Hurricane Creek a good hundred and fifty feet below. Irritated by the show-off, Stella had cautioned him more than once. She had just voiced her last remonstrance when Pom Pom ran by, pursuing a beautiful golden butterfly with black-laced wings. Neither the butterfly nor Pom Pom stopped at the edge of the precipice.

All three people on the bluff acted simultaneously. Stella screamed and rushed to the brink where Pom Pom had disappeared. Thornton, on the lip, made a dive to catch Pom Pom, and Paul made a dive to succor Thornton, who had one foot over the edge. As Thornton scrambled frantically and then went over, Paul hit the ground at the edge full-length and caught one of Thornton's flailing arms at the wrist with a far-reaching hand. Thornton's body slammed against the sheer face of the bluff, a knee striking a projecting rock, and Paul's head, arm, shoulders, and upper chest were dragged over the brink.

"Grab something—anything—other hand!" Paul gritted desperately, as his hold began to slip. "Try—help—climb!"

"Can't," Thornton gasped. "Hurt knee. Can't move it."

The boys stared into each other's white, strained faces. Then, as Thornton's wrist slipped out of his grasp, Paul released his hold on an embedded stone and reached his other arm frantically over into space. As Thornton dropped, Paul was so far extended that he would have gone over the edge if Stella had not landed on top of him and helped him struggle back to safety. Then Stella, lying prone on the brink, cried out in an agony of excitement. Thornton lay motionless on a ledge of rock fifteen feet below.

Paul crawled to the edge and, lying flat, looked at Thornton, who lay face downward with an arm and a leg hanging over the outside of the ledge. Paul's face lost its last vestige of color. If Thornton moved, as he would when he regained consciousness, he would go over and follow Pom Pom to death in the white-water rapids of Hurricane Creek—unless he was pulled back off the edge of that shelf of rock before he stirred.

"I can get down there," Stella said. "This slanting ledge just below is wide enough and goes most of the way. A three-foot step off the end to that big rock that sticks out about two feet and then one more three-foot-or-so step to the ledge, and there I'd be. I'm strong, Paul. I'm going— while you go for help. We need a rope and somebody to help you pull Thorn up."

"No," Paul said in an unsteady voice. "*I'll* go down."

"But you can help pull Thorn up better than I can," Stella protested. "You can reach that farmer's house back on the road pretty quick if you whip up that horse you're riding. Tell the man to bring a rope, even if he has to join two plow lines. Tell him—"

"You tell him," Paul said. "You're a girl, and you've got no right to shame me with that talk of you going down."

Stella studied him carefully. "All right," she said finally. "I'll wait till you and Thorn are settled on the ledge. Then I'll put Dan over some fences and shortcut it back to that farmhouse. You won't have to stay down there long."

From her prone position at the brink, she watched Paul inch his way down the slanted ledge on the seat of his pants, knowing that she would have moved down its length faster. Obviously he did not trust himself to stand. At the lower end he stood up on trembling legs, his face to the wall, and made his step to the projecting rock, teetered momentarily, then regained his balance and hugged the wall, shaking. Finally he was able to take the step to the ledge, where he sank instantly down to a sitting position before rising to his knees and dragging Thornton's inert body back from the drop-off edge of the shelf. Until Stella returned with a farmer and a strong slave, the latter carrying plenty of cotton rope, Paul sat hunched over Thornton, his head frozen with face to the wall, refusing to turn his eyes behind him into the gulch and down the sheer wall to the boil of rapids far below.

With Paul securing the lowered end of the rope, Thornton was drawn to the top, still unconscious; then the rope was lowered for Paul. When he was safe on the cliff at last, he was so weak and trembly that he could hardly stand. Free of the rope, he staggered farther back from the brink, white and sick, and lay down in the grass, clutching the turf desperately with his hands. The slave brought water from the nearby spring in a picnic container, and Stella bathed Thornton's face, noticing that Paul was not responding to the farmer's pleasantries. Both farmer and slave departed when Thornton returned to consciousness.

Sometime later Thornton whispered, "Stella, I knew I was going to drop. He was sliding over, and I knew he couldn't pull me up or even hold me, even if he stopped sliding. Paul knew it, too. But he wouldn't turn me loose to save his own life. I saw him make up his mind to die. I saw it in his eyes. And he has a horror of high places, Stella. Can't stand to look out of a third-story window to the ground. Claims that even when he stands back from a high place, he's afraid he'll run and jump off."

"He climbed down to that shelf of rock and pulled you back from the edge."

"God a'mighty!" Thornton breathed. "Wonder we both ain't dead. Where is he?"

Thornton crawled back to where Paul lay, and Stella stood over them, making an unstudied comparison of the two boys: Thornton, dark and rugged; Paul, slim and fair—both handsome, attractive to girls.

"You damned fool," Thornton growled, "how come you climbed down there?"

"What good would anything ever been if I hadn't?" Paul answered shakily.

Thornton shook his head. "You with your fear of heights! How'd it feel down on that ledge?"

"My insides crawled up in my chest, and my legs got weak and started aching. They still do. Reason I'm in such a funk. When they pulled you up, I thought I'd turn and jump off that ledge."

"Crazy!" Thornton exclaimed, aghast. "Feeling like that, I wouldn't have gone down there for a hundred dollars."

"I wouldn't have for a million," Paul murmured feebly.

Stella sat down beside him, her eyes suddenly brimming with tears. "Paul, I think you're the bravest boy I've ever known," she quavered, gently brushing a damp lock of hair back from his wet forehead, "or ever

will know." Then, impulsively, she added, "And the best-looking,"
and blushed furiously.

After that day Stella and Paul were often together. They gave up the
games, fishing jaunts, and picnics and confined themselves to riding and
walking by themselves. Toward the end of June they just went strolling—
not talking much and, more often than not, holding hands. Finally, one
evening at Belmont Grange, they stood face to face in the moonlight,
staring into each other's eyes while a garden full of roses was breathing
enchantment into the balmy air. Stella had the romantic conviction that
all it would take for her very soul to slide out of her body and fuse with his
was the contact of lips she had been expecting for more than an hour of
staring, stammering, sighing, and intermittent silences. Paul was leaving
the next day. He pulled Stella gently to him without saying a word, and
she came into his arms.

She'd been kissed before, at parties—the teasing, half-in-fun strug-
gle-and-smack kind of thing. But this pressing of lips was her first lover's
kiss; it lasted during a long, breathless madness of throbbing pulses, its
warm, intimate sweetness drawing an essence from the silver moonlight
and the fragrance of roses. It seemed almost to melt her very bones. From
her limited experience Stella judged Paul quite expert at kissing. She
remembered wondering where he'd got his practice. She remembered,
too, that she had not asked him. But she could not recall anything either of
them had said to the other that night—nor much that either had said all
the time Paul was at Thornton's house that summer. When he left, they
both assumed the other understood that they liked each other, and they
promised to write.

The next time Stella saw Paul was more than two years later, during
her last months at Belmont Grange. He was visiting Thornton during the
Christmas holidays at his father's request. She had had the story from
Thornton, since Paul did not want to discuss it. It seemed Paul's brother
Tennessee had been in a shooting scrape with some mountaineers who
had a feuding background, and there was an uproar going on in the hills,
including some bushwhacking attempts near McEveride Plantation.
Judge McEveride, who was conferring with clan leaders and trying to
keep Tennessee peaceful long enough to arrive at some kind of settlement
short of a prolonged feud, thought it was not a good time to celebrate
Christmas at home. Stella and Paul had taken up where they'd left off
when, as they both agreed, they were mere infants. He was taller now,
broader of shoulder, more self-assured, handsomer. But when he kissed
her on Christmas Eve, with snow falling outside, suddenly there was
silver moonlight all around her, and she was breathing the fragrance of

June roses. They sat close on the sofa as she unwrapped the gift he'd brought her—a beautiful pair of jade earrings.

"They were my mother's," Paul told her. "She died when I was twelve, and I have all her jewelry and all her—well, I guess you'd say her dainty treasures. I didn't think it was right, her leaving them all to me. But Father said she took a long look at Tennessee when he was fifteen and didn't figure he'd ever marry."

"Why? Is your brother so—so—"

"He's pretty wild, Stella. Father doesn't think he'll ever settle down." Then he added, almost absently, "Or love and respect a woman enough to make her his wife."

Stella got up and moved toward the blazing wood under the mantelpiece, keeping her back to him. "Then, if the jewelry's meant for your wife, you ought not, well, give it—"

He followed her and caught up in front of the fireplace. "It's mine to do with as I please." He chuckled, amused and faintly embarrassed, too. "I know what you're thinking—that I'm taking too much for granted, maybe. But I know how young I am, damn it." He turned her with a hand on her arm and looked into her eyes, grinning. "Don't worry. I'm sure it will wind up—most of it, anyhow—in the hands of my wife."

Then she was in his arms once more, whispering, just before his lips touched hers, "I'm going to keep it. You can't have it back."

Before she saw Paul again, a year later, the news of Jock Cameron's death had turned her world around and wiped out of her existence any lingering remnants of childhood. The first real darkness had come into her life with the death of her beautiful, gallant mother, who had reigned over Belmont Grange, knowing so well, perhaps instinctively, how to manage horses and servants and men. But after she'd lost her mother, Stella had had big, brokenhearted Jock to lean on and share her grief with. When Jock went down with the *Dolly Claybourne*, however, the second blinding darkness caught Stella totally alone. She hid in her bedroom behind drawn curtains, praying that she might die and join her father and mother wherever they happened to be. Then from somewhere—out of what her parents had left of themselves in her, she believed—came a contempt for herself for trying to give up. And with that contempt had come the strength to stand alone in the world.

After three days she emerged from her room into the light of day. "Mother, Dad," she whispered in her heart, "I'll never again quail and crawl and hide! So help me God, I'll never back off from anything that comes against me!"

Paul spent a brief two hours with her during the Christmas holidays that year and tried to give her an emerald ring from his mother's bequeathed treasure. But in many ways Stella was a changed person from the one who had accepted the jade earrings. She was eighteen now and not at all sure about where her choice might fall among a troupe of very eligible suitors.

"I can't accept it, Paul," she told him unhappily. "I'm not sure I oughtn't to return the earrings. The jewelry ought to go to your wife. The emerald ring's an engagement ring—or ought to be."

"That's why I want you to have it," Paul insisted, an undertone of hurt in his voice. "I love you, Stella. My God, don't you know that I want you to marry me?"

"But you see, Paul, I'm not certain about what I feel for you. We've been friends for so long. I love you—but, then, I love Thorn. I don't know how different those feelings are. I wish I were sure I *was* in love with you. Oh, I feel so sad! I'm not enjoying this at all!"

Paul had gone out of his way to see her on his way from Charlottesville, where he and Thornton were attending the University of Virginia. There had been a coolness between him and Thornton, she remembered. Lincoln had won the election, and both of them expected war. Paul, who opposed both secession and slavery, had already decided to brave his father's almost certain displeasure, if war did come, and join the Union forces. Thornton, who opposed neither, had decided to win the commendation of his relatives by fighting for the Confederacy.

As Paul was leaving, the couple stood alone in the dusk on the veranda of the house at Morrisburg. A streak of light from somewhere in the house turned his hair to silver and touched his eyes with dark shadows, giving him an almost spiritual look that reminded her of the gallant boy who had stood with her in the rose garden at Belmont Grange when they were fifteen. And again she felt as she had felt then: that if he were to hold her close and kiss her, her very soul would leave her body and fuse with his. Suddenly she was stricken by a premonition of tremendous loss. There was a good chance that she might be seeing him for the last time: that one of the noblest people who had ever loved her was on the verge of stepping out of her life forever.

She tried to shape a smile with quivering lips. "Don't—don't give that ring to the first girl you run across," she whispered. If he offered it to her again right now, would she take it or not? Merciful God, she still didn't know!

One or both of them then took a step, and they were in each other's arms. His kiss was long and hungry and somehow desperate, she thought. And then he was gone, though all at once there were a dozen questions she wanted to ask him and a dozen things she wanted to say. He was gone, and she felt abandoned and lost.

She stood in the dusk on the veranda, listening to the fading grind of carriage wheels on gravel and the diminishing scuff and beat of horses' hooves on the road. Her mind kept following Paul to the station, seeing him board the train, wondering anxiously when she'd see him again—or if she ever would. She was stirred and confused. If only she could identify each feeling in the strange complex of emotions aroused in her by his arms and lips, she might know whether she loved him. She had been kissed by other young men, but none of the suitors who had won the privilege through skill or persistence had caused her such disturbance and mystification—and, yes, enchantment—as Paul McEveride had tonight. Was she, then, as she had been three years ago, still in love with him? Shouldn't she, if she was, have taken the emerald ring? She had seen girls—lovely girls from impeccable families—watching him at parties. He was a catch of the first order, with or without the ring. If she loved him, she should have taken the ring and secured him from any female rival. *Did* she really love him? Maybe girls were vulnerable at certain times and under certain conditions, she thought. Maybe when a girl had been lonely, as she had been lately, she was stirred by the mere thought of a man—almost any attractive man. Or maybe when the moon was near the full, as it was tonight and as it had been in the rose garden at Belmont Grange three years ago, the arms and lips of any healthy, reasonably attractive man—not merely Paul McEveride—would rouse her to ecstatic response.

Stella concluded that there was, close at hand, a surefire means of finding out. She went inside the house and made her way to the library, where she found Thornton idly turning the pages of a book but obviously not reading. She gave him a thoughtful look. He was healthy, all right, and quite attractive—no doubt about that.

"Why didn't you go to the station to see Paul off?" she said absently.

"Let him see himself off," Thornton growled. "He's so damn sure of everything."

"Oh, I wouldn't say that," she mused. "Thorn, you can help me out." She stepped over close to Thornton's chair and stood looking down at him out of slanted, narrowed eyes. "Will you do me a favor?"

"Depends on what it is," he answered cautiously.

"The girls tell me you're a real menace in a rose arbor. Thorn, I want you to kiss me—you ought to know how. I've got my reasons."

He stared at her wide-eyed. "Now, hold on. We're cousins, but we've never been kissing cousins. What you want—"

"Oh, you fool, get on your feet," she said impatiently. "I told you I have a reason for this."

"Well," Thornton said uncertainly, "all right." He stood up and bent at the waist to get his face close. Then he touched her cheek with his lips.

"No, no, no!" she cried, her color mounting. "Not like *that*! I mean a *real* kiss." She moved into his arms and put her own around his neck, lifting her face.

He held her slackly and barely touched her lips with his. Then, suddenly, as if galvanized, he hugged her convulsively, and his mouth pressured her lips apart roughly. He held her close, his lips demanding, insistent. Stella tried to pry herself loose from his pressing body. "Tho-o-o-rn!" she mumbled, trying to shout. When she did get her mouth free, she yelled, "Damnation, Thorn! Turn me loose!"

He stepped back, sweating and red in the face. "God a'mighty," he groaned, "don't you ever ask me to do that again! Not even on the cheek!"

"You didn't have to overdo it, Thorn," Stella complained mildly.

"Didn't I?" The glaze had not completely left his dark eyes. "You don't know your own strength, girl."

"Mmmm," she murmured. "Well, I'm pretty sure I found out something, anyhow. I wish now I'd taken that emerald ring."

"I got to get out of here," Thornton said. "First time I ever wished you weren't kin to me. But, God, I sure do wish it now!"

Poor Thorn, she thought, killed on New Year's Eve in '62 at Stone River, dying among a thousand men who lost their lives in less than an hour in the Confederate attempt to crack the angle of the Union position between the river and the Nashville Pike. Paul, a fledgling lieutenant in Crittenden's corps, had been in that battle, fighting on the other side.

Before the battle, however, Stella saw Paul McEveride one more time since deciding that she should have accepted the ring. In October, after the battle of Perryville, Paul made a hurried trip to Morrisburg prior to joining the withdrawal of Buell's army from Kentucky to Nashville, where Rosecrans would take over the command from Buell. Having taken a long-range view of the possibilities, he came with the ring in his pocket and hope in his heart.

He rode up the driveway under the scarlet and gold of autumn foliage and turned a mud-splattered horse over to old Tobe in front of the massive white columns. Standing bareheaded on the veranda in his blue uniform, which set off his ash-blond hair and tanned features, he was, Stella thought, just about what every girl dreams of. How could she have doubted her feeling for him during the past year? But no more flirting with destiny. She meant to get the question between them settled before another hour had passed.

They stood before the cheerful fire in the drawing room, and he began at once, before she had time to suggest that they be seated. He couldn't know, of course, that it mattered little what he said in proposing marriage, since the young lady had already made up her mind before he had taken his place in the setting she'd arranged for the hearing.

"Stella, as you probably know," he recited, "I've loved you as long as I've known you." Then, momentarily, he left his obviously prepared statement. "Well, even before, as a matter of fact. Before you reached the barn the first morning I saw you, when you rode bareback over the fences. What a picture you made! I'll never forget it." He seemed to shake himself and returned to recitation. "I'll never love another woman. It's been my fondest dream that you'd marry me, but your happiness is more important to me than my own. If you aren't sure you can learn to love me, I'd rather you'd refuse—"

"I won't have to learn," Stella interrupted, her amber eyes aglow in her freckled face. "I do now." Then she added with some deliberation, "And I mean to have you."

He was stricken with shock. "You mean—you mean—what did you say?"

"I love you," she said, her voice beginning to quaver, "and I'll marry you." Then, in his arms, trembling, close to tears, she continued unsteadily, "I may as well warn you now, though. This is forever." A faint trace of her gamin grin appeared briefly. "Once I get that emerald ring on my finger, you won't get it back. So don't try." Then some spasm of feeling wiped away the grin. "Oh, darling, when I thought I might never see you again—oh, God, Paul, such despair! And now again— tomorrow—oh, this accursed, abominable war! Promise you'll come back to me, darling. I have such fears. . . ."

And her fears were justified. One year later, after losing far more than a leg at Chickamauga, Paul McEveride lay close to dying in Chattanooga and was trying his best to do so.

It was three days before Christmas of '63 when Stella heard that Paul had lost his leg in September. That year the mail service between Overton, Tennessee, and Morrisburg, Kentucky, offered a chancy, uncertain means of communication. Without the judge's influence with the

Union army, because of Paul, it would not have served at all. As it was, letters had to be routed by rail through Knoxville, Chattanooga, Nashville, and Louisville—all Union-held territory—and sometimes they lay around railroad stations and places serving as post offices for weeks before being picked up and moved along by some means. But Judge McEveride's letter came through with only a short delay.

The judge had not learned of the amputation until weeks after the operation, when an Overton soldier on a sneak visit home had dropped by to inform him that he'd better hurry to Chattanooga if he wanted to see Paul alive. Though Paul was at home when the judge wrote to Stella, the father having brought the son across the mountains in a light mattress-padded wagon three weeks before Christmas, the judge insisted that Stella remain in Morrisburg until he could assure her that her presence at McEveride Plantation would be beneficial. At the moment Paul was slowly regaining strength, but as yet was far from being mentally prepared for a visit from his fiancée. Judge McEveride hoped she understood.

After a while she did understand—but not before resisting the temptation to indulge herself in outbursts of wounded vanity and not before banishing such notions as dashing off a letter to Paul asking whether his writing hand had been amputated, too. She was being given a clear, unmistakable opportunity to avoid having a husband whose leg had been amputated halfway up his thigh and who would probably have to swing his body between crutches for the rest of his life when he wanted to cross a room or move from buggy to church pew or go to the outhouse. And from that thought a splinter of foresight leaped: She would be given no choice in the matter. Paul would make that choice for her. Suddenly she comprehended why Paul was not psychologically ready to see the woman who had promised to marry him.

But she was determined not to give him up. She loved him and wanted whatever was left of him, she told herself grimly. From Christmas through February, therefore, she wrote him letter after letter, at first begging and then demanding that she be allowed to visit him. She didn't know how many of her letters reached him or whether any of them did; she received no reply to any of them. Judge McEveride wrote that Paul's leg had healed completely and that he was moving about on crutches. The judge's letter was written in guarded language. Nowhere in it was there even a hint that his son had improved in outlook. When she realized that the judge, too, not knowing her personally, was helping provide her with an easy opportunity to discard a permanently crippled fiancé, she wrote *him* a letter about mental attitude—her own—and about good manners, in language which, unlike his, was not guarded at all. Finally, in March, evidently at the judge's insistence, Paul wrote her that he wanted to be freed from their betrothal. He had been having second thoughts about marriage and had decided that it was not for him. In any case, he had met another young lady who was monopolizing his time and thoughts. Near the end of the note, he wrote, "If things were as they were when I asked you to marry me, I would still ask for my freedom. For I cannot bear to think of being the cause of helpless children coming into this rotten, damnable world."

Afterward, for several years, Stella kept this letter and never reread it without weeping. Eventually, when it caused such pain in her heart that she could not bear to read it again, she destroyed it. But as soon as she'd finished reading it through that first time and had gained sufficient control of herself to speak, she summoned Lula May and they started packing her trunks. They packed every one she had. Then, in a wagon loaded high and drawn by a team of good mules, she and Lula May, with old Tobe handling the reins and whip, set out in as direct a route as could be followed, through the Cumberland Mountains toward Overton, Tennessee.

The judge, who met her on the road to the plantation, was astonished that Stella had dared such a trip, flaunting her possessions before the eyes of rogues in the laurel and guerrillas along the way; he was even more amazed that she had come through safely.

"Judge," she'd explained, "rogues and guerrillas were the least of my worries. I had a safe-conduct pass signed by Tinker Dave Beatty, which I showed to Union partisans who stopped us, and one signed by Champ Ferguson, which I showed to Confederate partisans. None of them dared touch us. I've had those passes ready since January."

"You know *them*?" The judge eyed her strangely. "Both of them?"

"Neither," Stella assured him. "But I know some mountain men who do, and who'd jump off a cliff to do my father's daughter a favor. And I laid out a little money here and there."

"You're a remarkable young lady," the judge said. "But—you look so—so young!"

"I've aged a lot, Judge, in the last three months."

"What are we going to do about him, my dear?"

"I don't know about you, Judge," Stella said. "*I'm* going to marry him. Then I'm going to make him forget that leg he lost and be a man again."

The judge looked down quickly so that she could not see his face.

"He's—why, he's a very lucky young man," he said, turning away, "if he only had the gumption to realize it."

She would never forget the ungainly, floundering retreat on crutches that Paul made from his chair on the veranda when the wagon drove up close enough for him to recognize her. Later, she had confronted him in the library, where he sat white-faced and stiff, a lap robe covering his good leg and hiding the empty, pinned-up trouser leg.

"Did you think you could fool me with that ridiculous letter?" she asked. "Paul, Paul, what have you to *say* to me?"

He shielded his eyes with a hand to keep her from seeing what was in them. "You promised to marry a man with two legs," he said, as if speaking by rote. "You deserve a whole man, not a hopeless cripple."

"I didn't promise to marry the leg," Stella said. "You're the same man I said I'd marry—the same mind, the same heart, the same personality. . . . Well, it *can*—and *will*—be the same personality again. You call yourself a hopeless cripple. Let me tell you about another soldier who lost his leg at Chickamauga—his right leg up close to his body—and he has to go about on crutches: General John B. Hood. And you know what he's been doing? Wishing he were dead? Wondering whether he's a man? Not on your life. He's been going to dinners and parties in his honor. He's the social lion in Richmond, where he went to recuperate. He's been planning war strategy with President Davis and courting the belle of Richmond, Sally Preston. My father did a lot of business with Mr. Wade Hampton, Sally's uncle. He's a general now, I think. I know Sally, and we've kept in touch. And I happen to know that John B. Hood, whom she calls Sam, had to jump in there, *with one leg*, and cut Sally out of a whole gang of two-legged suitors, the most eligible bachelors in Richmond. And he had to scrap for every inch of ground he gained with her. But he wouldn't take no for an answer and finally got a yes out of her. You know where he is now? At home indulging himself in self-pity? No, sir. He's in Georgia with General Johnston's command. He bled awhile and now has risen to fight again. What a man! And they say that one of his arms, hurt at Gettysburg, hangs practically useless. Of course, he's a Confederate soldier—though I still don't believe that Southern myth that one Rebel can whip five Yankees."

Paul dropped his hand, a painful grin twisting his thin, sensitive face. "All right, Stella, I'm sufficiently shamed. But allow me to say one thing. I still think both you and Sally Preston deserve better than one-legged husbands. And another thing. We don't know yet how well General Hood will do as a badly crippled general. In a moment of decision he may get to wondering how he looks hanging on crutches during a battle, and he may get to be a little careless about how many arms and legs *other* people lose. Ask the men under him, after a few battles, whether the surgeon didn't cut a little piece off his brain along with the leg.''

''Well, we can't know about that,'' Stella conceded, having made her point. ''But forget Hood. Let me ask you just one question. Do you love me?''

''Yes, Stella.'' Paul raised both hands to his face. ''God help me, I do.''

''Then I'm going to hold you to your word. If you leave me waiting at the altar, so to speak, you're no gentleman. And I'll have it printed in the newspaper that you did it because I'm an orphan girl who has no male relatives to protect her. I don't know how many challenges you'll receive.''

Paul chuckled, or meant to, but he came out with such a hollow, unamused sound that Stella would almost have preferred that he remain glum. ''You win,'' he said. ''But I'd hate to go flopping on crutches before a crowd of people to join you at the altar. Couldn't we hold the wedding here, in the living room?'' When she nodded, he smiled. ''Well, then, come give me a kiss—and welcome to your new home, Mrs. Stella McEveride-to-be.''

So they were married. After the ceremony, Paul got so drunk that he eventually had to be carried to bed. Stella slept in another room, denying to herself—and almost believing her own denials—that she felt any sense of relief that consummation was postponed for twenty-four hours. She knew, of course, that Paul had deliberately knocked himself out with alcohol, and his resort to this means of blotting out his wedding night confirmed what she had suspected about the nature of his problem. The next day was filled with humdrum and strained politeness. The judge spent the day in town and planned to spend the night there, too. Old Liza and Lula May appeared briefly to prepare and serve meals and then disappeared. She and Paul were alone in the house.

It occurred to Stella that if Paul were a less inhibited bridegroom, they might attend to that matter of consummation in the daylight. There was no law that required waiting for darkness. Such a suggestion, of course, if she were brazen enough to make it, would throw Paul into shock, since his problem, essentially, was that he couldn't bear to let the woman he loved see his stump. If only they could bring the whole thing out into the open and get rid of it once and for all. But she couldn't simply speak out and say, ''Paul, pull down your pants and let me see your stump.'' She paled at the thought. Actually, she was glad to postpone the confrontation until bedtime. She had her own concern. If she kept on worrying so hard about Paul's not being able to forget his stump, she might not be able to feel sensual, or whatever it was a woman felt that loosened her up and made her, well, penetrable. And if Paul was shaky and hardly ready and she turned out to be practically impenetrable, what a flopping horror of a mess that would be! . . . She was not encouraged by Paul's fluctuations between guilt and remorse on the one hand and despair on the other. Though they tugged at her heart, she dreaded the night.

At last it came, at the end of the longest, most nerve-racking day in her experience. Dressed in her most seductive nightgown, Stella lay under the covers of the big four-poster, watching the glow and flame of the fire Jubal had built in the fireplace to assure a warm room. As the door to the next room opened, she went rigid, then forced herself to relax as Paul worked his way through on his crutches and closed the door behind him. He kept his eyes on the floor as he swung across to the bed, his single white leg moving like a halting pendulum below the skirt of his robe. Taking his seat on the unoccupied side of the bed, he laid his crutches on the floor and slowly removed his robe. He was wearing a white nightshirt, which was, Stella thought, the most practical form of sleeping garment for a man in his condition. He sat still, holding his robe over the broken ridge of his covered stump. Then he let his head drop and groped blindly with his hands to cover his face.

"I can't—can't go through with this, Stella," he said in a hoarse, ragged whisper. "I can't *feel* anything but the horror of this—this—" He fell silent, shaking.

Stella's first reaction was a feeling of relief. She started to tell Paul to get in bed and forget it; there would be other nights. Then she felt shame at her own state of mind. This might be the most crucial hour of their life together. She wished she knew more about this man–woman thing. Somehow she felt that if Paul let that stump keep him from feeling "sensual" in bed with her on this night, his emasculation would be complete. She got out of bed and walked around to his side.

"Paul, let's drag this thing out into the open and whip it together." She sat down on the bed next to him. "First of all, darling, I love you. And that means all of you—even that—the injured leg you keep hiding so frantically. So we *must* not keep things from each other. Now show me that portion of leg God let you keep. Darling, I mean it."

He did not move for a dozen heartbeats. Then, very slowly, white of face and trembling, he put the robe aside and inched the bottom of his nightshirt over the red scar tissue and with one desperate jerk uncovered the segment of thigh. Stella mastered an impulse to cringe and said without batting an eye, "Well, what's so bad about that? It's a part of you, darling, as far down as it goes. Here, let me feel it." Steeling herself, she calmly laid her hand on the stump and held it there. "Honestly, Paul, how can you be so foolish? You have a handsome face and a superb physique with one flaw. After all, the beautiful body of the Venus of Milo has no arms."

"I don't know, Stella," Paul groaned. "I just can't *feel* anything. Maybe I'd better sleep in the next—"

"No, Paul. It's tonight or never. That isn't a threat. I just feel that's the way it will be." She stood up and studied him across the lower lids of her slanted eyes. "I wish I weren't a virgin. Then maybe I'd know more about—well, about this sort of thing. But I think the reason you can't feel—feel—well—sensual is that you're thinking about your leg instead of thinking about me." She looked down, her lips twisting in a nervous grimace. "And here I am, covered from shoulders to toes, when I've just got through saying we mustn't hide things from each other. Wait." She worked with hurried fingers at hooks and buttons, and the nightgown fell from her shoulders in a white silken heap around her feet. She hoped it looked like a pedestal from which rose a white, statuesque figure whose triangular patch of dark-red pubic hair would prove that it was not classic and whose freckled face and arms would prove that it was not marble.

"My God!" breathed Paul, with such sudden intensity that Stella wondered whether he was beginning to feel something, though, of course, she did not ask.

Crawling under the bedclothes, she said, "Paul, take off that ridiculous garment you have on and get in here with me." Then she came out from under the covers and blew out the light from the lamp on the bedside table. Behind her, as she blew, she heard Paul release a hard, uneven breath, and she wondered again whether he was beginning to feel what a man was supposed to feel after seeing what Paul had just seen.

Back under the covers, she watched Paul pull the nightshirt over his head and stand on his one foot beside the bed. Revealed by the dim, flickering firelight, his body bore out her judgment. He could have posed for a fleet Mercury that had lost one leg. As if reading her mind, he mumbled something about not being a statue as he came to bed. She hoped more than ever that seeing her naked had made things different for him.

She found out a few minutes later. With Paul close beside her, she sought again to dispel the horror from his conception of his stump. "I'll tell you, darling," she said, snuggling closer, "the feel of your hurt limb doesn't affect me any more than the feel of your hand." As she spoke, she reached across his good leg to lay a testimonial hand on his stump. But her reach was shorter than she intended, and somewhat less than accurate, too, and what her soft, feminine hand came to rest upon told her beyond question that Paul was *not* feeling "sensual." When he gave a great start, her impulse was to snatch her hand away. Fear of losing her direction and momentum in awkwardness, however, stalled the impulse. In the dull firelight, she hid her burning face against his shoulder and held her hand firmly where it was. When she felt him turn his head, she lifted her face and, finding his lips close, kissed him and held the kiss, too.

Slowly there came a stir of life under her hand. She wasn't certain at first, but then she could doubt no longer. For Paul was breathing harder, and she could feel his flaccid manhood stiffen and harden in the clutch of her hand. Languidly at first and then with a surge, it rose to stand as witness to his readiness. She took her hand away, almost frightened now by the transformation she had wrought—and worried, too, because she was not sure that she was feeling at all aroused herself.

She meant to say something like, "Paul, you'll have to help me out. You know, about where things go. Because I have no experience at this sort of thing." She didn't say anything, however, because she had already lost control of the situation and was getting all the help she needed. Paul had taken her in his arms and, with his groping mouth gone suddenly greedy and unrestrained, was finding her lips and mashing them apart. Then his hands were searching out the places where things went, and she was beginning to forget all about some of her former worries. . . . He had her legs spread and was between them and on top of her, and she found out that she need not have worried at all about whether she was penetrable. There was less pain than she had expected; but the shocking intimacy of having a part of him inside her, invading her private feminine recesses, was like nothing she had ever imagined. Before the end, as Paul struggled manfully, she was able, by an exertion of will, to keep from thinking about the jerk and slap of his stump against one of her buttocks. Gradually, however, the warmth and closeness of having her body melt and enfold the male flesh of one so dear to her urged upon her a special satisfaction and a pleasure that was unforgettable.

When Paul collapsed upon her, giving shuddering testimony that he was a whole man again, she held him tenderly in her arms and let the tears well up in her eyes and spill over. She hadn't reached those peaks of ecstasy that lively young widows sometimes spoke of in lowered voices behind their fans to enchanted maidens—maybe the prim, dry old ladies who called it a woman's duty and a man's pleasure were right—but she'd come through the ordeal of her wedding night victorious, and she wouldn't have exchanged her victory for any Ulysses S. Grant or William Tecumseh Sherman were likely to win.

Afterward, with Paul, now content, sleeping peacefully beside her, Stella lay awake. In retrospect she found her conduct with Paul hard to believe. All her mother's instructions, all her governesses' training, all her old black mammy's warnings—indeed, all her education in what was proper and modest had been forgotten in a moment. Actually, Stella decided, *ignored* was the word that fit. She'd simply acted like an absolute whore. Inside herself she winced at the word, but she knew she'd act the same way again when the occasion required such conduct.

And it would, she knew. She did not deceive herself; she'd won a battle, not a war. Paul would sink into despondency, would grieve himself into impotence again. And she'd play the whore again and woo him out of the shadows. Maybe her tight-corseted teachers at the Augusta Female Seminary in Staunton, Virginia, had dealt in generalities. She didn't *feel* like a whore, though she didn't know how whores felt. Maybe they, too—or most of them—had their compelling objectives, which had little to do with feeling sensual. She didn't know where all her thoughts were coming from, but she suspected there was a potential whore in every good woman. It *was* a matter of price, after all. Hers had been the restoration and salvation of Paul's manhood.

As she had predicted, Stella had had to dredge Paul out of the depths more than once over the past year. But not, she now recalled, in the past five months.

So it could be that she had finally won her war. And there had come a bonus in wooing Paul from the borderline of impotence: She'd learned how it was to feel those explosions in the loins that the young widows had described. Not often, perhaps—if women were supposed to every time—but often enough to know the pleasure of a feminine response in her body, over which she had no control, to the life-giving force of a man.

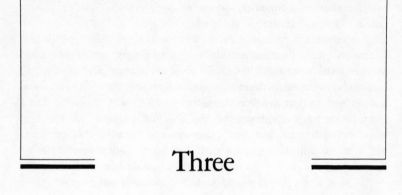

Three

True to Redwing's prediction, Jubal did return. Stella found him kindling a fire in the front room against the spring chill of the evening while Judge McEveride was eating a belated supper. Jubal was somber and uncommunicative, keeping his intelligent black face lowered to his task, his massive hands busy. All Stella could get out of him was that he'd ridden in with the judge. When he left the fireplace, he went directly to a closet in the back hallway; and Stella, on her way to the dining room, saw him duck out through the kitchen with the judge's double-barreled shotgun in his hands.

Judge McEveride stood up from the table with his usual meticulous courtesy. "Sit down, my dear," he said, "and have a cup of coffee. It tastes much better at a dollar a pound than at fourteen cents. It was the expense that made me an addict, I'm afraid." As Stella sat, he called back to the kitchen, "Lula May, a cup of coffee for Miss Stella, if you please."

"No, thank you, Lula May," Stella said, slanting her dark eyes against the old jurist's impassive face. "Judge, you didn't mention that Jubal was back."

"Didn't I?" he said without change of expression. "Your news must have crowded it out of my mind, then. Yes, I picked the poor boy up on the road. Homesick, I'm sure. After all, this *is* Jubal's home, you know."

"I saw Jubal with the gun, Judge," Stella said. "And don't tell me he's going on a possum hunt this time of year. Do you expect trouble tonight—before the troops can get here?''

The judge examined the dregs in his cup. When he looked up, his eyes were serene. "No, no, of course not, my dear," he said. "Why, the gun is Jubal's foolishness. He was stopped by several disreputable-looking horsemen, who *could* have been some of Parson Krull's men, and asked some peculiar questions about the McEverides of Smoky Water Cove. Now, Jubal has always been unduly suspicious. He came hotfooting it home with the idea of protecting us, of course—though I can assure you, my dear, we won't need Jubal's heroics.''

"I don't agree with you," Stella said. "We'll be lucky if we get through this night, Judge. And tomorrow, for your sake, we must move to town, and you must stay there until something is done about Parson Krull.''

The old man pulled at his handsome, iron-gray mustache, his eyes remote, speculative. "Stella," he said from that distance, "you've got the mind of a man. I've known that all along, of course, but I lose sight of it sometimes because, frankly, my dear, you're about the most female-looking creature God ever put on the earth—if you'll excuse the indelicacy. I don't think you'd panic in a crisis, so I won't hide any of the facts from you again." He produced a thin cigar and lit up at the lamp chimney. "We are indeed in very grave danger. Now—ah, I hear Paul's crutches on the stairs. I do wish that boy would follow your suggestion and move with you to the first floor. But all his life—pride, pride. Shall we go in to the fire, my dear? Now, mind you, not a word to Paul. No point to be gained by making him feel any more helpless, you know.''

Later, before the fire, the judge kept shifting and squirming in his chair; and Stella, who regarded the old man as a rock of calm fortitude, became restless herself until she remembered that the judge sometimes carried a bulky pistol in an enlarged hip pocket. After a while Paul commented upon the remarkable fact that the judge had mentioned no news whatever since returning home.

"A person would think you haven't even been to Overton," he said.

Judge McEveride kept his eyes carefully on the fire. "Well, I did hear one thing. It's all over town that General Forrest has finally surrendered. He's supposed to have signed the articles on May ninth at Gainesville, Alabama.''

"Why, that means Tennessee will be coming home, doesn't it?" Stella exclaimed.

The judge shook his head somberly. "Not for more than a flying visit, Stella. And at night. No, I'm afraid Tennessee can't come back to,

to, ah, Tennessee—that name! An office-seeker's demagoguery
and a mother's patriotism—what they won't saddle on a helpless infant! . . . You see, Stella, my elder son—against my advice and, I must
admit, against my will—fought with Champ Ferguson's guerrillas as a
partisan. Later, he rode with Morgan a few times and, finally, joined
Forrest's Independent Scouts—always as a partisan, never even on a
muster roll. There can be no parole for him, you see. He could—and
would, I have no doubt—be tried on several counts of murder that are,
ah, too well known to overlook, certainly by the military courts that will
be operating soon in Tennessee.''

"But Paul has influence," Stella protested. "And you, Judge—
surely you could help him. As for money, I certainly could—"

"Stella," the judge interrupted, "we couldn't help him." He
cleared his throat uncomfortably. "Frankly, I'm not certain that I want
Tennessee to return, under any circumstances. You've never seen him,
so you can't imagine such a man, Stella. He's an atavism of some sort, a
throwback to buckskin days, to long-hunter forebears. One crops up
about every third generation of McEverides. I had an uncle—but never
mind. When Tennessee was a little, short-haired lad, I used to tease his
mother about the dark streak down the crest of his yellow hair—white
then, of course. I called it his feral streak—the dorsal stripe, a sign of the
primordial you find on wildcats, wolves, panthers, most wild animals. I
wasn't serious, of course—then. But I've grown superstitious about that
mark. The plain fact is, Stella, that this state, where so much of the war
was fought, is still too civilized—"

The judge never finished. Before they looked around, the three
people at the hearth knew all at once that an alien presence was in the
room. When Stella turned, the swarthy savage she had shot in the woods
was standing in the entrance to the dining room, holding a Navy Colt in
each hand. His right ear was covered by a crude, blood-stained bandage,
and his eyes were black, glittering slits in the darkness of his face.

Coming to his feet, the judge demanded sternly, "To just what are
we indebted for this intrusion, you infernal scoundrel?"

"Don't move, old one," the savage warned. "I gutshoot you sure."
He started moving sidewise across the room to the front door.

"He's one of the Krull gang!" Stella said urgently. "He'll let others
in at that door!" She started walking toward the dining room, trying to
draw the man back from the door.

The savage did not change his course. "Go on, you want," he said
with a white-toothed grin, watching the men. "I don't spoil your meat
before the good time." Suddenly his left-hand pistol boomed, and a

bullet knocked splinters from the mantelpiece, causing the judge's hand to stop reaching under his coattails. "Move hand again, old one, and I don't keep for Pappy."

Stella ran into the dining room with some forlorn hope of getting into the backyard and calling Jubal, and crashed full-tilt into the waiting arms of a bearded giant who caught her up and held her clear of the floor. The big man studied his catch with small, red-rimmed, piggish eyes, then bent his shaggy head and smelled of her flesh with animal delight. Stella struggled frantically, exerting a desperate energy, and could not disturb the giant's strength.

From the room she had left came the stamp of heavy boots and the bark and growl of rough voices, and above them all Paul's voice, urging her to run, to save herself. "Listen," she said to the pig-eyed giant, "I'll give you a fortune in United States money to kill these men and set us free. Fifty thousand dollars, a hundred thousand. Think of it! I swear before God I have the money and will give it to you!"

"That goddamned Brownlow Krull!" the giant growled resentfully. "Swore you's a freckle-faced redhead, the half-breed bastard! I never would swapped my piece of this here ass for no loot could I seen you first." He shifted her to one massive arm, leaving one hand free to pull up her skirt and grope roughly up the silken smoothness of her thighs. "By God, I'll find out what I done traded off!"

Stella fought wildly, doggedly, hopelessly; then she quit. For the first time in her life she knew the sense of complete physical helplessness. Suffering stonily the indignity of the big man's questing hands, she looked into his glazing eyes and said, "I'll remember you! Damn you, the world's not big enough to hide you after this!"

Then Brownlow Krull, his face black with rage, was standing beside the giant, Navy pistols still in his hands. "Put down woman!" he snarled. "And pull out the hand! You make the trade, and you don't hump her! Not till after me." He nudged the bearded ruffian with one of the guns. "Turn loose!"

The giant dropped Stella, who fell to her knees and scrambled up. "You lying bastard!" the big man growled at Brownlow. "Freckle-faced!" He lumbered into the living room.

"Move," Brownlow ordered, shoving Stella back to the living room. "I don't miss Pappy kill the old one first. Then we have the good time, no?"

In the room Judge McEveride stood white-faced and impassive before the fireplace, regarding Parson Krull with eyes of death. Paul's crutches lay across the room, where someone had thrown them, and Paul was on the floor, bloody-faced and mute, scrambling around, trying to get up. He would rise to his hands and knee, and a slender, dark little mink of a man with a long neck and sharply receding chin would place a foot against him and kick him back down. The little man was dribbling saliva and making snuffling noises as if he were grieving or had a bad cold.

Stella cried out, "Leave him alone, you—you—dear God!" She tried to break across the floor to Paul, but Brownlow Krull held her back, wrenching one of her arms up behind her back with a cruel, punishing force.

"You don't go close to Jimpson," Brownlow said. "Might cut belly with the knife. Woman no good for Jimpson, you see, huh? That Jimpson one stinking bastard. You smell him, no?"

The ruffian followers of Parson Krull moved about, idly opening drawers and ransacking the escritoire and shelves, or merely stood listening with appreciative grins to Parson Krull. The guerrilla chieftain was a black-garbed, reptile-eyed old man, small-paunched and dew-lapped, with a high roach of possum-gray hair that reached to his shoulders and was held off his face by a black headband. He was delivering a grotesque jeremiad on the injuries he had suffered at McEveride hands. The strident whine of his voice ran on and on in the rhythm of a backwoods revivalist, malevolent and self-pitying by turns, painting pictures of proud persecutor and humble martyr.

"Stella!" the judge's voice cut through the parson's lamentations. "Whatever happens, you must live through this. I was wrong about Tennessee. Wait for him. Set him after these goblins. And—good-bye, my dear."

" . . . And I call, uh, on Almighty God, uh, to witness, uh," the parson was chanting harshly, sawing the air with one hand and holding a Navy pistol with the other, "that thy poor servant Krull, uh, would've freed thy black children, uh, from vile bondage and servitude, uh, if this here high and mighty, uh, John Freeman McEveride, uh, this disciple of hell, uh, this goddamned aristocrat, uh, this rich, slave-owning son-of-a-bitch, uh—if this here lawyering McEveride, uh, if he hadn't of drove the poor man, uh, the humble man, uh, the friendless Krull, uh, out from God-fearing, gospel-loving white folks, uh, drove him out into desert wastes, uh, into a savage land amongst redgut savage men, uh. I call on God to witness, uh, this here brand he burned, uh, with his own work-dodging, hell-serving, lily-white hands, uh, so the poor preacher of the gospel, uh, he'd have to seek refuge, uh, in wild, uncivilized—"

"Damn it, Pappy, you aim to wag your clapper all night?" interrupted an impatient ruffian, obviously the parson's eldest son, though he showed no trace of the dark blood that marked Brownlow and Jimpson.

"You want the horse soldiers to show up here so you can run like hell again, without taking nothing to show you been here?" All of a sudden he swung on his heel. "Damn this fooling around," he snapped, and took command. "Jap, you and Shep and Bull hump up them stairs and shake down the rooms up there. Grab everything will pack on mules and sell. Jimpson, take your knife and dig word out of your *mocho* there where-all they keep their money at."

"No!" Stella protested. "No! Don't! For the love of God, make that horrible creature quit torturing him! All our money's in a box in the desk at the head of the stairs. All we have here. Take it and leave us now, and we'll forget this outrage."

"Just forget *me*," the eldest son said callously, heading for the stairs. "I ain't interested in nothing but money."

Parson Krull stood dangling his black headband, his dewlap faintly quivering. He had yanked the headband off to reveal before all eyes the livid scar tissue of the *S T* on his forehead. The exhibition of his shame, intended as a justification for long-dreamed-of vengeance, had fallen flat—worse than flat. It had been contemptuously ignored. Now only the dark offspring of his banished years remained to shame him further by existing at all. They bore the Krull name. They carried the seed of future Krulls. They *were* Krulls—the produce of animal itch, filth, and despair in a godless land—and the proud man before the parson, who had caused these creatures to come out of savage red bellies wearing the name of Krull, would pay with his heart's blood.

"Parson, you can't honestly hold hatred for anyone here but me," Judge McEveride said, coming as close to pleading as was possible for him. "Do with me as you will. But don't harm my children. They've never harmed you. They—both of them, Parson—they were born *after* you left Tennessee."

Parson Krull bared snaggled teeth in a tortured grin. "So was mine, McEveride," he said bitterly. "So was mine." He waved his free hand. "These here two diseases your beautiful younguns are coming down with, McEveride. Like the Good Book says, the sins of the fathers. . . . You goddamned aristocrat, there was a time when the name of Krull didn't cause nobody to spit! There was a time. . . ."

"You come now," Brownlow Krull said impatiently, dragging Stella toward the closed door of the sewing room. "I don't wait no more till Pappy shoot. He talk all night, look like."

Boots drummed down the stairs, and the tall, ghoulish-eyed Shep passed Brownlow and Stella on his way to the dining room. "*Help me—please!*" Stella gasped.

"Why, I'll just pack up the silver stuff first," Shep leered. Then he paused, half-turned. "Tell you what, though, girlie. Soon's the half-breed gets you heated up, I'll see you get done some good by a white man."

Brownlow almost broke Stella's arm in a spasm of fury. "I'll see you burn on slow fire, you white-eyes bastard!" he snarled.

Shep swung back to face Brownlow squarely. "You don't mean right soon, do you, stud?" he asked, narrow-eyed. "Not right now?"

Hope flared in Stella as she felt Brownlow go tense. She was getting set to try to wrench free, even if the attempt snapped the bone of her arm, when a gunshot rocketed outside and went rolling through the grove and on into the distance. Shep lunged for the front doorway and leaped outside, gun in hand. The Krulls, with their victims, grew very still in the room, listening to brief, rough voices in the yard.

Shep returned, grinning. "The nigger come to and was running into the house with a shotgun," he announced lightly. "The captain smoked him. He says hurry up in here." He stalked on toward the dining room, winking lewdly at Stella's white face as he passed.

And all of a sudden Parson Krull's Navy pistol was slamming the enclosed air with concussion after concussion. Black-powder smoke piled up in a thickening, swirling, leaping cloud, obscuring the target as the old guerrilla fired until the hammer of his gun began clicking on bare nipples.

Jimpson was jumping and dancing, his watery eyes glistening red in the lamplight, as he shrilled a weird singsong of wild gabble. He whipped out a long-bladed knife and clacked some form of interrogation at the parson, who was turning away from his deed with eyes staring like those of some swamp creature out of a face mud-stained by sweat-moistened dust and grime.

When those eyes touched Shep, who had turned curiously in the entrance to the dining room, they seemed to whirl him out of sight. "I've got a list of the McEveride silver," the parson rasped after him, "and the last condemned piece of it better be turned in." The old man dragged a sleeve down his face, smearing the mud stains and making himself look like something emerged from primeval slime.

Then he turned his attention to Stella's fitful struggles against Brownlow's exertions of ruthless strength. He observed the woman's refusal to cry out in pain, to plead for mercy, or to collapse in hopeless weeping. Malevolence spread like a dark light out to his face as he recognized the marks of clean-strain breeding. "Well, well, Brownlow, I'm glad to see you've give up your share of the valuables for nothing," he whined sanctimoniously. "You'll store up credit in heaven for not harming her, boy. Why, it's better so, better so. Because she's for the canopied beds of rich white men, not for the blanket and dirt floor of some poor Krull. So I admire your turn to religion, my boy. It's what I been praying for. I thank God, though, *I* ain't young—like you, Brownlow—because God knows I never could turn down a proud-titted, hot-bellied white woman with red hair.'' The parson smacked his lips, even closed his eyes, to indicate an ecstatic lewdness. "The best of all, son, the *very* best of all! Oh, I *reckon* I'm too old. Why, now, may the Lord forgive these here sinful thoughts—though they're for your salvation, boy, seeing you never had nothing like this here proud McEveride woman, who—"

"You—foul—degenerate!" Stella panted. "You damned—monster!"

"My dear lady," the parson protested, "as God's my witness, I don't crave the sight of a scrub bull riding a pedigreed heifer. I aim to prevent it if I can." He showed his snaggled teeth in a frightful grin. "Brownlow, don't you take none of her clothes off. God knows, if she was naked in your hands—think of it, boy—why, even the Almighty couldn't blame you for losing your religion and—"

The parson threw out his hands in an elaborate show of resignation as Brownlow began heaving at Stella, dragging her in surges toward the sewing-room door. The half-breed wrestled her up against the door long enough to turn the knob; then, as the door suddenly gave inward, they both fell into the room, where Brownlow lost his hold as they hit the floor sprawling. Parson Krull closed the door and stood before it, listening to the crashing of overturned furniture within the room, the scuffling of feet, the bumping of bodies against woodwork, and finally the thudding of blows. After a while all sounds of struggle ceased.

"Jimpson," the parson said thoughtfully, "for your sake, I hope you ain't killed that *mocho* without being told."

The minklike little man whirled from his prey, whining shrilly, "*Mocho* sleep! Water throw at face make good—holler like hell."

"Drag him over here, then." The parson waited until Jimpson had dragged Paul's unconscious body across the floor. "That *mocho* would holler louder'n hell if he saw Brownlow on his woman in there," he said, as if thinking aloud. "Watching his woman get bred would cut him deeper'n that there knife, I can tell you. Being a servant of the Lord, Jimpson, I refuse to think of the *mocho* tied to a chair with a rope, and water throwed on his face to wake him up to see Brownlow on his woman, and her with her dress drawed up to her neck."

"Rope to the horses," Jimpson yammered. "I get *pronto*. Fix *mocho*, he holler good like hell. No, Pappy? No?"

"Before God, I wash my hands of it, Jimpson," the parson said piously. ''I forgive the *mocho* for all his injuries to me, if he ever done any, like the Good Book commands. If he said an unkind word to you, maybe, Jimpson, when you was bashing his head or sticking a knife into him, why, maybe he meant it for a joke, and you ought to forgive him, too. But you follow your own medicine, if it's right, and do what you got to do. Anyhow, the *mocho*'s yours. I got to get on upstairs and tone down that smart-aleck Wesley before he gets the notion he's top dog and starts trying to steal me blind.''

Jap and Bull, later joined by Shep, had already made several trips to the pack mules outside when the parson and Wesley finally descended the stairs with the remaining sackfuls of plunder. Before they reached the ground floor, they saw Shep come backing out of the sewing room, his face wry and perspiring.

''What you been doing in that room?'' rasped the parson.

Shep spat on the floor. ''Whatever I went in for, I never *done* nothing,'' he said. ''That one-legged feller got hung in there. Jimpson done it, I reckon. But, by God, I can't figure out *how* he done it! Got the feller to stand on a chair somehow. Propped him up, maybe. And got a rope on his neck, rope running through one of them quilting-frame hooks in the ceiling, other end tied to a doorknob. Feller come to, he didn't like what he seen, I reckon, and hopped off. Give me a turn, the woman trying to untie the damn rope at his neck, his eyes bugging and tongue out, and her looking like a beat-up, drowned rat.''

''Where's Brownlow at now?'' the parson demanded.

''Outside, I reckon,'' Shep grinned. ''Come out just before I come in, looking for Jimpson madder'n a wet hen—*and he was wet*! Haw, haw! Claimed Jimpson throwed a bucket of water on his head. Jimpson swore he was just trying to freshen the woman back to herself so she wouldn't miss nothing. Caught 'em both with the same water. Haw, haw, haw! . . . Hey, don't you aim to look in the room?''

''What for?'' the parson snarled. ''Get outside. We got to get moving.''

The Krull raiders sought their horses under the great oaks and mounted up quietly. Unrestrained indoors, they made barely a sound in the open. When the man who had shot Jubal from the shadows outside spoke a low, clear word of warning, therefore, every man heard him. The man had pulled his horse up at the edge of the moon-splashed driveway and was looking beyond the six loaded pack mules to the veranda. Heads swung, and a rough voice in the shadows whispered, ''Lord God!''

Stella McEveride had staggered out on the veranda. She was holding onto one of the veranda uprights in the moonlight, watching them with eyes that looked like black holes in her swollen, discolored face. Her hair was wet, matted, hanging limp and tangled about her shoulders; her dress, ripped to shreds, showed naked flesh in a dozen places. Yet, strangely, despite the evidence of her physical defeat, there was something in her that would not be beaten down, something that showed in the lift of her head, in the iron poise of her ravished body.

"You beastly sons-of-bitches!" she cried shakily. Then her voice steadied. "You'll regret this night, I promise you!" Finally her voice came with the strength of passionate hatred. "Before God, I swear that I'll see the last one of you dead! I'll follow you to hell, but I'll find you—and watch you die! And may God damn your souls to hell when you do!"

The man who had lurked in the shadows stood up in his stirrups to look around. "Now, this won't do at all," he said. "She's seen you, every one of you." The man's horse shifted restively and a patch of moonlight caught briefly on the polished-brass trappings of a U.S. Cavalry officer's uniform. "Brownlow," he said sharply, "you had the use of her. Now get up there and dispose of her. Knock her on the head. The rest of you fire that house. There's been too much foolery here. No telling what you've left lying around. Now, snap to it, and let's get out of here."

Brownlow Krull dismounted and moved reluctantly toward the veranda. Then, brightening, he ran up the steps, drawing a heavy pistol. Stella's eyes were like chips of black obsidian as he came close. "Dead cunt no good," he whispered rapidly. "You find me to hell, we have the good time some more, no?" Grinning, he swung the pistol with more motion than force, but struck solidly, nevertheless, dropping Stella to the floor unconscious. He knew the blow would not kill—unless the woman had a very thin skull, as some did. Bending over, he struck again savagely, hitting the floor instead of Stella's head. Pleased with himself, he turned back to the horses.

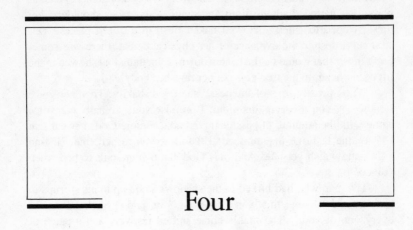

Four

Stella became aware of red light beyond her closed eyelids and of a roaring in her ears before she was fully conscious. She opened her eyes to what seemed a holocaust. As she had stood on the porch in that last moment, with death in the house and the half-breed coming toward her with drawn gun, she had expected to die, and now concluded that she had. She was vaguely surprised to find herself in a place of fire, since she hadn't considered herself all that bad, but it didn't matter much. Nothing mattered much.

Slowly Stella came to realize that she was lying on the ground under the seared, shriveling leaves of a great oak in the front yard. Then, all in a moment, both hell and the world in holocaust shrank to the flaming destruction of the McEveride farmhouse. Mounting volumes of leaping fire poured from all windows of both floors, swirling up the walls and merging in sheets of flame to sweep the roof. The seething, crackling roar of fire eating the house was unforgettable, and even back in the grove the yard was as light as a shimmering day in August.

Someone was kneeling beside her, bending over her, crying. Lula May? Yes, now she could see; it *was* Lula May. Between her and the burning house, limned against the searing light, the ex-slaves stood, together or singly, watching the house melt and crumble in the flames, holding protective hands against the heat. All of them kept moving from foot to foot, restless and uneasy, seeing in this blinding light something enshrouded and mysterious that was a dark aftermath of the Jubilee—the death of the big house. Some of the women were crying. Lula May's voice was a high-pitched murmur of syllables strung together. Finally Stella understood her words.

"You easy," Lula.May said. "You laying there on the porch. When Jubal come, we got the judge and Mist' Paul out. They laying over there under them blankets. Oh, God, honey, I thought you's dead, too!" She started crying again, then checked her sobs angrily. "We never got nothing else out. Everything gone. Them fetched, no-'count niggers ain't been here ten minutes. They scared them devils come back. Miss Stella, you ought to send them niggers down the road. They's any account a-tall, they'd done *been* gone—when the freedom come. All they do's eat."

Stella spoke out of a cloud laboriously. "Jubal? Where . . . where . . . ?"

"Jubal gone to lay down. He be dead he didn't have a hard head. That bullet knocked most of his sense out. I had to keep him from walking back into the fire. He say the judge sho want old Miss's picture out the library when he come to. And he keep asking what happen and where all the other niggers gone."

"Paul," Stella murmured vaguely. "Where's Paul? Why isn't he here? Did something—happen—to Paul?"

"Oh, Lawd God!" Lula May groaned. "Honey, you out of yo' head from a lick. You got a big bump on yo' head. Mist' Paul can't come now, honey."

Afterward Stella could never remember much about the fire. As the roof of the house caved in, she lapsed again into unconsciousness, and when she came to, she was in a bed in a cabin once occupied by Sebe and Liza before they were emancipated.

Somehow she knew where she was. By her bedside sat a rugged old man, the family doctor from Overton, with his closed medicine case on the floor at his feet. All that could be done for her had been done, and the doctor was waiting for her to regain consciousness so that he could talk with her. Stella remembered vaguely having talked from her bed about her plans. She didn't know when or to whom, but there were already decisions firm in her head.

"Hello, Dr. Broadus," she said faintly. "What's happened?"

The doctor had a bearded, kindly face and sharp eyes. "You've been comatose for three days," he said. "For at least the last eight hours, you've been asleep. Do you remember talking with me at all?"

Stella shook her head, and it started aching mildly. She felt also a dull pain between her legs.

"Let me save time by speaking frankly," he suggested. "You've been suffering from a brutal beating, concussion, and torn vaginal tissues. Your injuries have been thoroughly treated, and you're well on the way to physical recovery. The concussion was of most immediate concern, but I'm a little worried about the long-term effects of the last mentioned. I hope you won't suffer some psychological trauma from the knowledge that you've been raped. Some women do, and they're such fools! Probably afraid their market value with men will drop, or maybe that they'll be whispered about by other women. Tell you a secret, Stella. Reason I never married was women. Now, tell me. Your mind going to break up over that rape?"

Stella's face firmed. "No," she whispered. "Damn such men—my market value. Two things, though, about that rape—"

"You told me, in one of the moments when you seemed to make sense, that it was one of the guerrillas. Some Indian or half-breed. That right?"

"Yes. What about the chances that I'm pregnant or diseased?"

Dr. Broadus took a cup of coffee from Lula May, who had just come in from the lean-to kitchen. He turned his intent, dark eyes back to Stella. "I've done all that can be done to prevent disease," he said slowly. "When's your next menstrual period due?"

Lula May answered for her, "It due now. Maybe day or two past."

"Forget it, then. If you miss this flow, you *could* be with child by Paul, certainly not by the savage, nor by that bearded monster you mentioned, if he was involved sexually. That would be Bull Jakes, by the way, one of the most notorious murderers among Parson Krull's guerrillas. Now, if your period were two weeks off, you *might* be in trouble."

Stella closed her eyes. "Oh, God, I've got to make arrangements! The judge and Paul—" Tears of weakness seeped through her lashes.

"All attended to," the doctor said quickly. "We had to bury them, Stella. The funeral can wait on your decision. It can be private, or you can have most of the county. Just let me know, and I'll handle it."

"Dr. Broadus," Stella quavered, "after today, you're one of my best friends." Then her voice steadied. "So I'm going to ask another favor of you. Will you wire the Pinkerton National Detective Agency and have them send one of their agents here to see me? I don't know the address. It was in Chicago when my father had them do some business for him some years ago. And, Doctor, I'm not worried about the whispers. I don't care a jot what the women whisper—or, for that matter, what the men say out loud."

"I'm like the priest who hears confession." The doctor picked up his case and rose. "Nobody will hear it from me."

"I wasn't trying to swear you to—"

The doctor held up his hand. "Doesn't hurt to let you know, anyhow. I'll see you next week." He turned toward the door. "Need me sooner, send a pigeon to Betty Cravens."

When he was gone, Stella looked up at Lula May, exhausted. "How's Jubal? Did something happen to him? I seem to remember—"

"He got shot," Lula May said. "All right now, though. I told you he got a hard head." The comely young black woman thought for a moment and then looked directly at Stella. Almost defiantly she said, "Miss Stella, ain't nobody here now but us and Jubal. And maybe Mist' Redwing. He here this morning. All them trifling niggers done gone."

"Just when we might need them! Why did they leave?"

Lula May's eyes glinted. "Me and Jubal told 'em to hump their black asses down the big road, that's why!"

"Watch your language," Stella said. "I don't like to hear vulgar words. Why'd you run them off?"

"They didn't lift a hand when the big house burn. If I waited on them, you be dead as a burn-up crisp. They black trash, honey. All the quality colored folks done been *long* gone."

Two days later Stella decided to start things moving before she left her sickbed. "I want to see Jubal and John Redwing in here," she told Lula May. "Jubal must go to Overton. We need money from the bank, and we need a desk, rug, and other furnishings for this cabin. We'll need groceries. That dressmaker, Mrs. Lawson, will have to come out. You'll have to ride in with Jubal and see about other clothes. I can't keep on wearing your things."

"Doctor claim he going to move you to Overton when you able. You do that, we won't need all them things."

"I'm staying right here," Stella said wearily. "Redwing might as well bring the horses from Long Hollow, too. We won't be raided again. And I want him to go down in Alabama and look for Tennessee McEveride. Oh, Lord, I need the strength to get out of this bed!"

Lula May was picking up things, straightening the room. "What you want with that Mist' Tennessee? Niggers claim he soon kill a man as tell him hidy do."

"He'll come back here. I know it. And I'll be here when he comes. I just want Redwing to hurry him home before the trail gets cold."

"You aim to sick Mist' Tennessee on them Krull devils?"

Stella stared blindly at the ceiling. "I'll set him on their trail." Her freckles stood out harshly against the dead white of her face. "I won't let him stop. And *I* won't stop—not until every Krull that lives is back in the earth with rocks and skulls and empty shells."

The next morning there was blood on the sheets, on her nightgown, and on her. Stella's menstrual flow had caught her unprepared. She had attributed the discomforts of the approaching period to the manhandling she had received from Brownlow Krull. While Lula May cleaned her up and changed the bed, Stella wept bitterly. She had hoped during the last eighteen hours that she was pregnant with Paul's child. Now she knew that all living trace of Paul was gone forever. It seemed unfair that God should respond to the venereal itch of such horrible creatures as old Parson Krull and then erase from the earth such an intrepid, selfless, loving soul as Paul McEveride.

Lula May tried to comfort her. "Better be glad yo' womb cleaned out. Might had you one of them squinch-eyed papooses. Them doctors don't know it all. Guinea Mary claim she got big once when no man touch her till about three days befo' she due to pass blood. Better be glad, honey."

A week later Stella was up and doing—planning, executing, fretting. She sent a pigeon aloft, and Dr. Broadus arranged the funeral. It was held in the family cemetery at two o'clock on a sunny day when birds outside the dead-leaves area of the burned house were caroling in scattered chorus. As far as Stella was concerned, the minister's sermon consisted of meaningless words—meaningless because they could not pierce through her numb, wooden exterior to the tortured reality writhing inside. Yet she endured it, dry-eyed, her hands clenched hard to still their trembling, her teeth locked together to hold back her voice lest she suddenly shout out, "Stop it! Stop it! Stop this barbaric travesty!" Looking at the mourners gathered at graveside, she whispered in her heart, Oh, goddamn it, I know they mean well! Most of them. And they're sincere—some of them. But she also knew that many of them had their faces set in solemn shapes for the moment, acting before others and not even knowing they were acting. They would be laughing before night, joking, eating, thinking about making love. And Paul, and the judge, too, were lying there under the ground, breathless, still, like stones, slowly beginning to turn back into dirt. . . .

As soon as the service was over, Dr. Broadus drew Stella aside. "I've got to leave at once," he said. "I have an expectant mother waiting half out of her mind. Lula May tells me that you refuse to move into Overton because you're waiting here for Tennessee McEveride to come home. Is that true?" When Stella nodded, he asked gently, "Do you think that's wise?"

"He and I should discuss what's happened," Stella said. "He's the judge's son and Paul's brother."

"He's also an outlaw," the doctor said. "Do you know him personally?"

"We've never met."

Frowning, the doctor studied the toes of his Sunday shoes with troubled eyes. "Look at yourself in the mirror," he suggested, a tinge of red showing through the gray of his beard, "and then decide whether you think it's safe to be here alone with a man like Tennessee McEveride. I'm sure you've heard how deadly he is among men, but what you may not have heard is that he's just as dangerous, in another way, among women. He has a very bad reputation with women, Stella. And, believe me, it's not a case of the dog that's been given a bad name. Oh, I could tell you some things about that predatory young man—but then, as I told you, I'm like a priest who hears confession."

"Doctor," Stella said, "I appreciate your concern. You're a true friend. But I'm committed to waiting for Tennessee. Just before he was killed, knowing he was about to die, the judge gave me that commission. I must—I *will* fulfill it."

"I hope you aren't making a mistake," said the doctor regretfully. Then, after warning her against overtaxing her strength, he hurried toward his buggy.

After the last guest had departed, Stella went to bed, though it was several hours before dark. "It was a mistake," she told Lula May when she was under the covers. "It should have been private. With just four guests—you, Jubal, Redwing, and Dr. Broadus."

"Folks got a right to pay their respects," Lula May differed. "The judge and Mist' Paul, they quality folks. They ain't white trash, to pass out of mind quick as dead hosses do. Anyhow, you got it wrong. Me and Jubal's family. We ain't guests. And Mist' Redwing *couldn't* be here. He ain't got back from Alabama yet."

"We didn't have to hold it today. We could have waited for Redwing—and Tennessee, too, maybe."

"Who make the talk at the graves if you didn't have no preacher there?"

"Me," Stella murmured. "I'd make the talk."

"You!" Lula May scoffed. "You heard that preacher man. You know you couldn't match them big, fine words of his'n, and you couldn't match his tune. What you think you say, anyhow?"

Stella thought for a long moment, her eyes closed. Then she said in a voice hardly above a whisper, "I'd tell Paul and the judge to hang on and not be too restless. I'd say, 'One day I'll come and stand beside you, and

I'll tell you that all the goddamned Krulls are dead and in hell. After that, my dearest ones, you can rest.' ''

Lula May was scandalized. ''Miss Stella, a lady ain't got no business cussing like that! Why, you breaking one of them Ten Commandments! And you just come from listening to that preacher, too!''

Stella turned over on her stomach. ''When I say goddamn, I'm praying,'' she said. ''Want to hear the whole prayer? Now I lay me down to sleep. Goddamn Parson, goddamn Jimpson, goddamn Brownlow, God—God—oh, God help me! I'm right in the middle of hell, and I'm not even dead yet!'' Her muffled sobbing shook the bed for a long time, until finally, the agony of her grief having abated, she spoke again, her voice sounding half-stifled and broken. ''Anyhow, you don't catch me saying ass and shit and fuck the way *you* do. Now leave me alone.''

Awed and aghast, the maid headed for the precincts of the lean-to kitchen, which was a safe distance from the bed, she hoped, just in case there should come a stroke of lightning out of a clear sky.

A Pinkerton agent came and departed with a list of Jock Cameron's business acquaintances who might alert their connections in various parts of the South and Southwest to be on the lookout for men answering to Stella's descriptions of the Krull guerrillas. The Pinkertons' first move would be to search among the Seminoles of Florida for any information concerning the Krulls. The detective was businesslike, confident, and expensive.

John Redwing returned from Alabama in early June and reported failure in his mission. He had found no trace of Tennessee. On his way home, however, he had come up with an idea.

''I got to thinking about that Yankee officer who shot Jubal in the raid,'' he told Stella. ''He could've been the Krull's contact with the Union army. Champ Ferguson had connections with Confederate armies, and Tinker Dave Beatty was supplied with Yankee guns and ammunition to use on secesh folks and tear up the country. Way I figure, that officer had been serving liaison duty between some Union force and Union partisans. He likely saw profit somewhere with the Krulls after the war was over and was getting 'em on their way—just stopped by here because the Krulls wouldn't leave without taking their revenge. Now, maybe we could find us a Lincolnite guerrilla—say Tinker Dave, for a starter—and find out who that Yankee officer was. Then your army friends could tell you where he's stationed, and we'd find the Krulls near him, you can bet.''

''That's very good thinking, John,'' Stella told him, ''and if your idea leads us to the Krulls, I'll make you a wealthy man. So go find Tinker Dave and ask him. He's a tight-mouthed old hellion, though, and may not be willing to tell you what he knows. Tell him I sent you and tell him what the Krulls did here.''

The next morning Redwing was gone, and Stella made her daily trip to the cemetery, this time with something hopeful to report to Paul and the judge. It seemed to her they understood every word she said. Sometimes, too, they seemed to speak to her by making her recall vividly conversations she'd had with them in the past.

The family cemetery was located on a knoll west of the burned ruins of the house in a clump of venerable elms and shaggy-boled cedars that seemed to be gathered in a never-ending wake over the memorials of the dead McEverides. A picket fence, recently repaired with new poles where old ones had rotted away, guarded the sanctities of the plot from browsing livestock and suggested inviolability to thoughtless or callous humanity. Stella stood by the unmarked graves of her loved ones and told them of Redwing's idea and his mission. There was a good chance that soon she might find out where the Krulls had gone, she told them, and she remembered the judge's injunction to wait for Tennessee and set him after those goblins.

From the knoll, there was an excellent view of the road leading to the Overton Pike, and each day from the graveside Stella held vigil, hoping to see Tennessee McEveride riding toward her. ''Oh, why doesn't he come?'' she lamented. It was the first time she'd uttered aloud the silent cry that was repeated each day as she stood there. And Paul's voice, speaking in the closed chamber of her memory, seemed to answer her in the open air of the cemetery.

The conversation Stella now recalled had taken place in the library one day during the early months of their marriage, when Paul was still suffering periodic moods of depression. She had walked in and found him slumped in a chair, his chin on his chest, a book opened at random and lying on the floor at his foot. When he had raised his head and she had seen his face, she knew the blue devils were rending his vitals again.

''Why, Paul, what in the world?'' She had spoken almost impatiently.

''I was thinking about Tennessee,'' he said. ''From what you've heard, can you believe that I used to love him, Stella? Until I was eight or nine years old, I almost used to worship him. And until he was about twelve, I think *he* loved me. Then something happened that froze his heart, I think. I don't know what. Father does, but he won't talk about it. After that, Tennessee didn't seem to love anybody—not even Mother. Maybe he loved himself. That was the only company he kept—except sometimes, in the woods, with Jubal and John Redwing.''

''Didn't he have a sweetheart?'' Stella asked softly.

Paul shook his head, sighing. "No. He's never loved a woman. Oh, he's used women for his pleasure. There have been a few minor scandals. There could have been more, I think, if Tennessee had broken any hearts. But he didn't, since his attraction for women, I believe, is primarily physical. There's something about him—it's not his looks exactly, though he's handsome enough. Something else. Women and horses and dogs—he masters them with a touch. I've caught girls I was with watching him, wetting their lips. He never took a girl from me, but he could have—and would have, I'm convinced, if he'd cared enough. He could have taken any girl I've ever had. What haunts me, I guess, is the fear that he still could."

"You mean me," Stella said resentfully. "Paul, I'm getting a little tired of listening to hand-to-mouth whispers about this superbadman brother of yours. And I'm not flattered by the innuendoes you're edging into this conversation."

"I'm not being covert at all," Paul protested. "I'm saying openly that when Tennessee returns, he may very well want you. How could he help himself? And if he wants you, he'll try to take you. How can you know, never having seen him, that he won't be able to take you? How can you predict your feelings?"

"I won't listen to another word!" Stella cried, outraged. "Why, why, it's obscene, this talk of —of—why, you'd think I was a mare to be led into a stall! Oh, Paul, you fool, do you think marriage vows can keep a wife—a normal wife—from feeling maybe a twinge of desire when she looks at a handsome stallion of a man, even a stranger? Oh, I know wives deny that they're ever stirred by any man except their husbands. But they are—and they shrug it off and forget it unless they're sluts. What you don't remember is that virtue isn't measured by what a woman feels but by what feelings she restrains. You know what? I've got a good mind to slap your face."

Paul had grinned sheepishly. "Just don't want to have to shoot my own brother," he had murmured, leaning over to pick his book off the floor.

Stella fell on her knees beside the mound of raw earth and spoke to her dead husband gently, believing devoutly that he heard every word. "Darling, give me a little time—a few months or years. Then the last of those monsters will be dead, I promise you, and you and the judge can rest. And if you're still tormented by your last glimpse of life on earth—a savage violating your wife while you stood helpless—then hear me, darling, and this vow will erase that black vision and give you peace. I will never marry another man. I will never enjoy another man's body. I will never have another man's child. And may God strike me dead if I don't mean every word of the vow I've just made."

Then she rose and gazed somberly down the road toward the Overton Pike, hoping to see a dust cloud rolling up from the thundering hooves of a great black stallion with a tail of fire, bearing a tall, black-garbed rider with a satanic face.

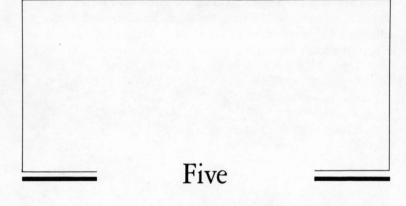

Five

Before ten o'clock in the morning, a sighing drowsiness in the hum of insects, somehow made drowsier still by the liquid wood-notes of a solitary thrush hidden in the deep shade of trees, promised an unusually hot day for late June in the Cumberlands. A timber rattlesnake, headed for water in a hollow below, started across a steep, winding road at a switchback, head weaving and rattles held clear of the ground. Then, almost across, the rattler's flicking tongue caught the vibrations of travel from uproad and down, and the snake crawled into a roadside straggle of weeds, coiled, and became practically invisible against a dark-brown mold of dead leaves.

The meeting of travelers occurred at the switchback. Five United States troopers, toiling upward on plodding horses, found themselves blocking the narrow road before a lone horseman—a big, yellow-haired man riding a magnificent line-backed dun and eating green apples from a hatful he nursed against his side with his left forearm. The dun gelding, finding his way blocked, stopped of his own accord; his rider calmly regarded the blue uniforms with cold gray eyes and kept on eating, plainly savoring the sharp acid taste of the green fruit.

In a land occupied by Federal military forces, where civilians—especially secessionists—were denied the right to bear arms, the horseman's appearance was enigmatic. Two .44 Army Colts rode butts forward, high on his hips in open-topped holsters, and the stock of a Spencer rifle protruded from a saddle sheath under the stirrup leathers of an expensive Western saddle. It was equipment that a well-to-do ex-Union officer might have brought home from the war. And the man *was* dressed in blue Union trousers. The shirt, however, was of butternut homespun, and the hat that held the apples bore an unmistakable resemblance to hats worn by Confederate cavalry.

The fiercely mustached young lieutenant in charge of the troopers came slowly erect in his saddle, frowning. "Howdy," he barked when it appeared that the man on the dun would not speak first.

The rider nodded. "Wouldn't have any salt, would you?" he said in a deep, soft voice.

"Salt?" said the lieutenant. "*Salt*? What the hell? Did you say *salt*?"

"Green apples taste better with salt."

The lieutenant drew himself up stiffly. "I'm Lieutenant B. F. Ledbetter," he announced shortly. "These are my men. You understand, sir, that I must have your name and service in the war."

"Why, no, I don't understand none of that." The big man bit into a new apple and gazed at the lieutenant with eyes as clear and unfeeling as those of a feeding hawk.

"It's like this," Ledbetter snapped. "We're contacting witnesses for the trial of Champ Ferguson in Nashville. Former guerrillas, partisans—folks like that. And here you are, armed to the teeth. You're not Occupation, far as I can see. You could be Tennessee McEveride! We've got reason to suspect that he may—by God, you *could* be him!"

"That's right," the man on the dun agreed, watching a bull-necked sergeant shift his horse to the edge of the road to move up abreast of the lieutenant. "And I could be somebody else. Now, before you make a bad mistake, you better get in touch with General George H. Thomas at Nashville and find out who I am."

"Lieutenant," the sergeant growled, palming the butt of his Navy pistol, "lemme put a gun on him and draw his teeth. Then we'll get some answers without a lot of—"

The half-eaten apple dropped from the big man's hand. Before it hit the ground, an Army Colt leaped, steadied, and thundered, black-powder smoke piling around the hooves of the sergeant's mount as they left the earth. The rearing horse crashed into the shying mount of a trooper to the rear, and the sergeant hit the ground on one foot and was knocked flat by a flying hoof of the lieutenant's horse. Of the horses on the road, only the line-backed dun remained under control, though his master had not bothered to speak a word or even touch the reins.

The sergeant surged to his feet with brute energy and plunged to the fore, where, clear of the horses, he stood on unsteady legs, his face dirty and wild. ''What the goddamned hell!'' he bawled.

The man on the dun pointed to the roadside with the long barrel of his Army Colt. Only now, as they brought their horses back to rest, did the troopers see the writhing coils of a dying rattlesnake in the straggle of weeds. The stump of the neck turned into view with the flat, wicked head hanging by a shred of skin.

''Why the hell couldn't you say something?'' snarled the sergeant.

The man regarded the sergeant without sympathy or interest. ''You fell off a horse,'' he observed, ''but now the horse ain't snakebit. No need to thank me, though.''

''That was damned good shooting, friend,'' the lieutenant said, his black eyes snapping. ''*Too* damned good, if you know what I mean. Now I *know* you, McEveride!''

''The hell you do!'' said the man, the barrel of his Colt resting idly on the pommel of his saddle. ''If there's anybody in the whole Union army you *don't* know, that somebody's me. Now, you look like a smart fellow. Figure it out. If I'm that Tennessee McEveride and you crowd me, why, I'll just have to pile bluecoats up on this road. Anything else don't make no sense. If I'm on a mission for General Thomas—who wants that Ferguson convicted, by the way—and you ball things up by taking me in, you'll sure catch hell, I promise you. So there ain't a damned thing you can do that makes sense but go on about your business and, when you get back to Overton, wire General Thomas for the facts about me. If I'm that McEveride you talk about, why, hell, you know where I'm going and can come after me. If I ain't, you can claim you showed sense by cooperating.''

In his moment of indecision, the lieutenant looked somewhat like a small boy wearing a false mustache far too large for him. ''I don't know,'' he said, pulling his face together in a scowl. ''I don't reckon—''

''Why, hell, he's McEveride, all right,'' the sergeant declared. ''And we're five to his one, Lieutenant.''

''Maybe I'm talking to the wrong man,'' said the man on the dun, his cold eyes fixed ironically on the sergeant. ''You carry this big-mouth around to do your thinking, Lieutenant?''

The lieutenant turned angrily on the sergeant. ''Mullins, when I want your advice, I'll ask for it. Until I do, you keep your damned mouth shut.'' He cut his eyes at the big man as if for approval, and straightened with authority. ''What the man says makes sense. Make way and let him by.'' Then he bristled his mustache at the man on the dun. ''Let me tell you something, friend. If you *are* McEveride, don't think we won't be after you.''

"You got sense," the big man observed, moving the dun past the troopers and on down the road, the long blue revolver held idly in his hand as if he had forgotten to thrust it back into the holster.

Two hours later the dun gelding was eating up distance at a running walk along a side road of the Overton Pike. Dipping down a low hill, the horse swept on toward Smoky Water Creek, slowing down as he came to the stream, and stopped before an old wooden bridge made impassable by rotten timbers and gaps where planks were missing. The rider glanced once at the bridge and, turning his eyes upstream, sat for perhaps two full minutes gazing at nothing, feeling the scorch of the sun against his broad back. Then he reined the horse off the road and down a wheel-marked bank to the shallows of an old ford and crossed the stream on a wide gravel bed in water that was fetlock deep. Instead of following the wagon trace back to the road, he headed the dun into a dark path that disappeared under creek-bank trees heavily interlaced with grapevines and infested with clumps of mistletoe and squirrel nests. Riding upstream, he observed that barely a trace remained of the old path he followed, which once had been well worn by the feet of white boys and slaves seeking freedom from supervision, drawn irresistibly to water for swimming, fishing, trapping, and gathering summer plums and fall grapes.

The man was little affected, however, by old, lost associations. Nostalgia, for him, had some faint existence, perhaps, in the remembered pleasure of swimming in a shaded pool, but his was primarily an animal's desire for the comfort of cool water against hot, sweat-fouled flesh—more anticipation than memory. An animal's, too, was the wariness that enabled him to observe the big Negro fishing from the opposite bank of the pool he sought before he sent the quiet horse around the point of a plum thicket.

The Negro rose slowly to his feet, speechless, white areas growing at eyes and mouth. The tip of his cane pole sagged and kept going down until a third of the pole's length was under water.

"Well, well, if it ain't old Jube!" greeted the man on the dun.

"Lawd God, he's here!" Jubal's voice rose like the open diapason of an organ. "Marse Tennessee, you done come home!"

Tennessee Smith McEveride stepped out of the saddle and slip-knotted the reins high on the horse's neck. Leaving the dun to graze on the bank, he walked down upon the gravel, moving with an habitual soft-footed ease like some great cat.

"May as well quit fishing, Jube," he said, dropping his shirt to the gravel. "I aim to bust that swimming hole wide open. You been in today?"

"Nossuh." Jubal lifted his cane pole to the bank and began winding his fishing line along its length. "I ain't hot enough for old Smoky Water. Ain't dirty, neither."

"You've changed, then."

"I sho changed, all right," Jubal admitted, a somberness shading his words. "Mo'n you think, Marse Tennessee."

Tennessee finished undressing and stepped to the water's edge. Though he was at least three inches over six feet, he looked only medium-tall because of the bulking proportions of his two hundred and twenty pounds, which lay primarily in breadth of shoulders and herculean development of chest, arms, and legs. So well distributed was his weight, however, that General Forrest had once commented to his brother Bill, after the latter had pointed out Tennessee McEveride standing alone some forty yards away, that it was remarkable how many men of average size in history had acquired fame for their almost legendary physical exploits. Captain Bill, the general's chief of scouts, had been delighted to point out that his latest recruit to the fabulous Forty Thieves outweighed the general himself by at least twenty pounds. . . . Tennessee's face, which was much darker than his brown-streaked yellow hair, was sculpturesque in the classic proportion of its features and in its immobility, looking as if it might have been chiseled from a block of select brown marble. The flaw of the whole man was revealed by the eyes—not by their size, color, or shape, which was prepossessing enough, but by their lack of a certain human warmth one expects to meet in the eyes of a man—any man, even an evil one.

"Jube, you don't have to call me Marse Tennessee," he said, wading out into the shallows of the bar. "You're free now."

"If I'm free, I'm free to call you Marse Tennessee," Jubal reasoned. "Who gonna stop me?"

Jubal stood on a high rock-buttressed bank where the creek swung in under overhanging branches of beeches and oaks and pooled in quiet, blue depths. Tennessee hit the water in a long surface dive and, turning down with powerful strokes, touched bottom, and came up to the surface, rolling, wallowing, splashing. Then he turned on his back and lay barely submerged, gently moving hands and feet like a lazy fish moving its fins.

"Aw, man, this feels *right!*" he said, water lapping his face. "I've thought of this pool, Jube."

"Yessuh," Jubal said. "Don't *seem* right, though. Look like you'd feel too bad to go swimming, Marse Tennessee."

"How come?"

"Aw, you know, suh. Just come from where the house burn down, graves of Judge and Marse Paul. Look like you'd feel sad."

Water closed over Tennessee's face. He came surging upright, coughing, treading water with a thrust that kept his head and shoulders above the surface. When he could speak, he said, ''You mean to tell me the judge and Paul are dead?''

Jubal gaped down at him. ''Marse Tennessee, ain't you been home yet?''

''No. I stopped off here for a swim first.''

''Lawd God,'' Jubal groaned, ''here we just been talking and you don't know! Never come to me you wouldn't gone on home first like folks—er, like they does gen'ally. You sho been outa pocket, though. Miss Stella send Mist' Redwing down in Alabama to see can he find you, but he claim he cain't. Where all you go to when Gen'l Forrest quit, Marse—''

''Listen, Jubal,'' Tennessee said quietly. ''Listen! By God, I don't remember you so mouthy! What happened to the judge and Paul?''

''They done got shot and hung. Yessuh, kilt by trash. And—and don't blame me, now, Marse Tennessee—they shot me, too.'' Jubal knelt down, holding his head sidewise over the bank. ''Here. See where it took me? Still touchy. And, Marse Tennessee, it ain't fitten for me to tell you what them hellish devils done to Miss Stella. Lawd God, they need killing, Marse Tennessee! They *need* killing!''

Tennessee sank back in the water. ''So it happened here, too,'' he murmured. He lay on his back again, his strange, cold eyes staring up into the leaf-thatched recesses of a great oak. ''I figured their politics and regular ways would bring 'em through. I looked to laze here one night in a bed and eat some victuals that was meant to taste, not just to keep a man going. But I ain't much surprised. It's an old story, Jube.''

''It ain't old to me,'' Jubal said darkly.

''That Miss Stella—she must be Paul's wife. Last word I had, Paul had lost a leg and married a rich woman. Man who told me was from close to here, a Union man I come on in a woods south of Memphis. His face looked so green, though, I figured he was telling me a pack of lies, trying to buy his life with news from home.''

''What you do to him?''

''Why, I thanked him kindly for the news,'' Tennessee said. ''Funny thing. That fellow went off without a sound for maybe a hundred yards. Then you could track him through the woods by ear. Sounded like a broke-loose mule reaching for the far side of a cornfield.''

Jubal fanned himself slowly with his straw hat. He shifted weight from one foot to the other. Finally he said, '' 'Bout time we getting on home, ain't it, Marse Tennessee? Po' Miss Stella, she spend her time looking down the road, waiting for you to come home. Co'se you didn't ketch on when I say they mistreat Miss Stella.''

"I know what you meant," Tennessee said. "But I sure as hell can't turn back the days and keep what's happened from happening. Now it's done, Jubal. And it ain't the first time in this war a woman's been raped."

"It the first time a McEveride lady has."

"All right," Tennessee said wearily. "Who was it? If they're still around, I'll kill 'em. That suit you?"

"The Krull gang done it!" Jubal declared, his deep voice rumbling with passion. "And if they *was* still here, I'd a-done took at 'em myself, nigger or no nigger! But they done shuck outa the country, look like. No telling where they gone."

"So that old bastard, Parson Krull, finally got even," Tennessee observed somberly. "Well, there ain't but one God's thing we can do, Jubal—try to forget it. I've got to 'shuck out' before another day's gone myself."

"You gonna leave?" Jubal brooled. "Why, you *cain't* leave! It take time to find where they gone. And—and, Marse Tennessee, you ain't heard it all. You *got* to change yo' mind! Miss Stella got a lot to tell you she likely ain't told no nigger like me. You wait till you hear—"

"I'll tell you one thing," Tennessee said. "Freedom has sure gone to your mouth. Damned if it ain't. A whole troop of blue-belly cavalry could move up under cover of your blasted bellering. Now, you shut up and let me swim in peace. You can tell me the whole thing on the way home."

While Jubal waited above him in brooding silence, Tennessee McEveride rolled in the creek, swimming for short spurts, enjoying the luxury of cool water enveloping flesh that remembered heat and grime and thirst. Finally he lay on his back again, thinking of the news he'd just received, his cold eyes blind now to the overhanging branches of the oak. At one time, the news would have been hard to bear. That was before he'd learned that his own life was not as important to others as it was to himself. He remembered well his first chilling lesson in self-preservation. Indeed, all the education he valued thereafter began that day fifteen years ago, when he was eleven years old. . . .

The three mountain ruffians had stepped from behind trees when he was squirrel hunting with Jubal. When the hulking red-haired man, grinning, had reached for the rifle, which was almost as long as the boy, Tennessee had handed it over, thinking the big redhead wanted to examine it with friendly interest. But then the man's two bearded companions grabbed Tennessee and held him while the man holding the rifle, still grinning, swung a huge, red-tufted fist to the boy's face and kept swinging until a merciful darkness closed in. When he regained consciousness, Tennessee was bound hand and foot in a cave back in the mountains, and the three mountaineers were passing a jug around a fire out front.

"Ain't nary a doubt in my mind," one of them was saying. "That damn judge will sure God turn Bobby Joe loose now the nigger boy done fetched him word we aim to kill his boy if he don't. Hell, he don't *dast* do nothing else. This here's his own child."

"I don't know, Luster," said a second. "Them McEverides ain't like common folks. They set store on high-toned ways of doing things. Be like him to hang Bobby Joe in name of law, then come hounding after us for killing his boy. If only Bobby Joe hadn't got funny and cut them corpses up like he done! If he'd just killed Clem Bivins when he catched him in the bushes with that gal he's sweet on and, if he was bounden to do *something*, maybe just whupped the gal—or even, if he was pizened complete, just shot her! Why, then the judge might could just penitentiary him for a year or two. But like it is now, I don't know. Course we'uns had to do what we could for Bobby Joe. What you think, Red Billy?"

"What *you* do. Bobby Joe's done bogged down in Shit Creek, looks like. Reckon now he's got to take his chances, and them chances ain't none too good. Way he cut off Clem's ears and nose and prick and stuck 'em around in the dead gal—why, folks in this here country would break in the damn jail and lynch Bobby Joe if the judge didn't sentence him to hang. No, I allow we done seen the last of Bobby Joe's ass. Lessen we go to the hanging."

"What'n hell we got the judge's youngun for, then," Lester growled, "if the boy won't do us no good?"

"Well, there's always some *speck* of chance," Red Billy conceded. "But Bobby Joe's our blood kin, my own brother and you-all's cousin. We got the judge's youngun as the eye for an eye, like the Good Book says. The judge hangs Bobby Joe, we kill his youngun."

"Naw, *we'uns* don't!" Lester differed emphatically. "That's *your* job. And you're sure God welcome to it. Palford, we'uns better get on our way. Trial's tomorrow. One of us'll fetch you word how Bobby Joe fares in court, Red Billy."

After their footsteps had faded down some rocky path, Red Billy wrapped himself in a blanket and stretched his hulking length across the entrance of the cave. Soon he was snoring; he hadn't even checked to see whether the boy had regained consciousness. But Tennessee was not frightened, not really worried. If Red Billy had thrown a blanket over him against the autumn chill and had removed the unnecessary bonds, Tennessee could have ignored the hurts and bruises from the beating Red Billy had given him and might have been able to rest. For the ruffians' talk of killing him did not trouble the boy at all. The judge would get him out of this. He was as certain that the judge would not let him die as he was that the sun would rise in the morning. The judge would turn over the world to keep him alive. So the boy lay sore and shivering on the cold ground in a cramped, tortured position, awaiting the dawn with a quiet mind.

Finally daybreak came, and soon thereafter Red Billy was tilting his jug and building a fire. When it was burning well, he proceeded to fry fat side meat and then cornbread in an old iron skillet and to boil coffee in a battered can. Only after he had eaten did he concern himself with the condition of his captive. He came back and, squatting down, began untying the boy's bonds.

"Let you go untied," he said. "Me, I don't aim to untie you every time you eat or have to piss." The habitual grin seemed stamped on his red-stubbled face. "Reckon you can take out your own peter—if you can find it." Then, clutching a handful of shirtfront, he dragged the boy's stiff, practically helpless body out of the cave and dumped it beside the fire. "All right, you little shitass, stand up. I aim to show you what'll happen, you try to leave this here cave today." Suddenly he stooped and jerked the boy to his feet. "Just come to me," he said softly with a cold grin. "You didn't yelp none when I whupped you yesterday. Better tune up now and lemme hear you sing." Then he knocked the boy down with his huge fist. He lifted Tennessee and knocked him down six more times before the boy lost consciousness, still without having uttered a sound.

Tennessee awoke in late morning to remnants of cornbread and pieces of side meat cold in congealed grease. Bloody and unwashed, under threat of having the scraps crammed down his throat, he ate them from the skillet on the ground near the fire. He felt like a dog—Red Billy's dog—and knew that he would likely be beaten again before dark, for there was not much around the camp to entertain Red Billy through a long, dull afternoon. But still he was not seriously worried. If there was a person in the whole world he could depend on, that person was the judge. . . .

It was dark and the fire was burning in front of the cave when a high-pitched halloo from down around the bend in the trail announced the arrival of the expected messenger. Red Billy came to his feet and moved out to the edge of firelight, facing down the trail. Instantly, behind his back, Tennessee whipped past a chunk of wood off to one side of the cave entrance, swept up the poleax leaning there, and carried it into the cave. He did not believe Red Billy would free him without giving him another mauling, and he meant to deprive the grinning mountaineer of that pleasure if he could.

The man who emerged from darkness was Palford. He stopped beside Red Billy at the shifting edge of light. "Judge sentenced Bobby Joe to hang," he announced, breathing hard from his walk up the trail.

"Well, by God, it don't surprise me none!" Red Billy swore. "Now, goddamn him, it won't surprise *him* none when I keep *my* promise! Didn't he say nothing in court about the boy?"

"Sure as hell did. Said his boy'd been took and his life threatened, but claimed he didn't have no choice. Said the law was clear and no getting around it. Allowed it was his bounden duty to sentence Bobby Joe to swing. But he swore he'd spend a lifetime tracking down them as taken the boy if they harmed a hair of his head. He's done swore out a warrant for your arrest, Red Billy."

In the cave Tennessee listened in a paralysis of shock. The meaning of the news was at first incomprehensible; the import seeped into his mind slowly. Finally he understood: The judge had refused to save his life. His own father thought more of a vague thing called duty than he did of his own boy's life. The small price—a little shame-faced bowing down of head in town—was a price too high to pay. So Tennessee must die. He must stop breathing and rot in the ground so that people would point to the judge, who had done his duty, and praise him for his character in upholding the law. He had thought he was safe because of his father's love, and now he found there was no safety from any source outside himself. He discovered that the judge loved himself more than he loved his son.

It was in these moments that a coldness entered the boy's heart, and the affections and trusting faiths of childhood were gone forever. Suddenly something cold and deadly grew behind staring eyes that were only eleven years old. He would save himself, or he would die. He gripped the handle of the poleax fiercely. Tonight he must act instantly; he must recognize the right moment.

"Piss on his warrant," Red Billy snarled. "There ain't a goddamned thing left to hold me in these here hills. Wait here a minute. I'll cut the little turdknocker's throat and go back with you. On my way out the country."

"*Hell*, naw!" Palford protested shrilly. "By God, you won't! You wait right damned here till I get to the bend in that trail and light one of these here Lucifers I got hold of in town. Soon's it strikes fire, I'm around that bend and long gone. I don't aim to be no witness to nothing."

"You chicken-gutted mule's prick!" Red Billy jeered. "Go on and strike your stinking match. By God, I hope it catches your rag-tailed britches on fire and singes your rusty ass!"

Now was the time. Red Billy's back was to the fire, and Palford was hurrying down the dark trail. Tennessee darted out of the cave and swept like the shadow of a great horned owl past the leaping flames of the campfire. En route, the poleax was lifted, moved backward, blade up. The wonder was that the boy did not strike too soon. The deftness with which he functioned in this moment of crisis, the native deadliness he revealed, would have frightened an onlooker. There was no lost motion. The boy swung the ax smoothly above his head with all the force he could muster. The blade struck with a thud and bit through bone where neck and shoulder met. Red Billy never knew what hit him.

Spreading the dead man's blanket on the ground, Tennessee piled skillet, coffee can, and what remained of the meager supply of side meat, corn meal, and coffee upon it and made his bundle, tying it with the rope they had used to bind him. Then, carrying the bundle over to where Red Billy lay, he stripped the body of powder horn and bullet pouch and picked up the rifle which had fallen from the big, red-tufted hands. He debated removing the ax from the dead man's severed spine and gore but decided he had enough to carry already.

"*You* don't have to sing *me* no tune," he muttered, shouldering his bundle, and trudged down the trail. He did not intend to go home, but he was only eleven years old, and the weather turned too chilly for comfort, and the scarcity of game where he was kept him hungry. So after ten days in the woods, he made his way back home, where he found his mother under the care of a doctor and not speaking to the judge and found the judge almost out of his mind with worry and despair.

"I wished I coulda took your place," little Paul told him solemnly.

"Don't ever take nobody's place," Tennessee advised him. "Nobody would take yours."

An army of searchers was still in the woods. The judge embraced him with tears in his eyes and tried to explain how anarchy results when law bends to blackmail and how it would have done no good to recuse himself and step down from the case, since another judge would have pronounced the sentence. The father tried to convince the son of his love and of the mind-breaking strain of not being able to help.

Tennessee had stood like a stone, feeling nothing. "I didn't need no help," he said finally. "I helped myself."

"I know," said the judge. "We found Red Billy."

The cold-eyed boy did not change expression, and the judge shivered. . . .

Tennessee waded out of the creek and dressed on the gravel bar without drying while Jubal went downstream to cross on spaced rocks at a shallow. Then, side by side, they set out for the home place of the McEverides, the big dun following at heel like a well-mannered dog.

"All right," Tennessee said, after waiting for Jubal to speak. "By God, are you pouting, Jubal? Get on with your story."

Jubal began talking with his eyes on the ground, his voice sullen and monotonous at first, then gradually warming until his words came with a smoldering animus that was barely restrained. He had finished before they reached the entrance to the driveway through the grove. Walking beside the last of the McEveride men, he waited with hope in his face for a McEveride's reaction.

"If I've heard that story one time, I've heard it a dozen," Tennessee said. "*Seen* the leavings of the same thing, too. I followed three Yankee foragers on the Mississippi once. Come on 'em in a clearing at a dog-run kind of house where they had a young fellow dead and his pretty wife raped. I left 'em hanging like fruit from a tree. One was a Northern senator's boy, so the Yankees upped the price on my head—and yearned after it harder, way it seemed. The boy was riding as fine a horse as I ever saw—this dun horse here. Reason I was following 'em, I wanted the horse."

Jubal looked upward with a downcast face. "They hanging for the lady or the hoss?" he asked.

They started up the driveway, walking in the cathedral shade of the grove. Tennessee looked to the end of the stretch of brown gravel, already catching fractional views of ashes, twisted metal, and one skeletal chimney of the dead house. "What difference does it make why they got hung?" he answered Jubal. "They couldn't follow me off, the wife wanted it that way, and I had the horse. Beats me why folks fret and stew over their reasons for doing what they mean to do in spite of hell, anyhow."

"Maybe them devilish Krulls got a hoss you want," Jubal said bitterly. "Maybe you listen to Miss Stella, then. She got *two* fine hosses."

Tennessee's cold eyes turned and steadied on Jubal, causing the big Negro to hold his breath for a long moment, then release it very slowly. Neither spoke again until they had reached the remains of the burned house. Tennessee looked once at the ashes and rubble, then raised his eyes to the backyard and out toward the barn.

"Where's Miss Stella staying now?" he asked.

"She staying yonder where Sebe and Liza live befo' the freedom come." Jubal dragged a sleeve down his face. "Sho hot. She likely inside in the cool. Ain't you gonna stop here and look at the house?"

"What house?"

"Uh, here where the house burn down."

"What for?"

"Some folks like to look," Jubal said uneasily. "They like to remember the good times, what all they done in that old house. When the home gone, they like to remember it. And their folks, too, when their folks gone."

"You talk like a damned fool," Tennessee said, and studied Jubal narrowly. "What *was* the house is just ashes now. What *was* the judge and Paul is just dirt, Jubal. And I ain't got no time to stand wringing my guts over a pile of ashes and two mounds of dirt."

Jubal backed up a step, shaking his head in resignation. "Yonder come Miss Stella," he said sullenly. "You go on talk to her."

The log cabin once occupied by the two house slaves stood in the shade of a mighty red oak at the farthest reach of the wide backyard, sharing the area with the well house, smokehouse, and two other small buildings, the identities of which had been changed several times over the years. The other Negro quarters were strung along a lane leading in the direction of the barn and toolsheds to the east, where the pastures began.

Tennessee had observed the woman come out of the log cabin and halt curiously at the sight of a strange man and horse in the yard. She stepped forward now, out of the shade, and stopped again to look, one arm raised with a hand shading her eyes from the glare of the early-afternoon sun. Above the full skirt and tight bodice of the white dress she wore, her hair was like flame in the sunlight. To Tennessee, even at this distance, she was a compelling sight that made his hands clench hard and the muscles of his stomach contract. Stella McEveride was not the sort of woman he had expected his brother Paul to marry.

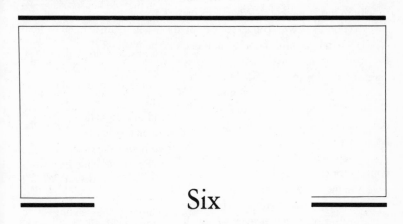

Six

Before she reached him, she said, "Oh, I knew you'd come!" in a breathless, unsteady voice. "I *knew* it!" There were tears in her brown, faintly slanted eyes, Tennessee saw, and at least one tear had rolled down a cheek of her fine-boned, freckled face. She struck at it with an impatient hand and smiled. "You're Tennessee."

"Yes, ma'am," he said, coming to a halt, "I'm Tennessee."

Stella walked in against him without pausing and hugged him hard around his big, hard-muscled body for a brief moment, her head pressed tight against his chest. "Don't call me ma'am," she said, and stepped back to look at him. "You're my big brother. Only one I ever had, too. You've come home!" She bit her lips to still their faint trembling. "*Big* brother is right. Nobody told me you were so big."

Her words came opportunely. They reminded Tennessee McEveride of what he needed to remember—that this woman was also a McEveride, his dead brother's wife, his sister, indeed, by law. Already, despite the fact that her embrace had been wholly natural and innocent, every square inch of his sense-starved flesh where her woman's body had touched him was aware of her. He avoided her eyes, the clean female smell of her vivid in his nostrils. He looked away toward mountain cliffs five miles to the east, seeing them through a shimmering heat that hovered over fields and pastures. He felt like a cougar chained close to meat and was afraid she'd see the beast looking out of his eyes.

"Now, *there's* a horse!" she said, and Tennessee recognized authority in the judgment. "What's his name?"

"I don't know," Tennessee admitted. "Taught him to mind without words when I got him. I don't call him by no name at all."

Stella gave him a strange, sharp-eyed look. "Will he let Jubal take care of him? I want to talk to you inside, out of the sun."

"He'll let anybody lead him off—if I'm in reach and don't mind." Turning, Tennessee called to Jubal, who had remained behind, looking down at the ashes and rubble of the big house, "Hey, Jube! Look after the horse, will you?"

They walked toward the cabin, but the horse stood in his tracks, waiting for Jubal. Stella kept looking over her shoulder. "I didn't see you give him the signal to stand," she said, "but you gave one, so don't lie."

"I never give no signal," Tennessee said.

Stella gave him that same strange look again. Then, once more, she glanced over her shoulder. "What's wrong with Jubal? Was he sulking back there?"

"That's right," Tennessee said. "He's mad because I told him I had to leave tomorrow. Wants me to stay and hunt down the Krull gang."

"I see," Stella said, her back to him as she entered the cabin. "Come in."

Tennessee followed her in, his eyes on her superbly molded back and shoulders, noticing that her lightly tanned, beautifully shaped arms were freckled almost as much as her face. She turned, almost bumping into him, and started back with a smothered imprecation. "Do you have to walk like a cat?" she asked brusquely. Then, before he could answer, her lips twisted in wry apology. "Sorry. Nerves, I guess."

The cabin was Stella's temporary living quarters and office, and it was furnished accordingly: white window curtains, a neat bed at one window, a heavy desk at the other, two straight chairs, a rocking chair, and a multicolored rag rug in the middle of the floor. Everything was spotlessly clean and neat. A door at the back closed the room off from a lean-to addition, which, Tennessee remembered, had been used for cooking and dining in Sebe and Liza's time. Stella turned the chair at the desk and sat down facing Tennessee, who chose the other straight chair, dropping his Confederate hat on the floor beside him.

"You've heard about your father and Paul, of course," Stella said, watching Tennessee with eyes that looked black from where he sat.

Tennessee nodded. "Jubal told me what happened here."

"You've known it just since—" Stella picked up a pen from the desk and studied it carefully. "You've taken the news in stride, I see," she commented, not looking up.

"I'm sorry they're dead," Tennessee said, half his mind on the pronounced contrast between her girl's waist and her woman's breasts, which were strutting the bodice of her dress. "If howling would bring 'em back, I'd howl. But if you want the truth, I'm so used to men killed in this war that the judge and Paul seem like just two more."

"You don't understand," Stella said, making a visible effort to control herself. "The judge and Paul were killed by marauders who *knew* the war was over. The Krulls were never soldiers. They'd be outlaws in war or out, and they struck here to get revenge for that damned Parson Krull, to get revenge on the judge—or, what I believe, on the very name of McEveride. That makes it private, Tennessee. That makes it my business—and *should* make it yours."

"Sure," Tennessee said, "that's the law of it. But the thing is, law don't fence in a war. You can't cram a whole war inside gray and blue uniforms. Measure it that way, I'm no better'n the Krulls. Matter of fact, you can find folks will tell you I'm worse."

"They might be right, too," Stella said bitterly. "Did you hate the judge and Paul so much? Is it because they were not on your side? Is that why you aren't interested in avenging their deaths?"

Tennessee looked at the ceiling. "I don't hate 'em. I never did." He was telling the simple truth. He distrusted hatred wherever he found it, for it destroyed the patterns of self-preservation he could recognize and understand, and it ignored a certain economy in violence that was instinctive to all creatures close to the earth. Anger and fear and greed were motives he could understand and trust—but not hatred. "Don't reckon I've ever hated anybody," he added. "Can't remember anybody, now that I think."

"I believe you," Stella said coldly. "From what I've heard, you've never *loved* anybody. That's why. You've got to love before you care enough to hate. I just hope you find that out someday."

"You're talking wild because you're mad," Tennessee complained. "Now, look. If the Krulls were still around here, I'd kill 'em for what they done. I told Jubal the same thing. But they *ain't* here, and I can't hang around. Only this morning, as a matter of fact, I almost had to shoot my way through soldiers to get down the mountain. Way I figure, they'll be showing up here by tomorrow night or the next day at the latest." He reached for his hat and settled forward with elbows on knees, studying the hat as if he had never seen it before. "Oh, I *could* take to the woods and stay on, I reckon, killing a few Occupationers now and then. I could likely stand a life like that better than most. But I'd rather go off where I can relax and be easy for a while or, if I've got to keep on fighting, go where there's a war and they're hiring soldiers. I've been thinking some of signing on with that French king down in Mexico. Maximilian, his name is. But what I mean is that I'm more liable to run across the Krulls away from here than I am here. And when I come on one, I'll get you word so you can mark him off your list.''

Tennessee thought he was making a farewell speech, explaining his strategic withdrawal from the neighborhood. Actually, his sole objective for the immediate future was to get away from this woman, for already he was having premonitions of disaster if he remained close to her. Merely looking at her filled him with unrest, made him sweat; his recurring impulse was to reach out and take hold of her, to crowd into her at every twist and turn with undeviating intent, like a dog wolf crowding a bitch. If he remained, one day when neither of them expected him to, he'd jump her as sure as death; and, as surely as he knew he would, he knew there'd be hell to pay when he did.

Whatever he meant to say, Tennessee found out soon enough that he had not said farewell. Stella had maintained a keen-eyed, thoughtful silence while he spoke. When he had finished, her whole face expressed a weary acceptance of what he was, as if she were thinking that she knew him now as well as she ever would. Then her face hardened with purpose; she straightened in her chair.

"Tennessee," she said, "I'm under no illusions about you. I can see now for myself what I've gathered from others—that you have about as much soul and heart as some predatory bird. Oh, I'll admit that I'd hoped to find in you more of a sense of honor, more pride, more loyalty—or even more good-dog qualities like simple devotion. But you're pure wolf, my friend." Suddenly she smiled, and Tennessee knew her thereafter as a very dangerous woman. "That's all right, though. It's a wolf, and not a dog, I mean to loose on the Krulls anyhow. I'll never forget your father's last words to me just before he died. 'I was wrong about Tennessee,' he said, meaning that he'd thought you were too uncivilized for the state of Tennessee. 'Wait for him here,' your father said. 'Set him after these goblins.' That's what the judge said, Tennessee, and, so help me God, that's what I'll do, one way or another!''

"Let me ask you one question," Tennessee said evenly. "Where *are* the Krulls? Do you know?''

"I do not," Stella said. "I've hired the Pinkerton Detective Agency to investigate certain areas, though, and I've hired men who know their own sections to watch for them. Believe me, I *will* know eventually.

Personally, I believe they're among the Seminoles in the Florida Everglades. Parson Krull and the Seminoles both have a history with runaway slaves, and the parson has two half-breed sons with him. He's lived among Indians, I know. But that's about all I do know right now.''

Tennessee stared at her. "What you expect *me* to do?" he asked. "Pick up tracks several weeks old and follow 'em straight to the Krulls? I may be a wolf, like you say, but my nose ain't that good.''

"I expect you to stay here until we find a trace of the Krulls," Stella said. "Now, I know, you're wanted by the Union army. But is that new? I know—better than you do, in fact—that you can't stay on here indefinitely. Believe me, I did my best. I tried to buy you a parole, but General Thomas is self-consciously honest, and Governor Brownlow is warped by fanatical hatred of all secessionists. I offered them their bribes in person—properly devious about it, too—but I got absolutely nowhere. Thomas politely excused himself, and Brownlow spewed poison for thirty minutes until I almost became a secessionist myself and took my leave. As I say, I want you to stay on here for a while, taking to the woods if you have to, until a Krull track comes to light somewhere. Then, as I say, I want somebody who's all wolf beside me, for that's a trail I mean to follow myself.''

"You know, I keep thinking you ain't serious." Tennessee stood up from his chair. "I can see myself stalking a camp of man-killers with you tromping brush behind me. Or do I go in and pack 'em out one at a time for you to cut their throats back in the woods?''

Stella looked at him with eyes suddenly turned black and deadly. "Don't ever think I won't cut their throats if I get the chance," she said coolly. "So don't waste your sarcasm on me." Her high-cheeked, freckled face looked angular and tough, making Tennessee wonder how a face could have so much wrong with it and still make every other woman's face he could remember now seem commonplace. "Sit down, Tennessee. I think I've got to tell you what happened in that raid.''

It was a twice-told account of wartime atrocity that Tennessee had heard many times and had a great reluctance to hear again. To forestall it, he said hastily, "I've done heard it all, from Jubal.''

"You haven't heard it from me," Stella said. "The way you act, it might all be something that happened in a book. Maybe I can make you realize why I won't rest until every man on that raid quits breathing the air of this earth. . . ." She told him about hiding the horses and meeting Brownlow Krull in the woods and about the raid on the McEverides that night. Gradually, as color seeped from her face, myriad freckles began to appear. They looked like a spattering of dirt from a handful thrown at her face. Her voice became dogged and monotonous. At least twice, while she was describing Jimpson Krull's treatment of Paul in the living room, she broke off, breathing with difficulty, and then continued in the same monotone. She told how Parson Krull had murdered Judge McEveride, how the parson had sought to inflame Brownlow's lust for her, though Brownlow would have ravished her without persuasion. Then she passed quickly to her loss of consciousness in her battle with Brownlow in the sewing room. Though she sat dry-eyed and staring, her voice began to shake as she told of returning to half-consciousness with water on her face, of either hearing or remembering a terrible cry from Paul that she would never be able to forget, and of catching one glimpse over Brownlow's shoulder of Paul's insanely stricken face just before it had dropped from sight behind Brownlow's intervening body.

At that point in her story, Stella stopped. She was through, her goal reached. By omission, she implied that he could draw on Jubal's account for the rest. But Tennessee had stopped at that point in the story, too. He was almost writhing on his chair in sweating, extreme discomfort. By God, he wanted out of this room into the open air! Never before had it occurred to him that a man's lust might be intensified by the thought of taking a woman in her grief and despair—as Brownlow Krull had taken Stella, as Tennessee himself wanted to take her now.

"How many of the others followed Brownlow in that room and— and—" Tennessee closed his mouth, silently cursing himself for blurting out every stray thought that came home to his chuckleheaded mind.

Stella stared at him for what seemed a full minute. "You fool!" she said finally, in disgust. "What difference does it make? You've missed the whole point of what I told you. Get out of here!" Then, as he crossed the floor and went through the door, she called after him, "I know you're hungry. So come back and eat when you've looked around—or learned some sense."

Stella remained in her chair, listening intently and hearing no sound of his departing footsteps. She felt discouraged and depressed. She had not been completely truthful when she'd told Tennessee that she had been under no illusions about him. Whatever she'd expected his attitude to be regarding avenging the murder of his father and brother, certainly it had not been complete disinterest. Obviously a desire for vengeance had never been a motive for any of his killings, and this knowledge made her shiver.

His attitude toward hatred and vengeance, Stella thought, was like that of some gold-streaked man-eating tiger, and it would be just as frightening—and exciting—to put one's hand upon him as to stroke such a tiger. Indeed, he was in some ways as dangerous as that same great cat—and dangerous in one way the cat wasn't. She was not so blind that she had not seen the lust in him. She knew now the danger that Dr. Broadus had had in mind. It was a danger of weakened will and female response to the male-animal life-giving force. Stella was not immune to her brother-in-law's physical attraction. She admitted to herself that she was stirred by his nearness, and was not alarmed. As she had pointed out to Paul, she was not a mare to be led into some stall. Neither was she a slut to stand for the first tumescent dog that stood on his hind legs. Her prickling nipples and quickened pulses at the sight of his hard-muscled body were normal in a healthy woman, things to be properly evaluated and restrained, but not forgotten. If she succeeded in keeping him with her, as she meant to, her vigilance must never relax. She must keep reminding him—yes, and herself, too, perhaps—that he was her brother-in-law. She must not let fear of the son keep her from meeting the terms of the commission the father had given her.

Outside, Tennessee drew a breath so deep that it molded the home-spun to his great torso for a long moment. What a woman! It was the first time he'd ever been around a woman who made him feel like doffing his hat, bowing low, and asking her pardon one moment and jumping her like a mare-crazed jack the next. He wondered what he had missed in Paul that had attracted her, and, remembering his brother, he suspected that Paul's ghost might prove more successful with the woman than Paul would ever have been. That ghost might have more influence on Paul's brother, too, he thought wryly; it might get him killed, in fact. For he was not the fool Stella thought, or claimed she thought; he knew, of course, which crime of the raid Stella regarded as the one never to be forgotten this side of hell, and it occurred to him that rape was a crime which might be more serious to husbands than to wives. Well, Stella was evidently rich enough to afford an expensive pastime like hunting down Krulls, so men would die because of a look on a husband's face when a wife was raped.

Tennessee moved across a corner of the yard and entered the lane—or old wagon path now, since long sections of the fence had been destroyed and never replaced. He crossed into the orchard south of the barn lot; then he halted, his eyes searching the area where the early-bearing apple trees once had stood, and whispered a savage oath. Ignoring thrifty late-bearers farther off, he waded unerringly through the weeds to a rotten stump that still showed traces of old ax marks. He was still standing there when Jubal rounded a corner of the barn and came over to him, walking fast.

"Marse Tennessee, I plumb forgot something," he said, pitching his voice low and glancing toward Stella's cabin as if he had no conception of what constituted reasonable earshot. "I got to tell you something Miss Stella don't know. Somebody got a roan mule up in them mountains was down here in the yard that night the house burn. Old Mose claim he seed a man riding a mule in the dark 'tween him and the light. Mose laid up with rheumatiz and watching from his back do'. He say the man look like he been hanging around all through the raid. When he pull out, he hit that briar patch back of the lane and scratch through to the pasture, then ride on around the barn and head for the mountains. Me and Mist' Redwing find white and red hair, like roan, on the briars. And, shonuff, like Mose claim, they *was* mule tracks. Mist' Redwing say don't tell Miss Stella 'cause she go up there and try to kill the man without asking him nothing. He sho right, too. Mist' Redwing up there now looking for that man. He been so stretched out, running for Miss Stella, he ain't had no time to look till now."

So long as he could hear the sound of Jubal's voice, Tennessee stood like a figure cast in bronze, never once looking up from the ground, never once asking a question. When the voice had ceased, he raised his cold eyes, somehow looking burly and savage without change from his usual expression.

"Who cut down this tree, Jubal?" he asked evenly.

"Whassat?" Jubal looked around vaguely. "Tree?" Then he saw the stump at Tennessee's feet. "Oh—oh, that there un! Why, sojers done it, suh. They come here looking for hosses one winter day I mean was cold. Made up a big fire right over there while they look. First, they burn fence rails. Then they start piling on fruit trees for the green wood that last better."

"The blue-bellied sons-of-bitches!" Tennessee growled. "Wouldn't been long before that tree would been loaded with ripe apples."

"Marse Tennessee," Jubal said cautiously, "them sojers was Confederate men, suh."

"I don't care who they were," Tennessee said. "I say goddamn 'em for sons-of-bitches! I counted on some apples from that tree."

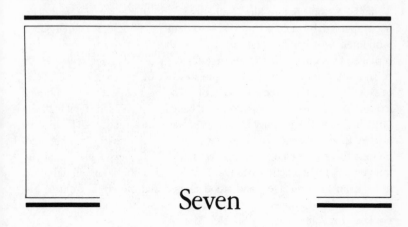

Seven

Tennessee leaned on the picket fence and looked at the graves, wondering what he was supposed to feel as he looked—what Jubal and Stella figured he *ought* to feel. It was God's truth that he had no interest whatever in either the new graves or the old ones. For him death had never had much dignity or mystery, and now it had none; it provoked in him no speculation. His was the realism of the beating heart; his only definite objective in life was to keep on living, regardless of the cost to himself or to others. For the most part, therefore, he'd come up to the knoll to have his look down the road toward the Overton Pike, knowing from experience that traveling bluecoats were usually careless about how much dust their horses kicked up.

In some way, though, he was visiting the graves because he knew that Stella and Jubal expected him to. He had no desire to hurt others and would not do so where his choice was even, as it was here. Anyway, he couldn't stand all day in one place. He was restless, at loose ends, eager to be gone from a place that had no living present and no discernible future, that had only the shattered and barren reminders of a dead past. Once he'd learned well the past's lessons in self-preservation, Tennessee McEveride had little further use for the past.

Tennessee's memories of his father usually called up the image of a handsome and dignified gray-mustached gentleman whose countenance was marked by a look of concern. Indeed, as the boy was growing up,

Judge McEveride usually had had reason to look concerned whenever
Tennessee stood before him. Sometimes, too, the expression had been
accompanied by a look of wary puzzlement, as if the veteran jurist
wondered whether his firstborn had not been whisked from crib and
replaced by a changeling in revenge for the judge's having sentenced to
prison some long-memoried lawbreaker out of his past. One of Tennessee's most vivid recollections of standing before those combined
expressions on the judge's face harked back to the day of his fight with the
Gilly boys and Buck Henry Lynch. Paul was thirteen and small for his age
at that time, whereas Tennessee was sixteen and nearly two hundred
pounds of cat-muscled youth six feet tall. But Tennessee had felt about
ten years old when he reached the front yard that afternoon, all lightness
gone from his tired feet, and stood ragged and bloody in front of his
father. Paul had stopped crying a mile or so down the road but still could
not keep back an occasional sniffle.

"Both horses came home," the judge said, obviously dreading to
hear what had happened. "I was getting ready to go look. How—what in
the world—"

"I told Paul to hold 'em," Tennessee said. "But he turned loose the
reins, and the horses run off."

"I—I was just—just trying to *help* you!" Paul started crying again.

"What happened?" the judge demanded sternly.

Tennessee shrugged wearily. "Reckon you got to know. Them two
Gilly brothers jumped me about a mile this side of Coley's Mill. Them
and that bully cousin of theirs, Buck Henry Lynch."

The judge's face darkened with anger. "You mean those three
grown men attacked you two boys?"

Tennessee shook his head. "*One* of us boys. Me. Mainly, though, it
was Simp and Buck Henry that come at me. Lew Gilly kept circling to get
at my back and never done much."

The judge eyed Paul's swollen cheek. "How'd Paul get hurt?"

"I hit him," Tennessee admitted.

"And I was only trying to *help* you!" Paul's voice was choked with
self-pity.

The judge sighed. "Why did you hit him?"

"Had to knock him out of my way. They's coming at me with knives
and Lew circling around with a club. Lucky I had my bowie knife along.
Just had it sharpened at the mill. I mean, I had to move faster'n I ever
done before. With Paul in my way I could've got killed. And *he* could've
got cut up bad. Because that knife of mine, it sure ain't got no eyes."

"*Hasn't any* eyes," the judge corrected him. "Are you hurt? All that blood—"

"It ain't *my* blood."

"*Isn't.*" Suddenly the judge seemed to brace himself. "Give it to me, Tennessee. The whole thing. How'd you get clear?"

"Well, I got lucky right off with Buck Henry Lynch. Then I had more time for Simp Gilly. And Lew Gilly took off like a dog-bit shote when he saw 'em both on the ground. He's lucky I didn't have no gun, or I'd got all three."

This time the judge overlooked Tennessee's defective grammar. The look of dread was more pronounced on his face. "Are you *sure* about what you did?" he asked with forced calm. "Are they dead?"

"Good chance Buck Henry is. Could've hit the big vein in his throat, way the blood flew. And I cut Simp up pretty bad. I never looked to see *how* bad."

Shaking his head dazedly, the judge half-turned and squinted down the Overton Pike as if he expected to see the dust of approaching horses. "Paul, go in the house and tell Liza to doctor your face."

When the boy had trudged off, Tennessee asked quietly, "You want me to leave home, sir?"

"You wouldn't mind that much, would you, boy?" The judge studied Tennessee's face with troubled eyes. "No, I'll stand by you. It had to be self-defense. When three men, all past twenty, attack a boy of sixteen, no matter what—" He broke off, obviously remembering an area he had not probed. "Tennessee, why did those ruffians try to kill you? What had you done?"

Tennessee's eyes dropped. The silence lengthened. Finally, still looking down, the boy answered in a low voice, "Simp caught me in the bushes with his sister. I didn't know how much he saw because he didn't do nothing then but order her home. But I reckon he saw enough. What he was waiting for was help—from Buck Henry and Lew."

A look approaching horror had been growing on the judge's face. "Tennessee, so help me God, if you've been scoundrel enough to violate that little Betty Sue Gilly—by God, and her a mere child!—I'll personally see to it that—"

"Not Betty Sue!" Tennessee protested angrily. "I'm talking about that other sister, Flora Belle."

"Why, she's twenty-two or -three years old!" the judge exclaimed. "And her with a husband killed by a falling tree less than two months ago." His face turned wry, as if he had bitten into something rotten.

"Ah, well, they're low-born, I reckon, those Gillys. Anyhow, that Flora Belle is too old for you to be fooling around with."

"Reckon I didn't have her age in mind," Tennessee said. "And she never mentioned mine."

"Son, son," the judge groaned, "what in God's name am I going to do with you? If you aren't off roaming the mountains for months on end without letting a soul know where you are—"

"Told you I'd tell you before I went on another long hunt." The boy's cold eyes met the judge's squarely. "And I'll promise you something else. I won't go off to the bushes with no twelve-year-old girl, neither."

"*Any* twelve-year-old girl, *either*," said the judge. But he was pleased by Tennessee's resentment, evidently thinking that he'd discovered an adherence to code or principle where he had not been certain it could be found. "I apologize, of course, for doubting your sense of honor, son."

"I don't understand how you could think it," Tennessee said. "That little old Betty Sue Gilly ain't hardly got no kind of tits even started yet."

The new mounds of earth were side by side. They were still unmarked, but for some reason Tennessee picked the one on the right as Paul's grave, and he wondered what he could possibly remember about his brother that would give meaning to that mound of earth under which Paul was rotting down to a one-legged skeleton. Nothing. Not a damned thing. Tennessee had never been quite certain of his feelings for Paul when the latter was a young boy. He'd liked the little fellow well enough, he reckoned, but no two brothers were ever more different. Everybody who knew them had pointed that out. Paul had been shy, sensitive, studious, with far more courage than strength.

Tennessee was better acquainted with his feelings, of course, after Paul had grown up so consciously and stubbornly noble that he became a damned Lincolnite and joined the Union army—one of the thirty thousand east Tennesseans to do so. But they'd shaken hands and turned their backs on each other without much bitterness. He *had* hit Paul with his fist again, though, after they'd gone their separate ways in the war. He'd had no choice. That second blow had been delivered in a Union encampment near Chattanooga a month before Paul lost his leg at Chickamauga.

For a month Rosecrans's war-worn army had been recruiting its strength at Stevenson, Alabama, in preparation for moving on Bragg's forces in mountain-locked Chattanooga. The eyes of Bragg's army were watching the mountain passes and valley approaches along the river, and Forrest's partisan scouts were scattered over the area, gathering and evaluating information on enemy movements. From the branches of a great oak high on Stringer's Ridge, Tennessee had looked down on some military action that he had found extremely puzzling. Northern artillery was throwing shells across the river into Chattanooga, and blue-clad soldiers were massing as if to force a crossing of the Tennessee River. But from the heights Tennessee could see what Bragg's men in Chattanooga could not—that there were too few men engaged in the action, or available for it, to make it a serious threat. He decided, therefore, to prowl the enemy encampment that night and try to discover what was afoot.

The size of the first sentry he encountered—and put to sleep with the barrel of a Navy Colt—suggested the dangers of a gray uniform among Union soldiers. So he risked hanging by wearing the sentry's Union blue and carrying the soldier's musket through enemy lines into the sleeping camp. Skirting pools of moonlight and keeping to darkest shadows where possible, he faded past dying campfires and recumbent figures, pausing under trees to listen to drowsy conversation. Taking his time, he moved unerringly to the area where orderlies had pitched the officers' tents. The soldiers were sleeping too soundly for men expecting a big river crossing under battle conditions on the morrow. He felt that if he could identify one officer here, he would have all the information he needed. Selecting the nearest tent, which had its flaps tied back because of the August heat, he slid inside out of the bright moonlight and bent over the single occupant, who was lying face upward, sound asleep. He stopped breathing at the sight of the face. It was clearly visible, and there was no mistake. It was his brother, and Paul was serving as a lieutenant under Crittenden, who, in his turn, was one of Rosecrans's generals. So the action here on the part of Crittenden's corps was dust raised to screen from view the movement of Rosecrans's main army. Suddenly Tennessee knew that Rosecrans was coming—horse, foot, and guns—straight up the back-breaking mountain slopes and across the precipices. If the Confederates caught him among those rocky funnels, they could ruin him. Tennessee knew also that it was time he pulled foot out of here and carried the word.

But as he started to move, he found himself looking down into Paul Smith McEveride's wide-open eyes.

"What is it?" Paul asked swiftly, and rubbed his eyes. Then he came scrambling up to his feet. "Tennessee!" he hissed.

"Quiet," Tennessee said softly. "Don't wake the camp."

Paul's eyes flared wide with alarm. "Why, I'll *have* to!" he moaned. "I've got no choice. Oh, God, Tennessee, are you mad? And in that uniform! Don't you know they'll hang you?"

"Not 'less they catch me first."

"But you're caught now!" Paul's face looked twisted with pain. "I can't let you go. Even if this weren't a secret maneuver, I couldn't."

"Since I'm caught, then, what's the secret maneuver supposed to hide?"

"If this were anybody but me, you'd cut my throat or crack my skull," Paul lamented. "But you aren't dedicated to your cause enough to do that, are you?"

"Reckon not."

"I *have* to give the alarm! It's my duty. And you'll *hang*, Tennessee! God help us both, for I'm going to yell!"

He opened his mouth, and Tennessee swung hard. Afterward Tennessee always thought that in the last split-second before the fist landed, Paul had leaned forward slightly; he had almost seemed to hold his chin out to meet the fist. Then he was flat on his back with what looked to Tennessee like the barest trace of a smile on his unconscious face.

That was the last time he ever saw Paul.

Now Tennessee's primitive urges were prompting him to get his horse and ride out, indifferent to what Stella and Jubal might think of him, since he would likely see neither again. He would have done so save that he knew he was not indifferent. He knew somehow that he would not want to leave if Paul were alive; he would attend Stella as single-mindedly as a stallion attends a mare in season, for the flimsy barrier of her marriage to Paul would mean nothing to him—if Paul were alive. He found it unreasonable to expect a man to feel a sense of kinship for a woman just because she was sleeping with his brother. With Paul dead, though, the widow occupied a chaste bed and claimed kinship with her brother-in-law, and somehow the claim stood against all logic, pointing an ancient taboo.

Turning his head, he looked up the cove to the great escarpment of the mountain, seeing an eagle swing down from the crags and sail out over lower timber. He thought of John Redwing up there somewhere—of John Redwing hunting a man who owned a roan mule. Something to do. . . . And there, all in a moment, without fitting the parts together, he had the excuse he sought.

He faded down the path to the edge of the yard, where a thicket of black locusts had sprung up and grown rank in the last four years. Instead of keeping to the path, he passed through the thicket and saw Jubal leaning against a tree up the yard, watching the knoll. Tennessee moved up behind the big Negro and said, "Jubal," in his deep, soft voice.

Jubal bounded into the air, wheeling, and landed in a crouch, his eyes flaring with shock. "How—how you get—know I seed—" He straightened up, breathing gustily. "*Lawd God*, you like to skeer the daylights outa me!" He groaned lugubriously. "Don't *do* that, Marse Tennessee!"

"What the hell's wrong with you?" Tennessee said. "You know I don't fool with folks like that. Good way to get a bullet or knife in your guts." He studied Jubal thoughtfully. "Don't seem like I come up that quiet, anyhow. Jube, you don't reckon your ears been failing some of late?"

"Why, I ain't no older'n what you is!" Jubal protested. "Twenty-six, ain't it? Nossuh, co'se they ain't failing." Then his eyes began to prowl uneasily. "Co'se, if I *don't* hear what I—don't hear—how I know if I ought to?"

"I was thinking about that night of the raid," Tennessee said. "About somebody slipping up and knocking you on the head. Man could left his mule and walked in, ready to claim business with the judge if you saw him . . . . But I reckon not. More likely one of the half-breeds done it—probably Brownlow Krull. From what I hear, Jimpson would killed you for the fun of it."

"It sho that devilish Jimpson, then," Jubal decided. "He done his best. I's so addled when I run to the house I run smack ag'in' that Yankee sojer on the hoss."

"You see that Yankee good?"

"I seed him plain as you while I look. Just had a face-looking kind of face. Mean eyes, though. Co'se I didn't have long to look. Mist' Redwing went to see that old Tinker Dave Beatty and ask if he know what Yankee sojer had truck with them Krulls in the war, but old Tinker wouldn't tell him nothing."

"Probably told all he knew," Tennessee said. "Tinker Dave had *his* truck with Dr. Jonathan Hale, Union army chief of scouts. But I don't think Dr. Hale ever used them Krull bastards. Redwing ought to checked out the small-time rogues. Like Hard Hampton, maybe." Tennessee glanced toward Stella's cabin. "Think I'll go up the mountain and help John Redwing find that roan mule. You got any idea where John's likely to be about dusk?"

"Ain't much telling where he apt to be." Jubal braced himself with a hand against a tree, head lowered in thought. "He camp sometime at the Rock House Cave—where us three sleep the night that old panther tom kilt half our dogs. Might pick up his hoss tracks, he gone from there." Then he straightened, dropping his hand from the tree. "Hold on. Seem like he did name it one day he aim to mosey over Fiddler Creek way first chance he get. Didn't say why. Get him a jug, maybe. Fox Wilkins, he got a still up on Fiddler Creek. He kept the judge in whiskey while the war going on. Brung it down regular."

Tennessee nodded. "Why, you've likely treed the damn redskin—at that still." He looked toward Stella's cabin again. "Jube, you go fetch my horse. Bring him down in front of Miss Stella's door. I aim to find that red mule before another day dawns."

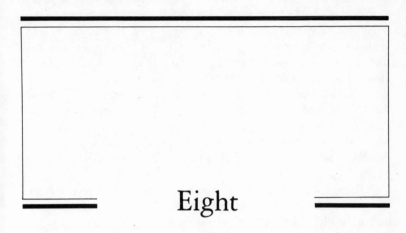

Eight

Tennessee rode out through the south pasture in late afternoon, taking the route the man on the roan mule had followed, striking directly for the escarpment. He was leaving temptation in the form of Stella McEveride behind him for good, he hoped. He sat loose in the saddle as the iron-mettled dun, freshened by grain and rest, stepped out through the weed-crowded grass as if fording a wide, shallow stream.

Dusk had thickened to near-darkness in the cove before Tennessee turned the last switchback and rode up through a break in the escarpment to the mountain plateau. A red bank of cumulus clouds in the west reflected the last light of day on top, and Tennessee gave the dun no rest after the climb. He wanted to reach the Rock House Cave while there was still light enough to check for signs if he failed to find John Redwing camping there. Heading the dun straight toward a point several miles to the southeast, where the cave formed the hollow foot of a broken ridge, he rode through the deepening gloom of oaks and pines, heeding an animal instinct for direction more accurate than any compass. He had never been lost in his life.

After an hour's steady progress, however, with darkness gathering rapidly under the trees, he pulled the horse up and sat there, making up his mind. Darkness would beat him to the cave, he knew now, and the thin edge of a low-hanging moon told him that he would do no trailing tonight. In any case there was a quicker way of learning whether Redwing was encamped at the Rock House.

Traveling due east, he rode to the foot of a pine-covered ridge that loomed high-backed above the surrounding country and sent the big horse along a steep, brushy slope, angling upward. On the crest Tennessee drew up under brooding pine trees and listened to the hooting owls as they hallooed back and forth across the dark woods, the hard, handsome cast of his face turning pleasant. The night life of the forest was beginning. Creatures that shunned daylight were stirring forth, moving abroad, the hunting and the hunted. Covered by darkness and remote from people, here was the old, beautiful land again—the old land before the war had come, with its trampling armies of heavy-footed men, its damned interference and regimentation, its wanton and massive change. . . .

Dismounting, Tennessee moved out in front of the horse. Holding his cupped hands to form a trumpet, he drew in his breath and suddenly hurled the high, blood-chilling scream of the Southern panther out over the shrouded forest toward the Rock House Cave.

"*Hiii-yeee-ahhoww!*"

The big dun crouched as if struck by a sudden weight, then stood trembling, and all save far-off voices of the night were stricken mute. After waiting a full minute Tennessee sent forth a second panther scream, then stepped back and placed a hand on the horse's neck. If John Redwing was in hearing distance, he would answer now. Tennessee stood listening, his ears ringing with what passes for silence in a forest, where stillness is never absolute.

Then it came—a far, faint "*Hiii-eee-yahh!*"

John Redwing had camped for the night at the Rock House Cave. Tennessee swung back into the saddle and sent the horse downslope.

Deep in the woods the trees thinned to a straggle over perhaps a dozen acres, forming a near-glade where soon the grass would be belly high to a horse. Tennessee reined in and sat his horse back in the shadows with the open before him. Soon John Redwing came riding out of the trees across the way.

"That cougar squall was real good," Redwing said as they pulled up. "Way it run the hollows without talking back, I wasn't sure. Timing on the second's what give it away. Followed too soon."

"You ain't changed," Tennessee observed sardonically. "The fact that cougars are mighty scarce around here—*that* never entered your head. It was the timing. Different with me. If I heard right, your cat hollered back and forth. Things get close, maybe you better screech like an owl."

The Cherokee grinned, a flash of white against the darkness of face.

"You got a cat's throat to go with the rest of you," he said. "I ain't. Tell me about yourself, Tennessee. Funny I never run into you anywhere. One day I swore I'd cut your trail for sure, but damn me if I didn't follow the sign right up to an epidemic of smallpox. Mrs. McEveride sent me down to Alabama. . . ."

"We can palaver some other time," Tennessee interrupted. "If you ain't found that roan mule, we got a long ride ahead of us. To Hard Hampton's house. I aim to shortcut this thing."

"Jubal told you, huh?" Redwing said. "Well, I've done found that mule. I hunted him down in my mind, and he was right where I thought."

"At Fox Wilkins's place?"

The Cherokee leaned out from the saddle, staring at Tennessee. "Now, how the hell did you know that?"

"It figured to be him."

"It never done no such thing," Redwing denied. "Not to you, it didn't. It took me weeks, and you don't know what I know."

"Well, Jube did mention you aimed to make a trip over Fiddler's Creek way," Tennessee admitted. "So I took over some of your figures. Fox Wilkins was one man in these parts the guerrillas left alone. He made regular trips down to the judge with whiskey. The Krulls wouldn't just ride in without somebody told them what to expect when they got there. So Fox looked prime to me."

"The bastard's prime, all right," Redwing swore. "He's got his cut of McEveride plunder stored in a back room of his shack. Room's packed mightnear full with household goods and stuff from no telling where all. He must've been trading or working with Hampton and Mizer and all the rest. The Krulls sure never took all that stuff. Tennessee, you'll swear he's a man turned pack rat when you see that room."

"I reckon he invited you in to see his collection," Tennessee said.

"He didn't have no chance to be sociable," Redwing explained. "I waited up on a ridge back of his place till he left with a mule-load of garden truck. Then I drifted down through a corn patch to the barn and found the roan mule. That mule, by the way—it was in the Krull pack string a couple days before the raid. Well, to make it short, Fox's woman went off to the spring with a water bucket after a while, and I sneaked in the house and found the room. Been trying to decide whether to brace Fox about the Krulls or go tell Mrs. McEveride. Truth is, I didn't expect you back. I'm right relieved."

"Well," Tennessee suggested, "let's go ask Fox where the Krulls are."

"What if he won't say?"

Tennessee's cold eyes surveyed Redwing briefly. "Now there's a fool question. You know he'll tell us."

"That's a thing I *don't* know," Redwing insisted. "My guess is he's the kind will purse up his mouth against all hell and won't give up the time of day."

"He's a new kind I never saw, then," Tennessee said. "You lead off. I ain't sure of the way to his place."

Riding east, they followed woods paths and old wagon traces until they struck a dirt snake of a road that had its head in the lowlands below the escarpment and its body and tail winding among the hills of the great mountain plateau. An hour later they turned off through the woods onto a side road that Tennessee would have missed in the dim starlight if he had not been following John Redwing. Finally they found themselves crossing and recrossing the narrow shallows of Fiddler's Creek. Tennessee could soon smell green corn and hear it whispering on the shrouded slopes of a wide, rough hollow.

Redwing pulled up his mount and waited for Tennessee to draw abreast. "We turn that outcrop of rock, you'll see the house and barn," he said. "You got your questions memorized good?"

In the dull light Tennessee's face was like a study in bronze. "He got a dog?" he asked.

"Had one," the Cherokee answered dryly. "Old shepherd kind of dog that was company for the woman. Seems he cornered a wildcat in Fox's chicken house once and lost both eyes. Still a big, strong dog, though—could smell his way good enough. But if he couldn't see, he could eat. So one day Fox went out to him with a knife instead of his pan of scraps. The woman was near crazy, begging and crying—the dog like as not being the only thing on the place treated her like a human. But Fox, he weighed the table scraps against the woman's grief and saw where he could feed the scraps to his hogs and get it back in meat. Naturally, a practical man like Fox, he didn't have no choice. They claim he had to knock the woman down to get past her. Then he cut the dog's throat."

"Damned if you ain't in voice tonight," Tennessee growled. "All I asked was did he own a dog. Let's hitch the horses somewhere and walk in."

"What for?" Redwing wanted to know. "He don't know we're after him."

"He knows what he's done. I don't want no stray bullet finding this horse of mine."

Where the road heaved up over the creek bank, they tied bridle reins to persimmon trees and walked toward the house. As they entered the yard, grotesque shapes began rising between them and the lamplight from the cabin—part of the litter Fox Wilkins had drawn about his nest: old wagons and wagon parts, a broken-down surrey, farm tools, piles of fruit jars, empty crates, and rubbish of many kinds.

Twenty yards from the door Tennessee touched Redwing's arm, and they came to a halt. "Make him think I come alone," he whispered. Then he yelled in a voice of iron, "*Hello, the house! You in there—Fox Wilkins!*"

From inside came the sudden bumping of a chair, as if someone had left a rocker hastily, setting it in motion. After a moment a woman's complaining voice droned a question that was answered by the hushed snarl of a man near the door.

"Fox Wilkins!" Tennessee bawled again.

Finally a cautious answer came. "Who's out there?"

"Tennessee McEveride. Open up. Want to talk to you."

Beyond the door there was breathless silence. The rocker's motion slowed and died. Then Fox Wilkins asked through the closed door, "Who's with you, Mr. McEveride?"

"Nobody. Who'd you expect?"

Inside, a loose board creaked, as if somebody were moving on stealthy feet. The creaking sound was followed by an audible expulsion of pent-up breath. But when Fox Wilkins spoke again, his voice was ingratiating and hospitable—and as false as the glowing animation of first fever.

"Hold on a minute, Mr. McEveride," Wilkins called. "I'm all stove up in here. Been too weak to tote out the slop all day. But don't you stir a step till Marthy fetches a light or you'll tangle your feet in them trading goods out there. God knows I'm too poor to roof 'em over right. Marthy, old gal, take this here lantern out to Mr. McEveride. Don't never get tied to your chair with miseries, Mr. McEveride. Damn blue-belly soldiers told me you's back. Proud you come a-visiting so neighborly. Want to talk to you about a piece of land down below. Might buy, you'd sell it reasonable to a poor man." Suddenly his voice dropped to a fierce, urgent whisper not intended for Tennessee's ears. "Ah, you trifling slut! *Move*, goddamn you!" Then, instantly, it was directed again to the outside. "Now, don't you move a foot, Mr. McEveride, till you get that lantern light. Then you come on in and sample this here jug I got beside my chair, without it won't cost you a cent, neither—and welcome as the rain, God knows."

Tennessee stood very still, listening with attention to the false, uneven voice, and knew that the man was moving in a sweat as he talked.

Finally, when the voice leaped away in the night, Tennessee knew that a door had opened at the back of the house.

Closing a hand on Redwing's arm, he said quickly, "Keep out of that lantern light," and wheeled away toward the corner of the lighted room. He slid around the corner and swept along the wall in a long, running dive, coming to earth near the far corner with barely a sound. So certain was he of Fox Wilkins's intentions that he felt no surprise whatever when the barrel of a long gun came snaking around the corner and the hunched shape of a man followed it stealthily into view. Rather, he felt a grim satisfaction in observing anew that fear and greed, especially when combined with a ratlike courage, made a wily man's conduct predictable in a given situation.

When the stalker was almost on top of him, Tennessee exploded up from the ground, knocking the gun skyward with one hand and wheeling the man savagely about-face with the other. Fire and thunder rent the night as both barrels of the shotgun were triggered by trapped fingers, and the gun fell away in the darkness. Whining and grunting, the man fought desperately as Tennessee caught him from behind by his right arm and left shoulder. He tried to stamp Tennessee's feet, kicked backward for shins, and swung his head with wide mouth and ready teeth. Holding the shoulder in a bear-trap grip, Tennessee jerked the man's arm back and up with all his strength, hitting the small of his back with a knee for leverage, and somewhere a bone broke with a dull crunch. The man howled like a dog and slumped, hung in Tennessee's hands, moaning and cursing brokenly.

The woman was standing in the open doorway with a lantern in her hand when Tennessee thrust Fox Wilkins around the corner and conducted him up the steps. Her graying hair was strained back to a sparse knot, and numerous escaped wisps strayed about her gaunt, sallow face. Her eyes, lackluster and expressionless, never seemed to leave her husband's face.

"You better step back, ma'am, and set that lantern on the floor," Tennessee said, practically lifting the groaning Wilkins up the steps. "Don't blow it out, though. You'll be needing it right away."

Mrs. Wilkins stepped slowly from the doorway and bent to set the lantern carefully on the floor. Then she straightened and stood with her hands rolled into her faded Mother Hubbard, watching Tennessee shove her husband into a straight chair before the cold andirons of the empty fireplace. Wilkins, a stocky man, had a long-jawed face marked by small, bright eyes and a wide, down-slashed, troutlike mouth that was partially screened by scraggly, rust-colored whiskers. In contrast to the standard mountain dress of his wife, he was wearing dark woolen trousers and a white silk shirt, though he had never been known to wear better clothes than denim or homespun on his trips to Overton. At the moment his face was greasy with sweat, twisted with pain; but his small, shrewd eyes were everywhere at once, evaluating, seeking some unseen avenue of escape.

"I couldn't noways get myself up to do it, Fox," Mrs. Wilkins explained in a dreary voice. "I just couldn't. I taken the lantern up, but the Lord held me back at the door. One thing I never done yet is help you kill a man, Fox."

"*Kill, hell!*" Fox Wilkins shouted in furious amazement. He lunged up against Tennessee's hand and fell back into the chair. "God a'mighty!... Look, I heared something out back as I answered Mr. McEveride. Thought a varmint was after my chickens. Goddamn it, woman, get out of here!... She ain't right, Mr. McEveride. Fact, she's crazier'n a damn Bessie-bug. You got a wife? Don't never marry no woman. They're cheaper rented, you take my word. You ain't stuck with 'em when they dry up and can't do nothing but eat, neither."

Tennessee looked down at him with cold, inscrutable eyes. "Ma'am, you got any folks you can stay with tonight?" he inquired gently.

"My sister and her man live over on Pine Ridge, Mr. McEveride," the woman said incuriously. "It's two miles to her house. I've rode it muleback at night before, though." She dropped her eyes. "When I've been drove out of my own house to make room for rogues and their camp women. I reckon I can ride it again."

"Ah, you lying bitch!" Fox Wilkins groaned. "She ain't responsible, Mr. McEveride. Marthy, I mean you better not stir a foot outside of this house. You do, so help me, I'll—"

"You get whatever wrap you need and light out, then, Mrs. Wilkins," Tennessee suggested. "You wouldn't want to see what's done here, ma'am. You can come back tomorrow and get your things or do what you want. But you better go right now."

The woman's dull eyes clung steadily to her husband's glistening, wet-haired face. "Do you aim to kill him for what he done, Mr. McEveride?" she asked tonelessly.

"I reckon so, ma'am," Tennessee said, studying the woman's grave-lined profile. "He helped the Krull gang raid my folks. That's why he thought he'd kill me tonight. I aim to get out of him what he knows

about the Krulls.'' He turned his cold eyes back to check Wilkins's
sudden stillness. ''After I get the information, though, I can't see my way
to let him live.''

There was no change whatever in the woman's gaunt face. ''Why,
no,'' she murmured, ''I couldn't ask you to do that. You got to do what's
the Lord's will, I reckon. Whatever happens, why, it's the Lord's will,
like the Good Book says, and I wouldn't have it no other way. You aim to
hang Fox, Mr. McEveride?''

Tennessee glanced at Redwing, who had followed them into the
cabin, and found the Cherokee jaw-locked and staring. ''Why, no,
ma'am,'' he said. ''I hadn't counted on going to all that trouble.''

Again Fox Wilkins rebounded from Tennessee's hand. Wind and
words filled his gaping trout's mouth, and his bright, cold eyes glittered
over the three faces, flashing about the room. ''*Hang me!*'' he cried in a
strangled voice. ''You see? I told you, huh? All I done for the hag, she
wants me dead! You want help, get money. Don't get no woman.''

The woman had never stopped looking at her husband's face. ''It's
the Lord's will, not mine, Fox,'' she said in the same toneless voice. ''I
don't grudge you none for all the whores and licks and cruel, mean ways
you've sorrowed me with. And I aim to see that your soul gets saved,
Fox. I've done spoke more'n once to Brother Harkins to preach you up
from the funeral. I vow it's worried me sick these last years, fearing your
meanness would get you killed far off without me knowing and no
preacher handy to lift you up. Why, it's better so. You tell Mr.
McEveride what he wants and lay down to your rest, Fox.''

''You want to help me,'' Fox Wilkins shouted, ''get the hell out that
door, you holy slut! Go pray naked in the bushes with that psalm-singing
Harkins bastard, for all I care!'' He dragged his good hand down his face
from forehead to chin and slowly rubbed it dry on the leg of his trousers.
Then he looked at Tennessee from under his brows, small-eyed and
cagey. ''Listen, Mr. McEveride, you claim I've knowed them Krulls.
Well, now, I don't admit it for a minute, mind you. But say I did. Seems
like what I knowed be worth money to a rich woman like Mrs. McEveride. It would *if* I knowed where they was, say—which I ain't admitting
nothing, you understand.''

John Redwing took Mrs. Wilkins by the arm and led her toward the
door. ''Come, ma'am,'' he said courteously. ''I'll saddle your mule.
You want me to ride over to your sister's with you?''

The woman shook her head and moved away from his hand. ''I'd be
scareder in the woods with an Injun than by myself,'' she said frankly.

"I'll thank you kindly, though, to saddle up for me. You go on while I get my coat." She trudged to the side door and stepped outside.

Tennessee looked at Redwing. The Cherokee opened his mouth to speak, then changed his mind and, turning, went out into the night. Tennessee drew up a chair and sat with elbows on knees, watching the sweating Wilkins with patient, ruthless eyes.

When Mrs. Wilkins reentered the room, she had a coat of some sort folded over an arm and was carrying a gallon jug. She set the jug down by Tennessee's chair. "There's the whiskey he promised you," she said, rolling her hands into the coat as if it were a muff. "Do you aim to burn the house over him, Mr. McEveride?"

"No, ma'am," Tennessee said, barely making himself heard above Wilkins's inarticulate cursing. "Never entered my head."

"You're right kind," the woman said. "If he was burnt up, I vow I don't know what Brother Harkins could do. I hope you won't bury him, neither, but just leave him lay, Mr. McEveride. It might be unsafe for him to lay in the ground all night before he's preached up and funeraled."

"I won't, Mrs. Wilkins."

"I thank you kindly," the woman said, taking a last look at the naked hatred crawling in her husband's eyes. "I reckon I'll be going now, Fox. And I ain't worried. Brother Harkins never fails to preach his men up to heaven, no matter how wicked and lost some of 'em was. So if it's God's will, I'll see you soon in a better place."

"I'll see you in hell before you ever set foot in *this* house again!" Fox Wilkins shrilled. Then, as the woman picked up the lantern and passed through the doorway into the night, he looked into Tennessee's cold eyes and came bolt upright in his chair, screaming after the woman in a voice as nerve-racking as the squealing of a stuck pig, "I see it all, goddamn you! You want my money—with me dead! Well, look for it—and pray for it—and be damned! You won't never find where a nickel of it's hid, by God!" Suddenly he closed his wide mouth, his eyes almost popping with the strain of trying to see beyond the open doorway into the darkness. Finally, when no response of any kind was heard, his voice came again, a voice that might have recalled a woman who had more concern for the material man and less for the spiritual. "Marthy, come back, for God's sake! We'll pay this McEveride killer off, Marthy. I'll get religion—join the church—be good to you. Please, Marthy. . . ."

Sometime later, after the sounds of a walking mule had passed in front of the house and died in the creek-bed road, John Redwing appeared in the doorway, stood a moment regarding Tennessee with somber speculation, then stepped into the room. "You tell her the truth?" he asked, as if Fox Wilkins were a piece of furniture. "You figure to kill him after he tells you all he knows?"

Tennessee nodded, without removing his eyes from Wilkins's pain-racked face, which had now faded to a fish-belly white. "Can't leave him loose. Why pack him down the mountain?"

"But how's this chinch-bug important? Turn him loose. He'll run right out the country."

"God, yes!" Fox Wilkins inserted quickly. "I will, so help me! I'll leave the country for good. But I swear to God I never went on no raid with them Krulls. First I knowed what happened to your folks, them Krulls come by here to trade and—"

"You mangy bastard!" Redwing snarled. "You think I'm interested in what happens to you?"

Tennessee stood up and moved to the doorway, where he stood listening for sound in the night. Then, reaching to a scabbard attached horizontally to his belt at the back, he turned with a long, thin-bladed knife in his hand. "Reckon she's far enough off," he murmured, and stepped toward the chair where Fox Wilkins cowered. "Fox, I ain't going to ask you but once. All I want from you is where the Krulls are and the names and descriptions of every man who had a hand in that raid. For your sake, I sure hope you know where they went."

Now, run to earth against solid rock, as it were, Fox Wilkins was undergoing a strange transformation. Slowly his wide mouth closed and pursed up thoughtfully. His bright eyes grew smaller, shrewd, and sly. He was the trader again. His confidence was returning in halting rushes.

"Oh, I know, all right—know where they claimed they was headed," he admitted readily. Then, as if frightened by his own boldness, he began a retreat. "Course, I just picked up a word now and then. I didn't have no real truck with them fellers, Mr. McEveride." Instantly, as if afraid he'd shifted to unfortified ground, he grew bold again. "But if I got something you need, it's worth money. Now here's my proposition, Mr. McEveride. Take it or leave it. You give me, say, a hundred dollars and a chance to pack my stuff and move out, and I'll tell you a heap more'n you ever allowed to get out of me. Refuse me either one, I won't tell you nothing. Oh, I'll admit you had my wind up a mite before I thought. But not no more. So don't give me none of that torture talk. You ain't one of them Krull half-breeds. *I* may be low-down, but you ain't. Oh, sure, you're a real bad one in a stand-up fight, but you're one of these here Southern gentlemen that puts a heap of store on honor and fair play and such like. You just ain't got it in you to feed a blade into a poor old man who's bone-broke and helpless and can't fight back. Why, come down to it, you're more like to doctor me up than murder me. Ain't I right, Mr. McEveride? Now, own up. Ain't I right?''

Slowly Redwing lifted his eyes from Fox Wilkins to the ceiling. Shaking his head sadly, he turned to Tennessee, who was left unmoved by the trader's choice. "Uh, look, Tennessee," the Cherokee said uncomfortably, "I better go check on the horses. Wait for you there." He turned quickly toward the doorway, then hung in his tracks, looking back, his hawk's face somber and wry. "Feller, if that preacher's medicine does get you off the ground, wish you'd tell an old chief named Talking Bear that I didn't have the stomach for this thing."

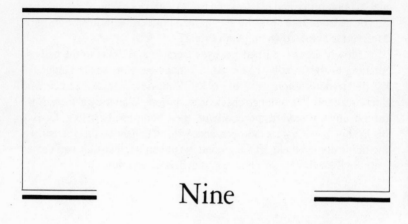

Nine

Somewhere in the cove a lone rooster was crowing to graying skies as Tennessee McEveride turned in at the entrance to the plantation and let his tired mount walk up the driveway. The big dun was no longer the cat-footed horse that had swept Tennessee down the driveway some twelve hours before. Now he was lifting his hooves wearily and letting them drop with a thud against the packed gravel. He was still strong and willing, however, and would be ready for the grind of steady travel after only a short rest, but prospects of his getting that rest were poor.

Tennessee himself had ridden all the way back from the mountain savage-eyed and grim, silently cursing John Redwing for causing him to head back toward the cove around midnight instead of camping some-where along the road to Chattanooga and the state line. The redgut son-of-a-bitch had gone whole-hog Indian back there on the mountain, harping on some fool blood-duty he owed his Cherokee kinfolks in North Carolina. Quitting the service of Stella McEveride cold, Redwing had refused even to ride down the mountain and inform Stella of the Krulls' whereabouts, thereby making it necessary for Tennessee to meet again with the woman.

Leaving the driveway, the horse crossed the backyard and came to a halt before Stella's door. Tennessee dismounted heavily, conscious of tight muscles in legs and hips. Though his deep reservoirs of endurance were virtually untapped, he was closer to weariness than it pleased him to note, since he knew well that a tiring quarry loses its vigilance and, soon thereafter, its life. Placing the blame for any drag in his movements on Fox Wilkins's raw whiskey, now gone dead in his system, he walked over to a window and peered into Stella's dark room.

"Stella!" he called. "Wake up!"

"I'm awake," Stella said distinctly. "I've been awake ever since you turned into the driveway." A faint metallic click in the darkness spoke of a gun-hammer lowered and brought back to safety. "That's a bad habit you've got, peeping in windows where nervous folks sleep."

Stepping hastily aside, Tennessee leaned against the side of the house. "Damned if it ain't!" he muttered.

"Just a minute," Stella called. "I'll light a lamp."

He heard her moving about, heard her bump into a table or chair and utter a low-voiced oath of exasperation. Then light bloomed inside, and Stella opened the door. Her disheveled hair looked a darker red in lamplight than it had in the light of day. It hung heavily about the shoulders of a pale-green robe of watered silk, masking her freckles with shadows and making her fine-boned face look like that of an ill-natured little girl.

As he stepped up into the doorway, Stella turned sharply away from him, her nostrils moving with distaste. "You smell like a whiskey still," she said. "Are you drunk? Damn you, Tennessee, if you've come here on some drunken whim this time of night—"

"Here's the whim I come on." Tennessee lounged in the doorway, a massive shoulder pressing the doorjamb. "I've found out where the Krulls are."

Stella whirled back to confront him, her face solemn with distrust. "What—did—you—say?" she demanded, spacing her words.

"I said I've found out where the Krulls are."

She stared at him in disbelief, her eyes darkening until they looked like black, rain-washed pebbles. Now, as her color faded, the freckles came swarming. Still she said nothing.

"What's the matter with you?" Tennessee asked irritably. "Didn't you hear me?"

Suddenly her face seemed to clench convulsively, as might a fist. For one fleeting moment it looked savage. Then her lips twisted in a grimace of rage and despair. "You lie!" she gasped. "We looked—everywhere! You go off—swill whiskey—come here—torment me with your drunken lies! You damn scoundrel, I counted on you, no matter what they said—"

"Will you shut up?" Tennessee snarled. "Nobody can tell you a thing. So you don't need me. And that suits me. Because, come good daylight, I aim to pull out of here, anyhow. Only reason I come back was to tell you the Krulls are in Texas, most likely on the Mexican border somewhere. Now you know. So you give me some breakfast, and I'll call the whole thing square and hit the road. Tell you what. You got some blue-belly friends coming here today. You listen to them.''

Stella raised a hand to her face, groping uncertainly. ''Are—are you telling me the truth?'' she said, her voice breaking with doubt.

Tennessee heaved away from the doorjamb and brushed past her, throwing his hat on the floor. He plucked a chair away from the wall and dropped upon it, swinging to face Stella hard enough to set the chair legs screeching against the boards. The cold, gray eyes below the tawny hair rejected her question. He said nothing.

Standing in the center of the room, Stella studied him carefully. ''All right,'' she said finally, ''so you're not drunk. But I still don't—it's still hard to believe. You mentioned Hard Hampton before you left. Did he tell you the Krulls were in Texas?''

''Never saw him,'' Tennessee growled. ''Fox Wilkins told me. Fox was the Krulls' undercover man around here.''

''Fox Wilkins?'' Stella stared hard. ''Why, he—why—*Fox Wilkins!*'' Turning slowly, she moved to her desk and stood with her back to him, thinking. Finally she said, without turning, ''Well, now . . . well, now, this begins to make sense. It fits—could explain a lot of things. It really could.'' She swung about, her face transformed by a hard, bright expectancy, and took her seat on the writing surface of the desk, resting her feet on the desk chair. Unconsciously she closed the robe over her legs, lapping the edges. ''Out with it, Tennessee.'' She gave him a small, stiff grin. ''So I apologize. Tell me the whole thing.''

Tennessee told her of a man's having ridden a roan mule in the yard on the night of the Krulls' raid, of John Redwing's search for the roan mule, of the discoveries in Fox Wilkins's house and barn. Then, as Stella came off the desk, he stopped talking and watched her stalk the floor, venting her anger against Jubal and John Redwing for withholding information from her. Tennessee was too little interested in her opinion of the Negro and the Indian to refute in detail her assertion that she'd been the victim of treachery at the hands of trusted employees, but he wanted to complete his mission and be gone; so he told her that they'd acted in her best interest, since Fox Wilkins would have given her no truths whatever.

''How can you say that?'' she flared. ''He told *you*, didn't he?''

''Come nearer *screeching* than *telling*,'' Tennessee told her.

Stella came to a standstill, staring blindly. ''Well, I know where

I'll go soon as it's light. When I think of that—that Fox Wilkins.... I'll kill him, Tennessee. This is the last day he'll ever see dawn."

"What makes you think I'd leave Fox Wilkins alive?" Tennessee demanded.

Looking into the cold flame of her brother-in-law's eyes, Stella did not recoil from what she found there, though her freckled face grew steadily more sober until it became blank. "Then, he's dead now?"

"Maybe you figured we had a drink together to show there was no hard feelings."

Turning away, Stella walked calmly to her chair by the desk and sat down. "I don't know exactly why I haven't assumed that you'd kill a Krull man if you found one. It's you, not the game, I need to understand, Tennessee." She faced him squarely. "What did you learn about the Krulls?"

Tennessee informed her that, according to Wilkins, Parson Krull and his gang had returned to Texas, where the Krulls had a long-established association with Indians and whence the parson had brought his gang to Tennessee during the war to loot and to pay off old scores. The Krulls had had some sort of liaison with a Union officer, whom Wilkins knew nothing about and couldn't describe since he'd seen the officer only in the shadows on the night of the raid. It was through this officer that the Krulls, like other gangs regarded as partisan, had received guns and ammunition from the Union forces. Wilkins had been necessarily vague concerning the Krulls' whereabouts in Texas, though they'd left the impression with him that their stamping ground was on the border of Mexico. He had named and described the members of the Krull gang. Then Tennessee had forced him to repeat the descriptions and answer questions about the four Krulls, Bull Jakes, and Shep and Jap McClanahan until he had formed distinct mental pictures and committed them to memory.

"May as well tell you now," Tennessee finished. "John Redwing's gone back to the blanket. You can't count on him no more for help."

"Done what?"

"Quit working for you. Gone back to his people."

"I'm sorry to hear that," Stella said without emphasis, her mind far out on another trail. "Why'd he quit?"

"Who knows what goes on under a fool redskin's feathers?" Tennessee growled.

"Feathers? John Redwing never wore a feather in his life."

"Might as well. Claimed he's due in North Carolina with his folks. I don't know what for. Maybe they all aim to gather around and eat a dog."

"Oh, now wait. Cherokees don't eat dogs."

"They get hungry enough, they'll eat worse," Tennessee said sourly. "Anyhow, after he visits there, he aims to drift out West to the Indian Nations, where he's got some more kinfolks."

"Well, that's just north of Texas," Stella pointed out. "He didn't have to quit. As a matter of fact, I may want him to scout around in the Nations for me. An army officer told me just the other day that ruffian whites from the South are flocking to Indian lands. Tennessee, I've a feeling we'll find the beginning, and not the end, of a mighty long trail in Texas. It seems to me the Krulls are galloping away from us at this very moment. I wish we were there."

"You want Redwing, leave him word," Tennessee said. "He'll come back through here on his way to the Nations." He started to yawn, then came suddenly to his feet, aware that daylight had stolen upon him, surrounding him in the room. "Stella, I can't wait no longer. Just throw some grub in a sack. I'll eat in the woods."

"You certainly will do no such thing!" Stella was on her feet, moving toward the doorway. "You sit back down there while I call Lula May. You'll eat your breakfast at a table like folks. Jubal can take care of your horse."

"Hold on." Tennessee was at the door with her, then outside at her heels. "I ain't got no time to wait for breakfast. Fox Wilkins told me the soldiers know who I am. Likely *he* convinced 'em." He caught her arm to emphasize his words. "Anyhow, they'll come piling—" He felt the sleek roundness of her arm, warm and firm in his great hand, and a wave of desire leaped inside him. He resisted an almost overpowering impulse to take her in his arms, and withdrew his hand as if he'd touched fire, his tired muscles swelling with a surge of bull strength.

Stella kept her eyes averted. Something hot and raw and animal had come through his hand into her body, and she wondered how it would be to move in against him and feel his arms close around her. Not that she was even tempted, of course. But why did she *have* such a thought? She didn't even like what she knew about this man. Even the reason she wanted to keep him near her was not reassuring: He was a skilled man-killer. Stella was beginning to wonder how well she knew herself. When she had time, she was going to think hard about that. Right now she had to devise a means of keeping this wolf-man from running away from her.

"Lula May!" she shouted across the yard. "Oh, Lula May!" Without a glance in Tennessee's direction, she nodded toward the big dun standing hipshot at the end of the cabin. ''You talk about riding that poor tired beast!''

''Tired or not, he'll move out of here,'' Tennessee said hoarsely. ''He ain't got no choice. I thought I told you—''

''*Lula May!*'' Stella shouted impatiently. ''So help me, if I have to go over there and wake up that—''

Jubal stepped out of the first cabin in the lane, still buttoning his shirt. ''She coming,'' he called, and came on toward them with uneven steps, shouldering his galluses.

''You come get Mr. Tennessee's horse,'' Stella told him. ''Rub him down and feed him good.'' She turned back toward the doorway, glancing quizzically at Tennessee. ''Fast fellow, that Jubal. He wakes Lula May up to come cook. Gets there so fast sometimes he can't get his clothes on.'' She lifted her shoulders. ''Oh, well.''

''Listen,'' Tennessee protested, beginning to sweat, ''I told you I can't wait. Now I'm telling you I can smell soldiers down that road.''

''Oh, damn the soldiers,'' Stella said over her shoulder. ''Come on in and sit down. If you're really uneasy, I'll send Jubal down the road to watch for dust.''

''Sure, *you* can be easy. They ain't coming for *you*.''

''What's bothering you, anyhow? You wouldn't breathe right without a few soldiers behind you.''

''That's where I want 'em—behind me.'' Tennessee followed her inside. ''But they won't stay behind, shape that dun horse's in—not if I wait to line up for an even start.''

''Leave him in the stable, then, and ride War Drum.'' Stella headed straight for her desk and began pulling open drawers, turning through papers impatiently. ''That's my Kentucky Thoroughbred stud. He's big enough to carry your weight and still run away from any army horse in the country.'' She pulled out another drawer and then slammed it shut without looking. ''I've got a map of Texas here somewhere. I never hired anybody to look out there. Somehow, I always expected to find the Krulls in Florida. That's a mistake I'll remember.'' Suddenly her freckled hand flew to a pigeonhole of papers under the rolled top, her fingers working nimbly through the stack. Snatching out a folded paper, she spread it on the desk. ''It *would* be the last one.'' She leaned over it on braced arms, her legs spread comfortably for balance.

Across the room Tennessee sank slowly to his chair, his eyes on the provocative mold of the woman's hips, his mind stripping away pale-green silk from freckled buttocks. He struggled feebly with his desire, losing ground. And then, finally, a stallion-mare image leaped in his brain, rearing and plunging with a hot brutality. Rising blood surged in his ears. He was aware of Stella's voice at the periphery of his attention, speaking words that formed and slid by and left no record. Crouched in the chair like some tawny beast, he expected each moment an impulse that might launch his great body across the room to close with its prey at the desk.

"... San Antonio's the only logical choice," Stella was saying, "... headquarters... Mexican border to the south... Indian country west and north... make arrangements... sell plantation or keep it... buyer in Overton... Northern man... in love with the country... plans to remain in Tennessee... buy horses and equipment... strong surrey might prove most comfortable way... take Jubal and Lula May along... be ready to leave in a week or ten days...."

Coming through the doorway, Lula May opened her mouth, perhaps to express her opinion regarding the ungodly hour of her summons, and then she saw Tennessee's face. She stopped short just inside the door, closed her mouth without speaking, and looked quickly toward the desk. Her eyes settled instantly on Stella's balanced, all-fours posture and molded seat. When she looked again at Tennessee, his face was glistening with sweat. Lula May marched past him with face set and eyes showing their whites. She showed him resentment in every motion, as only a former slave could, and disappeared through the doorway to the lean-to, where she continued to express herself by banging stove lids, skillets, and pans. The din she created was eloquent.

Stella swung erect, facing the lean-to. "For the love of God!" she exclaimed and, crossing the floor, stood in the lean-to entrance. "Will you stop trying to knock that stove apart, you—you—" She broke off, her face taking on an expression of deceptive blandness. "Well, now! All clouded up and ready to storm! Did I call you from anything except your sleep? Is this the first time you've ever had to cook breakfast before sunup?"

"I ain't said I mind—"

"Shut up. Let me tell you something, Miss Uppity. I'll have no frowning faces and banging stoves around here. Now, if I'm not asking too much, you get that breakfast and get it without knocking the house down. Do you hear me?"

Lula May muttered something unintelligible.

"What's that?" Stella demanded sharply. "So now, in these days of the Jubilee, you can mumble at me! Is that what you think?"

Lula may said nothing.

"*Answer* me!" Stella shouted.

"You get mad no matter what I say," Lula May wailed. "I ain't gonna say nothing."

Stella turned back toward the desk, shaking her head. "Yelling at servants!" she deplored. "My grandmother never raised her voice. But, then, no servant ever gave her cause. I never thought I had a common streak till lately, but that must be it. Oh, well, it's from my father's side, I guess. That's the side the money came from." She sat down and rested an arm across the map of Texas on the desk, tapping it with a finger. "Once we start, how long will it take us to get there, Tennessee?"

"Get where?" Tennessee said.

"Damnation!" Stella cried. "Have you been asleep? San Antonio, of course."

"I don't know," Tennessee said, dragging a sleeve down his face. "I don't know how long. No hurry, though. I'm going on right after breakfast, like I said. Time you get there, why, I'll have the Krulls already marked down, like as not."

Before he had finished Stella was gripping the sides of her head with freckled hands, her eyes shut tight. "*This is it!*" she moaned. "This is the day I found the Krulls' trail. Why, I won't survive it! Will you tell me why you're trying to drive me out of my mind?"

"Aw, Stella, talk sense."

"Yes," Stella snapped, "one of us ought to make sense. You can't leave today. There's sense. We've got business that must be settled. For one thing, what about Major Bronson's offer? Do you want to sell?"

"Whose offer?"

Stella stared at him narrowly, her face taking on its tough, high-cheeked look. "Major Bronson's," she said finally, with the elaborate patience of one who instructs an idiot, "the damned Yankee who's lost his mind and wants to settle in this graveyard he's helped build. Whatever *you'd* like to think he is, though, he'll pay as much as this place is worth. Now, listen carefully. Do you want to sell the place or keep it?"

"*Give* it away, for all I care," Tennessee said without interest. "It ain't my place. You know the judge never willed nothing to me."

"Did I say he left a will?" Stella asked. "If he had he might have left you some grammar. Why can't you talk one way or the other? About half the time you talk like a field hand."

"Well, folks don't have no trouble understanding a field hand," Tennessee pointed out. "In the war what a man meant counted more than the words he used. Take Bragg. He had the grammar, but nobody understood what he meant—not even him. Forrest, though, he used his words any way they jumped in his mouth, but his men jumped faster than the words. I've seen a schoolteacher with a bullet in his guts and a hillbilly couldn't write his name shot the same way. They both looked up at me and said about the same thing when I stopped by. I understood what they meant, too."

"What did they say?" Stella asked, in spite of herself.

Tennessee looked down at the floor. "That ain't the point," he said.

"Oh, come on," Stella insisted. "What was it?"

"Why, they goddamned me for a son-of-a-bitch and wished me in hell."

"No!" Stella cut off a surprised giggle, biting her lips. "Didn't they say something else, though—at the end?"

"I don't know. I went on."

"What? Without doing what you could?"

"I done what I could when I shot 'em in the first place. They were damned Lincolnites."

"Ah, you low hound!" Stella despaired. "You ought to be muzzled and chained up. Honestly, if I thought you were half the animal you seem—but let it go. Let the Krulls worry about your running loose." She squared herself in her chair, all business again. "All right. Now, Tennessee, here's what we'll do with the plantation. I'll keep it—mostly because of the graves on it—and give you half of what Major Bronson offered. But I won't hand you the money while you're trying to idle off the trail of the damned Krulls to chase rabbits or lie around in the woods, uh—well, scratching fleas."

"What the hell?" Tennessee protested. "First I'm a wolf! Now I'm a dog! Make up your mind, will you?"

"It's made up," Stella said firmly. "I know you pretty well, my dear brother-in-law. That's why I don't intend to let you out of my sight till you're lined out on a trail that's getting hotter by the minute. Tennessee, I'm a rich woman. You work for me and you'll make ten times what you'd make fighting a war in Mexico—yes, and probably get shot at a lot less, too, though I can't guarantee that last. Now, then. Have you any money to carry in your pocket?"

"What's money?" Tennessee growled. "I have to, I can do without it."

"Why, how can you do without money?"

"Like I've been doing. By taking what I need." He tapped the butt of an Army Colt at his side. "Using these when I'm heard taking. Which ain't often."

"Now, Tennessee," Stella said earnestly, "you listen to me. The war's over. You go about robbing people now, you'll be outlawed and hunted down by—by—"

"That's right," Tennessee agreed sardonically. "By soldiers. And, let me remind you, they won't *have* to hunt me down if I don't pull for the mountains right away. They know where I am. Oh, I'll sign on with you—even if you *are* trying to hire me for a dog. But I won't agree to stay in your sight. You'd weigh me down just about when I'd need to move like a scalded wolf. So you punch up your nigger at that stove and give me some traveling money, and I'll mosey on out to San Antonio and be there when you come. That way, nobody gets hurt that I can see."

Stella jumped up from her chair and started moving about the room. She halted by the lean-to entrance and stood scowling with indecision.

"Now, Miss Stella, ain't no call to look at me," Lula May complained. "I'm working as fast as I can."

"No," Stella said absently. "No. You can go faster."

"Don't need to. Breakfast be ready time you-all wash."

Turning back toward the center of the room, Stella stopped in front of Tennessee. "No, I don't like it," she said. "Tennessee, wait for me. You won't regret it, I promise you. I have the money for just such an emergency right here in this room. I ordered it from a bank in Philadelphia weeks ago. I can cut corners and be ready to leave in two or three days. Yes, three at the very latest. I'll have to see my lawyer in Overton, arrange for the care of certain—things. And we'll have to buy horses and a surrey. We can buy what else we need in the towns we pass through. Why, the trip will even be fun, with Lula May and Jubal to make camp along the way. Can you honestly think of a single reason why you shouldn't wait?"

"I can think of a dozen," Tennessee told her, "but one's enough. I'm wanted bad by the Union army."

"But only in Tennessee."

"That's where we are, ain't it? We got to travel on the earth in Tennessee. Anyhow, I'm wanted in Alabama and Mississippi or anywhere else I'm known."

"Well, I can't believe you're so afraid of meeting soldiers. You must have some other reason—some other place you want to go." She tapped the floor with a foot, watching him across the lower lids of her slanted eyes. "You know what your weaseling sounds like to me? That you've got a woman at the back of your mind. But if you have, why don't you say so?"

Tennessee studied the floor, his face impassive. "Here's what I got at the back of my mind," he said, "and the front, both. I got to travel the woods and the back roads and take to the brush to get out of this state. I got to travel alone to have much of a chance. Looks like you ought to understand that."

Stella lifted her eyes and stared in silence at the wall above the man's brown-streaked, leonine head. After a while she murmured, "I guess you're right," and a pulse beat wildly in her throat. Then her lips thinned with decision. "But if you think you're going to drift off on your own and leave the judge's ghost to haunt me, you can think again. Two can travel the back roads as well as one. I can send instructions to Overton by homing pigeon and by Jubal. In fact, I can leave the mopping up here to Jubal and Lula May. They can follow later. We'll leave in an hour."

Tennessee came to his feet and lounged to the doorway, where he slouched against the doorjamb. What the hell? he thought. Let her come—if she can keep up. She's kin—sort of, anyhow. One reason I signed up, maybe. Another is I done warned her. Hell, I'll warn her again! He felt the first movement of a hard swell of desire in his groin. She's a woman, and I'm a man. By God, she gets humped, she can blame herself!

"No decent woman in her right mind would do what you aim at," he said over his shoulder. "What you think folks are going to say? You ride out of here with me, something may come back—it won't be the same Stella McEveride. Could be, no man will look at you. You ought to get married again, even if it's to another Lincolnite. Now, I ain't going to argue with you no more. You done been warned. If you're bound and determined to be a damned fool—all right, then, I ain't responsible."

"You don't know me very well, Tennessee," Stella said evenly. "You'll learn, though, that I'll take my chances on this trip, whatever comes, and I can't conceive of what could keep me from taking them. If you're thinking of my reputation, let me remind you that I've been beaten and raped by a half-breed savage, though I don't think that's generally known. I saw my husband die with the sight of it bursting his heart. What else can happen to me? Damn my reputation, anyhow, and the men who might look at me, as you say. I want—and I intend to have—no man unless he be one of the Krulls. And I'll have *his* heart's blood. Now come in to breakfast."

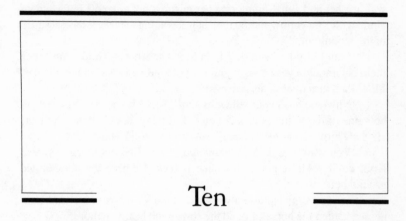

Ten

For several days they had ridden a winding course through the mountains, Stella astride a light-stepping cinnamon, or red roan, mare, Tennessee riding the big dun and leading a magnificent Thoroughbred stallion under pack. Once, for several miles, thay had followed the path of a great army's passage, its route through the hills marked by the bones of horses, cattle, and mules. In the upper Sequatchie Valley, wild-bearded ruffians, still pursuing partisan hatreds, had eyed Stella and the horses with predatory interest but had eyed Tennessee McEveride at the same time and passed on. Now, by eleven o'clock in the morning, they had descended the switchbacks of a road down Walden's Ridge and were walking their horses in sight of the blue-green Tennessee River in the great shadow of Signal Mountain.

Riding on the mountain under the green foliage of early summer forests, Stella seemed changed from the woman Tennessee had found nursing her hatred and grief at McEveride Plantation. Usually her manner toward her brother-in-law was now marked by an easy camaraderie and at times even by what seemed a sort of affection—the almost-cynical affection a sister might feel for a scoundrelly brother. Never once had she appeared to regard Tennessee as a possible source of danger to herself, though the menace he represented had been spelled out for her in unmistakable language before they'd mounted up at her cabin door, as Tennessee had reason to know.

He'd sent Jubal back to the barn for a sack of grain and come on past

Stella's cabin with the horses. Inside, Lula May was begging Stella to wait for her and Jubal, imploring her mistress not to go off in the woods alone with "no yellow-haired tomcat just waiting to make a she-cat squall in the moonlight."

"I ain't blind, if you *is!*" Lula May had wept. "Think I ain't seen them catamount eyes of his'n jump at yo' hind-end ever' move it make? Mist' Paul turn over in his grave—"

"Now you hush your vulgar mouth!" Stella snapped. "You'd think he's one of the Krulls, the way you talk. I tell you, he's Paul's brother. He's *my* brother-in-law. If I can't trust him—oh, just hush!"

"You wait," Lula May despaired. "You find out he bad as them Krull devils. All he got on his mind is fuck. He have yo' back on the ground befo'—"

Then came a slap and a wail and Stella's furious voice, and Tennessee hauled the horses around the corner and heard no more.

And she *had* been safe enough with him. What turned his recurring impulses inward was her apparent lack of any sex consciousness where he was concerned. He dreaded the expression on her face, the look in her eyes, when she would know him finally. Sometimes he'd fall behind to watch her supple woman's body move with the rhythm of her mare's motion, and he'd find his imagination conjuring up images of other women—whether comely or plain was unimportant. He was not fastidious. Only the previous night, while they were stopping at the house of a hard-faced mountaineer, he'd caught himself contemplating the probabilities of the man's leathery-faced woman—a snuff-mouthed slattern no longer young by mountain standards. The creature had given him some strange looks, too, had seemed to slough her old skin and shed ten years on finding herself watched. . . .

Beyond Signal Mountain they were soon winding through wooded hills. Where their road snaked over a ridge overlooking the valley, they pulled up and had their look at the town in its bowl of mountains. The river, sweeping in from the east past the foot of Missionary Ridge, cut westward through the valley like a gleaming scimitar and swung north at Moccasin Bend against the bedrock bluffs of Lookout Mountain. Sprawling down the valley from the south bank, in an area denuded of trees, was Chattanooga—a large collection of long, low, whitewashed buildings, government storehouses, shops, barracks, rows of huts, stock enclosures, and other such structures that spring up around an army's base of supplies. Cameron Hill rose from the western edge of the town, its summit flanked by forts with cannon still in place and crowned by the battery of a single huge gun, and a rifle shot upriver from the foot of its slope was the wooden bridge Grant's engineers had constructed in '63 during Bragg's siege of Chattanooga. On the near bank, immediately below where Tennessee and Stella sat their horses, makeshift huts and tents covered the flat on both sides of the north entrance to the bridge. Here some three or four thousand Negro refugees from farther south had lodged and settled. They were lining the riverbank, fishing with cane poles, moving idly or standing in small groups, talking and laughing, or just lazing about their humble dwellings.

"I visited here once with my father," Stella commented sadly. "Now all those fine trees are gone! What a shame!"

"Rosecrans's troops cut 'em for defense when they were hemmed in by Bragg's men," Tennessee informed her. "They had axes going all that Monday night after Chickamauga."

Stella flicked him with an ironic glance. "Now, how would you know that?"

"I heard 'em first, and then I saw 'em. I was in Chattanooga that night. You wouldn't believe a whole army could get so panicked. If that fool Bragg had pushed on in, he could've destroyed the Army of the Cumberland. But Bragg was so used to losing, he couldn't noways handle a victory." He studied the high places in the town. "Later the lumber and timber from them trees went into government buildings, blockhouses, and such. That bridge, too. It's all wood. Heard they didn't even use no spikes—just wooden pegs. Likely go out on the next big flood, though."

"Well, that won't be today," Stella said. "I'll take War Drum in tow and head on in. You wait here and then circle around to the foot of Lookout Mountain. I'll meet you there before dark." She reached for the lead rope, watching him with eyes that were suddenly dark and searching. "If I don't, you wait for me, anyhow. I'll be along." She took the rope and held it in her hand, waiting. "Well?"

"Well, what?"

. Her lips firmed, and then she said, "Can I count on you?"

"Sure," he said absently, his eyes on the town. "Stella, I been listening for church bells and ain't heard a one. And across the river things look about like I reckon they would any day of the week. But what we forgot is that it's Sunday."

"Damnation!" Stella exclaimed. "And we've *got* to get supplies here! Even crows can't live off the land west of here."

"Sutler's tent's probably open for business," Tennessee observed impassively. "What I heard, there *ain't* any churches fit to hold services in. Feds used 'em for hospitals and left 'em in bad shape. Like as not they don't even know when Sunday comes around. They don't need no churches, though. All them damned Lincolnites are infidels, anyhow."

Stella could hardly believe her ears. How Paul's brother could make such a blind, stupid charge against the majority of a nation, including Paul, was beyond understanding. And to her face! She was getting ready to roast him alive when she saw, or thought she saw, the faintest sort of a twitch at a corner of his mouth, and then she noticed the brightness of his eyes. So he was pulling her leg!

"Oh, I don't think so," she said with a straight face. "I've heard they're all Muhammedans. You know, so they can have a lot of wives here and a bunch of houris there. But I'll tell you what. If I can get into a sutler's place, I'll buy you some new clothes." And now, as the grin that had grown on his face vanished, a streak of humor swept openly across her face. "Unless you want Unionists bushwhacking your shirt while the secesh shoot at your pants."

"Don't you buy no man's clothes my size in that town," Tennessee warned quickly. "Pack horse behind you and your name McEveride, somebody's bound to figure me with you. And, by the way, from here on my name's Tennessee Smith. Smith was my mother's name. It's my middle name, just as it was Paul's."

Stella reined down the slope, followed by the powerful, long-legged stud. "I'll see what turns up," she said over her shoulder. "See you about dusk."

Tennessee watched her until she passed from view at a bend in the road. She was riding with a firm, sure seat, as straight-backed and confident as a slim, freckled boy. The cinnamon mare was a spirited horse, especially mettlesome in the mornings. Like any female that figured she was something special, she was skittish—not a safe mount for a woman riding sidesaddle, certainly not on rough mountain trails. But Stella, wearing divided skirts, defied convention by riding astride in Paul's McClellan saddle—that is, save when she would approach a house for a night's lodging. Then she would detach the right stirrup, snap it to a ring in the saddlebow, and let it hang short on the left side for her right foot; thus she could ride up to a door sidesaddle without offending a conventional hostess.

When Stella appeared on the bare ground at the foot of the hill, Tennessee saw with no surprise that she was again riding sidesaddle, sedately, even somewhat diffidently; and she was handling the led horse as if she feared he might climb up behind her if she relaxed for a single instant. Actually, the Thoroughbred stud was a marvel. Under pack, no matter what pace was set, he would follow on a loose lead and never overrun the horses ahead. Tennessee had been amazed to find such docility in a blooded stallion, though he had observed that War Drum had the large, soft eyes usually associated with evenness of temperament in a horse; yet, according to Stella, the stud could not abide a horse in front of him when he was ridden.

Watching Stella cross the flat toward the bridge, Tennessee felt like a buck that waits behind for the doe to draw into the open any danger that lies ahead. He wanted to find out whether the blockhouse that stood at the north entrance to the bridge was manned by soldiers now that the war was over and sabotage to the bridge extremely unlikely. As she neared it, two white men and several Negroes moved up to block her way, but they were not soldiers. They kept turning their heads and casting searching glances back toward the way she had come, obviously doubting that she was alone. *Scummy sons-of-bitches!* he thought, and whipped the Spencer from its sheath and levered a cartridge into the barrel. He hoped they had no more in mind than frightening a lone woman into giving them a little money. For if they tried to lay hands on her, then all their plans—theirs, his, and Stella's—would have to undergo a radical change. He couldn't afford to hang around and be questioned by the army about shooting a few refugees and camp followers. The men were worried, however; they kept turning their eyes up the hill, searching her back trail. They held her up only long enough, apparently, to answer a few of her questions, their leader gesturing as he gave directions. Then they moved back and let her pass.

Waiting until Stella was across the bridge and in the town, Tennessee rode leisurely down the slope and crossed the flat. As he approached the group that had stopped Stella, its leader, a lank, wild-bearded white man with long black hair, nudged his nearest fellow and gave them all a knowing look. The fellow was ragged—too ragged, Tennessee decided. To appear unhurried, in case the ragamuffin was a spy, Tennessee drew rein on the bridge and sat there, feeling the heat of the sun, studying the riverbanks and what he could see of the town. The Negroes who were fishing off the bank to his right had their heads turned his way, the whites of their eyes showing. Across the river a horseman, headed for town, was riding along the shore between Cameron Hill and the river. Tennessee sent the dun along the bridge, observing the still faces of the Negroes slowly turning. Feeling exposed at midstream, he tightened his knees, and the stealthy clatter of the quiet horse's hooves became a muted drumroll of sound. He came off the bridge and reined sharply to the right, passing in front of government warehouses and the post magazine. He continued on, following a road that ran along the bench between Cameron Hill and the river, observing the breastworks and batteries of hundred-pounder Parrot guns that commanded the river-bank and hills. True, the war was over, but the army was still here.

The roadway became little more than a wagon trace by the time

Tennessee had placed the miniature mountain between himself and the town. Thereafter, he had more hours than miles between him and his meeting with Stella. What concerned him now was the state of his belly, since it was unlikely that he'd find anything to eat west of Cameron Hill, where there were no dwellings, as far as he knew. He did come across one, though—a frame house with a narrow porch, set in a little hollow among the breaks of the Cameron slopes. It still bore witness to its original owner's ambitious carpentry, but it had been damaged in the war and recently repaired with rough lumber. What drew Tennessee's eyes, as an unpenned chicken draws the eyes of a hawk, was a man's black coat and trousers airing on a clothesline in the yard.

He pulled up in front of the house and measured the suit of clothes with his eyes, observing at once that it had been purchased for a big man, a man probably as large as he was. He surveyed the place carefully, feeling in a strange way that the suit had been hung out for him to take down and also that he was being watched. He thought he might just ride on past and then return on foot and take that suit of clothes from under its owner's nose; otherwise he might wind up killing this big man here, and then Stella would refer to him for weeks to come as some sort of animal or bird.

And then he saw the woman. There was movement at a window, and immediately afterward she appeared in the doorway—a tall, blond woman a full six feet in height, carelessly attired in a thin, low-necked housedress that had not been designed to conceal her full bosom, broad hips, and superbly molded flanks and belly. She had streaks of flour on her forearms and a trace of flour on one cheek, and she watched him with a bold, steady interest, her lips stirring faintly, as if on the verge of smiling. The flour on her cheek somehow kept her face from looking commonplace, but what interested Tennessee was the fact that she was a woman.

He removed his hat, letting the late-June sun beat down on his tawny head. "Ma'am, I'd like a word with your man if he's home," he said in his deep, soft voice.

The woman's lips moved against each other whimsically. "I'll confide in you, Mr. Man," she said pleasantly. "I would, too. Drunk or sober, roaring mad or laughing fit to kill, whatever the case might be—I would, too, and that's sure no lie." The movement of her lips, as much as what she said, alerted him. Her unabashed green eyes moved over him, approving the cold bronze of his features, the breadth of his shoulders, the girth of his arms and thighs.

"You mean he ain't here?" he asked uncertainly.

"Why, I mean the *real* men are petering out," she confided further. "And a woman don't forget a real one." Her lips moved, barely missed smiling. "I don't usually talk like this. But there's something about you—I guess it's just that these little men—well, they embarrass me. Always coming around. You know what? They remind me of little feist dogs tiptoeing up to smell a Saint Bernard bitch. Don't get the wrong impression, now. I may sound like a common—but what's talk? I've got no neighbors to scandal. Believe me, that's what keeps the skimpy little bustle-waggers watching their p's and q's—the neighbors. Well, there's nobody lives in hearing distance of *this* place. I'd be scared to live—but then, it's mostly the scrawny steers and little scrub bulls that drift by here."

Tennessee's eyelids drooped, hooding his feral eyes. "Was that the herd bull rode off awhile ago?" he asked casually.

"Who rode where?" The woman's eyes misted over as if with some secret mirth. "Don't be fooled by my talk. I'm alone in the house—if that's what you're trying to find out. So I can't invite you in, you being a man and me a woman." Her lips trembled, never quite smiling. "If you're waiting for an invitation."

Tennessee watched a hip round out as the woman leaned against the doorjamb. "Saw that suit of clothes on the line," he said. "Thought your man might sell it."

She looked him over again as if she were examining a slave on the block. "You really think you're man enough to wear that suit?" she challenged, and her lips were suddenly still.

Tennessee came off the horse in pantherish motion and crossed the yard. As he stepped upon the narrow porch, the woman came erect, stood poised in the doorway as if for belated flight. A frightened pulse beat in her throat, and she pressed one hand against her stomach as if to still a sudden tremor there. But her eyes watched him steadily, and in them was a knowledge that was older than Scripture.

"I'm always play-acting," she said, her lips quivering. "I was just teasing you. Seeing how you'd act when—"

He was through with talk. He moved upon her, reaching for her, but she warded him off with her hands, crying, "Wait! No, wait! Get the suit off the line!" And while she was talking, she was retreating, fading back into the room.

"Damn the suit!" Tennessee snarled.

"No, you've got to try it on," she said breathlessly, catching up a chair and swinging it around between them. "You've got to prove you're man enough to wear it. I wouldn't spit on less of a man."

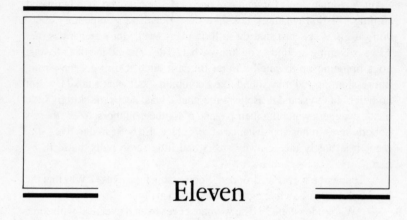

Eleven

As Stella left the bridge and rode south on Market Street, she began to get an idea of what some three years of almost constant military occupation could do to a small town. The thoroughfare was no more than a rough, deep-rutted roadbed covered with a heavy blanket of dust—the kind of street that a day's rain would turn into a quagmire, as was indicated by stepping-stones in place at street crossings and planks across ditches before business houses. All the structures that lined the street seemed to squat and to hug the earth in the valley; only the cupola of the one church on the street seemed to look up. The government storehouses, built by the quartermasters and commissaries and holding vast quantities of army supplies, were the most conspicuous structures in the community. Even they, though long and wide, contributed to the low profile of the town against the hills. Though something more than an army camp, Chattanooga was still a military town, Stella could see. It gave the impression that any resident could strike tent and leave in twenty-four hours.

The street was crowded, and the predominant color of apparel was blue. There were soldiers everywhere Stella looked—around tents on vacant lots, on occasional porches, on the street—and all their heads seemed turned in her direction. She began to feel a mounting tension. Suddenly it occurred to her that she didn't dare leave her fine horses— particularly since one of them was a Thoroughbred stallion under pack— exposed on the street to the inquiring eyes of the military while she made her purchases. She began looking for a livery stable, finally coming to one at the corner of the eighth cross-street on Market, one block short of the end of Market and, in some sense, the end of town, since practically all the commercial activity of the community was confined to Market Street. A sign announced Wells & Thompson's Livery, but Stella doubted that the raffish, somewhat jaunty old man who took charge of the horses in the runway was either of the proprietors. When he courteously assisted her to alight, she caught the spicy fragrance of cloves, which did not completely mask the rank, yeasty odor of libations taken periodically in some back stall to tide him through the day.

When she asked whether he was the owner, the man bent twinkling blue eyes upon her and grinned cheerfully behind a screen of iron-gray whiskers. "Why, honey, I ain't nothing," he said genially. "Y'see, I wore gray and followed the Stars and Bars in the late disagreement. This town favors blue."

"You're the very man I want to ask a favor of, then," Stella said rapidly. "I'm traveling with a relative who wore gray, too. He's waiting at the edge of town for a very good reason. Could I go out and buy supplies and have them sent here?" When the old man nodded and started to speak, Stella hurriedly continued talking, while thrusting into his hand a coin that would keep a bottle in the stall for a week or more. "And would you pack them on this horse and have the mare saddled and both horses ready to go as soon as it's dark? Will you be here that late? I'll have something extra for you if you're here when I come."

"I'll be here if it's midnight," the old man said earnestly. "I sleep here. And your hosses, ma'am—why, they'll be fed, currycombed, saddled, packed, and ready to go."

"Where can I buy supplies on Sunday?" Stella wanted to know.

"Sutler's tent across the street's open. Ain't much stock to choose from, though, Sunday or any other day." He gave her a rheumy, sidelong glance, pretending to hide a sly, teasing grin. "Lessen you're a *drinking* woman. Then he's stocked purty good."

Stella turned away, then faced the man again. "Oh, by the way, a man in blue may come looking for me. His—well, his attentions are not welcome. You understand? I'd rather he didn't get a look at my horses. Is there anywhere, possibly—any place—"

The old man brightened perceptibly. Solving this grand little secesh lady's problems was a real pleasure for him, and rewarding, too. "There's a two-hoss stall around behind the harness room you can't tell from a wall. Stables got their secrets, too, I reckon. In wartime, anyhow. I'll put 'em in there, and nobody'll lay eyes on 'em."

"See you after dark," Stella told him. "Hope you're awake. Hate for you to miss what I'll be holding in my hand."

The sutler's tent occupied a vacant lot across the street from the livery stable. One or two civilians were going through stacks of clothing on planks laid across sawhorses, and a soldier was leaving with a bottle of whiskey. Foodstuff was on display in boxes and crates on each side of the tent, but the sutler seemed in short supply of provisions that campers might require. Stella ignored the clutter of articles on either side of the entrance, a miscellany including brooms, chamber pots, axes, Dutch ovens, and cowbells. The sutler, a fish-eyed, paunchy man with a bloodhound sag to his sallow face, said he was sorry, but he was out of bacon and coffee and just about everything else on Stella's list. It was Sunday, and demands had been heavy during the week. Deliveries of new supplies were expected on Monday, or Tuesday, maybe.

"Why are you open?" Stella inquired. "To sell whiskey?"

Before the sutler could answer, two newcomers had entered the tent and were demanding her attention. "That's her," said the wild-haired ragamuffin from across the river. Then he grinned whitely through his black tangle of beard. "Well, lady, I see you found the grocery store."

A sergeant in blue stepped up to her and bowed. "I'm Sergeant Schuler, ma'am. General Thomas's compliments, and would you be so kind as to join the general for lunch at the Crutchfield House? I'll see to your horses, ma'am, if you'll tell me where you left them."

"I'm afraid I've misplaced them, Sergeant," Stella said coolly. "I don't have that information to divulge at the moment. Hasn't this—this—incredible person told you where I must have left them?"

The ragamuffin himself answered cheerfully, "They're not in that livery stable across the street."

"Tell the general I'm sorry," Stella said. "Another time I'd be delighted, I'm sure. Today I'm terribly pressed for time."

The sergeant looked down, his face taking on color. "I'm afraid I'll have to insist, ma'am," he said gently. "I wouldn't dare report back without you."

Stella felt the blood begin to seethe in her veins. "Let's get this straight," she said evenly. "The general told you to take me in whether I wished to go along or not?"

"Well, conduct—that's it!" The sergeant was red and sweating. "*Conduct* you, ma'am."

"Well, damn his leaf-fat arrogance!" Stella cried angrily. "If I'm under arrest, why didn't you say so?"

"No, no, ma'am! Not that at all—at *all*!" Sergeant Schuler, who was not used to hearing ladies swear, was round-eyed with shock. "It's just—he wants to see you. And—and, ma'am, you got to eat, anyhow, haven't you?" He stepped aside, bowing in the direction of the street.

Stella settled in her tracks, her chin lifted imperiously. "I will not budge one step on that street," she said coldly, "in the company of this abominable scarecrow. If you want me to lunch with his corpulence, get rid of this—this repulsive thing."

"Get back across the bridge, Rags," the sergeant ordered, unable to keep a small grin from twitching his lips. "You know what? You *are* repulsive."

Shrugging, Rags ducked out and slouched away. A few minutes later Stella saw him riding off on a horse so clean-limbed and fleet-looking that it made him look like a horse thief. The sergeant escorted her back across the street and on past the stables to Railroad Avenue, at the south end of which was the Crutchfield House. It was a three-storied frame structure set back from Ninth Street far enough to allow a spacious lawn, upon which, Stella observed, there was a bandstand. The hotel was a huge building for its time and place, running from street to street with ells at both ends.

In the lobby the sergeant left Stella with the proprietress and went in search of General Thomas. He had introduced the woman behind the desk as Madam Bastrop. She was a comely middle-aged woman, and somewhat shapely, too, in spite of the fact that she weighed, Stella guessed, not less than two hundred and fifty pounds. Mrs. Bastrop came around the desk with a feather duster in her hand.

"Will you lend me that duster for a minute?" Stella said. "I've just ridden into town. And then, too, your streets—I'm covered with dust."

"Permit *me*," the big woman said and, without any further formality, began stroking Stella's clothes with the duster. "Be glad, though, hon, it's dust instead of mud. Last year I saw a dispatch rider's horse sunk up to its knees in mud on Railroad Avenue. Rider got confused, I reckon, and turned off of Ninth a block too soon. Good thing. He'd sunk deeper on Market." She chuckled. "Got lost in a blinding rain. Just a kid. He hollered up to the balcony, 'I'm looking for Chattanooga.' So I hollered down, 'Well, step out of your saddle, friend, and you'll be in it up to your ass.' " Mrs. Bastrop delivered one more stroke and quit. "I guess that'll get you by. You know, hon, I don't understand how you can be so damned good-looking with all that mess of freckles on your face."

"Why, I can go you one better, Madam," Stella returned. "I was wondering how *you* can be so good-looking and be so damned big and fat at the same time."

Mrs. Bastrop shouted with laughter. "Why, you'll do, you saucy minx," she chuckled. "Come to my apartment and freshen up. There's a handsome young major with the general that'll make you stand at attention. I hope you set him afire and make him drool, my dear. But *you* must stay cool and dry. So come, now, and take a spit bath like the cat you are—unless I've lost my ability to judge another woman."

"No," Stella said, "but I'll take a room and stay here tonight. I'll have baggage when I can get back to my horses—if I get back to them. So let me sign the register, and give me a key. I *will* run up to the room for a few minutes before I go to the general."

Mrs. Bastrop moved behind the desk, reversed the register, and laid a key beside it. Her fine, dark eyes were amused and speculative. "Ah, you Rebel vixen, I'll bet you've left a world of wreckage in your wake." She sighed gustily. "And there's a world of sack and pillage waiting up ahead. I do wish you'd stick here awhile. I'd dearly love to watch you work."

On her way upstairs Stella pondered the woman's meaning. Finally it came to her and provoked the strained, wry grimace of a smile. Mrs. Bastrop, who was, herself, probably no better than she should be, had marked Stella down as a younger, smaller, Confederate version of herself—as a kindred spirit and, in addition, as something of a *femme fatale*. But Stella knew she had no time to think of such things. General Thomas obviously intended to keep her under surveillance, hoping she would lead him to Tennessee. Stella had to get loose, buy her provisions, get to her horses, and ride out of town unseen before Tennessee came prowling into town looking for her. How would she ever manage it all?

When she returned to the lobby after freshening up, General George H. Thomas was standing with another officer at the desk in conversation with Mrs. Bastrop. So, she thought, he knows now I've registered for the night. Stella's angry references to the general's corpulence were not exactly fair, she realized. True, he was large-proportioned, even massive, but his excess flesh, whatever there was of it, was symmetrically distributed over a broad-shouldered, six-foot frame. His head was large; his features strong; his hair and beard thick and brown and sprinkled with gray. Needless to say, the Rock of Chickamauga's presence was commanding. When he turned and stepped forward to greet her, Stella noticed again, as she had in Nashville, that his personal movements were slow and deliberate, sometimes even ponderous. She'd heard that he had sustained a spinal injury in a railroad mishap before the war. If this was true, the injury may have contributed something to his appearance of calm, impassive dignity.

"Hello, General," she said composedly and extended her hand. "I thought you were immovably stationed in Nashville."

"I go here and there, where duty calls. All of Tennessee is in my division of command, you know." Instead of bowing, he merely inclined his head over her hand. "Mrs. McEveride, it is indeed a great pleasure to see you again."

"A pleasure you made sure of, I notice," Stella said tartly. "Is Sergeant Schuler getting my cell ready?"

General Thomas blandly ignored her pointed sally. "Mrs. McEveride, may I present a valued member of my staff, Major Armistead Gordon Randolph? Armistead, Mrs. Paul Smith McEveride."

It was then that Stella looked closely at the general's companion for the first time. He was smiling, not at all politely, but with amused appreciation of her remark and of the fact that she had meant to sting the general with it. The smile crinkled the corners of warm brown eyes and made them shine; it set up a sharp contrast of white teeth against the black-and-tan background of a trimmed black mustache and deeply tanned face. Under coal-black hair with a slight wave in it, the major's medium-tall, muscular physique was revealed to advantage by a beautifully tailored uniform. But Stella's eyes had not left the chiseled features of his face before she made her judgment: He was, she decided, and never afterward changed her mind, the handsomest man she ever saw.

"Major Randolph," she murmured. Over his shoulder, as he bowed gallantly to take her hand, she caught sight of Madam Bastrop's broad, sly look and knowing smile. Their eyes met, the proprietress winked suggestively, and Stella felt heat flooding her face.

When they were seated at a private table in the dining room, they were served at once, Mrs. Bastrop having already chosen the menu and arranged the service. The food was excellent, though Stella, with her problems pressing and with no solutions in sight, hardly knew what she ate or who served the food. As soon as he'd settled in his chair, General Thomas reached slowly to a pocket of his uniform and finally produced two telegrams, which, he said, were relayed to him from Overton through his Nashville office. He read them to Stella. The first one asked the questions Tennessee had advised the soldiers he'd met in the mountains to ask and established the fact that Tennessee McEveride had made a visit home. The second one concerned the departure from home of Mrs. Paul McEveride in the company of Tennessee McEveride, her brother-in-law, both of them on blooded horses; their probable direction, Chattanooga; their true destination, unknown. The telegram mentioned also the death of Fox Wilkins at the hands of Tennessee McEveride.

The general fixed Stella with steady eyes. "Mrs. McEveride, if I may ask, where *are* you headed?"

"I have a list of supplies to fill," Stella said. "Right after lunch I'm headed back to Market Street in search of a sutler who sells something besides whiskey." She cast her eyes up in mock despair. "I haven't much hope."

The general smiled his appreciation at her nimble dodging. "See to that, Armistead," he said, without shifting his eyes from Stella. "Have the commissary fill her list at cost. The supplies will probably go to sustain Tennessee McEveride on his way, but let them. We know your brother-in-law is hiding in town or lurking on the outskirts, Mrs. McEveride. I want you to persuade him to come in and give himself up. For his own good."

"How would it be for his own good?"

"Although it is late, he still may come in under the terms of the order I issued on May first regarding bands of guerrillas—the same terms that Lee accepted from Grant at Appomattox. Come in, surrender, and be paroled; fail to surrender and be regarded as an outlaw and, when captured, be treated as one."

Stella began to feel a slow outrage at the situation in which she found herself; it bunched her freckled cheeks and steadily darkened her slanted eyes. She knew the Machiavellian ease with which generals could forget promises and justify the sacrifice of other men's lives to achieve "strategic gains" and "larger objectives." She knew General Thomas would try to have her supplies followed from the commissary to Tennessee McEveride. She knew, in fact, that the only things slow about the general were his physical motions.

"Colonel Blackburn, of your command, offered Champ Ferguson those same terms, in your name, General," she pointed out, her voice rising, "and then, when he surrendered, *you* ordered him tried for murder. And when you're done with him, he'll be swinging from the gallows."

The general nodded, his face impassive. "He may. Certainly he should. But you don't know the facts. Colonel Blackburn's men *captured* Champ Ferguson, promising him nothing."

"That's not what they're saying in Overton and through the hills. Nobody who knows Champ Ferguson believes that."

Major Randolph entered the conversation at this point. "I don't, either, Mrs. McEveride, as I've told General Thomas privately more than once. But look at the case as the general must. A trusted officer in his command swears privately and reports officially that the capture was made with no promises of amnesty or parole, no treachery involved. Now, I don't believe it, but General Thomas *has* to, whether he wants to or not.''

"No," the general denied firmly, "I don't *have* to. I *do* believe Colonel Blackburn's report."

"Let me ask you, then," Stella said rapidly. "Don't you have men out searching for Tennessee McEveride right now?" When the general nodded reluctantly, her next question tumbled quickly back at him. "What happens if they capture him before I have a chance to persuade him to surrender?"

The general lowered his empty cup and picked up his fork. He answered without looking up. "He'd be tried as an outlaw for murder," he admitted.

"You're a great man, General," Stella said coldly, "and great men are not free. Their hands are tied by too many things, and they're too quick to compromise the rights of others on terms of expediency. How can I trust you? How can I have faith in your promises?" She leaned over the table, her slanted eyes now black and unwavering. "I hope you won't mind some plain talk, General. You have a complex organization and vast resources at your command. Have you ever used any part of them to find out where the Krull gang went? Have you ever tried to identify the Union officer who was liaison between the army and the Krull guerrillas?"

Before the general could reply, she rushed on, her voice now even and cool. "One reason I've wondered why you won't concern yourself with any attempt to find the Krulls is that you're so diligent in your pursuit of Tennessee McEveride, whose only crime, so far as the war is concerned, is that he didn't sign his name on a muster roll. But you're consistent about muster rolls, General. I'll give you that. You're going to hang Champ Ferguson in Nashville for not having *his* name on a muster roll, either, which makes his wartime killings murders, according to your court-martial. But hold on! Did I say you were consistent? If you were, you'd have Tinker Dave Beatty on trial, too. Tinker Dave was on no muster roll and killed people all through the mountains. Civilians, too. Yet you people, I understand, plan to use Tinker Dave Beatty, of all people, as a witness to convict Champ Ferguson. As a matter of principle, that's incredible to me. You, a man of honor! Why, the only reason Tinker Dave goes free is that *he* killed Confederate sympathizers, whereas Champ killed Union people. Talk about being consistent, though— listen to this: The Krulls, though they had a Union officer with them, murdered my husband, who was a Union officer, and Judge McEveride, who certainly was *not* a Confederate sympathizer. And you—or your investigators—did nothing. Why? I went to *you*, and you weren't interested. So I got Tennessee McEveride to risk his life by coming home so that I could put him on the trail of the Krulls and see that they're brought to justice, and what's happening now? Instantly you've alerted your whole organization. To find the Krulls? Not on your life. To find Tennessee McEveride and capture or kill him—*and protect the Krulls!* You don't believe in justice, General Thomas. What do you believe in?''

As Stella spoke, the general had stopped eating. He waited her out to the end, his face impassive, his calm blue eyes steady upon her. ''Well, young lady,'' he said slowly, ''for one thing, I believe in your skill as a debater. The way you color facts and twist half-truths is very close to wonderful. Now let me correct some of your misconceptions. I won't discuss the Champ Ferguson matter. That's for the court-martial to decide. But you're wrong when you think I haven't concerned myself with the McEveride murders. We looked for the Krulls until we became convinced they'd lost themselves in the West, as so many criminals have. You understand the difficulty of seeking them there, unless there *was* a Union officer with them and he could be identified. Dr. Jonathan Hale, our chief of scouts, has exhausted all his resources in his efforts to identify such an officer and has come up with nothing. He thinks now that some guerrilla was wearing a captured uniform with officer's—''

''That's not what Fox Wilkins told Tennessee,'' Stella broke in.

''Fox Wilkins?'' A dawning light broke over the general's face. ''So that's why—''

''He was one of them. Had McEveride plunder in his house.''

''I see. We *could* mark that down as justifiable homicide, then, if your brother-in-law would give himself up. I wish he would. I really would like to do some service in memory of Paul McEveride. Nobody can appreciate his situation in the war better than I can—unless it's Major Randolph here. Both of us are Virginians. Both from families who were slave owners and Confederate in their sympathies. It's no little matter to a Southerner when the members of his family turn their backs and refuse to recognize him. At least your husband was spared the sorrow and bitterness of banishment from the family circle. And I hope he was spared, as I have not been, the suspicion and distrust of officials in high places simply because he was a Southern-born man who chose to remain true to his country. But it does not become me to speak of these things. Anyway, I have some pressing business and must tear myself away. Mrs. McEveride, I'll leave Major Randolph in your charge. Don't hesitate to command him. Armistead, get those supplies, and anything else she wants. Entertain her. And persuade her, if you can, to send that brother-in-law in to give himself up."

When he was gone, Stella looked at Randolph and found in his expressive dark eyes the reflection of some emotion that had not been there before. Before she could speak, he said, "You're a most unusual woman—beautiful in person and brilliant in mind. I haven't met many women who were both. The general also was quite taken with you. I could tell. You had him cornered on that Champ Ferguson thing. And I was absolutely amazed when he spoke to you of his resentment of the high command's treatment of him. He's usually very closemouthed about that."

"Then he *has* been discriminated against?"

"Oh, yes. General Grant has moved to take his command from him more than once. But he's the best general in the Union army, and they haven't been able to ruin him. He told me once that it was deeply gratifying to him that he'd never received a promotion they dared to withhold. They couldn't withhold a brigadier general's commission after Chickamauga nor a major general's after Nashville. . . . And speaking of commissions, what say we adjourn to the lobby, where Sergeant Schuler loiters, if he values his hide. I want to commission *him* to get those supplies for you and deliver them where you say." He rose from his chair and circled the table to make the gesture of pulling back her chair. "Turn over the list, lady," he said as he did so, "and tell me where you want delivery made."

"Here's the list," Stella said. "Have the purchases delivered to Wells & Thompson's Livery."

"I was told your horses aren't there."

"I'll send word where they are to the old man in charge sometime tonight. I want him to have the horses in front of the hotel at nine in the morning, in any case."

"Good," he said, as they walked out of the dining room. "That gives you time to have breakfast with me so that we can finish discussing what we'll discuss at dinner tonight."

"My, such ardent attention to assignment!" Stella murmured, and pointed across the lobby. "There, loitering faithfully, is Sergeant Schuler."

"Excuse me a moment," he said and went off toward the sergeant.

Stella rushed to the desk, where Mrs. Bastrop waited soberly, with no trace of her former somewhat broad humor. "Madam," Stella said hurriedly, "let me pay you for a night's lodging right now. I'm expecting a message that may take me away in the night. I hope not and don't really think I'll have to leave, but there's always that chance."

"Hon, there's no charge if you're not staying." Mrs. Bastrop patted her hand. "Why'd you let me run on with that fool talk? But how was I to know you were the widow of a Union officer? I thought you were some little secesh baggage on a manhunt and traveling close to the wind, as a sailor friend of mine would say. Maybe it's the freckles and red hair, or maybe it's the sexy look without the smidgen of a simper. But, damn me, hon, you just don't look like a lady."

"Thanks," Stella said. "I don't always feel or act like one, either. But take the money. I'll have to use your room until the night, whether I leave or not. I'm having supper with Major Randolph, though he calls it dinner, and it isn't at all convenient to collect my baggage. So I've got to wash this blouse and press this riding skirt. That is, if you'll lend me an iron."

"I'll send a maid who can do all that for you while you wait in your room." Mrs. Bastrop rejected Stella's money again with a wave of her hand. "Keep it. Tip the maid if you want." A suggestion of her former sly, knowing expression revisited her face. "So you're dining with the major. Handsome, isn't he?"

"I've never seen a handsomer man," Stella said. "He *thinks* I'm having breakfast with him, too. And I may. I certainly hope to. But if my luck doesn't hold, shall we let him discover I'm *not* when I don't show up?"

"I won't give you away, hon. Hmm, here comes your man. Lordy, now wouldn't that be something to pull up your gown to?"

Stella turned to Randolph as he approached. "I've got some things to do in my room. I'll see you later."

"Hold up a minute," he said. "Let's decide when. I can't wait till dinnertime to see you again, lady. Tell you what. There's a music concert this afternoon, and the army band that plays out front isn't half bad. I don't know when it begins, but when you hear them tuning up their horns, meet me in the lobby, and we'll listen from around the corner on the third-floor balcony. All right?"

"All right," Stella said, "if you think the general expects you to go that far."

"*I'm* doing the expecting," Randolph returned, "and I expect to go further than that. Much further."

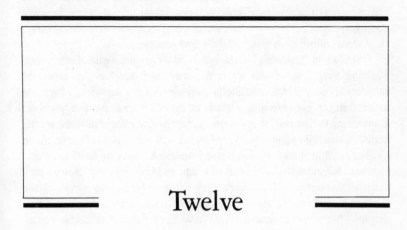

Twelve

It was past mid-afternoon and the musical program had been in progress for some time when Stella and Randolph settled into chairs on a balcony overlooking Railroad Avenue. Since the bandstand was out of their sight, the music did not interfere with conversation. Rather, its background of sound muted their voices and provided them with a kind of privacy that encouraged them to confide more personal details about themselves than they might otherwise have done. He told her about his people in Virginia: They were saved from ruin at the end of the war by investments abroad; nevertheless, they'd lost a fortune in slaves when the South was defeated, and they had not been happy about his decision to keep his oath of allegiance and fight with the Union. His course in the war, however, had not alienated his family, as General Thomas's course had alienated his. . . .

Stella told him about Jock Cameron and her childhood at Belmont Grange. Her story progressed to the night of the Krull raid on the McEveride plantation, and she told him as much about the raid as it was discreet to tell. She talked at some length about Paul, finding many likenesses between him and Randolph; for example, both were adamant in their adherence to principle, both tended to live by code, both were clean in thought and person. But she did not mention these likenesses, for already she was beginning to suspect that it might prove dangerous, no matter how much she was sworn to preserve her chaste widowhood, for her to converse in terms of love about her departed husband to a handsome, sympathetic, attentive young man—even *without* venturing into the intimacy of analogies. They continued talking after the musicians had put away their instruments and departed. When they left the balcony, they were calling each other by their first names.

Stella and Randolph left the hotel and went walking up Ninth Street. Meeting Sergeant Schuler along the way, they received his report of mission accomplished, and Stella paid him for the supplies, which, he assured her, were safe in the hands of the old man at the livery stable. Continuing their stroll, they followed a straggle of pedestrians toward the sound of martial music somewhere ahead—music with a different, much livelier rhythm than they had heard from the balcony of the Crutchfield House. They mounted a hill east of town, and from its crest, along with a surprising number of onlookers, they witnessed the dress parade of the Sixteenth Colored Tennessee Regiment. It was a remarkable military display. No white regiment could have been induced or compelled to attain such precision. At a barked command, a thousand muskets came as one to a thousand shoulders; a thousand gunstocks struck the ground with one thud along the lines....

"Is there anyone you're likely to marry?" Randolph asked out of a silence. "After a decent interval, of course."

The contrast of colors offered an unforgettable spectacle: the black faces, the white gloves, the blue uniforms, the bright steel—all moving or still in perfect obedience to gusty, soft-edged shouts; all caught up in the tom-tom rhythm of the colored band's drums; all seemingly ready to explode into dancing and chanting without moving a collective muscle.

"No," Stella said without emphasis. "There's no one."

"But there *will* be someone," Randolph said somberly, as they turned down the hill. "And soon. You're so young and so beautiful, and you're leaving in the morning—for God knows where. And I'm headed back to Nashville. This day is ending badly."

"You're gallant, Major," Stella murmured. "Quite beyond the call of duty."

"No," he said, frowning. "All of a sudden I feel frustrated. I want to see more of you, yet I've put in for a transfer to the army in the West. I was schooled and trained for the army, and I'm good at my job. Short of old age or death, I'll never leave the army, Stella. And I want some service against the Indians. They say the Comanches are the best light cavalry the world has ever known. I want to see them in action."

"Where will you be stationed, Armistead?"

"Temporarily at Fort Gibson in the Indian Nations, I think. General

Thomas is working on it for me. I'll lose my wartime rank, I guess, since the war will leave such a glut of officers in the regular army that there'll be gray-haired lieutenants and captains on every post. I'll be lucky if I don't slide below captain. And promotions will wait on funerals. But I don't care about the rank. I probably went up too fast, anyway, because I was in General Thomas's command. What I do mind is that I'll be about a thousand miles away from you. Oh, I know what you'll say. I've only known you five or six hours. I don't know. I never felt this way before.''

Stella was looking thoughtful. ''Armistead, look around for the Krulls out there,'' she said with sudden animation. ''Not that I take you seriously, but if you find the Krulls and let me know, and—well, I'll guarantee you one thing. Before you know it, I'll be as close to you as they are.''

''That's pretty grim, Stella,'' he deplored. ''And just about as unromantic as you can get.''

Stella lifted her shoulders. ''It's the way I feel.''

''You mean that you *and* that bloody brother-in-law of yours will be as close to me as the Krulls. We know, of course, that you're traveling with him. So you may as well quit denying it.''

''When have I denied it? You heard what I told General Thomas.'' She studied the puffs of Ninth Street dust their feet were stirring up. ''But about your being far away . . . maybe not. My brother-in-law and I may wind up somewhere in the West. Who knows? Maybe in the Indian Nations.''

''I don't get much comfort from the thought of you traveling with Tennessee McEveride, riding together, camping together. You're no blood kin of his, and I've heard plenty about that wild man.''

''Don't be ridiculous,'' Stella scoffed. ''I'd be as likely to get sentimental over a wolf-man in the full of the moon. By the way, aren't you going to try to argue me into persuading Tennessee to give himself up? That was your assignment.''

They found themselves before the entrance to the Crutchfield House. ''We'll talk about that at dinner,'' he said. ''I have some suggestions about your brother-in-law that may interest you. They're different from what you expect.''

He left her at the entrance, and she crossed the lobby toward the stairs. When she reached them, they were murmuring and creaking under the weight of Mrs. Bastrop coming down. ''Hon, I left one of my daughter's dresses on the bed in your room,'' the big woman said. ''It should fit well enough. Mine would've fit you when I was in my twenties. Can you believe that?'' She gave Stella a sidelong glance. ''Better not answer that. If you find you can't stay, just leave the dress in the room.''

The dress was white and had a form-fitting bodice with high neck and long sleeves. It did fit well, and Randolph thought Stella looked stunning. When she told him that she'd borrowed it from Madam Bastrop, he laughed, not believing, of course, that she and Madam could wear the same clothes.

Toward the last of the soup, she waited no longer. ''You had some suggestions about Tennessee McEveride's situation,'' she reminded him. ''Do you still have?''

''Yes,'' Randolph said. ''Don't let him come in and surrender. Not yet, anyway. And tell him, for God's sake, not to get caught. You were right about great generals. I guess it's true of practically all ambitious directors of large affairs, particularly those whose eyes are trained on history. What happened to Champ Ferguson could happen to Tennessee McEveride. And afterward, when the 'greatest good' has been served, the explanations will be reasonable and the justification irrefutable. No. Let's keep your brother-in-law out of Union hands for a while. Let me document his case with statements from General Forrest, General Wheeler, Tinker Dave Beatty, Dr. Jonathan Hale, a few others—and even General Thomas. If I can get them all to state that they regarded Tennessee McEveride as a Confederate soldier, whether he was on a muster roll or not, we may get him under the protection of the general parole before he places himself in the hands of the Union military.''

Stella looked at him with steady, glowing eyes for a long, still moment. ''Armistead,'' she said softly, ''I've got to tell you something. I've got to let you know what a fine person I think you are. You're the kind of man I like. You mentioned my getting married again. I won't. I've sworn in my heart and on the grave of my husband never to remarry, and I never will. But if I did intend to and God would hear my prayer, it would be to somebody just like you—a most excellent gentleman, handsome and good and kind. *You'll* never blink at injustice with your eyes on history, Armistead Gordon Randolph.''

''No, I don't suppose I ever will,'' Randolph agreed with a deprecatory grin. ''But, then, I'll never be a general, either, or a captain of industry or the President of the United States. Incidentally, I hope you keep on swearing that oath of celibacy in your heart till I meet you again. Then we'll both see what we shall see. If no woman had ever changed her mind, the human race would be extinct.''

When he conducted Stella to her door, she looked all around with exaggerated wariness and suspicion. "Where is he?" she inquired anxiously.

"Who?"

"The guard who'll watch my door tonight."

"You know better than that," he snorted. "See you at breakfast."

Constantly aware of her own plans, Stella had not always kept in mind the fact that Randolph did not know these were moments of farewell, so she had considered the possibility that he might try to kiss her. They had reached the door with her still undecided about whether she'd let him. She thought of their evening together and was surprised to realize that, in spite of her anxieties, she had enjoyed herself. She told him so, and he reached for her hand. She thought of him in the Indian Nations, where the Krulls could be, and of his plans to clear Tennessee of outlaw status and stigma, and she wanted to bind him to her. Consequently she decided to let him kiss her if he wanted to, whether her conduct would be ladylike or not.

Stella was disappointed, therefore, when Randolph merely raised her hand and touched his lips to it. Then he was gone and she was in the room, taking off the dress and preparing to get into her own clothes and venture outside to what awaited her. The dimensions of the task she faced made her head swim. She stood still in the room, considering what she must do in the darkness that shrouded the town and hovered along a road leading across blood-soaked ground, where she'd traveled only by rail, to Lookout Mountain. Suddenly she was sitting on the edge of the bed with her face in her hands.

Angrily she jumped up and began dressing. She was no forlorn maiden in a melancholy romance; she couldn't afford the luxury of loneliness and tears. Gradually it began to dawn on her why she had wanted Armistead to kiss her—for she *had* wanted him to. His kiss would have warmed her heart, allayed her uneasiness, comforted her. It would have given her courage to explore the deep shadows of the night and find her way to Tennessee. Now she must draw upon her own resources for courage. Her last act before quitting the room was to examine the caps and charges of her small revolver, spin the cylinder, and thrust the weapon back under her light jacket. Soon she was through the door, around the corner, and in a corridor of the ell on Railroad Avenue. Ghosting down a back stairway, she came to a rear doorway and went through it into a region of discarded things—barrels, boxes, crates, broken bedsteads, shattered chairs, an iron stove standing askew, and a small mountain of glass jars and tin cans. This enclosed area was the core of the block bracketed by the ells of the Crutchfield House.

Stella started running toward the nearest corner of Eighth Street, then tripped on some hidden piece of junk and fell down hard on her elbows. She crouched in the shadows, crying from the pain without making a sound; then she was up and running again. Hurrying along Eighth, she met three half-drunken soldiers and had to dodge from the grabbing hands of one of them, who wanted a trip with her into the nearest alley, assuring her there was a couple of dollars in it for her. "Lay off, Herman!" a companion warned. "That's the one we seen up on the hill with that major from Nashville." She hurried on and arrived at the livery breathless.

The old man had run out of cloves, and it occurred to Stella that the whole place might go up if a match were lit near his mouth. "Got something to show you," he said, leading the way to a stall in the rear, where a fully uniformed soldier lay flat on his back on manure-fouled straw, snoring loudly. "I ought to drag him out back. He's keeping the hosses awake."

"What's he doing here?"

"Stationed here as a lookout," the old man said. "Sergeant Schuler's man. He was to report quick, case you come for the hosses. They aimed to foller you, honey. So I kept offering the hog bottled comfort till he passed hisself out. Only trouble, he finished my last bottle, and now *I'm* plumb out of comfort."

Stella put a coin in his hand. "Bring my horses, and then you're free to go take on all the comfort you can stand. This fellow's horn will surely scare off any prowlers that might come around."

Sight of the coin jolted up the old man's head. "Why, honey, this here's a double eagle! It's *way* too much."

"You've earned it, my good friend," Stella assured him. "I'll remember you with a full heart. Now, if I could have my horses. I'm in a desperate hurry."

As she mounted the Tennessee mare in the runway, with War Drum's lead rope in her hand, Stella was attentive to the old man's directions for getting on the road to Lookout Mountain. Following them precisely, she headed the horses west on Eighth Street, retracing her own footsteps, and then turned south. Passing near the blockhouse where soldiers had been stationed to guard the railroad yard during the war, she was hailed by a loud, demanding voice. She waited tensely. If soldiers moved to intercept her, she'd whip the horses past them or over them and lose herself in the night. But she suspected that the voice belonged to a drunken loiterer, since she had no reason to believe that the government still manned the blockhouses. Then she was quietly past and moving on. All through town she'd been grateful for the heavy layer of dust underfoot, since it tended to muffle the sound of hoofbeats on the streets, and now she welcomed the dull moonlight, which provided sufficient visibility for travel by night but only enough to enable lookouts to spot travelers up close. Sooner than she expected, the black bulk of the mountain rose before her and stood giant-shouldered, overwhelming, and somehow frightening for the rest of the way. Then the slate-colored range of crags was hanging high overhead and swinging off to the left, and Stella rode up a steep, rough road that wound among trees and huge limestone rocks as it skirted the northern slope of the mountain. Where the road took a sharp turn around a great boulder, she drew up for a last look at the town. Nothing of it was visible save a few weak lights. But nearer at hand, on the dark water of the river, was a lurid, crimson glare from the flames of a government rolling mill that operated night and day. Stella shivered. Somehow the blood-red glow in the night seemed ominous. She reined around the boulder, still climbing; and there before her, silhouetted against the pale sky, a black-garbed rider sat on the great black shape of a horse. As she drew her pistol, Stella thought, I'm as spooky as the Tennessee mare tonight. Maybe with reason—even if it's who I think it is....

During first darkness Tennessee grew restless and was well on the way toward making up his mind to scout for Stella's whereabouts in the town. Chattanooga, he'd heard, was not a safe place for a woman alone. But by moonlight he caught the rumor of approaching horses on the road from town and, waiting patiently, finally recognized the mare's unmistakable style in the mixture of hoofbeats. He mounted and sent the dun downslope to the road. Soon a dark mass showed at the edge of a huge rock outcropping and continued on, changing shape. Then it separated into a rider and two horses that slowed abruptly to a walk and stopped. Dull moonlight caught on metal near the saddle of the ridden horse.

"Steady, now!" Tennessee called. "It's me."

"Who's me?" Stella answered in a guarded voice.

"Fine thing, can't tell your own brother's voice."

The mare jumped and came on with a scamper of hooves, the stud's pack bobbing behind her like the hump of a long-striding dromedary. Stella leaned out from the saddle, staring at Tennessee's black suit, white shirt, and black string tie. She was close enough for him to make out her set face and hard eyes.

"Well, now, just look at the fine gentleman!" she said bitterly. "Oh, you damned, brutal fool! Who's naked and probably dead up in those woods?"

"Wait a minute!" Tennessee protested. "Somebody give me these clothes."

"Here," Stella snapped. "Take this lead rope. We've got to get away from here." She wheeled the mare away and said no more until the horses were churning the dust and running before it along the road. Then, when the dun pushed up beside the mare, she lifted her voice above the pound and scuffle of hooves. "Know who's back there in that town? Great big Rock of Chickamauga himself—General George Henry Thomas! In all his flesh. Had dinner with him—lunch, rather. Remembered the time I went to see him in Nashville. And why. Read me two telegrams. You told soldiers to check with him at Nashville. Outsmarted yourself. They did."

"Knew they would," Tennessee said. "What else could I do, 'less I killed 'em all? Done that, one of 'em might got some lead in me."

"Wanted me to tell him where you were—for your own good. Wanted you to come in, surrender, be paroled. Had soldiers follow me everywhere, a major keep me company. So I got a room in the Crutchfield House and slipped out after dark. Now he knows for sure. Maybe he knew already. Said he did. But *you* were the one said don't buy clothes for you in that town!"

"You get the supplies?"

"You know I did. Don't try to change the subject." Suddenly Stella began hauling back on the reins. "Whoa, damn you! This mare's been spooky all—slow up a minute, Tennessee!" Stella reined the mare close to the dun, watching Tennessee's face intently. "Did I hear you right? Somebody *gave* you that suit?"

"That's what I said."

"Well, say something more. Who was it?"

"She was a widow-woman—that's what I think. She couldn't wear the suit herself. So she give it to me. That's the whole thing."

"Where'd you find this old lady?" Stella asked casually. "Not in town, surely."

"This side Cameron Hill—that steep hill down from the bridge," he growled. Then, encouraged by her use of the term "old lady," he added, "Only house I saw back there. The suit was hanging on a clothesline. I offered to buy it, but she wouldn't take no money."

"Of course not," Stella said understandingly. "She had *some* pride. How old would you say she was? Twenty-five? Thirty?"

"How the hell do I know?" he snarled, feeling betrayed. "What's her age got to do with giving me clothes?"

"Well, I'm relieved," Stella decided. "Certainly the good widow won't catch up her skirts and fly uptown to report entertaining a big handsome brute in her house. What kind of dinner did she serve? She a good cook, too?"

"All right, Stella." Hunching his burly shoulders, Tennessee pulled his hat brim over his eyes. "You know so much! I never said I set foot in that woman's house."

"If you hadn't eaten—and probably enough for three men, at that—you'd have broken open that pack before we stirred a step." Stella sounded coolly amused. "And don't tell me that poor, lonely widow didn't have you in to try the clothes on."

"What if she did? What good would they been too small for me? Anyhow, she claimed I put her in mind of somebody. She could had a boy my age killed in the war. That ain't unlikely."

Stella's shoulders jerked convulsively. "That—that's *very* likely," she agreed in a muffled voice. "But more than one, I'd say. Likely a dozen or so. Boys as old as she is, some of them— and older, too." Her voice stopped on the ragged edge of a giggle.

Tennessee surged upright in the saddle. "By God, there you go!" he exploded. "Will you just kindly tell me how in the name of God you're so sure some blasted whore give me this suit, and not some kind old lady?"

"Now, now," Stella chided unsteadily. "If some other blackguard used such language in front of your sister, you'd have to horsewhip him to hold your head up."

"Sister, hell!"

"For your information, brother," she continued cheerfully, "no 'kind old lady' in her right mind would give you anything but a wide berth. And ábsolutely *no* female would ever be reminded of a son or grandson—well, not unless you found one riding on a broomstick. Oh, those Hercules-hardcase Apollo looks of yours might unbalance some giddy featherhead of twenty. I guess they would. Or some lush wanton of thirty, or even some last-chance jade of forty, for that matter. But your 'kind old lady'—uh-unh! She'd look right past your muscles and profile. What she'd see is a tiger looking out of a man. And then, unless she froze in her tracks, she'd bolt the door and join the mouse traps under her bed."

"Just tell me one thing," Tennessee growled resentfully. "Why ain't you behind some door instead of out here in the dark with a tiger like me?"

"Why, if you were a stranger," she said lightly, "you'd scare the daylights out of me a dozen times a day. But then, I know you, brother. And I'm gratified to see you dodge and squirm when questioned about that woman. It proves that a wolf can be housebroken to feel *some* guilt when he soils the rug, even if the training *won't* make him a dog."

"Now I'm a wolf again," he observed sourly. "What if I started calling *you* a dog? Way you talk, there's a word you wouldn't like to hear."

Stella laughed briefly. "You touched me there, all right," she admitted, and fell silent. He could feel her mood change.

"I'm learning a few things about myself," she mused somberly. "Might as well face it. I've got more evil in me than I ever suspected. I know now that I'll pay a big price for those accursed Krulls. . . . Tennessee, do you know that I wouldn't convert you to a good, upright, God-fearing man if I could? That's how evil I've become. Yes sir, you may be a brutal, immoral, murderous rogue—and I suspect you are—but I wouldn't change one thing about you. . . . But I can't help it, Tennessee! So help me God, I can't help it! I've got one goal in this life and nothing beyond it. If I go to hell for it, I mean—to stop—the breathing—of every damned Krull that lives! Then, when Paul's honor—when his tortured face—" Her voice died out in labored breathing. When it came again, it was barely audible. "Then, at last, *maybe* I can sleep."

Thirteen

Traveling across north Alabama, Tennessee and Stella found themselves forced to camp out at night in a ravaged land that might as well have suffered the repeated visitations of a Genghis Khan or the occupations of an Attila. Under Sherman, the Federal armies had adopted sack and pillage as an official policy during the last years of the war, and all down the Tennessee Valley fire had reduced whole villages to lonesome-looking chimneys and blackened ruins. Bridgeport, Stevenson, Bellefonte, Scottsboro, Larkinsville, Woodville, Paint Rock, Decatur—all were practically wiped out. Farmhouses, gins, fences, and livestock were gone. By comparison, the attrition wrought in this land by repeated invasion and prolonged occupation made Sherman's "March to the Sea," since it occurred but once, seem mild. And famine, which had followed the armies in, had remained behind them in the land.

Stella was appalled by the general desolation. Her indignation mounted when she witnessed the brutal marks of starvation on the faces of people they passed on the roads. She offered them money, and they took it, too desperate for shame. Tennessee shrugged and rode on, apparently unmoved by the ruin of either the countryside or its people. Finally he protested against Stella's acts of charity, pointing out that such donations from one person would not get the country back on its feet.

"Damn the country," Stella answered hotly, "if you mean the proud counties and states that made the decision to secede! I'm putting a little food into the mouths of children and overburdened women and weak old men. What decisions did *they* make? And damn the barbarism of a government that would send great armies down on helpless people and then leave them homeless and plundered to starve and sicken and die! Look yonder at those fields. Sprouts and saplings taking them over—and why not? The beasts that were here have left their stinking tracks everywhere, defiling what they couldn't devour. It's time the wilderness *was* reclaiming its own.''

"Hold on, now," Tennessee said with a grin. "That's Confederate talk. Thought you were Union."

"Confederacy! Union!" Stella's mouth twisted wryly. "What do those words mean? I'm talking about people. If you want the truth, I had no politics in this war. I just wanted it over. What did *you* want? How come you fought for the South against the North?''

"Where you think I lived? They come down here. I never went up North.''

"The principles meant nothing to you, then?"

"What principles?"

"That's what I thought."

"Paul took all the principles off with him. None of 'em fit to eat, anyhow. Say, you ought to be passing out principles instead of money. Lot cheaper, and likely do you as much good when you look back."

Turning in the saddle, Stella braced herself with a hand on the cantle. "Tennessee, answer me honestly. No, look at me. . . . Can you sit that horse there and tell me that you aren't sorry for these poor people? Don't lie, now.''

Something flickered in the depths of Tennessee's cold eyes; but, whatever it was, it was not compassion. "Go on," he complained. "Call me a wolf again. You don't have to work up to it."

"No, no," she said, "I'm serious. When you think of what the Yankees did to these people, doesn't it make your blood boil?''

"What you expect? These folks lost a war, Stella. All this ain't new to me, because I saw it happen—saw their places burned and their stuff hauled off. You wouldn't believe what an army can get out of a neighborhood in just one raid. And it's smart war, Stella. Without that kind of war, we'd be fighting yet—with a good chance of winning, too."

Stella studied the bobbing ears of her mare thoughtfully. "I don't believe merciless force is ever smart," she said quietly. "The Krulls will find it wasn't. They had no mercy, and they'll receive none. And I'll pay for showing *them* none, I suppose. These people here—you think they won't pass their bitterness down to generations yet unborn? So how can any real unity result from all this devastation?''

"Pick any generation you want," Tennessee said with grim assurance. "It won't try secession again. That's settled. And that's all the unity Abe Lincoln was after."

Stella threw him an ironic glance. "That's what I like about you, Tennessee," she observed dryly. "You're never in the faintest doubt about anything."

It took them the better part of a week to cross Alabama to the hill country of north Mississippi. Their route across Mississippi was northwest, toward Memphis, along roads which often served them little better than as guides across passable terrain. They'd learned from their crossings of the Tennessee River that large streams were major barriers to horseback travel in the upper South, since practically all ferryboats in the western theater of war had been captured or burned. But at Memphis, if anywhere in their reach north of Vicksburg, they could count on ferry service in crossing the Mississippi River. They found lodgings at night in the cabins and dog runs of the hill country and, farther west, in the skull-like mansions of the cotton lands, where painfully hospitable planters in mended linen or homespun were learning that confiscation, unlike cannon fire and bayonet thrusts, apparently had no Appomattox.

Then, one afternoon, a day's ride from Memphis, with wind freshening in their faces and black clouds crawling up from the west, they came upon the burned-out ruins of plantation buildings where they had hoped to find shelter. Main house, slave quarters, barn, sheds, blacksmith shop, gin, warehouse, chicken houses—all were ashes and blackened debris, even the inevitable outhouse. Such thoroughness indicated that here a hatred beyond the call of service had fed with the flames.

"We're on the right track, looks like," Tennessee commented. "I reckon the Krulls sure stopped by here."

Stella gave him a withering glance. "You're very funny," she said coldly. "And smart, too. Now tell me where we go fast enough to beat that rain."

Southward stretched wide fields long used for growing cotton but now green with weeds, veined at great intervals by cane brakes spreading out from small streams. Tennessee pointed north toward distant eroded hills barely visible above the trees of a low, flat forest land.

"See that poor land?" he said, managing a certain smugness without change of expression. "Well, at the edge of it there's a shack of some sort. And in it there's a white-trash mouth feeding better'n it ever done before. Want to bet I'm wrong?"

"You've got nothing to bet I'd want," Stella said, as if she hoped he was wrong, and turned her mare toward the eroded hills.

Falling in behind her, Tennessee studied the graceful line of her straight, slim-waisted back, the swell of her hips and thighs molded against the saddle. It occurred to him that Brownlow Krull had not had anything she'd wanted, either. A familiar contraction of his belly muscles reminded him of Memphis. Stella might refresh herself for a day or so at the Gayoso Hotel, and he might run across a willing woman. And then he might buy himself some better traveling clothes—at least, some more comfortable ones. . . .

They found the squatter's place beyond the flatwoods in a gully-washed land of saw briers, blackberry bushes, scattered sage grass, and scrub cedars. Following a woods road apparently much used of late, they came first in hearing of the thin clapping of an ax and then to the edge of the woods, where they pulled up to look the place over before riding into the open. Near the end of a large-roomed log cabin with a kitchen ell, a man in denim trousers was chopping stove wood, his long gray hair whipping in the wind. In a barn lot made of unbarked poles, several big mules were crowding each other under a makeshift shed. Overhead the wind was roaring through the writhing, lunging foliage of the woods, but Tennessee was certain he'd heard the whickering of more than one horse in the barn, which was little more than a walled-up shed with a closed hallway.

"Mighty good mules for a place like this," Stella observed uneasily.

"Yeah," Tennessee agreed. "Good enough for the army to keep instead of shoot, anyhow. See one's got the US brand on him. Others, too, likely."

"You think he stole them?"

"Why, he never had anything he didn't steal." Tennessee watched the house with narrowed eyes. "Stella, what you say's in that house?"

"You mean furniture or people?"

"People."

"He lives by himself. If he had a wife, she'd be cutting that wood."

"That's where you're wrong." He looked up at low-flying banners beneath the seething darkness of the clouds. "Got a young, strapping wife he ain't sure of. Something making her stay inside, keeping her from watching the weather, feeling the wind. . . . Must be more'n one man in there, old man cutting so steady, not checking the door. Wasn't for rain coming, we'd pull back and ride on."

"Are you serious?" Stella asked incredulously. "You can't know all that."

"Where'd he get his ambition, then?" Tennessee wanted to know. "He's the shiftless breed lives on poor land all through life. So shiftless he waits to cut wood till the next meal's due. He wanted a place to live, you'd think he'd find an empty shack to burrow in. But here he's built a tight two-room cabin. Sure, the woman nags him and holds his age up, and she's too much for him to beat down and make do with nothing but hard-scrabble. And there's three different horses closed up in that barn. Maybe more."

"Well, you're cautious." Stella regarded him curiously. "Are you afraid soldiers are in there with her? Soldiers driving those mules somewhere?"

"Not soldiers." Tennessee reached under his coat and shifted his Army Colts farther to the front. "Old man's partners. Bushwhacking rogues. We get inside, don't get scared or mad at what they say. I tell you to do something, don't wait. Do it then."

"Now, wait, Tennessee!" Stella's freckles were registering alarm. "If you expect trouble in there, it's foolish to go in. Let's ride on."

"And get caught out and soaked?" He reached for the reins, took up the slack in the lead rope. "They ain't that important. Come on. Rain won't last long, all that wind. Could be wrong about the whole thing, anyhow."

The old man had laid aside his ax and was on one knee picking up an armful of wood when he heard the tramp and scuff of their horses. His head came over his shoulder like a snake's, and he leaped up, the wood clattering about his feet. Yelling something toward the door, he stooped and came erect with a stick of wood in his hand. He stood his ground, his eyes like black smudges above his scraggly white beard. He was robust and lithe for an old man—and not so old as he'd looked from the edge of the woods, either.

Two men with rifles hit the doorway, one coming through to the ground, the other stopping with his head almost brushing the lintel. They were dressed alike, in soiled dark trousers and sweat-stained blue shirts. Though one was tall and the other short, they were obviously brothers. Both had square, heavy-boned faces; both had thick necks, broad torsos. Their eyes rejected Tennessee instantly and fastened on Stella and the horses.

Tennessee was watching the door expectantly, and then she appeared beside the tall brother. He glanced at Stella, his face expressionless, and she bit her lip. The woman was almost as dark as a gypsy, shrewd-eyed, voluptuous—attractive in spite of coarse features and discontented mouth. She was wearing a light-blue dress that would have graced a belle of plantation society before the war. She looked at Tennessee and smoothed the fabric over her hips.

"Howdy," Tennessee said, drawing rein beside a snarl of uncut wood dragged up for fuel.

The woman gave him a slow, sensual smile that seemed deliberately provocative. He brought his eyes back to the old man's sinister, wolfish face. "Got here just in time, looks like," he said, nodding toward the sooty clouds piling out of the west. "That's a *rain* coming!"

Murky eyes crossed Tennessee's and would not hold. The old man set his jaw. "You got here in time to flog them hosses back the way you come," he said harshly. "That's what you done."

"Take a look at them clouds," Tennessee said evenly.

"Who showed you the way in here? What you looking for?" The old man's eyes clashed with Tennessee's and shifted again.

"Looking for what we found—the roof on that house," Tennessee told him. "We aim to get under it, if you got no objections." Then he added deliberately, "Or if you have."

"Lord God!" the old man snarled. "Here plantation folks done come a-visiting poor folks their biggity niggers used to look down on. Now *I* got the roof and *you* got the needfuls. Tell you what. Fair's fair. I'll tell you just what I been told. Get the hell offen my place and stay off!"

"Why, long as your roof's handy," Tennessee said, "we ain't too good to get under it with you. I reckon we'll stay."

The murky eyes jerked with strain, then shied again, and the old man flew into a rage. "By God, hump your asses out that road!" he shouted, and stamped the ground as if he had a cottonmouth underfoot. "Turn them hosses and get!"

"Tennessee!" Stella said urgently. "Tennessee, let's go! We've got more important business than this."

Tennessee stepped out of the saddle, placing the dun between himself and the house. "Old man," he said grimly, "you keep this up till that rain gets here, you won't make it to the door. We will, but you won't."

Then the woman spoke from the doorway, and Tennessee realized at once that he'd been wasting his time with the old man. "Abe, quit acting a fool!" she said sharply. "You got about us much manners as a boar hog—if you *ain't* as heavy hung. Now, you ask them folks inside to sit out the rain, or I will."

The tall brother leered at Stella. "Sure, Abe," he said. "What the hell? Want the lady to get her—uh, ah, herself wet?"

"I done told 'em to get!" Abe shouted, his murky eyes flaring. "I don't aim—" The utterance lacked force. "By God, I don't aim—"

"Time you did, then," the woman quipped cruelly. "You never do *hit* nothing, neither." She winked at Tennessee. "Maybe your old gun's wore out."

The tall brother stepped down from the doorway, grinning. "Rose, you got a tongue like a snake's tooth," he said. "You folks go in the house. Me and Zeke'll put your hosses in the barn." The brothers exchanged fleeting glances.

With her eyes on Tennessee, Rose said, "You know there ain't no more horse room in that barn."

For a moment the tall brother looked stricken. Then he swung his head toward Abe, without looking at Rose. "Goddamn it, Abe, when you going to learn this here slut of your'n—" He broke off, almost spraining his face with a rueful grin. "Mightnear right, though, at that. But I reckon we can make room."

"Just keep your hands off them horses,Tobe," the woman ordered, her black eyes wicked with anger. "And you watch how you talk in front of a lady, too, trash-mouth! You ain't at home with your sisters now." Ignoring the black scowl her words had not been designed to lighten, she looked across the big dun at Tennessee. "You can hitch your horses behind the house. Ain't no other place. They'll be out of the wind there, though. Better off than them mule critters under that shed, catching the slant of the rain."

A few large drops of water hit the yard. Tennessee recognized them as the outriders and knew that the rain host would not be far behind. He led the horses around the single-room end of the cabin, while Abe and the brothers trooped inside behind Stella, whose freckles were never more in evidence. Behind the cabin was a porch extending from the corner to the ell formed by the second room. As he tied reins to porch uprights and unsaddled, Tennessee observed the closed back door and the absence of a window on the near side of the ell.

Walking lightly, he stepped upon the porch and placed saddles and pack slowly against the wall. Then, instead of returning to the front by the way he had come, he cut around the end of the second room and discovered an open window on the north side. Hugging the wall, he moved toward it, prepared to swoop under it; and then he heard the voices inside—the old man's and Tobe's, pitched low.

Removing his hat, he brought one eye slowly to the nearest corner of the window, tilting his head to reduce the area of face he would expose. A kitchen range, a massive dining-room table, and a mahogany sideboard left barely enough space for the chairs against the wall and the human occupants of the room at the same time. Tennessee was in time to see old Abe thrust a Navy Colt inside his belt and cover it with his shirt. Tall Tobe was undecided, apparently, as to the choice of a heavy pistol in one hand or a long knife in the other.

"If I could work in behind him—" he began.

"Naw, damn it!" Abe snarled. "I done told you *not inside!* Get blood on that rug, Rose will jest . . . goddamn her, anyhow! Some-day . . . someday. . . ."

"When, then?"

"Wait till they get outside, leaving. And make damn sure his back's turned. Might be better we let him go. Son-of-a-bitch kill us all, he gets half a chance. I never seen no such eyes before in a human head."

"He ain't leaving with them hosses and that woman," Tobe declared. "And he ain't leaving without 'em, to come back with soldiers, neither. Ever see a freckle-faced woman look like that? Ain't pushed, I may keep her, she tames right, you know."

"Never looked," Abe grunted. "Couldn't see nothing but that big bastard."

"You must not looked at Rose, neither," Tobe said maliciously. "You'd saw she taken a shine. . . ."

Tennessee leaped away from the wall and whirled toward the corner, racing the rain for the front door. The first drops swept the yard like a rattle of musketry and caught him turning the corner; close behind them a great cloud-high tide of rain was surging across the land, a storming wind turned solid with water, it seemed. Tennessee hit the front door a split-second before the rain hit the roof with a crash that shook the sturdy cabin. He was standing on a Persian rug, hackles raised and eyes flaring, when the rain settled into one thrashing, continuous roar. In that moment of violated wariness, while he was adjusting himself to a place into which he'd been forced to rush blindly, it would have taken a more experienced rogue than the dour Zeke to oppose him.

Zeke gloomed over his rifle near the door, watching the rain; Stella was seated in the center of the room; and Rose was standing in front of the fireplace. Abe and Tobe were still absent from the room.

"Pick a chair and set, Tennessee Smith," Rose invited. "Mrs. McEveride claims y'all brother and sister, even if you *do* look more like man and woman. But sure glad to hear it." Though her smile was no more than friendly, her eyes were so intimate that Tennessee dared not look at Stella. "Hate like sin to break up a home, you know." She was game to handle him in front of Stella or old Abe or the devil, and Stella was sitting there marking down things to rag him with later. Now Rose was saying, "Tennessee. *Tennessee* Smith. There's a funny name."

"In Tennessee, maybe," he admitted. "Not so much in Mississippi. Which side the line this place on, anyhow?"

"Some claim one thing—" Rose began, then turned to Zeke. "You know for sure, Zeke? Which we in, Mississippi or Tennessee?"

Zeke said nothing. In fact, he gave no indication whatever that he had heard the question. But Tennessee knew the Zekes of this world. They pursed their words habitually, lest they inadvertently drop one that might accommodate some other human being.

Rose regarded Zeke with a disgust tinged with humor. "Now, ain't he something!" she said wryly. "Only case on record where the youngun died and the afterbirth lived." Suddenly her face hardened. "Shut that door, you dog's knot! Think you're the only thing getting wet? Look at that rug!" She glanced at Tennessee, nodding her head to the far side of the room. When he followed, she put her back to the wall and then stepped in close to him, brushing her hands down his coat until they struck gun butts. Then, screened from Stella's view by his body, one of her hands drifted casually through an opening in his shirt front where a button was missing, fingers digging into hard muscles. "Watch your back, big man," she whispered. "They don't aim for you to leave here. They want your horses, what else you got—her, too. . . . Aw, man, I bet you could lift a corner of this house!" She stepped around him just as the back-room door opened and Tobe came through, followed by Abe. "Set there." She indicated a chair backed against the wall.

"Have a drink," Tobe invited, holding out a jug. "Ag'in' the damp."

"Mighty loud damp," Rose commented.

"Hit's slacking off some," Abe observed sourly. "Wouldn't a-hurt 'em to flog on and get where they's going. Might been better off in the turnout, all you know."

"Better off, how?" Rose asked sharply. "You sound foolish—'less you know something we ain't heard. That the way of it?"

Tobe looked at Rose with puzzled eyes. "Rose, what the hell's gigging you?" he complained. "Abe don't mean nothing." Again he proffered the jug to Tennessee. "You want a drink or not?"

"After you," Tennessee said. "Might be poisoned." He felt Stella's black eyes staring and wondered whether her freckled hand had already gone under her riding jacket for her .36 Remington. She knew what kind of place they were in, yet she sat there without a tremor. By God, for guts and sense, as well as for looks, she beat any woman he ever saw.

Tobe's slate-colored eyes got small, and then he grinned tightly. "Might be, at that." He raised the jug toward his lips and drank briefly, but Tennessee heard whiskey gurgle out of the jug.

Tennessee took the jug and let the raw whiskey pour down his throat until he heard a restless stirring from Stella's chair. Then he handed the jug back and took his seat, feeling a glowing warmth radiate through him. He felt fine.

"Have a drink, girlie." Tobe offered the jug to Stella, his eyes cutting back at Tennessee.

"No, thank you," Stella said coldly, her voice stiff with restraint.

"Hey, Zeke," Tobe said, "you still nursing that rifle-gun? You watch it don't go off accidental and blow the head off our new friend here." He leered at Tennessee. "Maybe your woman's needful of a change, friend. Don't you allow her to have no kind of fun?"

"My sister," Tennessee corrected him. "She does what she pleases." He looked up at Tobe with a savage grin. "No more, no less." Still grinning, he turned his head and spoke softly to Abe, who had shifted over against the wall to his right. "Old man, you make me nervous over there. Move back to the fireplace."

Abe stiffened, thunderstruck. Finally, when he found his voice, he snarled, "You got your damn guts!" But he was moving as he spoke, and stopped with his shoulders against the mantel. "Ain't this here *my* house, by God?"

Tennessee lounged to his feet. "Why, I don't know, old man," he said, as if he thought the question merited consideration. "Whose timber you cut for the logs? Man's you burnt out? What place you burn to haul off this furniture here? Plantation other side the big flatwoods? You ever own anything before the war made it safe to steal things bigger'n a chicken?"

Tobe turned toward the fireplace, his motion too slow, too casual; he set the jug carefully on the floor, keeping his back to Tennessee. Abe stood rigid, his lupine face grotesquely drawn. Zeke had his head up by the door, listening, as if startled by the sound of quietness itself. Shifting the rifle to his left arm, Zeke got out of his chair and swung the door open. The storm had ceased. Though a light shower was falling now, the wind had blown the main force of the rain east and followed it out of the area. Low in the west, behind gossamer streamers of rain, the sun was shining.

''Who might you be, friend?'' Tobe asked, without turning.

''Might be anybody,'' Tennessee said, wondering how an obvious rogue like Tobe had managed to live so long. ''Calling myself Tennessee Smith right now.''

''Why, I was scared you might be *somebody*,'' jeered Tobe, and started turning.

''No, Tobe!'' Abe shouted, coming out of his paralysis. ''No!''

The trapped roar of Tennessee's right-hand gun was like a thunderclap in the room. The heavy bullet caught Tobe half-turned, slamming him back against the mantel. Instantly Tennessee swung the gun and fired through swirling powder smoke at Abe's upright shape, and the old man went down as if poleaxed. Leaping wide of the roiling smoke, Tennessee had Zeke under the muzzle of his eared-back Colt before Tobe had settled on the hearth, flailing the andirons, drumming his heels in the fireplace.

''Do what you want with that rifle,'' Tennessee said to Zeke. ''But do something.''

Zeke blinked like a stunned bulldog coming to. Throwing the rifle through the open doorway, he turned dull, opaque eyes back to Tennessee. ''Ain't armed,'' he said. ''Ain't giving you no excuse.''

''Snakes always armed,'' Tennessee said. ''Still got your teeth. Live to a hundred I'll never figure why you ain't down on that floor right now.'' Looking around, he found Stella on her feet, watching him with amazed eyes. Only her freckles kept her face from paper whiteness.

''*Why*, Tennessee?'' she asked, shaping her words numbly. ''*Why? What did they mean to us? What did they do?*''

''You missed something,'' Tennessee told her. ''It was them or me from the first. Didn't have no choice. Tobe had his gun half out.''

''But the old man!'' Stella protested. ''What did *he* do? *You just killed him!*''

''God's sake, Stella! They dropped me, you couldn't told him from Parson Krull. How could I see what he's doing behind that smoke, anyhow? Expect me to wait till—'' He stopped short, beginning to realize why Zeke was not on the floor with the others, where the bastard belonged. ''Stella, go saddle your mare and ride out. Slicker'll keep you dry now. Wait for me at the edge of the woods. Just take the mare—and hurry. Be along quick as I can.''

Rose straightened up after dragging Abe off the rug. ''He's right, Mrs. McEveride,'' she said, her voice thin with excitement. ''They aimed to kill him for the horses, and for you, if you know what I mean. I told Tennessee before he sat down.'' She tilted her head, passing Tennessee a crude, intimate message with her eyes. ''You couldn't do nothing else, Tennessee. I won't never speak a word against you for it.''

"Different with me," Zeke snarled. "Because I never was no Memphis whore.''

"Every lady's a whore to Zeke," Rose confided cheerfully to Tennessee. She looked at Zeke narrowly. ''That's all you never been, you trashy bastard. You've hated the guts of *people* ever since your mammy showed her eight tits to the litter.''

Stella paused in the doorway, looking back at Tennessee. In the last two minutes she'd dug down and come up with her old tough, high-cheeked expression. ''I won't say it,'' she said coldly, ''because it's just too brutish to think.'' Her lips curled scornfully. ''No! . . . No, I don't *really* believe you're low enough to put on a suit of clothes you'd find in this awful place!'' Turning, she stepped through the doorway and was gone.

''What she mean by that?'' Rose asked suspiciously.

''Damned if I know,'' Tennessee murmured, his mind occupied by the problem Zeke posed. He watched Zeke with cold detachment, balancing the cocked revolver in his hand. While Rose was going through the pockets of the dead men, he heard the mare cut out from behind the cabin and beat a tattoo across the yard, fading toward the woods.

Zeke's eyes were like two minie balls caught in the vises of his narrowed lids. His stare contained the dumb, enduring viciousness of a chained yard dog that hates everything that lives. He swallowed, and then he said, ''We ought to knocked you down out front.'' His voice was guttural, low. ''You had luck, bucko. Be different next time. Don't think I ain't coming after you.''

''I know,'' Tennessee said softly, ''and I ought to save you the trip.''

''Ten years, twenty years—if it's in hell, you look back. I'll be behind you, coming up.''

A response popped full-blown into Tennessee's head, and he almost made it before he remembered that Stella was waiting for him within hearing distance of a pistol shot. Instead, he said quietly, ''I'll mark you, then, so I'll know you when you come.'' Then he took one step and slammed Zeke across the forehead with the barrel of his heavy Colt.

Zeke crashed back into the wall and slid down rubber-legged to a seat on the floor, bowing from the waist and slapping the floor with his face. Rose was on her knees, watching Tennessee. Then she got up and left the room. Tennessee felt Zeke's jugular area and came to his feet with a muttered oath when his fingers registered the throb of a strong, steady pulse. He wished now he'd gone ahead and shot Zeke between the eyes, letting Stella hear the shot and misunderstand three killings instead of two. Well, he'd have it to do later, and probably with Zeke having the choice of circumstance. He was not at all pleased with himself; he was thinking too much about what he did. Thinking made simple things complicated, made action halting and uncertain. It wasn't natural, and it was a damned good way to get killed.

Rose reentered the room carrying a cotton rope and moved up beside him. "All his life the dumb bastard never said a dozen words a week," she mused, "and here, when he ought to just breathed, he come mighty close to talking himself to death. I saw *that*, and I was sure hoping . . . but tie him up good with this rope, Tennessee. You don't, he'll haul off everything here. I got a good friend down the road will turn him loose after you've gone." When he had Zeke bound securely hand and foot, Rose instructed him further. "Tie this cloth over his eyes, and stick this cotton in his ears."

"What for?"

"So he can't see what goes on," Rose said calmly, "or hear it, either. I'm a kind of a moaner, as you might say."

Puzzled, Tennessee did her bidding and stood up. "Reckon I might as well go," he said reluctantly. "Stella's waiting out there."

Rose hugged his arm and leaned against him. "Who you trying to fool?" she asked mockingly. "How come you sent your sister on? So you could tend to that business with Zeke?" Now she had her hand inside his shirt again. "Or that business with me?"

Tennessee looked down at Rose's black head, on past to the projection of her bosom with its deep, dusky cleft. "I ain't got the least idea," he said. "Ain't thought about it yet."

"Well, think now," Rose told him. "But don't take long. Your sister might come back and find you and your pants in different places."

Fourteen

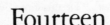

At the edge of the woods Stella dismounted, reset her saddle, and cinched it firmly. The rain had almost stopped. She stood for a while with the reins in her hand, still numb with shock. When Tennessee did not come, she tied the mare's reins to a sapling and sat down at the base of a tree with her back to the trunk, ignoring the drip from the rain-wet leaves, waiting and thinking about her brother-in-law.

Stella was aware that until now she'd been evaluating actions and experiences that were entirely academic. She hadn't seen Tennessee kill Fox Wilkins, who needed killing, anyway. She hadn't seen the "widow-woman" in Chattanooga nor heard her speak. It had taken the immediate reality of the past thirty minutes to turn her around completely. Now, at last, she had seen Tennessee in action and knew him for what he was.

She'd been incredibly naive. He was no wolf! Wolves killed instinctively to survive: They killed when attacked, when hungry, when competing with other dog wolves for bitches in the mating season. There was an animal, though, that killed from necessity but killed also, on occasion, from blood lust alone. She remembered seeing the dead chickens one morning at Belmont Grange after a weasel had visited the chicken house during the night. A great tawny weasel that would kill for the joy of killing — that's what Tennessee was. She shuddered, remembering how his gun had thundered in the midst of the conversation going on in the room. God in heaven, what must she do? Dare she continue a journey with a killer whom she could not restrain? Was he likely to take shots at just anybody they might come across just to keep in practice or to satisfy his weasel's lust for blood? She was terribly upset and knew she was being ridiculous: He hadn't been shooting at people on the road. But why kill these strangers here? He *must* have had a reason. . . .

She wondered what was keeping him. He couldn't be spending all this time killing Zeke. And he wouldn't be eating anything the voluptuous Rose might serve him by way of showing her appreciation—no, surely not in the presence of the men he'd just killed. . . . Slowly then, from the bitter aggregate of her tortured efforts to understand him, the idea of a possible motive for the killing of Tobe and old Abe began to take shape. She'd thought there had been some byplay going on between Tennessee and Rose over by the wall. Had Rose, with possessions and change in mind, asked him to kill her old husband and the lawless brothers, promising him something? And was she fulfilling that promise now? "I don't believe it!" Stella suddenly cried aloud, and was startled by the sound of her own voice. She tried desperately to think of some other activity that might be holding him inside the cabin, but there simply was none.

Maybe he *was* a wolf, then, not a weasel, she thought scornfully. Maybe he was eliminating the other dog wolves for the bitch in season. Rose was in season, all right; whores were always in season. Stella started shaking but not with weakness. A seething rage had been slowly developing inside her; now, with thudding heart and stifled breathing, she felt herself overwhelmed by wave after wave of impotent fury. And then her fury gave way to another powerful emotion. What if Tennessee, to whom nothing was sacred, ran out of chanced-upon women on this trip West? On whom would he fall when he had gone chaste too long and was constantly tumescent and blind with lust? She knew how she looked and knew her effect upon men. She'd seen men look at her; she'd seen Tennessee look at her. She knew where a hungry, aroused animal would turn—to the female closest at hand. And *she* would be that female closest at hand, unless there was an immediate, radical change in plan.

She'd felt his eyes upon her as she rode before him. She'd seen his eyes linger on her figure before lifting to add his approval of her face. Lula May had warned her. But it had never occurred to her that he was a source of danger to her. She'd never been afraid of him — until now. If he put his great hands on her, what could she do? She remembered her helplessness in the massive hands of Bull Jakes. It would be the same with Tennessee. No matter how much she begged and wept, no matter if she screamed, he could turn her, bend her, force her, open her to his will.

Stella jumped up and ran to the mare. Untying the reins, she got into the saddle. Her impulse was to gallop away toward the refuge of Memphis. She was afraid, and at first she refused to recognize a faint thrill of excitement that was an element of the fear itself. But honesty compelled her; she had to admit that fear of a man—at least, the fear of some man—held its own fascination for a woman, no matter how much the woman hated or despised the man. Maybe there was something a little trashy in all women where sex was concerned. Yes, there would definitely have to be a radical change in plan.

When Tennessee rode out to the edge of the woods, the Stella he found waiting in the shadows, with a stillness unrelated to patience, was not the Stella that had questioned him about the woman in Chattanooga. This one did not even show any curiosity about how he had solved the problem of Zeke. Nor did she require an explanation of what had detained Tennessee afterward. In fact, she broke her cold silence only to insist that they push on through the night and reach Memphis as soon as possible. Her refusal to camp in the vicinity was unreasonable and strange, since her need for rest had been evident before they had taken shelter from the rain. Morning revealed her tired, withdrawn face. Several times Tennessee observed her studying him with unreadable eyes. There were readjustments going on behind those eyes, he knew.

He learned the extent of those readjustments at the edge of Memphis, where Stella informed him of a revision in plans. She was going to arrange passage on one of the river packets and transport the horses by water to Fort Smith. When he asked for her reasons, she stated coldly that she had no desire to lay down across the breadth of Arkansas a trail of corpses attended by grinning whores.

Tennessee chose not to press for her other reasons. "Well, I don't know," he considered. "Had thought some I'd wait across the river for you to go on. Last year I rode a horse into that Gayoso Hotel. Captain Forrest and some of us scouts rode in after General Hurlbut, but he escaped in his nightshirt. Point is, I could run into some trouble here, folks know me still around."

Stella brushed him with a hard look. "Plenty of landings down the river where you can wait for the boat. Just name one, and I'll see you get picked up."

"How you know you can find a boat going?"

"Never mind. I'll find one if I have to charter it."

"Big change," he murmured.

She agreed curtly. "That's right."

"How you know I won't take the stud and keep on riding?" he

asked, his eyes fixed curiously on her high-cheeked, freckled face. It was like a face carved out of sandstone, he thought, waiting for her response.

"I don't," she said finally, "and right now I don't much care. I guess I can afford the loss of a horse."

"First thing you do, get some rest," he advised. "You look done in." He gathered the reins and shifted the lead rope. "I'll be at Kelly's Landing, thirty miles down. When you get there, I'll know you've come. Good-bye, Stella." He turned the big dun south, leading the Kentucky stud, and never once looked back to see whether Stella had ridden out of sight. Already he was looking forward to a lonely camp somewhere in the river bottom.

At Kelly's Landing he waited four days, camping in sight of river traffic. The landing was the cotton port of a deserted plantation, where canebrakes covered the ruins of burned-out buildings and gloomy woods narrowed the weed-grown fields. In the woods he killed a deer, a turkey, and a few squirrels; he caught catfish in the river on a throw-line. At night he listened to the great owls, foxes, and wolves, his wild blood responding to their haunting choruses; like him, they were hunters, content to kill their meat and eat it by themselves. The woods and the life in them were just about what they were before God began making mistakes, Tennessee reckoned, as he lay peacefully on his blanket, idly studying the form of the woman he always found in the moon. He'd tried to show that woman's shape to soldiers lying in camps at night, but the bastards had seen jack-o'-lantern faces or images like those on silver dollars.

Then late one morning the whoop and rumble of a packet upstream brought Tennessee up from the shade. For a moment he could think of no good reason why a steamboat should be blowing its whistle anywhere along this stretch of the river. And then, when he realized that it was blowing for Kelly's Landing, he stood looking upriver, grim and motion-less, not unlike some Pawnee sentinel watching Conestoga wagons crawl on the plains. He was aware of the motion of people on the decks, but his eyes remained fixed on something white that kept its position at the railing of an upper deck. Beside it stood a similar shape in gray that was harder to see. Almost from the moment he noticed it, he figured it was Stella McEveride in a white dress. And suddenly, for no reason that he knew, the odor of river-bottom vegetation grew much ranker; a faint trace of skunk musk in the air became pungent and overpowering; and the smell of his own sweat-staled flesh got stronger and stronger.

The stern-wheeler came on and finally thrashed in to the landing, paddles reversed, gangplank reaching out for the bank. Ragged black roustabouts were lounging about the freight deck, where for twenty-four hours of a day they ate and slept and fought and worked. Steamboat lines were now hiring labor they had been unable to lease before the war, and Negroes were beginning to put the Irish out of the stevedore business on the river. Because the three or four who came swinging over the gangplank were *not* Irish, because they were rhythmic and ivory-mouthed and idly bombastic, because they had the leached-ashes-and-rabbit-guts smell the horses could trust, Tennessee entrusted reins and lead rope to their reaching hands.

On board he lingered on the freight deck. He watched the roustabouts pen the horses in improvised stalls back under the overhang of the cabin deck and checked the condition of Stella's mare. Then Tennessee subjected the Negroes about the deck to a cold-eyed scrutiny and settled on a flat-eyed ebony giant who had more hide and less grin showing than any of the others. He beckoned, and the big Negro padded over.

"What's your name, boy?" Tennessee asked.

The Negro looked down, his jaw muscles bunching. After a long moment he muttered, "Sam," and obviously meant to say no more, until he raised opaque eyes from scuffed boots, soiled broadcloth trousers, and almost skintight white shirt to the quiet savagery of the white man's eyes. Then he swallowed hard and added, "Masta," dropping his eyes back to the deck in sullen anger.

"Want you to watch out for my stuff, Sam," Tennessee said. "This pack here, that saddle gear, them horses."

"Yassuh."

"Hand you something when I pick it up."

"Masta—"

"Masta, hell! Looks like I done picked the wrong nigger."

Sam kept his eyes on the deck, bull neck swelling past corded jaw muscles. "Said *mista*," he mumbled.

"Damned Lincolnites done freed you, Sam. So *be* free."

"Yassuh," Sam said with a swell of breath, his eyes beginning to rove, seeing the other Negroes watching him with this big white man. "Boss, how come you pick me out?"

Tennessee saw vanity working like a yeast in the brutal, wide-jawed face. "These other niggers, Sam," he said thoughtfully, "whatever they're doing, they keep you in the corners of their eyes." He shrugged his burly shoulders. "It ain't that I'll lose anything, they get in my stuff and scatter it out among 'em. Might get blood on it, gathering it up. That's the thing. So you keep it from scattering, Sam."

"You gets back, it sho God be here!" Sam swore. Then, overcome by admiration for himself and this white man, he grinned expansively.

"You know what, boss man? It just come to me. If I's you and you's me, you the very one I'd pick to watch *my* stuff."

"And you'd wind up with just what you got now, too," Tennessee assured him, and heard Sam's pleased rumble behind him as he departed for the companionway.

Stella had kept her position at the forward rail of the cabin deck as the horses were led aboard. Beside her stood a tall, striking young lady of about twenty in a modish dove-gray dress and a smart little hat that made a rakish angle on her dark head. She was a strong, shapely girl with firm red lips and level gray-green eyes. From the riverbank Tennessee watched the roustabouts handle the horses. As far as Stella or her companion could detect, he never once raised his eyes to glance higher than the freight deck.

The girl looked ashore with an alert, half-smiling expression on her face. The smile widened as her interest grew. Suddenly she said, "*Magnifique!*" in an amused tone of voice, thereby exercising in one quick breath most of the French she'd brought away from Madame DeWeese's Cincinnati School for Young Ladies.

"The mare or the stallion?" Stella asked, proud of her horses.

"Neither," the girl said coolly. "They're fine animals, of course, as you led me to expect. But I was referring to the man."

Stella half-turned, startled, to look at her. "*What* man?"

The young lady's smile was faintly derisive. "Have you and I been looking at more than one?" she asked. "If there's another on that bank, I've missed him." Then, watching Tennessee come aboard, moving like a young panther tom that smells the night, she added, "Or on this boat, who can stand beside him—or in Cincinnati, for that matter, or Memphis."

Unaccountably, Stella was irritated. "Why not just say the whole United States?"

The girl laughed. "Well, in all honesty, I can't. I'm not very widely traveled. There are places in the country I haven't seen any men from. So I must keep an open mind, you see. I believe in open things, Stella. Things like open minds, open seasons, open fields, open competition. How about you?"

"I don't follow that," Stella said, frowning. "Decipher it for me."

"That handsome brute of a brother-in-law—or whatever *in* law or *out* of law he is of yours—you wouldn't be trying to keep him all to yourself, now, would you?"

A thrill of fear quivered through Stella. The need to warn this young innocent was so urgent that she did not even trouble to deny a personal, feminine interest in Tennessee. "Listen, Nancy," she said rapidly, "I haven't got time to go into this right now. But will you believe me when I say that, for your own good, you must—you *must*—stay away from him? You'd be safer with a rattlesnake, believe me. Tennessee Smith's my brother-in-law, but I've got to tell you that he's a terrible gunman and . . . oh, Nancy, he has the worst reputation with women! If I told you—''

"Why, Stella," Nancy broke in, laughing, "you don't have to boost him to me. I liked his looks from the first glimpse. Come on, now, and introduce me.''

Stella had met Nancy Waterton in the lobby of the Gayoso Hotel in Memphis. The girl had been conversing with an army officer near the desk when Stella approached the clerk to inquire about the availability of transportation by steamboat to Fort Smith. While the clerk was floundering with vague information, the girl had come forward with the officer and introduced herself. She was en route home from school in Cincinnati and had booked passage on the *Tom C. Pyle,* which would leave for Fort Smith in three days. Nancy knew the captain personally, and she and Stella would look him up after dinner. The officer with Nancy was General Randolph B. Marcy, soldier and mapmaker of the Western Indian country, whom she had known as a child at Fort Towson, Fort Washita, and Fort Arbuckle, where her father, Colonel Joseph E. Waterton, had been stationed at different times before being ordered to the command of Fort Gibson. General Marcy, a tall, spare man in his early fifties, was not averse to sharing with the young ladies the benefit of his experience in locating fort sites in Texas and the Indian Nations, and had proceeded to do so throughout dinner.

After the meal, when the two women were alone, Stella had told Nancy that she was meeting her brother-in-law at Kelly's Landing. By the time the *Tom C. Pyle* had reached the landing, she regretted having told the army brat a damn thing. . . .

Tennessee found Stella waiting for him near the top of the steps. Behind her, at the top of the companionway, stood the girl in dove gray, who seemed to be waiting expectantly. The sight of Stella in a tight-bodiced, full-skirted white dress made his stomach muscles tighten and crawl as usual, but her face was set against him. She seemed remote, preoccupied, and asked him only one question. She was curious as to whether he'd murdered any husbands of any more whores since she'd seen him last.

Stella had asked the question as they were brushing past the girl in gray. She hadn't even glanced at the girl or lowered her voice. She told him nothing about her stay in Memphis. In fact, she gave him about as much of her time as it took to direct a white-jacketed Negro cabin-tender to conduct him to his cabin up in the texas, where the officers and crew were quartered. In the cabin, though, he found that she had given some thought to his needs. Laid out on the bunk were a tough corduroy suit, a pair of broadcloth trousers, flannel shirts, white cotton shirts, socks, underwear, a light-tan planter's hat, and a razor. In a box on the floor by the bed was a pair of black shoes that fit him. How Stella had determined what size to get, Tennessee never knew. In the middle of the floor was a tub of water with soap alongside; he reckoned, by God, that she was telling him she'd smelled him along the way.

At Napoleon the packet entered the mouth of the Arkansas River and headed upstream, passing one end of a house that was sagging over a high alluvial bank. Tennessee, lounging on the hurricane deck, reached for the bottle beside his chair and let the whiskey gurgle down his throat; then he waited for the crawling heat to warn up his belly. Actually, he didn't much care how long this boat trip lasted.

"Hello," said a feminine voice behind him.

Before turning, Tennessee cursed himself for sitting with his back to the companionway like a damned fool. There was many a bastard still above ground who'd like nothing better than to catch him in the open with his back turned. What had dulled his sense of wariness, he figured, was the whiskey in his belly and the illusion of security that a boat on water gives.

Tennessee looked around and saw the girl in dove gray standing on the deck at the head of the companionway. At her back the sun was a crimson disk sinking behind the shining water of a far bend. On either side of the incandescent water at the bend were the bleached and slate-colored trees and black shadows of a rotting swamp. "Hello," he said, dropping his hat over the whiskey bottle and standing up. "You're the girl with Stella at the rail when the boat landed."

"Yes," she said, coming closer. "Since she forgot to introduce me, I'll have to." She told him who she was, looking him straight in the eyes the way a man would. "You're Tennessee Smith, of course."

"That's who," Tennessee said, stepping aside to reach a nearby chair and placing it alongside his own. "Have a seat and help me finish—" he saw her glance quickly at his hat—"some loafing before supper."

She laughed. "You deliberately paused after you said *finish*," she accused. "Were you trying to find out whether I might take a drink with you?"

"Well?" He raised his brows.

"No," she said emphatically, "of course not." She sat down in the chair he had placed for her, a troubled look clouding her face. "You know, no man—not even a man like you—would think of offering Stella McEveride a drink of whiskey—''

He held up his hand. ''One did less than a week ago.''

''What happened?''

''I killed him.''

''Oh, no!'' She stared at him, wide-eyed.

''But not for that,'' Tennessee explained. ''He was a bushwhacking rogue. He tried to kill me.''

''Oh, I see . . . hmmm,'' she murmured, thinking. ''Then that's what Stella meant when . . . wasn't there some kind of woman—''

''Stella thinks there was,'' Tennessee said easily. ''She's wrong about the whole thing but won't listen to a damned—sorry—thing I say.''

''Well, what I started to say is that men are always getting the wrong impression about me. I'm as virtuous a woman as Stella McEveride is. Men who know me know I'm, well, a 'nice girl.' But strangers think otherwise right away. Why is that? Only a stranger can tell me. A strange man, I mean. *You* tell me, Tennessee Smith.''

All of a sudden Tennessee found that he liked this girl—liked her wholesome good looks, her honesty, her frankness, her lack of feminine guile, her refusal to stand on ceremony. ''I ain't used to thinking much about whether a woman's nice or not,'' Tennessee said slowly. ''I don't go much further than noticing whether she *looks* good or don't. You *look* good, all right. You sure you want me to think up an answer?''

''Oh, I mean it, all right,'' she said. ''I don't fool around with words.''

''Well, I think this is it,'' Tennessee told her. ''When you look at a stranger and he looks back, you don't drop your eyes or look away. Usually—and you won't like this—there are three kinds of women that keep on looking without any holdback when a strange man meets their eyes: a squaw, a woman willing to have truck with a stranger, and a woman who sells herself—you know—''

''You mean a whore?'' Nancy asked, unabashed.

''Well, yes,'' Tennessee said uncomfortably. ''And maybe I should add a fourth kind. The Nancy Waterton kind, who will look and look away when she damned pleases.''

''You've given me something to think about,'' Nancy said thoughtfully. ''Funny nobody ever told me that before. No, maybe not so odd. I was reared by men, grew up among soldiers, was told the facts of life—probably in stable terms, too—by an old sergeant. But, you know, I believe you've hit it. And I've got a problem on this boat because of it. A professional gambler named Ace McQueen was on my boat out of

Cincinnati. I thought he was a gentleman. I didn't know he was a gambler until the captain of this boat told me. Anyhow, he steadied me against a rail and kissed me by surprise one night, and after that his attentions became persistent and offensive. I'm sure he got on this boat to follow me, and I'm getting a little afraid of him. I don't know what he might do. What really drove me up here awhile ago was that I saw him in wait down by my cabin.''

Tennessee wasn't sure where all *his* wisdom was coming from, but he figured that what Nancy had learned about men as a sexless little girl was mainly how men are with men. She knew their strengths, loyalties, and rough chivalry and admired them; she knew their vices—their drinking, cursing, fighting, and occasional resorts to bad women—and regarded them with affectionate tolerance. She might have learned more about them that was pertinent to herself by being around women and studying *their* ways with men. If she had not thought that she knew more about men than she did, Tennessee thought sardonically, she would have been more attentive to Stella McEveride and, Ace McQueen waiting or not waiting, would not be up here hobnobbing with Tennessee himself. Not that she wasn't safe, but . . . that Stella! Damned if she wasn't a case, now, with her suspicions and doubts.

''Don't worry about him, Nancy. I'll eat supper with you and Stella tonight.'' A hard grin reshaped his bronze cheeks. ''Whether I'm welcome or not. I'll push back before you leave the table and drift down near your cabin. He tries to waylay you tonight, I'll have a little talk with him. Maybe I can show him how it don't pay to push his luck after it's all run out. So give me the number of your room, and then you run along. We'll let Stella introduce us, by the way. She finds out we're already friends, she'll be plumb out of charity before the niggers deliver the soup.''

They stood up, and Nancy looked directly into his eyes, smiling, and did not look away. Reaching out, she touched his big, hard-muscled arm. She could not know that the absence of the usual coldness from his clear gray eyes was a rare and special tribute to her. ''I believe you mean that,'' she said softly. ''We *are* friends already, aren't we? The number is 210. That's on the starboard side. I'll go now so you can get that bottle out from under your hat.''

Tennessee watched her until she was out of sight down the companionway. He'd never before thought of a woman as a friend. But this girl *could* be a real friend to a man. His friend? By God, he liked the thought of that! Funny. Stella McEveride could never be his friend. She could be his enemy—and seemed halfway that already. She could be some other things, too—things that made him uncomfortable and aroused—but not a friend.

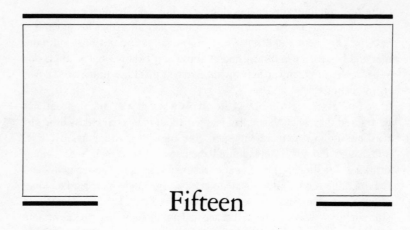

Fifteen

Tennessee moved into the dining-room entrance and stood there awhile, observing the diners. Most of the places at the tables were occupied, but he was interested in only the small table near a window where Stella and Nancy sat looking at their menus. He started threading his way toward it, ignoring the turning heads and suddenly guarded voices. He was accustomed to eyes following him across a floor or in the open and could usually sense whether the attention he was drawing was menacing, curious, or sometimes even flattering. Sensing no danger here, he attributed the interest to the fact that two big Colts were riding butts forward high on his hips for all eyes to see, since he was not wearing a coat with his white shirt and dark broadcloth trousers.

Stella looked up and saw him coming. She became suddenly motionless, feeling the physical impact of his presence in the room, remembering Nancy's half-humorous, impulsive exclamation, "*Magnifique!*" The girl was right, she thought; if judged by appearance alone, the bloody, unprincipled scoundrel *was* magnificent. Not so handsome as Armistead Randolph, she decided, but just as likely to draw feminine eyes, and much more likely to make a woman—she remembered Paul's words—wet her lips and become restless where she sat. Stella felt herself coloring and hardened her face to greet him, noticing that Nancy was as close to looking demure as it was possible for her to look. Stella wondered if Nancy would be the next woman for Tennessee on this trip.

"Hello," she said coldly. "Are you joining us for dinner?"

"Guess I better," Tennessee said with a faint grin. "All these folks piled up here, and—well, you know how shy I am around strangers."

"Yes, I know." Stella's voice dragged with irony. "I noticed that at Abe and Rose's place. But those guns at the table ought to make you feel more relaxed. Tennessee, this is Miss Nancy Waterton, whose father commands Fort Gibson. Nancy, my brother-in-law, Tennessee Smith."

"Mr. Smith," Nancy murmured.

"Pleased to meet you," Tennessee said, his hand on the back of a chair. "Seems like I've seen you before. Funny thing. All pretty girls look familiar to me. Ugly ones look like strangers. . . .Miss Waterton, could I sit where you are and you sit here? Easy to see the whole room and through the window from your place. Don't want my friends slipping up to surprise me. You mind?"

Nancy stood up. "Not at all—after that nice compliment."

When they were reseated, Tennessee busied himself with the menu. Fancy meals on steamboats, apparently, were not confined to the floating palaces of the big rivers. The bill of fare on the *Tom C. Pyle* listed two kinds of soup, two kinds of fish, four sorts of roast, five entrees, several choices of cold dishes, numerous desserts, and a variety of candy and fruits—all part of a distracting elegance designed to compensate for the hazards of a boiler explosion, a pilot's mistake, an unseen sawyer, or any kind of floating object that could rip a bottom and sink a boat. . . . When Tennessee came to himself, a waiter was standing by, and Stella's slanted eyes were mocking him with a look of derision.

"What he'd like to order," Stella commented to Nancy, "is everything listed."

"You forgot to say, 'And served in a trough.' " Tennessee looked at Nancy. "Stella can't make up her mind which I'm more like—a hog or a wolf."

Nancy laughed. "Which do you feel more like?"

"Depends on what I'm about to eat." He gave his order, showing a proper restraint. "So you live in the Indian Nations. How many forts do the damned—excuse me—does the Union army have in the Nations now?"

"Only one—Fort Gibson," Nancy said. "Confederate forces held the others during the war, and the army hasn't returned to them yet. Dad thinks Towson and Washita won't be reoccupied because they're too far east. Actually, Gibson's too far east, too, and might as well be in Kansas or Arkansas, since it's way up in the northeast corner of the territory. So you can see that the Nations haven't got much army protection right now, and lawlessness is the one sure thing travelers in the territory can count on. Are you paying attention this time, Stella?''

"I hear you," Stella said. "Tennessee, I listened to Nancy and General Marcy talk in Memphis. Both tried to warn me away from the Indian Territory because of the bands of white outlaws there. Well, what I say is that one of them could be Parson Krull's gang. I just hope to goodness one is. If not, the Krulls still may come, for cutthroats and ruffians and ruined Confederates of the worst sort are drifting into Indian Territory all the time. General Marcy thinks this outlaw element will take up where Stand Watie left off.''

Waiters came, delivering food to the table, and conversation lagged for a while. Then, when the edge of hunger was blunted somewhat, Tennessee said, "Two things. Who is General Marcy, and who is Stand Watie?''

"He's General George B. McClellan's father-in-law, *was* McClellan's chief of staff until President Lincoln fired McClellan after Antietam. You and Marcy would get along, by the way. You both share a low opinion of Lincoln.''

"You're wrong about me, as usual," Tennessee told her. "Always admired Lincoln. Knew what he wanted and didn't let the Constitution and a lot of crying get in his way. Swap Davis for Lincoln, the South would've won the war. How come this Marcy thinks he's an expert on the Indian Territory?''

"He served there with the army for years. He explored that whole country between the Cross Timbers and New Mexico Territory, locating fort sites and blazing trails. He's one of the few white men living who have traveled over the Staked Plains. Such a trip was possible only because he had an impressive escort of soldiers with him. It seems the Comanche Indians won't allow any other people but the Kiowas to set foot on their hunting grounds. Nancy will have to tell you about Stand Watie.''

"You listened closer to General Marcy than I did," Nancy observed, then looked closely at Tennessee. "During the war the civilized Indians split up in about the same way the nation did. Those closer to Kansas than Texas sided with the Union, and those closer to Texas joined the Confederacy. Stand Watie was a Cherokee general who became the scourge of the territory. He tried his best to exterminate all Indians— even his own tribesmen—who sympathized with the Union. He raided through the territory with torch and knife and gun, driving thousands of Indians into Kansas. Thousands more ran to Fort Gibson for protection.

They're still there—Cherokees, Creeks, Delawares, Seminoles. But the Confederate Indians are no better off. The Choctaws and Chickasaws and some of the Cherokees lost the war, and now they're waiting for the federal government to punish them. All their governments are gone. All policing has stopped. And now that they lack the organization for protection, the wild Plains Indians have started raiding them again. In fact, Dad says—''

"Excuse me, Nancy," Stella interrupted, "but that man going out—is that the McQueen fellow who's been bothering you?''

Tennessee's eyes settled on the man leaving—a tall, slender, black-haired man in a dark suit and white shirt—and heard Nancy say, "No. He could almost pass for him if he had a black mustache. But that's somebody else. Ace McQueen isn't in the room tonight. And that worries me. He may be waiting—''

"Tennessee," Stella said, "stroll down by 210 on this deck, and if a man with a black mustache is hanging around, tell him—well, you know—tell him he needn't wait. Something like that. Anyhow, speak to him.''

Tennessee prepared to depart. "Enjoyed it, ladies," he said, pushing back his chair. "See you later.''

"Tennessee," Stella said, "just speak to him. No guns.''

"No guns," he said, heading for the entrance.

As he padded along the narrow promenade between staterooms and outer guardrails, Tennessee thought about Stella's injunction. He bared his white teeth in a hard, grim smile. A riverboat gambler with a short-barreled hideout gun, with a derringer up his sleeve, and with no scruples whatever against using them, and Stella says, "Speak to him. No guns.'' Her guideline in violence seemed to be unless you kill a Krull, don't kill. That Stella was something else! He pictured her sitting at the table in her trim dark dress with white lace at her throat. He couldn't remember what Nancy was wearing; something pretty. But that Stella!

The gambler was lounging at the guardrail in front of the stateroom door bearing the number 210. His mustache was a trimmed black line in a pale, hard face that a certain kind of woman would consider handsome. A pair of glittering black eyes swept a malign glance across Tennessee and turned away into darkness, dismissing him as irrelevant to his concern. Tennessee saw at once that the bastard was as deadly as a rattlesnake in dog days. He walked on past, turned the corner, and leaned against a stateroom wall. There'd be a short wait, he figured; Nancy would be along soon. He pressed the wall with a burly shoulder, getting used to the sound of the paddle wheel below him so that he'd hear the tapping of Nancy's approach along the deck.

Soon he heard it. There was no hesitation in her footsteps. "What are you doing here?" she said.

The man's voice was a snarl. "Open that damn door and get inside. I'm through fooling with you, missy. No woman alive can blow hot and cold with Ace McQueen."

"I'm warning you!" Nancy cried angrily. "You'd better leave me alone. You—you stay back!" There was fear in her voice now. "Don't you dare touch me!"

"I'll—just have a touch—of those—lips again." Feet scraped and shuffled, and the girl gasped for breath and uttered a muffled cry. "Guess you hid—that key—down in your bosom. Don't mind—reaching down—in there between—"

Two steel-corded hands closed on the gambler's right arm and neck and jerked the dark man loose. Nancy fell against the cabin door and stood propped there, sobbing. Tennessee turned the gambler with his great hands, exerting his strength to quiet the slighter man's struggles, then looked calmly into the mad, wicked eyes. The man's face had lost what little color it had and was now a dead white.

"You must not hear good." Tennessee grinned savagely into the malevolent face. "The lady told you to leave her alone. Now I'll tell you the same thing. Listen close. Leave—the lady—alone. Want me to holler it in your damned ear?"

"You bastard," the gambler gritted, "you're a dead man right now! Nobody lays a hand on Ace McQueen and lives."

"Thought I'd speak to you," Tennessee said. "Promised to. Leave this little lady alone. Don't come around her no more. Now you done heard me. And I mean, by God, you better mind me."

"Why, goddamn you," McQueen snarled, "I never obeyed an order in my life! Not from my old man. Not from any sheriff or marshal. I wouldn't take an order from any son-of-a-bitch that lives. Or from the devil. No—and not even from God."

"You got a mighty bad attitude," Tennessee told him. "You ought to go off in the dark by yourself and think." Setting his feet, he raised his great hands high, with Ace McQueen in them, and heaved the gambler over the guardrail far out into the black water of the Arkansas. There came a splash from out in the darkness off to one side of the rough wake of the paddle wheel, but no outcry at all came back to those on deck. The man's pride would not permit his locked lips to part wide enough to let a sound past them—not even if death was the price of silence. Tennessee, listening for some sort of yell, shook his head. He could have slipped a knife between the bastard's ribs before stuffing him in the black hole of a swamp-country night. Now there were two of the same breed of dedicated haters behind him to dog his trail: Zeke and Ace McQueen. The woman would get him killed yet; that was sure as hell.

Nancy rushed straight into his arms, and he was kissing her before he had a chance to think. Well, hell, what was he supposed to do with a good-feeling woman in his arms? Then he pushed her out to arm's length and turned her loose, but she came right back in against him, her arms rising to encircle his neck, her softly cushioned body shaping itself against his. He tried to limit his kisses to gentle contacts, but already he was beginning to feel the hard swell of a mounting desire and was rapidly losing control. . . . Suddenly, feeling exposed, he pushed her back.

"We're out here on this deck," he said, breathing heavily. "Better get inside. How far do you want this to go, Nancy?"

Nancy stood with head hanging for what seemed a full minute. Then she looked up. "No further. You can't come in." She laughed shakily. "We might wind up in bed together. And I won't go to bed with you. No matter what I'd like to do, I'm not a fool. I think it was the reaction of seeing you throw that—holy Moses, Tennessee, do you realize what you did? Why, I can't believe it! Do you reckon he could swim?"

"If he could, he still can," Tennessee said. "Riverboat gamblers better be able to swim. Don't trouble your head about him. Good night, Nancy."

Standing in the shadows at the corner near the aft companionway, Stella watched Tennessee ascend the steps to the hurricane deck. She'd come around from the starboard side to see whether the gambler had lain in wait and what would happen if he had. And she'd seen it all. She'd seen the gambler thrown overboard and the embraces and kisses that followed. Stella was shocked that Nancy could be so forward and intimate with a man she'd met for the first time at dinner. But the one she was furious with was Tennessee, who would be in bed with Nancy this minute if the girl had let him past the door. She'd heard all they'd said to each other and knew that Tennessee would get past Nancy's frail defenses and have her at his will the next time they were alone together or, possibly, the next time after that. It was just a matter of time. Stella told herself it was her duty to protect the girl from a wolf-man she'd brought along with her to loose against the Krulls. Then she questioned why it hurt her to see him hug and kiss another woman after what she knew he had done with Rose. Did she want him to hug and kiss her? The very violence with which she rejected such an idea left its trail of doubt. She went to her stateroom on the starboard deck, confused, uncertain, and unhappy. It was the next morning before she recalled the gambler's departure from the scene and thought to wonder how he'd fared in the water.

From Napoleon to Pine Bluff the packet beat its way through a flat alluvial land of miasmic sloughs and cypress swamps—a dreary land remembered by river travelers for mosquitoes in dark places, buzzards in dead trees, and cottonmouth moccasin snakes on grounded driftwood. Occasionally the monotony of swamplands was broken by wide expanses of island weeds and tall, coarse grass identifiable as plantation fields by blackened chimneys standing alone or by weathered mansions standing upright on crutchlike columns.

Stella left the boat at Pine Bluff and was gone for the better part of an hour. Then, through a haze of dust from freight wagons, Tennessee saw her picking her way back down the river hill. Near the gangplank she slowed to a halt and, standing just out of the path of the stevedores, lifted her face toward the hurricane deck, where Tennessee and Nancy sat watching the freight handling. Her eyes found Tennessee and fixed darkly upon him. He thought she would call up to him, but then she turned in behind a stalwart roustabout showing off under a two-man crate of goods and came aboard. A few minutes later the texas-tender brought Tennessee a message: Mrs. McEveride wanted to see him in her state-room immediately.

Stella admitted him and, motioning toward a chair, seated herself on the bed. Then she gave the impression of looking at him for the first time. Either new freckles had popped out on her face or dust from outside had settled there, he thought. He wondered why she was in such a hurry to discuss something that could wait until she had freshened up, even if the something was a Krull in the town.

"I've just had another disappointment," she said, without preamble. "In Memphis I was told of a man in Pine Bluff who could put me in the way of hiring some men. Well, I've just been to see him, and he can't. So now I'd like your opinion on where to turn."

"Hire men for what?"

She studied him in silence. "Tennessee," she said finally, "if you've forgotten, we're looking for the Krulls." She was unable to keep the irritation from her voice. "I've become more and more convinced that we should search in the Indian Territory. In any event, I'll need the company of fighting men beyond Fort Smith."

"Who you aim to fight in the territory?" Tennessee asked. "The Krulls ain't there."

"You don't know that," Stella said sharply. "I told you what

General Marcy said. He thinks that's where they'd head for. He suggested that I get in touch with a Delaware Indian named Black Beaver or a Cherokee half-breed named Jesse Chisholm. Both are old men who've spent their lives in the Indian Territory and on the High Plains, hunting and trading and scouting for the army. Black Beaver was General Marcy's guide on the Staked Plains. Marcy thinks both should know a lot about the Krulls—where they were before the war, where they'd likely be now. Tennessee, he just may have given me the best lead we'll get on this manhunt.''

"Maybe," Tennessee grunted. "Maybe not. We'd hear from Jesse Chisholm, like as not, in time, anyhow. Know who he is?''

Stella's eyes were suddenly intent. "Well, only what I said.''

"Kinfolks by marriage to old Sam Houston. Chisholm's mammy was some sort of kin to old Sam's squaw. Sister, I think. Rogers, their name was. Reason I know, John Redwing told me. Jesse Chisholm's an uncle or cousin to John Redwing. Come to that, wouldn't surprise me to find that damned Redwing ain't more'n a half-blood Cherokee himself.''

Stella stared at Tennessee. "You know," she said darkly, "you amaze me. Here you've known about Jesse Chisholm all the time. Yet you would have ridden through the Indian Nations without saying a word. I wonder—I *wonder*—what else you know! I wonder if you'll *ever* get interested in hunting down those damnable Krulls—what could happen to *make* you interested!''

"Stella," Tennessee complained, "how many times I got to tell you I aim to find them Krulls and kill 'em? It ain't hard to find a man. You figure who knows, and then you ask him where the man is. Then you go to where the man is, point a gun at him, and pull the trigger. That's all. I don't understand why you have to get up an army and go marching up and down the country. You figure Black Beaver or Chisholm knows where the Krulls are, I'll find 'em and ask 'em. Then I'll go to the Krulls and kill 'em. So forget the Krulls. Why can't you do that? Why can't you ease up for a while and enjoy this boat trip?''

"Just a matter of pressing a piece of metal, pulling a trigger!" Stella said bitterly. "Killing Krulls or forgetting them—both are the same, a matter of perfect indifference to you. Let me tell you one thing, Mr. Tennessee Smith! The more I see of you, the better I understand that I *need* an army around me!''

A deep, uneven breath convulsed her blouse, then molded the fabric to her bosom. Again Tennessee was struck by the contrast between the taut fullness of her woman's breasts and the slimness of her girl's waist. His eyes trailed down, out of control, to the gentle curve of female belly and became engrossed in the contemplation of her hips, seeing them rounded against the bed into voluptuous contours by their sitting posture. He imagined the silken smoothness of skin where freckled thighs brushed, and his great hands jerked in a violent spasm, grinding themselves into fists that could have crashed through the stateroom door without feeling even the satisfaction of pain. Slowly he dragged his eyes up from her hips to her waist, to her bosom, to her slender-columned stem of a neck, to her fine-boned freckled face—and found her eyes looking straight into his.

Instantly he sought with hooded lids to hide the loll-tongued, humped-up thing staring out of his eyes, knowing that he was too late. He saw Stella's eyes heat up and then cool. He saw her complete recognition. When these moments were past, she would keep on claiming to be his sister, of course; but both of them would know that the flimsy taboo behind the claim would go like powder at the first touch of flame. She realized now—he knew she must—that she'd been expecting a flare-nosed, heavy-hung studhorse to nod along like a plod-hoofed gelding in harness with a mare that was giving off scent....

Stella felt his eyes along the length of her body and was distracted, thinking, How can such cold eyes generate such heat? Suddenly she became intensely aware of herself as a female, conscious of erect, tingling nipples, a tide of heat, a condition of thaw and melt down in her belly, and a pervasive, will-sapping weakness that was stealing through her. Finally, with naked, brutal impact, Tennessee's eyes met hers and held there, searching deep inside her, violating the secret places of her being. How could she have thought this man's eyes were cold?

Seeing the open lust in him, she responded to it against her will, with an aching desire that she could neither prevent from developing nor banish once it was in her body. I'm in no danger, she told herself, seeking refuge in the rationale with which she had soothed Paul's doubts and fears. *I'm not a mare to be led into a stall. A normal woman, a faithful wife, can feel a twinge of desire when she looks at a handsome stallion of a man and shrug it off and forget it—unless she's a slut.* Was this just a twinge, though? And beyond what point did a woman become a slut? As for the mare in stall, she might not be a mare, true enough; nevertheless, she *was* in season, apparently. And she was not at all certain that she could not be led to stall—to bed, that is, or pushed over on one—since she was already on the edge of a bed.

Angered by her thoughts, she whispered an imprecation in her heart. What she was beginning to fear desperately was the erosion of her willpower to the point where her traitorous female body would open its defenses to invasion by a man and then—when its hollowness had been filled, when its yearning had been assuaged, when resolution had been restored—what wreckage to all her hopes of avenging Paul and the judge would there be? She didn't know, but she had glimpses of disaster and wasteland ahead. And she hated Tennessee passionately for what he was doing to her, even though he had not reached out a hand to touch her nor taken a single step. Not yet, he hadn't. But he would. She could see the urge mounting, the decision forming, the impulse hanging breathless. . . .

"You damned animal!" she said in a low, ragged voice.

There was something in her voice that gave her away, that belied the words uttered and the old, tough, high-cheeked expression that accompanied them. The words sounded as if they'd been shaped by tremulous lips. It was a sound that excited Tennessee. By God, he'd rather try Stella and get slapped, maybe force a kiss, than outright hump Nancy Waterton, pretty as she was. He came out of his chair and moved upon her, his big hands reaching wide to possess her and drag her into his arms. Stella jumped up, her eyes flaring with fright, and moved to escape him by sidling frantically along the bed, her hands lifted to fend him off. She was desperately anxious to get clear of the bed.

"You st— stay back!" she chattered. "Don't you touch—"

He caught her near the foot of the bed and pulled her in against him. She fought him with a silent ferocity and surprised him with her strength. Twisting, kicking, trying to bite, she arched backward to extricate herself, her eyes wide and black and filled with despair. Again he pulled her in, using force now, and rendered her helpless. He turned her, seeing her face, her wide black eyes and parted lips, hearing her labored breathing, feeling the drumming of her heart. Then he lowered his head and caught her soft, half-opened lips with his mouth. Her instant response was startling. Her arms came up, out of captivity, and her hands clutched his brown-streaked blond hair at the back of his head. Hauling his head down, she ground her lips savagely, fiercely against his, while pressing all the soft, warm length of her body against him. . . . Then, when she was lulled for a moment by her passionate response, Tennessee sought to move her toward the bed. Suddenly memory came ringing into Stella's mind like the chiming of a silver bell: *Women and horses and dogs—he masters them with a touch.* Paul's words . . .and then her own: *I will never enjoy another man's body.* . . .Tennessee's great hand closed over one of her breasts, and she felt herself pushed one step, then two steps, closer to the bed. She wrenched her mouth loose and, with a sudden writhing, frenzied effort, struggled free and struck him wickedly across the face with a full-arm swing.

"Get out of here!" She kept striking furiously. "Go to your whores in Mississippi and Chattanooga!" She ran to the head of the bed and, reaching under a pillow, turned with the .36 Remington in her hand. "Go on!" Her voice was almost a scream. "Get out that door, goddamn you! And I mean *now*!"

When the door had closed behind him, Stella dropped her pistol on the rug and flung herself face down on the bed. She thought she might seek relief from her wrought-up state through unrestrained weeping, but found herself dry-eyed and reflective as her fury quickly subsided.

Her case with Tennessee, she decided, was not as bad as she had imagined while he was still in the room, nor did she regard his usefulness to her as irreparably damaged. Now that she considered the matter, she didn't know that he should be greatly faulted for his attempt upon her virtue. The pulsating sensuality that had sprung up between them in the intimate confines of the steamboat cabin could not be blamed exclusively on him, since both of them had been caught up in it. And the life-giving force, which nature had entrusted to the male, demanded that he be urgent and aggressive and, to a degree, unscrupulous. She'd known almost from her first sight of Tennessee that he could stir her physically. She was not surprised, therefore, by the fact that her loins were still yearning with the hunger he had awakened from slumber deep inside herself. Actually, she took some comfort from the belief that she could feel this way about a man safely. For now, she told herself, she had a monitor to warn her in times of sexual excitement—her vow to Paul at graveside. She need not fear Tennessee's lustful aggression nor her own body's treacherous response to it so long as that vow was kept green in her heart and mind.

At Little Rock the packet's stevedores put on their usual show. Making every motion an exaggeration of freight handling, the recently converted field hands sang and capered under loads they would have refused under threat of the whip in their plantation days. From his chair outside the texas, Tennessee observed that the pageantry of a steamboat at the landing was wasted on one segment of the audience. Up on the bank a collection of westering Confederates were taking the shade of a water oak. Even in postwar Arkansas their hard-used, desperate appearance set them apart, and would, in fact, guarantee them privacy just about anywhere they gathered. Tennessee had seen such men before, had seen their shaggy beards and ghoulish eyes. They were men who wore the badges of long-nursed hatreds ground to jagged edges by the hard travail of war.

As Tennessee's cold eyes probed idly among them, a stalwart youth arose from their midst and walked out to the edge of the bank. Tennessee ducked his head with a muttered oath, his hand leaping to drag his hat brim down.

"Tennessee McEveride!" the youth shouted. "Hey, Tennessee! What the hell you doing on that boat?"

Tennessee kept his seat, hat brim shading his face. "Name's Smith," he snarled. "Hollering at strangers get you in trouble, boy."

The big youth motioned the shaggy ones back as they started up from the ground at the mention of the word *trouble*. "Reckon I made a mistake, stranger," he said with a grin. "Don't make no difference, though. Crave a word with you, anyhow. Won't take a minute." His eyes dropped suddenly to the cabin deck, and his rag of a hat came off in a flash. The boy's hair was as red as Stella McEveride's, and he wore it long. "Reckon I'd rather come aboard," he leered, "now that I done come up with the second sight."

Tennessee got to his feet and took a step toward the edge of the hurricane deck. Stella and Nancy Waterton were standing at the railing below, watching the big youth curiously.

"Stay where you are," Tennessee ordered roughly, and padded down the steps to the cabin deck.

"Who's your friend?" Stella wanted to know. These were the first words she'd spoken to him since she'd driven him from her cabin.

"Fellow named John Greenwood," he said without pausing. "One of Champ Ferguson's guerrillas." He lengthened his stride, moving toward the stairway to the main deck.

"Wait a minute," Stella said. "This Greenwood—"

"Not now, Stella." He dropped down the steps and leaped across eight feet of water to the shore. So casual seemed his choice of route and so unhurried his swift motion that his actions attracted no particular attention.

John Greenwood came bounding down the bank, digging in his heels. His companions remained in a row at the top. Tennessee knew Greenwood well. At nineteen, the boy was six feet and two hundred pounds of veteran man-killer. He was bright-eyed, grinning, wicked. Significantly, Greenwood did not offer to shake hands.

"Bet that redheaded gal comes from good milking stock," he grinned. "Got nice tits. Other'n ain't bad, neither. Good-shaped ass."

Tennessee thought of going through the motions of knocking him down but decided against the effort because the boy was strong and fast and the knocking would require more exertion than it was worth. "My sister-in-law and her friend," he said irritably. "Mind your damned tongue. What you want with me, anyhow, you son-of-a-bitch?"

"Hey, don't call me that!" Greenwood whirled, looked up the bank, then turned back. His face appeared longer, thinned by strain. "They heard you, I'd have to—hell, I ain't sure I *can't* take you, come to that!"

"You goddamned fool!" Tennessee snarled. "How come you called me down here? Tell me now, or get your ass back in the trees with that pack of baboons."

"Keep your voice down!" Greenwood hissed. He looked up the bank again. "Boys, this here's that Tennessee McEveride you done heard about. Great josher. Don't pay no attention to what he says." He whirled back to Tennessee, sweating. "By God, you looking for trouble, it's up that bank! Three of them bastards rode with Quantrill. Others are worse, though—hungrier, lost more, don't give a damn for nothing. Listen, Tennessee, I need a stake bad. We're stuck here—no horses, no money, not enough guns to go around. You got something working, let me in. You need men won't flinch back from gunsmoke or arrers, neither one, here they are."

"You ever know me to need any men?"

"Say you never did before," Greenwood admitted. "You need 'em now."

"How come?"

"Ain't hard to figure," Greenwood said quickly, "if one of them women's your brother's widow, like you claim. Heard tell back home Parson Krull's gang killed your folks, and it's suspicioned they done shame to your brother's wife. Ain't known for sure. But it figures you and her are trailing 'em West. So you'll need men when you hit wild country, and you'll need men when you come up with them Krulls." A conceited grin came sneaking back to the boy's hard face. "Am I right?"

"I ain't decided yet," Tennessee told him. "What if you are? How do I know you own these brush piles? Maybe they ain't been told you're doing their thinking."

"Well, I won't lie," Greenwood confessed. "One of the Quantrills been objecting to what I say. But I speak for the rest, and that's all there'll be by sundown, you say the word."

Tennessee laid his ruthless eyes against the boy's confident face and kept them there until the brash grin faded. What can happen? he thought. Stella wants men. They have to be unhired, I'll cut 'em loose. They ain't immortal.

"All right," he decided finally. "Here's money for guns and grub while you get organized. Kill the bastard giving you trouble and come on to Fort Smith. This is all I got in my pocket." He counted out fifty-three dollars into Greenwood's hand. "But don't stir a foot until you're the boss—or dead."

"This here's a heap of money," Greenwood said shakily. "How you know I'll show up?"

Tennessee looked at him. "Boy, you spend a dime of that money, you *better* show up!"

"Damn it all!" Greenwood flung an arm in exasperation. "I still ain't sure I couldn't take you if I tried!"

"You know what you sound like?" Tennessee said. "A shirttail boy." He shook his head in disgust. "Damned if I don't believe I just threw fifty-three dollars to them baboons!"

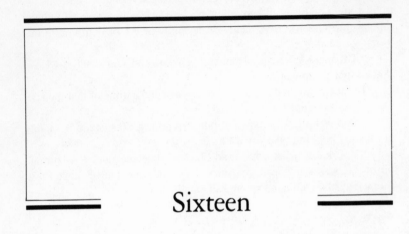

Sixteen

Far out on the South Canadian River, in Indian Territory, Tennessee had been encamped among the ruins of Camp Arbuckle for nearly a week. He'd touched here several times during the past month. Indians around Fort Gibson had informed him that Black Beaver and a band of Delawares had occupied the buildings before the war, and that during the past several months Black Beaver had been in and out of the camp on trips down from Kansas. Rumor had it that the old Delaware scout was planning to move back. Twice Tennessee had stopped by Jesse Chisholm's abandoned trading post on the North Canadian, and he had eaten plums and game meat along a hundred miles of new wagon road after learning from an Osage Indian that Chisholm had marked down the trace some months before in order to establish wagon communication with the Osages and the Poncas, with whom he was trading.

Finally Tennessee had damned the endless sweeps of sun-scorched prairie and settled down at Camp Arbuckle, where deer and turkey often came in among the old log buildings. He'd decided that the surest way to get in touch with Chisholm and Black Beaver was to let them come to him.

It was there that Stella's messenger reached him. From a corner of the double log cabin Marcy had built for his wife, Tennessee watched Stella's cinnamon mare come in off the prairie with a stranger in the saddle. When the man stepped warily to the ground and went down on one knee to feel for heat in the ashes of the cooking fire, Tennessee stepped into the open, causing the mare to swing with a stammer of hooves and blow a startled breath.

The man froze. Without looking around, he said with a quiet urgency, "Smith?"

The man was trying to hold off a bullet or arrow momentarily by not turning his head. In about two seconds, if he received no reassuring response, he would be rolling or leaping one way or another with a pistol jumping in his hand; so Tennessee said, "That's right."

The man turned his head, showing a wolfish jaw and bleak washed-out eyes under a low-drawn hat. Slowly he got to his feet. He was a lanky, middle-aged man dressed in good range clothes and wearing a Navy Colt very close to his dangling right hand.

"Reckon they ain't no cause to pull that pistol," the stranger said coolly, "if that's what you got in mind. Allowed you'd know me."

Tennessee's hand remained inside the buckskin jacket he was wearing. "How come you riding that mare?"

"Mrs. McEveride figured if I couldn't find you, you'd find me, you ever crossed the mare's tracks. Miss Waterton, back at Fort Gibson, told me where to look."

Reference to Nancy Waterton already had Tennessee convinced, but he thought he'd go one step further just for the hell of it. "Stella wouldn't trust that mare to no stranger."

"Thing is," the man returned, a rasp edging his voice, "I ain't no stranger. I work for her. Another thing is, a hoss—any hoss—is safer with me than with her." A cold flame was licking at the surfaces of the man's pale eyes. "Or with you, come to that."

"Reckon I place you now," Tennessee said. "You've shed and washed since I saw you. One of the Quantrills, ain't you?"

"Rode with Quantrill once. That ain't my name."

"Well, what *is* your name?"

"Call me Missouri."

"Missouri what?"

The man looked at him, bleak-eyed and resentful. Finally he answered, "Smith," and a streak of sardonic humor changed his face. "Trace back, maybe we're kinfolks."

"You made your point," Tennessee conceded. "What you come to tell me, cousin?"

"Mrs. McEveride wants you down at old Fort Washita. She's headquartered there now. Says drop whatever you're eating and come the hell on in."

"Eating?" Tennessee gave him a hard look. "You sure *she* said that?"

Missouri moved into the shade of the house and squatted on his heels. "I never seen you eat," he said indifferently.

"Well, what else?" Tennessee growled irritably. "What she doing down there?"

"Things been happening." Missouri rose up far enough to free a plug of tobacco from a hip pocket, then sank back and wrenched off a section with his teeth, saying no more until the plug was pocketed and the chew was comfortably lodged in his cheek. "We combed through them Yankee Injuns up at Fort Gibson, like you done, and then we combed down through the Cherokees and Chickasaws and Chocktaws, what we could find, and we ain't turned up no redskin or breed east of the Cross Timbers ever heard the name of Krull. Right away then Mrs. McEveride allows she might as well not crossed the Mississippi River as stay cooped up back at Fort Smith. So she sent us looking out in the territory for a place to set up headquarters."

"Headquarters," Tennessee grunted. "Why, them Krulls may be a thousand miles from her damned headquarters."

"Well, we couldn't found no better place," Missouri informed him. "We's following word of a bunch of hoss thieves down on Red River. They was decking out in feathers and paint and whooping down into Texas after hosses or whatever they seen and then dusting back to hole up at old Fort Washita. It sounded a little like Krull work, so we hunted 'em up at the old fort. We aimed to talk, but they taken one look and jumped for their guns, so we had to unlimber our'n and start smoking. There *was* one half-breed with 'em, but he swore he wasn't a Krull every time we let him down and slacked the rope. Finally we figured he wasn't and left him up. And in all them doings, you know what we done? We never lost but one man—Kentucky, we called him."

"Another cousin, I reckon."

Missouri spat at a large black ant coursing through the grass like a miniature hound. "Why, no," he said thoughtfully. "His name was Jones. Likely he done something regretful back in Kentucky. Didn't seem to mind dying. Didn't talk much. Don't reckon he said a hundred words all the time I knowed him."

"That ain't proof," Tennessee said. "Way you run on, he likely talked every chance he got."

Missouri glared up at Tennessee. "What you rather have, sign language? I got to tell you what I come to, ain't I?"

Tennessee was watching a flock of crows settle back on the prairie where Missouri had ridden them up. "You done told me Stella wants me down at Fort Washita," he said. "You been talking, but I can't find out what she wants me for."

"Who knows why a woman wants something?" Missouri said sourly. "*She* don't know. All I know is that a soldier stopped by Fort Washita and claimed he seen you up at Fort Gibson. Said you was riding around and going on picnics with the colonel's daughter. Well, right away, then, Mrs. McEveride starts getting restless as grass in wind, and nothing would do but that I should ride to Fort Gibson and tell you to leave them picnics—why, hell, maybe that's what she meant you was eating—and get the hell on down there and start earning your pay. Damned if I know what she wants you for. She don't need you. You're extra now that she's got Greenwood and me."

"She won't have you long, you keep busting over the rises and trailing dust clouds in Kiowa country."

"I been out here before," Missouri said, turning his head to spit. "This here's Chickasaw country, with Wichitas and Creeks living close neighbors."

Tennessee's cold eyes moved slowly over a quadrant of prairie to the west. "You ought to catch up on the news," he suggested. "The Wichitas are in Kansas. Creeks, too, what ain't hugging the walls at Fort Gibson. And I question the Chicks ever lived in this country. They ain't here now. Kiowas and Comanches pass through here when they please." He gestured toward the west. "Ought to scout out there a piece."

Coming to his feet, Missouri swept the prairie with eyes squinted and skeptical. "How long you been acting like Old Bill Williams?" he wanted to know. "You had any brushes with Injuns out here?"

"No, cousin. Never been dead, neither, but I know the smell of dead meat."

"Maybe it ain't Kiowas you're expecting," Missouri said casually. "Maybe it's Cheyenne—just one Cheyenne."

"What's that mean?"

"A Cheyenne squaw made them buckskins you got on."

"Is that a fact, now?"

"Tribes got their ways," Missouri informed him. "That's Cheyenne work. But it's a half-breed outfit—jacket instead of shirt, whole pants instead of leggings and breechclout—like something a Cherokee trader or a white man might hire a wild squaw to make up."

"Cheyenne squaw, huh?" Tennessee gave the matter consideration. "Maybe so. Or a Cherokee woman. Or a white woman. I figure somebody made 'em." Tennessee's eyes were moving along a straggling growth of trees and brush that marked the course of a far coulee. "So happens I took 'em off an Osage buck up on the Cimarron. I was eating plums inside a thicket, and he come snaking up a wash to steal my horse. But he had trouble with the horse, and then he had trouble with a .44 slug that got in his eye. I took 'em because I had on corduroys that kept whispering where I was every step I took. Funny thing, though. That Osage didn't fit the buckskins, and he was packing a new Spencer on a wore-out broomtail. Hard to figure. He ought to been riding a real horse.''

"Why, that ain't hard to figure,'' Missouri said. "What happened was he shot low, his first shot, and killed the other feller's hoss. So he used up what was left of his own nag getting his distance. Then he seen you and allowed he'd save his powder and lead for the hard ones. What he didn't figure on was a smart *hoss*. Likely he got to jumping and stumbled just when you pulled the trigger. Else how would you hit his eye when you was aiming at his belly?''

"Now, that's what I call real tracking.'' Tennessee was studying a thick patch of buckbrush spreading out from a motte of trees in line with the far coulee. He judged the distance at less than two thousand yards. "You're about as good as the fellow could track a three-year-old mustang back to the stud that got him.'' His eyes lifted to the coulee again and then leaped to the motte of trees, where all but the tag end of some movement had escaped his sight. "Cousin, let's haul ass out of here. Saw a flash of white just now, like a deer flagging through brush to beat hell. And that hawk ain't acting right. Ought to be setting on the dead limb of that lone oak this time of day, but he keeps away from it. Acts like he ain't hunting, just waiting to come back and light.''

"Seen it happen before,'' Missouri said dryly. "You done spooked yourself.''

"Could be,'' Tennessee admitted, "or could be I noticed the edge of something don't fit any whole thing ought to be here. Like a smell— something about that coulee—'' Suddenly he wheeled to face the north prairie and sent forth a low, weird ululation that sounded like some nameless animal's whistle or cry. His confidence in the sound's carrying quality must have been great, for he stepped through the doorway of the cabin without repeating it. When he emerged, he had his roll of camp gear already strapped behind the saddle and his rifle in the saddle sheath. He held close to seventy pounds easily, ready to saddle and ride. Then he repeated the ululation, and almost instantly, as if waiting just out of sight for the second call, the big dun lunged out of a swale beyond the tumbled-down stables and came into the camp yard at a gallop.

"Why, now, I call that a hoss,'' Missouri said, and there was something like reverence in his voice. "Used to wonder why you-all troubled to fetch these hosses West. Not no more, I don't."

They left the yard at a dead run and swept out on the prairie to the south, then pulled the horses down to a running walk.

Missouri turned in the saddle and had a long, squinting look back at the camp. The cluster of log buildings stood deserted in the sunshine. He turned back to the front and said, "Nothing. Honest to God! I won't never tell this here if you won't."

"Tell what?"

"Why, they ain't no Injuns back there."

"Guess not," Tennessee agreed. "Wasn't when we left, anyhow. There was two on the way, though. One bellied down behind that lone oak." He nodded toward the west. "And one coming through that buckbrush off there by that clump of trees. Main bunch hanging back in that coulee mile or so behind."

Missouri looked suspicious, but shaken, too. And then he was outraged. "You got the guts to set there and claim you seen two Injuns back there?"

"You know better'n that," Tennessee said. "Told you what I saw. A hawk and a deer. And then there was something about that coulee—a sort of haze in one place. Could been dust floating in the trees, and that's sure as hell what it was. If we'd *seen* the ones coming after your hair, we wouldn't be out here now. You can bet on that."

"Why mine and not your'n, too?"

"You're the one rode in. They saw you from the coulee—you or your dust."

They were rolled in their blankets that night before Missouri could bear to admit the likelihood that hostile Indians had been in the vicinity of the old cantonment, for being lessoned at his age, especially by a man new to the West and twenty years younger than himself, was a painful experience. He much preferred the role of teacher.

Out of the silence that precedes sleep, he suddenly asked, "You don't take no chances, do you?"

"None I can help."

"All right. Let me ask you this, then. Why you wear them Army Colts high up on your waist and hind-end before?"

"Keep 'em out of the way horseback riding."

"But you're taking chances you don't have to," Missouri persisted. "Come against a man wearing his pistol low down, like mine, your hands got too fur to go and back on a cross draw. Ain't handy."

Tennessee groaned, interested only in sleep. "What difference it make? I know where they're at."

The route to Fort Washita lay generally southward through wide, lonely stretches of undulating prairies. Their view of the country seemed limited only by occasional groves of oak on high ground, but the appearance of the terrain was deceptive. Once, as they rode along on what appeared to be an empty prairie as flat as the surface of a lake, eight or ten grazing buffalo seemed to rise out of the ground in front of them. It was observations of such phenomena that Tennessee marked down in his memory almost subconsciously. Where buffalo could not be seen, Indians or white men could wait in force to interfere with his plans for survival.

Two days after they began their ride, they struck a wagon road which Missouri said was five miles from their destination. Beyond the next rise they overtook a wagon drawn by good mules and driven by a man who looked forty but was probably ten years younger. Although he was bound to have recognized Missouri over his shoulder, the man was still nursing a .50-caliber Sharps when they drew alongside. He pulled up and looked at them with brooding, melancholy eyes.

"Shen, this here's Tennessee Smith." Missouri almost shook his head at Tennessee, so urgent was his expression of warning. "Shen's short for Shenandoah," he explained, and the odd inflection of his voice sounded a tocsin that was unmistakable.

"Howdy," Tennessee said. "Your last name ain't Smith, is it?"

"God's sake, Tennessee!" Missouri almost shouted.

The man stared at Tennessee without answering. His eyes were no longer melancholy; they were like the eyes of a cottonmouth trapped in the mud of a drained swamp.

"Hey, Shen," Missouri said in a voice too loud. "What's the news, Shen? Where you been?"

"Fort Smith," Shen answered in a voice that sounded as if it were stiff and rusty from disuse. His unwavering eyes hung on Tennessee's face with deadly intensity.

Missouri jerked his head toward the wagon bed, where a tarpaulin covered half the freight and leafy branches covered the other half. "What's that noise?" he asked in a strained voice. "You got a baby under them leaves or a sow and pigs?"

"Pigeons." Shen's eyes held to Tennessee's face like a snake's eyes watching a dog. "You goddamned smartass."

"Oh, yeah, I forgot!" Missouri cried, his lupine jaw dripping sweat. "Hey, Tennessee, Mrs. McEveride aims to stock Fort Washita with homing pigeons. Sent off, and they come by boat."

"Lost her mind." Tennessee shook his head.

Shen seemed to gather himself. "How come you think you're so damn smart?" he rasped. "I seen smart bastards like you before."

Tennessee brought his cold eyes to bear on Shen's dour face. "Fellow," he said quietly, "I was joking about that name of Smith. I don't give a goddamn what your name is. What I do mind is you sitting back here with that Sharps when I ride off and get out there where my Spencer won't reach back. So before I budge a step from here, you got to give up your grudge against me or give up that Sharps or give up breathing, one of them three. Because you got an eye would make my back itch for half a mile."

Missouri had listened without a word. Now he spoke quickly. "Shen, hand me the Sharps." When Shen hung motionless, he said, "I ain't asking you, Shen."

"No," Tennessee said. "He's the one got to choose."

Shen turned slowly and placed the Sharps on the tarpaulin behind the wagon seat; then he turned back, taking his time. "Man apologizes, that's all he can do," he said stiffly. "I got no grudge."

"See you at the fort," Missouri told him and was turning the mare away when Shen cleared his throat as if to free it of rust.

"Greenwood got shot last week."

"Hell you say!" Missouri exclaimed. "He ain't dead?"

"Don't know. Not when I left."

"Who shot him?"

"Feller named Cullen Baker. Leads a gang over in Texas."

"Yeah, I know. Ambushed him, I reckon."

"I never seen it. Others claim he beat Greenwood fair."

"John's gun stick?"

"They claim not."

"By God, I don't believe it!" Missouri touched the mare with his heels. "Come on. We'll get the straight of it at the fort."

They rode the quarter-mile to the next rise in silence. As they started down the long slope on the other side, Missouri looked at Tennessee, his washed-out eyes gleaming from the shade of his low-drawn hat. "Don't never tell *me* you don't take no chances. That Shen's got more pizen stored up in his head than a rattlesnake, and he don't sing before he strikes neither. Don't know why I never warned you before we come up."

"Yeah," Tennessee agreed, shaking his head. "Got to watch my damned tongue. Might had to drive that wagon in this sun. Hate like hell to done that."

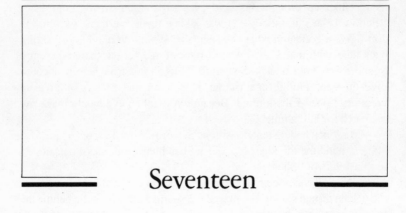

Seventeen

Old Fort Washita stood on a slight elevation in the midst of a succession of rolling prairies. The sand-colored stone buildings, with their upper and lower galleries and clapboard roofs sagging and broken by decay, were arranged in the general order of a rectangle enclosing a weed-grown parade ground. A corral fence and the long roof that covered one of the stables had been repaired, as had the roofs and galleries of two large, two-storied buildings facing each other across the parade ground. The others were left in ruins. There were horses in the corral—good ones, Tennessee observed—and half a dozen men were lounging on the gallery of one of the repaired buildings. They got to their feet as the line-backed dun and the Tennessee mare came off the prairie.

After a few pleasant insults had passed back and forth, Missouri introduced his companion. "Boys, meet Tennessee Smith. Know you-all seen him before, but *he* don't know you, now that you fell in the creek once or twice and covered your asses with whole breeches."

Tennessee nodded, and several of the men grunted. All of them were studying him with that intense curiosity, poorly veiled and speculative, usually reserved for national heroes, celebrated athletes, famous whores, and notorious man-killers.

"Mrs. McEveride lives over yonder." Missouri indicated the other repaired building. "You go report while I put up the hosses."

Tennessee stepped down and crossed the parade ground, moving with a cat-footed litheness that was remarkable to his observers, since they figured that he'd just spent about ten hours in the saddle. And then

Stella McEveride stepped through a doorway and stood on the gallery, waiting to welcome him.

Again, as so often happened when he caught full sight of her after an absence, something inside him lurched, and Tennessee wondered what the damned thing was. But if he didn't know what, he knew why. To him, this woman was continuously in season and constantly unaware of the fact. The scrub stud Brownlow Krull had teased her in, and Tennessee Smith was the stallion held back to stamp and kick the stall and go mad with waiting and itching for the real business. His impulse was to run up and yell the truth into her ears—that she was *woman*, helpless to change her condition by thought and wish—and then grab her up and rush her inside to a bed, hips squirming, legs kicking, tits jumping. . . .

Stella moved out to the edge of the steps, where the late-afternoon sun turned her hair to flame. "What you blowing and sweating for?" she said, a gamin grin making her freckled face look mischievous and satirical. "Got too fat to walk a hundred yards?"

"Reckon so," he said. It was all he could think to say.

They sat on the edge of the gallery, feet on the steps, while he made his report, which consisted primarily of the fact that he'd situated himself to establish contact with Jesse Chisholm and Black Beaver when next they came down into the Canadian River country from Kansas.

"That won't be necessary now," Stella told him. "I'll send somebody up there, though. I won't be satisfied until we check with those scouts. But I'm ready now to go on to San Antonio, and I want you with me."

"You giving up on Indian Territory?"

"Well, it looks now as if the Krulls aren't here," Stella admitted. "We haven't found a trace of them east of the Cross Timbers, and we've questioned Indians, traders, drifters, outlaws, settlers in north Texas. But what decided me was something Colonel Waterton wrote me about. It seems he had a clerk go through the official files at Fort Gibson to see whether armies afield had ever mentioned the Krulls in their reports. He said dispatches often contained mention of renegades and white meddlers among the Indians. Well, the clerk found many references to the activities of a Seminole chief named Wild Cat. Seems this chief was removed to Indian Territory after the Seminole war in Florida and caused trouble by wandering about the plains, trading with the Comanches and inciting them to all sorts of mischief. And listen: There was a renegade white man with his parties more than once. We've thought from the first, you remember, that Parson Krull had a connection with the Seminoles. Well, in the early fifties Wild Cat appeared in Texas with a party of Seminoles, runaway Negroes, and about a hundred Kickapoo warriors and their families. He defied an Indian agent named Rollins, who ordered him to move out of Texas, but finally he did move his party to Piedras Negras, across the Rio Grande from Eagle Pass. They never returned to Indian Territory, so—''

''So we're right back where Fox Wilkins left us,'' Tennessee finished for her. ''And you're leaving here. Is that right?''

''That's correct.''

''Then, Stella, why in the name of God are you building up this place as some sort of headquarters?''

Stella gazed off between sand-colored ruins toward the prairie to the south. ''This Wild Cat lead is pretty tenuous,'' she said. ''There may be nothing to it. So we can't afford to leave off investigating the territory. We've hardly touched the wild Indian country, and we haven't reached Jesse Chisholm and Black Beaver. That's a job for John Redwing—oh, by the way, he's on his way out here, bringing Lula May and Jubal.''

''That's fine,'' Tennessee observed dryly. ''Maybe you could start a town here.''

''Tennessee, this place is ideal,'' Stella insisted. ''We can occupy it indefinitely. The army will never regarrison this old fort. Too far east of the Plains Indians. Fort Arbuckle *will* be occupied, though—not that old camp where you've been. I'm talking about the permanent fort Marcy built in the Arbuckle Mountains. And it's only a day's ride up the Washita from here. So this makes a perfect headquarters for my scouts. It's a good place to raise pigeons, and I may need a lot of homing pigeons before I'm done. And it's a place to hold my warriors together until I need them. Cut loose, they'd turn outlaw in no time at all.''

''What do you care what they turn? I don't see—''

''I know very well what you don't see,'' Stella interrupted. ''And what you do.'' Her lips firmed, and then she said, ''Tennessee, I've told you the way it will be. Even if I had no more use for these men, I'd still feel a responsibility—why, that Missouri is a jewel. I'd intended taking him along to San Antonio until that fool Greenwood got himself shot. Now I'll have to leave him in charge here.''

Tennessee had convinced himself that he knew how to converse with Stella McEveride without feeling any excessive discomfort: All he had to do was keep his eyes off her. Now, after he'd wrenched his eyes away and fixed them on a tree, the damned breeze had swung, and he was smelling her clean, fresh female scent. He had to do something to get his mind off it. ''Greenwood dead?'' he asked, though Greenwood's condition was a subject that did not interest him.

"No," Stella told him. "He's in bad shape, but he'll recover. And I think he'll get busy and track down some brains when he does. There was no earthly reason why he should try to kill Cullen Baker. But he'd heard of Baker's skill with a pistol, and he couldn't resist measuring himself against him. Can you imagine anybody doing that?"

"Can Greenwood," Tennessee said. He felt Stella's eyes on him.

"How's Nancy?" she asked quietly.

"Don't know," he said. "Been nearly a month since I saw her. Meant to go back by Fort Gibson, but Missouri said you wanted me to hurry down here."

"Yes," Stella said, gazing off across the parade ground. "Are you in love with her?"

Tennessee looked at her, puzzled. "Why, I don't reckon so. I like to be with her. She's like being with another man, sort of. A good friend, I mean. I ain't sure I understand what it means to be, as you say, in love with a woman. How would I know about that?"

"Yes, of course," Stella said, with deceptive gentleness. "How would you know? But, then, how would you know about friendship with a woman, either? Would you go to bed with a woman friend? Is it friendly to risk getting her with child?"

"I ain't been to bed with Nancy. You know better'n that."

"Why do I?" Stella argued curtly. "I know you pretty well. I've had a little experience with you. I haven't forgotten your Rose of Memphis or the 'old lady' in Chattanooga."

"You know Nancy, too," he reminded her coldly. "That's why. You ought to know she wouldn't do that—if I tried to get her to."

"I don't know why not. She was more than half in love with you before the boat landed at Fort Smith, and I understand you've paid court to her since."

"You understand a damned lie, then," Tennessee told her shortly. "I ain't paid no court to Nancy or to any other woman. Why the hell would I? Can you see me married? What the hell's got into you anyhow, Stella?"

A good question, Stella thought darkly. What the hell *had* gotten into her? Pure selfishness, maybe? Was she afraid of losing her wolf-man just about when she might strike the Krulls' strong spoor? She remembered Nancy's face that last morning before they had left the boat. The girl had come to Stella's cabin in a state closer to tears than the occasion of parting warranted. Suspecting the cause, Stella had the unreasonable desire to slap her face before she spoke.

"Stella, I—I think I'm in love with him," the girl quavered, tears standing in her level eyes. "And I'll prob—probably never see him again."

"You'll be lucky if you don't," Stella said in a strange, flat voice and turned back to getting her clothes arranged for departure. "There'd be no future for a girl with that man. You'd be better off with Ace McQueen."

"I don't agree with you," Nancy said resentfully. "I think he's everything a girl could want in the way of a man, and I—I'm going to get him if I can."

"What would you live on?" Stella snatched up a garment and threw it down. "Tennessee has nothing. Not even the ambition to have anything."

Nancy was dry-eyed now and already sorry she'd come to see this hard-eyed woman. "I have money," she said firmly. "My mother left it to me. We could buy a ranch. In the meantime, Tennessee could scout for the army. I can get Dad to hire him."

"Got it all worked out, haven't you?" Stella tried to control herself with an effort that left her weak. "How does Tennessee react to your plans?"

"He doesn't know them yet. And won't until—afterward. All right, maybe he doesn't love me yet." She set her jaws with determination. Her lips firmed. "But he could learn to. And there are things a woman can do. There are ways to get a man."

Finally Stella was calm and beginning to feel sorry for the girl. "You're thinking of only one way," she said gently, "and that way's not for a girl like you, Nancy. It wouldn't work with Tennessee, in any case. He'd get up off you and go his careless way, probably leaving you with child, and never think twice about the trouble he'd caused you. Tennessee's the mountain-man kind born too late. What would suit him in the way of a wife is an Indian squaw—a woman who'd wait and slave and get on her back cheerfully twice a year when he showed up and have babies that he wouldn't recognize from year to year or really care whether they were his or not."

"Oh, you're horrible!" Nancy cried indignantly. "He isn't like that at all! You wait! You just wait! You'll see!"

Maybe the uncertainty in her mind as to whether Nancy had stumbled upon the thorny way to Tennessee's heart was what had gotten into her, Stella thought. Apparently, however, her wolf-man was still heart-whole and fancy-free, still available for duty on the Krull trail. Stella dropped her head in shame, although she still believed that the truth about Tennessee lay entirely in the shadow of her own opinion. Whatever he was, she'd found out what she'd wanted to know, and it was time to change the subject.

"I've been admiring your buckskin suit," she said, in lighter vein than she'd been using. "Tell me, did you and the squaw bury the buck before you tried it on?"

A white-toothed grin broke the cast of Tennessee's bronzed face. "Aw, this ain't Indian work," he said, deciding to bear no tidings of blood to Stella's freckled ears. "Bought it from a trader out of Fort Smith. Likely made in Memphis or Saint Louis or Santa Fe. Once I left Fort Gibson, I never laid eyes on no squaw. Thought I'd run on one in the Cross Timbers once, but it turned out a side of spoiled bear meat somebody hung in a tree."

Stella giggled, then made a wry face and got to her feet. "Too bad it was spoiled," she said. "You could have eaten it, once you found out you couldn't—" A mounting wave of color blotted her freckles. She hitched her shoulders and took a half-step. "Now, listen. We're leaving here in the morning if the horses are in shape, so I want you to check the condition of the horses we brought from Tennessee. And pick out a good pack mule." She turned toward the door, then turned back. "Tell Missouri I want to see him before supper. And—oh, say, I forgot—" She came back to the edge of the steps. "Won't you come in and speak to John Greenwood just for a minute?"

"You looking after him in there?"

"Of course."

"Thought you fired him."

"That's no reason to let him die. Anyhow, I can hire him back. He'll learn some sense—already has, I think." She started tapping a foot. "You coming in?"

"What for?" Tennessee growled. "Want me to tell him he's a damned fool? We got nothing to talk about."

"Don't talk so loud," she snapped. "If he's awake, he might hear you. For some reason I'll never understand, he looks up to you. I thought he'd like to know you came inquiring after his health."

"I done inquired," Tennessee reminded her. "I asked was he dead. You told me, so I'll be on my way."

Stella caught fire. "Well, go on, you insufferable brute!" she flared. "Someday you'll find yourself kicking a circle like a poisoned wolf. And, believe me, you'll be all alone. Maybe then you'll remember that you're supposed to be a human being, but I doubt it."

They did not leave the next day. Though not much thinned down by travel, the Tennessee mare would derive solid benefit from a day's rest.

Then, too, Stella was reluctant to leave before the final touches had been added to her pigeon loft, which occupied the space of two second-story rooms in one of the buildings; she wanted to be certain that Shen, who claimed some experience in raising chickens, understood her instructions regarding the care of pigeons. Missouri had relieved her mind concerning the nursing of John Greenwood. Once he was certain he could not persuade Stella to take him with her to Texas and leave Tennessee in charge at Fort Washita, he confided to her that he was a "qualified expert" in the care of gunshot wounds.

Tennessee and Stella rode out from Fort Washita in the first light of morning, the Tennessee mare dancing ahead, the Kentucky stud on lead behind the line-backed dun, the pack mule following free. Like most males of his breed, the mule would follow a mare anywhere, and he was fast enough to keep within rifle range if for any reason they had to call forth all the speed their horses possessed—a contingency Tennessee thought unlikely, since their line of travel would be somewhat farther east than Comanches and Kiowas usually ranged.

They crossed the southwest prairie, and the ruins of Fort Washita sank slowly into the shrouded earth behind them. Then they trailed down a long south slope and plodded to the crest of the next rise, and nothing lay behind them but the wide sweep of rolling grassland.

"Like the ocean," Stella said. "Tennessee, men could hide forever in the distances of this wide country." Her shoulders drooped. "How will we *ever* find them?"

"Easier to find somebody in wide country," Tennessee said. "You can see where you don't have to look."

"Thanks," Stella said. "I'll spend the rest of the day on that one."

Before the morning was over, they struck post-oak woodland and turned west on a wagon road. This narrow strip of country was not unlike the scrub-oak barrens of middle Tennessee, and Tennessee wondered whether Stella had the feeling, as he did, that they were riding down to Chattanooga, instead of down to some lonely ford on Red River. Since she was ahead of him on the narrow woods road, he couldn't see her face, but he could see her squared shoulders and lifted head. He could see also the slenderness of her waist and the spread of her hips against the saddle. The Remington .36 hung in a holster at her right hip now, and she'd been taking lessons in marksmanship from Missouri. Well, she could use a few lessons, after missing Brownlow Krull at point-blank range. That lucky Brownlow Krull! He'd kill Brownlow if they ever met, of course; but a man had to admit that the bastard knew what the real loot in the house was.

Leaving the woods around noon, they turned south, the road now lining out through expanses of sun-browned grass splotched at widening intervals by patches of brush and straggling growths of timber. The searing heat of the sun against her thin cotton shirt soon drove Stella back into the jacket she had removed in the woods. At last, in mid-afternoon, they came to the foot of a short prairie, followed the road over a low, timbered ridge, and saw below them the limpid pools and glittering shallows of the Red River.

"That's the Red River you heard about," Tennessee commented. "They call creeks and little branches rivers out here. Call dry gullies creeks."

Stella had her hat off, fanning her flushed face. "It's river enough for me. I feel like jumping in it right now, clothes and all."

They watered the horses at the ford and rode on into Texas. The character of the country remained unchanged, and the air was still laden with its day-long heat. Before the afternoon was over, Stella turned in the saddle and looked back at a few shimmering miles of the way they had come.

"This is that Texas you heard about," she mimicked him. "Have you got any comments to make about *its* size, too?"

"Why, the Texas folks all lie about it," Tennessee said. "They claim it's big, but you can see for yourself it's a hell of a lot bigger."

At dusk they off-saddled at a water hole in a dry creek bed, and Tennessee put the horses on grass, picketing the mare and hobbling the stud, letting the dun and the mule go free. Stella cooked supper—bacon first, then hash-browned potatoes, then pan bread, all in the same frying pan. By the time the bread was done, the coffee pot had come to a boil on coals beside the fire. Tennessee observed Stella's economy of motion with approval, remembering her first awkward attempts to cook on a campfire. She cooked enough for three people and then watched Tennessee eat enough for two.

"Good thing I'm not poor," she said. "Way you eat, I'd have to let you go."

"Nope," he grunted. "I wouldn't be here. You, either."

Her fork was stilled. "That's where you're wrong. I'd be out here in this West, looking for the Krulls. I'd be here."

"Stella, you wouldn't. You never been pushed back on yourself—just yourself. Being a woman and poor would've stopped you."

"I'd have found a way." She looked at him, her lips fixed in a small, cold smile. When he made no answer, she added, almost as an afterthought, "You would have been here, too. You just might have been the way I'd have found."

"You'd found *me* going every which way," Tennessee said.

"Hungry man can't spare the time for revenge. Never understood revenge, anyhow. Don't understand you, Stella."

"I know. You told me back in Tennessee." She set her tin plate aside and leaned forward intently. "Do you think revenge—the kind of revenge I'm after—is wrong?"

"Sure, it's wrong." He reached for the coffee pot. "Man after revenge don't look but one way. Wants to get his bullet in the other fellow's guts. Forgets all about his own hide. So he winds up taking two bullets in his own guts for the one he sends. A trade that bad is wrong as all hell, you ask me."

"Honestly!" Stella sighed. "Sometimes I think you talk in parables, even when I know you don't. Tennessee, it's taken me a long time, but I know now what's wrong with you. You have no soul. That's it. You haven't got the whisper of a soul."

Tennessee could have eaten more. He was still scraping his plate after the last morsel was gone. *Soul!* he thought. That Stella! He set his plate aside and lifted his cup of coffee off the ground.

"So I have no right to condemn you for what you are—you know, for what happened in Mississippi. Because you're innocent, really."

Tennessee put his cup back down, feeling now as if he were groping in the dark for a bear trap he'd set and then misplaced. "Told you that all along," he said cautiously.

"No, I don't mean that." Her eyes reflected briefly the light of a flaring ember. "I know you lied. I mean innocent like a wolf. A wolf can't be immoral because—"

"Well, by God," he groaned, "there you go again!"

"Oh, be still. I'm serious about this." She looked down into the coals of the dying fire. "Tennessee, do you believe in God?"

"Stella, sometimes—" he began. "Stella, I wish you'd get it through your head. I ain't a bit different from other folks."

"Then you *do* believe God exists?"

Tennessee shifted his bulk. "Why, I never claimed He don't," he growled. "Reckon I'll take the word of the preachers and the medicine men. They follow that line of—well, business or work or whatever you want to call it. I sure don't."

"Has He ever stood by you in times of trouble?" Stella persisted. "Ever helped you through a bad time?"

"Not me." Tennessee was on solid ground now. "And I question He did anybody else. Been told the medicine men claim He gives them power to turn bullets. They get a lot of Indians killed with that kind of foolishness."

Stella stared at him with puzzled eyes; then, apparently giving him up once again, she dropped her eyes back to the coals. "Well, I believe in God. I believe—almost I know—that the soul of a man is tuned to God. So I've had to consider the verse 'Vengeance is mine; I will repay, saith the Lord.' If the injury had been only to me, I'd never gone looking for Brownlow Krull. If I'd been single and the hurt all mine, as God is my witness, I could have dug up the strength even to forgive Brownlow. But I can't—and I won't—wait for God to repay Jimpson and Parson without any help from me. So I may lose *my* soul, too, before I get through with the Krulls. But there's a kind of morality in vengeance—some vengeance. My vengeance may not be aimed directly toward making the world a little bit safer for gentleness and decency and honor, but it will have that effect. It's aimed, I know, at wiping a horror from my mind that will destroy me if I give up and go home. It's hard to be honest with oneself—it's impossible, of course—but I keep wondering how God will judge a soul that's willing to sacrifice itself in a cause, good or bad, that will save many souls. Because the Krulls of this world destroy not just bodies but souls, too. Their outrages warp the souls of the survivors with hatred and bitter despair. Oh, I know in my heart why I'm after the Krulls. It all comes back to the black horror they gave Paul as his last impression of life. So if I do lose my soul in the pursuit of vengeance, why, then, that's the price I'll pay . . . . Now, God knows, if you don't, that I haven't really been talking to you, Tennessee. So spare me the rest of your damned skin-saving philosophy and go roll in your blanket. I'll sit up awhile longer and talk some more to myself."

In the gray light of morning Tennessee rolled out of his blanket and, acting on impulse, took the razor and soap from his saddle roll and then, stripped to the waist, padded down to the water hole and shaved, using water trapped off to one side in a little gravel bowl. Coming back near the cooking fire, he kicked up Stella's gun belt and holstered Remington, where she'd let them drop to the ground. He reached down for the gun belt, walked over, and dropped the weight of leather and steel on Stella's blanketed form.

Stella moaned softly, stirring feebly; then she sat bolt upright, clutching the blanket close. "What—what—" she cried out. She looked groggy and defenseless, drugged by sleep.

"Time to get up," Tennessee told her. "And look here. Watch where you let that pistol lay around on the ground. Dew'll rust it. Might need it some night."

She rubbed her eyes and tossed back her hair. "I slept like a dead one," she said, and sat watching him build the fire. It was the first time she'd seen him without a shirt on. Gradually, as she watched, she became aware of her breasts, of a faint flutter of feeling in the pit of her stomach, and of a spreading warmth. Well, here I go, waxing in heat again, she thought. Certainly Paul's brother should be the last—but no, she'd wrestled with this problem and knew finally that she could not blame herself. It was simply that the size, the muscular strength, the power of the man were enough to stagger the self-possession of any female. She shook her head to clear her mind. "My father had a big Negro blacksmith before the war. . . ." She fell silent, then started up again. "But he swung a sledgehammer for years and years. He *worked* for his muscles. Tennessee, how much do you weigh?"

"Don't know for sure. Two twenty-five or thirty, somewhere in there."

"Good Lord! Why, how can you move so quick and light?"

"Maybe I practiced at it; I don't know. Always did walk light, and I ain't fat now. Gained back ten or fifteen pounds, but that's what I lost in the war."

"Well, you're an awesome physical specimen," Stella observed, her whole face blurred by a dreamy speculation. "I wonder—Tennessee, that Bull Jakes is bigger than you. I'd say he's stronger, though I have no way—" Her sleep-flushed face suddenly tightened perceptibly. "What I mean is—that Jakes walks like some monstrous bear—a grizzly. So I just wonder—"

"Whether a wolf can whip a grizzly?" Tennessee asked sardonically. "Well, he can't."

"Whether a big, fast man could kill a big, slow man with his bare hands," Stella finished thoughtfully.

"How you know he's slow?" Leaving the fire, Tennessee moved over to his blanket and started donning his shirt. "I question he's fast enough to beat a .44 slug out of a pistol barrel, though. So I reckon he's slow enough."

"What if he were unarmed, though, and challenged you?"

"I'd shoot him."

Stella protested, "Somehow, I can't see you refusing to fight him."

"What you care how, long as he winds up dead?" He crossed between her and the fire, headed out of the creek bed toward the grass. "Get up and cook while I bring in the horses. We got a long, hot day to ride. Ought to get far as we can in the cool."

When the heat came down, piling up on the prairie in shimmering masses, Tennessee swore that Texas folks got their hope from looking to better weather in hell.

"Them Krulls ain't in Texas," he said once. "They got scalded out by the last rain."

Stella ignored him, though usually she would not tolerate humorous references to the Krulls. Her face looked as if the blood had boiled out of her veins and banked up behind her skin, and she was breathing through her mouth like a hot bird.

Now that the post oaks and blackjacks of the Eastern Cross Timbers had dropped back out of sight, trees were just about as far apart as water courses down the vast stretches of shriveled, sun-browned grass. Stella would point the mare straight toward a ragged motte of trees anywhere near their route and was hard to turn back when her judgment was bad. Tennessee allowed she was getting punished for being a woman and getting raped and giving a damn once the fellow got off her and went away. He allowed, too, that she'd suffer more, and not from summer heat, for denying she had a woman's body—for denying her female belly and leaning too heavily on her man's brain. They rode on, Tennessee looking for sufficient water for a tolerable camp. The time of day they found it didn't matter to him, nor the time they left it, either, so long as their supplies lasted.

They found water, but only after the sun had done its worst and was hanging two hours high over a grove of trees that looked six inches tall. Tennessee had thought at first that only a line of timber lay ahead, but when he caught sight of a patch of black-stemmed, small-leafed brush, he headed straight for the thicket. Then, as a faint breeze stirred briefly, all three horses and the mule as well brought up their heads and, of their own accord, broke into a heavy, jogging run.

"Well!" Stella exclaimed. "How'd you know? Smell it, too?"

Tennessee gestured ahead. "Plum thicket. Might be some plums."

"Might've known. No complaints, though. Not this time."

Skirting the south end of the thicket, they followed a path through the brush down to a little creek and, dismounting, moved upstream from the horses to drink at a shaded pool that nestled in the elbow bend at the bottom of a ten-foot bank. They drank like animals, flat on their bellies. Tennessee got up, tossed his jacket aside, and jerked off his shirt. Then, going back on his belly, he crawled in far enough to submerge head and shoulders and chest. He pulled back, letting the water stream where it would, grinning like a hard-faced boy.

Every freckle on Stella's face envied him. Then she jumped to her feet. "Come on! Let's pitch camp. I can't wait to take a bath in that pool, and I'm going to—while you go yonder behind that thicket and eat plums till I call you."

They made camp in a clump of cottonwoods west of the creek. Leaving Stella rummaging in the pack for fresh garments, Tennessee crossed the creek to the lower edge of the thicket and started browsing through a thin scattering of plums somewhat past their prime. By the time better plums just out of reach had drawn him into the thicket, he heard Stella splashing under the bank. But he had no mind for her now. Like a damned fool, he'd come to the thicket without putting his shirt back on, and now he was getting thorn-scratched and snag-cut every time he moved. But he kept going, fending off the stiff brush with bare forearms and whispering curses, for the prize collection of good plums was deep in the thicket on the bend of the creek bank.

When he'd worked his way to the good plums, he discovered that some of them overhung the creek. Reaching for a plum waist-high, he found himself looking down beyond his hand at the pool—and at Stella lying with only her head above water. It seemed a casual sight at first. He thought absently of calling out to ask whether she wanted him to toss her a plum. And then he froze, hardly daring to breathe. Under that water, Stella McEveride, whose shaped-out clothing had been suggesting almost more than he could bear, was as naked as the day she was born.

He knew, of course, that it was next to impossible for her to see him, even if she chanced to look straight at the little opening in the leaves through which he saw her, but he figured, by God, that he had to find a way to move back out of sight without stirring a single leaf. He wrenched his mind this way and that, trying to shake it loose from Stella, knowing all the while that he'd never free it long enough to move himself back a single step. And then it was too late to move back—ever again to move back to where he'd been before this day—for all of a sudden Stella sat up in the pool, her dripping breasts milk-white and boldly outthrust, independent, proud, and shameless. Each breast seemed at home in the open air, completely absorbed in a life of its own; and Stella, divested now of heat and grime, seemed unaware of their existence. Tennessee's outstretched hand closed in a hard fist, and juice from crushed plums dripped down on the leaves to the ground.

Reluctant to quit the water, Stella lay back for one last moment, then scrambled to her feet and stood knee-deep in the pool, a figure marble-white save for wet red pubic hair and brown freckled arms, face, and throat. She stood on one foot and with the other moved the water in slow swirls. Tennessee hung jackknifed, rigid and aching. He had somehow imagined her all of one color, had even conjured up an illogical image of freckled buttocks more than once; now he was looking on a female form so white that the wet red triangle of hair looked black against it. When

Stella waded ashore and started dressing, he watched her with the unthinking fixity of purpose that holds an old battle-scarred panther tom crouched and motionless ten yards distant from an unblemished young female groveling capriciously in her maiden season. When the groveling ceases, the tom breaks into motion, and the maiden cat screams against the night; that pattern is fixed, as the cycles of the moon and stars are fixed.

Now fully dressed, Stella looked up toward the thicket, examining it in some detail for the first time. She tilted up her head, obviously listening; then she called out, "Tennessee! I'm finished. You can come on down." Without waiting for a response, she walked off down the creek toward camp.

Tennessee tried to straighten up, and a brier marked him with a streak of red fire from shoulder to kidney. To ease his aching jaws, he opened his mouth like a trapped beast, sucking wind with a low, snarling sound. Then blindly he lumbered around and started wading through the thicket, lurching into waiting snags, careless of the slap, swish, rake, and scratch of plum-thicket brush that drew blood and raised stinging welts in a score of places. Breaking through to the path, he came sidling down the bank and lunged into the creek.

Stella was on her knees by the pack, removing the provisions for their supper. The coffee pot and the frying pan had been placed upright on the ground beside her. She heard his heavy-footed approach and should have wondered at it, but she did not look up. The thud of his holstered Colts against the ground did not alert her. Only when his boot struck her own gun belt and holstered pistol and the Remington went skating past her across the ground did she turn her head. Then she whirled about, catching at the ground to keep from falling on her face. She made no attempt to rise. She looked up, big-eyed and solemn with astonishment.

"What—what—oh, good God!" In her stricken face now was stamped the recognition of what she saw—what she had thought she'd seen from the first but had never really seen until now.

"Tennessee!" She found her voice. "Tennessee, listen—listen—" Freckles were swarming in her white face, and there was horror there and, at last, a strange and desperate sort of fear—a fear that went far beyond the bounds of physical dread. "No! Oh, no! Tennessee, wait a minute! Listen—" Her voice had a stifled, shuddering sound. Her hand was feeling about on the ground in search of a stick, anything. Then she started backing away on all fours. "Please, Tennessee! Don't—please don't—"

Though she'd fought Brownlow Krull in desperate silence and

silently struggled with Tennessee in the steamboat cabin, she screamed when his great iron hands reached her this time. Once before, in the hands of Bull Jakes, she'd known complete physical helplessness, and now she knew it once again. She fought as she'd fought Bull Jakes—furiously, desperately, as best she could—and then, since she could do nothing else, she quit. As her riding skirt was dragged over her hips, she begged Tennessee to spare her, gasped out something about Paul, mentioned incest. In a voice that shifted from fury to despair, she threatened him and cursed him as long as there was cloth between her and the ground. Finally there was none, so she gave up her last poor hope and set herself to endure the violence of another lust-crazed male. And perhaps she set herself far better than she intended; for sometime during that hard-thrusting invasion of her body, while a remorseless occupation was still in force, her lips turned mobile and responsive under his savage mouth. Her arms came up and embraced him, straining him to her in a sudden, wild abandon.

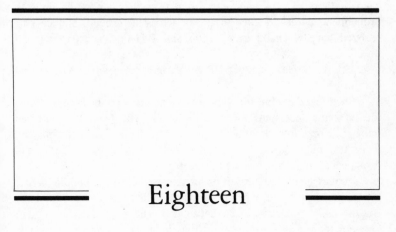

Eighteen

Tennessee padded aimlessly about the camp. Stella lay motionless, face to the ground. Her nakedness, from waist to boots, induced in him now a disturbance far different from what he had felt at the pool: He wanted her up and dressed, but he dreaded the moment when she would turn over, get up, and let him see her face. He felt like walking off down the creek, but some instinct held him there. What he had no instinct for was understanding *why* Stella lay unmoving, careless of exposure; therefore he had no regret for the violence he'd subjected her to, though he did regret something lost that he sensed vaguely but could not identify.

Taking a blanket from the pack, he walked over to Stella and covered her nakedness. What prompted such a gesture, he never knew, but her reaction to it convinced him that it was a mistake. When the blanket came down on her bare skin, Stella moved convulsively, came scrambling up to all fours, her head turning from side to side as if she were looking for something. Then she started crawling toward the place where her gun had come to rest. When the blanket slid off and dropped to the ground behind her, she kept on crawling. She reached the pistol and, turning, sat flat on the ground, the Remington in her hands. Then she pulled the hammer back. Her freckled face was smeared with dirt; it was ashen under splotches and streaks of brown. Without a word, she raised the pistol, took deliberate aim at Tennessee, and pulled the trigger.

The sharp click of the hammer on a bare cap nipple restored Tennessee's sense of reality. Before Stella could get the revolver cocked again, he reached her with a bound and took the gun out of her hands. Two of the five caps had been jarred from the nipples, he noticed, probably when he'd kicked the pistol across the ground. Suddenly he realized that Stella had meant to shoot him. By God, she had tried to kill him!

"God a'mighty, Stella!" His voice was a muted yell. "What you do that for?"

She looked at him, through him, hating the space he occupied. She looked at him once, and then, climbing slowly to her feet, she saw him no more. She bent to pick up her riding skirt, undergarments, and blanket; then, still naked from waist to boots, she walked out of camp and disappeared in the brush along the creek.

Tennessee busied himself by breaking up wood and building a fire. He cooked supper and, when it was ready, called Stella to come and eat. But she made no answer and did not come. Let her pout, then, he thought, knowing there was no whine of self-pity in Stella. For once his food had all the savor of heated sawdust, and he stopped eating, wondering what the hell was the matter with him. He was sure she'd come around by morning. Of only one thing about Stella, though, was he certain: She was all woman when she let go, and any woman after her would fall short of her mark.

Dusk deepened to darkness, and Stella remained away. Tennessee lay down on his blanket, head turning on his saddle uneasily. No telling where she'd spread her blanket, he thought—maybe a yard from a coiled rattlesnake, the state she was in. A snake might crawl in her blanket before it was light. Damned if he meant for some snake to plow that lush flower of meat back into the ground. Maybe he ought to go find her; maybe she'd cooled off by now. Anyway, she had no gun with her to shoot him with.

After a time he came to his feet, like smoke rising from the ground, and went into the brush after her, moving like that same smoke caught in a shifting current of wind. He found her in a little opening on the creek bank and went to the ground several yards away. Lying on his belly, he listened for her breathing. A full minute passed before he thought he heard a catching of breath, a faint gasping sound. He figured she was awake and thinking. Then, finally, even if she was Stella McEveride, he swore that he heard a low, muffled sobbing inside the blanket. It lifted him up and pushed him back silently the way he had come.

Stella had gone straight to the little opening because it was in the direction of two things she required immediately—a screen of brush and water. Dropping her clothes and blanket on the ground, she had waded out into a shallow run of the creek and squatted to wash herself, dipping and splashing water up against her genital area. As she cleared herself of the smears of secretion that her own willful and defiant body had issued to make his invasion of her easier, she wished she could as easily wash out what remained of Tennessee inside her. She wished, too, with a dull wretchedness, that she could wash out of her mind all memory of his brutal and unrestrained lovemaking, and of her own abandoned response to it. All she really wanted at the moment, though, was refuge and privacy. Leaving the creek, she made straight for the blanket and got into it without putting on her undergarments, without even drying herself. She covered her head and wept, keeping it covered as long as she could stand the heat and the increasing need for air. She pressed her face against the tear-wet wool in an agony of self-hatred and despair.

Stella writhed in shame when she remembered that while he was undressing her, even as she cursed him, a benumbing weakness had already gripped her legs, and heat was thawing and melting her loins. She had sought to preserve the spirit of her graveside vow by denying her hungry body the pleasure it was clamoring for. But the quickening motion had gathered and come rushing into open storm, and she had yielded to a guilty, explosive sensuality that could no longer be denied. She tortured herself by reliving the moment when he had withdrawn his hot flesh from her after the first time but had kept his hands on her. She had lain in his arms and made no attempt to get up; she had responded to his kisses and thrilled to the touch of his caressing hands as she waited like a patient, chained-up bitch in heat for him to get hard enough again to reenter her.

But the most difficult memory she would have to live with was of her wholehearted participation in that second coupling. Death would never again have terrors for her. All she'd have to do when threatened would be to recall how she'd heaved and lunged up under him and how she'd groaned and cried aloud when the racking pleasure could be borne no longer in silence. What she would hate him for most was that he'd turned her into a complete animal and let her see herself in that state.

Turning on her back, Stella pushed down the blanket and looked up at the stars. She *was* an animal, she realized, as all human beings were; and she had to act much as all animals did when moved by the basic drives, one of which was sexual desire. She was a female animal, and a healthy one; it was only natural that she should respond as a healthy female would while being bred by a virile male of the same species. And she had to admit that Tennessee, damn him, was a virile animal. She didn't think she should blame herself unduly for being undignified while in the throes of sexual ecstasy. She knew now that one of her vows to Paul at graveside was unrealistic, since she had no power to keep it when circumstances were beyond her control. Where the blame should fall for transforming her mental and emotional state to that of an animal was upon that goddamned Tennessee Smith McEveride. And she'd hate him for it until her dying day.

What she had to decide before she faced him again was whether she was going ahead with the quest as planned or whether she should get rid of him. Why should she fire him? Nothing had changed about him; he had merely proved he was what she knew he was from the first—a wolf-man whom she needed to help her find the Krulls. She had to see that he didn't attack her again, but she didn't think he would. If he did—well, she was no virgin. She would be thrice raped instead of twice. It wouldn't be the end of her life. But if he did carry her that low again, she would kill him—even if she had to hire a killer to get it done.

And then she thought of having to look into Tennessee's face in the morning, both of them remembering her passionate, breathless grinding and her ecstatic cries, and she ground her face into the blanket again. The blood seethed in her veins, and a red fog clouded her mind. *Oh, goddamn him!* She lay there, hating him bitterly, shaken by helpless rage.

Though he stirred late, Tennessee managed to have breakfast cooked by sunup, but the horses were still out on the grass. He called Stella and then stood idle until he heard her coming through the brush. He had her plate of food ready and coffee poured by the time she appeared. While she was still some distance off, he noticed the smudgelike shadows under her eyes, but he thought her face looked serene and pleasant. Then, when she stood by the breakfast fire, he saw that he was mistaken. Her face was set in a half-smiling mask that was not at all out of tone with the bitter darkness of her hard, unforgiving eyes.

"Why, how considerate!" Her voice dragged just enough to make her satire unmistakable. She took up her plate and, without sitting down, began eating. "You know, as a rule, brothers don't show the same consideration for their sisters they do for other women. But you're an exception, brother. And, believe me, I'll never forget you for it. Maybe it's usual, I don't know, for brothers to call on sisters for more than they ought to expect of them." She kept her eyes on her plate. "As you did last night, brother." Her lips started shaping, as if by rote, a cold smile. "I'm sure you'll be more thoughtful in the future." She lifted her bitter eyes and looked at him. "I know that you'll die before you do it again."

Tennessee could think of no response whatever. "Got to bring in the horses," he said. "I've done eat."

He was turning as he spoke, losing no time, but she stopped him before he could get away. "Just a minute, Brownlow." She sipped her coffee, taking her time. "Give me my pistol."

Tennessee stood thinking. "What you want with it?"

"To take my life with, of course," Stella said. "Surely you don't expect me to live after suffering a fate worse than death. Why *would* I want my gun?"

"Shoot *me*, maybe," Tennessee suggested. "You tried to last night."

"The light was bad," she said, "and I took you for a wolf. Don't worry. I intend to leave wolf killing to the wolfers from now on. In fact, I—I intend—I—" Suddenly she blew up, her face crumpling and then re-forming, shifting, all in a moment, to an expression of fury that bunched her freckled cheeks and set a fire in the depths of her slanted eyes. "Damn you," she flared bitterly, "give me my pistol, you—you despicable, low-life son-of-a-bitch!"

Without a word Tennessee walked over to his saddle, took the Remington from one of his bags, and tossed it on the ground at her feet. Then, still unable to think of anything to say, he walked through the clump of cottonwoods and out upon the prairie grass.

Riding the big dun bareback, he drove the horses into camp and started saddling. Stella watched him with burning eyes, slapping her quirt against her riding skirt. This nervous flicking of the quirt was something new; Tennessee figured that what she really wanted to do was cut the hide off him with that plaited leather. She moved over behind him as he loaded the pack mule and started securing the pack.

"When I *think* of the times I worried for fear you'd leave me—" Her voice sounded half-choked, starved for breath. "Damn you, there never was a chance you'd leave! Biding your time! That's what *sickens* me! You had one thing on your mind from the first."

"No, that ain't the way it was," Tennessee denied. "Not till I saw you naked. Hadn't been for that, it wouldn't happened."

"As God is my witness," Stella swore, "you're more of a beast than Brownlow Krull! At least he mentioned the matter to me first. Of course, you knew that—and knew that he got an ear shot off for mentioning it. So you took the shortcut."

"I never thought anything. You're making it out worse—"

"*Worse?*" Stella raged. "Will you tell me what's worse than getting bred like a sow in a chute? What's worse than being made ridiculous? Why, that's what I am! I'm comical!'' Her voice broke and died, and then started up again. ''Yes, sir, my husband dies, and I give up men. I make a vow by his grave and in my heart as truly as ever a cloistered nun took an oath of chastity. So what happens? Why, I can't get off my knees before I'm busier than a whore on Saturday night! There *must* be a sign on me somewhere like a free lunch, but where is it? I admit that I'm guilty—I must be—but *how* am I? I don't dare go ask a preacher about it. He might throw me down on a pew and get me with bastard before I could explain why I'd come.''

Tennessee left the mule and stepped to the head of the mare. He turned the mare into position for Stella to mount. ''You're talking foolish,'' he said. ''You ain't ridiculous. Here, let me help you up.''

''Keep your hands off me!'' she snapped. ''Go on! Back away from that mare! If you ever again so much as lay a hand on me, I'll kill you. Do you understand me?''

''Sure,'' he said, his face impassive. ''All I aimed to do was help you up.''

''I don't want any help from you. You helped me last night. You helped me out of my clothes. You helped me stay down when I tried to get up. And then—then you—helped me—goddamn you, I've a mind to see you dead before the week is out!''

Leaving the little creek, they went back to the old wagon road and headed south. They were riding on a great prairie where the wide expanses of grass were sometimes nearly level, sometimes rolling and broken, where every hill and settler's cabin and strip of timber seemed always at least five miles away. During the day they exchanged perhaps a dozen words, none that they could help. Stella rode out in front, her head hanging when it was not weaving from side to side or tossed high above squared shoulders. She rode like a woman in physical pain. Once, while she was swaying and hitching in the saddle, she gave the mare a sudden cut with her quirt, for no apparent reason, and was snatched halfway to the horizon before the mare would agree to terms.

Then, in late afternoon, they forded a clear, sparkling stream at the crossing of an east-west wagon trail and rode up a long rise to Fort Worth, a dreary little village that had grown up around an old army parade ground high on a bluff overlooking the Clear Fork of the Trinity River. They followed the dusty path past log dwellings scattered here and there east of the square, which was ringed by stores boarded up during the war and still in disuse. The roads around the courthouse served as the town's only streets, and the courthouse itself, a stone building begun before the war and never finished, had no roof.

Stella pulled up at the edge of the square and waited for Tennessee to ride alongside. ''Tennessee, I have a somewhat delicate favor to ask,'' she said, all expression ironed out of her face. ''Will you do me a very special kindness?''

''Sure,'' Tennessee said, hoping Stella was beginning to realize that he'd done her no real harm back at the last campsite. ''What you want?''

''After you slop up here in town, and swill all the whiskey you can hold, you won't have a doubt that you're the herd boar and the sow's delight. I want your promise that you won't come grunting and chopping at me on the street, where people can stop and watch. I'm not used to an audience yet. It would embarrass me.''

Tennessee had not had an easy day. He swung his head, searching the square with smoky eyes, hoping to find some man, any man, at a standstill watching them pass. He wanted to break some bastard's bones. Giving a savage haul on the lead rope that set the stud dancing, he wheeled the big dun into the square, silently cursing Stella, the horses, himself, and the town. He drew up at the hitching rail in front of a hotel that was obviously converted from a stable of the old fort. Dismounting, he secured the horses, letting Stella climb down by herself.

The proprietor of the hotel came up to them and took charge of the horses. ''Hotel man these days got to be fixed for man and beast both,'' he told them. ''Well, I am, and I ain't crowded. Go on in and pick any room you want. Wash up and go on down the hall to the dining room. Supper be ready when you are.''

''Why, thank you,'' Stella told him. ''We may leave in the morning, and we may not. I've got to think about it.''

''Hope you stay a year.''

Wanting to see Stella no more until morning, Tennessee barely paused by a water pitcher and wash bowl in a room selected at random, and went to the dining room. When Stella arrived, he'd been waiting a good half-hour for his food. They were the only guests, so they had supper together, eating in silence. Tennessee was the first to push back his chair.

''Knowing you have no conscience,'' Stella commented, ''I have to ask. What's happened to your appetite?''

''Saving room,'' Tennessee said, coming to his feet. ''Time I was slopping up. Got to get at that grunting and chopping.'' Turning, he stalked out of the dining room.

The First and Last Chance Saloon occupied the one small, dingy room of a crackerbox building west of the courthouse on the east-west road. A few shelves on one wall held rows of jugs with corncob stoppers, and here and there were signs announcing peach brandy, gin, and whiskey for sale. Tennessee came through the doorway and, ignoring several loungers on a bench against the wall, leaned on his elbows at the plain, varnished bar. At his elbow was a wooden bucket of water, floating a dipper, for customers who required a chaser.

A husky young man of simple eye and nondescript face was standing behind the bar. "What you want?" he asked the burly figure in buckskins.

"Peach brandy," Tennessee said, turning his cold eyes up at the bartender's face without lifting his head.

"You don't say?" the young man snorted. "Tell me where some is, and I'll beat you to it." He grinned toward the bench, hardly glancing at Tennessee. "We ain't got nothing but whiskey here. Red-eye or rotgut—take your pick."

Tennessee said nothing. He stared at the young man until the latter's eyes focused on him. When they did, they suddenly flared wide open and then got small and guarded. Tennessee's lips drew back from his teeth in a savage grin. "Why, then, I just won a bet from myself," he said, and quit grinning. "Why the hell don't you take them signs down? The First and Last Chance Privy, that's all you got here. You know what? I mean, this is the worst dog's ass of a town I ever been in."

The loungers were suddenly still. The bartender scowled with an effort that beaded his forehead with sweat. "Yeah?" he said, picking up a rag and starting to wipe the bar. "Well, them signs ain't mine. I'm just staying here today for Ed Terrell. I don't own this place."

"Sure, you don't," Tennessee sneered, dropping a coin on the bar. "Only thing you own is that rag. You don't own the town, neither. See if you own enough strength to hand me one of them jugs."

A jug and a tin cup were placed before Tennessee in silence. He reached over and plucked the lone chair in the room from behind the bar. Then, carrying the jug and cup in one hand and the chair in the other, he retired to a corner and settled down to an evening's drinking. The whiskey tasted like a mixture of kerosene, lye, and soured vegetable juice, but it had a raw authority that was irresistible.

After his third cup Tennessee began wondering why in the name of God he'd found it necessary to humiliate the bartender. He had drunk enough to admit that he'd entered the saloon hoping to find any excuse at all to smash some human face or even blast somebody's guts out with a .44-caliber slug of lead. If he'd addressed himself to the loungers on the bench, instead of to the bartender, he just might have had to kill one of them, although none of them offered any possible threat to his safety. So why had he harassed the bartender? Why, for the pleasure of seeing fear of himself sour another man's life, of course. He had enjoyed ruining the day and the week and the month for the bartender. It was the kind of pleasure that kept a man with a taste for it looking for trouble. By God, he'd better watch out! He knew, if any man knew, that a trouble-hunter's road is a short one, with a step-off into space at the end of it.

As the evening wore on, bearded men in rusty-looking clothes straggled in and filtered out, drinking the raw whiskey, seeing for themselves the big stranger with the jaguar eyes crouched over a jug in the corner. Their talk was of the galling restrictions imposed on loyal Southerners by carpetbaggers in east Texas, of the despotic military orders denying the franchise to men of the county, of young couples afraid to marry lest the license issued by a *de facto* county government be invalid, and of the increasing Indian raids.

Tennessee had no idea how much he had lowered the contents of the jug when he decided that he'd had enough. He got to his feet and lumbered toward the door. Two men were entering, and he brushed them out of his way with a swing of his arm. One of them rebounded, snarling something like, "Who the goddamned hell you think—" Tennessee picked the speaker off his feet and brought him close to look at him. He couldn't make the fellow out.

"You lucky bastard," he said. "Never saw you before." Suddenly, in a frenzy, the man started windmilling his arms and legs. Tennessee raised the fellow high and, turning, heaved him through the doorway. The crash of the landing and the wild howl that followed brought some measure of peace to Tennessee's heart.

He crossed the square with lurching strides and entered the hotel. If there were people in the room he entered, he did not see them. He somehow found the hallway and opened the first door he came to. Without undressing, he fell on a bed, which happened to be unoccupied, and was asleep almost as soon as he hit the top cover.

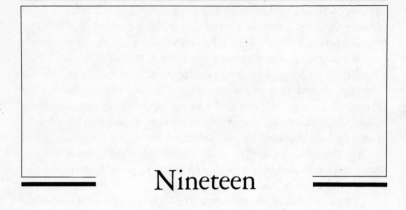

Nineteen

When Tennessee awoke at eight o'clock in the morning, his head felt as if he'd been poleaxed in his sleep. Groaning, he eased out of bed and made his way to the washstand, where he lifted the pitcher out of its bowl and drank with a raging thirst. Swearing off whiskey forever, he poured the remainder of the water over his head.

As if walking on eggs, he crept to the dining room for coffee and found Stella there eating breakfast.

"We're going on as soon as you can eat and saddle up," she announced, hardly glancing his way. "We need to leave here at once. I had to pass around some money about an hour ago. Some soldiers came here to arrest you. Seems you broke a man's leg last night."

"Stuff was in a stone jug," Tennessee complained. "Couldn't see how much I was drinking. Anyhow, it was doctored up with pepper and tobacco juice and rattlesnake heads, what I think. Maybe some arsenic, too, way I feel."

"You'll live." Stella sipped her coffee. "What had the man done?"

"How the hell do I know what he done?" Tennessee held his head with both hands. "Maybe just breathed."

They rode out of Fort Worth within the hour. Many a time thereafter Tennessee would dredge his memory for the physical features of the land within a day's ride southwest of Fort Worth and come up with nothing. On the second day's ride, however, he was alive to the wide sweep of a great, rolling prairie and the occasional broken hills and ravines which showed dark clays in their raw-earth exposures.

Around noon of the third day, as they were ascending a rise of prairie, Tennessee swung in the saddle. "You smell smoke?" he called to Stella, who was several lengths behind.

She inhaled deeply and shook her head.

"Thought I did," he said. "Here. Hold the stud back while I look."

When she reined the mare near and caught the lead rope, Tennessee moved the big dun up the rise; he pulled to a halt when his eyes could see over the crest. After a while he motioned Stella to come on. "House burned," he said as she came up. "Two riders there. Don't know. Maybe they set the fire."

Stella threw him a dark glance. "Let's hold back," she suggested, "or ride around."

"Ain't but two there," he objected. "Let's keep on the road."

"You damned savage!" she said bitterly. "You're just itching to kill somebody. God help them if one is a woman."

"May be two of the Krulls," he reminded her sardonically. "Ought to look 'em over."

A mile north of the tree-lined Colorado River, the smoking ashes of a house, barn, and sheds were visible in the center of a wide valley, the gray-black areas reduced by distance to small, rectangular patches. Two saddled horses stood at the edge of the scorched yard, and two human figures moved about near the ashes. Soon the figures came to attention, looking toward the newcomers, and moved to their horses, drawing rifles from scabbards; then, apparently after consultation, putting them back. When Tennessee and Stella were a quarter-mile away, one of the two men in the yard mounted his horse and came riding toward them at a gallop. The man pulled up in the wagon trace ahead, causing them to halt. He was a clean-cut young man with a deeply tanned, still face and level brown eyes, and he was armed for whatever the plains offered—rope and rifle on saddle, bowie knife and Navy Colt belted at waist.

"Howdy," he greeted them, touching his hat to Stella. "We seen you had a lady along," he explained to Tennessee, who concluded at once that if they had seen that well, one of them had to have a telescope, "and we 'lowed she ought to hold back a spell. The Perkins family, what was left behind, was massacreed by Injuns this mawning." He looked at Stella. "They sure ain't a pretty sight, ma'am. You might hold back till we get 'em buried."

"I've been through this sort of thing," Stella told him. "Anyhow, I don't keep things from myself. I have a strong stomach."

"Ma'am, I sure don't—"

"She ain't only got a strong stomach," Tennessee informed him.

"She's got a bull head, too." He ignored Stella's dark stare. "Let her look."

At the edge of the yard, the young plainsman, having told Tennessee and Stella his name was Dick Weatherford, introduced his graying, roan-mustached companion as Jeff Slaughter. Beyond Slaughter in the yard, a man, woman, and infant lay dead. The man and woman had been scalped and horribly mutilated. Their faces looked sleepy and melancholy because of sagging skin loosened by scalp cuts. The infant had merely had its brains knocked out. Slaughter had hastily covered the woman's body with his slicker as the riders pulled up. She had been a comely woman in her early thirties, and, unless she'd been very lucky, every buck in the raiding party had enjoyed himself with her, the last one "throwing her away." They buried the bodies, Tennessee helping to dig the shallow graves.

According to Slaughter, the attack had been made by a party of Kiowas. Comanches would have carried the woman off into captivity, he thought. "But them cussed Kiowas couldn't wait to start their devilment," he said. "I sure wish poor Ellie was laying here with 'em. They taken her and the boy. He's only about seven and may adjust to Injun ways, but Ellie's thirteen at least. Touch and go whether they take her to raise or entertain themselves out there a few miles. Either way she's in for hell and won't last." He looked down at the mounds of dark earth. "No finer folks lived than these here. Seems a shame just to throw dirt on 'em and ride off. We'll notify the nearest neighbors, though, and they can hold a funeral later."

Stella produced a small Bible that Tennessee had not seen before. "May I?" she said.

They stood by the graves, Slaughter and Weatherford with bowed, reverent heads and Tennessee with his hat off after receiving a hard look from slanted black eyes in a high-cheeked, freckled face. In a low, clear voice Stella read from the Scriptures and said a short prayer. Tennessee, still smarting from the look she had instructed him with, hoped that the bodies, beginning their slow, sure trip back to the earth, got some comfort from her words, but he doubted it.

When she had finished, Slaughter said gravely, "Thank you, ma'am. You sure been a big help here." He took a step toward the horses and then turned back. "We're headed for San Antone after we report this to some folks about five miles from here. Glad to have your company but sure don't want to push ourselves on you." He was speaking to Stella, while keeping her big, cold-eyed companion in the corner of his eye.

"Push yourselves on us?" Stella exclaimed. "After this?" Her eyes swept Tennessee. "You don't know how much safer I'll feel in your company."

Slaughter and Weatherford explained that they were ex-Rangers who had served in the Frontier Regiment, under Captain Jack Cureton, fighting Comanches and Kiowas on the Texas frontier during the Civil War. Now, with Texas under military occupation, there was no longer any Frontier Regiment or Ranger companies, either. The only protection against marauding bands of Indians in west and northwest Texas was the feeble resistance the retreating settlers were able to muster on their own. Like many other ex-Rangers, Slaughter and Weatherford had plenty of time at their disposal and not much else except their horses and guns. Tennessee saw an idea slowly forming behind Stella's speculative eyes.

And as they rode along through the day and rested in camp that night, Tennessee also saw ideas rapidly taking shape behind the eyes of Slaughter and Weatherford. By the end of that first day together, Stella could easily have persuaded Weatherford to commit a murder, and she was making Slaughter feel younger by the hour. The two men looked back at her from whatever direction they turned, as filings toward a magnet. And they watched Tennessee with reserve, sensing a strained relationship between Stella and her brother-in-law. Though they did not suspect the truth, both felt uncomfortable around Tennessee. They had been Rangers, used to running with the hounds; they recognized a curly wolf when they saw one.

In their first camp together Stella explained that she and her brother-in-law were in the West to find the Krulls, murderers of her husband and father-in-law, and bring them to justice. She wondered whether white men, instead of Indians, might have raided the Perkinses, since she understood that Indians usually did not raid that far east.

"Well," Slaughter answered, "maybe it *was* a mite far east, but you folks had done got off the main road and drifted some miles further west than you allow. Injuns depredate pretty regular along the San Saba, a day's ride west of the Perkins place. No, that massacree can be marked up to the Kiowas. In three or four years west of Fort Belknap, we never run across no raiders fits them Krull descriptions. Reckon your best bet is that Eagle Pass country on the Rio Grande. I seen that Wild Cat once. He was sure one wily devil. And there's still some of them Seminoles in Piedras Negras, 'cross the river."

In mid-afternoon they left behind them low limestone ridges and became immersed in a billowing gray-green sea of mesquite that smothered the distances of a wide land. They began to meet occasional lean-faced riders wearing big hats and *chivarras* and riding small mustangs.

The riders, headed for brush-country cattle ranges and sheep pastures, passed with reserved salutes and side glances that were veiled and curious. They passed small burros walking sturdily under huge loads of knotty mesquite firewood and Mexican *carretas* drawn by oxen that ignored the cartmen's constant shouts of *"Ándale! Ándale!"*

San Antonio seemed at first a town lost in the brush as its low, white and cream-colored buildings came rising into view above the thinning foliage of mesquite thickets. The first buildings along the road were huts made of mesquite poles daubed with mud or adobe. Dirty, half-naked Mexican children, goats, lean hogs, and mongrel dogs all played together in the road. Dusky slatterns with slick black hair and magnificent eyes shrilled entreaties and imprecations at the children and chattered across the yards to one another. Men in *serapes* and Mexican hats, apparently endowed with plenty of leisure time, smoked brown-paper cigarettes and ignored the clatter of domesticity around them.

As the riders made their way along the road, the houses improved, becoming predominantly adobe and stone; the grounds grew neater, roses and other flowers appearing in the yards; and old Germans smoked long pipes on the galleries. Then they were in Military Plaza, with its old parish church, its Spanish Governor's Palace, its sprinkle of Spanish-German-French people, its chili stands, its vendors of unusual foods.

Near one of the chili stands, three girls, coquettes from the cradle up, turned roguish eyes on the passing strangers. One of them said to the others, speaking in English for Tennessee's ears, "W'at you theenk? Me, I peek the beeg one. Ees *hombre del campo*, that one!"

Feeling Stella's eyes upon him, Tennessee kept his face impassive, as if he had not seen the girl nor heard her speak. Weatherford grinned ruefully. "Well, Jeff, that sure puts us in *our* place." He was not entirely pleased.

"Don't feel bad," Stella consoled him, her cool eyes brushing Tennessee. "Tennessee's a real ladies' man. He overpowers them. Wait till he gets into his new Mexican suit."

Tennessee and Slaughter stabled the horses in a combination wagon yard and livery stable just off Military Plaza on South Flores Street. With Weatherford as escort to bring the mare back, Stella rode on a half-mile further to the Menger Hotel in Alamo Plaza. As the two men were leaving the stables, a long-haired, slightly buck-toothed youth dressed in buckskins stepped up and spoke to Slaughter in the entrance. The boy's wild appearance was accented by the fact that the buckskins were leggings, that his loins were covered only by a bright red breechclout. On his right hip was belted a very businesslike knife, and on his left sagged an

Army Colt .44, very similar and in as good repair as Tennessee's own.

"You him man name Roan Stud?" the youth asked in a voice which sounded as if it would be more at home with another language.

"I hear I'm called that by the Comanches," Slaughter admitted, glancing sheepishly at Tennessee.

"You good man. Talk straight. Me see you one time."

Slaughter nodded. "I know. I remember you, Kid. What can I do for you?"

"Got hosses out in brush. Where me sell? What man talk straight?"

"See Ed Johnson down this here street a piece," Slaughter advised. "He'll treat you square. Mightnear too late now, though. Better wait till morning."

"Big bay stud," the Kid said, his flat, gray eyes coming alive with love of a fine horse. "Me want him *caballo entero*. Trade good ponies." He held up the fingers of both hands.

Slaughter shook his head. "He ain't mine, but I can tell you he ain't for sale."

The Kid waved his hands to clear the rejected offer, then closed them and opened them twice, making an offer of twenty ponies. Again Slaughter shook his head, and the Kid turned without another word and was gone.

They walked toward the plaza, Slaughter frowning thoughtfully. "Twenty ponies for the stud," he mused. "Hope he don't get to figuring that busting out on War Drum would be a sight easier'n running off twenty or thirty common hosses. Smith, you just laid eyes on one of the few white men the Comanches will allow on the Staked Plains. Spotted Hoss, they call him. Whites call him the Polka Dot Kid. Rides a little Appaloosa stallion and hunts wild hosses—and tame ones, too, if they're Appaloosas. That's how he got his name, I reckon. Captured as a child and raised by Comanches. Broke loose from 'em finally to hunt wild hosses on his own but still visits 'em and keeps in touch. Like as not some young Comanches helped drive his hosses in and then disappeared. I don't feel easy about that War Drum, no closer watch than the night man at that livery keeps. Did you see him after we first got there?"

Tennessee shook his head. "I'll keep an eye out. May sleep in the loft and save Stella a hotel bill. How'd you get the name Roan Stud?"

"Hair," Slaughter explained uncomfortably. "Enough gray in the red to suggest roan. Stud because Injuns got hosses on their brains, and I sure hope I wouldn't remind 'em of a mare."

Tennessee suspected that Slaughter had not told the whole story. They went past the old parish church between the plazas and ate supper at a restaurant on Main Plaza. They were joined there by Weatherford, who informed them that Mrs. McEveride had advanced him some money for his and Slaughter's lodgings and had requested that he and Slaughter come to see her at the Menger in the morning. His expressed opinion was that they were working for Mrs. McEveride now. Tennessee's unexpressed opinion was that Stella had more money than sense. He reckoned, by God, that she aimed to hire up all of Texas before she was done. Serve her right if she hired up a few Krulls along with the rest.

Leaving the plainsmen in front of the restaurant, Tennessee stopped by a saloon, purchased a bottle of whiskey, and, with it under his arm, went back to the livery stable on South Flores Street. It was the last of dusk before darkness cloaked the town. Around the corner from the livery entrance, he found the Mexican night man cowering against the wall.

"*Ah, Diós, señor,*" the hostler whispered hoarsely. "*Los pistoleros* are inside with the stud. *Pués*, they are the bad ones. I would not go in, *señor.*"

Motioning the man to silence, Tennessee stepped inside and faded down the hallway to War Drum's stall. In the light of a hanging lantern, two heavily armed, rough-looking men were leaning over the stable door and subjecting the stallion to a detailed inspection. "Why, hell, le's get him out here where we can see him good," one of them said as Tennessee came into position. "By God, I'll swear it now, though—that there's the stud, all right."

Tennessee set the bottle of whiskey on the ground of the hallway and straightened. "You won't take anything out," he said pleasantly. "Somebody, though, may have to drag your asses out of here."

The men whirled, stricken with dismay, and stared at him with ghoulish eyes. They were tall and well built, but they bore the marks of brutish blood and wolfish lives. "Who the hell are you?" one of them bristled.

"Go by the name of Tennessee Smith," Tennessee said, picking out a target button on the speaker's faded blue shirt, but not missing the startled exchange of glances that passed between the two roughs. Suddenly, faintly, a warning bell was ringing in his mind. There was something familiar about the men that he could not identify. Maybe he ought to get these bastards on the ground where he could examine them close. "What they call you scrubs when they throw your feed over the fence?"

"That's *our* business!" one of them snapped.

"Even scrubby sons-of-bitches like you got *one* name," Tennessee said.

"You calling us sons-of-bitches?" the one in the blue shirt snarled. "And what was that there 'bout dragging our asses out? If you want—"

"Shut up!" his companion barked urgently. "Use your head . . . . We ain't got no quarrel with you, Smith."

"*I* got one," the rough in the blue shirt persisted. "Cain't nobody call me—"

"Will you shut your goddamn mouth!" his companion shouted. "We're leaving, Smith. Ain't touching no gun. Reckon you won't murder us."

"I catch you sons-of-bitches fooling around this stud again, you'll reckon wrong. Ought to drop both of you just for luck. Thieving bastards like you expecting fair play!"

He watched them hurry from the livery barn, then picked up his bottle of whiskey and took a long drink. Calling to the Mexican that he was sleeping in the hay, he climbed into the loft and made himself comfortable. He took another drink, feeling a warmth spread through his belly.

There was something about those roughs he ought to remember. Why, though? He'd never seen them before; he knew that. They weren't shaking in their boots in front of him, either. They wanted out because they had other, urgent business. Maybe they had something to tell somebody, something to report. To hell with it, he thought.

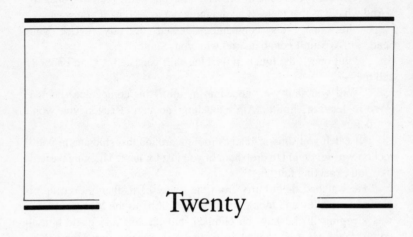

Twenty

After an early breakfast Tennessee was standing in front of a clothing store on Main Plaza when the merchant opened the doors. He bought a sand-colored sombrero, boots, and a pair of brown fringed Texas leg *chivarras*. Just for the hell of it, since Stella had mentioned his ''new Mexican suit,'' he wore them to the Menger Hotel, where he went to find out what Stella's immediate plans for him were.

He walked through the narrow entrance of the wide, two-storied Menger and found himself on a flagged patio surrounded on three sides by open galleries and shaded by big cottonwood and mulberry trees that lifted their branches to the cloudless blue sky overhead. A clerk at the desk directed him to a dining room just off the patio, and there he found Stella, beautiful in a crisp green dress he had never seen before, having breakfast with a young U.S. Cavalry officer.

A shadow of disturbance swept her fine-boned face when she noticed him. He winced when he saw the old high-cheeked, black-eyed expression beginning to form on her face. She schooled herself almost to civility, however, and introduced him to the officer as her brother-in-law, Tennessee Smith. Captain Boone Romine was a dark-complexioned man of medium build with a face made completely inscrutable by heavy-lidded, slate-gray eyes. In the depths of those eyes, Tennessee observed briefly, there was something that suggested the cold murkiness of a shaded swamp.

''What do you want?'' Stella asked curtly, her civility waning.

Tennessee scowled. "What you reckon?" he growled. "What you want me to do?"

"Tennessee, as you can see, I'm engaged at the moment. See me some other time—later in the day."

Stella would regret her conduct later, he thought. He was seeing a childishness, an irrational female contrariness, or some sort of warp-assed bitchiness in Stella that he would have sworn was alien to her nature. Well, he'd give her plenty of room to get over it.

"When you want me, send one of your damned hired hands to find me," he said. "I'll wait till you do." He stalked out of the dining room and out of the hotel. Heading for Main Plaza, he kept thinking about that swamp-eyed captain. Slaughter and Weatherford had been told that Tennessee's last name was McEveride. But Captain Romine, a U.S. Cavalryman sitting at a table with a Mrs. McEveride, had not turned a hair when introduced to her brother-in-law, a man named Smith, whose first name was Tennessee. A stranger—practically any stranger—would have shown some puzzlement, would have asked, or would ask, some questions. He would check with Stella about that when he saw her again.

Later in the morning Tennessee ran into Weatherford on Commerce Street between the plazas. The young plainsman was burdened with worry and lost no time in trying to shift his concern to other shoulders. "Tennessee, I sure wish you'd speak to Mrs. McEveride," he said at once. "She met a Yankee officer last night and ate supper and breakfast with him and seemed like she couldn't wait to get back to him when she seen Jeff and me. Just told us we was working for her and that she'd see us later and then skedaddled back to that fellow. Me and Jeff don't trust that Captain Romine any further'n you can spit. We seen him talking to the Watson brothers, and there sure ain't no doubt about *them*. They're murderers and hoss thieves from way back yonder and used to be wanted bad when there was Rangers. Like I say, somebody's got to speak to Mrs. McEveride."

"You do it, then," Tennessee said. "She won't listen to a damned thing I say."

In late afternoon Tennessee, who was not pleased with the day he had spent, was having a moody drink in the saloon he had been frequenting on Main Plaza when Slaughter came in and crossed to the bar with hurried steps. After ordering whiskey he lowered his voice for Tennessee's ears alone. "Look sharp! Trouble heading your way. Watson brothers. I passed 'em and heard 'em mention your name and something about coming here. I looked back just now, and they was talking to Mrs. McEveride's new army friend, that Romine fellow. Say the word and I'll back your play."

"No," Tennessee said. "Stay clear. I sure don't want no partners to worry about."

"You'll know 'em when you see 'em," Slaughter said. "Alike as two peas. Tall fellows, rawboned, wide-shouldered. A sort of slimy look. Spooky eyes."

There it was. At a word Tennessee's memory turned over. Out of the sweat, blood, and agony of Fox Wilkins, after all hope had been abandoned, had come the image "spooky eyes" with all the hard purity of Scripture, and the tumblers of reason all fell into place at once. The Watsons were the McClanahans Wilkins had described. He turned and ordered another whiskey. Slaughter had taken his drink to a table.

Suddenly Tennessee realized that he was feeling better. This day might turn into something, after all. He wondered whether he was getting to the stage in a gunman's life where he killed for the love of killing. He shrugged his burly shoulders. What *should* he do—cringe and whine and beg these bastards for his life? No—not unless he was ready to die, and he sure as hell wasn't. So he leaned on the bar, feeling loose and relaxed.

So sure was he of the pattern of events that was about to unfold that he was thrown off balance momentarily by the entrance of the Polka Dot Kid. Here was a thing out of its place. The Kid crossed the floor self-consciously and stopped by Tennessee. "Mexican boy say you send," he said. "Say come here him saloon. You sell him big bay stud?"

Tennessee studied the wild youth carefully. Who'd want him and the Kid together in the saloon, and why? Who but the Watsons? "Kid," he said in his deep, soft voice, "I didn't send for you." Suddenly his eyes narrowed, and then he smiled, for at that moment he thought he knew what was shaping up. "But maybe the Watsons did. Sure, now—think I see their play. You're in trouble, Kid. They'll pick a quarrel with *you* and kill me, too, the innocent bystander, with a stray bullet. Now, don't you move a hand toward no gun, no matter what, and when I tell you to step aside, *you move*."

The Kid wet his lips over his prominent front teeth. "Drink him whiskey?" he asked in a slightly strained voice.

"Later," Tennessee said, just as Captain Romine came through the doorway. "You can't afford to start feeling rich right now."

"Will you drink with me, Smith?" Romine asked genially.

"Sorry," Tennessee said curtly. "Done bought my own."

"I'll take the bottle to a table," Romine told the bartender and left the bar, carrying a bottle and a glass.

The two roughs Tennessee had challenged in the livery barn hit the swinging doors together and entered, their ghoulish eyes searching right and left, placing the scattering of men at the tables, looking everywhere except at Tennessee. They stalked across the floor, their hands brushing gun butts. One of them kicked a chair out of his way, sending it across the floor and drawing a smothered oath from someone at a table where it banged to rest. At the bar they ordered whiskey in rough, snarling voices, and two customers alongside Tennessee and the Kid gulped their drinks and departed hurriedly. The brothers tossed off their drinks, and then it was time to murder a man—a man they had not looked at once, a man who was watching them with cold, remorseless eyes. They stole embarrassed glances at each other, all expression ironed out of their stiff faces. They were groping for a way to begin their act. Before witnesses they dared not just whip out their guns suddenly and shoot their turkey cold.

Finally one of them nudged the other and gestured toward the Kid. "Here's that goddamned Comanch' hoss thief!" he blared, playing his role before the audience. "We got the goods on you finally, Kid, and we sure aim to collect your hide for it. You brung in six of *our* hosses. Last we seen, Comanch' run 'em off up on the Salt Fork of the Brazos. What you got to say, you thieving red nigger?"

"All lies!" the Kid shouted angrily. "Me catch him hosses wild. No brands. Don't steal no hosses."

"Reach, you red-gut bastard!" the other rough snarled, stepping away from the bar to confront the Kid, who had shifted from the bar and moved off to one side of Tennessee. "That's all the chance you get, by God!"

"Forget the Kid." Tennessee did not raise his voice, but it interrupted the drama, and all motion ceased. "You know it's me you come for." He did not so much as glance at the Polka Dot Kid. "Get out of here, Kid." He watched a momentary uncertainty break over the brothers' faces. "Why beat around the bush? We all know who you are— Shep, Jap. We know you're the McClanahan boys. Where's Parson Krull, boys? You might as well tell. You know who *I* am, and you know you're both dead men. Where's Brownlow and Jimpson, boys? Make a clean breast before you go out in smoke."

"Damn you, Shep!" Jap yelled. "You see now? Told you we'd ought to gone back and gunned him down. But you's always the smart one. Now come in, goddamn you, and help me beef him!" His hand leaped down and up with a Colt that exploded half-drawn as he collapsed with a bullet hole where a button on his blue shirt had been. Shep was faster, actually fanning Tennessee's cheek with a bullet before Tennessee turned him with a second shot and killed him with a third. As the shots boomed, Tennessee leaped clear of the swirling black-powder smoke and, holding a .44 Colt in each hand, watched the McClanahans settle to the floor, struggle convulsively, and finally become inert.

Men from the tables crowded forward to look down at the dead men, talking excitedly. A few, curious as to where the bullets had struck, knelt to examine the corpses closer. The spectators would tell the story of this gunfight and build on it: It had happened right before their eyes! Tennessee Smith, having run from Southern history, had entered Western history of the same kind. He turned to the bar and wryly ordered a drink.

"On the house," the bartender said. "And I'll join you—on the house."

The doors were swinging as people were drawn in by the sound of gunfire, and with them, as if on cue, came four policemen in the uniforms of soldiers—three Negro troopers and a white lieutenant. The lieutenant stood over the dead men a long moment, then raised his head.

"Who committed these murders?" he demanded harshly.

"Murders, hell!" Tennessee said. "This was self-defense. They reached first, and I beat 'em to a gun."

"Then you're under arrest," stated the lieutenant with cold finality.

Jeff Slaughter spoke up, "Self-defense is all you got here, Lieutenant. We can prove these men come here to kill Mr. Smith and that they tried to draw their guns first."

"I'll swear to that," said the bartender. "Smith was faster, that's all."

The lieutenant was not impressed by Rebel witnesses; he braced himself to oppose them, actually turned his head to order the troopers forward to disarm Tennessee. Before he spoke, however, Captain Romine stepped forward.

"These men are right, Lieutenant," he said in the voice of a captain speaking to a lieutenant. "I saw the whole thing. Smith had no choice but to defend himself. And I can add to the evidence that they came here to kill Smith. Several months ago they gave me a ride to town after my horse went lame out in the hills. Since they knew me, they questioned me today about Mrs. McEveride and Tennessee Smith. To tell the truth, I thought they were interested in Mrs. McEveride's fine horses. Evidently, they were pursuing a feud begun before they came West."

Instantly the lieutenant lost interest in the whole affair. "Well, if you say so, Captain," he murmured. "Since you saw it yourself." He turned to order the troopers out.

"How come you got here so quick?" Tennessee wanted to know. "You waiting around the corner for it to happen?"

"We happened to be passing on other business," replied the lieutenant stiffly, following his troopers back to the street.

Tennessee stepped over to Captain Romine. "Much obliged," he said. "Take that drink with you now, any left in the bottle."

"You flatter my capacity," Romine chuckled, but the murkiness of his slate-gray eyes remained unchanged. "By the way, that Shep claimed to be greased lightning. Smith, you're as fast with a gun as I ever saw."

"I better get faster," Tennessee said with real feeling. "That bastard almost tagged me. I made a bad mistake. Picked Jap for the dangerous one."

When Weatherford found Tennessee that night, he was eating a steak in a restaurant on Military Plaza and listening to a Goliad cattleman who wanted a rustler in his neighborhood made "honest." The rustler's name was Black Jack Tumlinson, and the cattleman told Tennessee he would go as high as five hundred dollars for the missionary work.

"Ain't interested," Tennessee told him, speaking around a mouthful of juicy beef. "Got a list of my own. All I can handle. Better not say no more. Here comes a fellow used to be a Ranger. He don't cotton much to settling out of court."

Casually the cattleman left the table as Weatherford approached. "Congratulations," the ex-Ranger saluted him. "Wish I'd seen you down them Watsons."

"McClanahans," Tennessee corrected him.

"Yeah, McClanahans." Weatherford sat down. "Why I come. Stella wants to see you quick as you eat."

"So it's 'Stella' now."

"All right, Mrs. McEveride, then. That suit you?"

"If it does you." Tennessee lifted his great shoulders and let them settle back to rest. "I don't give a goddamn what you call her." He wondered briefly whether he was speaking the truth, but gave it up. That was a bone he'd have to gnaw further another time.

Stella's room was off the balcony on the second floor of the Menger. She was in a state of excitement. "Captain Romine took me down to look at them," she announced at once. "They're the McClanahans, all right. It means we're hot on the trail. There's five thousand dollars in gold in that sack on the table. Take that with you when you leave. I may never see you again after tonight. I—I—really, I hope I don't, frankly—unless you find the Krulls or have something important to report. Anyway, if I don't, that money is for your part of the McEveride farm. If I do, I'll pay you back for any money you've spent in my service. Whatever the case, I'm sure now—and Captain Romine agrees with me—that the Krulls are on the Rio Grande, possibly in Mexico. So now I'm ready at last to turn loose that wolf I've brought along, nurtured, tolerated, and been attacked by. Now you know why I kept on with you after—after—'' She was breathing unevenly, and her brown mottle of freckles stood out against the white of her face.

"Reckon I'll be on my way," Tennessee said in a voice devoid of feeling. Then his words began to drag with ironic emphasis. "You need any advice while I'm gone, ask Romine. He may know more than you think."

"I'll do that," she snapped, the old high-cheeked, black-eyed look back in force. "And if *you* get lonesome for *me*, find Brownlow Krull and compare notes. You've both had the same experience."

"There's a lot of bitch in you, Stella," Tennessee said, "and you do some lying to yourself. Not much, but some. So just this one time you think back. You enjoyed that 'experience' much as I did once you got in the swing."

He would never forget the look that came into her eyes. Just maybe, by God, she really did hate him as much as she claimed to. "I don't deny it," she said in a broken voice. "Is that so strange? I'm a healthy female. If a mare in season is bred on a forced stand even to a jack, doesn't nature make her feel pleasure? How do you know Brownlow Krull wasn't a better stallion than you?" Her voice settled, then rose on a note of despair. "Whatever I say, you'll never know whether I got more pleasure from Brownlow Krull, will you?"

He lunged and caught her, seeing her eyes flare in quick alarm, her mouth open wide as if she were about to cry out. He looked deep, deep into her eyes, feeling the thrust of her breasts against his body before the pressure of his arms flattened them. Then he kissed her lips for a long time while an emotion rash and headlong went crashing through his veins. Raising his head, he looked back into her wide, shocked eyes, watching a flame of golden fire kindle and leap in their depths. Afterward he could not remember whether she had put up any sort of struggle.

"You're not a mare," he said softly. "That Brownlow Krull never give you no pleasure. But I aim to find the bastard and kill him, anyhow. Slow. I'll make him screech out a high song without words. Then I'll find Parson and the others. After that I'm coming back. . . . Yeah, and when I do, I'll rape you again if I have to." He kissed her once more, hard, then released her, picked the bag of money off the table in passing, and went out the door.

Behind him Stella stood with heaving bosom, feeling the throb of her racing heart. A tide of heat permeated her slim-waisted body, and a familiar weakness was making her legs tremble. She no longer sought to deceive herself as to the cause of that weakness and, therefore, was left with no defense whatever. Damn him, her loins were aching with desire. If, instead of leaving the room, he had pushed her over to the bed. . . . Her mouth twisted bitterly. ''Even to a jack,'' she whispered, and knew in her heart that she lied.

Twenty One

Dick Weatherford, who had grown up in and around San Antonio, kept trying to promote the town and the brush country as a land of opportunity. He was hoping to interest Stella in settling there permanently. She was aware that he had other plans regarding her and didn't mind, since she expected him to develop into one of her most valuable employees; so she listened. As for real estate, Weatherford pointed out, nothing was so cheap as Texas dirt. There was no gold in the land save in the sunshine; yet several million head of cattle crowded the grass in all directions, just waiting for somebody with capital to find a way to get them to northern and eastern markets clamoring for beef. But Stella listened unmoved. What had a market for cattle to do with finding and destroying the Krulls?

Stella was strangely at odds with herself and had been ever since her brother-in-law's departure from San Antonio. She kept wondering what Tennessee was doing, kept wishing she had a report of his progress. Had he found track of the Krulls? Was the trail getting hotter, carrying him far out? Did he think of Nancy Waterton beside his campfires at night, wondering how it would be with *her*, comparing how he imagined *she* would act with how the freckled slut had groaned and shouted in her ecstasy like an overpaid whore? . . . Dick was talking about opportunities for the future. But what future? She saw an objective of completed vengeance, but nothing that gave her joy and zestful expectations.

And then, after she'd been in San Antonio for two weeks, she missed her menstrual period. She waited several days and still was not surprised—or alarmed—when she still failed to pass any blood. The shocks her nervous system had recently sustained were enough to disrupt any woman's cycle, she told herself.

Nevertheless, she became even more restless and didn't know why. Nothing pleased her. Everywhere she turned, it seemed, there was something to depress the spirit or disgust the eye. And in early September of 1865 there was much in San Antonio that justified her jaundiced impressions. She went about the mesquite-thicketed town in the company of Weatherford, who continued trying to interest her in the locality, pointing out areas where values would increase dramatically in a few years. Stella judged sardonically that any change should increase values. The predatory carpetbaggers, in control of taxation, had left no money for public utilities or public works; the gas works were idle, leaving the streets dark at night and forcing people to carry lanterns to avoid mud-holes in the streets. The streets and plazas were unpaved, and almost any kind of rainy weather quickly reduced them to quagmires. People threw their garbage and trash into their backyards and into vacant lots, and this refuse, along with the grain waste and horse manure from the livery stables, drew great multitudes of rats and flies. The trigger for pestilence was set in the drinking water, which came from shallow wells and irrigation ditches, both open to contamination from outhouses; typhoid fever, malaria, and cholera were inevitable.

One day, after visiting the livery on South Flores Street where War Drum and the Tennessee mare were stabled, Weatherford was conduct-ing Stella back to the Menger Hotel along a shortcut of back streets when two dogs came kiting around the corner from the rear of a feed-store warehouse. Drawn by weird squealings from behind the building, they moved to the corner and found what must have been nearly a thousand rats, some of them as large as house cats, eating grain waste and garbage from piles of refuse brought there, either openly or stealthily, by home-bodies and businessmen of the neighborhood.

Stella whirled away in revulsion. "Invest in a place where dogs have to run for their lives from the rats?" she exclaimed. "No thanks!"

"Won't be this way long," Weatherford protested.

"I'll wait," Stella said.

When they arrived at the Menger, Jeff Slaughter was waiting in the lobby. "Got some news I 'lowed you might ought to hear," he began at once. "Word's come up from the border that Tennessee Smith killed an outlaw named Beef Kramer down in the Brasada. Story's sure mixed up, though, way it's told on the street and in the saloons. Some claim a hard young cowboy calling himself Nueces Riley done the killing and would sure paid for it if Tennessee Smith hadn't throwed his guns on Kramer's crowd and taken Riley out of camp to save the boy's hide. Sure ain't no telling how it really happened."

"Let me tell you," Stella said coolly. "Tennessee did the killing. I can't see him passing up the chance to shoot somebody any more than I can see him going to the trouble to save somebody else's life. Who *was* this Kramer, anyhow?"

Both ex-Rangers eyed her strangely, wondering at the feeling of hostility she obviously had for her brother-in-law. "Well," Slaughter answered, "Beef Kramer was a hoss thief from way back, but he was run into Mexico by the Rangers six, seven year ago for murdering a woman—a woman named Riley, by the way, so this Nueces could been some sort of kin. Kramer wasn't normal some way, I don't reckon. He was suspected of murdering two other women, but one was enough if we could of got our hands on him. So, as a criminal, Kramer was sure well known in Texas, and now the name Tennessee Smith stands for a mighty bad man with a gun, whether he done the actual killing or not."

"He's a bad one, with or without the name," Stella said. "But I'm glad to hear he's associating with the right kind of people. Maybe he's on the trail of the Krulls."

Stella had been consistently rejecting Captain Romine's invitations to go riding, visit the mission ruins, or dine with him. She much preferred Dick Weatherford's company. Though Romine was, in his own way, charming—smooth, gracious, and somewhat mysterious—Stella sensed a coldness about him. She suspected that somehow he'd smelled out her wealth and was attracted more by dreams of it than by thoughts of her; even his passions, she guessed, were cold. Finally, informing her that it was his last night in San Antonio, Romine asked her to have dinner with him, and she accepted.

They ate in the Menger dining room, since nowhere in San Antonio was there better fare. Even during Reconstruction the hotel's cuisine was widely renowned, particularly for its wild-game dinners. To make conversation Stella asked, "Where are you being stationed, Captain?"

"Fort Bascom, in New Mexico Territory," he said. "Already stationed, not being. Thought I'd mentioned that before, and that I've been here on fôrt business. As you know, San Antonio's a supply base for United States forces in the Southwest. One of them, that is. Now I'm due back."

"Have you—" Stella broke off, dipping a spoonful of turtle soup thoughtfully. "I almost asked if you'd ever heard of the Krulls in New Mexico, but I'm sure you'd have already told me if you had."

Romine's spoon left his mouth and was still. "Not necessarily," he said slowly. "You see, I can't be sure. If I had, among a hundred other names, they wouldn't have meant much. I heard of them from you, of course. But I've been wondering, from the little you've told me about them, whether the Krulls might be associated in some way with the *comancheros*."

Instantly he had Stella's complete attention. "*Comancheros?* Who're they?"

"Mexicans, mostly, but sometimes Anglo-Americans, too, who go out on the *Llano Estacado* and trade with the Comanches. At one time they were small-time *pelados* who drove their carts and pack burros out on the plains and traded bread, beads, trinkets, maybe some bright-colored cloth for household goods, horses, captive women and children—whatever the Indians brought back from their raids. But in recent times the trade has changed radically. The little cart men now drive big wagons for big-time *comancheros* who finance the trade but don't deal with the Indians personally, and the trade now is trinkets and rotgut whiskey, primarily for cattle."

"Wait," Stella said, a thread of excitement coming into her voice. "Let me understand this. Why are cattle so valuable in New Mexico when they're worth so little in Texas?"

"Well," Romine began, warming to Stella's interest, "at Fort Sumner, in the Pecos Valley, the government is issuing some thirty thousand pounds of beef each day to around ten thousand Navajos, Apaches, and soldiers. I saw a Texas cattleman sell a small herd there for sixty dollars a head a month ago as I came through there. Then, too, there's a demand for beef at the other forts in the territory, and much of it is supplied through the *comanchero* trade with cattle stolen in Texas by Indians. Stella, would you believe that during the past five years over three hundred thousand head of Texas cattle and over a hundred thousand horses have been run off by Indians and sold or traded to New Mexicans? Wealthy Anglo-Americans are now in the trade. They're providing the capital to poor Mexicans who deal directly with the Indians. Why, I've heard of instances where the *comancheros* have gone to Comanche camps and loaned their guns and horses to the Indians and then waited in camp until the Indians could go to Texas and return with cattle."

"Why, that's terrible!" Stella cried indignantly. "No wonder the Texas frontier is flaming from one end to the other with Indian raids! I heard Jeff Slaughter say just the other day that whole counties are being stripped of settlers, who are driven out or killed or women and children carried away into captivity. There ought to be a law against that damnable *comanchero* trade."

"Oh, there is." Romine smiled, and his hooded, somber eyes showed a brief gleam of light. "But the army doesn't enforce it. Nor do the New Mexican courts. You can't get a conviction against a *comanchero* in New Mexico—at least I haven't heard of any. Texans aren't popular in New Mexico. And since the war the army isn't fond of Texans either. Might as well admit it. I'm telling you all this in confidence, of course. The forts, by the way, won't buy beef directly from Texas cattlemen. The few who run the gauntlet of Indians and survive the long dry stretches to the Pecos have to sell at Fort Sumner through contractors."

"Well, it's a mighty sad state of affairs, if you want my opinion," Stella said. "And good men will go along with that *comanchero* trade, too, without a qualm, all in the name of business. How many respectable men have you already heard say that if you can't lick 'em, you might as well join 'em? I know enough about business to know that plenty have said it."

"Well, of course, I've heard—no, I won't hedge. I'm embarrassed, but I have a confession to make, and I'm going to make it." The waiter arrived to remove the soup dishes and replace them with dishes of wild turkey, dressing, and quail. Romine claimed personal credit for the quail, informing her that he'd killed them at a water hole deep in the brush.

When the white-jacketed Mexican had departed, Stella said with a smile, "I'm pretty sure I know what you're about to confess."

"Oh?"

"That you've bought cattle from *comancheros*. I'll bet you've stocked a ranch with bargain-priced cattle."

"On the Gallinas River," Romine admitted. He had the grace, she observed, to take on color and look ashamed. "Do you despise me for that, Stella?"

Stella laughed. "No," she told him without hesitation. "I certainly understand the desire to buy low and sell high. Actually, you're more honest than I thought, and I like you better. In fact, I think I'll call you Boone from now on instead of Captain, now that you've admitted to the most human and, I suspect, the most common of all weaknesses."

"What's that?" Romine asked quickly.

"Avarice," Stella said. "What else?"

"You're not very flattering," Romine complained.

"Oh, drop the art, Boone," Stella said. "Stick to substance. Surely you didn't confess a fault to get flattery. You've always struck me as a purposeful fellow, if not even a designing one. So it occurs to me now that you may have a reason for telling me that you've been encouraging

Indian raids in Texas by buying cattle from *comancheros*. If so, why not just come out with it?''

Romine did not have wincing eyes, but his face lost its impassivity momentarily and showed ruffled feeling. ''That's pretty hard,'' he judged, ''and devious, too, in a way. I see now that William Lloyd Garrison, Harriet Beecher Stowe, and John Brown encouraged slavery in the South by buying and wearing cotton clothes. Would you call Eli Whitney the father of modern slavery?''

''Maybe I would, at that. But you did have a reason for the confession, right?''

Romine admired her with his somber eyes. ''Well, as a matter of fact, I did,'' he said. ''I want you to enter into a partnership with me—go partners with me in buying and selling cattle on a big scale. Don't say no right off. Think it over. You've got the makings of a shrewd business-woman in you, and you've got capital at hand. I'm situated in New Mexico to do a big-scale trade with *comancheros*. We could get the business at the forts and sell stock to ranchers in Colorado, where ranching is making headway. I'd get rich, and you'd get richer. What do you say, Stella?''

His offer was unacceptable, but Stella did not tell him so. He was situated to do a big business with *comancheros,* was he? Then he might well be situated to find out for her where the Krulls were and be able to lead her to them. The Krulls had connections with Indians; they had had contact with the army and might still have; and if they were not on the border, they were in New Mexico Territory. If they were in the territory, they were *comancheros.* . . . Suddenly she wished that Tennessee was back from the border. She had an urgent premonition about New Mexico and *comancheros.*

''I'll have to think about it,'' she said. ''You know, of course, that I'm in the West looking for the Krull gang that murdered my husband and father-in-law. I won't be diverted from that quest—completely. But *comanchero* business sounds like Krull work to me. So, Boone, think back through your contacts with *comancheros*. Isn't it possible you may have heard some mention of Parson Krull?''

Romine looked down at his plate. ''As I've already told you, I simply don't know,'' he said finally. ''I've heard the name, but who from? You told me about them when we went down to view the remains of the Watsons, or McClanahans, or whatever their names were. I may have heard of Parson Krull just from you. On the other hand, I could have heard the name in New Mexico. The Krulls *could* be *comancheros*. There are some bold and hardy scoundrels among them, I can assure you.''

"Will you keep on the lookout for them and let me know if, well..." Stella lifted her shoulders, then gave him one of her gamin grins. "If I could find them, get them in a pocket, sort of—if you understand me—I'd be free then for some other kind of business."

Raising his brows, Romine said with a faint smile, "In other words, if I brought you their heads in a sack, we might become partners?"

"I'd have to be sure they were the right heads," Stella told him cheerfully. "Not that I don't trust an enterprising fellow like you. Your best bet is to find them and let me know where they are."

The next morning after breakfast, Stella sent a Mexican boy with a message and summoned Slaughter and Weatherford to the Menger Hotel. They arrived together, and Stella admitted them to her room, gesturing toward chairs.

Slaughter beat her to the first word after the greetings. "Fellow named Jake Wilson, from up on Cripple John Creek, come to town and heard about Tennessee Smith killing Beef Kramer. Sure did shake him up. Seems this here Wilson married Beef Kramer's wife. They thought he was dead. So he was some grateful to Tennessee for boring Beef, as any white man would be. Looked me up and left a note for Tennessee. 'Lows he may have a lead on some of them Krulls. . . . Something strange about the way them Comanches lets him and his wife, both of 'em white, live and raise stock in Injun country. Here, Stella. Reckon you better read this here note. It ain't sealed up noways confidential, and we ain't got no idea when we'll see Tennessee again. Good chance we never will."

Reaching for the note, Stella froze with hand outstretched. "Why do you say that?" she demanded in a quick, sharp voice. "What have you heard?"

"Why, I ain't heard a thing I ain't told," Slaughter said in surprise. "It's just that a gunman like Tennessee's liable to go out in smoke any day. You don't see many old gunmen, Stella."

Stella took the note with trembling fingers. It read:

Dear Tennessee Smith,
    Me and my woman want to thank you from our heart for killing that dam Kramer. Now we will marry agin soon as a preachers handy. Think we seen 2 of them Krulls your hunting riding with the commanch. Come see us we got a little ranch on Cripple John Creek mightnear in shadow of the caprock.

Your true friend,
Jake Wilson

"This is right in line with what I wanted to talk with you about." Stella moved to Weatherford and handed him the note. "Better read it, too." She crossed to the bed and sat down on the edge. "I'm afraid Tennessee's on a wild-goose chase down there on the border." She told them what she'd learned from Captain Romine about the *comanchero-*Comanche traffic in Texas cattle and concluded by saying, "So I think there are Krulls among the *comancheros* in New Mexico and Krulls raiding with the Indians out on the plains. Now comes the big question: If there are, how do I get *to* or *at* them?"

Slaughter was shaking his head. "Stella, believe me, there just ain't no way a-tall," he said emphatically. "We know plenty about them cussed *comancheros,* and we ought to know plenty about Comanches. Talk about a wild-goose chase—why, girl, you ain't never seen one till you start looking for somebody who'll admit being a *comanchero,* and it's sure suicide to follow Comanches out on the plains. Like I say, there just ain't no way to—"

"Now, hold on, Jeff," Weatherford interrupted. "There was a key word in what she told us, and looks like you done missed it sure'n hell."

"What key word?"

"Sixty."

Stella laughed. "Hey, Dick, you're pretty sharp!" she exclaimed, highly pleased with him. "Now let's see if you can tell him what's in my mind."

"*Sixty?*" Slaughter said. "Sixty what?"

"Sixty dollars a head," Weatherford said, grinning. "Maybe more. Cattle at Fort Sumner. Cattle you can buy for five to ten dollars a head around here. If we deliver a herd to Fort Sumner, we run a good chance of swapping lead with *comancheros* and Injuns. A market for cattle and maybe a chance to kill Stella some Krulls. Sort of a loose plan, but it's better'n none a-tall."

"That's not bad, Dick," Stella applauded. "Not bad at all. Jeff, do you know of anybody in the vicinity who wants to sell his brand and range rights? Some place where we can hold the cattle we buy? I've decided to go into the cattle business."

"Well," Slaughter said, "all I got to say is, what with Texas overrun with longhorn cattle, which ain't worth stealing, way things are, you sure can get stocked up cheap. And if there ain't no heading you off, reckon Ma Daniels has got a brand and range she'd be willing to sell. It's about ten mile from here, with enough cattle on it to base a claim on all the mavericks we can brand—which sure will be plenty."

Weatherford's face was knowing. "That the Hourglass brand?"

"You know it is." Slaughter's face colored slightly. "Ma's late husband, Joe Daniels, who was some uncurried and rough enough, I reckon, he registered his brand as the Hourglass in honor of his wife's figure. In *his* honor, she never changed it—the brand or her figure, neither one." He grinned. "Ma might could be talked into staying on to keep house and cook, seeing we'll need somebody to do them things."

"She might listen to talk like that," Weatherford agreed, "if *you* done the talking, Jeff."

"The boy's romantic," Slaughter confided to Stella, "and sees things where they ain't. I'm interested in her cooking, son, not her shape. Which, now that I think, she sure can cook them dried-apple pies."

"By all means talk to her, Jeff," Stella said. "Buy her out. The ranch will be a good base of operations, of course. But I want you men to remember that the Krulls are the consideration behind all my plans. So what I'm thinking of is trailing cattle to market, not ranching—trailing to Fort Sumner in the Pecos Valley. On the other hand, my father's blood keeps coming out in me, I guess, and I keep wondering what's wrong with buying cattle cheap in Texas, trailing them to market, and selling them high. What's wrong with making money, Jeff?"

Slaughter reached for his pipe, looking thoughtful. "Maybe nothing—if you got a pile of money and can afford the gamble, which you sure can. But that Pecos country!" He shook his head. "Long dry stretches. Eighty mile without water or graze, for one. Stampedes, drownings off the high banks of the Pecos, poison springs, Comanches and Kiowas and Apaches, *comancheros,* outlaws, crooked officials—great Lord, girl, you could lose your whole investment!"

"That could happen," Stella conceded. "If it does, we'll start all over and try it again. It won't be easy. That's why I want you two to handle it. Buy the ranch and hire some good men. We can hire extra hands for the trail drives, but right at once get a crew of ex-Rangers and tough cowhands who can read the minds of wild cattle and aren't afraid to jump right into the middle of hell if they're a-straddle horses with ropes or guns in their hands. I borrowed that description from an old cattleman who stopped at the Menger last week. He was talking about the brush hands of the Nueces country. Called them brush poppers. . . . You know, suddenly I feel alive again. I was beginning to feel mossed over, sort of run-down—thought more than once I was coming down with something."

In the next few weeks Ma Daniels's ranch was purchased, cowhands were hired, and the Hourglass brand was slapped on calves that followed Hourglass or maverick cows and on every maverick that hit the ground at the end of a rope. Stella was buoyant but still felt run-down.

And then, one morning in October, after Tennessee had been gone from San Antonio for more than a month, she took one look at the breakfast of fried eggs and bacon that a waiter set before her, quickly covered her mouth with her handkerchief, and hurried out of the dining room.

A middle-aged Mexican maid came into the room while Stella was still retching over the slop jar. The woman held a hand under the wet, freckled forehead, making crooning sounds of compassion, and Stella leaned her head weakly against the palm of the dusky hand. Then, with the woman steadying her, she got to her feet and, moving to the bed, sank down to a seat on the edge. The woman wet a towel at the washstand and gently washed her face.

"You don' feel so good, eh, *señora?*" the woman said kindly.

Stella shook her head, smiling wanly.

"What make you sick, *señora?*" the maid asked gently.

"Well, I'm not sure," Stella said, puzzled. "The smell, maybe. You know, the grease from the bacon."

"Grease, *sí*," the maid said. "But I don' think it grease from the bacon. I think it grease from the man. Grease that slide the little *niño* into the *madre*—that what make you sick, I think, *señora*. And me, I have seven *niños*. It much hard to fool me, *señora*."

God in heaven! Stella thought wildly. What if she's right? Suddenly she remembered the missed period weeks ago. She knew then, without much doubt, that she was pregnant. A wave of nausea surged upward, and foam entered her throat. She went to her knees on the floor, hugging the slop jar, retching weakly. Again the maid was holding a hand under her forehead. She wished that after one breath, with the next one forever due, she could die.

"Help me undress," she said in a voice that faded to a whisper. "I'm going back to bed."

The woman made her as comfortable as a queasy stomach would permit. "You feel better soon," she said, and started out.

"Wait!" Stella opened her eyes when the maid returned to her bedside. "Not a word about this. My husband is not with me in Texas. There would be talk. I'll make it worth your while."

The woman shook her head, backing away toward the door. *"Por nada, señora,"* she said earnestly. "I don' tell nobody nothing."

Later in the morning, feeling better, Stella got up and dressed. There might have to be serious readjustments in her life ahead, but she willed such considerations out of her mind until she could see a doctor. She might have eaten something that didn't agree with her, she told herself, but had no real faith in her own reassurances.

She chose a doctor with a Spanish name and an Indian face whose office was on a side street that was convenient to the inhabitants of the Mexican quarter. The doctor saw all his Mexican patients, whether old or new, before he admitted Stella to his inner office, for he was not one to be impressed by any *gringa*. In fact he sought to discourage their coming to him. He told her quickly and callously, therefore, and in the most indelicate terms, that she was indeed pregnant.

It was a long walk back to the Menger. Stella stopped at the Commerce Street bridge to rest a moment, half-sitting on the low wooden rail, her head hanging. Below her eyes a bloated rat and a white, putrescent fish floated close together, hardly moving on the surface of the sluggish stream. Smelling the dingy, polluted water and the exposed muddy banks, Stella felt a kinship with this river. She had begun life full of hope, almost constantly on tiptoe in expectation of some rare excellence in her existence. But then the war had dimmed the luster of her days and, in its aftermath, wrecked her hopes. Settling for justice, therefore, since there seemed little enough left in the way of happiness to hope for, she had persevered diligently with total commitment of her heart and mind and purse. And finally, just when light was beginning to show, she had been destroyed by the very weapon upon which she had exerted so much time and care, in which she had placed her first hope and strongest confidence—Tennessee. She looked up at the sunless sky in the waning light of day and then closed her eyes, whispering raggedly, ''It isn't fair. . . . It just isn't fair. . . .'' This was a moment of crisis in her life; her existence seemed at its nadir. She could see no hope in any direction—only darkness. Suddenly she understood, as never before, how a person bogged hopelessly in some black pit of wretchedness might reach the decision to take his own life and find the will to act on that decision, too.

Wearily she left the bridge and walked on toward the Menger. One thing was certain: Either she had to leave San Antonio at once, or the time of the baby's arrival would announce that her brother-in-law had sired a bastard on her. She would have to go back East, give up the quest for the Krulls, let injustice reign in the world without lifting a finger, discard all her plans involving Jeff and Dick and trailing cattle to New Mexico, get word to the men at Fort Washita that they were on their own, then stifle her aspirations and wait with a swelling belly in a slave cabin back in Tennessee for a bastard child to come out of her and grow up to be a killer who would master women and horses and dogs with a touch, making the women moan and cry and heave up under him while they were receiving his hot grease and becoming great with bastard young. What lay beyond the walls of that slave cabin, beyond the agony of giving birth? A gray wasteland, nothingness, a joyless waiting for the long, breathless stillness that was the only peace? Just up the hill from the cabin, Paul lay cuckolded in his grave, unavenged, unquiet, restless. A mounting rage at her helplessness sent hot blood storming through her. Helpless? She? Give up? She stopped dead in the street, shaking with fury.

"I'll be goddamned if I will!" she cried aloud, not caring who might hear. "I'll see the Krulls in hell before I'm done! And Tennessee, too, goddamn his soul!"

That night, still warmed by an anger that never quite died, Stella thought long and hard about what she should do. She was certain she'd never mentioned the date of the Krull raid and, therefore, of Paul's death to any of her employees in the West. Nevertheless, as a precaution, she'd return East to have "Paul's posthumous child" and then come back West and take up where she'd left off—with ranching, trailing cattle into the land of *comancheros* and Comanches, and hunting the Krulls. She'd stay in Texas another month, making the arrangements, if she felt well enough and didn't start showing. That would give her time to have funds transferred and come to an agreement with a San Antonio businessman of Slaughter's choice—possibly Ed Johnson, the livery man on South Flores Street—to act as her private banker, the custodian and dispenser of money for the purpose of paying cowhands, buying supplies, expanding the Hourglass range, and getting her brand on all the unbranded, slick-eared cattle in sight. She would have War Drum and the Tennessee mare taken out to the Hourglass, since she planned to travel East by stagecoach, steamboat, and train. Certainly she would not need those horses any time soon for any trips across country. She was absolutely through with Tennessee Smith McEveride forever . . . unless she got to thinking about what he'd done to her and sent some wolf hunter. . . .

She shook her mind loose from that thought and shunted it back on track. Before she went to sleep she had her forseeable future fairly well organized. One thing still loomed as a problem: Dick Weatherford's reaction to her leaving. She was aware that Dick thought that he loved her, and she knew that he desired her. She doubted, however, that Dick would make much distinction between the two emotional states; she'd seen his appraising eyes drifting off to other shapely women they encountered about the town. Nevertheless, Stella needed him to continue working for her. She didn't want him wandering off when she left Texas.

Three weeks later all her arrangements were made save one. She wanted to bind Dick Weatherford to her before she left; on the day before she was scheduled to leave, therefore, she suggested a visit to one of the missions.

"Which one?" Weatherford asked.

Stella said with a quiet, enigmatic irony, "*Nuestra Señora de la Purísima Concepción.* I memorized that."

"The Mission of the Immaculate Conception, huh? Well, it's sure the closest. Ain't close enough for no woman in your shape to walk, though. I'll bring a buggy around."

"What's wrong with my shape?" Stella demanded with spurious ire. "No," she decided, smiling wanly, "we won't discuss that subject. Just get the buggy. I'll be ready."

Stella was strangely moved by her first sight of Mission *Concepción.* From a distance the twin towers and impressive dome of the old church stilled her pulse with some indefinable expectation. She hardly listened to Weatherford, who had explored the vicinity countless times as a boy, as he pointed out the shallow pits across the road from which came the light, porous limestone used in building the mission.

Then, as they drew near, she saw the large cactus plants growing on the cupola and the openings that yawned without doors or windows, and apprehension began sipping at the hope in her heart. Weatherford stopped in front of the mission and helped her alight. They stood before the doorway. Above them, in delicate lettering, was a Spanish quatrain that meant, according to Weatherford's translation, "This Mission serves with these arms its Patroness and Princess, and defends the doctrine of her purity."

A heightened awareness came to Stella at this moment; it seemed to her that she was entering the mission with an eagerly groping spirit. She had an idea that a woman in her condition might be comforted by something that had to do with the mother of God. Yet the floor of the nave, where cattle were penned periodically, was covered with manure a foot deep in places, and suddenly bats—scores of flying, mouselike creatures—were flitting about on slithery, membranous wings overhead, chattering and squeaking.

Stella whirled and fled from the nave. She burst through the entrance and headed straight for the buggy. She should have expected something like this, she thought. The moonlight and roses and wide bluegrass had all gone out of her life, leaving her nothing in their stead except bats, bloated rats, rotten fish, and bullshit. . . . She climbed into the buggy, and when Weatherford followed, taking his seat beside her, she burst into tears, turning her face against her arms on the back of the seat.

He put a hand gently on her shoulder. "What's the matter, Stella?" When she made no answer, he took her in his arms. "You're hiding something surer'n hell. You ain't been right for weeks now. Come on, honey. What's happened?"

Stella spoke against his shirt front in a muffled voice. "Oh, Dick, I feel so awful, and I have to tell somebody." She became motionless, tense in his arms, like someone listening for a dread sound. "I—I'm going to have—a—baby, Dick."

"God a'mighty!" Weatherford said numbly. "Oh, Jesus!" Then he was silent, thinking. When he began to grow rigid with some violent emotion, Stella looked at him. His face was pale beneath its tan, and his eyes were black and hard and deadly. She had forgotten that he'd been a Ranger. Given provocation, this man would kill.

"Dick, what?"

"The man—the baby's father?" he asked quietly. "Tennessee Smith?"

"Oh, no, no, no!" Stella cried wildly. "Why would you think that?"

"I reckon you'd lie about it," Weatherford said grimly. "I feel like killing that damned curly wolf. He done it by force, didn't he, honey? Why, hell, course he did! Your own brother-in-law? You wouldn't let him done that except he never give you no choice. Ain't that the way of it, honey?"

"Stop it, Dick!" She clutched his shoulders, shaking him. "Stop it, now! Listen, Dick. . . ." She told him that she had begun to suspect that she was pregnant a few weeks after the death of her husband, and then had been certain that she was before leaving home. But she had thought she could manage well enough on her trips and on her stay in the West. Recently, however, as he knew, she had found that she could no longer do so. She concluded by saying, "Now, Dick, you're the only person in Texas I want to know this. You're the only one I've told or shall tell. And when Tennessee Smith returns to San Antonio, don't—let—him—know. Some of my reasons for this secrecy are business consider-ations, and some are personal. In the case of Tennessee they are very personal. I'm through with Tennessee for good. I saw him kill some men needlessly on the way out here and, well, I don't want Tennessee around my child. I don't want the child—particularly if it should be a boy—making a hero out of a killer, even if the killer *is* his uncle."

"What you want Smith told when he gets back?"

"Tell him he can go to hell, for all I care."

Reaching with some confidence now, Weatherford pulled Stella back into his arms. "Let me go back East with you, Stella," he said urgently, in a voice rough with emotion. "I want to marry you. A woman with a little baby needs a husband, and a baby needs a daddy. I'll love your baby like it was my own." Quickly he found her lips, his kiss heavy and deep and hungry.

Stella knew that she could grow pleasantly accustomed to such kisses from this clean-cut, brown young rider. She knew, too, that if she married him, a day would come when she would find contentment by his side and pleasure in his arms. But marriage was not in her plans.

"Please, Dick," she said, disengaging herself not too abruptly. "I've got to go back home, where my family doctor and my servants can look after me. But I'll come back West. And I want *you* here, you and Jeff, looking after my interests. I want trail herds on the move next year. You do, too. I don't know what the future holds for me, Dick. A big involvement with cattle, I hope. And if so, I expect Dick Weatherford to be a man I can lean on in the running of that business.

"Now, you asked me to marry you, but I'm not ready to give you a firm answer now. There are things I want accomplished before I give you a yes or a no. So you'll just have to wait on that decision, Dick."

Stella excused her deviousness on the grounds that she thought he was no one-woman man who would love once only and greatly. Not Dick. He would be attending some young woman before Stella reached the slave cabin in Tennessee. She hoped she was right.

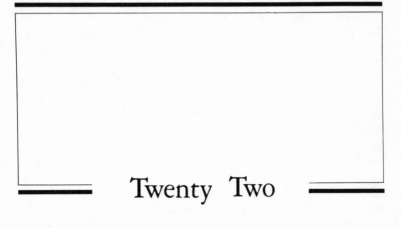

Twenty Two

Two hours before sunset Tennessee rode up the eastern slope of a mesa and sat in his saddle at the edge of the west-side cliff to have a look at the country. Before him stretched a vast, rolling red-and-green land of grass, sprinkled with mesquite and cactus and scarred by red-clay earth exposures. A winding line of deeper green marked the course of a stream that looked like segments of a silver cord dropped in the valley by a child wandering after flowers. An increasing number of buttes and mesas bulked in the west, casting in the valley shadows that crawled steadily away from the lowering sun. He thought he could make out along the western horizon a dark line that had to be the escarpment of the Staked Plain.

From what he'd heard, Tennessee figured that save for the camps of the wild Quahadi Comanches, there was only one trace of human habitation between the cliff edge of the mesa and the eastern settlements of New Mexico Territory, several hundred miles away: Jake Wilson's ranch. In the distance he made out what he judged were cattle and, nearer at hand, a dozen antelope grazing with the buffalo. Finally a rectangular spot of darkness caught his eye. "Reckon that's it," he decided, and reined down the mesa the way he had come up.

The succession of events that had led Tennessee here smacked of destiny. Marshaling them in his mind, he saw again the gross, bestial face of Beef Kramer in the horse-thief camp, where Texans and Mexicans had met in the Brasada to exchange stolen horses so that they might then turn back to their home ranges with horses to sell or trade and no questions asked. Kramer had captured a young *pelada* woman on the road and had been with her up in the brush. Finally, when the camp cook yelled, Kramer came straddling into view, dragging the stumbling woman by one arm as if he were leading a cold-jawed horse. He had torn the woman's dress off a shoulder, and she was trying to cover an exposed breast with her other hand and not having complete success. She was somewhat broad across the cheekbones, and her nose could have stood higher to better advantage, but her face and her body, against the setting of the wild brush, had a kind of beauty. She was crying.

"By God, Kramer," objected the leader of the white crowd, "I don't like this here woman business no little bit!"

"Why, you can sure'n hell lump it a little bit, then," Kramer rumbled ominously. "This here woman's my catch, and I'll sure God do what I want with her." He stood with spread legs, swinging his head like some great beast searching the shifting currents of an unclean wind.

Then, all of a sudden, Kramer's mood lightened, the scowl leaving his brick-red face. "Aw, I'm just joshing you, *hombres*. I don't aim to mistreat this little *señora*—or nobody else. I aim to take her back to Mexico, and after a while I'll send her home." He pushed the woman down to a sitting position on the ground, commanded her to be still, took a long gurgle of tequila from a pint bottle, and threw the empty bottle into the brush. Then he sat down on the ground. "Listen," he confided in greasy vein. "Lemme tell you about women. My own wife's the one showed me that women ain't serious. Aw, they're like butterflies—as like to light on a turd as on a flower. We's living up on the Brazos in Injun country when she got big—with my kid, I taken it for granted, until she had it and I seen the redgut look of the half-breed whelp. Well, we's both blond, so she was caught and had to give me a story. She claimed that while I's on a trip after hosses, the Comanches raided the place for stock, and a buck come in the dugout and covered her by force. But I knowed for a fact they would taken her captive if she'd been caught in a raid. I know Injuns. Why, she got to itching and throbbing 'tween her legs, and some damn redgut was the only man handy. That's what happened. But I sure paid her back, by God! I sent word for the Comanches to come and get 'em both. Then I hauled ass away from there. Later I heared that the Comanches taken only the redgut baby, so I got word to the woman that I's dead. She married up with a *hombre* named Jake Wilson, and I heared tell not long ago that that Wilson done built a house and is raising cattle right under them damn Injuns' noses. Someday I aim to get back up in that Brazos country. I can just see the look on their faces when I take back that ranch, long enough to sell it, and that wife—"

He looked around, grinning, his coarse, red face a mask of brutish lewdness. "Well, I reckon I know better how to treat a woman now, eh, *hombres*?

Maybe that statement had been the last straw in the mind of Nueces Riley, Tennessee thought. If Kramer hadn't said those words, he might have lived longer—but not much longer. In any event, the response to Kramer's challenge was deafening, but Kramer didn't hear it, nor see the flurry and boil of black-powder smoke that accompanied it. He simply fell over backward and was dead.

Riley, a slim, sandy-haired youth, stood white-faced and grim, his cedar-handled Colt ready in his hand, wisping smoke. He knew he was in trouble. "I sure ain't sorry," he said hardily. "I been looking for that son-of-a-bitch on both sides of the river. He killed my sister. Now I aim to ride out of here. Anybody going to stop me?"

"*Sí*, we weel stop you, *señor*," answered a scar-faced Mexican under a peaked sombrero. "We don' have no choice. It is the example, *señor*. Next time some *gringo* might shoot me. Unless these other *gringos*, with the *caballos*—" He turned toward the white crowd with a sneer on his sinister face.

"He ain't with us," the white leader said.

Tennessee moved his hands and held two guns pointing at nobody in particular. "He's with me," he said, showing his white-toothed, savage grin. "Met on the road together. Reckon we'll ride out together." He gestured toward the leader of the white crowd with a pistol barrel. "You low-life bastard, order one of them dogs you pack with to saddle our horses, and you stand there and keep looking silly. And saddle one for the lady, too, goddamn you! I wouldn't leave a scrub mare with you sons-of-bitches—unless I wanted her to foal a diseased mule." He pinned the scar-faced Mexican with his ruthless eyes. "*Example!* By God, I got a good mind to leave your yellow hide on the ground as an example to that greasy huddle of sneak thieves behind you."

The three rode out together; then, after the woman was delivered to the door of her *jacal*, having confided along the way that *Señor* Kramer was not the *mucho hombre* he thought, they were two hunters on the same trail; for Nueces Riley had decided to join forces with Tennessee—or, rather, had insisted on remaining with Tennessee. Riley was a man who paid his debts. Having paid the one he owed Beef Kramer, he was now ready to set about taking care of another that was equally compelling, this one owed to the man who had saved his life.

They had searched for the Krulls along the river and back in the brush up to Del Rio and down to Laredo and then on down to Browns-ville, not overlooking many long shots; and the days and weeks and months faded along their back trail. Finally, after they had been in the border country six or seven months, they heard of an old Seminole-Negro woman in the Santa Rosa Mountains. This *anciana,* according to their aged Seminole informant, was a medicine woman, a *curandera,* who had many years and knew many things, some of which she had no means of learning.

"This old man claims she was old when he was a boy," explained Riley, who had been conversing with the old man in Spanish. "He says most folks think she's dead. He did, too, but he heard the other day she's still kicking. If anybody on the border can tell you anything about the Krulls—or anything else—she can, he says."

When they saw the old woman sitting in front of her *jacal* at sundown, Tennessee and Nueces were prepared by her looks to believe anything she said. She sat in a straight chair on the bare, hard-packed ground, looking like a piece of black earth crowned with hoarfrost. Since she spoke no English, Riley had to do the talking in his border Spanish. She covered their presents—tobacco and *mezcal*—with a piece of cloth and then, as Riley talked, studied his face intently with eyes that were as bright as glass beads. Before Riley finished speaking, she turned her black, wrinkled face toward Tennessee, and there, in the hard, beady eyes, Tennessee caught a flicker of something that jarred him with a sense of the grotesque. It was, he thought, like finding a gleam of amusement in the eyes of a snake. She started talking in a clacking falsetto. She talked on and on; then, abruptly, she stopped.

Riley looked at her in wonder, a slow grin forming. "Tennessee, give up the idea this here's one of them sweet old church-going, mellow-laughing black mammies you hear tell of." He chuckled. "Listen to this. She says a white man was with Black Cat about twenty-five years ago. She says she saw this man in Florida before that. He had hot-iron marks under his headband in Texas but not in Florida." Riley's grin broadened. "She claims this here fellow was always trying to hump the girls. He'd follow any ass that wiggled down the path to the water hole. She thinks Black Cat may have run him off because he was after some stuff Wild Cat had done marked down for his own. She claims, too, that the fellow wanted some of *her* stuff bad." Here Riley laughed outright. "Ain't she something, claiming to been a good piece at seventy? At least seventy. Says she wouldn't let him have none because she had her a big heavy-hung buck—she don't leave nothing out. Listen to these here measurements she gives—"

"All right, Nueces." Tennessee's burly shoulders stirred impatiently. "Get her back on Parson Krull. That the last she heard of him?"

Riley questioned the woman further and listened to her answer. "Parson Krull hooked up with Plains Injuns," he reported. "Comanches. She claims this here Parson Krull raided into Mexico with Comanches more'n once. With some other white men. *Comancheros,* maybe. She gets hazy along in here, thinking the parson lived with Comanches, raided with 'em, and traded with 'em. She don't make it clear whether he done 'em separate or all at the same time. Me, I doubt if he done them things. Don't sound reasonable he done 'em all."

"Maybe he did, though. Nothing much would surprise me that bastard done."

"Don't know whether I ought to tell you this." Riley looked half-way embarrassed. "But *she's* the one said it. *I* sure didn't. She says she hopes the red-haired woman's ass is worth all the trouble you're taking for it."

Tennessee's eyes turned to slits of cold flame. "By God, you made that up!"

"The hell I did!" Riley protested. "Wait a minute. Who told me anything about any red-haired woman? What woman you know's got red hair?"

"Ask her how she figures the woman's hair is red."

As Riley talked, a toothless grin writhed among the wrinkles on the woman's face. She clacked out a brief answer. "Aw, hell!" Riley threw up his hands. "We wind up in hoss-shit. She says the woman's color rubbed off on you when you humped her. Says she can see it on you."

Tennessee eyed the old woman's dried-up and shriveled face, and he felt his hackles prickle and lift. You're looking at a goddamned witch! he thought. They actually do exist! "Let's get away from here," he said and turned toward his horse without waiting for Riley's company.

"I can figure out part of it," Riley said, as they were mounting up. "Cut that old woman's head open, all you'd find is one thing humping another thing's ass. That red-haired part, though—that beats me."

Tennessee had returned to San Antonio alone in the first full flush of spring, Nueces having veered off toward Dog Town, in McMullen County, to visit his people. Riding into Military Plaza at sunset, he breathed the balmy air of springtime and thought of Stella as he listened to the strumming of guitars and the heartbroken voices of despairing lovers in song. The girls around the chili stands were never lovelier; they, too, made him think of Stella. But, then, so did a soft breeze off a field of bluebonnet and Indian paintbrush, and the yap and yammer of coyotes in early darkness, and the medley of wild geese wavering north against a brightening sky. Almost anything made him think of Stella.

He had not seen her in some nine months and could hardly wait to reach her.

Suddenly, inexplicably, he was as nervous as a fourteen-year-old stripling calling on his first girl, when he asked for her at the Menger.

"Mrs. McEveride?" the clerk said. "Why, I don't believe—oh, yes, Mrs. McEveride: red hair, freck—freck—*very* high-class lady! . . . Why, sir, Mrs. McEveride went back East, I understand. As a matter of fact, I got the impression that she was returning to Tennessee for good."

Later Tennessee ran into Jeff Slaughter and asked why Stella had gone. "I don't know, and that's gospel," Slaughter said. "She started ailing, seems like, several weeks after you left. She looked sick, and she sure was down in the mouth. Nothing pleased her, and she didn't seem to have no hope in nothing. Then one day she said, 'Oh, to hell with the whole damn thing!' and pulled out for the East. Taken the stage for Austin. A few weeks later a fellow called Missouri come down from Fort Washita and picked up the Tennessee mare. He come for the stud, too, but War Drum was done gone—just plumb disappeared. I've got a powerful hunch it was the Polka Dot Kid taken the stud—without leaving no trace a-tall, so I sure ain't got no proof. The kid ain't showed hide or hair in San Antone since you saved his skin by gunning down them Watsons or McClanahans or whoever hell's spawn they was. A fellow come down with Missouri—I *reckon* with him—named John Greenwood. Right away he went down to Goliad and picked a fight with Black Jack Tumlinson. Word is, he didn't give Jack no choice, then beat him fair to a gun. Being's he didn't *know* Jack, who was named a rustler by some, it sure had the marks of a hired killing. Since then he's been hanging around the saloons, backing down tough cowboys and doing a lot of talking. Claims he knows you from back East and that you done a lot of killing back in Tennessee. But he claims he's faster on the draw than you. You reckon somebody's done paid him to push a fight on you like he done to poor Jack Tumlinson in Goliad?"

"Don't know," Tennessee said. "Could be. Did Stella—when she left—did she leave any word for me?"

Slaughter would not meet his eyes. The roan-mustached ex-Ranger looked embarrassed. "Like I say, Smith, she wasn't herself. I wouldn't put no stock—"

"Listen," Tennessee said. "Tell me what she said. Her very words."

"Nothing, to me," Slaughter said. "But Dick Weatherford asked her particular what she wanted you told, and she said, 'Tell him he can go to hell, for all I care.' "

Tennessee drew a deep breath. "Well, that's that, I reckon."

Despite his calm words there was such a wild, destructive anguish writhing and clawing inside him that it scared him. "Where's Greenwood hang out?" he asked, wondering already whether it was possible that Stella had hired Greenwood to kill him. The pythonlike muscles of his burly shoulders stirred sleepily and grew still again. "If the son-of-a-bitch wants trouble, he can have it. All I want to know is whether he still works for Stella and why he stayed here when Missouri left."

"Help you look for him," Slaughter said. "Wait a minute. Almost forgot." He started searching himself. "Got a note on me somewheres. Meant for you. Picked it up when I heared you's back in town. From a fellow named Jake Wilson who lives up on Cripple John Creek. . . . Here it is. Allow you'd best read it."

Tennessee found Greenwood in the same saloon in which, many months earlier, he had killed the McClanahan brothers. Greenwood was wearing a green silk shirt, yellow scarf, and tight dark trousers with braided seams, the legs of which were thrust into gleaming, hand-carved boots. Two ivory-handled Colts hung low in tied-down holsters.

Tennessee poured himself a drink. "I can see blood money in that outfit you got on," he said evenly. "Black Jack Tumlinson's blood. Do you deny that you been paid to gun *me* down?"

There was a momentary glint of admiration in Greenwood's eyes; then it was gone, leaving only a brash self-confidence. "Hell, I don't deny nothing," he said in a lowered voice. "I don't know how you found out so quick. Got to hand it to you. But hearing it from me won't do you no good because you ain't going to live long enough to tell no tales."

"Then you won't mind telling me," Tennessee said, keeping the urgency out of his voice with an effort. "Was it Stella McEveride hired you?"

Greenwood looked startled. "Well, I'll be goddamned!" he whispered. He relaxed, a wicked grin slashed white across his face. "Damned if you ain't sharp," he said. "Tennessee, I got to tell you something. You used to have me buffaloed. But not no more. All you used to have on me was more practice with a gun. Now I done caught up and passed you. So I'm glad for you to think about this here: While you're rotting in the ground, I'll be playing with them freckled tits and humping that freckled ass of sweet Stella McEveride—like I done before I left Fort Washita." Greenwood straightened and stood ready for action, expecting Tennessee to reach for a gun.

Instead, Tennessee held him motionless with cold, inscrutable eyes. "Since you're about to die," he said softly, "you can take this news to hell with you: They ain't freckled."

The killing of Greenwood continued to be a matter of regret to

Tennessee. Not the killing, actually, but the quickness of Greenwood's dying. For the bastard had tried to prove worthy of his hire—without ever saying who it was that had hired him. . . .

Tennessee used up most of the two hours before sundown riding around mesas and through draws, detouring to avoid canyons and a large herd of buffalo grazing upwind. Coming into a cattle trail, he followed it toward what he knew would prove to be a ford on Cripple John Creek. Then, a mile ahead, he saw a small, square, sod-roofed house back on a high bank across the creek and, farther to the right, a barn surrounded by a high-railed corral.

Splashing into the shallow waters of the ford, Tennessee pulled over to a pool of greater depth and let the big dun drink. In the vicinity of the barn, a red-bronze game rooster and several brown hens were leaving their scratching in the brush above the creek bank and drifting warily away before the intrusion of the strange horseman. Now a man was standing before the doorway, resting the stock of a rifle on the ground. If he'd been wearing a blue uniform in a different setting, instead of open vest, rusty woolen pants, and scuffed boots on a Comanche-patrolled buffalo range in west Texas, Tennessee thought, he might have passed for Ulysses S. Grant. Behind him a woman in a cotton dress stared with a steady, curious interest. She was a golden-haired blond, in figure reminiscent of the sharp-tongued Rose whom Tennessee had widowed back on the Mississippi-Tennessee border. He felt a twinge of something like regret, remembering Stella's reaction to Rose. It was a good bet, however, that the similarity between this woman and Rose stopped at their figures.

Tennessee raised his hat in deference to the woman. "Looking for Jake Wilson's place," he called.

"You done found it, stranger," the man answered. "Ride up here and light."

The big dun splashed out and climbed the bank. Dismounting, Tennessee dropped the reins and removed his hat. The woman's eyes were as direct as a man's, and they flared with sudden discovery.

"Jake," she cried, "you know who this here is? Why, look at them eyes, that streaked yellow hair, that cold-chisel face a lot darker'n the hair, them pistols wore back'ards, that there dun hoss—"

"Why, sure!" Jake exclaimed. "You're Tennessee Smith!"

Tennessee stared. "How come you know me?"

"Jake, he got a word picture from Jeff Slaughter," Mary Wilson explained. "We been going over it, though it don't do you justice. Jake, you put Tennessee's hoss in the barn. I aim to call you Tennessee, and you call me Mary. You made a friend out of me when you gunned down Beef Kramer. Someday I may tell you why. Come on in. We'll eat a bite 'fore long.''

The one room of the house had all it needed for comfort in the way of fireplace, stove, tables, chairs, and bed. There was a fire against the chill of the spring evening, and supper was on the stove; its aroma clutched like hands at Tennessee's throat.

Mary's observant eyes watched Tennessee survey the room; then she consoled him with an amused, faintly mischievous grin. "You won't have to sleep with Jake and me. We got a guest house, as you might call it, backed into the bank outside—the dugout we lived in 'fore we got rich and built this here mansion. It was a bunkhouse for a while. Jake hired two drifters to help him keep buffalo off the grass. But then they seen Injuns and give us the first real proof they sure was riders.''

When Jake came back from the barn, he backed up to the fire, his eyes alight with pleasure at Tennessee's presence. "I'll swear they ain't a man in Texas I'd rather see,'' he said finally.

"Got to set you straight on one thing,'' Tennessee said. "A young cowboy friend of mine killed Beef Kramer, not me.'' He proceeded to narrate the border incident involving the horse thieves, telling more about Kramer's treatment of the *pelada* than he would have if he could have kept clearly in mind that Mary had been married to Beef Kramer. That fact he found hard to believe.

Before he had finished, however, Mary was nodding her head in recognition of a thing familiar and distasteful. "Why, it's enough to make a body throw up!'' she declared. "But maybe it's fit and right he should get killed while blowing off about what he didn't have no under-standing of at all. His whole life was spent in mistaking—and hating—women. I always suspicioned he thought his mammy somehow cheated him. He doubted he was as much of a man as he ought to be with women, and he had some reason to think it, too.'' Suddenly color suffused her face. "Lord God, I never meant to say that! A body can't talk about Beef, though, without talking trash. That Nueces Riley sounds like a real nice boy.''

"He sure is,'' Tennessee confirmed. "Expecting him out here in a few days. Jake, if you'll put up with me till he comes, I'll be glad to help you shove them buffaloes back off your grass.'' He paused, then added, "Or shove off the cattle. Which you raising—buffaloes or cattle?''

Jake smiled. "Why, I'll take you up on that offer.'' His eyes brightened. "Funny you should mention what I'm raising. You won't believe this here, but one of my cows had a half-breed buffalo calf last year. So I ain't plumb sure which I'm raising.''

"You know, I've wondered if that couldn't happen," Tennessee said. "Well, we know white women can have half-breed Indian babies. Ain't the same thing, though, I don't reckon." Quickly then he became aware of Jake's blank face. Mary was facing the stove, presenting only her back. She seemed caught in a moment of stillness. By God, he thought, when will I learn to watch my damned tongue?

During the next several days Tennessee learned from the Wilsons that the Indians had departed from their long-time practice of stealing only horses off the range; now they were raiding for cattle. Less than a year before, a large number of Indians had conducted a massive raid on Elm Creek and run off a herd of about two thousand cattle which Charles Goodnight had put together for a trail drive. Already this spring three different parties of Indians had been sighted driving stolen cattle across the Wilson range toward the Cap Rock. Plains news, or gossip, somehow made its way to remote cabins in out-of-the-way places as if borne on the back of the constant wind, and recent word had it that Charles Goodnight was making up another trail herd back down on the Clear Fork of the Brazos. Jake had been considering the possibility of gathering some of his steers and old dry cows and throwing them into Goodnight's herd for marketing in New Mexico and Colorado. What had been keeping him from doing so was the difficulty of making the gather and trailing the cattle by himself.

"How come, with buffaloes so handy, Indians run off cattle?" Tennessee wanted to know.

"Trade with *comancheros*," Jake told him. "A cow for a loaf of bread, maybe. A small herd for a keg of rotgut whiskey. They steal cattle because the *comancheros* tell 'em what they want."

"You know any *comancheros*, Jake?"

"Two—Juan Trujillo and José Tafoya. Know 'em purty well. I done both of 'em good turns one time or other. I come from New Mexico original. Never got no further into Texas than this here.''

"You see one of 'em, ask where I can find Parson Krull." Tennessee described the parson and then went on to describe the parson's offspring, emphasizing the description of Brownlow. "That's the bastard I want most," he said.

"You know what?" Jake exclaimed. "I'm mightnear sure I seen that Brownlow and Jimpson about three weeks ago. They was with a party of Antelope Comanch', helping drive a bunch of cattle toward the Cap Rock. Reason I remember what Injuns so good, their leader was a bad Injun named Broken Fang. Talk about a mean son-of-a-bitch! Makes me flinch just to look at him.''

"You know this place is watched, don't you?" Tennessee said. "Yesterday an Indian was sitting his horse on a mesa over there to the west. Bold as hell. Say we should get a bunch of cows together, why wouldn't Indians run 'em off?"

"Well, I don't think they would." Jake's hooded eyes revealed nothing. "Course they ain't no way to tell for sure what Injuns will do, but they's a Quahadi peace chief who's told them Antelope Comanch' to lay off us. I reckon they will."

"How come a Quahadi can tell an Antelope what to do?"

"They're the same," Jake said. "*Quahadi* is Comanch' for *Antelope*."

A week later Nueces arrived. While working the broken mesa country to the west, Tennessee and Jake missed the brush hand as he crossed the great flat east of Cripple John Creek. When they rode into the yard in late afternoon, he was in the corral, removing the pack from a mule. Mary had accompanied Riley to the corral and stood watching him work. She turned reproachful eyes on Tennessee as he and Jake dismounted.

"You never said nothing about gunning down no hired killer in San Antone 'fore coming out here," she complained. "The boy rode in right uneasy about you."

Tennessee turned his cold eyes on Riley. "Why come yapping about that out here?"

Riley straightened with an unabashed grin. "That set-to with John Greenwood, him trying to rub out your mark—why, it give me a chill," he said. "Thought some other hired gun might of followed you out of town for a second try. Jeff Slaughter's dead certain somebody's after your hide. Tennessee, I aim to keep you alive if I can, till I get a chance to save your life and pay my debt." His eyes glinted derisively. "Course, after that, some *hombre* wants to take a crack at you, it won't be no big thing." He turned to the pack that had been stripped from the roan. "Jeff Slaughter and Leck Franks, by the way, they sent you a present." He turned from the pack, extending belts and holsters containing two gleaming, ivory-handled .44 Colts. "They figured you had a better right to Greenwood's guns than them soldier-policemen in San Antone with their taking ways."

"Who's Leck Franks?"

"That barkeep that served up drinks on the house after you piled up the Watsons, then done it again when you punched Greenwood's ticket. Way he tells it, they was three shots—*brrrup*, like that—and them Watsons was kicking on the floor. He claims that Greenwood—"

"Ease off, Nueces," Tennessee interrupted. "You take them fancy pistols, Jake, and hang 'em up or use 'em. My wooden-handled pistols suit me fine.''

Tennessee and Riley rode north the next morning, Tennessee astride the big dun, Riley riding his buckskin and leading his roan under pack; the mule, heavily burdened with the pack of trading goods, followed free. They intended to pace their mounts with an eye to weeks of hard riding, for they were headed for the canyon country on the branches of Red River a hundred miles or more to the north. The Polka Dot Kid had a wild-horse camp there, according to Jake Wilson. Though the Kid's camp was likely to be in sight of Comanche campfires, Tennessee wanted to ask him some questions concerning a number of things, not least among them the whereabouts of Brownlow Krull.

As they rode into the shade along the west side of Long Mesa, they looked back at the lonely little ranch house on the bank of Cripple John Creek. ''Don't take no imagination to see a pile of ashes where that house is now,'' Riley commented.

''I don't know. Jake claims they got a peace chief on their side.''

Riley squinted into the distance. ''Only trouble is, that peace chief might hear an owl screech after daylight—something or other—and get spooky. I'd trust a Comanche peace chief 'bout the same way I'd trust a March breeze not to turn into no blue norther.''

Tennessee looked toward the west, then turned his face to the fore and looked quickly toward the west again. A thread of smoke was climbing into sight above distant red hills. He nodded toward it. ''You reckon them bastards are getting ready to come after us?''

''No telling what Injuns may do,'' Riley said after a long look. ''But my guess—and it's sure a guess—is we're looking over some redgut reporter's shoulder while he whips out an item for, say, the *Comanche News-Sentinal.* 'Messrs. Tennessee Smith and Nueces Riley, who have been visiting the Wilsons on Cripple John Creek, left this morning on business in the north.' My itching scalp tells me we won't see no smoke when them Comanches jump us. We won't see nothing but a swarm of redguts behind a cloud of arrers.''

''How come you're such a knowing lad about Indians,'' Tennessee sneered mildly, ''at the ripe old age of twenty-three?''

Riley grinned meagerly. ''Where I growed up,'' he said, drawling his answer, ''you got ripe quick around Injuns, or you didn't get to be no twenty-three.''

They camped that first night in a clump of willows on a thread of spring water that emptied into a creek. They dug a pit to hide the hot flame of their tiny fire, boiled coffee and fried bacon, which they ate with cold biscuits. Rolled in his blankets against a chill wind that seemed fresh off the wastes of Canada, Tennessee listened to the voices of the Texas night. Riley slept like a brush cat, without snoring, the sound of his even breathing lost in the swish and rasp of the swinging willows. The yammering of coyotes came from some unseen red-clay hill to the west, and the mournful wail of a lobo wolf drifted down the wind from a high, lonely mesa. A screech owl quavered a few times from a cottonwood down the creek and then was silent. In the wind there was a tinge of musk from some distant skunk.

As he lay wide awake in his blanket, Tennessee felt sorrow well up in him at the thought of Stella, frustrated, sick, and desperate. Jeff Slaughter had said she was sick, but a mere illness would not have stopped her—not Stella. Her sickness, Tennessee guessed, was merely an outward show of an inner illness that was worse—a sickness of the mind, caused by him. When he considered that he was the one who had frustrated all her plans and wrecked her hopes, he was forced to the conclusion that she had hired Greenwood to kill him. He cursed Greenwood for dying without telling him.

Somehow Tennessee could not blame Stella. She had brought him West to kill Brownlow Krull, and he had turned out to be worse than Brownlow. Yes, worse, for she had trusted him, regarded him as a brother, and he had brutalized her the way Brownlow had. He tortured himself with a recurring fantasy, seeing Brownlow Krull humped between Stella's velvet-smooth, lovely white legs. . . .Tennessee turned over with a groan, breathing the first genuine prayer of his life. "Aw, goddamn his soul to hell!" he whispered. "Lord God, just bring me in sight of that black-assed son-of-a-bitch! I won't ask you for no more favors, I promise you."

They were in their saddles by daybreak, across the Wichita River by mid-morning, and pushing ahead on the divide toward the North Fork of the Pease in the afternoon. When they reached Red River, they found the stream swollen with the rainwash from the red canyons to the west and looking like a river of blood. Traveling westward, they entered a country of deep gorges branching in all directions, a land of jagged cliffs and broken hills. Gradually the escarpment of the Staked Plain rose up frowning in the west until it stood a thousand feet above the rolling plains. Now, in their camps at night, one of them stayed awake to guard their hair and their horses while the other slept. Slowed by rocky ridges and deep ravines, they worked their way along a fork of the Red through prairie-dog towns, past the long stretches of water running on a sand bed bitter with gypsum, and finally they were at the Cap Rock, where Palo Duro

Canyon began and where the water flowed on a bed of colored rocks and was clear, cool, and fresh.

The walls of the Palo Duro dropped sheer from the Cap Rock, several hundred feet in places, then shouldered out and descended in slopes, which in turn had their own precipices and declivities and were marked by jutting rocks, eroded hummocks, and ravines. Below the Cap Rock were bands of sandstones and shales, their colors fading into one another; but the slopes, with their rust-red earth exposures, caused the memory of the beholder to forget the varied colors of the cliffs and carry out of the canyon an impression of red walls splotched by green clumps of juniper and white streaks of gypsum.

"Heard an old mountain man claim the walls of Palo Duro burned like the fires of hell." Riley's face had a wooden look. "He sure wasn't lying."

Very few white men had seen the Palo Duro and lived to describe it. It was the heart of Comanche country, and the Quahadis were its keepers and its watchdogs. According to Jake Wilson, they allowed the other bands of Comanches free access to the canyon, as they did their allies, the Kiowas, and, under certain unusual, specific conditions, the Cheyennes and Apaches. But woe to the Navajo, Ute, or Wichita who left a moccasin print that could be followed in the red clay of the canyon.

"Tennessee, if you'll listen to me and haul ass back the way we come, I'll consider that debt I owe you paid up in full." Riley's eyes were constantly in motion, like the eyes of a bird in snaky brush; they darted up and glanced off a slow-gliding buzzard, then bounced back to the Cap Rock. "We don't watch out, we may fly out of here inside a bunch of damn feathers 'fore we get done visiting. You had any pride, you wouldn't stay where you ain't wanted."

They crossed Tule Creek a mile or so above its junction with the Prairie Dog Town Fork, and beyond that crossing they came upon the tracks of unshod mustangs running hard. Instinctively their eyes leaped, as they did to the tracks of all disturbed animals in this country. The broad path of the horses came out of Tule Canyon and headed up the Palo Duro, the outside hoofprints crowding over the top of those inside the turn.

Riley dismounted and knelt to examine them. "They ain't *rode* hosses, way they crowded and packed on that turn. I'd allow they's wild hosses and sure something running 'em to beat hell." Suddenly he bent low and coursed ahead for a dozen yards, then dropped to one knee. By the time Tennessee had dismounted to join him, Riley was stretched full-length on the ground. "Big hoss driving or chasing 'em—stallion, likely. But here's what's funny—the damn stallion's wearing Apache rawhide shoes. And something else. You ever hear tell of a mustang, stallion or any kind, with a stride of twenty-five or thirty feet?'' Slowly he got to his feet as Tennessee answered with a shake of the head. ''Me neither. What I think, that big hoss ain't no mustang, and somebody was riding him, maybe trying to run down and catch him a wild mustang.''

Tennessee stiffened. ''The Polka Dot Kid, by God!'' he exclaimed. ''Nueces, we're right on top of the man we come looking for—and him riding War Drum. How old you say them tracks are?''

''One day,'' Riley said, coming up to saddle. ''Made sometime yesterday.''

Before the two men were well on their way, however, Riley discovered that the stallion had reversed his direction somewhere up-canyon and come back down in the company of two unshod horses. The trail of the three horses turned back into Tule Canyon, the walls of which bracketed a range extending southwestward along Tule Creek.

They trailed through the late afternoon, until dusk had erased the colors of the escarpment and filled the great canyon with mysterious shadows. Soon they would have to camp for the night or follow the canyon in darkness, gambling that the trail would not turn off into some side canyon. Then, from beyond a lone, shrouded butte turned ghostly by the gloom of dusk, came the nicker of a horse.

Instantly they were out of their saddles and at the heads of their mounts to prevent answering nickers. Riley handed his reins to Tennessee and faded back to keep the mule and the roan company. The horse that had whinnied was answered by several horses farther up the canyon and off toward the eastern escarpment.

''Could run our heads in a hornet's nest,'' Tennessee said in a quiet voice as Riley came forward with the pack animals. ''You hold the horses back here while I move in and make the count.''

Riley's face looked thin with strain in the thickening dusk. ''Why, I'll have the damn jitters worser'n a nervous goat waiting back here. How 'bout me doing that moving-in part?''

Tennessee was already removing his boots in order to replace them with a pair of moccasins from his saddlebags. ''Nueces, you can show me things about reading mustang prints. Ain't no wild horses back in the old South. But nobody, white or red, can teach me a damned thing about scouting an enemy camp. I used to get my rations in Union camps at night. You know where they kept the best whiskey? In the generals' tents.''

When he walked away from Riley and the horses, Tennessee seemed to merge with the dusk, moving like a small patch of fog drifting along the ground. He faded into the gloom that shrouded the butte and then, bent low, made his way through the scattered boulders and fringe of thin brush along the shouldered-out base of the butte. Then he stopped stone-still in the deeper shade of a huge boulder. Beyond the butte, on high ground above the creek, there was a large buffalo-hide tepee standing among flickering shadows cast by the flames of a supper fire under a suspended iron pot. Tennessee flashed across the space and pressed against the rough bark of a gnarled old cottonwood that stood wringing its leaves halfway between butte and tepee. From here he studied the camp and the land beyond, making certain that no other tepees were visible in the vicinity.

There was the sound of movement in the tepee but no talking, no single utterance; so Tennessee figured there was only one person inside. He left the tree, a long-barreled Colt sliding into his hand, and took his post beside the entrance flap of the tepee.

When a long-haired man in breechclout and buckskin leggings came through the tepee entrance and straightened up, Tennessee placed the muzzle of his pistol against the man's spine and said softly, "You start hollering, Kid, you won't finish."

The Polka Dot Kid seemed stricken. Without looking around he whispered in a voice that was like a muted shout, "*Quién es?*"

"Look around," Tennessee invited.

The Kid paled when he saw the big man with the gun, but his gray eyes did not waver. "You take him War Drum," he said in a despairing voice.

"Who told you his name?"

"Me hear Roan Stud call him War Drum. Me hide in barn day borrow him War Drum."

"Borrow?" Tennessee said with a hard grin.

"Me *need* him big stud!" the Kid gestured passionately. "Want two wild hosses no can catch. War Drum fast enough to catch. But not yet. Goddamn! Let me keep *poco tiempo*. Me keep him good. Kill any *hombre* come steal."

"How many Indians are camped around here?"

":No Injuns." The Kid's drawn face, with lips parted over prominent front teeth, revealed intense strain. "*Me* camp here. Keep hosses here. Comanche on Quitaque."

Tennessee thrust his Colt back into holster. "Nueces!" he shouted down the canyon. "Come on up. Supper's ready."

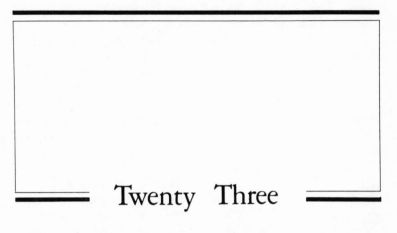

Twenty Three

They had eaten and were sitting around the fire, the flames whipping the darkness back from their faces. ''Kid,'' Tennessee said out of a brief silence, ''I never come after the stud. May let you keep him awhile. That depends. What I did come for is two sons-of-bitches I aim to kill.'' Patiently he described Brownlow and Jimpson Krull, delivering himself of every detail concerning them that either Fox Wilkins or Stella had been able to provide.

Before he had finished the Polka Dot Kid was leaning forward, his eyes bright with recognition. ''Comanche call him Brownlow Humping Brother,'' he said, eager to please. ''Him raid with Broken Fang warrior.''

''Humping Brother?''

''Screwing Brother,'' Riley explained. ''Brownlow sucks around, scraping up friendship with the bucks, until the redguts declare him a blood brother. Then he borrows the bucks' wives. Reckon he does that with enough bucks, he ain't ever likely to run short of squaw meat.''

''He will, though,'' Tennessee said softly. ''When I catch up, the bastard will run out of everything all at once—even breath.''

''No see him Jimpson much,'' the Kid said. ''Comanche call him What Buzzard Drop. Stink when—when—um, *nervioso*. Comanche make him stay out of camp *con los renegados*.''

''What the Buzzard Drops?'' Tennessee studied the Kid's face in the flickering light. ''Buzzard Shit?'' he said doubtfully. ''They call him that?''

The Kid nodded. "*Sí*, him, too. Him Buzzard Puke, Buzzard Mouthful Stinking Meat, Buzzard Louse, Buzzard Molt Feather—What Drop From Buzzard, him Jimpson's name."

"Humping Brother and Buzzard Droppings!" Tennessee murmured sardonically. "Where can I find 'em, Kid?"

"Don't know. Maybe Earth Daughter know. Come morning."

"Who's Earth Daughter?"

"Quahadi girl ride War Drum catch wild hoss." Trying to expand this statement, the Polka Dot Kid soon tripped on the roots and bogged in the mire of his English and suddenly plunged into the Spanish he had learned from his foster mother, a Spanish woman brought back from a Comanche raid in Chihuahua.

"I do hope," Tennessee remarked sourly, "that just once we can run across some bastard somewhere who can speak English."

"Me *write* English," the Kid informed them. "Schoolteacher learn me good. White squaw. Wolf Waiting take her off—um, off him stagecoach." He continued with his story.

"What'd he say, Nueces?" Tennessee asked.

Riley translated. Earth Daughter, it seemed, was the daughter of Horse Walking, a peace chief of the Quahadis. Horse Walking had opposed one of Broken Fang's recent raids and, having failed to win Chief Bear's Ear's support in that opposition, had pulled out of the main camp on the Quitaque and was now sulking in Bull Bear's camp up on the plain. Bull Bear was a Kotsoteka chief whose hatred of the white-eyes kept him with the Quahadis most of the time. When her father's camp was in reach, Earth Daughter rode War Drum for the Kid in his pursuit of wild horses. There was no better rider on the plains than the Polka Dot Kid, but he weighed a hundred and seventy-five pounds, too much handicap for War Drum in races with the very fastest wild horses—and these were the ones the Kid wanted. Earth Daughter, at fourteen, weighed only eighty pounds. She was wiry and strong and fearless.

Though the Kid's tepee was comparatively luxurious, with buffalo robes, bear skins, and other hides covering the ground, Tennessee and Riley preferred to sleep in their blankets outside. Tennessee awoke during the night. Scudding clouds, black against the sky, were fleeing up the canyon before a rising wind. There would be rain behind those clouds, he predicted with a silent oath, pulling his blankets tighter.

They were up at dawn, building a fire, starting breakfast; the Kid did not appear until they heard the barking of a gray fox. Suddenly Tennessee became motionless, listening. The barking came against the wind; he could not be certain. Riley came up from the fire and, with sudden, quick motion, stepped behind the tepee. Then the kid was standing before the entrance flap, barking like a dog fox answering a vixen.

"Earth Daughter come."

The girl rode up to the fire and sat her pinto mare, watching them, her brown, shoulder-length hair blowing in the wind. Tennessee recognized her instantly. She was brown-skinned, probably less than half Indian, and she was studying them with Mary Wilson's blue eyes. Her face was thin, unlike a Comanche squaw's, and she lacked the stolid, level-eyed wariness of a squaw before strange white men; but then this young squaw had not been kicked about by some brutal buck nor loaned out to his friends. She lacked also the stature of a squaw. When she kicked out of her metal stirrups and slid down from her sheep-pad saddle, Tennessee observed that she was taller than he had expected; she was lithe and poised in her thigh-length, split-bottom doeskin skirt and buckskin leggings.

The Kid indicated his visitors with a vague gesture. "No come take War Drum," he told her. "Come kill him Humping Brother, What Buzzard Drop."

The girl looked from one to the other, and then she smiled. "Good," she said. "Humping Brother always try to put his hand here." She touched the doeskin over her crotch with an unabashed finger. "He try to get me to night-crawl. I tell Spotted Hoss. I think he kill Humping Brother. Hah! Spotted Hoss no kill."

"Me kill him one day," the Kid growled. "You little. Wait."

"For why I wait?" She tossed her head. "Knife Eyes kill Humping Brother." She turned bright eyes on Tennessee. "Knife Eyes big man!"

Well, by God, I don't reckon they're ever too young! Tennessee thought. So now they'll be calling me Knife Eyes. "Where are they now?" he asked the girl. "I mean Humping Brother and What Buzzard Drops."

"Don't know where What Buzzard Drop. Humping Brother in Blanco Canyon with Broken Fang. They bring cattle and hold there."

They had barely finished breakfast before the rain came sweeping up the canyon and drove them inside the tepee. Tennessee curbed with difficulty his impatience to be on his way toward Blanco Canyon and Brownlow Krull. He reminded himself, however, that the horses had been worked hard and could use the time spent out on the grass. During the course of the morning he learned, with surprise, that Earth Daughter knew that her mother was Mary Wilson and that she had visited her mother more than once when the Quahadis were in riding distance of the cabin on Cripple John Creek. Earth Daughter knew also that the Wilsons were under the protection of Horse Walking. In fact, the quarrel between her father and Broken Fang had been caused by a raid in which Broken Fang had swept up some twenty head of Wilson Cattle on his way back to the breaks of the Cap Rock and had refused to give them up. Earth Daughter was in favor of Knife Eyes' killing Broken Fang, too, if he got the chance. His death, she thought, would improve the earth.

It was noon before the rain ceased and the clouds dispersed. Soon thereafter Tennessee and Riley set out, reaching for the High Plain shortcut to Blanco Canyon. Since they might find themselves among Comanches at any time, they had both the roan and the mule on lead, the roan carrying their camp gear and supplies and the mule loaded with *comanchero* trading goods.

They reached Blanco Canyon in mid-afternoon of the next day. One minute they were riding on an apparently endless plain, and then, minutes later, with only the briefest forewarning, they were drawing up at the edge of a bluff with the floor of a wide valley lying hundreds of feet below them. Blanco Canyon, like Palo Duro, was a water-cut gash in the High Plain, though it was not so deep and raw as the latter nor so vivid in color. The red clay earth exposures were there, but the fires of hell did not light the canyon walls with so red a glow.

At a break in the Cap Rock a quarter-mile down-canyon, they found a trail leading under the bluffs and across the slopes into the valley. It was heavily marked by signs of animal traffic—the tracks and droppings of buffalo, cattle, and unshod horses. They put the horses on the trail in single file, finding the descent easy enough. Tennessee noticed that all the cattle tracks were pointed uptrail and that only horses had left tracks on the trail since yesterday's rain. There were bound to be other paths leading over the Cap Rock, however, so he could not be certain that Broken Fang's warriors were still holding cattle in the canyon. Nevertheless, those fresh horse tracks caused the fine hairs on Tennessee's skin to prickle.

Suddenly he knew that Quahadi scouts were above the Cap Rock, watching his and Riley's descent into the canyon, and he knew also that the scouts would stay out of sight as long as he and Riley kept moving on toward the Quahadi raiding party waiting somewhere below. He glanced over his shoulder and saw the strained composure of Riley's grim young face. The brush hand knew they were committed and believed they were already in trouble.

On the canyon floor Riley brought his buckskin up beside the big dun. With his eyes looking straight ahead, he said in a toneless voice, "If you look over my head at the foot of that red cliff, you'll see a Quahadi redgut in the damn flesh.'' Tennessee looked at the south wall and kept looking, seeing nothing unusual. ''Look straight down under that big yellow rock,'' directed Riley.

Tennessee's eyes found the rock and ran down the face of the bluff to the foot, where the slope shouldered out, and there they stopped. An Indian, naked save for breechclout and moccasins, lay in full view, motionless and practically invisible against the red clay of the slope.

''You got eyes like a buzzard!'' Tennessee murmured.

''He's passing on the signals from scouts up on the plain.'' Riley pointed ahead. Half a mile away the willow-fringed stream of the canyon disappeared around the point of a broken ridge. ''Them Injuns with Broken Fang, they're behind that ridge. They knowed we's on our way 'fore we come off the plain. Tennessee, I'll tell you this last time. We're going to graze the edge of hell on this here go-round.''

''What we got to do,'' Tennessee said, ''is keep talking trade. What I want is to trade 'em out of the cattle, then hire Brownlow Krull to help drive 'em a few miles off. Ought to work.''

As they neared the point of the ridge, Riley took a quick look over his shoulder and then faced around slowly. ''If you've give some thought to jerking around and getting out of here,'' he said woodenly, ''you can forget it. We got company.''

Tennessee glanced back. Four Indians were walking their horses down-canyon a thousand yards to the rear. Herding us in like sheep! he thought grimly. Soon they saw the cattle, loose-herded between ridge and creek, and beyond the herd two Indians idled on the backs of ponies standing out in the grass. Other horses stood among the cottonwoods and willows along the creek. At the edge of the trees, where two cooking fires had been started, the Indians, dark, bronzed figures in breechclouts and moccasins, were facing up-canyon, with their weapons in their hands, awaiting the approach of the strangers. Several had feathers in their coarse black hair or hanging from plaits; most had none. One of them, standing forward in haughty isolation, wore a buffalo-horn headdress.

At a distance the riders suspected that the savage with the horns was Broken Fang; close up, they knew that the cruel, evil face could belong to no other. He was taller than his squat, stocky warriors and equaled any of them in breadth of shoulders, depth of chest, and herculean muscular development. He stood with folded arms and gave no sign of welcome in answer to Riley's talking hands that kept saying, ''Peace . . . friends . . . trade . . . gifts. . . .''

They pulled up in front of the Indian leader and sat their horses, awaiting an invitation to dismount. It was not given. With a muttered oath Riley stepped out of his saddle and stood at the head of his horse. He spoke at some length in Spanish and then was silent, standing expectant before the horned Comanche. Tennessee knew that Riley had explained that they were *comancheros*, that they had gifts, that they wanted to trade for cattle. The snarled reply was in the ugliest Spanish Tennessee had ever heard, and it was accompanied by a scowl of contempt and hatred.

As they talked, Tennessee looked beyond the horned headdress, studying the faces of the Indians who stood with ready weapons in a loose, shallow semicircle behind the leader. Most of them had wild, harsh faces highlighted by eyes that looked like chips of black rock. One had the small, glinting eyes of the savage humorist.

Brownlow Krull was not among them.

The wind stirred briefly, and pink dust came whirling up the creek bank, veered sharply, and died in thin grass. Suddenly Tennessee was smelling a feral mixture of things: buffalo tallow turned rancid on greased skin, decayed particles of blood from slaughtered animals, fetid armpits, breechclouts fouled with horse sweat, smoke from buffalo-chip fires, uncured scalps. . . . It was the stench of death common to arid country.

"Tennessee, listen close." Riley's face was drawn thin by strain. "This here bastard's that Broken Fang, all right, and he says he won't trade no cattle. He's holding these cattle for a *comanchero* from Puerto de Luna. But he'll trade us our lives, maybe, he says, for the goods and the mule."

"Keep hold of yourself, but be ready to jump on that horse, too. Ask him where's Humping Brother. Tell him we're partners with Parson Krull. Tell him the parson told us to trade for the cattle."

Riley talked in slow Spanish, using his hands. Broken Fang listened, his wide trout mouth changing from sneer to vicious grin. Slowly he unfolded his arms and made a contemptuous gesture toward a part of the canyon south of the creek. He said something in Comanche to the warrior with the fixed half-smile, who whipped out a knife and ran a mahogany thumb along its edge. Then Broken Fang addressed Riley in a Spanish that sounded like a series of oaths.

"By God, we're walking on eggs!" A fine sweat glistened on Riley's face. Listening, Tennessee heard, behind the cowboy's voice, a murmur of hoofbeats from south of the creek. "This son-of-a-bitch says they'll eat the mule now and maybe trade later. Maybe not. So we may as well forget them goods and that mule." The hoofbeats across the creek were drawing closer.

The warrior approached the mule and, with deft motions, cut ropes and straps and pushed the pack off the mule's back. Then he turned and went into a comic dance step, flourishing his knife in mimic battle. His audience applauded him with gobbles and brays of laughter, flashing looks at the strangers. Tennessee ignored him. A small bunch of cattle, pushed by two Comanche horsemen, was crossing the creek fifty yards downstream. Stricken by a sudden premonition, Tennessee observed with only half his attention the Quahadi comedian, who came to the end of his dance with a dramatic sweep of his knife and cut the mule's throat, then leaped aside to avoid the gush of blood. The mule plunged to his knees, held there for long moments, his head drooping sleepily, then fell on his side, kicking feebly. The Indians were on him with their knives, butchering him before all motion ceased.

The two newcomers drove the bunch of cattle into a loose herd and turned their horses toward Broken Fang and the others. With a sudden, unthinking savagery, Tennessee locked his eyes on one of them and never thereafter looked at the other. The Quahadi came on, riding his black-and-white buffalo horse with his knees, his black eyes at peace with the world and his perfect teeth shining white against his dark face. He was naked from the waist up, and his shoulders, chest, and arms were powerfully muscled. This savage was one of the handsomest men Tennessee had ever seen. *Brownlow Krull!* When he was thirty yards away, he faded into a familiar fantasy. Tennessee saw him rise, handsome as a devil from hell, stinking of death and spent lust, from between Stella McEveride's perfect white legs, and he heard again Stella's anguished voice: "How do you know Brownlow Krull wasn't a better stallion than you? Whatever I say, you'll never know whether I got more pleasure from Brownlow Krull."

The roar and buck of his right-hand gun came almost as a shock even to Tennessee himself. "By God, Stella," he groaned in his heart, "you sure as hell got it done!" Even before Brownlow Krull struck the ground in a loose-limbed sprawl, Tennessee was swinging both guns, firing into the Indians.

"Holy Jesus!" Riley yelled, and came surging up into his saddle. Instantly his gun joined the clamor of Tennessee's. Two or three Indians were down, and the others were leaping for cover. Tennessee snapped a shot at Broken Fang, who was dodging over the creek bank, and saw him go spinning into the creek, looking as if he'd clapped a crimson mask over his malign visage.

"Hiii-yeee-ahhowww!" Tennessee's panther scream set the Indian ponies to plunging and kicking and surging this way and that. "Head at 'em!" he roared. "Ride over 'em!" The big dun ran over an Indian and

plunged into the creek, coughed, and stumbled; then he righted himself and scrambled up the opposite bank. It was while the horse was struggling up the bank that Tennessee felt the shock and heard the thump of the first arrow driving into his back, but he felt no pain and was able to rise in the stirrups, grasp the reins, and lift the horse over the bank. As he did so, three more bullets or arrows hit him, and something like a red-hot iron struck his head, almost sweeping him from the saddle. He could feel the instant leap of blood greasing the left side of his face. He heard the thud of another bullet striking the big dun. Then they were in the open, running down the canyon.

"God a'mighty!" Riley despaired, pushing the buckskin alongside and reaching over to steady Tennessee in the saddle. "Tennessee, you can't die on me in this place! By God, I won't let you! You hear me?"

Blood from the big dun's nostrils was spattering Tennessee's face as he bent over in the saddle, and the horse's stride had lost some of its wonted smoothness. Tennessee looked back, almost going off the horse, and saw a half-dozen Comanche horsemen burst out of the willows behind them. These were the scouts and cattle guards; the others had been delayed in mounting up, but that delay would be brief. Riley whipped out his rifle and threw a shot back to discourage any Indian who wanted to win this race.

Tennessee had lost one of his Colts; the other was empty, and suddenly he did not have the strength to handle his rifle. Now his wounds were on fire. He had never been hurt before, not like this. His life blood was draining out of him. All he wanted to do was rest his head on the horse's neck. By God, he couldn't see! It was the big dun's rough, faltering stride that caused everything to blur in front of his eyes. He dropped his empty Colt. . . .

Twenty Four

Stella did not go back East. She started out, traveling by stagecoach to Austin. Then she had several trying days of delay in Waco, where she found the hardships and uncertainties of travel in a land hardly beginning to recover from the war too much for her. After hiring a rider to deliver a message to old Fort Washita, she waited in Waco until Missouri came for her. They rode to her headquarters in a buckboard, the hard-bitten Missouri at the ribbons and a trio of ex-Confederate warriors riding escort. Stella arrived sick and despondent and found Lula May, Jubal, and their newborn baby boy already in residence. In Lula May's arms she wept out her tale of woe and was comforted, receiving effusive assurances that she was going to be taken care of and loved.

It was months later, in her apartment at the old fort, that her pregnancy had run full course. She awoke in the middle of a May night, having been conscious even in her sleep of grinding abdominal pains, and found herself drenched in soaking-wet bedclothes and unable to keep the water from running out of her. Before she was fully awake she thought despairingly that she had reverted to early childhood and was wetting the bed. Then, lifting her head off the pillow, she saw the huge mound her gravid body made under the bedcover, and she knew what had happened.

"Lula May!" she wailed, feeling herself start trembling.

One call was enough. Almost instantly bedsprings creaked in the adjoining room, where Lula May and her six-month-old boy had been sleeping of late so that the black woman would be on call. She came through the doorway, hanging a robe about her shoulders, not taking time to put it on. "What, honey? What—"

"My water broke. I'm all wet, and I can't keep it from running out."

"Oh, my Lawd!" Lula May's voice was ragged with fright. "And we's counting on at least one mo' week. That doctor man in Fo't Smith sho God ain't gonna be here like he promised." She caught her hands together to keep from wringing them. "We do without him, though, honey. Sho, we don't need him. We do fine. Now, don't you worry yo' head—"

"Hush, now," Stella said in a shaky voice. "Stop your chattering and get me on that chamber pot." She raised up on her elbows until her chin was as high as her mountainous belly. "There's a time to be scared, and this is *my* time. You had yours six months ago."

Lula May helped Stella to the floor beside the bed, where she stood bent over, her arms cradling her stomach. She looked as if she were trying to carry in her arms a great prize-winning pumpkin concealed under her nightgown. The maid toed the chamber pot into position and lowered Stella into place upon it. "You say, now, when it all done run out."

Lula May went to a cedar chest in the next room and came back with a blanket. She wrapped it around Stella and proceeded to change the bedclothes, pausing now and then to brush away tears she could not hold back. Finally she burst out, "Woman go through this oughta be happy! You ain't happy. You never *have* been. You mis'able. Honey, why *couldn't* you listen to me? I told you what that yellow-haired catamount do to you!"

Lumped ungracefully under the blanket, head hanging and hair in disarray, Stella looked like a tired squaw who was no longer hopeful of anything worthwhile in a brutish, warrior-dominated world. "Paul's hair wasn't yellow," she said without animation. "Fair, but not yellow."

"Who talking 'bout Mist' Paul?" Lula May said darkly. "Mist' Paul been dead a year. You know who I's talking about. That big mean-eyed devil who hold you down and pump that baby in you, that's who. Mist' Tennessee."

"Paul's the baby's father," Stella said in a colorless voice, as if credibility were the least of her concerns. "All the water's run out now. Get me a dry gown and help me back in bed."

When Stella was in bed and dry again, Lula May leaned over her. "Honey, you ain't got no idea how you gonna start hurting just any minute now, and I got to have some help. You rest easy, and I won't be gone mo'n a minute or two."

"What help? Who—"

"Get Jubal to boil water and look after the baby, it wake up, and get Mist' Missouri to help in here. He good with mares having colts, and he got a way with sick folks. He claim he better'n a midwife and good as a doctor—even if he do have to listen at yo' chest with his naked ear."

"No men in here! You and I can manage—" Suddenly something shifted inside her, and her uterine walls began contracting. She had a long spasm during which every nerve in her swollen body seemed to turn white-hot with pain. Stella's face twisted, and a whimpering sound escaped her. As the pain was subsiding, she gasped, "Go get the help. Anybody. Anybody at all."

Lula May was gone not much more than ten minutes, and Stella was in the grips of another contraction when the maid came hurrying in from outside. Freckles seemed to be swarming in Stella's red, contorted face. When they settled to rest, the maid asked, "How you feeling, honey?"

"Like the worst hell!" Stella moaned. "Lula May, that—that damned animal—*he* did this to me! That low-down, low-life—goddamn him! If I don't die I'll have him hunted down and shot like a dog!"

"Mist' Paul done dead," Lula May reminded her gently. "You say *he* the one."

"You know who I mean," Stella chattered wildly. "You *told* me he'd put my back on the ground! Well, he did, damn him! I—I mustn't die, Lula May. He mustn't get away with it—to—to rape and ruin other women. *You* keep the baby. You've got milk. More than your baby needs. I'll pay you well. I don't even want to see it—ever. I'll shut my eyes when it comes out. I must be free to run down that—that damned woman-killer—who—who couldn't *love* any woman. Or anything about her except what's between her legs."

"Now, Miss Stella, you can't turn yo' back on that li'l baby. Sho, I got enough milk for two babies, and I *mean* to let yo'n suck when it get hungry and you gone or ain't close by. But, honey, you got to give it suck, too, so it love you the way a baby supposed to love its mammy." Lula May kept glancing nervously toward the door. "I do wish them men come on! That's the way, though, when a woman need—"

The men came in, Jubal tiptoeing, Missouri looking self-assured, almost professional, in fact. If he'd had a medicine case, he could have passed for a renegade doctor escaped to the ranges of the Indian Nations. He went straight to the bedside.

"How many labor pains she done had?" he wanted to know.

"Two in not mo'n fifteen minutes," Lula May told him.

"We got a baby in a right smart hurry to get here."

Feeling trapped by circumstance, Stella was prepared to be displeased with everything. "How would you know?" she sneered. "Did the mares count their pains?"

Missouri grinned sourly. "Why, I've delivered a few babies in my time. Not as many as colts, I don't reckon, but more'n enough to tell the difference between a woman and a mare. Case you're afraid I might start giggling, may as well tell you right off I delivered two of my own brothers. Done what Maw needed done, anyhow. Paw, he was a mountain man and touched home just often enough to keep Maw in a family way mightnear the teetotal year around. He was like a stock raiser whose stock was kids. Soon as Maw'd drop one, he'd breed her back. And twice they wasn't anybody there big enough to help except me. Course, by that time, Maw didn't need much help. Don't reckon you'll believe this here—because nobody else never does—but once I brung a fourteen-year-old girl through a breech birth. White girl, too. And the baby lived. Now, Stella, them's my credentials, and I'll lay you odds my hundred-percent record of live deliveries is better'n that of any four-eyed rumpot you could toll down here from Fort Smith with money. And you heard me right when I called you Stella. Time we get through this here, I won't never be able to call you Mrs. McEveride again. I sure ain't *that* professional."

Looking up into the bleach-eyed, wolfish face with its tobacco bulge at cheek, Stella gradually became aware of something that was shocking. In the ex-guerrilla's pale eyes, which usually registered on their chill surfaces no feelings whatever, there was deep compassion. Suddenly she felt as if she were becoming acquainted with this man for the first time. She knew somehow, in this moment, that Missouri, for all his bloody years as a guerrilla, was a more highly civilized man than Tennessee, the son of a learned judge. She believed firmly—she *knew* by intuition, she told herself—that here was a man who remembered his mother's hardships and understood, therefore, how difficult it was to be a woman in a world where brute strength, more often than not, determined the way of life, deciding who would rule and who would serve. Her rebellious soul almost cried aloud for justice against men who preyed upon women simply because they were physically stronger. Actually, she thought, the civilization of a land could be evaluated almost completely in terms of the way men treated women in that land. Missouri, unlike Tennessee, respected women, deeply honoring them for their courage, endurance, and sacrifice. And because of this new insight into Missouri, she felt drawn to him as she had never been before; from this moment she trusted him completely, confident that he would see her safely through her ordeal.

"You call me Stella," she said gently, "or I'll call you *Mister* Missouri."

Grinning wryly, Missouri turned his head toward Jubal and Lula May, who were shifting from one foot to the other, nervously awaiting orders. "Go build a fire and boil some water. We may not have a whole lot of time. Don't know yet. Lula May, you better fetch in some cloths—towels and sheets—and we ought to have a bed pad of some sort. I got a buffalo hide will do for that." He turned back to Stella as the Negroes headed out. "Stella, this here Lula May don't know nothing about birthing. All she knows is she had a baby herself, so a cow would know as much—more, likely. Anyhow, we can't count on any examination she could make. How a darkie raised in slavery could know so little about having a youngun—"

"My father gave her to me when we were both little girls," Stella explained in a rapid voice. "As my maid, both of us single, how would she learn—see—see what you've done! The poor thing went through that door cry—cry—oh, God have mercy, here it comes again!"

The sweat on her mottled face ran in rivulets in the wrinkles of her contorted features. Missouri knew Stella McEveride as a beautiful woman, but he saw no vestige of beauty in her desperate countenance now. Then, as the pain subsided, her features relaxed and settled into place, smoothing out into the wet, mottled face of Stella McEveride again.

"Honey—" Missouri began, and stopped. "Reckon now I done galloped around the whole track. I've gone from Mrs. McEveride to Stella to honey all in about ten minutes. But, honey, what I want to say is that I'm old enough to be your paw. And even if I wasn't, why, you sure ain't the sort of woman I'd pick for myself, anyhow. I never went in much for red hair and freckles. And the shape you're in—well, what I'm getting at is that I got to examine you, honey, and see can I tell what we got on our hands. Now, you going to flinch when I touch you under the covers? Case you allow you might, why, just think of yourself as a mare in foal. Then likely you can look on me as a doctor."

"All right, go ahead, you—you horse doctor," Stella groaned. "The examination won't be any worse than listening to your talk."

The baby was born at dawn. Before gray light, when the contractions were almost incessant and the agony was no longer to be endured silently, Stella moaned or sobbed or screamed, whichever expression of anguish harmonized best with the chords of feeling produced by the vibrations of her quivering nerves. She did not choose to be brave. She didn't give a damn what impression she was making with her cries on the others in the room; they were in her employ, paid to fetch and carry and serve. Afterward the most vivid part of having the child would become the dimmest memory—the almost unbearable pain. But she would remember what it pointed up—her rejection of the baby forced upon her and her hatred of Tennessee Smith McEveride. She cursed Tennessee in gasps between her moans and cries. She did not call him by name, but her calls upon God to do his damnedest in afflicting somebody who sounded very much like the father of the baby put an odd look in Missouri's eyes.

Then the baby was out of her. She knew it was out because of the tremendous relief, and she closed her eyes, telling herself she would not look. But she had no choice. By a strange compulsion, as naturally as the contractions had come, her eyes opened, and she was horrified. Missouri had come up with a double handful of what looked like a squirming rabbit skinned alive and covered with blood, a mucous slime, fragments of broken waterbag—all the fetal membrane of the afterbirth. The gory mass was made additionally unsightly by the glob of placenta still in Missouri's hands. In Stella's mind the repulsive mass stood as the true image of Tennessee's predatory lust, the visible evidence of his criminal violence upon her. He had crammed this horror into her belly, pushing it up under her heart with his unrestrained hunching, without any love for her, merely for the dirty, greasy thrill in his flesh, careless of the cost to her. But he'd find out what the cost was. He hadn't counted the cost yet. He hadn't begun to count it.

Dimly she heard Missouri's voice asking Lula May to hand him the sterilized pair of scissors so that he could cut the umbilical cord, ordering cloths with which to wipe the infant clean. She heard him say, "We need some oil to grease him with. Ain't you-all got no oil?" And Lula May answered, "*Coal* oil? Lawd God!" Missouri snorted, "No, no. Oh, hell, fetch me some lard. That'll do fine."

Gradually Stella became aware of a sound that was *not* coming from Lula May's baby in the next room, as she had assumed without really thinking. It *was* coming from Missouri's hands there in the kitchen: an infant's lusty squalling. It was *her* baby crying. And the fragile wall she had so carefully built around her heart with words began to crumble and then came tumbling down.

Before she could stop herself, she cried out, "Bring the baby to me!"

Lula May was beside the bed. "We got to get you cleaned up and that bed dry first. We do that while Mist' Missouri in the kitchen fixing up the baby. Now you done had the baby, ain't fitten to change yo' gown and wash you with a man in the room." She beamed upon Stella. "Honey,

you done fine. You got you a big fine boy. 'Bout eight pounds, Mist'
Missouri think. Jubal claim closer to nine.''

"He felt like a *hundred* and nine and about twelve years old.''

Lula May leaned close. "I done told Jubal not to tell nobody how
long Mist' Paul been dead. I don't know what Mist' Missouri gonna
think, though.''

"Leave him to me," Stella murmured. "Nobody must ever know
who the father was. I'd rather folks would think it was some drifter
passing through than know the truth.''

When the baby, wrapped in a blanket, was lying beside her, Stella
leaned on an elbow, looking down upon the tiny face. The red, swollen
little features were contorted in an angry grimace, and the blinking eyes
looked blearily at nothing. And out of the depths of her being there welled
an unreasonable and irresistible love for this ugly atom of humanity. She
thought he was one of the wonders of the world.

"Oh, he's beautiful!" she cried softly. "Isn't he beautiful, Missouri?''

"Sure ain't no doubt about that. What you going to name him?
Missouri?''

"Not on your life." Stella glanced up with her old gamin grin back
in force. "Folks might get the wrong idea. I'm giving him his father's
name. He's Paul Smith McEveride, Jr., and we'll call him Smitty.''

Jubal had moved up beside the bed in time to hear the name. Nobody
met anybody's eyes. Missouri said something about looking in on his
patients later in the day and left the room, motioning Jubal to follow.
From the sound of their voices, they must have stopped walking just
beyond the gallery. Stella motioned Lula May to silence, and they both
hung motionless, listening, hardly breathing.

"How long's Paul McEveride been dead?" Missouri's voice was
pitched low, but not as low as he intended it to be.

"Lessee here, now." They could picture Jubal scratching his head.
"Hum-m-m . . . Lawd God, man, how you 'spect *me* to know that? Ain't
nobody ever told you a nigger can't tell the time of day lessen the sun
shining? And that he live from day to day and don't remember nothing?
Can't be mo'n nine months, though, from what Miss Stella just got
through saying.''

"Jubal, you ain't fooling me none by playing stupid," Missouri
said. "I been around niggers all my life. So I'll tell you this here for what
it's worth. I got a man in mind that sure God needs killing. And I aim to
keep him in mind, too.''

The women barely heard Jubal's soft-voiced reply. "If you thinking 'bout who I think you is, don't reach for no gun or knife in front of him. You a good man, Mist' Missouri. It wouldn't pleasure me none to see you dead."

"I always been able to take care of myself."

"I seed you pull yo' gun and shoot a rabbit once. You a right good shot. But, man, you couldn't live in front of him, and it take a black cat on a dark night to slip up to his back." They moved on, their voices fading.

Later, in early afternoon, Missouri made his call, hat in hand and stepping softly, for the baby was sleeping inside his mother's arm. Something about Stella and her baby made him think of a slim, young female cougar guarding a sleeping cub between her paws. He asked how she was getting along, in a voice barely above a whisper.

Stella assured him all was well and thanked him with gracious warmth for taking care of her. Then she changed her tone and said, "Missouri, I want you to listen carefully to me, now. This is important. As you know, I'm going into the cattle business. Actually, I'm already in it, but I've got bigger plans, and I want you with me all the way—as my bodyguard, personal advisor, ranch-headquarters manager, whatever comes up. So I need you, and I most desperately do *not* want to lose you—ever. So," she held his eyes with a sober, steady gaze, "I want you to forget any suspicions you may have about Tennessee Smith. If I've guessed what they are, you're wrong. Take my word for it. I want your promise that you won't have trouble with him. Believe me, I'm concerned for *you,* not for him."

Missouri's wolfish face softened. "Why, honey," he said gently, "reckon you been holding yourself up to have this here talk with me. You want a promise, you got it. Now you can go on to sleep and get some rest. You look plumb wore out, and no wonder, all you done today."

Three weeks later Slaughter and Weatherford arrived at the old fort and were ushered into Stella's office by Missouri, whom she had instructed to remain in the room for the business meeting with the Texans. Stella was seated in a rocking chair holding the baby. She was wearing a low-cut coral-pink dress, obviously designed to permit easy breast-feeding. Weatherford and Slaughter shook hands with Stella, who remained seated, the baby asleep in her lap. Never had they seen her look more beautiful, a freckled arm around the baby, a misty happiness in her amber eyes, her whole face softened into the matchless mold of the eternal young mother. Weatherford gazed with enchanted eyes, and knowledge of what was working in the young plainsman's head put a deeper shade of color in Stella's cheeks. Then Lula May appeared and carried the baby out, and the compliments on the beauty of her infant son became less restrained as the men found chairs and made themselves comfortable.

Stella proceeded at once to explain at some length her reasons for leaving San Antonio and her change of mind about going back East. Most of her explanation was for Slaughter's benefit, a part of it for Weatherford's. She was pregnant when Paul died but had come on West with her brother-in-law anyway, thinking her condition would not trouble her greatly. She had found in San Antonio, however, that she could no longer manage alone and had started back to Tennessee. Traveling had proved too much for her; so she'd come back to Fort Washita, where she had Lula May, Jubal, and Missouri to look after her. There was another reason, too, for staying in the West: She wanted a herd of big steers put on the trail for New Mexico this spring and another herd following it by fall.

"Before you get into that," Slaughter said, "I got to tell you that John Greenwood ain't with us no longer. He traded his gun for a harp—or maybe swapped it for a pitchfork."

"Hey!... Hey now!" Missouri exclaimed. "What happened to John?"

"Why, he chose Tennessee Smith in a Main Plaza saloon—the place, by the way, where them McClanahans made the same mistake. Done it for money, what Tennessee told all of us that seen it, but all Greenwood collected was lead. I never seen no faster gun work."

Out of a shocked silence Missouri said, "Reckon I ain't surprised that John turned hired killer. Seen him drifting toward it. He never had his mind off his gun after Cullen Baker beat his draw, and he practiced the Lord knows how many hours a day. The world's better off with him dead."

Stella's slanted eyes had a veiled look. "You mean," she said slowly to Slaughter, "that Tennessee thinks somebody hired John Greenwood to kill him?"

Slaughter nodded. "That's what he allowed."

"Who does he think did the hiring?"

"He never said," Slaughter replied. "Course, I never asked."

Stella sank back and let her chair rock gently. "Strange," she murmured.

"Now back to trailing cattle," Slaughter said, reaching for his pipe. "Your plan to gather and trail *two* herds to Fort Sumner by fall just ain't practical, Stella. One, sure—with luck. But with hands to hire and some cattle to buy and road-brand, if you figure on more'n one herd, then, allowing a month to a month and a half on the trail—"

"Wait, Jeff," Weatherford objected. "This here means too much. We ought to push it hard. Look." He leaned forward on the edge of his chair, looking dynamic, impressive, and downright handsome, Stella thought. "Good hands are mightnear begging for any kind of wages. Cattle are swarming like locusts on the grass. Hell, why not double the hands we aimed at, or hire many as we need, and gather two herds, sending you on with the first and me following on later with the second? Why don't that make sense?"

Stella answered, "It makes all the sense in the world, Dick. And we'll do it just that way—*next* year. Like Jeff, I had one trail crew in mind. And one trail boss—you, Dick—to trail the first herd, sell it, and return for the second. If there isn't time for two before winter, we'll trail only one herd this year. I want Jeff to supervise another project of mine that must be carried forward without delay." She got up and walked to a window, looked out, and then turned back.

"I might as well be back in Tennessee as stuck here in this old fort," she declared. "So I'm moving my headquarters, bag and baggage, down to the Clear Fork of the Brazos River in Texas, about thirty-five or forty miles southwest of Fort Belknap. It's beyond the westernmost advancement of settlers, in Indian country, but I've been talking with Colonel Waterton at Fort Gibson, and he says the government is pretty certain to build a line of forts down across west Texas to protect the settlers. Talks about that are going on in Washington right now. Well, Rome Dixon, whom I sent down there to scout out a location, has found a place in line with such forts—unless Colonel Waterton doesn't know what he's talking about. We'll be between Fort Belknap and Fort Chadbourne, both already manned, to some extent, by soldiers. With my own warriors around me, I'll make out until the forts are built." She took a step and turned her warmest smile on Dick Weatherford.

"You hurry on back to San Antonio, Dick, and get that Hourglass herd on the trail," she said. "Hire any extra men you need. Jeff, I want you here for several days to discuss plans and get things moving. You'll have to hire carpenters—you'll know where—and purchase lumber, tools, and building materials. And you'll need men with guns for protection against Indians. Later in the summer I want you back here to help Missouri move us down there. I intend to be settled in those new quarters by fall, and I won't listen to any arguments about that."

Later, after supper, Stella permitted Weatherford to see her alone, since he would be leaving early the next morning. He lost no time in pulling his chair close and capturing her hands; then he proceeded to press for a decision on his proposal of marriage, which had gone unanswered for seven months. So far as he knew, Stella had not made up her mind about what answer she would give him.

"Dick, how *can* you be doing this to me?" Stella protested, somewhat amused by his heated assertions. "Why, it's unseemly, if not downright obscene, for a would-be lover to be pressing a proposal of marriage upon a woman with milk in her breasts. Think of it, taking hold of a mother, trying to embrace her—and her with a baby at her breast! Shame on you, Dick! I'll tell you what you'd do. You'd mash the helpless infant, smother it, that's what!"

Weatherford sank back in his chair, amazed. "Hellfire," he ejaculated, "surely to God your little 'un won't be hanging on a nipple twenty-four hours a day!" Then he saw that she was not wholly serious, save in her determination not to give him an answer until it pleased her, and a sneaking grin widened on his bronzed face in spite of his efforts to suppress it. "And if a fellow got caught up in his work outside, maybe, and run in where you was, say, in kind of a rush, why, surely the baby could be laid aside while—while—long enough to—" Suddenly he burst out laughing. "Stella, I swear you're the damnedest woman ever I seen. You can think up more ways of keeping me hanging and guessing and—oh, hell, let me have ahold of you. You can't claim I'll mash your little baby this here time. And if a kiss is all I can have, I'll sure'n hell take that. I ain't proud."

She let him kiss her, knowing that a day would come when she'd have to tell him that she wouldn't marry him. Wholeheartedly she wished he'd find some eligible, worthy woman and transfer his affections or desires or whatever his feelings were for her to that woman. Suspecting that he was inflammable around attractive females, Stella had thought more than once of finding one for him and setting her in his way. Nancy Waterton would be ideal, she thought—not that she particularly cared about seeing Nancy married safely to some clean-cut young man. Stella never expected to see Tennessee Smith again. Certainly she hoped she wouldn't.

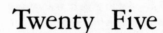

Twenty Five

The first sense to awaken from long darkness was that of taste. Opening his eyes, Tennessee discovered Mary Wilson sitting beside him, holding a spoon of beef broth against his lips. Her face was heavy and patient, her eyes dull. When she carefully tilted the spoon and withdrew it, Tennessee swallowed, finding the broth as good as honey must be to winter-starved bears in the spring.

"Tastes good," he whispered, struggling feebly to shape the words.

Slowly Mary's empty eyes came to focus; then, suddenly, they opened wide. "Lord God," she breathed, "I believe you knowed what you said then!"

"Always know—what—" His weak voice failed him.

Mary smiled, her eyes at once tender with a woman's tolerance of a man's blind assurance. "If you do," she told him, "then you know you been in hell these past few weeks. And I reckon you know that you ain't got no secrets from me no more."

"How come you here—Blanco—Indians—"

Mary studied him with puzzled eyes before she understood. "Tennessee, you're back here in our house on Cripple John Creek, and you're safe. Now, you done talked enough, I reckon. Best you eat this here soup and . . . ."

He awoke at long intervals and remained conscious briefly. Then one day he awoke to find Mary, Jake, and Riley eating breakfast in the early morning. Save for a general lassitude and a sore, itching back, he felt good. He studied the ceiling, orienting himself. Lifting a hand to his bearded face, he started streams of pain in the channels of his upper body and observed with wonder how weighted his wasted arm felt. When he knew who he was and where he was, the tumblers of his mind settled into place, and he remembered. How in God's name had he ever got out of that canyon, he wondered. More incredible still, how had he escaped a swarm of stirred-up Comanches across fifty miles of badlands and got back to the Wilsons' place?

He tried to speak, making an inarticulate sound, and a minute later Mary was standing over him, still chewing. Behind her were Jake and Riley.

"You back with us now, Tennessee?" Mary asked cautiously.

"Reckon so," he said, in control of his voice. "How I get here?"

"Why, we figure hell wasn't ready for you, hon," Mary told him, her eyes glinting with humor, her face solemn. "It looks like the devil withdrawed his help from them Injuns. Nueces got you out of Blanco Canyon and hid you in them badlands at the foot of the Cap Rock. He ain't clear how he done it. He rode in here all shot up, and Jake went out there and packed you in more dead than alive. Don't never be afraid of nothing else, Tennessee. If you'd been five other men, them five licks you taken sure God would killed you all."

"Why ain't Nueces in bed?"

"He's well now," Mary told him. "He *was* in bed—a week, nearbouts."

"Tennessee, I got to tell you," Riley said. "That big dun saved your life. How he beat them Comanches to the mouth of that canyon, I'll never understand. He was mightnear dead all that last half-mile. I want to file the name of *that* hoss in the back of my mind."

"He didn't have none, far as I know." Tennessee turned his face toward the wall. "Don't reckon I ever spoke half a dozen words to him. He just knew what was right to do. Wish now I'd talked more to him. I won't see his like again."

The others exchanged glances, sharing some secret knowledge which they looked forward to imparting. Mary and Riley deferred to Jake.

"Maybe not," he said. "Then, ag'in, you might come closer'n you think. Maybe we done got your next hoss out there in that corral—big sorrel stud, caught wild, a picture hoss with speed and bottom. The Polka Dot Kid brung him down as a gift when he heared the big dun was dead. Didn't want you coming after that Thoroughbred stud, likely. He sure never caught this here hoss with that Kentucky stud, though. Claimed he trapped him in that box-canyon pasture of his. This wild stud jumped in there after the mares. The Kid brung your saddle, too. Got it off one of them Comanch'. Said you could settle for it later."

"What the Kid say about Brownlow Krull?"

Again the Wilsons and Riley exchanged looks. "The Kid claimed they was a sight of squaw howling in them Quahadi tepees," Jake said carefully. "You-all killed maybe five, six Comanch'. Shot up a few more. But I got to tell you, Tennessee, you never killed that cussed Broken Fang—just shot about half his face off."

"Just so I got Brownlow," Tennessee said wearily.

"Aw, you bored him plumb dead center," Riley said, measuring each syllable carefully. "I seen him hit the ground flat. Ain't no doubt about that."

Again Tennessee slept and then awoke to eat and sleep again, and the hours passed into days. Slowly his strength returned, some of it; so slowly that sometimes he wondered whether he had survived his Stone Age wounds or whether he had survived Riley's and Jake's crude surgery; great, jagged patterns of scar tissue would go with him to the grave. Then he began to sit up in a chair a part of each day. He would sit on the gallery with Mary in the afternoon while Jake and Riley were out on the range or in the corral working with the wild stallion. He and Mary would talk as they watched butte and mesa shadows crawl across the great flat beyond Cripple John Creek.

Mary was about thirty-five years old and shapely, a good-looking woman who was honest and plainspoken to a fault. In disposition she reminded Tennessee of Nancy Waterton and, as he did Nancy, he found he liked Mary very much as a friend. Mary told Tennessee things about herself he was curious to know and a few things he would rather not have heard. When she was a motherless little girl, her father, a Forty-Niner, had stepped off the old California Trail and become a nester on Red River in Cooke County, squatting on land claimed by a cattleman whose three sons equaled their father in reputation as bad men. The handsomest and worst of the boys had sought her out in her teens, made her think she loved him, and gotten her pregnant. Discovering her condition, her father had strapped on his gun and ridden to the cattleman's ranch, where he had been shot down in the yard—in self-defense, according to the cattleman, who may well have told the truth.

Thrown on her own, Mary had gone to the county seat, where, in her condition, she was in such desperate circumstances that she attempted suicide. The only person bold enough to come to her assistance when she had a miscarriage was a dance-hall girl with a kind heart and no reputation to lose. When Mary was well again, the only job she could get was in a saloon as a dance-hall girl. In the eyes of the "good" people of the pastoral West, girls who worked in saloons were chippies. Actually, more often than not the judgment was accurate. Because of pressures from both employers and patrons, dance-hall girls on the frontier were rarely allowed to function merely as dance-and-drink entertainers, and Mary was drifting toward the cribs when she met Beef Kramer, a desperado from Indian Territory, and married him to stay out of them.

"Beef was sort of finicky about sex," Mary said. "So, in spite of his loud mouth, I thought he was sort of gentlemanly. Lord God, I found out! If I'd had it to do over, I'd found less shame in selling it than giving it to Beef."

She came to her part in the story of Horse Walking and Earth Daughter one day in late afternoon when bullbats were swooping after insects above the long butte shadows across the creek. From the corral came the trample and pound of a pitching horse, now and then overridden by a wild cowboy yell. Occasionally Jake's voice rose above the drumming hoofbeats, bawling advice or shouting with laughter.

"It's like yesterday that I looked up and seen him standing in the doorway of the dugout. Not bad-looking, neither, for an Injun. But Lord, I reckon my heart near stopped at the sight of him. 'Well, it's come, like I been fearing,' I recollect thinking. He stood there looking at me, and I heared Injun yells and the hosses running out of the corral. But no other buck followed him in. He was a chief. Then his moccasins come whispering across that dirt floor, and he stopped in front of me, and I was smelling the smoky, wild-leather smell of him. Lord God, I thought I'd faint when he put out his hand and combed his fingers through my hair the way you'd fool with the mane of a hoss. That's what I was to him. Most of an Injun's thoughts centers on hosses. He could speak a little English, and he told me I was a palomino mare and he was a sorrel stud, and that if I'd help him make a colt, he wouldn't take me captive. He pushed me down to all fours, and I reckon he wanted to see if I had a straw-colored tail to go with the mane. Because, I mean, he sure had his look."

Mary surprised Tennessee—and probably herself—by blushing. She would not look at him. "Lord God! . . . Oh, well, I've gone this far! Tennessee, think what you want, but I'll tell you one thing—I tried to live up to a mare in heat. I aimed to keep my hair if I could. And I got to admit that, as a lover, he sure was some stallion. Well, Beef was gone for months, and that Injun come back a few times before I got pregnant, and then he didn't come no more till he come for the child." Something akin to pathos was in her voice as she concluded, "Earth Daughter's come here a few times. I like her well enough, but somehow I can't feel no kin to her at all. It's like I had a baby girl and she died. It would been different if I'd raised her. When Hoss Walking come and taken the baby, I stayed on here, trying to figure some way to turn. Then Jake come by and stopped. He'd just had a try at trading with Injuns and give it up. So when we got word that Beef was dead, we decided to get married.''

Tennessee studied Mary's face through half-closed eyes. ''Looks like, risky as it is out here, you would've moved back to settled country, baby gone, feeling the way you did.''

''You don't know how Texas folks are about Injuns.'' Bitterness crept into Mary's voice for the first time. ''Beef, everywhere he went, he never talked about nothing else, I don't reckon. He loudmouthed me and my Injun baby all over the range. And folks remembered what I was before. Back in the settlements women turned their heads and drawed their skirts aside when I walked past, and men waited around corners with their dirty offers. They still would if I went back.''

''By God,'' Tennessee said softly, ''I'd like to walk down one of them streets with you.''

''I know you would,'' Mary said somberly. ''You'd likely kill somebody. You kill mighty easy, Tennessee. A man don't deserve to be killed for wanting to breed a woman—or for breeding her, come to that. Might be good to beat him when he goes at it like a hog, but not *kill* him. Tennessee, I don't hold no grudges against the men who've come at me, even them that done me wrong. The hard meat of a woman-hungry man ain't got no conscience, my friend. And I reckon that's about all I ever learned from any man before I met Jake.''

''I know a woman who wouldn't agree with you,'' Tennessee murmured.

''You think not?'' Mary swept his face with a knowing glance. ''You mean Stella McEveride.'' When Tennessee said nothing, she spoke again, her voice gentle. ''I think you're wrong about her. You talked out of your head about her, and I can guess more than you said. She didn't come looking for Brownlow Krull for what he done to her.'' Mary's eyes were suddenly curious and penetrating. ''And I don't be-lieve she hired that gunman to kill you. She probably knew you was in love with her.''

He was shocked, even appalled. ''She *didn't* know it, and I wasn't,'' he growled.

''You are now.''

''Love!'' Tennessee scoffed. ''What's that?''

''I ain't sure what it is,'' Mary told him, faintly smiling, ''but I know what it ain't. It ain't what me and the bitch dogs had before I met Jake. It ain't what *you* had before you wanted to kill Brownlow Krull so bad you was willing to give up your friend's life and your own to do it. Don't tell me you ain't in love with her.''

Her words struck deep. He hadn't given a thought to the danger he was subjecting Riley to in Blanco Canyon, and he knew that he'd risk the brush hand's life again to get at Brownlow Krull if the latter were still alive. Why? Not because Brownlow had been a member of the gang that had killed the judge and Paul, but because Brownlow had enjoyed the beautiful body of Stella McEveride. By God, he could almost wish the bastard were alive so that he could kill him again!

Was he done with the vengeance trail, then, now that Brownlow was dead? He knew that Mary was right about Stella's view of Brownlow; she had thought of Brownlow merely as a Krull among Krulls—all marked for death, of course. And he knew that Stella had always preferred the deaths of Parson and Jimpson to that of Brownlow. Well, he'd kill them, too. He believed that someday he'd see Stella again, even if he had to make a trip back East. He'd walk into her house, where she was surrounded by her husband and a swarm of her goddamned kids, and he'd say, ''I just come to tell you I done killed all the damned Krulls. So now you can sleep—though looks like you been in the bed pretty steady, like it is. But don't worry. I don't aim to kill this son-of-a-bitch you been screaking the bed with.''

He dragged a shirt sleeve over his sweating face. He suspected, by God, that his chuckle-headed mind would torture him by dreaming up a series of nameless bastards to put on top of Stella, now that Brownlow was no longer handy. Did he, indeed, love her? He didn't know. All he knew was that she was in his blood like a disease, burning him with fever, making him sweat, dulling his instincts for survival. He reckoned that if the devil were willing, he'd swap the rest of his life in hell for a week with Stella in his arms, her voice—soft and sweet, for a change—whispering the damnedest things in his ear.

Steadfastly Tennessee refused Riley's and Jake's invitations to go out to the corral and see the big red stallion. After he was strong enough to walk a reasonable distance without tiring, they could not understand his continued refusals to look at the horse. And they did not understand him—nor believe him—when he explained that he wanted to be strong enough to ride the wild stallion when he first approached him. Riley shouted with laughter and asked Tennessee what made him think he could ride that big red bolt of lightning when the best broncobuster in McMullen County couldn't stick on. Tennessee explained patiently that he would ride the stallion, where Riley had failed to, because the red stud would not try to buck him off. They would see. Riley and Jake glanced at each other without laughing and walked softly out of the house, probably wondering what was under the fresh scar of their friend's head.

When Tennessee was able to ride the range again, he had Riley bring a saddled horse to the house, where he mounted and rode out; when the day's riding was done, he dismounted before the house and turned the horse over to Riley or Jake. By late summer he was fully recovered: His muscular power was back; his steps were light and controlled, as quiet as falling snow again; and when he daily practiced, John Greenwood's ivory-handled Army Colts, which he had reclaimed from Jake, whipped out of their holsters up into his hands faster than the striking heads of stepped-on diamondbacks. Then, finally, he was ready to claim the red stallion as his mount. Before heading for the corral, he instructed Riley and the Wilsons to stay at the house so that the horse would have only one person to think about—himself, Tennessee.

Amused and skeptical, Riley wanted to know whether Tennessee still claimed that the wild horse would not buck with him.

Tennessee grinned. "Well, not today, anyhow."

"What sort of medicine you aim to use?" Jake was equally skeptical; he had rescued Riley from the stallion's trampling hooves more than once.

"Aw, you know, Jake," Mary grinned. "Scent. Tennessee's bottled him up some mare juice."

"Come on," Jake insisted. "What you aim to do?"

"How the hell do I know?" Tennessee said. "I ain't there yet."

He turned and walked off, not toward the corral, but away from it, circling to place a thicket of mesquite between himself and the horse. Coming downwind, he reached the thicket and faded through it to the edge nearest the corral, a hundred yards away. Downwind, the horse would catch his scent and associate it with whatever calls or sounds Tennessee made. Nesting down, he broke off a frondlike branch of mesquite before his eyes and had his first look at the red horse.

The corral was deer-high and buffalo-strong, and the stallion was standing at the far side of it, head lifted to look between the top rails at the distant plains beyond the great flat across Cripple John Creek. Tennessee's view was confined almost exclusively to the horse's rump, and it made him wonder: It was blocky and massive with muscular power, suggestive almost of draft-animal proportions. Then the stallion turned, and Tennessee's heart leaped. The massive rump had suddenly become an unobtrusive part of a clean-limbed conformation that guaranteed great strength, speed, and staying power. Tennessee thrilled to the knowledge that he had seen few horses that could stand in judgment beside this one. Why, the mustang stud would stand close to sixteen hands, Tennessee judged. Some ''mustang!'' So why had the Polka Dot Kid parted with him? According to Jake, the Kid was skinned up and limping. Maybe he'd figured that riding this horse was costing too much skin.

Tennessee quit thinking. Shaping a trumpet with his hands, he called to the horse in a low, clear, far-carrying voice. It was an unpremeditated, unrehearsed articulation, merely his call to a horse—the strange, wild ululation to which the big dun had never failed to respond. Its effect on the red horse was instant and electric. The stallion wheeled, his head tossed high, nostrils flaring, ears pointed alertly. Tennessee called again, and the stallion trotted halfway across the corral and stopped, blowing, tossing his mane. Then he whirled, trotted back, and started stamping the earth in great disturbance.

Tennessee sent forth the weird ululation a third time, and the stallion came storming down the corral, squealing with rage. He halted in a cloud of dust and stood on hind legs, ears flattened, teeth bared, forehooves flashing in the air as if striking at an unseen adversary. Tennessee drifted back through the thicket and circled to the house.

Riley and the Wilsons were lounging on the gallery, listening to the stammer and pound of hooves from the corral. Riley turned his ear to the excited bugling of the stallion. ''He ain't the gentleman that big dun was, eh, Tennessee?'' he grinned. ''But why you reckon he gets mad as hell when you holler like a wolf or an owl or, now that I think, maybe like a ghost tearing loose from a dying redgut witch doctor?''

''Expected him to,'' Tennessee said. ''He hadn't, I wouldn't go back.''

''How you make that sound, Tennessee?'' Mary wanted to know. ''What you trying to sound like?''

''I ain't got the least idea, Mary,'' Tennessee said. ''I just open my mouth and holler.''

''Maybe.'' Mary gave him a curious look. ''Maybe you do, at that.''

At the same time each day for a week, Tennessee nested up in the mesquite and called to the horse. At first the stallion trampled the earth, snapped at the air, and squealed with rage. Then he ran back and forth, blowing, and shaking his mane. Finally he began hugging the fence, as close to Tennessee's position as he could get, whickering excitedly his answers to the call. At the end of the week he was waiting at the fence, trying to see through, when Tennessee arrived.

The next day Tennessee invited his friends to watch him ride the stallion, instructing them to hold back until he was in the corral, then to come on and drop his saddle and bridle over the fence. The stallion was waiting at the fence again. When Tennessee sent forth his eerie, feral cry, the big mustang whickered a greeting and bobbed his head as if beckoning. Tennessee came out of the thicket and crossed the open. Seeing him for the first time, the stallion whirled and thundered to a remote corner of the corral, then whirled back, curveting like a colt. Tennessee swarmed up the fence, chuckling, and dropped to the ground inside. Thirty yards distant, the stallion kept rearing, jerking his front hooves a foot or so off the ground, blowing through distended nostrils. His flat-eared head had a wicked look that was belied by the soft eyes.

Tennessee took a step forward, the animal in his throat whimpering softly, and the stallion whirled and careered deep in the corral, then cut back straight at the intruder, plunging to a halt and kicking the dust not six yards away. Tennessee moved in on the wild horse, giving voice to a mewling yammer that was beginning to have a crooning sound. The horse tossed his head but could not move away. And then Tennessee's hand was stroking the horse's neck, and the red stud was snuffing at the man's buckskin shirt with an inexplicable, equine delight.

Tennessee grasped a tuft of mane and led the stallion over to the bridle and saddle. He had not heard them drop. The big stud jerked his head a time or two before taking the bit; but after the bridle was slipped on, the saddle was something else. The red horse shied away from the saddle, remembering, no doubt, his contests with Riley. As he sidestepped, however, Tennessee followed him with the saddle dangling from one hand. Thirty minutes later the saddle was in place, and two hours after that Tennessee was in the saddle, making his mewling, crooning sound. The big red mustang swung his head, snuffing at the rider's leg, then whirled down the corral, danced around the enclosure, and finally straightened out, walking as if barely restrained from kicking a trail of stardust across the sky.

The faithful gallery was still in attendance, perched on a top rail of the corral. As Tennessee rode past, his face pleased and somewhat smug as well, Jake called out, "By the Lord, I still don't know how you done that!"

"I done told you," Mary said. "Mare juice."

"Open the gate, Nueces," Tennessee called over his shoulder.

Riley jumped to the ground. "You-all watch! This time that hoss will jerk old Tennessee's backsides clean over the Cap Rock!"

"At least you hope so," Mary observed with a knowing smile.

"Course," Riley admitted cheerfully. "I got my pride, lady."

After his next lap around the corral, the red stallion shot through the gate and stretched out toward the open range, running with a drumroll of sound like distant thunder. He was racing with abandon, not at all averse, apparently, to carrying the man with him into the freedom of the open country. In seconds the horse and rider disappeared in a rolling dust cloud that was soon lost behind Long Mesa. They were back in an hour, the horse sweating comfortably after running down the long, hot miles, the rider wide-eyed and grinning.

As they passed the house and headed for the corral, Jake yelled, "How was it?"

"Why, he never touched a dozen blades of grass the whole way!" Tennessee swore blithely. "His name is Grassfire."

By the time late summer had merged with fall, Grassfire and his owner had learned the skills of working cattle, the big red stallion proving the more talented student. Jake and his two helpers were gathering Jake's cattle on the range, planning to throw them into a herd going over the Goodnight Trail to market in New Mexico Territory. When the sweeping wind was turning the cottonwood leaves to glittering gold along the draws, the riders gathered some five hundred head of cattle, about half of what Jake figured he had on the range, and Grassfire became practically a finished cutting horse. He reminded Tennessee of a smart shepherd dog working sheep. He was quick as a cat, and he used his teeth on straying or lagging cattle.

"Give me another week," Tennessee boasted to Riley, "and when I say, 'Buffalo,' why, he'll go among the cattle and cut out the buffaloes."

They were riding toward the house just after sundown, following a cattle trail through a forty-acre patch of mesquite that already was looking like a dead orchard. "Well, you won't get that week," Jake said. "It's too late to trail this year, boys. Winter's mightnear on top of us. Starting tomorrow, reckon we better drift our gather into them canyons west of here. Maybe we can hold 'em together till spring."

"That ain't smart, Jake," Tennessee said. "Them red bastards been watching us steady from the mesas. Like putting a flock of chickens out in front of coyotes."

Riley took a darker view. "We might be lucky if them redguts don't come down here after nothing but cattle. I keep on wondering why that damn Broken Fang ain't drummed up a vengeance raid and come down on this place before now."

"Yeah," Tennessee agreed, "after you and me. Sure didn't do you no favor coming here, Jake. Nueces, we've got to get away from here.''

"You want my opinion, it's already too late for just us two to leave. What I think, all *four* of us ought to slide out of here. And soon—like tonight."

"No," Jake said, "if there was a vengeance raid shaping up, we'd likely heared from a peace chief up there named Hoss Walking."

"That Hoss Walking!" Riley shook his head. "Maybe so. And maybe *his* medicine's done gone sour."

It took them three days to place the cattle in the canyon country. It took one long night for about forty Comanche raiders to spirit the cattle out of the canyons and vanish with them into the breaks of the Cap Rock. Jake rode out the next day to check on the cattle. Tennessee came out later to be with Grassfire, though he swore he was riding just for the hell of it, and Riley went along without giving a reason. When they were a mile or so west of Long Mesa, they saw Jake heading back. Instead of pulling up and waiting for them to come to him, he kept coming. When they met him, he drew in and sat slumped in his saddle, watching them narrowly without speaking. Then he rolled the tobacco in his jaw, squeezed it with his cheek, and spat off to the side.

"Well, they're all gone," he said. "Comanch' run 'em off."

Tennessee stared. "The cattle?"

"Ever' goddamned head."

"Well, hell—let's get on back there, then."

Jake's jaws worked steadily. He spat again. "What for?"

"Why, get on that sign. Follow 'em."

"Follow forty Comanch' into the Staked Plains?" Jake shook his head. "Uh-unh; might catch up. And not if there was just three or four." He straightened in the saddle and lifted his shoulders, trying to pull himself together. "Listen, boys, this here's the way she shapes up. We can't figure them Comanch'—don't know whether Hoss Walking knows about this here raid, what he'll do, or *can* do, when he does hear, whether he's losing out to that son-of-a-bitch Broken Fang. It may be he's still high in the saddle and this here's the closest to a vengeance raid Broken Fang can get away with. If he *don't* dare more, he won't *do* no more. We follow these here and kill a Comanch' or two or get back the cattle, next time they'd sure God come after our hair. Whichever, though—and take this right—maybe in the next few days you fellows ought to take that trip you been planning over in the Pecos Country. Them Comanch' might settle back once you two are gone. Like I say, talking like this makes me feel bad. It's just that I got Mary to consider—''

"Why, Jake, don't say no more!" Tennessee said. "We'll leave tomorrow. Tell you what you might do, though. Write out a description of these Comanche-stolen cattle, giving me power of attorney to take possession of 'em wherever I find 'em. May not be legal, but might give me a handle on Parson Krull in Puerto de Luna or wherever I find him, and we might get your cattle away from them *comancheros*. There's a chance—not much, but some—they're driving your cows to market for you free."

Twenty Six

Locating Jake's cattle was a hope that did not materialize. The only evidence they ever found that the cattle had reached New Mexico was a cowhide hanging on a high adobe wall of a great corral in Puerto de Luna. The hide carried the straight-iron burn of Jake Wilson's Tepee brand, but Tennessee and Riley could find nobody who had seen a Tepee herd or knew from whence the rotting hide had come. The Mexican village, however, was reported to be an important *comanchero* base. They were destined to find in this land of white sunlight and black shadows that the smiling, sun-baked people they questioned would profess knowledge of almost everything save one thing—*comancheros*.

After several days of learning nothing in the village, they tired of the tequila in the *cantinas* and rode back to Fort Sumner. From the little Mexican settlement of Punta de la Glorietta to the fort, they rode between two rows of cottonwoods which bracketed four miles of broad, smooth thoroughfare. Soldiers, probably using bayonets as pointers, had directed the Navajos in planting these cottonwoods in a largely treeless land. The trees ended abruptly at the edge of Fort Sumner, though the thoroughfare continued southward, separating the stores, saloons, and shops backed against the Pecos River from the big parade ground that was surrounded by barracks and officers' quarters off to the east.

The *cantina* of Juán Lopez stood near the river not far from the last cottonwood. Here Panchita Candelaria, the owner's sister-in-law, nightly kept her magnificent black eyes on the ebb and flow of *pesos* from pockets of customers to cash drawer of *cantina,* and on the conduct of the *cantina* girls with the *hombres* who came to the place of Juán Lopez for tequila, pulque, and women. And the *hombres*, in their turn, kept their eyes on Panchita—on all of her, to their great discomfort. For Panchita's sinful-looking body, with its proud, firm breasts, slim waist, and curved hips, was shaped for bed, and Panchita did not drink or leave the room with any of the *hombres*.

On his first visit to the *cantina*, Tennessee had caught Panchita watching him. While he was paying for the drinks, she had found occasion to inform the big, tawny *gringo* that she was part-owner of the *cantina*, that she was not a *cantina* girl, and that she was very strict with her morals. On his second visit, Panchita had managed to lose her balance and fall against Tennessee's burly shoulder, and one of her hands had caught his arm to steady herself. When her fingers had dug into his upper arm, Panchita had not been able to repress a faint moan at the feel of his might. Tennessee thought that this third visit might prove the charm. He was getting desperate for information.

It was not long before closing time when they hitched the horses in front of the *cantina*. "There's a *vaquero* or *comanchero* or some kind of greaser passing news to that Panchita mightnear every hour of the day," Riley commented. "So she sure knows plenty, and the other girls swear Panchita ain't sleeping with no man. Reckon you done seen how she looks at you. Surely you ain't so stupid I got to draw your picture on top of her."

"All I want from her is information," Tennessee said. "If I have to get it in bed, all right. Looks like I can't count on you. Might as well geld you for draft stock."

Only half a dozen customers remained inside. Panchita was getting into her cloak, preparing to leave early. At sight of Tennessee in the doorway, she ceased all motion. She stood half in and half out of her cloak, a look of wariness in her eyes. He moved up to hold her cloak, feeling a tremor run through her as he touched her shoulder.

"Leaving now?"

"*Sí*, I—I mus' go," she said uncertainly. "My modder's brodder, he is ver' sick at my house."

"Let me walk you home," Tennessee suggested. Then, as she caught her breath in alarm, he added, "If you want, I'll leave you at the door."

"Before then, *señor*," she said quickly. "My modder's *familia*, they are ver' strict. You can come but little way weeth me, *hombre*."

As they passed Riley on their way out, Tennessee said, "Hang around. Be back in a few minutes."

Behind the last of the business houses, with the troubled Pecos gurgling a few yards away, she halted. Here the air was heavy with the not wholly unpleasant rankness of a stable, but under it he caught the elusive fragrance of a delicate perfume that unsettled him. Her face was a patch of lighter shade in the darkness as she whispered, "*Señor*, another night—*quién sabe*? But you mus' not go no fodder. I weel kees you good night, though." She moved in against Tennessee and opened her soft, warm lips to him, and there was some light, fleeting tongue-play—learned, perhaps, by observing the strokes of butterfly wings. With studious body motions and gently grinding precision, she checked out his essential qualifications. "Oh, *hombre, hombre*," she moaned, "I pray that you don't peeck me up and carry me off!"

"By God, I got a better idea!" Tennessee was in a genuine sweat. "I'll kill your damned uncle, and then we'll get in your bed."

For a moment she seemed to consider his suggestion reasonable; then she was against it. "I don' want nobody keel in my house," she decided.

Tennessee drew her back into his arms and kissed her urgently. "Panchita," he demanded softly, "where's my best bet to find that old *comanchero* Parson Krull?" He held her arms and looked in her eyes. "Won't do no good to claim you don't know." He kissed her one more time. "Tell me now."

After a silence in which she appeared undecided, Panchita whispered raggedly, "You mus'—not say—who tell you. Five mile from Tucumcari Mountain on Plaza Larga Creek. The Parson Krull and Wes, they have the *rancho* there." Suddenly, from a whisper, her voice rose with a fierce intensity. "Keel them, *hombre*! Keel them both!"

"So you know Wes, too, huh?" Tennessee said.

"He is a peeg!" she spat.

"Well, I hope your uncle gets better soon."

"He is a peeg!" Panchita repeated and, turning, walked away.

The building behind which they had stood was the livery stable where Tennessee and Riley had been keeping their pack horse and, when not in use, their saddle mounts, too. Dawn was a graying promise over the distant *Llano Estacado* when Tennessee turned a corner of the stable and eased into the runway. He found Riley asleep in the hayloft and reached to nudge him awake. Before Tennessee's hand touched flesh, however, he found himself looking down into wide-open blue eyes that were staring coolly upward.

"A 'few minutes,' huh?" Riley grunted. "Damned if our ideas of that match up a-tall. That greaser gal wear you out?"

"Get up and grab your saddle. I saw Wesley Krull ride north awhile ago. I figure he'll lead us to the parson—up near Tucumcari Mountain, from what I heard."

"The hell you say! Then Panchita did—"

"Yeah. Claimed Wes was a sick uncle in her house. But you got to admit she's pretty strict. She run Wes out of her bed before daylight."

Riley sank back in the hay, groaning. "Well, if Wesley Krull's done gone," he pointed out reasonably, "she's sure'n hell lonesome now, Tennessee. What she needs is a heavy-hung fellow like you as a follow-up. Why don't you go on back—"

"Me ride a wet saddle?" Tennessee's lips shaped a faint, wry smile. "Get your ass up. We're on our way."

Some seven miles north of Fort Sumner, the tracks of Wesley Krull's horse left the Pecos road leading to Puerto de Luna and took a northeasterly direction across country. In this change of direction Tennessee detected the spoor of a fox. Why had Wesley gone out of his way for seven miles along the river road? He could have traveled the Fort Sumner–Fort Bascom road that passed within five miles of Tucumcari Mountain and within ten of the ranch on Plaza Larga Creek. Whom was he trying to deceive as to his destination?

They rode steadily through the day, holding to the northeast, and Tucumcari Mountain was rising on the horizon before deepening dusk closed it off. Soon thereafter, two miles ahead of them, a big greenhorn fire blazed up and steadied, burning like a beacon in the night. Tennessee and Riley made camp without a fire, chewing jerky and hardtack and drinking water. The big fire worried them. Nevertheless, Tennessee found himself dozing off between bites.

"I'd swear that Wesley Krull knows we're trailing him close," Riley said finally. "Still, he builds that tenderfoot fire. You sure Panchita didn't tell him nothing?"

"Figure she told him something or other. Didn't tell him I followed her home and waited outside to watch him leave. She didn't know that." Tennessee looked around sleepily. "Sort of sorry for her, Nueces. He's got her scared half to death."

"You think she lets him in her bed because he's got her scared half to death?"

"Well—" Tennessee was unrolling his blanket. "Well, yeah, I'd say that's one reason. She's got another'n, though. One of us ought to go check that bastard. Be like him to pull foot and soft-hoof off in the dark while we're watching his fire.''

Riley got up and passed between Tennessee and the distant light; he walked off into darkness, and then he came back, standing close. Tennessee turned in his blanket, looking up from the ground.

''What's the greaser gal's other reason?''

''Strict woman like Panchita,'' Tennessee said drowsily, ''she can enjoy herself with a man she's scared to death of. She can claim no choice and get on her back with a good conscience.''

Riley grunted in agreement, or perhaps disagreement; Tennessee didn't concern himself with the brush hand's opinion. He was aware, in the back of his mind, that there was something he was forgetting . . . some damned thing . . . something almost in reach. . . . To hell with it, he thought, and, for the first time in thirty-seven hours, went to sleep.

Around midnight Tennessee sat bolt upright. Suddenly he came scrambling out of his blanket and leaped to his feet. ''Goddamn it,'' he snarled, ''wake up!''

''What the hell!''

''What you see at the fire?''

''Seen Wesley Krull. Who you think? Him rolled in his blanket and his horse picketed close.''

''There you are!'' Tennessee sounded as if he were in physical pain. ''The son-of-a-bitch is long gone!''

''You just woke up. You don't know that.''

''Hell I don't. If he aimed to get in his blanket instead of cook, why'd he build the fire? What we forgot—what I forgot—is that he's Indian raised. Much as Brownlow and Jimpson, if he *is* white himself. He knew we's trailing him, knew we'd scout his camp. That fire was to mark his camp and show him and his horse settled for the night. Smart bastard's got a three-hour start on us. Only excuse I got for missing his trick is that I's so damned beat I didn't have no sense, and I reckon you were, too. Now we can't trail him, and we don't know where to go on Plaza Larga Creek. What we got to do is head for Tucumcari Mountain and scout for tracks. Be light enough to see by then. From here on he'll make his tracks hard to follow.''

Wesley Krull was indeed long gone, leaving only the ashes of his big fire. Later they figured that he had turned due east in darkness from his false camp, made a wide circle, and come in to the parson's wet-weather ranch on Plaza Larga Creek from the east, thus leaving no tracks between Tucumcari Mountain and Plaza Larga Creek. Just before dark they stumbled on the ranch—a dugout, a barn that was little more than a shed, and a makeshift horse corral. The only sign in the vicinity that cattle had been held on the range was months old. There was evidence around the dugout and the corral of the hasty departure of five riders, three besides the Krulls.

"Reckon the parson wanted better odds than five to two," Tennessee complained bitterly. "Son-of-a-bitch might've made a stand if he had twenty men."

"You're looking at them odds from *your* viewpoint," Riley said. "Take a look from the parson's and that five to two means five *co-mancheros* against Tennessee Smith and some fellow good enough with a gun to side him. If I's the parson, I wouldn't like them odds, neither."

They spent the night in the parson's dugout and rode out the next morning as soon as it was light enough to get their direction from the tracks of the five ridden horses. The hoofprints pointed north, toward Fort Bascom on the Canadian River. And the tracks touched base at the fort, as the pursuers learned from Captain Romine before noon. Romine was standing on the steps at headquarters, as if waiting for them, when they rode into the fort. He was at Tennessee's stirrup as Grassfire came to a halt.

"They were here, Smith!" he said excitedly. "Finally I've laid eyes on old Parson Krull!" There was a shine in Romine's eyes. "I even spoke with him."

Tennessee dismounted and shook hands. "He know I'm after him?"

"*Does* he! He and that son of his agreed that you'd be close on their trail. The son, by the way, seems to be the leader of the bunch." Suddenly a wide grin of amusement made Romine's face look like the mischievous countenance of a wicked schoolboy. "You wouldn't believe what terror you've inspired in those hardy ruffians! They're in a panic—all except the son. If it weren't for him, I believe the old *comanchero* would seek refuge with the Comanches, where two of his sons already are, I understand."

"One," Tennessee corrected. "Brownlow's dead."

"Oh, really?" Romine was surprised. "I hadn't heard. When was he killed?"

"Back in the spring," Tennessee said, glancing at Riley, who had his back turned. "In Blanco Canyon."

Something—some kind of uncertainty—withdrew into the deep shadows of Romine's eyes and was gone. He did not ask for any details concerning the killing, and Tennessee assumed the reason he didn't was that he simply was not much interested in Brownlow Krull as a person.

"You get any lead on where they're headed?"

Romine nodded. "Maybe I did—where the two Krulls, at least, will come together eventually. I just caught the tag end of talk between Wesley and the parson. My impression is that somebody in Santa Fe's holding some money for them and that they'll meet there in a month to pick it up. They rode off in opposite directions, the parson toward the Staked Plains and Wesley toward Puerto de Luna or maybe Albuquerque. Anyhow, he rode west. The other three scattered off like flushed quail, no two together. You see, Smith, that scattering into five trails instead of one is the favorite dodge of Indians when hotly pursued. Wesley's idea, of course. And make no mistake about that. Oh, they're wary as wolves."

"Thanks," Tennessee said. "Now, if you'll make it right with your cook, we'll grab a bite and head out."

"Follow me," Romine said genially and walked toward the mess shack. "Tennessee, the Krulls got fresh horses here. The colonel permitted the exchange over my protests. What I wanted was to throw that bunch of villains in the guardhouse." A frowning seriousness roughened his brow. "But the colonel wouldn't hear to it." He cut the air with a hand. "Of course, you can't get a conviction against a *comanchero* in a New Mexican court. Really made me feel bad, though, to watch those scoundrels ride off without lifting a hand."

"Didn't expect you to lift a hand," Tennessee assured him. "I'll lift the hand when I catch up."

When they had eaten and were preparing to mount up and ride out, Romine suddenly snapped his fingers. "Why, I almost forgot! Congratulations, Smith, on becoming a—ah—an uncle, isn't it?"

Tennessee looked at him hard. "What the hell you talking about?" he demanded harshly.

"Why, Stella's—Mrs. McEveride's baby. I assumed you knew she'd given birth. At old Fort Washita. An eight-pound boy, I understand." Under the lift of the officer's brows, his slate-colored eyes were probing intently. "Doesn't that make you an uncle?"

Slowly, numbly, Tennessee pushed back his hat, as if it had become too tight for him, but his hard face remained impassive. He had the faculty of suspending his emotions in moments of shock or stress. At such times his perceptions remained sharp and his judgments objective. This faculty, as much as any other, had enabled him to keep alive. It had failed him only once—in Blanco Canyon. Only an iron schooling kept it from failing him now.

"I ain't heard a word from Stella since she left San Antone," he said. "I thought she went back to Tennessee."

"Then you don't know that she's quit the vengeance trail, apparently, and started ranching and trailing cattle. She has a ranch, the Hourglass, a few miles from San Antonio and has already trailed and marketed one herd at Fort Sumner—at top prices, too, since she has influential army connections. Trail boss was Weatherford, that good-looking ex-Ranger she had hanging around in San Antonio. Mrs. Mc-Everide has surrounded herself with a hard-case crew, and I mean *hard-case!* Civil War guerrillas, brush poppers from Brasada country, and a whole bunch of ex-Rangers Jeff Slaughter came up with. And Weatherford has a collection of curly wolves riding between those steers and any would-be raiders on the trail. Really, I'm surprised she doesn't have you, since I'm quite sure she doesn't have anyone like Tennessee Smith—that is, unless she hired that Fort Smith gunman. What's his name? Mysterious Pete Epps. She probably hired him *and* his gun. She meant to. Went to see him, I know that. I saw her coming out of his boarding house in Fort Smith."

Tennessee's face might have been cast in bronze, but his eyes were flaring with a pale, cold light that grew brighter and brighter. "The baby, goddamn you!" he said very softly. "What about the baby?"

"What—what—" Romine's dark face roughened into a scowl, but he seemed more puzzled than offended. "Why, it's a boy. I said that. Somewhere, I judge, around eight or nine months old. It's, well—oh, I don't know! What the devil can you say about a baby?"

"Where'd you hear all this? From Weatherford?"

"No." Romine watched Tennessee narrowly, as if searching for some symptom of internal bleeding. "Some of it from Mrs. McEveride herself. I had to make a trip to Fort Smith last summer. I told you I saw her there. She and one of her men were there buying wagons, supplies—outfitting to move down into Texas, to new headquarters on the Clear Fork of the Brazos. She's down there by this time. My other informant was a friend of mine who's stationed at Fort Gibson—Captain Armistead G. Randolph. Incidentally, he's head over heels in love with our rich young widow, as is Weatherford, and would be delighted to hear that Weatherford was on the trail with cattle twelve months out of the year. He confessed a fear that the lady had made some sort of commitment to Weatherford and—oh, yes, he thinks there's a good chance that a new fort, to replace Belknap, will be established on the Clear Fork, and he's all set to pull strings and get transferred down there where the lady is. He just might win out over the Ranger. An officer and a gentleman from an old family in Virginia would make an excellent father for that boy. Don't you think she'd consider *that*, Smith?"

Tennessee was preparing to mount Grassfire, hiding his face from

Romine lest its stiffness reveal the murderous passion that was slugging the blood out of his heart. He said in a voice strained to neutrality, ''I don't know what she'd consider. I don't have no word from her. I told you that. You want the truth, she hates me. The day she hears I'm dead, she'll celebrate.''

''But why? Man, what did you do?'' Romine asked.

''Nothing,'' Tennessee said, rising to the saddle. ''Not a god-damned thing. She's a woman. She don't need no reason to hate a man.''

''Let me ask you this.'' Romine raised his voice as Tennessee reined away. ''You intend to keep after the Krulls, now that Mrs. McEveride's quit?''

''If she *has* quit. So long.'' Tennessee swung Grassfire alongside Riley's mount, and the two horsemen rode on past headquarters, heading out toward the Canadian crossing.

Before they reached the river Tennessee said thoughtfully, ''Wait a minute,'' and pulled up. ''No reason to doubt Romine, I don't reckon,'' he said, ''but we better check out the Krulls' horse tracks before riding a hundred miles out of our way. Let's go round the fort a couple of miles out. You ride back the way we come and circle east around to the north. I'll cross the river and circle east to south. When we meet, we ought to know pretty well whether them tracks kept on going the way they started.''

Several hours later they rested their horses in the shade of a huge cottonwood near the lip of a dry wash, each reporting that Romine's account of directions taken was accurate.

Finally Tennessee turned to Grassfire. ''I won't need you any longer, Nueces,'' he said over his shoulder, and rose to the saddle. ''Not hunting Krulls. Let's head back south.''

Riley mounted all in one motion. ''What you cutting me loose for?'' he wanted to know. ''Getting tired of my company?''

Tennessee grinned. ''Done took up too much of your time, and after today, seeing how that foxy Wes scattered them bastards every which way, I can see that it's going to take a long time to run 'em down. Years, maybe. Tell the truth, Nueces, Mary set me thinking. I almost got you killed without giving a single thought to it. But I won't forget Blanco Canyon. I can't pay you for that. Just remember this, though: You ever get in trouble anywhere at all, holler, and I'll do whatever needs done and get you out of it.''

Riley studied the pommel of his saddle. ''You don't owe me nothing,'' he said gruffly. ''I owed you what I done in that canyon. We're just even, that's all.''

"Will you tell me what you did do?" Tennessee asked curiously. "All you've told me is sketchy and don't half make sense."

"I done told all I aim to," Riley said with a sheepish grin. "It's sketchy in *my* head, too. I's hurting and bleeding and nearbouts addle-headed half the time. I will say, though, what I think—them redguts quit before they had to because they thought their chief was dead and their medicine had done gone sour. Tell the truth, I don't want to think no more about it, Tennessee. Turns me sick at my stomach to remember just how goddamned scared I can get. I didn't know before."

"Well, I ain't cutting you loose complete," Tennessee said mildly. "Not a man that gets scared exactly the way you do. I aim for you to take a note to Jeff Slaughter at San Antone. Stella McEveride's hiring every other son-of-a-bitch in Texas, looks like. She might as well hire you."

"No need to write no note," Riley said quietly. "Jeff Slaughter tried his best to hire me when I seen him in San Antone. I been out to that Hourglass."

Tennessee, with a blank face, considered this new evidence of the boy's integrity. He realized that Riley could have been working under the protective umbrella of Stella's hard-case crew, with an excellent chance of getting ahead in her expanding cattle business, and had turned it down to put his life on the line against the worst Indians in the West because of a debt only *he* thought he owed.

Tennessee reined Grassfire around, unable to think of a comment to make about Riley's actions that wouldn't embarrass an uncurried brush hand from Dog Town, Texas. "Let's head back toward Fort Sumner," he said. "Before I stretch out on a long trail behind them Krulls, I want a talk with that Panchita. Maybe I can get lucky and cut that fox off from his den."

"Good place to hunt," Riley agreed.

Riding south, Tennessee could not keep his mind on the problem of catching up with the Krulls; his thoughts kept harking back to what he'd heard from Romine. He knew he was a father, not an uncle. He remembered a trip to the bushes in an overnight camp in north Alabama, remembered a bloody rag Stella had probably covered with leaves and sticks and some roaming dog had found and dropped in the open. She was *not* pregnant before reaching Texas. She *was* pregnant before reaching San Antonio. Her hatred for him, then, was understandable and reasonable. So was Greenwood's attempt to kill him. So would be the presence of Mysterious Pete Epps in New Mexico Territory; Tennessee laid a bet with himself on that.

He knew he had destroyed both Stella's physical ability and her will to continue her quest for revenge; he had opened a channel that had drained off most of her hatred in his direction. But the fact remained that the wrong with which the Krulls had blackened her life was still unavenged. He would avenge her—unless one of the Krulls or one of her own assassins stopped him. And in that event she might feel an even more gratifying revenge, he reckoned. By God, he would serve her in another way, too. He would stay the hell away from her and that baby.

He kept thinking of Stella and her commitment to Weatherford, of Stella and Randolph, the army officer who was jealous of Weatherford. "My husband dies, and I give up men," he remembered her saying. "I take a vow of chastity as truly as ever a nun took one." Well, he could thank himself—or curse himself, rather—for changing her mind. "I'm a healthy female," she had said. "If a mare in season is bred even to a jack, doesn't nature make her feel pleasure?" Aw, goddamn me for a fool! he thought. He closed his eyes tight. I've got to get that woman out of my mind! I'm as close to her right now as I'll ever be.

Twenty Seven

In 1868, the year the Indian reservation at Fort Sumner was abandoned, the Navajos returned to the Canyon de Chelly country beyond the northwestern edge of New Mexico Territory. When the army left Fort Sumner, along with the Indians and the soldiers departed also the biggest, steadiest cattle market in New Mexico. Stella McEveride had to determine what to do about the holding grounds for her Texas herds, which were on the Pecos below Bosque Grande. For over a year now Dick Weatherford had been in charge there. It was from this range that cattle, trailed in from Texas, had been fattened on the grama grass and then driven to market at the forts, primarily Fort Sumner, or trailed north to Stella's swing-station ranch in Colorado, where new ranges were being stocked and miners were in need of beef.

On a day in late spring, Stella rose and went to her office in the largest of the log structures, save for the huge barn, in the complex of buildings which formed her headquarters on the Clear Fork of the Brazos River. The room had the equipment common to business offices, but it was unusual, too, in its sheer, white curtains and green drapes at the windows, its gold-colored cushions in comfortable chairs, and its Argand round-wick lamps with white-and-green shades that picked up the colors of the curtains and drapes. The room had been designed, of course, as a setting for Stella, whose red hair was a light in the room. She was conducting a man's business in a man's world, and she wanted all the advantage she could get. Here Stella kept the records of her far-flung cattle interests and projected most of their directions of growth and their conditions of change.

Today she had three decisions to make: Whether to give up the range on the Pecos; whether to answer yes or no to Armistead Randolph, who was at nearby Fort Griffin, the new fort on the Clear Fork, still under construction; and whether to give Dick Weatherford a single firm and final answer to his multiple proposals of marriage. Expecting Weatherford to arrive at any hour of day or night to confer with her, she was determined to have her answers ready before he arrived.

Stella knew, of course, which one of her decisions Dick was spending around a full month of round-trip riding to hear. She would have given him her answer by homing pigeon and ordered him to remain on the Pecos, save that she was afraid he would quit her service when he learned the whole story unless she was with him to talk him into staying. For she was not merely rejecting Dick; she was seriously considering marrying another man. Then, too, she had only one pigeon left that would home back to the Pecos, and Dick couldn't have more than one or two on hand that would fly back to headquarters. The supplies of homing birds at both ends needed replenishing, and Dick's trip back and forth would take care of that need.

She got up and moved casually to the window and then to the door. Down the length of the quadrangle, two of her men were pitching horseshoes near the barn, and three more, atop the corral fence, were offering derisive advice to Missouri, who was making a point of ignoring their very existence as he gentled a skittish, unbroken horse. A breeze stirred, bringing a fragrance that reminded her of summer, or maybe it was the cicadas throbbing in the trees of the quadrangle that reminded her of summer.

She hurried back to the desk and, reaching far back into a drawer under a stack of papers, drew forth a brown envelope. Raising the flap, she removed the contents and spread them on the desk before her. They were slips of paper—carefully selected messages flown from New Mexico by homing pigeons—and they all concerned the activities of Tennessee over the past year and a half.

She arranged them chronologically on the desk and leaned forward in her chair, elbows on desk, studying them somberly, though she could have quoted every word of every one of them from memory. The messages read:

Tenesee Smith run them Krull comancheros clean across country and down Rio Grande and back across to the Steak Planes. Dont know whether he killed any of them scannels or not cause he aint passed a word about what he done. But they dont dast to steal no cattle or do around much no more cause he has got them too scared to spit.

Dick

Misterios Pete Epps a hard killer come to Sumner to kill Tenesee Smith. He drawed on Smith in Murphys saloon. If he didnt collect his mony fore he come he sure will be broke in hell.

Dick

A feller got off a comanchero waggen in Puerto de Luna and taken a shot at Tenesee Smith which he didnt have no time left to take no othern. And no time left to breathe neither. When the smoke cleerd Tenesee looked down and called the feller Zeke. Far as I know he didn't have no other name.

Dick

Fore Tenesee Smith could get out of town after they planted Zeke a bad kid lookin fer rep and glory chose him on the street. The kid never made no rep but he shore went to glory in a cloud of smoke.

Dick

You said pass along news about Tenesee Smith cause hes yore kin. Well I met him and a mitey purty lady hossback ridin tween Las Vegas and Fort Union. He innerduced her as Miss Nancy Waterton and said shes visitin the cunnels daughter at the fort. They was so wrapped up in each other I swear they would of rode me down if I hadnt hollered.

Dick

I hadnt no moren got home than word follered me down the trail from Las Vegas that Tenesee Smith and a gambler name of Ace McQueen ennertaned at a get together. Some say the cardsharp follered Miss Waterton far as Vegas. Others claim he was trailin Smith. When they got together for two handed draw Smiths pair of 6s beat McQueens ace high. So the tinhorn folded.

Dick

Tenesee Smith wownded a wildhare fool lookin fer rep last
week. Done it a purpos. And next day he buffalod anothern.
Claimed he was runnin low on powder ann lead.

                                                    Dick

What had once been a myth-making whisper concerning a big,
tawny rider on a wild red stallion—the man called Tennessee Smith—
was now sweeping the New Mexican ranges in open voice. Stella had
heard this voice in the mouths of drifters and outlaws and cowboys riding
chuck line. It had traveled with the drovers back to Texas along the
Goodnight Trail and gone back enlarged by narrations of exploits involving the Watson brothers, John Greenwood, and Beef Kramer. It had been
enlarged by credit for dead men whom Stella would swear he had never
heard of. Stella was beginning to believe that the only man-killer in the
Southwest too modest to announce his killings on far-flung, lonely trails
was Tennessee Smith. Gradually, too, stories of bloody deeds committed
before and during the war were coming out of the Old South and lending
their dark accretion to the growing legend.

He won't live the year out, Stella predicted darkly. She recalled
Mysterious Pete Epps, the deadly little gunman with the corpse-white
face and sick, mad-dog eyes, and shuddered. But obviously Tennessee
was more deadly still than that little hired assassin had been. What if
Tennessee came back someday to claim the child as his son . . . and her as
his. . . . She felt his hard-muscled arms holding her, his savage mouth
crushing her lips, his brutal flesh hot inside her. . . . She shook herself
free of a memory that too often came close to fantasy. If he ever came
close and got his big hands on her, she knew she would be lost. So she had
resolved long ago that whatever she had to do to protect herself and the
boy from Tennessee, she would do.

Now Stella found herself, as she always did, returning to the two
messages that mentioned Nancy Waterton. She brooded over them, not at
all amused by Dick Weatherford's sardonic levity nor by the plainsman's
discovery in himself of a bent for turning a phrase. Strangely enough, it
had never occurred to her that marriage between Tennessee and Nancy
would prove the best possible safeguard in keeping Tennessee and his
"big hands" far removed from her own person. She fiercely opposed the
development of any romance between Tennessee and Nancy and told
herself that her objections reflected concern for the girl's welfare and
happiness. Wondering how Nancy could keep in touch with Tennessee
and arrange their visits together, Stella wondered at the same time how

far their relationship—whatever it was—had carried them. The girl could reach him by letter at Fort Sumner, if he knew to call for mail, she figured; and their relationship had gone as far as Tennessee wanted it to go; she had no doubt of that.

She felt a sinking sensation inside her as she tried to envision Nancy Waterton successfully repulsing or even attempting to resist one of Tennessee's amatory attempts upon her virtue. According to news brought down from Fort Gibson by Armistead, Nancy was back home now from her visit to Fort Union, where the social life was famed in army circles and along the Santa Fe Trail for its variety and liveliness. She'd had a wonderful time, if Armistead was any judge, and seemed perfectly happy.

Armistead Randolph, as handsome as a captain as he had been as a major when she'd seen him in Chattanooga, had not remained long at Fort Gibson. His desire for action in the field against the Comanches and Kiowas had caused him to pull every string he could as soon as he'd learned that Fort Griffin was being established only four miles downstream from Stella's headquarters ranch. The result of his appeals to influence was a recent transfer, and now the gallant and soldierly Randolph was the captain of a company of cavalry at the fort. He came to see Stella regularly—as often as possible—and he was a welcome suitor.

A change in the pitch of voices outside caused her to go to the window and look out again. Weatherford was riding past the house with two pack mules in tow, headed down one side of the quadrangle toward the barn and corrals. Stella rushed back to the desk and, almost guiltily, returned the slips of paper to the envelope and the envelope to the drawer. The men at the barn were converging upon Weatherford with handshaking and loudmouthed badinage. They took charge of his animals, and he came striding toward Stella's quarters. He was eager to reach her, still charged with hope, she knew. She knew also that he would try to take her in his arms; so she stayed inside, out of the men's view, to greet him. She opened the door for him and stepped back, smiling, speaking a greeting. But he did not even pause. He kept coming, dark eyes burning and white teeth flashing in his bronze face. Then he reached for her, and she was in his arms.

She had been thinking of Tennessee's powerful arms about her, and now, with this man's strong arms holding her close, some perversity within her made her think of her brother-in-law's arms again. A moment's weakness swept her, and she made no attempt to avoid Weatherford's kiss. She melted against him, feeling defenseless and half-willing, until she felt him stiffen with passion and grind his lips against hers with elemental abandon. She brought up her hands and pushed away from him until he released her.

"Now, just calm down, my friend," she said unsteadily. "Let's not get carried away."

"Stella, you ain't got no idea how I been looking forward—" Weatherford was breathing as if he'd just run a mile footrace against Apaches. "Yes, by God, and to getting hold of you! You *know* how I want you. And I got to have you. Stella, give me my answer. I want it now."

"Business first," Stella said crisply, back in possession of herself. "Your answer later. My father used to say that two heads on a pillow are *not* better than one in making business decisions."

"Two heads on a pillow!" Weatherford exclaimed. "You mean— you mean, Stella—"

"No, I don't," Stella said, coloring faintly. "It was a manner of speaking. Have a seat, Dick." She reversed her desk chair and sat down facing him. "Now to business."

In the discussion that followed, Stella gave him her decision to replace the dugouts on the Pecos with permanent adobes and retain the range as holding grounds for Texas herds. Weatherford wholeheartedly approved. They could still supply army and Indian beef to other forts in New Mexico, but more and more they would direct herds from the holding grounds to Stella's ranch in Colorado, from which steers could be driven to the mines and sold for beef, and from which stockers—cows, calves, and bulls—could be trailed on and sold to pioneers in the cattle industry, which was just getting started on the ranges of Colorado, Wyoming, and even Montana. At the moment Jeff Slaughter was in Colorado with a herd of bred cows, and Nueces Riley, whom Slaughter had hired down in the brush country, was in south Texas putting together a trail herd destined for the holding grounds on the Pecos. Stella wanted Slaughter to come to her as soon as possible. Nueces Riley could replace him as manager of the Colorado ranch. She was planning the establishment of a fortified ranch farther west near the Cap Rock, deep in Indian country, and she wanted Slaughter to supervise the building of that stockaded ranch.

"Dick, you'll have to send a messenger to Jeff," she said. "I can't spare a man because of security. I have so many men on far-flung errands! These accursed distances! How long did it take you to get here? Two weeks? More? No matter. Someday, when I can find the man or men who can travel this wild country and set up my stations for me and afterward make deliveries of pigeons, I'll have homing pigeons flying all over, saving men and horses. Vast ranges to the west will be settled by first-comers in the next few years, and I don't intend to wait for the Indians to fold their tents and retreat to reservations. When I first heard the army was building Fort Griffin almost in shouting distance of here, I started thinking of a ranch farther west. I've got Rome Dixon down on the upper Colorado River looking for a place. He was the one who scouted out the site for this place, you know.''

"Sure thing." Weatherford was sweating lightly, waxing restless. "I'll send for Jeff." He came forward in his chair, prepared to leap up and move upon her. "Now, I done asked you about a hundred times to marry me, and you keep on putting me off. Well, your time's up. I want my answer."

"All right, Dick." She looked him in the eyes, dreading his anger, not his pain. It would be anger that might take him from her. "I won't marry you."

"By God, I seen it coming!" He slumped back in his chair, then surged upright again, color beating into his scowling face. "But why, damn it? *Why* won't you?"

"Dick, I do intend to marry again—for my child's sake, more than for my own. If I had no child, you'd have as good a chance with me as anybody I'm likely to marry. For you *can't* know how much I value you. As a man suited to the Western frontier, you can't be beat. But all this buffalo country won't remain a frontier. One day Smitty will be a man of means and large affairs. His education must fit him for life in the East as well as in the West. What I've hoped for in a husband—for Smitty's sake—is a man of education, breeding, and, if it can be had, cultural family background. I'm describing Smitty's father, of course.''

"Reckon that lets me out," Weatherford growled.

"Yes, Dick," Stella said in a soft, steady voice. "I don't like to talk like this to you. But it does, as you say, leave you out. I'll double your salary. I'll triple it. But I won't marry you."

"You pay me much as I'm worth." Weatherford's mind was hanging on something else. "You found the *hombre* yet that's got all them frills?"

She did not pretend to misunderstand him. "Maybe I have. I haven't given him an answer yet, but I may marry Captain Armistead Gordon Randolph."

"Yeah, I seen him once," Weatherford remembered. "He come down to Fort Washita from Fort Gibson to see you when I was there time you was moving. Right pretty soldier."

"Pretty?" Stella raised her brows. "He's handsome, educated, gentlemanly, cultured—true, Dick. But he's all man, too. I wouldn't settle for less."

"Well, all I got to say is he's one lucky son-of-a-bitch. I ask your pardon for the language, ma'am, but I won't take none of it back."

Stella laughed, and Weatherford could not suppress a grudging smile. "Dick, let me tell you something about yourself," she said impulsively. "You're not bad-looking and undoubtedly attract women. You can't make me believe you're not attracted back. Maybe to one woman at a time, but you're no one-woman man. Now you can get me off your mind, and I predict you'll have someone else in my place within a month." Seeing Weatherford preparing to register some feeble denial, she headed him off. "Why, I'll bet you've already *got* one on your mind. Dick, don't pretend that you've spent month after month on the Pecos just thinking about me and never about some Spanish girl in Fort Sumner, maybe, or—hah, I can tell by your face! Come on. Admit it."

Weatherford twisted uncomfortably in his chair, an almost rueful look on his face. "Well," he admitted lugubriously, "there's a girl named Panchita in Fort Sumner that just tore me up the first time I seen her. Stella, you never seen such fetching eyes, soft black hair, such curves—such a—" He broke off, turning red. "But let that go. She's Mexican, but that wouldn't made no difference to me. Yeah, reckon I'll have to own up. I tried every dodge I knowed to make up to her. But she wouldn't have no truck with me a-tall."

"Why not?" Stella asked, casually interested. "Is she married?"

"Might as well be. She won't see nobody but your curly wolf of a brother-in-law. So he might as well have her locked up. Funny thing, too. I may be the one caused him to take up with her. One day I's talking to Tennessee and seen her on the street. I said something about how graceful she walked—what it meant, anyhow—and he taken a look and asked me why I didn't try my hand if I wanted her. I told him I'd done asked *you* to marry me and I allowed you'd say yes, seeing you'd done let me kiss you a time or two. I said that before I thought and could bit my tongue. And—well, he taken offense at something or other—maybe at what I said, you being kinfolks. He mumbled something grouchy like and walked off. But after that day nobody but Tennessee Smith could get close to Panchita, and he sure was close to her every night he was in town. What I think, and try not to think, is that he sleeps with her."

Stella had come out of her chair. She stood with freckles stark in her face, staring blackly. Slowly she turned her back on Weatherford and leaned on her arms above the desk, letting her head hang. Only the coil-binding at the back of her neck kept her thick red hair from cascading over her freckled arms. "Don't mind me," she gasped. "I feel a little dizzy."

Oh, goddamn his rotten heart! she thought. He's everything that's wrong in my life. That's why I hate him, hate him, hate him! I leave the Krulls to God, my life begins straightening out, I'm finding some contentment in my child and my work, and then I have to hear his name—and learn that all the time I've been sweating my way out of hell, he's been taking his pleasure, without a care in the world, from the body of some Mexican slut! She could envisage him lying on top of Panchita— the unfreckled, brown-skinned Mexican slut—kissing the dark red lips, feeling the chocolate nipples of the chestnut breasts go taut, feeling the brown belly wriggling . . . and, damn him, he never remembering a fleeting moment of pleasure derived from a freckle-edged white body beside a water hole overhung with wild-plum brush a day's ride north of Fort Worth. . . . She shut her eyes in pain. She *did* feel faint, but after a long, choking moment she could breathe again—and could hear Weatherford behind her.

"You all right? Want me to call Lula May?"

She straightened and turned. "No, no," she said, and managed to move her lips into the shape of a smile. "I'm all right now. Let's go eat lunch. I want you to see Smitty." She led the way through a side door into a dog run that separated office from living room. "We're eating in the dining hall today by order of Lula May, who's doing a washing." As they crossed the quadrangle toward the east row of log houses, Stella touched his arm, showing for the first time, with touch, look, and tone of voice, some genuine compassion for her rejected lover. "Dick, don't give up on Panchita. You'll get her yet. I have a feeling that Tennessee won't be around her much longer. As sure as God is just, somebody will shoot him down before the year is out."

"Way you sound," Weatherford said, "you don't like him much, even if he *is* your kin. A fellow might allow Tennessee ain't no one-woman man, neither, huh? Course, since you're my boss-lady, ma'am, I don't allow nothing."

"What utter nonsense!" Stella murmured. "What's it to me how many women he goes to bed with?"

Weatherford left for New Mexico the following morning. Normally he would have remained for several days in order to rest his horse and pack mules, but Stella provided him with fresh animals so that he could depart at once. He was in a hurry to get back to Fort Sumner, he said with a grin, so that he might catch a distant glimpse of Panchita. Now that the uncertainty had gone out of his suit for Stella's hand, he seemed cheerful enough. It was the hope that was never more than one breath away from despair that had kept him unsettled.

Stella wanted Weatherford on his way back to the Pecos because she was expecting a visit from Captain Randolph. They were going on a picnic the next day. The two men under one roof or treading the same sod could not possibly prove a combination that would promote her interests.

When Armistead arrived, Stella knew she would not show the same reluctance to greet him in public that she had in the case of Dick Weatherford. Strangely, she thought, he had proposed marriage more than once but had made no attempt at all to take her in his arms and kiss her. She had not accepted his proposal, and did not plan to until they knew each other well enough to give and receive caresses.

At Fort Washita briefly and then on the Clear Fork, Stella and Randolph had enjoyed many hours together—horseback riding, eating dinners for just the two of them served by Lula May, discussing books each had read, and conversing companionably about many things. On several occasions she'd expected him to kiss her and had been surprised when he had not done so. She wondered wryly whether he was a "gentleman of the old school" who made formal and stilted proposal before even dreaming of any sort of familiarity more intimate than helping a lady into a carriage. Whatever the case, she'd meet Armistead at the hitching rail careless of watchers, for he was a man of controlled actions and faultless conduct. She doubted that any impulsiveness would ever break through his reserve far enough to threaten decorum—though sometimes she wished it would.

Randolph rode in the next day around mid-morning, leading a dun pack mule bearing a piled-up burden covered with canvas. Stella came out of her office when Lula May, who was outside with Josh, her own child, and Smitty, called her to announce the captain's arrival. Randolph had both animals tied to the hitching rail by the time Stella reached him.

Smitty's treble voice rose above the flurry of adult greetings. He was pointing at the top-heavy dun mule. "Camel!" he piped. "Camel!"

Randolph's white teeth gleamed under his carefully trimmed black mustache. "No, Smitty, you're mistaken," he said. "That's a mule."

But Smitty had greater faith in a picture he had seen. "No!" he shrilled, jumping up and down and falling on the ground. "Camel! Camel!"

Stella laughed. "Well, at least he has a hump." She took Randolph's arm and turned with him toward the office. "Why the pack mule?

Bringing your duffel? Don't tell me you've been transferred to Fort McEveride.''

He looked down at her with a smile that was belied, in part, by the intentness of his fine, dark eyes. ''Would you approve the transfer, Madam Colonel? Could you find a place for me in your regiment?'' It was a serious, earnest inquiry delivered in the style of persiflage.

She replied, ''Why, I can always use an ambitious young captain.'' For very shame, she tried not to look arch. Nevertheless, there was a sudden break in his expression, and she sensed the gust of strong feeling that swept him, and that he quickly brought under control.

''The mule's carrying pigeon crates,'' he said, ''and a few pigeons that Corporal Snyder assures me will home back to Fort Griffin now. I want to take some back with me that will return here.'' He gave her a grin that made him look very young. ''Then we can have *billets-doux* coming and going like mad.''

''Lula May!'' Stella called. ''Tell Jubal to take this mule to the barn and have Shen exchange the pigeons for some that will fly back here. And tell Jubal to saddle up the Tennessee mare and bring her to the office.'' She led Armistead up the steps into her office. ''Come on in, Armistead.''

''You know, Stella,'' he said gently, ''we wouldn't need those pigeons to carry messages if you'd marry me.'' He stood there with his heart in his eyes and took not a single step toward her. ''We could forget the picnic and ride to the fort and have the chaplain marry us. I could get a week off, and we could just be together, having fun, getting acquainted. What do you say, Stella?''

Still he did not reach for her, when he could have won her consent by merely putting his arms around her. Did he have a bet with himself that he could get her without touching her? No, she had to admit he was one man who did not seem at all vain about his good looks. Indeed, he was a puzzle—one that she was determined to solve. She moved up close in front of him and put a soft, freckled hand on his arm.

''Armistead,'' she said in a soft voice, ''are you determined to storm the last of my defenses?'' She hoped her eyes were starry and filled with misty allure. She despised herself, but she just wanted him to kiss her. It wasn't that she was aroused or in heat; it was simply that she needed to check the man's firepower and know how his lips felt before definitely deciding to sleep with him for years to come. And in this moment of moments, a small wicked voice from deep inside her whispered insidiously that Tennessee Smith would already have had her jiggling on her back, skirt up to her neck, and groaning and shouting to wake the dead. That goddamned Tennessee! The thought of him was so hateful and unwelcome that she almost spat an oath into Armistead's handsome face.

Where her hand rested, she felt Randolph's arm go rigid. But his reserve held; he did not make his move. "You haven't given me your answer, Stella," he said. "Will you ride to the fort and marry me?"

Dropping her hand, Stella shook her head. "No, not that. I couldn't get around to doing that. Not for a while, anyhow."

"Be honest. You ever intend to marry me?"

Stella turned away and moved toward a chair. "I don't know. I thought I did. But I just don't know."

Around eleven o'clock they mounted up and rode out on their picnic with no particular destination in mind. They pulled up on the crest of a hill and sat there talking. Stella was aware of a strangeness in the day. The sun was bright and hot, as usual, but there was no wind stirring; none at all. An hour or so past noon, they found themselves walking their horses beside the sparkling waters of a small creek, enjoying an unexpected breeze that had sprung up. It came sighing out of the west, disrupting the dead calm. It cooled their flushed faces and gladdened their hearts with the smell of growing things.

Their picnic site turned out to be a grassy flat stretching north and south between a thick grove of oaks and a high-banked bend in the creek. Across the stream a mockingbird was singing in a lone cottonwood, sublimely ignoring the loudening disturbance of leaves in the steadily freshening breeze. "Let's eat here," Randolph suggested, "where we'll have music with our meal."

Stella spread the picnic cloth back from the creek in a patch of close-lying green grass agleam with spangles of yellow, red, and purple flowers. Before securing their horses, Randolph led them down to a water hole in the elbow bend of the creek and let them drink. Then he built a fire for boiling coffee.

Stella was strangely restless. There was something in the air or the day or the place or some eerie combination of all three that made her feel uneasy. As they ate, the feeling persisted, though Armistead was never more entertaining. Finally they were finished, and Armistead packed his pipe while Stella sacked up the coffee pot and empty food containers.

"Wish those plums were ripe," he said, looking toward the bend in the creek. "But they're green as a gourd, of course."

It was as if the single pealing stroke of a silver bell had pierced Stella's brain. She flashed a glance where he was looking, and her eyes froze on the high bank crowned by brush overhanging the water hole. Her heart stopped, or seemed to, for a long, still moment; then followed a clamor of blood. No wonder she'd been feeling uneasy! Why, she'd ridden past this place before, had even watered her horse in the bend of the creek—though not when the plum thicket was in leaf, she now recalled. It was strange that she'd never noticed its similarity to the water hole north of Fort Worth where she had camped with Tennessee—not until she'd come on this picnic with Armistead. Could there be some kind of prophecy in this coincidence?

Suddenly a great, dark shadow, having moved up behind the screen of the oaks at her back, fell over the water hole, casting the high bank and the plum thicket into deep twilight. Stella stared in almost superstitious awe. Then she whirled and looked up.

"Armistead," she cried, "we're going to get soaked! You chucklehead! Where *were* your eyes, soldier?"

"On *you*, of course." Randolph looked up, laughing. "Good God! Well, let it rain. Who cares?"

"I do." Stella grabbed the sack of picnic utensils and ran for the horses, shouting over her shoulder. "There's a hay shack a mile down this valley."

They raced down the valley under lowering black clouds, the seething darkness of which reminded her of the storm clouds that had driven her and Tennessee to shelter on the Tennessee-Mississippi line, where Tennessee had widowed and then pleasured himself with the ex-Memphis whore. Damnation, must everything remind her of Tennessee and his brutal lust? . . . They beat the rain to the hay shack, which stood in a motte of elms and cottonwoods at the edge of a wide meadow.

As they tied the horses in a lean-to behind the shack, they were made frantic by the shout of the wind. They ran out under writhing trees and circled the shack to the front door. Snatching the wooden peg out of the hasp, Randolph crowded Stella's heels to the inside and slammed the door.

When the door was blown open again, having no catch, Stella said quickly, "Bar it with that slat of wood. We use this shack only a few nights a year to shelter hay crews. We take hay off that meadow."

Only a minute or so after the door was securely closed, the rain raced in, sounding like a locomotive coming wide open, and hit the shack with a massive thump, then leveled out into one continuous roar.

The shack had a rusty stove at one end of the room and bunks strung with rawhide strips built into the other three walls. There was a rough-plank table, but no chairs or benches. Stella found a lantern that still had some oil in it, borrowed a match from Randolph, and struck a light. She set the lantern on the stove.

"We don't need a fire, but the light will cheer us up," she said.

Randolph had taken his poncho from his McClellan saddle and now spread it on the packed-dirt floor in front of the stove. Removing his hat and coat, he tossed them on the table and took his seat on the poncho, looking up. "We can sit in front of that lantern and imagine it's a fire in a fireplace. Come down, my dear."

There was something in his voice that Stella had never heard before, and she wondered what he had on his mind. She gave him a slanted look from lowered eyelids and found him much different from the man who had hurried into the shack. What was the reason for the change? Was it the isolation with a woman, the coziness of shelter in a rainstorm? Whatever the cause, his stiff reserve was gone. She saw the open admiration standing in his dark, expressive eyes and sensed the hard roll of feeling that his unguarded looking kicked up in him. She loved the way his soot-black hair swept back from his forehead and grew softly down to offer its contrast to the deep tan of his clean-shaven cheeks. He was well-formed, lean, and supple. He was clean and brown and gentle. He *could* be the antidote to all the poison that was afflicting her mind and heart—if—*if* he could make her forget. And there was Smitty's need. . . .

She came to him, murmuring, "Do you think this is quite proper?"

He chuckled softly, leaning toward her. "I don't know," he said, "but I do know it'll be proper to shove you out into that storm if you don't promise to marry me."

Sitting beside him, she turned her head and looked into his eyes. And with no hesitation whatever, he drew her into his arms. His kiss was all she had wanted it to be—gentle and tender and, as she assured herself critically, sweet. She clung to him, liking the way his lips felt, though her body was in a strained position. When she did not break away, his lips grew fiercer, more demanding, though never approaching the unrestrained savagery of . . . of. . . . She made her mind go blank.

Then Randolph pulled back. "This position is damned uncomfortable," he said unsteadily. "Here, since there's nowhere to sit." He pushed her down on her back and lay on his side beside her, his length pressing her right shoulder, hip, and thigh. It occurred to her that Tennessee would already have been on top of her, holding her down, and getting ready to enter her, and she almost reared back upon her seat in anger at herself for having such a thought. A body would think she was critical of Armistead's restraint as a lover—that she wanted him to be otherwise. She knew that she was not sexually aroused; she was on her back, she told herself, because she was more comfortable than she would be sitting twisted around and nearly breaking her back.

He was propped on an elbow. "Are you going to marry me, Stella?"

"I surely am," she murmured. "I wouldn't miss it for the world."

His face came over hers, and then his arm came over her waist, tightened, and drew her closer to his side. When his lips locked on hers, such peace came into her troubled heart that her mind went blank, and she was afraid she might embarrass them both by going to sleep, as one might who has been tempest-tossed and finally comes to safe harbor. She could feel the rataplan of his heart against her right breast. His lips grew more elemental, more insistent. Yes, he *was* that antidote. He was a sweet, sweet man. . . .

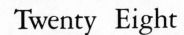

Twenty Eight

When Tennessee heard that the army had abandoned Fort Sumner and let the Navajos return to their old home grounds, it occurred to him that Stella might move all her cattle business out of New Mexico—not that Stella's plans would affect his own, of course. But Dick Weatherford, whom Tennessee met on the street in Fort Sumner one golden autumn day, told him at some length about the permanent adobes on the Pecos, the swing-station ranch in Colorado, the sale of beef to the mines, and the trailing of breeding stock to pioneer ranches getting started in several states of the Northwest.

"Going at this thing big, ain't she?" Tennessee said.

"She'll sure'n hell wind up the cattle queen of the West," Weatherford predicted. "Buys cheap in Texas and sells high out here. She's already richer'n grease and getting richer."

"I figured you two'd be married by this time. When's the wedding?"

"Ain't going to be none for me." Weatherford's eyes were narrowed on distance, as if he were trying to make out some speck on the horizon. "She turned me down. Told me she aims to marry an army officer named Randolph. I seen him once. Captain Armistead Gordon Randolph. *Was* stationed at Fort Gibson. Now he's been transferred down to that new fort they built down on the Clear Fork of the Brazos, and Stella's done moved her headquarters down there. Already got some houses and corrals up a few miles from the fort."

Tennessee's eyes revealed nothing. "Stella follow him down?"

"No. She moved down before the fort was built." Weatherford's brown eyes were curious. "But it don't make no difference who followed. That Randolph's sure what she wants. West Pointer. Real gentleman, not no ex-Ranger who don't know nothing but cattle and is fair slick with a gun. Fellow comes from an old slave-owning family in Virginia, even if he did fight with the North in the war."

"So!" Tennessee murmured sourly. "A goddamned turncoat! I ain't surprised. She always had a weakness for Southern Lincolnites."

"She ain't never turned away from the grave of the first one, you want my opinion. She ain't in love, as you might say, now, lessen it's still with the daddy of that boy. There's *something* about the daddy of that boy—" Weatherford shook his head. "I don't know. A feeling I got. Anyhow, she aims to get that boy a proper daddy. And that there ain't just my feeling. She plain-out said so." He looked up and down the street, ignoring the passersby. "Tennessee, you ain't busy, walk down to that *cantina* with me. Meeting one of your old friends there—Nueces Riley. Been working for Stella over a year now."

"Rode the river with Nueces," Tennessee said. "He'll do."

"Yeah," Weatherford agreed, his mind on something else, something that heated his eyes with a reddish glow.

In front of the *cantina* Weatherford stepped ahead and walked on in, while Tennessee hung in the entrance for a long moment, his cold eyes sweeping the room. Near the end of the bar a *vaquero* in *charro* jacket and big Mexican *sombrero* was leaning over a table in intent conversation with Panchita Candelaria, who was mostly listening with a troubled face. As they circled near Panchita's table, the *vaquero* turned his head and saw Tennessee close up. He wheeled aside and backed into the bar, his caught breath sounding like an exclamation. Then he snaked away and slid fast through the doorway and was gone.

Weatherford looked amused. "What the hell?"

Tennessee shrugged, his face impassive. He was used to nervous reactions to his unexpected appearances. Then, too, gossip about his and Panchita's relationship was bound to be making the rounds in this small town, inspiring young buckos who might otherwise lust openly after Panchita to a special kind of wariness. He moved on to the wall, where Riley stood up, grinning, to shake hands.

"Same old Tennessee," Riley said. "Scaring hell out of folks. Set down and help me out with this here bottle. Two drinks of that stuff, and over there's the prettiest greaser gal you ever seen."

"Prettiest girl in town *without* a drink," Weatherford said when they were seated. "Where's your eyes?" His own eyes were burning. "Well, now, what you know? Here she comes!"

"Dick, if Stella gored you deep as you let on," Tennessee observed dryly, "damned if you don't heal quick."

Panchita came up beside Tennessee's chair and set two glasses on the table, politely declining Weatherford's invitation to sit down and have a drink. She leaned against Tennessee with an arm resting on his burly shoulder. "*Hombre*, I mus' talk weeth you," she whispered. "The *vaquero* you make jomp—he bring the bad news for you. I mus' see you alone."

"How about tonight, then?"

"No. It mus' be now, before sopper."

Tennessee lifted the glass Riley had filled and drained it. "Panchita," he said, "meet two friends of mine, Dick Weatherford and Nueces Riley. You can talk in front of them, Panchita. Comanches couldn't make 'em talk, and they'd side me with guns if I needed help."

"You weel need it, *hombre*." Panchita looked around. It was a slack period of the afternoon, and behind the bar paunchy, dewlapped Juán Lopez kept blinking to stay awake. There were no girls working and only a few customers drinking at the bar and tables, none nearby. Pulling out the chair between Tennessee and Weatherford, Panchita sat down and leaned on her elbows.

"Bend close and talk low," she said. "Listen, *hombre*. The Parson Krull *comancheros*—Wes Krull—they 'ave set one trap for to keel you. Tonight, tomorrow night—when you come to the *cantina*. Guns, they 'ave fail weeth you, *hombre*. Now they weel try the bare hands of a ver' beeg soldier from Fort Bascom. Bool Jecks. He is more beeg than you, *hombrecito*. Bool Jecks, he has keel men weeth his hands. If Bool Jecks, he don' keel, they weel 'ave one who is skill in the *cuchillada* to throw a knife. You weel 'ave no chance, *hombre mío*."

"Hey, I know that soldier," Weatherford said. "Brute's a grizzly bear shaped like a man. You can't fight him, Tennessee."

"I know him, too," Riley said. "By sight. Seen him clean out a dive in San Antone once. Throwed men around like they was sacks of straw. Ain't no two men could whip him, Tennessee. We got to think of something."

"Use a gun on him." Weatherford's eyes were trading curiously between Tennessee and Panchita. "That's what I'd do."

"Can't," Tennessee decided. "Shoot an unarmed man in public, I'd have to run or could get lynched. Ain't much law here, specially now the army's gone, but there's more than that." He reached absently for one of Panchita's small brown hands and held it like a captured thrush between the palms of his great fists. "Big sergeant," he said. "Saw him in San Antone when I got back from the border. Loading a wagon at the Alamo for Captain Romine, who'd come from Fort Bascom for something or other. Showing off how stout he was. I remember—by God, there *was* something then—" He looked at Panchita. "What you call him?"

"Bool Jecks."

He shook his head. "Well—no, I don't reckon—"

But the border-bred Riley was nodding. "That's his name. Bull Jakes."

Tennessee stiffened. "Bull Jakes!" he whispered hoarsely. "The hell you say!"

"That's what I say," Panchita said, snatching her hand away. "Bool Jecks."

Now, under the streaked tawny hair, Tennessee's diamond-hard eyes glittered palely in his dark face. "Why, I reckon that irons the whole thing out, then," he murmured. "Bull Jakes was one of the old Krull gang that murdered my father and brother. He's one I been hunting. Now I've found him. So all I got to do is show up here tonight and let him deliver himself. That simple."

"That's all, huh?" Riley jeered. "You show up and fight him barehanded—and get killed. *That's* simple enough."

"Well, I got to admit I had something different in mind," Tennessee said. He remembered, though, how he'd told Stella that a wolf couldn't whip a grizzly. She'd wondered whether a big, fast man could kill a bigger, stronger, slower man with bare hands. She'd been talking about him and Bull Jakes. "We know this Jakes is stout as a mule. No doubt about that. But is he quick, too, or slow, would you say, Nueces?"

"Quick as hell. Strong as a grizzly and quick as one. Don't fight him naked, Tennessee."

Tennessee observed the unruffled curve of Panchita's dusky cheek with speculative eyes. You never knew what went on under the jeweled combs, mantillas, and lustrous black hair of women who loved matadors and avidly watched them enter arenas against the kill-set horns of quick, mad bulls. "What you think, Panchita?" he asked, smiling faintly.

"I theenk you keel that Bool Jecks, *hombre grande*," the girl answered calmly. "But when you keel him, what of the *hombre* with the knife? Who weel keel *him* when you are dead?"

"*My* job," Weatherford judged. "Reckon I can pick the snakes out of a crowd. I've sure done that sort of thing before. You might could stand by me at the fight, Panchita, and show me who to watch."

"*Sí*, I can do that." Still she looked troubled. "But where weel Wes Krull stand? Not in the light. *Hombre*, the word of this trap come from Wes. He act like he theenk we are still—what you say—friends. But you theenk they 'ave not watch my house? You theenk Wes, he does not know you come to my house, *hombre?* So Wes know that I weel tell you of this trap. Why for he send the word, then?"

"Because he's a fox," Tennessee said. "Bull Jakes, one way, is bait. Wes knows I'll be there ready to fight him soon as I hear his name. And Wes hopes—and likely figures—that Jakes will put me down for keeps. If he don't, the knife man might get a blade in me. Main thing, though, is that any help I call in will be looking close up for the knife man. The real backup man will be a sharpshooter with a good rifle further out in the dark. After the fight starts, he can pick his spot in the town. He'll watch Bull Jakes invite me outside and then demand lanterns for light. Wes expects me to tell you to have 'em ready, Panchita. So have 'em ready."

Panchita shook her head, frowning. "Maybe I miss it. How it weel do Wes some good for *us* to know. I don' onnerstand it much."

"It fixes the time—sets the thing up. No telling when I might ride in or how long I'd stay gone. Wes can't keep the soldier and the knife man coming here every night for a month, six months, a year." He scowled, thinking intently. "Backup man with the rifle, that's the third step in this thing. Wes, he's watched me on his trail and knows I know how he works. Maybe he figures I can count up to three. What worries me, there may be a fourth step. Got a hunch, but can't see it."

"Maybe it ain't there," Riley said. "Man gets started, he'll get to figuring mighty cute. Maybe too cute. Gets so the trickiest thing is the simple thing. Could be there won't be no rifleman out in the dark. But I allow there will be, and he's mine. Soon as I get outside, I'll figure the likeliest spot for that backup man to nest up with a rifle."

"Wes, he weel be that one out in the dark," Panchita said. "He is ver' proud of his rifle shot. Sometime he weel lie up half the night bragging."

"How you know that?" Weatherford asked, resentment in his voice.

"Wes used to be her uncle," Tennessee told him.

"That is so," Panchita said. Then she laughed. "How you know that?"

"Because you're very strict with your morals," Tennessee said gently. "Who else *could* a pig like Wes be?"

Weatherford scowled in puzzlement. "What—what kind of talk—"

Riley grinned. "They ain't talking to you, Dick," he said lightly. Then his face turned sober. 'If it *is* Wes out in the dark, I'll have to be sharper'n a damn weasel. Only thing is, I hate like hell to miss that fight.''

"Watch it over Wes's shoulder," Tennessee suggested.

Two soldiers entered and ordered tequila. Immediately Tennessee was on his feet, as wary now as any hunting wolf, wondering whether the presence of soldiers in the town had any special significance. His hand closed on Panchita's shoulder briefly; then, patting her on the back, he departed. Weatherford was at his heels, and Riley joined them outside a minute or so later, having learned from the soldiers that they were from Fort Bascom. There were yellow-leg troopers on the street and eight or ten cavalry mounts hitched to the rails in the vicinity of Murphy's saloon.

"Somebody must sold tickets up at Bascom," Riley commented darkly. "I ain't got no whole lot of faith in coincidence." He turned away. "So long. I want to scout the back of them buildings."

"Try the feed store above the old ford," Tennessee called after him.

Halfway to Murphy's saloon Tennessee heard his name called and, swinging his head, caught sight of movement in an alley. Instantly he lunged into the passageway and flattened against the wall, a gun in his hand. He was pleased to find Weatherford against the opposite wall, a gleaming Colt poised and hammer-fanged.

"Back here, Tennessee," the same voice called again, and Captain Romine showed himself and then stepped out of view at the end of the alley.

Tennessee nodded to Weatherford, and they walked down the alley, their guns held at the ready. Romine and a sallow-faced, bone-poor soldier in blue uniform were standing together behind Kelton's general store. Ignoring the drawn guns, Romine spoke both their names and shook hands quickly. He seemed almost desperately hurried.

"All right, Private Greaves," he snapped, a throb of impatience in every syllable, "this is Tennessee Smith. Tell him exactly what you told me."

There was, unaccountably, a sly malice in the soldier's shifty eyes. "Bull Jakes and Wes Krull, they aims to kill you, fellow," he said, baring his yellow teeth in the reflex of a nervous half-grin. "Tonight at the Lopez *cantina*. Bull aims to get real fresh with that there greaser gal you took away from Wes—maybe slap her ass or handle her tits, maybe try to buy a piece, talk to the gal like she's a whore—right there in front of ever'body. When you acts up, he'll kill you. He won't have nary a weapon on him—gun or knife, see? So you'll have to fight him with your hands, or back off. Well, they 'lows you *won't* back off, and no man that lives can stand up to Bull. So you're in a hell of a bind, fellow.''

He told them what they had already heard in a whining voice that contained a strange assurance. He either knew something, or hoped something, that he was not putting into words. The soldier did add a detail that was new, however, by naming two ''greasers,'' instead of one, that would do the knife work, though obviously he thought the greasers would never be called on to demonstrate their talents. Then he told them what they had surmised but had not heard: Wes Krull himself would back up the murder attempt with a rifle from the darkness.

At this point Romine dismissed the soldier, who slid around the corner. They could hear the beat of his running feet going up the alley. Finally Romine seemed to breathe easier.

''I risked that poor devil's life,'' he said, now more like himself. ''They'd kill him before night if he were seen talking to either one of us, Tennessee.''

''Why's he unloading on Bull Jakes and Wes Krull?'' Tennessee asked.

''It's Bull he's paying back,'' Romine said. ''I'm not sure what for. Until recently he and Bull were bosom cronies. Always together in some greasy business. Now he claims Bull did him dirt. Tennessee, my hands are tied in this whole affair. This brute Jakes ought to be arrested and court-martialed. I know now that he's a complete villain, a former associate of old Parson Krull—and, I suspect, not just a *former* one. And even though the Krulls have now joined the Comanches and should be hunted down as renegades, my commanding officer at Bascom won't let me move against them. He won't take a stand against *comancheros,* and he's blinking at this whole treacherous business here. He found out who you are, but then he discovered that for some reason the army is no longer interested in Tennessee McEveride. He prefers to regard this murder attempt as a private vendetta among outlaws and man-killers—the Krull *comancheros* versus the man-killer Tennessee Smith. *His* words, Tennessee. So what I think you should do is ride out of town. You haven't been challenged. Don't go near that *cantina* tonight.''

Once or twice in the past Tennessee had wondered about Romine. Now he was convinced the man was honest. ''How'd you find out Jakes used to run with the Krulls?'' he asked.

''Last year I was in Fort Smith and visited an officer I knew during the war. At one time—in '63, I think—he served liaison duty between the Army of the Cumberland and Union partisans in the mountains. His

Southern background and Union sentiments fitted him for that service in east Tennessee. I had Bull in my detail at Fort Smith, and when this officer saw him, he told me he'd seen Bull Jakes with Parson Krull's guerrillas in the mountains.''

"What's this officer's name?'' Tennessee held his breath for the answer.

"Randolph,'' Romine said. "Captain Armistead G. Randolph. *Was* stationed at Fort Gibson.''

Romine did not notice, apparently, how still the two men before him had become, nor did he notice Tennessee's great hand gripping Weatherford's arm and the grimace of extreme discomfort on Weatherford's face before the hand loosened and fell away. He had a question he wanted answered. "What will you do, Tennessee? Leave town?''

"I'll handle it some way or other,'' Tennessee said. "Much obliged for the warning. I won't forget it.''

Later, on the street near the hotel, Tennessee said to Weatherford, "Dick, forget what Romine said about Randolph. May mean nothing, but don't think I won't check it out. You let *him* be the one tells Stella he used to work with bastards like the Krulls.''

"Reckon that's your business.'' Weatherford felt of his arm where Tennessee had gripped it. "Maybe you *have* got a chance against that big bastard. Have you, Tennessee? What you really think?''

Tennessee dropped a hand on Weatherford's shoulder and drew him closer. "I'm going to kill him, Dick,'' he said confidentially. "I'll tell you something. You know where to hit, a man kills easy. But say I don't make it.'' He was talking almost in Weatherford's ear, grinning now. "Well, look on the bright side. You'll be free then to go at Panchita like a biting sow at a gatepost.''

Weatherford jerked away. "Aw, goddamn you, Tennessee!'' There was real misery in his voice. "You're sleeping with her, ain't you?''

"You know better'n that,'' Tennessee said. "Panchita's very strict. She'll tell you that herself.''

"She already has,'' Weatherford groaned. "What if you win that fight? How free am I then with Panchita?''

"I won't be here much longer,'' Tennessee told him. "Not often, anyhow. Far as I'm concerned, you got an open road with her, Dick. That ain't saying much, though. Always figured any man's got an open road with any woman.'' After a long pause, he added, "Long as he gives her a choice.''

Nueces Riley made his appearance in time to join Tennessee and

Weatherford for supper in the hotel dining room. "He'll nest up on the feed store," he told them, "where he can drop in the alley after the shot, grab his hoss, hit that ford, and be gone west in the mountains."

"It *will* be Wes Krull, all right," Weatherford said. "We done found out for sure." He went on with the account of their meeting with Romine.

"Hellfire!" Riley groaned. "What if I miss that slick bastard?"

Around a mouthful of steak, Tennessee mumbled, "You won't miss."

"By God, I don't know when I been nervouser! Well, maybe once, now that I think—in Blanco Canyon—but we sure'n hell won't go into that, or my nerves will never loosen back enough for me to hold no gun steady enough to hit anything."

They finished eating and walked out to the street. There Riley left them, heading for the livery stable, where he'd left his rifle in a saddle sheath with his riding gear. Tennessee and Weatherford strolled north on the sidewalk in the cool, crisp autumn dusk. Maybe, just maybe, Tennessee thought, he had reason to be as nervous about the coming battle as Riley claimed to be. But damned if he believed Bull Jakes could kill him with his bare hands. Instead, he expected to kill Jakes with his own bare hands—and do it quickly, too. He had meant what he'd told Weatherford. Once he'd seen a big man killed by a much smaller man, and he wanted Stella to hear someday that he had taken Bull Jakes with *his* hands, as he believed she had wanted him to. He wanted her to know that he had remembered.

Lanterns were hanging from the top of the adobe front wall of the *cantina* and from poles erected along the hitching rail. The fifty feet of space between the two rows of lanterns offered ample room for fighting and watching the fighting, Tennessee reckoned, observing at the same time that it was in plain view and in good rifle range of the flat feed-store roof. Inside, the bar was enjoying unusual patronage for so early in the evening. Panchita was giving several girls hurried instructions in a voice that was high-pitched and uneven. She saw Tennessee at once and came to him, her eyes wide and black in her pale face.

"*Diós*, I weel not get through this night!" Then she moved in close, whispering, "Nobody 'ave seen that Bool Jecks. Maybe he weel not come. Oh, *hombre, hombre*, you mus' come to my bed before this night is finish."

It was a long wait. In spite of the crowded space, the table between the end of the bar and the table against the wall, where Tennessee and

Weatherford nursed their drinks, was unoccupied. Tennessee felt the continuous flicker of glances, but few eyes remained longer than seconds in his direction.

At nine o'clock the arrival of Bull Jakes was announced by raucous voices outside and by the hurtling form of a soldier that came crashing through the doorway and sprawled on all fours halfway to the bar. Close on his heels came another soldier, not a small one, either, with his arm gripped and twisted by a hand of the massive Jakes. Other soldiers, with grins on their faces, came trooping in the giant's wake.

"Leggo, Bull!" the soldier groaned, his face twisted with pain. "What you doing this for? Christ, you're breaking my arm!"

"Let the folks see a man," Jakes mumbled. "Here!" Suddenly he shifted grips and caught the soldier with both hands; then he heaved the man aloft, held him at arm's length above his head, gave him a little heave, and tossed the soldier up higher, catching him with one hand. Then he stood, with no excessive strain on his oxlike face, holding the soldier at balance with one hand raised to arm's length above his head.

Panchita turned to the old *cantina* swamper, who had been holding himself ready. *"Pablo, ve y enciende los faroles."* The old man maneuvered himself outside to light the lanterns.

Weatherford began to sweat. "That soldier has got to weigh a good hundred eighty, and that damned Jakes ain't even taxed. How much you think he'll run to?"

"Two seventy-five, if an ounce," Tennessee guessed. "Watch him now. He's a mean son-of-a-bitch. No need to, but he'll hurt that soldier before he lets him go."

When Jakes decided that he'd finished his demonstration, instead of lowering the soldier gently, he jerked his supporting hand from under its burden, and the soldier came crashing into the floor, slamming down on knee, elbow, and chest and plowing the floor with his face. Desperately the man pushed himself up to all fours and started crawling into the crowd, whimpering and cursing. Jakes watched him crawl with expressionless, porcine eyes, then spat contemptuously in the crawler's path.

"Shoot him and take your chances, Tennessee," Weatherford said. "Don't fight him with your hands. Don't be a fool."

Jakes took two giant strides toward the end of the bar, his great mouth stretched in a lewd grin. He turned Panchita with one hand and ponderously slapped her shapely backside with the other; then he released her. While she was staggering to regain balance, the giant cut his eyes toward the table against the wall, where Tennessee sat relaxed and motionless, with a half-smile on his hard brown face. Jakes looked back at Panchita, grinning obscenely.

"How much you greaser whores getting for ass these days?" he inquired casually.

There was no ribald laughter from any spectator; no single guffaw, no snigger. Not even a grin showed, save on the giant's broad face. The onlookers sensed a sinister purpose in Jakes's mind and recognized the lewdness as a stratagem.

Panchita righted herself and looked directly at Tennessee. "Weel that be enough, *hombre?*" she asked coldly. "Or mus' I speak to the *cabrón?*"

"He asked you a question," Tennessee said. "Give him an answer."

Panchita looked up at Bull Jakes, her sculptured face containing no mark of fear. "Go ask your whore modder how much she charge you, *chingamadre,*" she said in a voice that carried to all corners of the room.

Tennessee lounged to his feet. "That's a good answer," he said.

Jakes turned his eyes and was still. Tennessee expected the surly brute to hang a quarrel on his comment, but Jakes suddenly laughed. "Never knowed my mammy. She may of been a whore, at that. But get your price right, *puta*, and I may buy a piece. Wes Krull allows it ain't half bad."

"What you do with a woman, boy-lover?" she said. "You pay him good, maybe some *hombre* unbutton his breeches for you."

There was a burst of laughter, and all of a sudden Bull Jakes lunged. Snarling oaths as feral as any boar's hoarse grunting, he caught Panchita in the vise of his great hands. Before he could move her out of her tracks, however, Tennessee was standing beside her, a .44 Colt coming to full cock with its muzzle looking the giant squarely between his red-rimmed, expressionless eyes. Jakes had appeared angrier than he was.

"It's either your hands off her," Tennessee said softly, "or your brains on the floor."

The giant released the girl and stepped back. "I ain't armed," he said. "You got a gut in you, you'll shuck them guns and fight me fair." He looked at the front window, which was aglow with lantern light, and added, "Outside—where we got room."

Tennessee stepped back and motioned toward the door with mock courtesy. "After you."

Outside, surrounded by a hundred burning eyes, Tennessee handed his guns to Weatherford. "Shoot anybody who horns in on this," he said in a voice that reached all ears. "No matter whose side he's on." Then he stripped to the waist, as had Jakes before him, and stepped out into the center of the lighted area to face his opponent.

Rarely would the frontier offer more remarkable physical examples of the animal man than the opponents here. The contrast was that of an Atlas to a Hercules. They were of equal height—about six feet three— though Jakes outweighed Tennessee by forty or fifty pounds. The massive torso, sleek with solid might; the cable-thewed arms, as large as average thighs; and the thick bull neck that had contributed to the man's nickname—these evidences of brute power explained only in part why Jakes had never been whipped by another man. The little red lights that were now showing in the porcine eyes offered a better explanation for the mauled and broken dead men along his back trail.

Tennessee was equal to Jakes in breadth of shoulders, smaller of waist, better proportioned—for pleasing the eyes of beholders, perhaps, but not for strength, though he exhibited extraordinary muscular evidence of that. As he stepped toward the slightly crouched Jakes, Tennessee said, "You made a mistake, fellow. You'd had more chance with a gun." He swayed gently on planted feet and lowered his voice. "While you can still hear—my name is McEveride. You felt of a McEveride once. She was redheaded, freckle-faced." He stepped forward, then back, weaving snakelike before the stolid, waiting Jakes, who was grinning now. "See how you like the feel of this McEveride." Then he moved in fast, feinted high with his left, and, as Jakes straightened up, swung a whistling right to Jakes's midriff, putting surge into it, plenty of arm, shoulder, and back.

It was like hitting the earthen bank of a deep gully. Bull Jakes laughed, hardly moving from the force of the blow. Then, with amazing speed of foot, he made a short, quick, fighting-bull charge and almost caught Tennessee flat-footed, grazing the latter's fading body with a reaching hand that left a foot-long crimson trail of abraded skin behind it. Tennessee side-stepped and whirled, catching Jakes half-turned. Before the giant could set his feet and get his guard up, Tennessee sent a smashing right to his broad, heavy-boned chin. It was the hardest lick Tennessee had ever delivered. He would not have believed any man alive could remain conscious after receiving that lick. Yet it did not completely wipe the brute grin off Jakes's wide mouth, though it did change the grin to a sort of grimace with a stamped-on look. Instead of falling, Jakes shook his head and came with a quick rush, and reached Tennessee with his hands.

The next moment they were on the ground, lunging and rolling, knocking down spectators who could not escape them against the press of banked onlookers, crashing against the hitching rail and sending a lantern flying. In the steadily tightening crunch of Jakes's great arms, Tennessee came closer to panic than he had ever come before. Wherever he clutched at Jakes, his hands seemed to be trying to grip the bunching mass of muscles across a draft horse's rump. Slowly, steadily, his ribs were being folded back on his bending spine. His breath was a noise in his throat; it seemed never to reach his starving lungs. Unless he broke the giant's hold and got back on his feet, he was done. No man could live more than minutes in this grizzly's embrace.

"I like—the feel—of this—McEveride—fine!" Bull Jakes gritted, surging and heaving, and still tightening his arms slowly, inexorably. "Break—your goddamn—back! . . . Before—it pops—tell you where—that little—freckle-faced—bitch—felt good." He seemed to gather himself for a mighty effort. "Her cunt! . . . Yeah—her cunt."

Suddenly Tennessee reached Jakes's eyes with his great talon of a right hand and held there, thumb gouging wickedly, remorselessly, fingers clawing savagely. Nevertheless, Jakes held on with brute tenacity, hoarsely groaning, brooling curses. Then Tennessee worked into position and drove his knee viciously into the big man's groin, heard the man's bawl of agony, and wrestled himself from the loosened arms. He scrambled to his feet.

Bent over and reaching deep for breath, Tennessee watched Jakes slowly master himself and climb to his feet, pawing at his blood-masked eyes. When the big man was almost erect, he dropped his hands from his eyes, and Tennessee swung the edge of a hand as if it were the blade of a hatchet and chopped Jakes hard across his exposed throat. The giant went back to the ground, convulsed, choking, strangling. He started back up, making frantic, grotesque motions, and Tennessee aimed a kick at his throat—and hit it, perhaps by chance. Then Jakes was back on the ground, struggling convulsively, making such frightful sounds that a few of the weaker stomachs among the spectators began to turn queasy. Tennessee got a handful of Jakes's hair, lifted the man's head, knocked down his big clutching hands, and gave him another carefully measured chop across the throat. As he did he heard two pistol shots a few yards away, a commotion among the spectators, and the clear voice of Weatherford ringing with menace and command.

Tennessee stood there, momentarily exhausted and numbed, watching Bull Jakes choke to death. Somewhere in the town a rifle cracked spitefully once and then again, and a wild, high-pitched yell of triumph sounded. When Jakes was finally still, Tennessee looked around. There were two Mexicans motionless on the ground, and Weatherford stood over one of them, holding Tennessee's .44 Colts in his hands. Panchita moved up, her beautiful black eyes wide and savage and proud, and Tennessee felt the pressure of her hand on his arm. Down by the feed store, Nueces Riley would be standing over the dead body of Wes Krull, he knew. The meaning of that yell was clear enough. A few spectators were moving off to investigate the rifle shots. But most of the onlookers remained, stricken motionless, mute—men in *serapes* and peaked *sombreros*, soldiers in blue uniform with yellow stripes down the legs, Texas cattlemen in open vests and Levis or woolen breeches thrust into high-heeled boots, *cantina* girls in low-cut blouses and colorful skirts designed to swirl.

Tennessee's eyes swept the still faces blankly. The people here were not looking at Weatherford, at the dead Mexicans, or at the body of Bull Jakes. They were looking at him, and there was something shrunken back in their eyes that looked like horror. It was a strangely bitter moment of his life; for he saw, with a slowly growing resentment, that these frontier people, even the rugged soldiers and cattlemen, were afraid of him—as they would be afraid of a ravening lion standing over its kill.

Twenty Nine

In late winter Tennessee lay rolled in his blanket with his head on his saddle, looking up at the low-hung stars that glittered down coldly. From a shallow swale nearby came the steady rhythm of Grassfire's teeth cropping the rooted fodder of buffalo grass, and further out on the plain half a dozen coyotes threw medlied voices at the stars. Both sounds were comforting in Comanche country, and they kept Tennessee relaxed, though he was not consciously listening to either. He had off-saddled a mile or so back from the drop-off edge of Tule Canyon after dark, reluctant to ride blind into the Polka Dot Kid's camp at night. He would scout the canyon in daylight.

The parson had disappeared. Since the death of Wes, Parson Krull had not been seen at Las Vegas, Santa Fe, Puerto de Luna—at any of the New Mexican *comanchero* bases. With the passing of Wes, the strictly *comanchero* end of the Krull cattle business was finished. At Fort Bascom Captain Romine had expressed the opinion that the parson was now with the Comanches and would remain with them while Tennessee Smith was still alive. At Las Vegas some of the "reformed" members of the Krull *comancheros* were of the same opinion.

It was from these *comancheros* that Tennessee first heard that the great Comanche warrior Parruwa was on his trail. According to word that had sifted down from the Cap Rock, somebody had offered Parruwa one hundred selected ponies to track down and kill Tennessee Smith, and the Great Bear had decided to collect the hundred-pony bounty, less for the wealth in horseflesh than for the honor of killing the great white-eyes man-killer. Out on the plain and in the canyons, this news was as bad as that concerning Bull Jakes had been in town—maybe worse.

Later, while passing through Fort Sumner, Tennessee had seen Panchita briefly, and she, too, had warned him about Parruwa. He found himself thinking about Panchita, remembering the odd conflict of feeling on her face as she had stood in the alley, looking down on the sprawled body of Wes Krull. Suddenly, on impulse, she had knelt and gently brushed the black hair off the dead man's forehead. When she got up, Tennessee had seen tears standing in her eyes and observed at the same time the wry, disillusioned expression on Weatherford's face. Later that night Panchita had tried to explain, but he had stopped her, telling her that he understood, that she was much woman, and that he respected her. He did not tell her, as he could have, that he wished he could love her. Slowly now she would turn and spread her hands to Weatherford's heat. Tennessee knew she was much like Weatherford in that she had to have near her all the time another's fire to warm herself by; so long as it was there to offer its comfort, she would tend it faithfully.

At daybreak Tennessee saddled up and went into the canyon, seeing no recent sign of Indians. When he rode into the Polka Dot Kid's camp, he found the Kid and Earth Daughter at breakfast. The Kid had recognized Grassfire from afar and stood by the breakfast fire, watching horse and rider come down the canyon, his face bright with admiration. He was grinning in buck-toothed wonder when Tennessee reined in at the fire. Earth Daughter got to her feet, and Tennessee stared. In three years the girl had grown into a real beauty.

"Ho, ho!" the Kid exclaimed. "Me no think you *ride* him bad one! Damn hoss try him best kill me. Mightnear do."

"Likely took you for an Indian." Tennessee dismounted and ground-hitched the stallion well back from the fire, speaking over his shoulder. "Earth Daughter your squaw now?"

"No give him ponies to Hoss Walking," the Kid said cautiously. "No do him yet."

"What's she doing here this early?"

"Run him hosses after dark too late for ride far. Earth Daughter sleep here."

"You-all ain't been night-crawling, have you?" Tennessee asked severely, thinking of the girl as Mary Wilson's daughter.

"No night-crawl," the Kid said, strangely defensive. "Earth Daughter too little for blanket yet."

"Hah! Too little!" the girl spat. "Spotted Hoss too big fool for night-crawl! All he know is hoss. What Knife Eyes think? Earth Daughter too little for blanket?"

Tennessee gave her a brief appraisal. "Well, hum. . . ."

"Humping Brother, he think Earth Daughter big for blanket. He try make me night-crawl when he see me sometime," the girl said.

Something coiled inside Tennessee. The girl, he told himself, was remembering Brownlow Krull's attentions when she was fourteen years old. And yet . . . and yet. . . . There was that strange, thoughtful look that always came to the face of Riley or Mary or Jake whenever Brownlow Krull's death was mentioned. And there was that cold wind of premonition stirring the hair at the back of his neck right now, pushing him forward, lifting him to the balls of his feet.

Dreading to hear her answer, he had to ask, "When did you see Humping Brother last?"

"Three suns go down," the girl said.

Slowly Tennessee turned murderous eyes on the Polka Dot Kid and held him in their frightening grip for a long moment. "Is Brownlow Krull—is Humping Brother still alive?" he asked in a flat voice. "Thought I killed that son-of-a-bitch in Blanco Canyon three years ago."

"No comprendo." The Kid was genuinely puzzled. "Me tell him Nueces, Jake, Mary tell you. Say him Humping Brother shot bad but get well. Me ride down Cripple John Creek take him wild hoss no can ride." He gestured toward Grassfire. "Me talk loud for them hear good." He shook his head. *"No comprendo."*

"Well, I do!" Tennessee snarled. "I *comprend* the hell out of it. Goddamn 'em all! They looked me in the face and lied like dogs."

Then came worse news. Just the morning before, the Kid had seen Brownlow Krull on Quitaque Creek with a party of Broken Fang's warriors. They were off on a raiding trip to Cripple John Creek to run off Jake Wilson's cattle, and they might hump the woman and collect both scalps, if their boasting meant more than wind from their mouths. Broken Fang was a full-fledged war chief now, riding high in the saddle since Quanah Parker had become war chief of the Quahadis following the death of Bear's Ear. Horse Walking had no influence with young Quanah and could no longer protect the Wilsons from Broken Fang, who for three years now had longed to lead a vengeance raid against the Wilson place.

"I got to get down there quick as I can," Tennessee said. "Kid, I need another horse to side the red stud—one with bottom to run all day and all night, carrying me, off and on, half the time."

"My hoss—El Tigre!" the Kid decided instantly.

"No, no, goddamn it!" Tennessee groaned. "I don't want no stud or mare, either one, alongside that stallion there. What I need's a strong gelding. Don't need to be too well broke. I *mean* for him to run." As the kid ran toward the barn against the bluff, Tennessee said to Earth

Daughter, "I need some grub I can eat without a fire. He got anything?"

"Pemmican," she said. "Jerky." She disappeared inside the Kid's big tepee.

The Kid rode his Appaloosa stallion up the canyon and returned thirty minutes later with a rugged-looking, quick-footed mustang on lead. In the open sunlight the mustang was crane colored, with a grackle sheen; then, coming into a long, early-morning shadow of the cliff, he turned blue-black. Over the bozal end of a ten-foot hair rope, the Kid had fitted a bridle and had tied the reins out of the way over the grullo's neck.

"You want him bozal for lead him red stud?" he asked, handing over the lead rope.

Tennessee shook his head. "Me straddling that blue pony, Grass-fire'd have his nose on my shoulder if he was running loose." He reached for the Kid's hand and put two double eagles in it. "Give Horse Walking a few ponies, and get Earth Daughter on a new blanket." Earth Daughter was putting a package of food in Tennessee's saddlebags and did not look around, but a bunching of one visible cheek showed that she heard. Tennessee added, "She's big enough for the blanket."

Ten miles out on the plain, Tennessee switched his saddle from Grassfire to the grullo and found himself moving across the great table-land of grass with a sweep that let him know how much the blue mustang liked to run. Grassfire ran alongside on a loose lead, his nostrils flaring— as much from indignation, Tennessee suspected, as from an increasing need of more oxygen. Every two hours or so Tennessee switched the saddle and changed mounts, and at every switching stop he sponged out the mouths and nostrils of the horses and poured into his hat only enough water from his canteen to wet their throats. In mid-afternoon he watered the horses and gave them an hour's grazing in Blanco Canyon, sixty miles from the Kid's camp on the Tule. He figured he was about halfway to Cripple John Creek.

When he rode past the place where he had shot Brownlow Krull, he thought again bitterly of how the Wilsons and Riley had lied to him. He knew why, of course. They all wanted to keep him from going back into the canyons and broken country along the edges of the Staked Plain in search of Brownlow. They wanted him to stay alive. And Riley didn't want to refuse to accompany him back into Comanche country.

Tennessee did not expect to meet Indians in his sweep down the canyon—certainly not Broken Fang's raiding party—since the Indians would have to work Jake's range all day to gather enough cattle to justify the hard push over the long miles. Nevertheless, he breathed easier after the horses had carried him out of the canyon and into the gnarled redlands below the Cap Rock and were pushing the escarpment of the Staked Plain back along the trail. They wore the afternoon out, a sagging man and two slogging, sweat-foamed horses moving at a snail's pace—or so it seemed to his dulled senses—through the vast distances of a crimson land of sentinel buttes, broken hills, raw stream beds, and gypsum water. He rode on into dusk and then into darkness, riding without hope. Two white-eyes, especially those marked by grudge, would not last through a whole day in the hands of Broken Fang. He knew Jake and Mary would be dead by now, but he had to find what remained of their bodies and bury them.

Finally Long Mesa was looming above the mesquite flat ahead. Tennessee came through the mesquite and along the foot of the mesa, riding Grassfire, and already he was aware of lingering traces of wood smoke and the smell of charred wood in the air. He stopped and tied the grullo to a mesquite. He wanted both hands free and a horse that knew and hated the smell of Indians for the next half-mile of this trip. There was always a chance that Jake had been away when the Indians attacked and that one or more Indians had remained behind to collect his scalp when he came in.

Remounting, Tennessee rode on into the site of the cabin and sat looking at the ashes and charred, smoking fragments of wood. The barn and the rails of the corral nearest the barn had gone the way of the house. Tennessee reined away to begin his search for bodies, and immediately Grassfire blew an alarm. Following the direction of the horse's ears, Tennessee rode on some forty yards and dismounted to examine what remained of Jake.

He struck a match, and when it burned out, he stood away. Somehow—there was something about the way Jake had bled—Tennessee found himself believing that Jake had died early, before the knife work had started. The mutilation had been done by cruder hands than those of the Comanche humorist of Broken Fang's band, whose artistic efforts, Tennessee figured, required the inspiration of a living victim.

Tennessee hoped that Mary had died as quickly as Jake, but it was a forlorn wish. He had to figure that somewhere in this darkness she was lying, thrown away by the last sated buck after every member of the raiding party had taken his turn on her. He rode the quiet-footed stallion over the area for an hour, cursing the clouds that shut off the moonlight. He found where the Comanches had camped, where they had butchered one of Jake's horses for meat. Then he decided to look east of the creek. Riding over to the high creek bank, he pulled up and looked down upon the ford. As he sat there, the moon finally came out of hiding, and it was the sudden, bright moonlight that enabled Tennessee to see the Indian war pony tied in the willows by the ford.

By God, she just might not be dead after all! he thought. He pulled back and rode to the corral fence, where he tied Grassfire. Then, taking his rifle, he drifted over the bank like the shadow of a wind-blown patch of cloud and went down a leaf-covered path through the brush along the creek, looking for bare ground that might show tracks in the dim light. He had gone the better part of a hundred yards past the place above the bank where the barn had stood when he came to what he sought at a shallow little rain-water channel across the path—two sets of moccasin prints, a large one partially overlapping a small one.

Tennessee was familiar with Mary's practice of wearing moccasins about the place, and he was sufficiently acquainted with Mary's moccasin prints to distinguish them from some Indian boy's or squaw's. He knew then that Mary had gone down this path and that later an Indian warrior had followed. Squatting by the prints in the path, he finished the search in his head and found Mary, treed by a Comanche warrior, he guessed, in a wolf den a quarter-mile down the creek. It was the only place along the creek he could think of to hide from raiding Comanches.

Before he came to a bend in the stream, Tennessee heard wolf-howling around it from the vicinity of the den. He listened carefully. No wolf would be howling around a hole in the ground occupied by a human being. He decided, more from logic than from sound, that the howling was coming from an Indian. His objective was a salt-cedar bush on the bank at the bend of the creek in full sight of the wolf den. He came up behind it silently and, when his breathing was regular and shallow again, looked through a gap between the evergreen branches. The wolf hole was there, about thirty-five yards down the creek, and the Indian was there, too.

The little cave was large enough for the Indian to crawl in and pull the woman out, but he was enjoying himself. He was sitting to one side of the hole, howling mournfully. When he stood up and turned his face in the moonlight, Tennessee saw that he was a handsome young brave and that he was grinning with delight at the thought of the trapped woman's horrible fear. Pretending to be a wolf, the Indian sank to all fours and crawled to the edge of the opening, growling ferociously. Then he rushed into the opening and out again with such a burst of snarling, roaring, and brawling that the sound was very much like that of an attacking wolf. Tennessee knew the image of quivering fangs would be in Mary's mind. He was not surprised to hear a muffled cry from the den-hole.

Since the warrior drew no shot, he knew now that the woman had no gun with her. He stood and grinned with self-appreciation, and it was at this moment that Tennessee's rifle bullet tore into his chest and out his back, knocking a handful of dirt and a puff of dust from the high bank beyond him. He was dead when he hit the ground.

Tennessee stepped around the bush and ran to the den-hole. He went to one knee, calling, "Mary, it's Tennessee! Come on out."

He was answered by a faithless silence. "Mary," he called again, "this is Tennessee Smith. You're safe now, honey. Come on out."

Back in the hole, a choked voice began sobbing, "Oh, God, Tennessee! Oh, God!"

"Come on, now," he coaxed. A muffled rubbing, scuffling sound of movement came from back in the hole. Soon Mary's dirty, uncombed hair showed and then her shoulders, covered by one of Jake's old coats. Tennessee pulled her out and lifted her to her feet. Under the coat was a shapeless old flannel nightgown, and on her feet were worn-out moccasins. That was all she had on, and that was all she had in the world. He held her close as she clung to him, sobbing wildly, on the edge of hysteria. He let her cry, merely holding her.

Finally she grew quiet and then stepped back, wiping her face on the sleeve of the man's coat she wore. "You—you shoot—that—that wolf?" she asked in a shaky voice.

"Yeah," Tennessee said. "Big red one." He nodded toward the dead Indian.

Mary stared, her red, swollen eyes distended with horror. "Lord God!" she whispered. "I—thought—" She turned her strained, tear-muddied face back to Tennessee. "Jake!" Her lips started trembling. "They killed him, Tennessee."

"I know, Mary." Tennessee took her arm and started leading her up the path toward the ford. "Bear up, now, honey. We got a hell of a lot to do."

At the ford Tennessee untied the Indian pony and lifted Mary to the bearskin saddle pad. He adjusted the buckskin straps attached to the metal stirrups and walked ahead, leading the pony. At the dugout he helped her down and led the pony on to the corral fence, where he tied it at a safe distance from Grassfire. Unsaddling the stallion, he carried the saddle, blanket roll, and saddlebags to the dugout. He cooked a meal out front, while Mary, whom he would not permit to go look for Jake, told him what she knew of the raid.

In the afternoon she had been repairing her chicken pen behind the barn, piling rocks and earth around the bottom where coyotes had been digging, and had come away before finishing. That night she had left the gate open. She awoke before daylight, remembering the gate, and couldn't sleep for worrying about her chickens. Finally she got up, slipped on her house moccasins and the old coat she wore for outside chores in bad weather, and went to the barn to see about her chickens. She was behind the barn when the Indians attacked. She heard Jake's shout, telling her to hide and save herself. Retreating to the wolf den, she waited until she heard Jake hollering. She came running down the creek path toward the ford, not knowing what she intended to do. Under the bank below the house, she could make out Jake's words. He was taunting Broken Fang about the latter's wrecked face with its great gaping mouth and teeth laid bare, telling the chief that squaws got sick when they looked up at his buffalo grinders. Then Jake's voice stopped short and never made another sound. When she was convinced that he was dead, she fled back to the wolf den and crawled into it.

"Jake was smart," Tennessee said. "Made Broken Fang lose his head. He knew what was in store and got it over with quick. They cut him up pretty bad, but they done it after he was dead. I know that for a fact, Mary."

After they had eaten, Tennessee handed Mary his blanket. "Get in there and try to sleep. Something I want to get done tonight. You have a shovel out at the chicken pen?"

Mary nodded. "I left it laying there," she quavered. Then she bent her face to the blanket and stumbled into the dugout.

Tennessee found the shovel, still usable though only a blackened half of the handle remained. Beside Jake's remains he dug a shallow grave and put all he could find of Jake in it. He took one last look at Jake's scalped head with its droopy, sad-looking face and started shoveling dirt upon it. When he had finished, he tossed the shovel aside and stood there a long moment, his shoulders and back aching with strain and weariness. He was so tired that he felt like lying down by the grave and going to sleep. But before he could rest he had more to do.

Walking heavily now, he made his way to the corral fence, untied the Indian pony, and mounted him, letting his feet hang past the stirrups. He rode out to Long Mesa and pulled up where the grullo the Polka Dot Kid had given him was a still, black shape. Stripping the pony, he turned the little horse loose. As was so often the case with Indian war ponies, this one was uncut, and Tennessee wanted no stone horse constantly inviting Grassfire's teeth and hooves on a trip through Indian country. Transferring the bearskin saddle pad to the mustang, he rode back to the corral, picked up Grassfire, and picketed both horses out on grass. Then, finally, he was ready for whatever sleep he could get in front of the dugout under the partial covering of his saddle blanket, with his feet to a fire that would not last until daylight.

Mary was already out at the grave when Tennessee awoke the next morning. On her way past she had covered him with the blanket she had slept under. She returned while he was cooking breakfast and stood by the breakfast fire. Her face was molded by sadness and by a sober thoughtfulness.

"It might of been better if they'd took me," she said drearily. "Hoss Walking might could of give me some sort of life up there."

"You didn't have no choice, Mary," Tennessee told her gently. "They aimed to have their fun and then kill you."

She stared at nothing. "I don't know where to turn," she murmured. "You know what folks think about me. They'll draw their skirts aside like they might catch something. I ain't welcome nowhere. Not in Texas. I don't know where—don't know what—"

"Don't worry about it, Mary. You're my responsibility now. We got a long ride ahead of us."

"Where we riding to, Tennessee?"

He had known where he would take Mary from the moment he had rescued her at the wolf's den. "To Fort Griffin, Mary," he said. "I'm taking you to Stella McEveride."

Mary's face came alive with alarm. "She'd hear what I been. I'd have to tell her myself. It ain't no use, Tennessee. She wouldn't let me stay." Her eyes shifted to space with a fugitive speculation. "Anyhow, what could I do for my keep?"

"Something or other," Tennessee told her. "Housekeeper, maybe. Stella's got a little boy to raise and a big business to run. She'll have a place for you, Mary."

"I'd work hard," Mary said, some light returning at long last to her face. "I'd sure help her out every way I could."

"You'll be yourself," Tennessee said, not understanding the choked feeling that this woman's plight and her helplessness brought to his throat. "And that will be enough."

They rode east in mid-morning, Mary on the grullo, sitting astride on the bearskin saddle pad with the blanket folded over her bared legs like a rider's lap robe. A line of slate-gray brush receded behind them at the Salt Creek crossing, and ahead of them the gray-brown plains stretched rolling into the purple haze of distance. They rode through the day and descended a timbered slope into the brakes of the Double Mountain Fork of the Brazos River, where they camped under cottonwoods on the riverbank. Though tired and stiff from the unaccustomed riding, Mary was in control of herself again and insisted on doing the cooking.

After they had eaten, she was soon in the blanket, leaving Tennessee at the fire dreading the ordeal of roughing it through the chilly night under the makeshift cover of a saddle blanket. He didn't expect to get much rest, and Mary didn't seem to be getting much in the blanket. He heard her shifting and turning, and then he noticed the blanket shaking. At first Tennessee thought she was shaking with cold; then he heard the gasps of stifled sobs and knew that she was weeping.

He went over, pulled back the blanket, and got under it with her. Putting his big arm around her, he drew her back against his chest, feeling her stiffen. "Mary, Jake would want you to get hold of yourself," he murmured. "Don't worry no more about your future. You won't be alone. You're safe." He felt her turn loose all holds. "Go to sleep, now, and get your rest."

When she was fully relaxed and breathing regularly, he started to crawl from under the blanket, but her hand tightened on his arm. "Stay, Tennessee," she said drowsily. "Keep me warm."

"That goes both ways," Tennessee said gratefully and was asleep almost by the time he had said it.

Tennessee and Mary rode into the civilian settlement at Fort Griffin, called the Flat, well before noon and made directly for a general merchandise store, for Mary preferred death to appearing before Stella McEveride in a soiled flannel nightgown and a man's cast-off coat. Inside the store, the proprietor, a heavyset man with a graying Vandyke and protuberant, expressionless eyes, got out of his chair and looked them both over without any apparent curiosity, waiting expectantly.

"Comanches killed this lady's husband and burned 'em out," Tennessee told him. "Can you outfit her with a dress, shoes, what a woman wears?"

The storekeeper nodded. "Who was the man killed?" he asked.

"Jake Wilson on Cripple John Creek," Tennessee said, and saw something move back in the fat-rimmed eyes as the man turned slowly to examine Mary more closely. Then Tennessee added, deliberately, "I'm Tennessee Smith."

The storekeeper froze with his head canted in Mary's direction. Very slowly, very carefully, he turned his eyes back to Tennessee. A very slight tic in his left cheek now became perceptible. "I got room in back where she can try on the garments," he said. Then he added, with some diffidence, "And—er, ah—freshen up, if she wants."

"Good," Tennessee said. "Mary, I'll be back in a couple of hours. Get what you want." He glanced at the storekeeper. "Pay you when I get back. Can you tell me how to find Mrs. McEveride's layout?"

"Up the river three–four miles. Follow the road and cross the ford. Bunch of log houses in a grove of trees. You can't miss it."

"I'll leave Mrs. Wilson in your charge," Tennessee said, making every word distinct.

To his credit, the storekeeper looked straight back into the cold eyes of the tawny-haired bad man whose bloody exploits were dramatized on the streets of the Southwest by urchins with wooden pistols. "She'd be treated like a lady in *my* store," he said, "if your name was Quanah Parker."

The road led Tennessee sometimes along the edge of river timber, sometimes through the trees, several times in sight of the Clear Fork. Then it turned down to a ford, and Tennessee felt the tension beginning to mount. He knew he was riding into an hour of crisis in his life—one of those times when he must suspend his emotions and do his bleeding later.

The log buildings of Stella's headquarters, he found, were arranged around a tree-grown quadrangle in a grove of cottonwoods, elms, and pecans; and the north, or river, side was occupied by a large two-story structure, in which he assumed Stella had her office. When he rode up he saw an army-branded horse under a McClellan saddle at the hitching rail in front of the building.

He had dismounted and taken a step toward the hitching rail when an army officer backed out of the door and was followed by Stella herself, in white shirtwaist and navy-blue skirt. Since they had eyes only for each other, they trusted their feet to find the way down the steps to the ground. The officer was a handsome man in his thirties, with wavy coal-black hair and a gallant mustache trimmed over firm lips and white teeth. His tailored uniform molded a set of shoulders, back, and legs that would find favor in any woman's eyes, Tennessee suspected. Obviously they found favor in Stella's. Her eyes were a shining amber as she looked up into the man's face. Now on the ground, she moved into his arms for a leave-taking kiss, which lasted too long for Tennessee to shrug it off as a token gesture of farewell.

Stella stepped back and, letting her hand drop down to the officer's arm, turned with him toward the hitching rail. It was then that her eyes settled on the tall, burly shape standing motionless beside the red stallion. A shock of fright hit her face, causing all color save a mottle of freckles to recede from it. Then Tennessee noticed something in her slanted black eyes that sent a wave of bitterness through him: He saw that she, too, was afraid of him.

"Tennessee!" she gasped, shaking her head as if rejecting his presence. And suddenly, too quick for thought, she took a step and stood in front of the trim cavalryman, her arms lifted defensively.

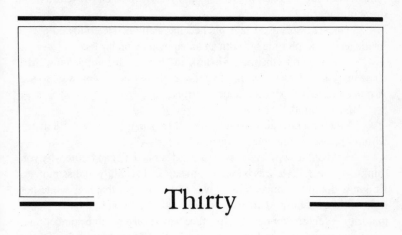

Thirty

The cavalryman set Stella gently but firmly aside, apparently puzzled and not at all pleased by her reaction to the sudden appearance of this big, wild-looking stranger in buckskin jacket and Levis. The man's shaggy, streaked hair and three-weeks' growth of beard proclaimed the plainsman, but his cold eyes and face, as much as the way he wore the ivory-handled .44 Colts, proclaimed something additional and more deadly. "What—what—" he said, before he was interrupted by Stella, who had regained much of her self-possession.

"Armistead, this is Tennessee Smith, my brother-in-law. Tennessee, I want you to meet my fiancé, Captain Armistead Gordon Randolph." She searched Tennessee's face with intent black eyes for reaction to the word *fiancé*, but he remained impassive.

Randolph stepped forward and would have offered his hand, but Tennessee merely nodded and let the hitching rail between them excuse him from shaking hands. Stella noticed. Her lips firmed, and a flush beat up into her freckled cheeks. Tennessee led Grassfire to the rail, then stood undecided.

"If you're leaving," he said to Randolph, "might ride with you far as the ford. Been wanting to discuss something with you."

"Certainly," Randolph said, reaching for the reins of his mount.

"No!" Stella whipped under the hitching rail and caught Tennessee's arm, holding it firmly. "No you don't, Tennessee!" She had lost color again. "You can speak to Armistead some other time. Come inside.

I must talk with you. Go on, Armistead. I'll see you when you return from the scouting trip."

Tennessee shrugged and hitched the stallion. He followed Stella inside as Randolph rode off with an unhappy look on his face.

Stella moved to the massive desk and turned. She nodded toward a chair but couldn't wait for him to get seated. "What do you want to see Armistead about?" she demanded sharply.

"Never mind," he said.

"You have no claim on me!" she said in a ragged voice. "I'll marry whom I please! Damn you, if you dare to hurt—"

"Hold on, now," Tennessee said. "Damned if I can figure why you think I'd object." He was beginning to admire his ability to dissimulate. He knew that this woman's mark was on him deeper than any white-hot iron could ever burn. Three years and motherhood had given her more maturity, even greater beauty. Her face was stronger, more somber than he remembered it; her bosom was as full, her waist still young-girl slender. Her hips—a gust of desire swept him. He had to keep reminding himself that she hated him, that she had repeatedly tried to have him killed. "Stella, I told you in Tennessee you ought to marry again. Still think you should." Then, as the pythonic muscles of his shoulders stirred faintly, he murmured, "To the right man, of course."

Her lips twisted with scorn. "And you think you're that right man."

"No, I don't. But don't start feeling too damned proud. I wouldn't be the right man for any woman." He studied her face. "How does Jubal take to Captain Randolph?"

"Why—why, he likes him, I'm sure. Respects him. I'm sure I've heard Jubal say so."

"Good enough." He grinned sardonically. "Go ahead and marry him, then, with my blessing."

"Why is Jubal's opinion important to you?" He read suspicion and distrust in her face. "Do you think you know something about Armistead I don't?"

"Forget it, Stella." Tennessee picked his hat off the floor and held it in his hands. "Look . . ." He kept his eyes on the hat. "You mind if I see the boy?"

She was silent, leaning back in a sitting stance against the top of the desk. She did not so much as move a foot on the floor or stir a paper on the desk. Her voice, when she finally answered, sounded flat under the control she was exerting.

"It's not what you think."

"What do I think?" he asked gently.

"That he's yours. Maybe he favors you. You inherited that dark streak in your hair from McEveride ancestors. He did, too. Well, I'm telling you now. *Paul* was Smitty's father. I ought to know."

Tennessee nodded. "I'm his uncle, then. And I want to see him."

Without another word Stella left the room through the side door, and Tennessee heard her calling from the hallway. He heard enough to know that she was directing someone, evidently in the room across the dog run, to bring Smitty to the office. She did not return until Lula May opened the door and led into the room a little boy who almost took his breath away. Then Stella came in behind them and drifted across to the west window. Lula May was not as pleasant-looking as Tennessee remembered her. Her quick black eyes observed Tennessee carefully, missing nothing.

"Hidy, Mist' Tennessee," she said, with no trace of a smile. "This here's Smitty."

The little boy had a seraphic face crowned with pale golden hair streaked with brown from a line of light-brown hair in the middle of his head. And he had his mother's freckles—or would have when he saw more of the sun. He walked toward Tennessee, looking up, and the big shaggy man came down to one knee before him. "How's your pup?" Smitty asked and moved to Tennessee's bent knee.

"He's been bad," Tennessee complained. "Run off and played in the woods."

Smitty's laughter was like the tinkling of silver bells. "Mine done that, too," he said. Then he reached an elfin hand and tugged at Tennessee's beard. "You're a bear!" He laughed merrily. Then his face sobered, his sky-blue eyes dancing with glee. "Are you a bear? Do you eat li'l' chillun?" He came in against Tennessee, who closed his big arms around the little fellow and hugged him gently.

He figured Stella didn't want him holding the boy, but he didn't give a damn. By God, he couldn't keep his hands off the kid! With infinite tenderness he held the little body close. "Yeah, Smitty," he said, "I'm a bear, all right. But I just eat honey and horses."

Smitty put his hands against Tennessee and pushed back so that he could look into the big man's face. "I wanna live in a tree, too!" he shrilled. "Lemme go home with you!" He began bumping his forehead against Tennessee's chest. "I'll eat—a li'l'—ole—horse."

"Smitty," Tennessee said, "tell you what." Smitty was still with a fey expectancy. "I got a red horse nobody can ride but me. I'll let you ride him with me."

The little boy gazed with ecstatic eyes. "Are you my daddy?" he asked, now drawn across the threshhold of a dream. "*You're* my daddy! *You're* the one!"

Without turning from the window Stella said sharply, "Lula May, take Smitty out! It's—it's time—it's time for his nap." Her voice was shaking with emotion.

"Oh, lawdy, I clean forgot!" Lula May reached for Smitty. "Come on, honey. Time for yo' nap." Her eyes brushed Tennessee's close up. They were softer now, touched with kindness.

"Feed your pup good," Smitty urged in treble as he was ushered out. "Don't forget."

"My pup's a coyote," Tennessee called after him. "He eats rabbits and fried chicken." He heard Smitty's delighted laughter tinkle across the dog run and stop at the sound of a door closing.

Tennessee remained on one knee, his eyes on the door where Smitty had vanished. Stella remained at the window, her back still turned. One thing was certain: He would never again be sorry for Stella because of the trouble he had caused her; he was glad now that he had violated her for his pleasure. How can she hate me, he wondered, when she looks at Smitty? God, what a boy!

Finally she said in a cool, steady voice, "I wonder if you will ever cease to amaze me. How can you talk like that to a little boy? You who have killed so many men. You whose very name frightens the boldest ruffians. You who have wallowed in the mire with the worst women."

Tennessee stood up and stepped to his chair. He sank back in it and closed his eyes, letting the silence run.

"You can't stay here, Tennessee." Her voice sounded flat, without feeling.

"That's right," he agreed. "I can't stay."

Stella turned and faced him squarely. "No. I want it clear. I knew this would happen." There was strain behind the resolution in her face. "It's not for you to decide whether to go or stay. You must go. You've been in my service to hunt down the Krulls for the past three years. Now that service is over. I've lost faith in private violence, private vengeance—most of it, anyway. When this Indian-raiding and *comanchero*-trading are stopped, the Brazos country and the Panhandle will bloom as cattle country. Only the army can handle the Indians. The forces of law and order will follow the army in. So I'm planning to cooperate with the army's campaigns against the Comanches and Kiowas. I have some definite plans . . . but let that go. The point I'm making is that I no longer have any use for the services of a—a man like—like—"

Suddenly Stella's eyes looked sick in her freckle-mottled face, but she took a moment's bearing and went doggedly on. "Like you, Tennessee. Smitty will be a rich man someday. He'll be an important man in Texas affairs if his values are sound and—well, if he doesn't turn wild and irresponsible on the frontier. I intend to give him a stepfather who can teach him to be a gentleman. But what chance would any man have to teach him anything if you were here? I won't have Smitty making a hero out of a gunfighter, following him around, imitating his ways of moving and thinking, grieving his heart out in a little while when that gunfighter comes to the end of his bloody trail. So I'm discharging you, Tennessee. I advanced you some money in San Antonio. We'll regard that as expense money. Now I propose to pay you a sum of money that will make you independent if you invest it properly. I don't want to appear unkind unless I have to, but—"

"Ain't a matter of being unkind," Tennessee interrupted finally. "Just of being wrong. You paid me five thousand dollars for my part of the farm. I been spending it hunting down Krulls. My choice. I ain't worked a day for you since I left San Antone. So forget the blackmail. I never had the least notion of staying, anyhow."

She walked to the desk and stood again with her back turned, absently straightening objects on the desk. "Not blackmail." Her voice was low, schooled to evenness. "Do *me* the kindness and take the money. I'm sending you away because of your bloody record. And I caused it. Do you think my conscience ever lets me rest?"

"Stella, let me ask you a question." He sat up, watching her turn toward him. "Does your conscience really have much say when you're arguing with yourself about what to do?"

Her black eyes regarded him somberly. "Not always. You know that. Some things have to be—even if they tear your heart out. In every life there's one thing a person will give up everything else for. Sometimes it changes, as it has in me. I have to give up a lot, but I don't plan for happiness—or expect it."

At last, Tennessee thought, he had the clue as to why Stella had hired the assassins. It was possible that she didn't hate him at all. But whether she did or she didn't proved nothing. Even if she felt for him what he felt for her, she would still be quite capable of doing whatever she had to do to keep him away from Smitty permanently. Not that she did care for him, of course. But he had to admit a grudging admiration for her determination and strength.

"If you think you made me a killer, you're wrong," he said. "Think back. I was wanted by the Union army before I ever heard of you. Let your conscience rest. You can forget you ever laid eyes on me after today.''

She continued to stare at him, her slanted eyes narrow and cool. "Tell me something," she said finally. "Why did you kill that monster Bull Jakes with your bare hands?" In the corners of her eyes, he thought, there lurked a memory of their first camp in Texas, where they'd speculated about the outcome of a fight between him and Jakes.

"It was a setup," he said, "with Bull Jakes unarmed to force me to fight him bare-handed. If I'd shot him when he was unarmed, I could've got lynched for murder."

"I heard it was over a Mexican girl."

"Hard to believe you'd hear that," Tennessee said shortly. "If you did, you heard a lie. Weatherford understood the situation. In fact, damn him, he's been trying to cut in on the girl himself."

"Cut in? Then you—then there *was* a Mexican girl there?"

"Yes! Yes! You know there was! Stella—what the hell?"

"Tennessee," Stella said, very coolly now, "why did you come here today?"

Tennessee scoured his beard-grown face with an uncertain hand. He reckoned that poor Mary Wilson had a sorry advocate in Tennessee Smith at the court of Stella McEveride. "Well, there's this woman, Mary Wilson, needs help the worst way," he began guiltily, expecting Stella to think the worst right off and, from the expression on her face, not being disappointed. Grinding his teeth, he plowed ahead, holding nothing back—Mary's teenaged pregnancy and miscarriage, the killing of her father, the cruelty of small-town society and frontier women, her experience as a dance-hall girl, her marriage to the outlaw Kramer, Earth Daughter, the protection of Horse Walking, his own debt to the Wilsons for saving his life, his responsibility for the attack, Mary's defenseless position. . . .

When he had come angrily to a close, Stella said stiffly, "Seems to me this girl has had an incredible run of bad luck."

"Well, she couldn't *hide* none of it," Tennessee said sarcastically. "All that happened to *her* is known. She couldn't hide the Indian rape because of the half-breed baby and Kramer's mouth. Then, too, she wasn't rich. She had to live the best way she could. And she didn't have hell in her heart nor any desire at all for revenge nor a killer for a brother-in-law nor a—"

"All right, Tennessee," Stella said coldly. "You don't have to *try* to be crude. For the record, though, what does this girl look like? Is she pretty?"

"Yes, she is," Tennessee snarled. "But she's not a girl. She's crowding up toward forty. Will you talk with her? Find a place for her? She's got to be safe from them goddamned harpies that pull their skirts aside before I can go on with my business."

"Not so fast." Stella pulled a chair up squarely in front of him and, from it, looked him in the eyes. "All she brought away with her was a nightgown and a man's coat?" When he nodded, she said, "Last night was cold. What did she sleep under?"

"My blanket." Sweat began to cover his face.

"Where did *you* sleep?" she asked softly. "Under the blanket with her?"

"That's right," he said. "I'd tell you it's none of your business, but you'd manage somehow to ask *her*, and she'd tell you. Mary Wilson is the best woman I know. I love her like a sister, and I'd as soon breed a sister if I had one."

"I don't believe you," Stella said bitterly. "Damn you, can't you remember whom you're talking to?"

"We were under the same blanket to keep warm and get some sleep. All we done was sleep." He leaned forward, his cold gray eyes locked in a struggle with her hard black ones. "Now, listen close. I want to be sure you understand me." Reaching a long arm, he tapped out each word on her knee. "I didn't breed Mary Wilson. I didn't hump her. I didn't screw her. I didn't fuck her."

She struck his hand from her knee. "That'll do, Tennessee! Is there no end to your vulgarity?"

"While you're asking me questions you got no business asking, let me ask you one. I saw how much you enjoyed kissing Captain Randolph out front." Then, as her color mounted high, he asked, "Have you been to bed with him?"

Instantly she slapped him with a full-arm swing. For the sake of diplomacy he chose not to dodge the blow or catch her wrist. He was glad he had not shaved before making the visit; his whiskers offered some cushion against the shock of her palm. When he merely looked at her, she caught her breath and bit her lip.

"I'm sorry," she said. "I really am. That wasn't exactly fair."

"Shrewd, though," he pointed out cynically. "Slap me, and it looks like you're too proud to deny it. But the slap could be a lie, too."

"All right. I'll answer your question. I enjoy kissing Armistead." Suddenly a furious blush was blotting her freckles. "He's nice to kiss, but I haven't been to bed with him. When I kiss him, I don't think about that."

He closed his eyes wearily. "Why lie about it?"

"Believe it or not, it's the truth," she insisted. "I really don't."

"Ought to forget him, then, and find somebody who does make you think of bed. I know your mettle. Randolph will bore hell out of you in six months. He'll wind up running little errands for you."

"Hush!" she said. "Quit it, now! Armistead is what I need. He's what I want."

"What about Mary Wilson?"

"Go get her. Actually, I need a housekeeper, and I hope she'll do. But go bring her and let me talk with her."

Stella followed Tennessee outside, where her eyes lit on Grassfire. She had been too emotionally wound up to notice Tennessee's mount before. "Oh, Tennessee, what a magnificent stallion!" she exclaimed. "But—but that great horse—the dun? I never heard. Where—what—"

"Dead," Tennessee said. "You ought to see this stud when he's fresh and in good flesh. He's wore down to the bone right now. You wouldn't believe the miles he's run in the last three days. He was caught wild." He turned the stallion away from the rail and stepped into the saddle.

The virility of the picture they made put a gleam in Stella's eyes. "You certainly make a pair," she admitted, and then, for no apparent reason, the color rose once more behind her freckles, changing the tint of her face.

"Wish I hadn't promised Smitty a ride on Grassfire with me. Won't matter, though, what he thinks of me. Don't reckon I'll see the kid again. Don't aim to."

"When are you heading out?"

"Tomorrow morning before daylight. Got to let this horse get some rest. Hope you can loan me a horse for the rest of today. Going back to Fort Griffin after I bring Mary out."

"Why?"

"Well," Tennessee said slowly, looking over her head, "I ain't been in a town for a month. Few things. . . . And I might run across Smitty out here."

Stella dropped her eyes. "You can have the horse, and I'll have somebody wait up and show you to a cabin when you come in tonight."

"Tell him to stay out of the shadows," Tennessee said quietly. "Tell him to stand in the light." Then he rode out, leaving Stella gazing after him with puzzled, unhappy eyes.

She stood where she was a considerable while, now wishing she'd told him that Nancy Waterton was visiting Elizabeth Evans, the colonel's wife, at Fort Griffin. Why hadn't she? Nancy would come hotfooting it out here if she learned of Tennessee's presence—and she *would* hear of it, from Armistead. Or had Nancy known Tennessee was coming before he arrived? Were their simultaneous visits to the Clear Fork really a coincidence? Or were they having another of their rendezvous? Stella knew she was being ridiculous. Since it was Mary Wilson's trouble that had brought Tennessee here, she could hardly think that he and Nancy had planned to meet in Fort Griffin. Why, her mind was working for all the world like that of a jealous, suspicious wife! Why did she feel threatened by Nancy Waterton, when the girl was in love not with her fiancé but with her brother-in-law? What were her real feelings? . . . Disturbed by all these questions she'd been asking herself, Stella turned suddenly toward her office door, went inside, and attempted to forget about Tennessee by immersing herself in her work.

At the general store near the fort, the storekeeper, whose name was Buck Harris, had outdone himself. He had gone to the big store on Government Hill and found an attractive dress that had been ordered for an officer's wife who had tired of life in Fort Griffin and gone back East before the dress arrived. It had been tried on by a dozen women and fitted none of them. Then Mary, with every intention of making do with whatever size it was, put it on and found it a perfect fit. The dress was a robin's-egg blue, with puffed sleeves, tight waist, and full skirt; it showed off Mary's good, slightly voluptuous figure to flattering advantage.

The storekeeper had also come up with a cape of darker blue that went well with the dress; it had been pawned to him by a young prostitute. And, finally, the amazing Harris had dug out of a storeroom at the back a sidesaddle, which he had placed on the back of the grullo.

When Tennessee rode up to the hitching rail in front of the store, he saw the sidesaddle, and he noticed that the horse's coat was sheening in the afternoon sunlight from a fresh grooming. The elbow grease had to come from the storekeeper, he figured. What the hell? he wondered.

Inside, he found the storekeeper a changed man. There was animation in the man's face and a gleam in his eyes. He swung about and moved toward Tennessee with an alacrity that somehow did not seem characteristic.

"Listen," he said in a lowered voice, "before the little lady comes out. The outfit I got together didn't cost me much because of one thing and another. No offense, but I won't take no money for it. Ain't unusual to contribute when folks get burnt out or scalded out by Injuns."

Tennessee studied the man narrowly. "Well, when you put it like that," he said slowly, "what can I say?"

Then Mary stepped out of a back room in the outfit, and Tennessee thought he understood. She had washed and brushed her golden hair, and the knowledge of how she looked in the blue dress had colored her face with pleasure. She made a picture that tugged at the heart, and the storekeeper felt as if he had painted it. He had groomed the grullo to complete the picture. The beauty he had created had no price, and he would not cheapen his creation by putting a price on it.

"Mary, you're beautiful," Tennessee said, and Mary blushed self-consciously. The storekeeper was actually beaming as he fidgeted around the room. What the fellow wanted to do, Tennessee thought, was step forward and touch up the puffed sleeves or tug a fold of cloth, maybe, and then step back and admire the effect.

"I'll bet you're starved," Tennessee said, suddenly remembering that he hadn't had any food since breakfast out on the Double Mountain Fork.

"Oh, no," Mary said. "I eat dinner with Mr. Harris, and it sure was good, too." She walked over and shook hands with the storekeeper. "Mr. Harris, I won't never forget your help. You're a good man."

"Glad *you* think so, anyhow," the storekeeper said. "You come back, now." He cleared his throat. "If you ever need anything—anything in the store or help of any kind—why, I'd take it kindly if you'd let me know."

Out on the Clear Fork road, Mary began to droop in the saddle and grow somber. Tennessee knew she was dreading the meeting with Stella McEveride. He was dreading that meeting, too. By God, he hadn't known what a beautiful woman Mary was when she was all fixed up! Her meeting with Stella might not go as well as it might have if she had worn the soiled nightgown and man's coat, especially now that Stella knew that he and Mary had shared the same blanket last night. Sometimes Stella puzzled Tennessee with what appeared to be a woman's jealousy in her remarks about his relations with other women. He couldn't understand how her hatred of him left any room for jealousy.

"Mary, don't worry about meeting Stella," he said finally. "After she knows you, she'll love you." He grinned. "Unless she gets jealous. By God, you're beautiful!"

Mary's lips began to tremble. "What good is it?" she whispered brokenly. "Jake—Jake—he can't see me."

"He didn't want you to die with him, honey. Told you to hide and save yourself. So buck up and look proud. I got a feeling you're about to begin a new life."

There was a saddled horse at the hitching rail in front of Stella's office, and Missouri came through the door as Tennessee and Mary rode up. When Tennessee dismounted, Stella appeared in the doorway. Neither she nor Missouri had eyes for anything save the golden-haired woman in blue on the crane-colored mustang with the blackbird sheen. Tennessee helped Mary to the ground and turned toward Stella, who was now walking over to them.

"Howdy, Missouri," Tennessee said.

"Later, later," Missouri replied, never removing his eyes from Mary.

"Stella, this is Mary," Tennessee said.

While the women were talking, he nudged Missouri aside. "Where's the horse she promised me?"

Missouri was bleach-eyed and cool. "There he is." He nodded toward the horse at the hitching rail and spat an amber missile at a stone three yards away. "Hitch your hoss to the rail and ride off any time."

"Maybe I better put the stud in the barn."

Missouri spat again at the stone. "No need. I'll take care of him."

Tennessee studied Missouri a long moment. For some reason the ex-guerrilla was not friendly, and Tennessee did not want to linger. "All right," he said, his voice hard-edged, "I'll let you. He's so wore down maybe he'll let you lead him. But don't try to ride him. He's a wild-caught stallion and won't let nobody ride him but me. That ain't advice. I'm telling you. I don't want him breaking loose after he throws you."

Tennessee turned from the hostility in the bleached-out eyes and stepped back to the women. "Mary"—he touched her arm and felt the quick brush of Stella's dark eyes—"I won't be seeing you before I ride out. Remember now. You ever need me, let me know. Ain't much I wouldn't do for you."

Mary's eyes began filling with tears. Suddenly she pulled Tennessee's head down and kissed him. "Folks claim you ain't got no heart," she said, her voice shaking. "They don't know. They don't know you at all."

He walked toward the horses and heard Stella tell Missouri to show Mary into the office. She moved up behind him as he unbridled the horse. He felt the hard rake of her eyes and looked at her, feeling a wave of anger engulf him at the sight of her high-cheeked, black-eyed look.

"Like a sister!" she said, bitterly sarcastic.

Sick with rage, he waited until he could control his voice. "When will you know whether she suits you?" he said coldly.

"As soon as I talk with her."

"If she don't, leave word with the man waits up, and I'll ride out with her in the morning. If she suits, I reckon this is good-bye, Stella." He swung up to the saddle and started to rein away.

"Is that all?" Stella asked.

He looked at her, puzzled. "Yes."

"You've developed a pretty deep dislike for me, haven't you?"

It might make her bleed a few drops if he told her he had, but he thought he ought to be honest here at the last. "No, I can't quite manage that. Wish I could. I don't trust you. Don't think you're honest. Not after the lies you've tried to hurt me with. I don't want to stay around you. But—no, Stella, I don't dislike you." He saw her face register shock, and then he had the horse in motion and was drawing away.

Thirty One

Tennessee rode back to the grove and crossed the quadrangle at Stella's place at nine o'clock that night, having spent a short time in a barber shop, a short time in a restaurant, and the rest of the time in a saloon. He was, therefore, close-shaved, medium-shorn, and slightly more than a third drunk. As he dismounted at the corral gate, a shadowy figure came off the ground at the base of a tree and lounged forward. Then came the mellow organ notes of Jubal's voice.

"Mist' Tennessee! This here Jubal. Watch out yo' thumb don't slip offen that hammer, suh."

The gun had come sliding to hand as if it had a mind of its own. Shoving it back into his holster, Tennessee said, "Jube! Hellfire, Jube, I wanted to see you today. Why'n't you come speak?"

"White folks business." Jubal accepted Tennessee's hand with a brief, horny-handed pressure. "I's waiting around, though, see if you-all holler. Then you gone. Miss Stella say wait up and show you where to sleep. Say put you in that cabin on the end." He gestured toward the northernmost cabin in the west row. "Bed made up. You go on and pile in. I'll look after the hoss." Jubal shook with silent laughter. "Like old times. Smell like you done took on a man-size load."

"Stella leave any word about whether the lady I brought will do?"

"Sho ain't no doubt about that. She do, all right. See that light upstairs in the big house? That Miss Stella and Miss Mary talking. They been at it all evening and all night."

"You mean they ain't stopped even once?"

"Oh, no! Oh, no! I don't mean none of that. They sho stop *one* time!" And suddenly Jubal broke up. A white man might have shouted at the top of his voice and bawled with hilarity; Jubal shook and staggered and lurched with subdued, almost soundless mirth. Finally he mastered himself enough to speak. "You 'member Miss Stella's favorite saddle hoss, that Tennessee mare? Well, suh, we got her in a pen by herself 'cause she coming in heat, and Mist' Missouri turn yo' wild stud in the corral next to that pen. Co'se the stud oughta gone in the barn and been fed. Don't get me wrong, though. Mist' Missouri a good man. But he so mad he ain't thinking after that stud pile his ass on the way to the barn.

"Well, shonuff, soon as that mare switch her tail and the season smell hit that stud's nose, I mean he just riz in the air and bust over that fence, knocking them top rails ever' which a way, and come down in that pen with the mare. Man, you never heared such a racket! We swore the mare was just coming in and wouldn't noways take no stud yet. Lawdy, how a man gonna know? And she do try to keep him off. She whup around and turn herself away 'cept when she kicking. She bite and squeal, but that devilish stud—lawd God, he like a man won't listen when a woman say no. When she come up on her hind legs, he riz up and took her in his fo'legs and turn her. Then she back on her feet, and him on her, hugging her up close. Mist' Tennessee, when he start humping her, you oughta seed that Tennessee mare. She just stand under him, looking sorta sorrowful and sorta pleased, too. . . .

"Well, suh, Miss Stella sho musta heared that stud knock rails when he lam over the fence. Maybe she look out and seed the stud in with the mare. No matter how it happen, Miss Stella come flying out the back do' with a rifle in her hands. She the maddest woman you ever seed! She cussing and hollering how she gonna kill that wild son-of-a-bitch. 'Fo' she get to the corral, though, the stud done hit his shortrows, and she just stop and watch that mare try to make up her mind whether she gonna bust out crying or start singing. When the stud come down, Miss Stella turn tow'd the house with a funny look on her face. She glance back once with a look at that mare like she thinking, 'Well, missy, now you knows!' She pass me without seeing me 'cause I done step behind that cottonwood tree over there. But I seed her face. She sorta frowning and biting her lip. Look like she trying like hell to keep from grinning 'fo' she get inside the big house."

"That was Missouri's fault!" Tennessee snarled. "And I told the son-of-a-bitch to keep his ass off that stud."

"Don't blame him too hard, Mist' Tennessee," Jubal said earnestly. "He love a good hoss and think he can do mo' with 'em than anybody else. But he the best man Miss Stella got."

"Bastard's got something he's holding against me, Jube. You know what it is?"

Jubal hunched his shoulders. "I knows, all right."

"Well, what?"

"If I tell, I got to talk up to you. Sound uppity. You get mad, likely."

"Talk up."

"Mist' Missouri suspicion you done Miss Stella wrong." Jubal squared his shoulders resolutely. "Me, I got to tell you, Mist' Tennessee. I done suspicion that same thing, too. Lula May claim she *know* you done it. Co'se I ain't zackly *mad* at you, suh. Us colored folks, we got mo' onderstanding of that kind of thing than what white folks do."

Tennessee had had no doubt as to who had sired Smitty and did not need this confirmation from one of the three people who had been closest to Stella during her pregnancy and who, obviously, shared her secret. "Whatever I done," he said, "I've paid for it, and I'll keep on paying, looks like."

"How many of them scannels you done kilt, Mist' Tennessee?"

"Ain't but three Krulls and the army officer left," Tennessee told him. "Jube, I'm having trouble with that soldier. Think back. Think how he looked."

Jubal became very still, apparently thinking. "He mighty dim," he said finally. "His face don't come out. If I seed him, maybe it might ring—"

"Could Captain Randolph be the man?"

Again Jubal was motionless. "What you do if I say he the one?"

"I'll kill him."

"Even if I say he a good man now and Miss Stella aim to marry him?"

"Even if you say that. He was rotten once. He wouldn't be right for Stella. Smitty, either."

Jubal sighed. "He ain't the man," he said. "If he is, I done clean forgot what that Yankee sojer look like. How come you think Cap Randolph might be the one?"

"Just wondering—seeing he's a damned Lincolnite." Tennessee yawned. "Think I will turn in. Really didn't need that last drink. Funny thing about liquor, Jube, last quarter of a bottle ain't got much taste."

He cut across the quadrangle and entered the end cabin. A fire was going in the fireplace, and shadows flickered along the whipsawed boards of the floor and on the mud-chinked logs of the wall. There were three bunks in the room. He was vaguely aware of other furniture—chairs, a table, and a desk—but all that interested him was the bunk that was made up for him with top covers turned down. He hung his guns on the back of a chair and took off his clothes, letting them drop to the buffalo robe that served as a rug; then he got into bed, pulled up the covers, and went to sleep as if sandbagged.

In a bedroom upstairs in the big house, Stella and Mary were still awake. Stella kept thinking, as the two women talked, about what had happened that afternoon with the Tennessee mare.

She and Mary had been in the bedroom when they had been interrupted by a great commotion from the direction of the corrals.

She had taken one look and flung open the window. Leaning out, she started shouting, "Missouri! Jubal! Somebody! Get in there and stop that stallion!" She whirled from the window. "Oh, that wild brute son-of-a-bitch!" She hurried from the room, trailing words behind her as she headed for the back stairs. "I'll kill that red son-of-a-bitch if it's . . . the last . . . ." She raced out the door toward the quadrangle.

Later, when Stella had returned, she had found Smitty in the room with Mary. "The hussy!" she cried, heaving a gusty, lugubrious sigh. Her face had a flushed look and her lips were twitching with a fugitive grin that she was having difficulty repressing. "Squealing like that! Why, she enjoyed it. What a magnificent brute of a stallion! No wonder she—no wonder—" Suddenly the tint of her flush deepened. "Did you ever see—you know what? I'm *glad* it happened. It's her first time. I never would have her bred. Oh, but *this* colt, now—why, it should prove *very* interesting."

"Is he a sumbish?" Smitty said.

"What?" Stella threw Mary a startled, guilty glance and looked at Smitty. "What did you say?"

"He heard what you called the stud," Mary explained, smiling. "Wanted to know what the hosses was doing. Wouldn't noways let me off without I told him something. So I claimed they was wrassling."

Stella nodded. "Good enough." She reached for the child's hand. "Mary, I'm going to let you rest awhile before supper. Tonight, if you aren't too tired, we'll talk some more. But I can tell you now, Mary, that I want you with me. I can't begin to tell you how glad I am you came to me. And I promise you one thing. No small-town house cats will ever again draw their skirts aside when you walk past. If they do, damn them, they'll sure pay for it."

Mary took three steps and had Stella's free hand against her cheek. She shut her eyes against the blur of the room, whispering brokenly, "Oh, Mrs. McEveride, thank you, thank you, and—and thank—thank God, too! For the first time—I can't remember when—somehow, all of a sudden, I feel safe! I feel so *safe!* . . . Oh, Mrs. McEveride, you sure won't never regret it, I promise you! There won't never be anybody that'll work harder—"

"Hush, now, Mary," Stella said, her own voice not quite steady. "Hush, now. You *are* safe. From now on you'll be safe. And don't ever let me hear you call me Mrs. McEveride again. Call me Stella. That's your first order in your new job."

After supper they had retired to the same bedroom, which Stella had assigned as Mary's permanent quarters. They took up where they had left off, occasionally refilling their cups from the coffee pot kept warm on the small wood-stove heater in the room. They told each other their life stories with a remarkable frankness, laughing over some of Stella's growing-up embroilments, weeping over each other's misfortunes and abuses. . . . Then, finally, when the moon had become an old story to coyotes and wolves and hunting owls, they arrived at the subject that had been at the back of both of their minds.

"Well, Stella, I'm convinced now you do want me here," Mary began, moving toward confession. "So I'll make bold to admit at first I was some scared you'd hired me to make sure I didn't ride off in the morning with Tennessee Smith."

Stella came alert, startled. "Why on earth would I care who rode off with him?" she snapped.

"Reckon I always was a fool for taking chances," Mary said, almost as if to herself. "But here goes again. Stella, I nursed Tennessee for over a month when he was mightnear killed by Injuns once. Well, he was out of his head a lot of the time and—"

"When was this?" Stella cried. "Why, I've never heard—"

"Sure, you haven't. It must been two, nearly three year ago. I'll begin at the beginning. Him and Nueces Riley went into them canyons of the Staked Plains, looking for a bunch of Comanches that Brownlow and Jimpson Krull was knowed to run with. But it was Brownlow that Tennessee hoped to find and kill. Surely I don't have to tell *you* why. Well, they aimed to pass themselves off for *comancheros* and buy cattle from the Injuns and hire Brownlow to help drive 'em off. Then, when they was far enough off to make it safe, Tennessee aimed to kill Brownlow Krull. That there was their plan. Well, when—"

"Mary!" Stella burst out. "Did all this *really*—did you say Nueces Riley was with him? The same Nueces Riley that works for me?"

"There sure ain't but one Nueces Riley," Mary told her. "Stella, let me tell the whole thing. When they come up to them Injuns in Blanco Canyon, it was a bunch led by Broken Fang, a mad-dog Comanche that Jake always claimed was just the worst Injun in the whole world. Well, like I say, when they come up, Nueces was trying to talk Broken Fang out of them cattle, him talking Spanish, when Brownlow Krull rode up. When Tennessee seen that handsome buck and knowed who he was, why, all he could think of was you, Stella McEveride, down on your back with that good-looking stud between your legs a-having his way with you and you telling Tennessee later on that Brownlow Krull, for all he knowed, was a better stallion than Tennessee himself was. . . ."

Observing with evident satisfaction what she was doing to Stella, Mary continued talking. She recounted the shooting down of Brownlow Krull in the midst of his fellow Comanches and the close-to-mortal wounding of Tennessee, emphasizing the real heroism of Nueces Riley in the rescue of his companion. She told of nursing Tennessee and of listening to his delirious revelations. Coming to Tennessee's violation of Stella, she defended Tennessee on the grounds that a man "stone-blind" with lust was in no condition to count costs to himself or anybody else. She ended by saying, "But it come to mean more than that to Tennessee, Stella—so much more that he was willing to throw away his own life and his friend's life to kill Brownlow Krull. He loves you, honey. He loves you so wild he'd swap the rest of his life in hell for just one week with you in his arms, whispering sweet words in his ear."

"I don't—don't believe you!" The anguished, muffled cry came from the bed, where Stella lay prone, her face hidden from Mary's eyes. She had jumped up and moved about during Mary's narration, finally winding up on the bed, moaning softly, as if in protest, toward the end. "You *can't* know that—that last! What he'd give—and for what!"

"*He* sure don't know it," Mary replied serenely. "But he *told* me what he'd give and for what. Out of his head, sure—but that's when folks say what they got shut up tight in their minds and hearts. He loves you, Stella. Make no mistake about that one thing. Trust a woman to recognize what it was she seen and heard. Now, Stella, I don't aim to tell you no more of what he said. It ain't my right to tell it nor yours to hear it, and there ain't no man living I'll ever be loyaler to than Tennessee Smith."

"You've said—said quite enough." Stella came off the bed with a tear-stained face but with eyes in which banked amber fires were glowing. "But go one step further, Mary. You're a beautiful woman, and I know a few things myself about Tennessee Smith. What is he to you? What are you to him?''

"Oh, I do love him, Stella, and I think he loves me—about the same way I do him. If I's foolish, I reckon I'd claim your question didn't have no bearing, seeing I'm about ten years older'n Tennessee. But you know, and I know, that a woman my age can have a mighty good time with a man ten years younger and give *him* a mighty good time, too. But I don't reckon I could bring myself to dirty up my feeling for Tennessee by no lovemaking—not that lovemaking's got to be dirty. It just ain't *that* kind of love, and any sort of trashy sex mixed in would sure kill it. And I'd allow Tennessee feels about the same way. Stella, listen to this here, which sure don't flatter *me* none, one way you look at it, but it ought to set your heart and mind at rest once and for all. I slept with Tennessee last night. It was cold, and we didn't have but one blanket. Well, with his big arms around me, I felt good and warm. But for all the notice he taken, I could been a funny-shaped boy he was holding. All he wanted was sleep. Does that answer your question, honey?''

"Yes," Stella said. "Yes, it does. You're an honest woman, Mary." She started walking about the room, her eyes gleaming. "Much more honest than I am." Clasping her freckled hands, she brought them up against her forehead. "Oh, I have plans for a lot of people! You, Mary—always with me. Big ones for that grand cowboy, Nueces Riley. But the best ones, the biggest ones"—she brought her hands down, revealing eyes that were shining through mist and lips that were trembling on the verge of a smile—"are reserved for Mr. Tennessee Smith McEveride. He'll never leave me again, Mary. I'll bind him to me and hold him for the rest of his life. You'll see."

"May not be easy," Mary said laconically. "You got some fences to mend."

Stella turned, stood still. "What do you mean by that?"

"Why, he allows you hate him, and that hurts him some. Or if you don't *hate* him exactly, he allows you ain't got no more feeling for him than if your heart was stone and the rest of you was made out of wood, and that—"

"Why, that's crazy!" Stella cried. "It isn't that way at all!"

"There's more," Mary charged. "He's sure in his own mind that you been putting hired killers on his trail. John Greenwood, for one. And there's others. He swears you want him dead."

"Why, that's the most ridiculous—" Stella was aghast. "And yet, thinking that, he kept on after the Krulls—after Brownlow!" Suddenly she clutched at her head with both hands, her eyes shut tight. "Oh, Mary,

Mary, Mary!'' Then her eyes flew wide open. ''Damnation! What time is it?''

Mary got up and moved to the window. ''Why, it's got to be around four o'clock,'' she said, turning back. ''Would you believe, now, that we done talked mightnear the whole night away?''

''We'd have heard that stallion move out, wouldn't we?'' Stella cried anxiously, catching up her coat from a chair. ''Oh, God, Mary, if he's already gone! I'm going over there. I just hope I have to wake him up.'' The last of her words came from beyond the door.

At four o'clock in the morning, Tennessee awoke dully to a sense of profound depression. He got out of bed and pulled on his Levis; then, naked from the waist up and barefooted, he sat back on the edge of the bunk and slumped there. It seemed to him that he was caught in a maze of aimless existence, that he had steeped himself in blood to no purpose. In this moment he was sick of bloodshed and could see nothing else ahead of him. He would head back to the Staked Plain and try to cut a Krull out of the Comanche herd and lay down some tracks for Parruwa. And he would grab his horse and leave now, before breakfast, before he came in contact with any member of Stella's household. He hung there, muscle-locked by a hopeless inertia. By God, he would move, he would stir himself, he would shake himself loose!

Suddenly he raised his head with dull expectancy. Outside, a pad of light, running feet accompanied by a rustle of skirts approached the door. It flew open, and a woman's silhouette showed briefly in the doorway. He recognized the shape of Stella McEveride. She closed the door and put her back to it, waiting for her eyes to adjust to the darkness of the room.

''Ought to knocked,'' he growled. ''Lucky you didn't get shot.''

''Let's strike a light.'' She felt her way across the room and shook a spluttering match to flame. Then she raised a chimney and lighted a lamp. When she turned, her wide, dark eyes told him that she was keyed up to a high emotional pitch. ''I was afraid you'd already gone. And I don't know who could've run you down on that wild, terrible stallion. You smell like—you aren't drunk, are you?''

''What you want?'' he demanded harshly.

''Take it easy.'' She moved toward him. ''That Mary's a jewel. I'm in your debt for bringing her to me. And I give you my word that I'll protect her with everything I've got. . . . Let me look at your back.'' She put a hand on his burly shoulder and pushed him around. He heard her gasp.

''Oh, Tennessee!'' she cried softly. Then, moved by compassion, she brought her softly cushioned body impulsively against his back and clung to him, her face against the side of his neck. When he turned his head, she kissed him softly an inch from his mouth. "Why, Tennessee? *Why?*"

"Why what?"

She traced the scars with gentle fingers, infinitely compassionate. "Why did you have to shoot him down in the middle of those Indians?"

He sighed. "Don't know. Reckon I lost my head."

"Because it was Brownlow Krull?"

He couldn't see her face behind him. "You done talked to Mary," he murmured. "What *you* think?"

Her answer was a long time in coming. When it did come, it was in a voice barely above a whisper. "I don't just think. I know. Mary's opened my eyes to you, Tennessee. There were so many things I didn't understand about you. Why you became such an avenger after San Antonio. Why you developed such a hatred for Brownlow Krull. You who'd never hated anyone, never trusted hatred. Yes, I agree with Mary about the whole thing."

"You think I'm in love with you?" he asked numbly.

"Yes, Tennessee," she said gently. "I think you are. No, don't turn around. Not yet." She gripped his shoulder and braced it firmly with a stiff arm. "I know, too, that you've been thinking I hate you. And I don't, Tennessee. I never have. Not even at the water hole that next morning after what you did to me. Oh, I was angry! Because you'd turned me into an animal. Mary said that in those moments when you can believe I don't hate you, you still think I have no feeling for you at all. Tennessee, you're so terribly wrong."

Tennessee sat hunched on the side of the bunk, motionless, silent. He was gripped by a paralysis of uncertainty, not knowing yet where he and Stella were heading. Then her hand left his shoulder, and she came from behind him fast, reaching toward the chair where his holstered guns hung. Her hand closed on the ivory handle of a .44 Colt and brought it up level. Deliberately she pulled back the hammer. Her high-cheeked face was bereft of all color save for slanted black eyes and stark mottle of freckles.

"Tennessee, would I kill you if I had cause?"

"Yes," Tennessee said, eyeing the muzzle of the Colt. "No doubt about that."

"All right," she said, suddenly breathless with excitement, "I'm going to tell you how far from indifferent I am. Why? Because I've got my reasons, that's why. And when I tell you, Tennessee, if you come at me—if you lay a hand on me—I'll kill you. Do you understand?"

Tennessee nodded. "You don't get your finger off that hair trigger, you may not wait to see what I do."

"There's this physical thing when you come near me. A man thing. I come in heat. It was that way before we got to Texas, and I fooled myself that it was something else. And then at that camp in Texas when you forced me. Such unbearable pleasure! And then such shame and remorse! And now do you know what I'd like to do more than anything else in the world? I'd like to pull off my clothes and get in that bed with you."

Tennessee started up from the bed. "Stella! Stella—"

The gun muzzle tilted with his movement. "I mean what I say," Stella murmured. "I can't miss at this distance."

Sinking back on the bunk, Tennessee tried to understand her. He remembered her hired assassins. This woman was capable of lust, maybe even a kind of love, and—at the same time and influenced by neither—a remorseless purpose. "You don't need the gun," he told her, somewhat grimly. "I'll never touch you again. Unless you ask me to—and I don't expect you'll ever do that." He reached for his shirt, watching Stella lower the hammer of the Colt and thrust the gun back into his holster. "I'll never get the chance to, anyhow, seeing I'm riding out of here quick as I can throw saddle on horse."

"No," Stella said. "No, I don't want you to leave. Why do you think I ran over here before you got out of bed? I want you to stay—and work for me."

He stood up, barefoot, amazed. "You forgot about Smitty watching me wipe my mouth on a sleeve while Armistead's showing him how to use his napkin? Where's the change?"

"In my mind, mostly," Stella said, calmly now. "I didn't know you cared for me, Tennessee. I know it now, even if you deny it. So I know now that you'll work harder for my good than for your own. I'd be a fool to let a man like you get away from me. Now that I know I can trust you, I know that you won't be bad for Smitty. Anyway, what I have in mind will keep you away from Smitty most of the time. You see, I'm brutally frank."

"I'll be, too," Tennessee said. "I told you yesterday I didn't trust you. I still don't. I don't want you knowing where I am or sending people to find me."

Stella studied him narrowly with slanted eyes that gave her face a mysterious look in the shifting lamplight. "Yes, I know," she said slowly. "Mary told me about that, too." She fell silent, as if considering what more needed to be said, then burst out, "Tennessee, I simply can't believe you seriously think I hired John Greenwood to kill you! That's the most ridiculous—ask Missouri why I *fired* Greenwood. He'll tell you—if you won't believe *me*—that it was because of his obsession with those guns.'' Her eyes shifted to the ivory-handled Colts hanging in their leather on the chair. ''Those right there, as a matter of fact.''

''*Somebody* hired him. He admitted it to me before he reached for his gun. But forget Greenwood. What about Mysterious Pete Epps? Somebody hired *him*. You went to see him. Did you hire him?''

He could see her face darken and, for a shaky moment, was afraid he had her cornered. ''You're well informed,'' she admitted. ''I was thinking of somebody to head a security force here at headquarters or to serve as a bodyguard. I plan to be back and forth between headquarters and the ranch west of here a good deal, and Missouri can't be in two places at once. But when I went to speak to Mysterious Pete Epps, I saw what he was and shied off. If you'll believe me, it should help you come down to someone more likely to want you dead—if you have any others on your list. Do you?''

''Might help, when I get time to think. Right now I don't know *what* to think.''

Stella shivered. ''Let's build a fire,'' she suggested. ''We've got a lot more talking to do before breakfast, and it's cold as hell in here.''

''Hell is cold?''

''It thrives in all weathers. Anything else you want to know about hell, though, you ask me. I'm an expert.'' She stood behind him while he shaped the wood in the fireplace and nursed a match flame to light the kindling. ''Tennessee, I need you terribly, as you'll see when I explain. You aren't leaving me, so just start getting used to the idea. . . . With that out of the way, you've got to understand a few things about, well, about our relationship. After all this frank talk, you might get the wrong idea about what it will be. Nothing's changed about that, Tennessee. I'm sure I'll keep on coming in season when I'm near you, but I'm going to marry Armistead Randolph—and be faithful to him, too. He's what I want for the years ahead and what Smitty needs.''

''Pretty damned cold-blooded,'' Tennessee said bitterly. ''You ain't in love with him.''

''Well, not starry-eyed or panting, maybe''—her eyes were glinting in the firelight as he looked up—''but I really am fond of him. And Armistead's nice to kiss and will be pleasant to sleep with. I won't mind that part of it, I know.''

''Go on, damn you!'' Tennessee snarled over his shoulder. ''Enjoy yourself! By God, I haven't said I'd work for you!''

"Why, what's the matter?"

"You know what! An Apache wouldn't do what you got planned for me. Sure, you want me around. To see it all. You kissing that bluecoat bastard. Holding hands and laughing. Your window curtain come down and the light go out, leaving the window dark. Them little bedroom smiles you give each other in the daylight. Your belly start swelling up. Oh, I believe every goddamned word you say! You won't mind sleeping with Armistead at all—or mind watching me wring my guts, either."

There were dancing devils in her eyes. "I had to be frank so you wouldn't misunderstand. This is a one-time conversation about our feelings for each other, to clear the air. You don't have to be so damned crude."

"Who's crude? Me?" He got to his feet and picked up his boots. He kicked a chair nearer the fire with a bare foot and whispered an anguished oath at the contact. Stella was drawing up a chair, a faint smile curving her lips.

"Talk about crude!" he said bitterly. Now she was seated, openly smiling. He was angry and stung and beginning to fear that she was playing him, much as she would a medium-sized trout. He wanted to hit her hard. "What'll you talk about to me after you're married? Tell me what a stud Armistead is on his first night home after a month in the field? Tell me how many times a month, by actual count, Armistead is pleasant to sleep with? And will you tell me how many times he wilted and quit before you got warmed up good?"

She was laughing at him, making no effort to disguise her amusement at his efforts to shock and anger her. "Why, I wouldn't think of confiding such intimate details of married life to a bachelor," she protested, with a smile not wholly free of malice. "What we'll talk about is the cattle business, long-distance communication, and scouting for Comanches—particularly those sheltering the Krulls. And your part—a key part, too—in all that. Because, Tennessee, I want you to set up a homing-pigeon system of communications with stations in the Staked Plains, New Mexico, Colorado, Indian Territory, maybe even Kansas, since I'm beginning this spring to send cattle up the Chisholm Trail, as well as over the Goodnight-Loving route. Don't you see what it will mean if—"

"Wait! Wait a minute!" Tennessee dropped his boots and sank into a chair. He held his head, which was aching dully, with both hands. "All right, I'll do what you want me to—for a while. Until you marry Randolph. Then I leave." He raised his head and looked at her. "When you marrying him?"

"I don't know," she said, her eyes searching his face. "Not soon, though. Maybe not for a year or more. Smitty doesn't need him yet. I'll tell you in plenty of time for you to pack your gear. But why? What difference does it make—I mean, *really*? I can't believe—"

"Guess you can't. The loop missed *you* and dropped on *my* horns. I ain't sure I like you a whole lot, Stella. But that ain't much help, along with what you're doing to me other ways. I might could stand watching you and Armistead cozying up in the open. But when your belly starts swelling with a weaker, duller, lesser brother or sister for Smitty—"

"Why weaker or duller?" she flared instantly. "Why lesser?"

"You know more about stock breeding than that," he said grimly. "The bull contributes as much as the cow."

"As a matter of fact," she returned defiantly, "Armistead is much like Paul. One of his attractions for me, I think, is that he reminds me of Paul."

"What's Paul got to do with Smitty? Why in the hell don't you quit lying? I stumbled across the bloody rag you got rid of in the woods in north Alabama. You couldn't been pregnant when we left Tennessee." He had wanted to sting her, and now he had. His words drove the color from her face, leaving it with a slack, defenseless look.

"I was sorry for you and for what I done at that camp by the water hole until I saw Smitty," he went on. "Then I was glad. And now I'm proud." He paused, glaring, then reached all the way back to his *McGuffey's Reader* days to one of the few characters in literature that had ever aroused his interest. "Paul couldn't got a kid like that on Helen of Troy. Armistead won't get much better than average on you. You think I don't know whose get Smitty is! He's mine! Mine, by God!"

Slowly Stella straightened, her face tightening. When she faced around in her chair, her eyes were gleaming with confidence. "You poor, ignorant Simple Simon!" she said. "That bleeding is called spotting. Not at all unusual after a two- or three-month pregnancy." Now she was smiling, her eyes glinting with malice. "You sowed your seed on planted ground, my friend. What a waste! Of course, you can believe what you want to."

"I do," Tennessee assured her. "I believe you're a damned liar."

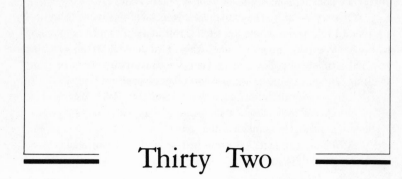

Thirty Two

Tennessee and the Polka Dot Kid picketed their horses in a saucer-shaped depression half a mile back from the edge of Palo Duro Canyon and, carrying rifles, canteens, blankets, and a buckskin satchel of food, made their way on foot to the verge of the great earth rift. Already the gray light of approaching day was improving visibility by the minute up on the High Plain, where they stood listening to the cheerless whispering of the raw, incessant wind against the greening earth. Then, faintly, they heard the yapping of dogs in the canyon.

The Kid pointed into the darkness. "Him Quahadi down there," he said.

Tennessee wrapped himself in his blanket and stretched out on the ground; the Kid followed his example, and they made themselves as comfortable as possible as they waited for light to show them the Indian village in the canyon.

It was a day in the red spring of 1870 in *Comanchería*. During the past fifteen months Tennessee had ridden thousands of miles in the service of Stella McEveride, establishing homing-pigeon stations at dwellings or business posts of paid informers who were either full-time or part-time employees of Stella. Establishing a pigeon loft at one of these stations consisted of the delivery of young birds from Shen's great loft at headquarters with instructions on how to train the birds to return to their new lofts when they were released at varying distances; it included also the delivery of older, mature birds that would return to headquarters at Fort

Griffin and others that would return to Stella's stockade on Cibolo Blanco Creek, which drained into the Colorado a hundred miles southwest of Fort Griffin. Periodically, as these pigeons homed back to Stella with messages, Tennessee had to replace them at the stations with others like them. At the same time he had to bring birds trained to return to the station back to headquarters, or to the ranch for sending messages to the station.

Driving a light spring wagon drawn by a team of fast, rugged horses, Tennessee supplied Stella's fortified ranch on Cibolo Blanco Creek; Dick Weatherford at the holding ranch on the Pecos; Jaime Valdez, one of the "reformed" *comancheros*, in Las Vegas; Benito Candelaria, one of Panchita's several brothers, in Santa Fe; and Nueces Riley at the swing-station ranch on the Arkansas River in Colorado. Then, riding Grassfire and using pack horses with speed and bottom under packsaddles especially designed to hold bird crates level, he serviced the Polka Dot Kid in Tule Canyon, John Redwing at Stella and Redwing's sheep plaza on the Canadian River in the Panhandle, Eagle Horn—a kinsman of both Redwing and Jesse Chisholm—at a chancy little trading post in the Antelope Hills, and Eagle's brother Buck on the Little Arkansas in Kansas.

Tennessee remembered well Stella's announcement of a new pigeon station on the Pecos. It was back in early winter that Stella had hailed him from an office window as he was riding past on his way to the barn. He pulled up and waited. The hitching rail was lined with saddle horses, and the rumble and murmur of men's voices came through the window. Stella had come down the steps and crossed to him. "When are you leaving for the Pecos?" she wanted to know.

"Tomorrow morning before daylight," he told her.

She said very casually, "This time leave only half the usual number with Dick Weatherford and deliver his other birds to Panchita Candelaria in Fort Sumner."

Before Stella's watchful eyes, he schooled his face with an iron control. "When you sign her up?" he asked mildly.

"About the time we doubled Dick's allotment of pigeons. He's been supplying her. . . . All right, I'll answer your next question. Dick's been trying to win Panchita's love. But supplying her through him was *my* idea. What chance would he have had if she were seeing you? They're married now. I've just heard. But she won't join him at the ranch until the summer. Her interest in the *cantina*—"

"I could've been trusted with this information," Tennessee said coldly. "You went to a lot of trouble for nothing. You'd already ruined Panchita for me. And I knew she'd turn to Weatherford. Didn't you expect Weatherford to turn to somebody else when you turned from him to Randolph?''

A wave of color swept her face. ''I didn't turn from Dick,'' she murmured warily. ''I never regarded him as—as a—''

''You mean you never encouraged him at all? You never let him kiss you?'' A sardonic smile gleamed white against his hard, brown face. ''You told him no right off, I reckon, when he asked you to marry him.''

''He kissed me once or twice,'' she admitted defensively. ''One of those moments—I don't know—a meaningless kiss—easier than—than—oh, pushing him away and hurting his feelings.'' In a flash she was angry. ''You've got your gall, blaming me for one or two harmless kisses, permitted out of kindness! You who have slept with God knows how many of the worst sluts! You who—who—what do you mean I ruined Panchita for you? Tennessee! . . .''

He had ridden on toward the barn. She had called after him, but he had kept going and had not looked back. . . .

The sun moved up from the underworld and peeped over the horizon. Then it had moved into full view, and the gray light was gone like a sucked-dry mist. And even as sunlight flooded the High Plain, a gloomy shade filled the canyon. Through it, however, the Comanche village was visible, made small by distance, with miniature tepees scattered about the canyon floor. It was a large village of several hundred lodges and, Tennessee reckoned, upward of two thousand people.

As he and the kid watched, they held their heads close to the base branches of two junipers that grew on the rim of the canyon wall. They knew, however, that the chance of being discovered by the Indians was remote, for Comanches in camp were not vigilant. They posted no guards, sent out no scouts for purposes of defense, and paid no attention to the barking of their dogs.

The warmth of the early sun, as it strengthened, began to ease the bite of the cold, and Tennessee felt his muscles slowly relax. He would have more of that sun than he needed before the day was done. Then he smiled, thinking of Smitty. . . .

Returning to headquarters one afternoon, he had followed his pack horses past Captain Randolph's horse at the hitching rail and on toward the barn. Then, behind the big house, he had seen Smitty standing stiff and defiant before his mother and his future stepfather. Jubal and Shen stepped out of the barn to take charge of the pack horses, and Tennessee reined Grassfire over to the group behind the house, since it looked as if there was some kind of problem. Randolph was scowling and angry, and

Stella looked serious and concerned. Tennessee had only a back view of Smitty.

"Private fight?" he asked lightly. "Or is everybody welcome?"

Smitty whirled, a frightened, baffled look on his little face. Slowly the look faded. He pressed his lips tightly together, trying to repress a tremulous grin. He knew a friend had arrived.

"Smitty's been cursing," Stella snapped. "And I can imagine where he learned it."

Tennessee leaned from the saddle, caught a handful of Smitty's clothing, and brought the little boy flying to the saddle before him. "If you mean me, you're way off. I ain't swore a single oath in front of him. What'd he say, anyhow?" He looked at the severe countenance of Randolph, feeling Smitty burrow into his shirt front inside his jacket.

"Ask *him*," the officer said, a white, pinched look around his nostrils. "Ask him what he called me."

"All right, Smitty," Tennessee said. "What did you call Captain Randolph?"

"A sumbish," Smitty said against Tennessee's shirt. "I called him a sumbish."

Stella glared at Tennessee accusingly. "And who's always calling people bastards and sons-of-bitches?" she demanded.

"Stella, this boy needs discipline," Randolph insisted. "We ought to be married at once. Then I could take him in charge. He's not too young for a firm hand. What I say is that if you train a child in the way he should go, he won't depart from it."

"I don't know," Stella said. "You may be right."

"You keep pointing at me, Stella," Tennessee said. "Let's pin this thing down. Smitty, who'd you ever hear say sumbish?"

The boy wriggled against Tennessee's shirt. "Mummy called Grassfire a sumbish."

"When was that?" Tennessee asked with a savage grin, watching Stella's face go blank. Her eyes became veiled and wary. She was looking ahead and dreading the rest of the conversation.

"When Grassfire was wrassling with the Tennessee mare," Smitty said around the edge of Tennessee's jacket. Stella lifted a hand vaguely, her mouth open in silent protest.

"When did you call Captain Randolph a sumbish, Smitty?" Tennessee asked coolly.

"When him and Mummy was wrassling," Smitty shouted in treble.

"Where were they doing it, son?" Tennessee murmured gently and saw Stella wince.

"In the bedroom. They was wrassling on the bed."

"Tennessee!" Stella said swiftly. "It's not what it sounds like!"

"All this is beside the point," Randolph complained. "The circumstances aren't the issue. It's what the boy said. He needs to be disciplined for saying the word. I insist on that point."

"Never mind, Armistead!" Stella said in a ragged voice, watching Tennessee. "You have no children, so you're an expert. Let it go."

"Oh, I don't know," Tennessee said sardonically. "What he says makes good sense to drill masters. And it's the way you train a dog." He lifted Smitty up before him and looked into the elfin face under the brown-streaked golden hair. "Smitty, you made a mistake. A sumbish ain't somebody who wrassles. A sumbish is a bad person that you don't like."

Understanding grew on the little boy's enchanted face. "He's a sumbish!" he shrilled, a seraphic smile shaping his cheeks and touching his sky-blue eyes. "Captain Randolph is a sumbish!"

"Go ask Mary for a cookie." Tennessee set the little boy on the ground and watched him scamper away. Then he turned his cold eyes on the two adults before him. Randolph looked greatly offended, and Stella had a forlorn, pleading look on her face. Tennessee did not spare her. "Let me give you some advice," he said with a stinging quietness. "Next time, lock your bedroom door if you don't want Smitty growing up too fast." He turned Grassfire and rode on to the barn.

An hour later he cut across the quadrangle toward the cabin in which he slept when he was at headquarters. He had spent a longer time than usual in rubbing down Grassfire, hoping to avoid Stella. The encounter outside had left him feeling bitter. He thought she might be waiting for him, and he didn't want to see any more of her until he felt kinder toward her—if he ever did. He had wasted his time, however; she was still waiting.

She came out from a corner of the big house and intercepted him in the middle of the quadrangle. Randolph's horse was gone from the hitching rail. Her freckled face showed strain and embarrassment and some suggestion of a slowly developing storm that might reach the surface at any moment. "Wait a minute," she said curtly. "You can at least hear how it was, damn you!" She drew a deep breath. "I had Armistead in the bedroom to help me hang a curtain. We pulled out the bed to stand on, and I lost my balance. He caught me, and we both fell on the bed. Well, it was so ridiculous that that—well, we were laughing, and all of a sudden he pulled me close and kissed me. Wallowing on the bed with him wasn't my idea of proper fun, I guess. Anyway, I was struggling a little to get loose when Smitty walked in. Honestly, I hadn't given it a thought—''

"Stella, you don't need to explain anything to me," Tennessee said wearily. "You ain't obligated to concern yourself with my feelings. What I feel about you and Randolph, well, that's my grief, not yours."

She drew herself up, stiff with resentment. "You mean you don't believe me."

Tennessee scowled. "Well, why should I? You been lying steady about who sired the boy. Why not about going to bed with Randolph?"

She gazed at him blankly. "I told you the truth," she said numbly. "Believe what you will. Paul was Smitty's father, not you."

A stirring of his burly shoulders was Tennessee's only response to this reiteration of what he knew was a lie. When he spoke again, he was coursing a trail more dim and distant than it appeared to be. "Stella, you may have to rethink this fellow Randolph. Maybe you ought to look over some other husband material."

"He did sound like a perfect fool a while ago," Stella admitted.

"No. Something more serious. Stella, either Randolph or Captain Romine is the cavalry officer who raided McEveride Plantation with the Krulls. Now listen. Romine told me that Randolph saw Bull Jakes in Fort Smith and told him that Jakes was a member of the Krull gang. According to Romine, Randolph used to serve liaison between the Army of the Cumberland and Union guerrillas in east Tennessee. He said Randolph saw Bull Jakes in Parson Krull's camp on one of his visits. Has Randolph ever said anything that makes you think this might be so?"

The color had washed out of Stella's face. "Good Lord, Tennessee!" she whispered, appalled. She was silent for long moments, thinking. "He knew Tinker Dave Beatty. I know that because he got Tinker Dave's name on a statement about you. He got statements from General Forrest and General Wheeler and others that they regarded you as a bona fide soldier in the Confederate army in spite of the fact that your name wasn't on any muster roll. That's how we got you included under the general amnesty for Confederate soldiers. Of course, he did it for me, but you'd still be an outlaw if it weren't for him. But he said he'd just *heard* of the Krulls when I told him about them. So if Romine told the truth, Armistead may well be the one."

"News to me, that about the amnesty. Reckon I owe you for that. And him."

"Now that you know what you owe him, what will you do if he's the one?"

"You know what," Tennessee said. "But Romine's my pick. I

think he's the one hired the killers. He was close enough to things every time—even in Fort Smith in time to hire Mysterious Pete Epps. It was him saw you come out of Mysterious Pete's boarding house. He eased my way for me and was so helpful and seemed so frank he could've fooled me easy. Like when he fed me Wes Krull in Fort Sumner—guess he was getting rid of partners, planning to quit. If Randolph convinces us Romine lied, I want Jubal to see Romine. If Jubal recognizes him, that's it. Randolph could lure Romine to Fort Griffin, maybe. Him or you, one, could set him up for Jube to see. Now, can I trust you to handle this thing? Can I trust you to question Randolph and find out which officer lied?''

''Yes,'' she said without a moment's hesitation.

''What if you wind up convinced Randolph's our man?'' Tennessee asked.

''A man that treacherous? I wouldn't protect him.''

A week after he and Stella had this conversation, she told him that Randolph, when questioned, had freely admitted to her that for a short time he had served liaison between General Thomas's army and Union partisans in east Tennessee. His service in this capacity had been limited to just three contacts with Tinker Dave Beatty's irregulars. After that his work with partisans, rogues, and guerrillas had been taken over by Captain Boone Romine, who was more experienced in the field. Randolph said he had heard of Parson Krull but had never seen him or any of his men. So far as he knew, he had never laid eyes on Bull Jakes.

Stella had taken a longer look at Randolph and decided not to burden his gentleman's conscience with any complicity in the entrapment of a fellow officer nor burden his mind with any knowledge of the matter, either. She had learned from Randolph that there was a big military conference shaping up at Fort Richardson, in Jack County, for late March. The purpose of the conference was to unify and coordinate military policy afield in the protection of settlers against marauding Comanches and Kiowas. Army personnel at the forts in New Mexico, particularly at Fort Bascom, because of its proximity to Texas, were urged to attend the conference at Fort Richardson. Randolph said he expected Captain Romine to be there.

Immediately Stella sent a message to Dick Weatherford in the Pecos. Four days later a pigeon, released by Weatherford at Fort Bascom, arrived at headquarters with the information that Romine would attend the conference at Fort Richardson and would visit Stella at Fort Griffin to discuss Stella's offer to buy two thousand head of cattle, to be delivered at Romine's ranch on the Gallinas River. Stella's tentative offer, if confirmed on Romine's visit, represented a profit that no clear-thinking cattleman would have passed up. Certainly for cattle acquired from Indian raiders at *comanchero* prices, it was an offer Romine could not turn down.

Tennessee blinked to stay awake, remembering the Kid's relief at the sight of him when he had ridden into Tule Canyon the day before. The Kid had been holding a message from Stella for two days and, with time running out, was preparing to watch the Indian village alone. Briefly, the message had stated that Romine had recognized Jubal and the trap set for him and had panicked. He had fled northwest, straight into Comanche country. The orders were to intercept him. Nothing else. Nothing else was needed in this lawless land.

It didn't surprise Tennessee that Romine was revealed as the Krull guerrillas' army connection. He'd been figuring for some time that the swamp-eyed bastard was the one. Now, if he could only get his hands on the damned renegade. . . .

They ate cold food, and Tennessee went to sleep, the Kid having promised to wake him if anything of interest happened in the village. When the Kid roused him by tossing pieces of sod, the sun was an hour past the meridian. Tennessee blinked and looked into the canyon.

"Him *hombre* come now," the Kid grunted.

A mile or so from the village, a white man was riding up the canyon on a tired horse. Tennessee put his field glasses on him and, after studying him a long time with squinted eyes, decided the rider was Romine. Tennessee saw a party of young warriors go racing down the canyon, riding bareback with weapons in their hands. They plunged to a halt before the lone white-eyes and then accompanied him to the village. A shift of the glasses to the middle of village showed a group standing before a large tepee, waiting for Romine and his escort to ride up. Tennessee had the impression that the white man had been expected; word had probably been brought by a scout or transmitted by smoke signal while he had been sleeping.

The center of attention in the group was a grim-looking, hawk-faced young warrior in beaded vest and fringed leggings. Since he was wearing a feathered headdress, Tennessee judged that he was a chief and that he considered Romine's visit to be in the nature of a state occasion. At the young chief's elbow, talking and gesticulating, was an old white man with long white hair held off his face by a black headband. The Kid had a look through the glasses and identified the two as Quanah Parker and Parson Krull. Before the riders reached the plazalike open space where the big tepee stood, the Kid had identified others: Broken Fang, Bull

Bear, Humping Brother, Singing Wolf. . . . Parruwa, whose quests for entertainment and glory were solitary, was not there, the Kid said; nor was Jimpson Krull, who was an outcast from the Comanche dwelling areas.

Despite the years he'd spent on their trail, Tennessee was little moved by sight of the Krulls. Though he'd hunted them diligently and would kill them remorselessly when he caught up, for Stella's sake, he'd never really yearned to kill any of them except Brownlow, upon whom, for over two years, he'd thought that he'd inflicted final vengeance. Now there was little fire left in the ashes. In Tennessee's changing conception of the half-breed, Brownlow had used Stella's body for a sort of masturbation, since she had not participated in the act nor given him anything—except, of course, terrible revulsion and deadly hatred—and now Brownlow was rapidly shrinking to the proportions of just another dirty, savage Comanche buck. Actually, Tennessee was weary of the long trail, weary of too many lonely nights kept awake by an empty belly and a starved heart, weary of killing brutish men who regarded skill with the tools of murder as the most desirable mark of distinction. So he watched Parson Krull and Brownlow, along with Quanah and the other Indians on the floor of Palo Duro, with cold, dispassionate eyes.

The white man and his escort came up to the group before the big tepee and stopped. Then followed a show of waving and jerking of hands on the part of Romine and Quanah Parker while the others in the enlarged group stood watching. After a while the group that had awaited the white man's arrival conducted Romine into the big tepee and closed the flap. The mounted Indians rode off toward a herd of horses grazing up-canyon from the village, leading Romine's mount, and the other onlookers drifted off.

Tennessee and the Kid settled down to wait. Several hours passed. Then, when the sun was a flaming disk balanced on the flat crest of a cliff across the Palo Duro, several Indians erupted from the big tepee and went hurrying about the village, their high-pitched cries reaching up to the watchers. Soon there was commotion in the village. Warriors and boys were running their horses on the floor of the canyon, wheeling and careering among the tepees. Squaws were hard at work, with boys on horseback helping them now, dragging or carrying wood to a growing pile in the center of the open space near the big tepee.

"What they doing?" Tennessee asked.

"Get ready him big war dance," the Kid said.

Why, hell, it figured, Tennessee thought grimly. Some big raid, cooked up by Romine to advance or secure his own interests, was shaping up. And what was Romine's interest of greatest moment? Keeping Stella McEveride from making his villainy known to the public, disgracing him in the army, and possibly causing him to be court-martialed. But more important than these considerations was keeping Stella from informing Tennessee Smith of what she knew about him. So what was Romine's immediate objective? It stood to reason, Tennessee figured, that Romine would be best served by having Jubal killed and Stella killed or captured. Romine could lie himself clear of the hearsay evidence of any others Stella had told. He would go free on the frontier, especially in New Mexico Territory.

What Tennessee had to find out immediately was where the Comanches were planning to hit and when. That meant he had to go down to the village and persuade some Comanche to tell him or send the Polka Dot Kid to do the same thing in a different way. But Tennessee knew it was likely that Romine was aware of the connection between himself and the Kid. In San Antonio Romine had seen him apparently go to the rescue of the Kid against the McClanahan boys and would undoubtedly have followed up with some sort of investigation of his acquaintanceship with the Kid. Romine was bound to have learned through the Krulls, for example, that the Kid had War Drum. So Tennessee reckoned he would have to go into the canyon. He wondered why everything he did had to be done the hardest way there was.

"Got to find out where they aim to raid," he said. "After dark we'll injun down there and catch us a Comanch' out on the fringe."

"No catch him Romine?" the Kid inquired.

"No way to. Too late, anyhow. With pigeons already come down on the Pecos, Romine's same as a dead man now. A pack of cowboys and *vaqueros* will be waiting for him below the west Cap Rock."

They started for their horses when the bonfire was a faintly shifting spot of red deep in a sea of black, and the drums and rhythmic chanting cries of dancing Indians were rising in the canyon to fade in the upper air of the High Plain. They followed the rim eastward, the Kid leading the way on a paint gelding toward a buffalo-path descent into the canyon somewhere ahead. The trail down was winding and long and obscured by darkness. It took the loose-reined horses a long time to make their way to the canyon floor. Finally they were at the foot of the slope, picking their way around and between dark hummocks, skirting a shadowy butte, moving ahead in quest of the unseen river. The drums and wolf voices of the Comanche warriors sounded faintly from far around a bend of the great canyon wall.

Like a darker lace against a dark cloth, the willows along the Prairie Dog Town Fork showed in front of them. Tossing his head with angry intolerance, Grassfire followed the rump of the Kid's gelding down to a ford. Riding up the opposite bank, the Kid suddenly hissed like a cat and hauled back on the reins, which made the gelding back into Grassfire. Only Tennessee's instant jerk on his own horse's reins kept the flat-eared stallion's teeth out of the gelding's rump. Alongside Tennessee, the Kid said quietly, "Him tepees over bank."

They pulled back across the stream and tied the horses in the willows. Then they crossed back on foot and went up the bank like the shadows of two hawks flying low over brush. There were three tepees set forty yards away. They heard no movement, no sound; evidently the lodgers had deserted the tepees for the war dance at the bonfire. They went to the ground under glittering stars and snaked their way slowly, silently toward the nearest dwelling. With his chin on the ground, Tennessee watched the Kid inch up to the grounded buffalo hide and saw his head disappear through the open flap. After a while the Kid came to his knees and crawled back to squat by Tennessee's prone bulk.

"Injun go him dance," he said softly. He gestured over his shoulder. "Him tepee there belong What Buzzard Drop."

"Jimpson Krull!" Tennessee breathed. "How you know that?"

"Smell," the Kid grunted. "Him stink."

"How many sleeping here with him?"

"Maybe ten. Maybe him dozen."

"You think they'll all come back from the fire with him?"

The Kid shook his head. "Him Buzzard Shit come back quick." He waved his fingers to suggest flight. "Him stink bad. Slobber like sick skunk. Hurt him children. Comanche kick him ass out."

"All the goddamned Krulls ought to look and smell like Jimpson," Tennessee said. "Way they are inside." He came up on an elbow. "Well, by God, he's the one! Kill two birds with one stone. We'll step back and wait for that weasel-faced Mr. Buzzard Droppings."

They came to their feet and faded back into the brush of the riverbank. Not much more than an hour later, Jimpson Krull came riding down the canyon. He dismounted and staked his horse near the tepee the Kid had looked into; then he stooped under the flap and slid inside. Tennessee and the Kid moved in on whispering feet, like wind sweeping through grass, and stood like sentinels with the entrance flap between them.

The half-breed's horse had its head up, ears pointed, nostrils flaring. Tennessee reached into a pocket for one of the water-rounded stones he had picked up at the ford and threw it, hitting the horse and causing an outraged snort and a great stammer and trample of hooves. The little weasel of a man came through the opening and whipped erect, looking toward his horse. Then the barrel of Tennessee's Colt crashed down on his head, causing him to crumple and fall into the Kid's arms.

"Why you hit him?" the Kid complained, dragging the dead weight toward the horse. "Why you don't cover him mouth with hand, make him walk?"

"Might've bit me," Tennessee said, walking up the rope toward the frightened horse. "Or got slobbers on me. Anyhow, pack better this way. Damned if he don't stink, at that!"

Tennessee quieted the animal with gentle hands and soothing murmur, and they tied Jimpson Krull across the horse and led it off toward the river. Three hours later, at midnight, they were several miles up Tule Canyon. Their captive was conscious now and riding astride with his feet lashed under the belly of his horse. He had amazed his captors by a fearful mewling and weeping intermingled with pleas that they would not hurt him, though they had made no threats of any kind. Tennessee called a halt near some scattered boulders at the base of a broken hill, where a rock-bound enclosure, like a room without a roof, offered a confinement which should, he felt, contribute to the sort of mental concentration he had in mind for Jimpson Krull in case the bastard required persuasion. Tennessee unloaded the captive and marched him into the enclosure, turning deaf ears to the snuffling pleas as he rebound the little man's ankles and sat him down with his back against a boulder. The Kid came in from the horses with enough wood for a fire. When the flames were highlighting the bunched wet mouth and beady eyes of Jimpson's chinless face, Tennessee was ready for business.

He drew a long, thin-bladed knife from under his jacket and held it in his hand, testing its edge. Squatting in front of his captive, he said quietly, "Jimpson, I'm Tennessee Smith. My real name's McEveride. I been on your trail for five years. You tortured to death a one-legged man in Tennessee. He was my brother. Ain't no reason I can think of why I shouldn't work on you with this knife."

Jimpson's head swung from side to side on his sleek neck. "No! no! no!" he cried desperately. "Please no hurt Jimpson! Jimpson no can stand hurt bad. Jimpson do anything no hurt. Anything! Please! Please no hurt Jimpson!" The minklike little man's stench was growing from a sickening staleness to an oily, nauseating vividness that was overpowering.

Tennessee rose and walked out of the enclosure. He went over to the Kid, who had preceded him, and took a long breath of air. "Hard to believe," he murmured. "By God, you wouldn't think a live man could smell that bad! Ain't sure what he's saying, either. That goddamned yammering. . . . Go ask him in Comanche what them Indians got in their minds to do.''

Tennessee stood there, listening to the Kid's bark and murmur and Jimpson's mewling. He hated the very thought of what he had to do. But he knew he could never face Stella and admit to her that he'd had Jimpson Krull in his hands and had let him go. Then, too, he could not have Jimpson running back to Romine and the Comanches with news of Tennessee Smith and the horse-hunting white Comanche called Spotted Horse. And he knew very well that the world would be better off without Jimpson, who was worse than a squaw when given the freedom to torture some helpless captive: Jimpson, who could not bear pain himself, became ecstatic at the torture of others.

Nevertheless, the feeling that Jimpson was one of nature's obscene jests shook Tennessee's faith in the seriousness of creation. If, indeed, there *was* a Creator, as people claimed, maybe He had a warped sense of humor. It would be a joke on men to send the soul of a murderer into the world in its own flesh . . . a hell of a joke, he decided. Whatever the point of Jimpson's existence—and he suspected there really was none—he dreaded the moment when he must plunge a knife into this Krull's corruption.

The voices in the enclosure stopped, and there came a pad of moccasined feet. The Kid moved up beside Tennessee, mopping his face with a piece of cloth. ''Him war dance get ready him big attack on fort-ranch down on Cibolo Blanco Creek,'' he said. ''Him all Comanche tell. Him Buzzard Shit get ass run off. Don't know nothing else.''

''When will they attack?''

''Don't know. Maybe him Comanche start sunup. But you know Comanche. Maybe not.''

Tennessee raised his eyes from the knife in his hand. ''Well, if that's all he knows. . . .'' He kept wondering why turning Jimpson back into earth was any different from what he had done to Fox Wilkins. ''Well, hell, I got it to do.''

The Kid touched his arm. ''Why you no like kill him Buzzard Shit?''

''I don't know, Kid.'' Tennessee dropped his eyes to the knife. ''But somehow—look at him, smell him. God! You get to thinking. Jimpson sure as hell didn't make himself. He ain't what he planned. It sort of hit me hard. By God, he ain't what he'd *like* to be. He's what he's *got* to be. . . . Don't matter, though. I can't let him live.''

''Give me him knife,'' the Kid suggested casually. ''Stay here. Me give him new mouth under him old one.''

"No," Tennessee mused softly. "If there's a goddamned jinx or something in this, it's mine. I got no right to smear you with Jimpson's stink." Then, turning, he swung into the enclosure, shutting his ears to Jimpson's whimpering, which began as soon as he entered the rock pen.

Moving fast now, Tennessee whipped out his left-hand Colt and brought its barrel down upon the little man's sloping head and, close upon that blur of motion, cut Jimpson's throat from ear to ear with the knife in his right hand. He jumped back to avoid the gush of dark blood, feeling as if he had made an opening through which poured a black wave of poisonous acid that could destroy the world. He looked down at the bloody knife, and Jimpson's stench blossomed out until it was like a dense fog in the night, tainting the air. Suddenly, for the first time in his memory, his stomach churned and a sour something pushed up into his throat. Tennessee flung the knife away and whirled aside, falling to one knee. He braced himself with a hand against a rock and was sick against the wall.

When he rejoined the Kid outside, the night air was cold against his clammy face. Now he was filled with shame and guilt. "Let's get on to your camp, Kid," he said. "We got pigeons to send—one to headquarters and one to the ranch. We got to let Stella and Jeff Slaughter know that Romine's sending the Comanches to attack the stockade ranch. Maybe we better make sure by sending two birds to Jeff at the ranch."

"No can make him sure," the Kid reminded him. "Got plenty pigeon fly him headquarters. Only one fly him ranch."

"Yeah," Tennessee remembered, "we were short on ranch birds. Well, we'll send two headquarters birds. Make sure as we can."

They moved toward the horses. "Well, I'm through with it," Tennessee said, as if thinking aloud. "I've done killed my last Krull."

"What about him Humping Brother?" The Kid paused before mounting, the lead rope of Jimpson's mount in his hand.

Tennessee rose to the saddle and settled in the seat. "He can live till the hair turns white on his black ass, for all I care."

"Him different me," the Kid said. "Him try night-crawl with Earth Daughter. Me get him knife sharp. Maybe cut out him balls. . . . Yeah! Sew him rocks up in bag." He chuckled. "No hump no more squaws. Fix him good."

Reining up-canyon, Tennessee murmured sardonically, "Kid, if I ever called you a white man, forget it."

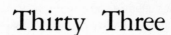

Thirty Three

After stopping at the Kid's camp only long enough to send the three messages and choke down enough food to keep himself going, Tennessee rode out of Tule Canyon around midnight and headed south on the High Plain. His task was to make, unseen, a race against time through Indian country and, assuming that the Indians would ride at dawn, stay well ahead of the Quahadi war party, with its spare ponies for each warrior. Twice his decision to leave his pack horses behind and not bring along a spare horse served Tennessee well. Once he sat the still, wary stallion under a cutback in a draw while a party of Penateka Comanches slowly passed; and again, from a clump of brush in Blanco Canyon, he watched a large party of Kiowas crossing the valley, headed north.

By the end of three days, he was emerging from the butte- and mesa-shadowed redlands east of the Cap Rock, and after another half-day, with the broken hills behind him, he was descending the long, almost imperceptible slope of a wide, shallow valley that had been formed by centuries of drainage into Cibolo Blanco Creek. Stella's stockade was a dark, rectangular shape with a coral center far down the valley—a wall of upright half-logs surrounding an adobe ranch house. East of the stockade a mass of loose-herded cattle, the beginnings of a trail herd destined for the Goodnight-Loving Trail, was slowly spreading out from a high-banked bend in the creek, and several riders were drifting along the ragged edge of the fan, keeping the cattle from scattering over the valley.

As Tennessee approached the west gate of the stockade, a lookout waved a greeting from the nearest of two towers on diagonally opposite corners and signaled for the gate to be opened. Tennessee entered along a short alley formed by the log walls of two dwelling rooms that were built against the inside of the stockade wall. Toward the east end of the stockade, the dwellings gave way to storerooms, smokehouse, black-smith shop, harness room, and wagon sheds, ending with the corrals and barn occupying the entire east end of the stockade, including corral-deep stretches of the north and south walls. The doorways of all these struc-tures opened on a wide court, in the center of which was situated Stella's pink adobe ranch house.

A detail of some thirty blue-clad troopers were lounging about the court, clumped here and there playing cards or pitching horseshoes, rubbing shoulders with Stella's cold-eyed ex-Rangers and former Con-federates. Several of the brash younger men called greetings as Ten-nessee rode past, asking when they might expect the redguts and whether they might capture a few squaws. Some of them watched Tennessee with awed speculation; most observed him with still faces. They all knew that this big man in buckskin shirt and Levis on the gaunted wild stallion was the man-killer Tennessee Smith, who rode the wild Indian country where no white men, save renegades and Comanche captives, were supposed to leave tracks without leaving also the feet that made them. Tennessee rode on, raising a hand in a general greeting. Beyond them, on a second-floor deck of the adobe, Stella McEveride stood waiting between two tall men—Jeff Slaughter and Captain Armistead Gordon Randolph.

The two men nodded, lifting casual hands. Tennessee saw that for some reason Stella's face had tightened as he approached. She was completely absorbed, her dark eyes narrowed and intent, as if she would see inside his brain and heart before he opened his mouth. Then she turned and, followed by the two men, walked through an open door and upstairs to her apartment.

Jubal was at the stallion's head. "Miss Stella say you come on up. I'll take care this here old Grassfire."

"How long you-all been here?"

"Got in last night 'bout ten o'clock."

Tennessee dismounted. "Tell me about Romine, Jube."

"Man, I still got the shakes!" Jubal stood holding the stallion's reins up close to the bit, shaking his head. "Well, suh, I's outside changing the dirt in Miss Stella's flowerpots, like I does ever' spring, when I heared this hoss leave the road and come tromping up behind me. Lawd God, I *sho* oughta took a look! But there I's caught on my knees a-shaping dirt around them flowers, and I just *knowed* one of the hands was riding up to devil me 'bout doing woman's work. They does it *ever'* spring that come. So I didn't aim to give whoever coming to give me a hard time no satisfaction of looking up and paying him mind. Then I heared a voice say, 'Mrs. McEveride pay you for doing that?' So I say, without looking up, 'Miss Stella, she don't pay me for what I *does*. She pays me for what I *knows*. Now, I don't know a damn thing. And she don't pay me a damn thing. And I don't *do* a damn thing.' Then I look up, and a cold chill hit me. Oh, Lawd, *there he was*—just like in the moonlight at McEveride Plantation! Lawd God, like a fool, I come boiling up—I don't know how far up I *did* jump! But I seen them hoods flying up off them snake-swamp eyes of his'n, him clawing for his pistol, and then I's running and yelling to beat hell. . . . Well, suh, it sho some hazylike from then on. Dust was jumping from his bullets, my feet flying, men running out the barn, Miss Stella in the dog run with a rifle. Then he riding off, shooting back—at me and Miss Stella both—her emptying that Spencer after him 'tween the house and the ford. Look like she miss him, though, ever' shot."

"By God, she's the worst shot in Texas!" Tennessee swore.

"We pile on hosses quick and push him hard. Got close enough one time for Mist' Shen to cut loose with that .50 Sharps of his'n. He claim he got lead in him, but I don't know. The man strong enough to go on and outfox *us*. He gone without much sign in them badlands by morning."

"He reached the Indians," Tennessee said. "Saw him three or four days ago. Didn't look to me like he was carrying lead. See you later, Jube. Lead this horse, now. Don't try to ride him."

"Sho, now, you done forgot my mammy didn't raise no foolish child?"

In Stella's living room, the two men rose to shake hands with Tennessee. Stella kept her seat, motioning to a chair. Tennessee gave them a bare, factual account of what had happened in Palo Duro Canyon, barely conscious of the growing wonder in their strained, intent faces. When he had finished, Jeff Slaughter commented briefly, "Smith, you sure beat me. Wouldn't thought a man could scout a Quahadi camp that close and come away."

Tennessee shrugged. "Ain't hard. They feel safe in camp, home free. Don't look out much."

Randolph's admiration was open. "What an army scout you'd make, Tennessee!" He shook his head regretfully. "I guess that breaks it. We can no longer doubt Romine's villainy."

"Mind telling us," Stella asked carefully, "what happened to Jimpson Krull?"

"*Ley de fuga*," Tennessee said with a bitter smile, remembering Slaughter's use of the term "law of flight" in explaining the Rangers' executions of rustlers in the brush country, where there were no jails to hold prisoners, and their reports to Austin that the prisoners had been killed while trying to escape.

Stella's eyes dropped to her clenched, white-knuckled hands. Suddenly she raised her head and held Tennessee with a full, wide look. "What's troubling you, Tennessee? We're ready for these Indians. Armistead has thirty-odd troopers, and one of my trail crews is here, along with our regular ranch crew. We can muster close to seventy well-armed men. They oughtn't to have much trouble beating off two or three hundred Indians. That's the most you figured. The men are ready, even eager. But I can tell you've got a burr under your harness. Why?"

"Can't figure this thing," Tennessee growled. "The smell ain't right. Romine's behind it, but what's he after? Not cattle; not now. Not revenge. Can't afford it now. He ought to be aiming at stopping your mouth and Jubal's. Why's he attacking this place? You and Jube are in Fort Griffin, far as he knows."

"Could be simple enough," Slaughter said. "If he keeps her busy enough with Injun trouble, she can't go after *him*. Would give him time to think up something better."

"May be it. Don't seem Romine's style, though, somehow. After his long ride to the Palo Duro, he wouldn't *need* more time to think. He's never run short of ideas yet. By the way, Armistead, does Romine know about Stella's pigeons?"

"Oh, yes. And very much intrigued by them. As a matter of fact, he even insisted on inspecting my little loft at the fort." Randolph glanced at Jeff Slaughter, almost shyly, color rising in his face. "Stella and I— well, we exchange little messages sometimes. A Corporal Snyder tends the birds for me."

That Stella and Randolph had pigeons going back and forth between the fort and headquarters was news to Tennessee. He looked at Stella and found her watching him with steady, inscrutable eyes. "The purpose," she said quietly, "was to have a quick call on the fort in case of emergency. No need to trouble you about supply, with Armistead coming and going."

Tennessee studied the intricate pattern of the Oriental carpet underfoot. Then he raised his head slowly, his eyes narrowed with thought. "That may explain it," he said softly. "That loft at Griffin could explain why he didn't aim the Quahadis at headquarters. Hate to say this—could be wrong and might cause some slack here. But the Comanches may not do much more than put on a show here, mostly out of range. Might make a stab at the cattle. Romine didn't know me and the Kid were watching him in Palo Duro. He didn't know we sent pigeons from Tule Canyon. So the Quahadis may wait here until enough time has passed for a pigeon to fly from here to headquarters and another one from there to the fort. Then they may just fade back into the redlands. Romine expects Captain Randolph to lead a detail out of Griffin, pick up Stella and Jubal and maybe a few of the headquarters warriors, and come hotfoot down here to the rescue. So probably what he's got set up is an ambush—at the Elm Creek crossing, like as not—with Broken Fang and his warriors under orders to shoot at nothing but the red-haired woman and the black man. When the army don't show, Broken Fang will pull out and go home to find out what went wrong."

Randolph brought up a point. "Don't see how Romine could plan on killing Jubal in the ambush. How would he know Stella usually has Jubal along on her trips to the ranch?"

"Comanches would told him," Tennessee said. "They keep buzzard-eyed scouts bellied down out there on the rim of the valley. Lucky your troopers rode in after dark, but you better keep 'em behind stockade walls if you don't want the Comanches to find out there won't be no ambush."

"Question is when do you expect the Injuns to show," Slaughter said, "and what kind of a welcome ought we to be preparing?"

"Expect 'em in two minutes or two days," Tennessee said. "Prepare for 'em like it's a last stand. No other way to plan against Comanches. You and the captain know more about how to defend a fort than I do."

Slaughter and Captain Randolph got up and departed through a side door, their footsteps fading down the stairway to the first floor. Tennessee turned his head and found Stella watching him. "Now you can tell me what's sticking in your craw, Tennessee," she said calmly.

"Reckon I might as well," he said wryly. "Something about killing Jimpson Krull—by God, Stella, it turned my stomach! I'm sick as all hell of killing folks just because the sorry bastards ought never been born. I'm through, Stella; I'll never hunt down and kill another Krull."

His announcement affected Stella strangely. There was disturbance in the tilt of her chin and the turn of her head, in the glance she whipped at him before dropping her eyes. "Not even Brownlow?" she murmured in a voice that was barely audible. Then she was still, hardly breathing, waiting for his reply.

"Reckon not," he said. "Look, Stella. That God-awful Jimpson Krull wasn't noways responsible for what he was. God a'mighty! Why, he'd been *anything* else if he could. Same thing goes for Brownlow—maybe a little bit less. What he done to you was natural as rain for a Comanche buck, and that's all Brownlow is—if I *did* look at him different once." Her eyelashes were long and dark against her bunched, freckled cheeks, and Tennessee felt somehow that when she looked up, he would see again the old, familiar, high-cheeked, black-eyed look of anger and hostility.

She got up without looking at him, however, and moved across the room to lean against the jamb of the doorway opening on the deck. She spoke with her back turned. "Guess I flattered myself, after all. If I've been a fever in your blood, you're cured now. No doubt of that. So I may as well go ahead and marry Armistead. You won't mind that any longer."

"You got my permission," Tennessee said harshly. "I'm still hooked, but I won't be around to watch your belly get big. I'm riding out of here for good soon as we get shut of these Indians."

She came about with a flushed face and hot eyes. Tennessee recognized all the signs of the old, familiar storminess boiling under the surface. "But why, Tennessee? I *told* you I'd lost faith in private vengeance—though I'll admit I'd be happier if that old Parson Krull were dead. But my business is mainly trailing cattle and will be ranching more and more. I need you, Tennessee—need *you*, not just your guns. Why can't you stay?"

"Law and order's too far off, with this part of Texas rawer'n hell. It's got to get worse, too. And I'm a known man. Live long enough, I'll wind up killing a dozen more men in the next five years."

"Maybe," Stella agreed. "God, how you've changed! But say you do kill a dozen brutish cutthroats—murderers, thieves, human wolves. Sure, killing them will leave scars on you—on me, too—but we'll all be better off without that dozen predatory scum. And your idea that a wretched goblin like Jimpson Krull didn't design himself won't stand as proof of anything. If you'll feel better, don't *blame* him. You don't blame a rattlesnake for being a rattlesnake, but you kill it. I'm just beginning to understand how much blood it takes to mellow a frontier. You may have to spill a lot of blood on this land—even your own, Tennessee—before it's ready for Smitty."

"My nephew?" Tennessee asked sardonically.

She studied him with slanted, cooling eyes. She started to speak, then swung back to her place against the door jamb. Finally she murmured, as if to someone outside on the deck, "Does it make so much difference who sired him?"

After a while Tennessee spoke to her back. "No. Reckon it

wouldn't change me now if I found out he was Brownlow Krull's.''

The melancholy of loss and regret and imminent loneliness was affecting them both, but in Stella it honed an edge of frustration that sharpened her voice. "You won't have to ride all the way to Fort Gibson," she said, with her back still turned. "Nancy Waterton's visiting Elizabeth Evans again at Fort Griffin. Or did you know that already? Maybe her messenger reached you in Palo Duro Canyon."

Tennessee made no answer, having nothing to say about Nancy's visits that would do any good; but he wondered why Stella seemed so upset about his leaving her. They'd been apart most of their lives. She wanted his talent for violence to serve her, of course. Was she simply determined to have her way?

She spoke again, over her shoulder, without looking around. "You *are* going to her, aren't you? You'll wind up marrying her, won't you?" Her voice began shaking with some emotion that sounded to him like repressed fury. "She'll buy a ranch, and you'll settle down with her, raising cattle and—and babies, I suppose." She whirled to confront him. "Oh, damnation, haven't you sense enough to see that it won't do? She's not *right* for you, Tennessee!"

"Why not?" he snapped.

"You don't love her!"

"I think a lot of her," he argued angrily. "I respect her. She's honest and loyal and true. Hell, she's a lady.... And I'll tell you something else about her. If she was going to bed with Armistead Gordon Randolph, she'd tell me if I asked her. By God, she wouldn't lie to me!"

"I *didn't* lie to you! I tell you, I haven't! Tennessee—"

"You haven't lied to me?" He laughed sardonically.

"Not about that! Not about *that*!"

"All right, you say I ain't in love with Nancy and that makes her wrong for me." He lounged to his feet and moved toward her. "You ain't in love with Randolph, either. I don't give a damn what you say. What makes him right for you?"

"A woman's different from a man," she said earnestly. "She can go to bed at night with necessity better than a man can, and she can find more contentment with necessity from day to day. That's because a woman doesn't have the choice and must take the best man she can get and do the best she can with him. I've picked a man I'm fond of and may grow to love. He suits my purpose. The difference between you and me is that I have a son to rear, while, well, you—you—"

"I *don't* have a son?" he asked with biting irony.

Momentarily bereft of her usual certainty, Stella seemed to sag, her face gone suddenly slack. And then a high, clear yell came from the lookout in the corner tower of the stockade. Stella straightened up and stepped quickly out on the deck.

"Come here, Tennessee!" she called, a throb of excitement in her voice.

Tennessee followed her out to the deck, wondering, by God, whether the Comanches had been this close on his heels. In the court troopers and trail hands were milling about, some of them moving out at a trot to take their places on the long, flat living-quarters roof below the top of the stockade wall, where they were being assigned their battle stations by a sergeant under the supervision of a lieutenant. Randolph and Slaughter were hurrying back inside.

Off to the west the rim of the valley tumbled into broken hills and rose to jagged buttes and flat-topped mesas. From the top of a far mesa, a slender column of smoke was rising like a pale snake lifting its head high in search of a distant piper. Tennessee moved up beside Stella, hearing the quick beat of footsteps on the stair, and then the column of smoke broke into a pattern of puffs. Stella's eyes whipped up to Tennessee's face and back to the puffs of smoke. Slaughter and Randolph came through the doorway behind them.

"Could they been following right behind you?" Slaughter wondered. "Or is that smoke talking to Injuns back in the redlands coming on?"

"They ain't here yet," Tennessee said. "Could be that last. Damned if I know what it means."

It was some thirty-six hours later, however, before anything was heard or seen of the Indians. In that darkest time of morning before gray light begins to show in the east, Captain Randolph came through the doorway of a room against the stockade and squatted beside Tennessee's bunk. Tennessee's eyes opened at the touch of the officer's hand.

"Come outside," Randolph whispered, careful to avoid waking the other sleepers, and turned back toward the door.

Tennessee dressed and stepped outside. Pup tents, each designed for two soldiers, had been set up in the court. They looked white under the stars, which filled the court with dim light and shifting velvet shadows; a sharp-edged morning wind complained among them, whipping loose flaps and jerking slack ropes, testing the stakes with pressure against the stretched canvas. Over by the captain's tent, which stood removed from the pup tents, Randolph was talking with Lieutenant Baker and Jeff Slaughter. Three paces apart from these three stood Sergeant Bullen and Red Dog, war chief of the Tonkawa scouts.

"They're out there," Randolph said as Tennessee joined them. "Least, that's what Red Dog says. All the Tonks haven't come in yet."

Tennessee swung aside. "Who's out there, Red Dog?"

Red Dog spoke English with a deep-voiced Texas drawl. "Big war party, sure'n hell. Snake people."

"How you know?"

"Smelt their smoke. Seen the shadows of their campfires in the clouds." He jerked his head toward the west. "Over yonder rim. Many hosses moving, blowing. Stone hosses whistling. Mares nickering. Camp awake. Maybe Snake warriors gitting their paint on. Hanging ribbons in pony manes. Tying up hoss tails. Gitting ready for big fight come mawning."

"How you know they're Comanches?"

"What we here for?" Red Dog grinned. "Maybe you expecting Navajos or Wichitas?"

Turning to the officers, Tennessee spread his hands. "Well, there you have it. If Red Dog's right—and I got no doubts—we can expect either a fight or a horse show in the morning. If it's a fight, it'll come in gray light. If it's a show, it'll come after sunup, when we can see the bastards all foxed up in their paint and feathers and doodads."

Without a moment's hesitation Randolph made his decision. "We'll prepare for the fight."

Slaughter nodded. "Got no choice. We might as well get everyone fed and start moving 'em to their stations. That gray light ain't none too far off right now."

"Half the men better go to their stations now while the other half eat." Randolph was rapidly proving to Tennessee that he was more promising as an army officer than he was as a stepfather. "Jeff, if you'll roust out the cooking staff and get breakfast started, we'll start moving the men. Mr. Baker, you and Sergeant Bullen wake them up, soldiers and cowhands alike. Better count them off and post a man at every other station. On the double, now."

By full gray light, before any tinge of pink began to show in the east, every man had been fed and was at his post. Tennessee was drinking a cup of coffee on the deck outside Stella's apartment when the Indians appeared—small moving objects, little black ants atop big black pissants, fanned out in a quarter-mile line. They showed briefly, outlined against the starlight on the western rim of the valley, then dropped out of sight against the slate-gray plain. A murmur ran along the roofs, and Captain Randolph's voice rang out sharply. All was quiet again—with a difference. The general grayness had thinned, and the Indians could be seen now, jogging their ponies at a mile and a half.

"Better come look," Tennessee called over his shoulder, and Stella crossed the room from her bedroom door and moved up beside him. She was dressed in blouse, riding skirt, jacket, and boots. "Looks like they may fight. Man can live his life, I reckon, and never learn a damned thing about Indians."

Then Stella saw them and clutched Tennessee's arm. At a mile the Indian ponies broke into a gallop, and shortly thereafter they came racing in an all-out charge. And now, for the first time, the war cries rose screeching and whooping in full chorus above the pounding hoofbeats.

"They mean to swarm in here!" Stella sounded breathless.

"Bastards fooled me," Tennessee admitted. "I'd swore they meant—what the hell?"

At a thousand yards most of the Indians brought their ponies to a plunging halt, while about a third of their number—some seventy-odd low-lying, stripped-down warriors on horseback—continued the charge. Tennessee thought they might be young glory-hunters intent on touching the stockade wall before turning back. Or maybe they simply hadn't listened when the chiefs were talking. Whatever the case, they ran into a blazing, crackling roar of gunfire that took a heavy toll: Horses somersaulted, their riders scrambling like frantic crabs to get behind downed horses still kicking; riderless ponies ran about aimlessly, leaving inert warriors on the ground; all the ponies bearing riders swung wide and circled to join the main force of mounted Indians that had stopped at a thousand yards. The whole war party drew back another five hundred yards and stopped again, this time to give full sway to an altercation of some sort that involved a great deal of shouting, head-jerking, and angry gesticulation.

"What are they doing?" Stella asked.

"Don't know," Tennessee said. "You got a telescope or field glasses up here?"

Before Stella brought the glasses fifty or sixty Indians had turned their horses and were riding away toward the west, a number of them not forgetting to bid their adieus with hand gestures that obviously were not friendly. Stella handed Tennessee the glasses, and he studied the loose horses and the departing Indians. Finally he recognized a horse, or thought he did, and then a back-turned face above the rump of a claybank pony. A name came to his mind from somewhere—Dancing Eagle.

"Kiowas," he muttered, and kept shifting the glasses until he discovered, by chance, the hawk visage of an Indian he had seen once at Eagle Horn's little trading post in the Antelope Hills and again, several days before, north of Runningwater Draw—a Penateka war chief named Wild Goose Calling.

"What?" Stella questioned, watching his face.

"The Quahadis picked up a bunch of Kiowas and a party of Pena-
tekas on the way down. They had scalps, coups, and hell on their minds,
so they wouldn't agree to stall and play-act. Quanah Parker's young and
inexperienced. They took over the battle plans—or thought they had. So
Quanah played 'em for fools, and now they're leaving in a huff."
Tennessee stepped over to the edge of the deck and called toward the
corner tower, "Hey, Armistead! That's it. Get ready for the horse show.
At sunup."

"Maybe," Randolph called back. "We'll hold our places."

"Where *is* Armistead?" Stella asked.

"Up in the tower. Been relaying orders through the lieutenant down
on the roof. I been wrong about Armistead, Stella. He's a good officer.
Damned good."

Stella was silent for so long a time that he thought she would not
comment. Then she said, "You restore my confidence in my judgment of
men." Her words seemed designed for light irony, but they were delivered in a voice that sounded more nearly flat than light.

"He's more man than I thought."

"You think, then, that he might get much better than average—in
case we decide that Smitty should have a brother or sister?"

"Hell, I wouldn't go that far! Reckon, though, I will feel a whole lot
better about leaving you in his hands." When she made no answer, he
finally looked around and found her gone. Then he heard her bedroom
door close. He thought for a moment about the sound of that door closing.
He decided that Stella had no reason to slam a door and, therefore, hadn't
done so. But something was bothering her, for she did not reappear until
after sunup, when the Quahadi horse show was in full swing.

A scouring wind seemed to catch the tight roll of the sun beyond the
curve of the plain and whip it over the horizon, unrolling a great banner of
golden light all at one crack and flinging it over the breadth and length of
the wide valley. Suddenly the floor of the earthen saucer was pastel
green. And suddenly, in the full flush of light, better than a hundred and
fifty warriors, arrayed in all their barbaric splendor, were sitting their
horses in a long, straight line a mile and a half away. The Indians were
armed with rifles or short bows and lances, and were carrying heavy
shields of thick buffalo hide. Bronzed, half-naked bodies were highlighted by glittering ornaments of yellow and silver-colored metal, and
bright feathers danced in the wind from war bonnets, bare heads, pony
manes, and tied-up tails of horses. Ribbons and strips of colored cloth
fluttered; scalps dangled from bridles and lances. War paint was gen-

erously splashed over warriors and horses alike, its colors running predominantly to red, vermilion, and ochre.

Jeff Slaughter called up to Tennessee, ''What you think now? They aim to fight?''

''Not today,'' Tennessee answered. ''Not with scalps hanging from lances. All them gewgaws on. Start worrying when they strip down.''

The Indians pulled out in mid-afternoon. They rode in a body toward the east, skirting the stockade just out of range, and crossed the creek to Stella's cattle—a herd of some seven hundred head fairly well bunched in the bend of the creek. They got around the cattle and began pushing them across the creek with an insolent leisure that was maddening to the defenders of the stockade.

It was then that Captain Randolph came down from the tower. ''Now!'' he barked at the lieutenant. ''Tell the bugler to hit boots and saddles! Now, by God, we'll do what we came to do—go after those heathen!''

When the bugle notes sounded, the soldiers exploded from the long roofs with one solid yell and, with Stella's cowhands among them, went running toward the corrals and barn.

''Abe Woods!'' Jeff Slaughter yelled, and a stocky red-mustached cowhand stopped running and turned. ''This here's your orders. The trail hands can go with the soldiers. The ranch hands stay here. Go on, now.''

Stella whipped past Tennessee and hurried to the edge of the deck. ''Armistead!'' she cried. ''Armistead!'' The officer stopped short of his tent and lifted his handsome face. ''Let them have the cattle, Armistead! They're not that important. Don't go after them.''

Randolph's face darkened. ''Don't interfere, Stella. We're chasing Indians, not herding cattle. Why do you think we're stationed at Fort Griffin?'' Before she could answer he whirled and hurried into his tent.

Stella turned a flushed, mottled face and raked Tennessee with a dark glance. ''He'll end up running little errands for me!'' she jeered bitterly.

Tennessee's burly shoulders moved and were still. ''Maybe some big ones, too.''

''They might need a scout,'' she said waspishly. ''Aren't you going with them?''

''Nope. They got the Tonks. Anyhow, I ain't lost no Indians. Cattle, either.''

Stella watched him with brooding eyes, searching her mind for words to beat him with. Before she found them, however, saddled horses and riders, some of the latter mounted, some afoot, were crowding the space unoccupied by the pup tents in the court. A trooper acting as orderly delivered a saddled horse to Randolph's tent, and the officer mounted and worked his way to a place near the gate. Responding to the bugle, the riders hit their saddles and sat, still-faced and motionless, to hear the orders, which Captain Randolph, in this instance, chose to deliver personally. Then he led the troopers and cowhands out the west gate and aimed them at a dust cloud that was moving rapidly toward the western rim of the valley.

The Indians had reacted to the bugle notes with as much energy as had the troopers. Now they knew that the army had arrived before them and that troopers, poised for battle and pursuit, had been inside the stockade all the time. So they were running the cattle, hoping to reach the redlands, where they might fend off the troopers and keep the cattle, too. Tennessee and Stella watched the pursuit until there was nothing to see beyond the dust cloud fading above the rim of the valley.

Almost exactly one hour later all the stockade pigeons arrived from headquarters. None of them bore messages. Tennessee was deep in a nap in the room against the stockade wall when Stella shook him awake. Her eyes looked haunted, and her freckles made a smear on her pale face. She tried to speak and could not do so.

Finally she was able to gasp, "All—all—the pigeons from—from headquarters just flew in. Without messages." She clutched at her throat. "What—what does it mean?"

"Somebody turned 'em out."

"But who?" she moaned. "You don't think—"

"Could been Jubal's boy, playing up there."

"He's not there. Lula May took him to visit Britt Johnson's family over at Fort Belknap."

"Maybe Smitty—"

She was wringing her hands. "Tennessee, you know Shen won't let anybody near—something's *happened* to Shen! How many other pigeons are flying—flying—"

Tennessee sat up, staring. He saw them then, taking shape in the back of his mind: copper-colored faces stretched by grins and childish laughter; copper-colored hands opening cage doors; moccasined feet kicking cages apart—happy, savage, wanton black eyes watching the birds fly. . . . He'd had an itchy feeling of uneasiness about Romine's reasons for sicking the Indians on the stockade ranch even before he'd left Tule Canyon. Romine was attempting to decoy Stella and her army escort and kill her and Jubal, Tennessee had decided, since he could think of no better explanation; but the itch of dissatisfaction had not been wholly eased. There were too many loose ends, too many things based upon guesswork and left to chance. Stopping Stella's and Jubal's mouths would not call off retribution in the form of Tennessee Smith. Nor would it prevent the ruin Captain Armistead Gordon Randolph could bring upon Romine through the Virginia Lincolnite's influence in the army. There was only one sure way of stopping all mouths at once. Now Tennessee saw, too late, what he should have seen from the first. The Indian show had been designed in part—perhaps in large part—to decoy Stella from headquarters in order to keep her alive and free, for Romine knew that Stella must live and swing her weight of influence to guarantee his safety.

"Aw, goddamn my stupid soul to hell!" he whispered, and grabbed his head with his big hands.

Stella was beating at him with her hands, crying, "What—what—oh, God, Tennessee, what—"

"The Indians—Broken Fang's warriors—they've hit headquarters!" he ground out. "They've got Smitty!"

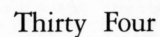

Thirty Four

They rode away from the stockade with a blood-red sunset hanging over the western rim of the valley, beyond which, somewhere, the troopers and trail hands were pursuing the Indians with the cattle. They rode through the dusk and through the night, dimly aware of the shrouded features of the land. Accompanying Tennessee, Stella, and Jubal were ten heavily armed ranch hands, including Jeff Slaughter, who had left the stockade ranch in the charge of Abe Woods, his second-in-command. They rode spaced apart to allow running room for twenty-six horses, for each rider had a spare mount on lead. Every hour or so they stopped briefly to switch saddles and change horses. Tennessee, on Grassfire, set the pace from the start; it was a hard pace designed for a long-haul speed that would wear down the horses just short of ruining them.

Once, at a saddle-switching stop, Stella moved up beside Tennessee and touched him with her hand. When he looked down into her pale face, she did not speak, merely gazed at him with tragic black eyes that twisted his heart.

"Stella, I'll get him back," he murmured. "He's tough. He's part of you and me. He'll live till I can get to him." Neither of them seemed aware that he had assumed what had been controversial between them.

He was so sure of what they would find at headquarters that he wanted Stella to prepare herself before they arrived, to face the fact that Smitty would not be there. At sunrise they were about twenty miles from headquarters, and Stella, who may have been hoping against hope, was holding up well. Then, ahead and off to the left, several buzzards circled down toward some small carcass on the ground, where three or four of their grisly fellows were already at work.

Tennessee tossed his lead rope to Jubal and reined Grassfire straight toward the carrion birds. "Stay back!" he called harshly over his shoulder.

But when the buzzards had awkwardly taken flight and he had pulled up and was looking down at the carcass of the Tennessee mare's little colt, he heard Stella's horse pound up and plunge to a stop. Tennessee dismounted to examine the feathered half of an arrow protruding from back of the colt's shoulder, knowing beforehand that it was a Quahadi war arrow, not a hunting arrow. Stella had alighted and stood shaking beside him, looking down at the little stallion colt she had named Flame because it had inherited Grassfire's flaming sorrel color. Suddenly she turned to Tennessee, clinging to him desperately. Tennessee put his big, hard-muscled arms around her, holding her close.

Stella knew now, against any forlorn hope, that the Indians had attacked headquarters, that they had the Tennessee mare, all the horses—and Smitty, too. But Tennessee believed that her thoughts were centered momentarily on the baby stallion. She had always had a special feeling for the colt, had never tired of watching him frolic about and then come in to nuzzle his mother. He thought he understood, therefore, why Stella was stricken now with a passion of weeping. Finally her grief seemed to burn down to its bed of coals, and he heard her anguished voice, muffled against his chest.

"This proves it," she said. "Smitty's dead, Tennessee. They've killed him, too."

Tennessee shook her gently. "Nothing to that. They had their orders from Romine. The boy's alive. They shot the colt because it couldn't keep up." He was speaking with far more confidence than he felt, for he knew how easily a Comanche like Broken Fang could be moved to kill by anger and how easily the bare-toothed Quahadi could be roused to anger.

"Will you ever forgive me for lying about Smitty?"

"How's that?"

"Smitty's yours, not Paul's. I got pregnant that day by the water hole when you forced me. I'm telling you now because I can't face the loss of Smitty alone. I've got to lean on you."

Screened from the eyes of their companions by the horses, Tennessee pushed Stella back to arm's length and soberly studied her tear-stained, freckled face. "I never doubted whose he was," he said. "But no matter. I'll always remember you told me." He drew her back into his arms and kissed her lips slowly and tenderly. Then he set her back on her horse, and they rejoined their party.

They rode on, backtracking the Indians toward headquarters, all of them now expecting the worst. Ten miles beyond the carcass of the colt, they saw buzzards again. This time the gracefully sailing birds numbered in the dozens; they were drifting and circling beyond the crest of a rise a mile ahead, spiraling down to something out of their sight. A terrible dread drove the last remnant of beauty from Stella's face; she clutched at her saddle horn, desperately trying to maintain her balance on the galloping horse. All the riders had strained, tense, dust-grimed faces. Already, before they knew what was drawing the carrion birds down, they were sick at heart with premonition.

Gradually, almost imperceptibly, some distant object began to push into view above the crest of the rise. It puzzled them all at first. Then, as they urged their tired horses on, it began to look like the head and shoulders of a person standing just over the rise. As they drew nearer, the figure of a woman slowly came into view. She stood with the wind whipping her skirt against her body, her head bowed as if she were inspecting the flock of ungainly black fowl on the ground at her feet. She looked like a farm woman standing in her backyard, feeding her fowl.

A strangled curse came from Tennessee as he sent Grassfire shooting ahead, the lead rope attached to his spare mount flying free. He closed the remaining distance rapidly, and the buzzards labored off the ground and flapped away, rising quickly to sailing heights. Tennessee leaped off the stallion and staggered toward the motionless figure of the golden-haired woman.

"Mary!" Stella screamed, swaying in her saddle. "Mary, look up! Oh, God, Mary, look at me!"

Jeff Slaughter swung his horse alongside and steadied Stella with a long-reaching hand. "She can't hear you, Stella," he said huskily. "Get a-hold of yourself, girl."

Tennessee could not look at Mary's face as he stepped forward and touched her. Her flesh was hard, cold, rigid. Putting both hands on her, he found her body somehow attached securely, immovably fixed in an upright position. Perplexed, he stepped back and looked at her face. What he saw then in the stark features—the frozen reflection of her last moments of agony—he would never forget. He leaned his forehead against her unyielding shoulder for a long moment, his eyes closed over the flames of hellfire that burned in his soul.

Mary had not been scalped, mutilated, or stripped of her clothing, since her appearance was designed to give the impression of life until the last moment of discovery of her death. He remembered the small glinting eyes and fixed half-smile of the Comanche humorist who had cut the mule's throat in Blanco Canyon. He knew then, all in a flash, the grim jest of her posture and just how she had died. Bending his knees, Tennessee put his arms around the hips and straightened, lifting the body high, removing it from the trimmed and sharpened bole of a mesquite tree, upon which it had been impaled. He glanced once at the long, crude, blood-smeared wooden spike sticking up from the roots and laid the body gently on the ground.

His companions had pulled up and dismounted. Most of the riders stood looking down with murderous eyes. Stella knelt beside the body and started weeping. Tennessee gave her a moment, then helped her up.

"We got no time for this, Stella," he said. "Jeff, drop off two men. Have 'em load her on a spare horse and bring her to headquarters. We better push on."

When they reached headquarters, a surprising number of people were already on hand, moving in the quadrangle, looking around the barn, standing near the empty corrals. Lula May, just arrived, came with a rush, openly crying. She was followed more slowly by an attractive black woman, Britt Johnson's wife, who only a few years before had been rescued, along with two of her children and two Elm Creek white women, from captivity among the Comanches—rescued by the heroic black plainsman she had married. The two women took Stella in charge and conducted her immediately into the house. Tennessee stood holding Grassfire's bridle reins, listening to somebody tell him about the massacre, how a freighter who had business with Buck Harris had rented a livery-stable horse and followed the storekeeper to Stella's place, arriving only minutes after the Indians had left, apparently, and had brought the word back to Fort Griffin. Afterward Tennessee could never recall whom he had been listening to, but he remembered other things he had seen while leading a plodding Grassfire toward the barn: Jubal's tear-muddied face as he held his son Josh tight in his arms, the seven blanket-covered victims of the raid laid out in a row on the gallery of a log cabin, the long row of pigeons lining the ridge of the barn roof. These were homing birds, already at home, headquarters pigeons. All the others had flown.

Coming back from the barn, Tennessee stopped by the gallery where the dead men lay and, as several spectators stepped back, lifted the edges of blankets. Under the covers were the bodies of four headquarters hands besides those of Shen and Missouri. All were scalped, but the hurried Comanches had left off the art work in this instance. They had waited until they were ten miles away for that, Tennessee thought grimly. The last body was that of the Griffin Town storekeeper, Buck Harris. As Tennessee looked into the stern, melancholy white face, he knew somehow that Buck Harris was where he would have chosen to be during the raid if he had been given a choice.

Tennessee straightened and found Colonel Farris Todhunter Evans, commanding officer at Fort Griffin, standing beside him. The graying, ruddy-faced man was drawn to the scene of the massacre by a knowledge of Stella's wealth and influence, Tennessee knew, but he knew also that the colonel had a genuine sense of obligation to protect the settlers from hostile savages.

"I don't see how the storekeeper got into this," the officer said curiously.

"Kept company with Mrs. Wilson," Tennessee told him. "Every chance he got. Missouri—there next to him—was his rival. She liked 'em both. Didn't lean toward either one, far as I know."

"We found 'em both dead in her room," contributed a lanky, bearded man in rusty store clothes. "And they sure God taken some redguts with 'em. The stairs to where her room was, it was just slick with Injun blood."

"I understand the Indians carried off Mrs. Wilson and the little McEveride boy," the colonel said. "I'm personally leading troops in pursuit as soon as I can get back to the fort. I've been waiting—"

"Like to talk to you about that," Tennessee said. "In Mrs. McEveride's office. Right now—if you'll come along with me."

For the next hour Tennessee was busy persuading Colonel Evans to leave the rescue of Smitty to Stella's men and Randolph's troopers at the stockade ranch. He informed the officer of Mary Wilson's death and clarified the terms of Smitty's captivity sufficiently to emphasize the point that an army attack on Broken Fang's camp, wherever it might be—and they didn't know yet where it was—would doom the little boy. The Indians would kill Smitty at the first sign of an attack upon them from any source. Finally the colonel's reason conquered his desire for action in the field. He agreed to hold off and, further, to dispatch within the hour a courier to the stockade ranch with an order for Captain Randolph to hold his troopers in readiness to implement Tennessee's plans for rescuing the boy, and also with a message to be relayed by pigeon to the Polka Dot Kid in Tule Canyon.

Later the bodies of the woman and the seven men were buried on a little knoll overlooking the ford. By some odd chance, unless the men who dug the graves and placed the blanket-covered corpses in them were guided by sentiment, Mary was laid to rest between the two men who had respected her, loved her, and died for her. At the graveside service Stella stood beside Tennessee with a hand holding his arm. The chaplain spoke of a time in west Texas when the war drums would throb no longer and the battle flags would be furled. He spoke also of resurrection, of a brighter day and a happier life to which the eight loyal souls would awaken. . . .

Tennessee hardly heard what the man said. He observed that Stella was dry-eyed, whereas Lula May and Britt Johnson's wife were weeping copiously as they remembered the dead ones. He knew then that Stella's mind was where his was—with a little four-year-old boy who had to endure the brutality and savagery of captivity in a Comanche war camp ruled over by a half-insane war chief named Broken Fang.

Stella tried to listen to the chaplain's voice. Shamed by the two black women's tears, she tried to concentrate on the deaths of Mary, Missouri, and the other unfortunates who had died in her employ. But she could not. She knew that she was not callous, that in the months and even years ahead she'd still be grieving over the deaths of these people. It was simply that thoughts of Smitty kept drawing her mind away from the service. Memories of Tennessee and Smitty together kept torturing her—memories she fully expected would break her heart when these next few days were past. There was one that persisted in distracting her. . . .

Randolph had come to see her one day in mid-morning, bringing news of another forthcoming visit by Nancy Waterton and the colonel's lady. Stella had boldly suggested that he might do the girl a great service by paying her some attention and charming her out of a dangerous obsession with such a disreputable ladies' man as Tennessee Smith— not, she had insisted, that he needed to pay court to her beyond the extent of showing her that another, even more handsome man, a gentleman, found her attractive. Her suggestion had put an odd look in Randolph's eyes, but she could tell he was flattered. While he was thinking it over, the angry voices of brawling children outside drew them both to the west window of the office.

Smitty and Jubal's son Josh were tugging and striking at each other, shrilling furiously. As Stella and Randolph reached the window, Josh, who was six months older and proportionally larger than Smitty, brought Smitty to the ground and came down astride him.

Randolph turned. "I'll put a stop to that," he said severely.

"Wait a minute," Stella said quickly. "I want to see how well Smitty takes a licking."

"What?" Randolph was incredulous. "You don't want him fighting with a Negro, beaten by one."

Stella was gazing through the window, a half-smile lighting her face. "Why not?" she asked. "He plays with Josh, doesn't he? What's the difference?"

Josh was astride the heaving Smitty now, beating him with his small black fists and crying. Good boy, Smitty! she thought, noting the boy's stoic fortitude: no tears, no pleas for quarter, no cries for adult rescue. That last arrived, however, as Jubal came striding from the direction of the barn. By the time he reached the struggling children, Tennessee was crossing the quadrangle.

"Here, now! Here, now!" Jubal plucked Josh off Smitty and set him on his feet. "Doggone yo' time, Josh! What you mean beating on po' li'l' old Smitty?" Josh held on to his father, wailing louder than ever.

Tennessee came up, grinning, closely followed by Lula May, who had a switch in her hand. Smitty climbed to his feet and stood watching Josh cry, solemn-faced and silent. "Hey, Josh, what you crying for?" Tennessee said, with an amused glance at Smitty. "You whipped him, didn't you? What you got to say about that, Smitty?"

"Josh whupped me," Smitty said matter-of-factly. "He done that."

"What you fighting for, Josh?" Lula May demanded sharply, holding the switch. "Answer me. You knows I don't allow none of that."

Josh turned his tearful face around briefly. "He—he *peed* on me!" he wailed. Then, with face hidden, he added in a muffled voice, "He done it on purpose."

Tennessee ironed out his grin with an effort and went down on his knees before Smitty, looking the little boy in the eyes soberly. Smitty tried to move in against him, but Tennessee held him at arm's length. "Smitty, you don't pee on your friends," he said gently. "Your enemies, maybe. But not on a good friend like Josh. Why'd you *do* that?"

"I's trying to wash his black off," Smitty explained simply.

Lula May laughed, tossing her switch aside, and reached for Josh. "Ain't no meanness in that child," she said. "Ain't been a week since he trying to *kiss* the black off of me. Come on, Josh. I ain't going to whip you for fighting this time."

Tennessee hugged Smitty close, then transferred the elfin fellow to his shoulders and went off down the quadrangle, laughing. And inside her office, Stella stood still, facing the window, off in a warm, personal world of her own, where Randolph's feet had never trod and never would. Her eyes were shut tight against an exquisite agony of tenderness that was wonderful and terrible and almost unbearable. . . .

After the funeral Tennessee walked back to headquarters with Stella. "When are you leaving?" she asked him. "Oh, Tennessee, how will you go about finding Smitty in all that wide country? Where will you look? What—"

He told her about the army courier on the way now to the stockade ranch. "Got to wait here till I hear from the Polka Dot Kid," he concluded. "Got no choice. The Kid's run out of pigeons for the stockade. So I'll stay here till he lets me know where they took Smitty."

"Come sleep with me tonight," she said, as if she were inviting him to dinner.

He was stunned. "What did you say?"

"You heard me. Will you sleep with me tonight?"

When she raised her eyes to him, he shook his head and was amazed at his own resolution. "Means too much to me now. It's gone a hell of a lot further down the road than a one-night stand with me, Stella. I won't sleep with you because you want to be comforted. Not while you're promised to Randolph."

"You're getting mighty finicky, seems to me," Stella said.

That night, however, Tennessee almost changed his mind. He needed comforting himself. When one of the ranch hands—Ryan McGuire, who had taken over Shen's work—was getting the homing pigeons back into their section of the loft, he found one pigeon carrying a capsuled message. This is what it said:

> Hung Romine. Died pore. No marker. Spilled guts, so we're on our way.
>
> Dick, Nueces, Redwing, others

Tennessee's scalp prickled. Now he had to get to Smitty before Broken Fang found out Romine was dead. As soon as he discovered that his *comanchero* connection was gone, the war chief would kill Smitty with the greatest pleasure in the world. As it was, Broken Fang, not hearing from Romine, would start getting restless and fractious. Any vicious thing could happen on a brutal whim.

He did not voice his increased fears to Stella, who was puzzling over the phrase "on our way." She thought Dick meant that they were on their way across the Staked Plain to the stockade ranch, but she wasn't sure. He could have meant that they were leaving the scene of the lynching, feeling justified after hearing Romine's confession.

"Why's Nueces Riley in New Mexico?" Tennessee asked.

"He brought a crew down from Colorado to pick up a herd Dick's been holding. I just hope he brings the crew—if they *are* on their way to the ranch. Let's make sure of that, Tennessee. Tomorrow, when the horses are rested, we'll send five of the men back to the ranch. I'm leaving Jeff in charge here, and he won't need more than four with him. Anyway, the men can carry a message to be sent by pigeon to Dick on the Pecos, just in case. We *do* want them at the ranch, don't we?''

"Yeah, reckon so. If what's shaping in my head works out, we do.''

The next morning the Tennessee mare was back home with a war arrow tangled in her mane. She greeted Jubal with a nicker from the corral gate when he stepped out of his cabin. A broomtail stallion had followed her scent almost into the quadrangle before shying back to open country.

When Jubal reported to Stella, she jumped to her feet and struck out spasmodically with one hand. "That's it,'' she breathed. "That's it. I've been waiting—''

"I done shut her up in a stable off to herself.''

"Is she in season?'' Stella asked quickly.

"Ain't quite. She coming in, though.''

"Good. Watch her close. I want her bred to Grassfire the very first moment she'll take a stud.''

Five days later Ryan McGuire came to Stella's office, where she and Tennessee were drinking coffee and hiding from each other behind desultory conversation. "Pigeon come in with a message.'' The poker-faced redhead laid the capsule on Stella's desk and departed.

Stella picked up the capsule and extracted the note with trembling hands. She glanced at it and came to her feet as if stung. "It's from the Polka Dot Kid,'' she said breathlessly, and Tennessee came out of his chair fast enough to help her read it. The Kid's printed letters were barely legible, but both readers could make them out:

BROKN FNG AN BOY IN YELOHOUS CANON ME WATE DUBL
MOUTN TIL YU CUM

SPTED HOS

Tennessee could feel the drumbeat of his heart along his bloodstream. "Ain't so far out of reach,'' he said. "Now we know where he is. Yellow House Canyon. Maybe they're holding him close enough to the ranch to deliver quick as Romine makes his deal. But now, no Romine and no deal.... I'll know what to do when I see the Kid at Double Mountain. Stella, I'm on my way!''

"No, Tennessee, goddamn it! Give me time. An hour. I'm going, too. Never think otherwise."

"All right," he agreed. "But not on that horsing mare, you ain't. Every scrub stud on the plains be following us."

"She's already bred to Grassfire," Stella said. "I don't need her along anyway. Go pick out the horse you want me to ride."

Tennessee selected a zebra dun gelding that looked as if it could run faster and keep running longer than any Comanche pony on the plains. They left in late morning with sandwiches, bread, sliced raw bacon, frying pan, and coffee pot rolled inside blankets behind their saddles. They rode hard through the afternoon, not sparing the horses, and after darkness had settled over the land, they came into a grove of elms and hackberries along the east bank of the Double Mountain Fork of the Brazos River. Here Tennessee stripped off the saddles and picketed the horses, then built a fire somewhat larger than was necessary for boiling coffee, since a spring chill had become steadily more pronounced after sundown. Meanwhile Stella had been laying out the prepared food on a blanket. They ate and then looked at each other over tin cups of coffee.

"Tennessee," she said somberly, "what can you do now, with Romine dead? Why couldn't we send another *comanchero* into Yellow House Canyon with the offer of a ransom?"

"Too chancy," Tennessee said. "No, not even that. No chance at all. Broken Fang wouldn't deal with any trader unless Romine had Quanah Parker tell him to. And if he finds out Romine's dead, he'll kill Smitty. He'd rather have revenge than ransom any time. No. I got to go in and bring Smitty out. Ain't no other way."

Stella shook her head in despair. "All right. So you walked into Union camps at night. But these are Quahadi Comanches! Walk into a hostile *Indian* camp? Tennessee!"

"In camp they're just people. I don't expect much trouble. Maybe someday, after they get hurt enough, they'll camp nervous, but that ain't yet. Getting Smitty out's a matter of timing. Hell of a lot depends on the Polka Dot Kid and Earth Daughter. I'll know better after I talk with the kid tomorrow. Got an idea of holding an early-morning wedding—the Kid and Earth Daughter. Ought to be married, anyhow. Then, while the bucks and squaws are gawking, we'd stampede the Indian horse herd through camp about the time your men come down the trails to attack the camp and Randolph's troopers come charging up the canyon. There'd be Fourth of July everywhere. During it I'd snatch the boy and run like hell, leaving the others to do the fighting. Only problem is getting to the tepee where they're holding Smitty before the wedding starts."

Tears spilled over Stella's lower eyelids and coursed down her freckled cheeks. She raised a trembling hand to brush them away. "You're going to leave me alone in this sorry world," she said in a voice that faded to a shaky whisper. "Oh, Tennessee, you're going to die if you go in there! And yet—and yet—you must, I know! You *must!*"

Tennessee showed her nothing beyond his old savage grin. "They do find me dead in that canyon, tell 'em to turn me over. Smitty will be under me. And he'll be alive, too, by God!"

"Somehow . . . .I believe you. I've *got* to believe you. If anybody can get Smitty out alive, you can. That's the only reason I—I can bear—" She rose without finishing, picked up the blankets, and carried them off into the shadows.

"Don't go off too far," Tennessee said. "Indian gets by Grassfire and crawls in to carry you off, I got to hear him."

"Hear him? You're more apt to *feel* him."

He thought vaguely that her voice was pitched strangely. Then, when he stood and stepped over to pick up his own blanket, he found it gone. "Damn my soul!" he growled. "Maybe some redgut bastard's already—" He broke off, rubbing his jaw with a great hard hand, feeling the hammering strokes of his heart. "Stella, did you take my blanket?"

"I'm cold," she complained in a shaking voice. "I need your blanket, too. With you in it. Come help me get warm."

He walked into the shadows and looked down at her. She had his blanket pulled up to her chin, and her eyes were closed. Suddenly they were wide open and very dark, and she was smiling. "Stella," he groaned, "I can't sleep with you."

"You slept with Mary, and that was all right. You can sleep with me."

"It was different with Mary."

"How different?"

"I'm in love with *you*, Stella. I can't sleep with you just to keep you warm. By God, I'm hotter'n hell right now just thinking about it!"

"Well, don't waste all that heat. Get under here. I'm *cold,* I tell you!" As he came down to his knees, she cried sharply, "Not in your pants, damn you! Unless it's your idea to rasp all my hide off."

"All right, you damned Jezebel!" He began taking off his clothes with a surging impatience. "Don't claim you didn't have no chance to draw back. But that chance just slid past, Mistress McEveride, and you sure as hell won't get no other—"

"You talk too much," she chattered, as he crawled under the blanket and reached for her.

"No wonder you're cold!" he breathed raggedly, as one of her full, firm breasts stood under his hard hand. "You're naked as a jaybird!"

But when his lips sought hers, she pulled her head aside. "Wait!" she said urgently. "First, I've got to tell you something. Then you can take me— like a whore if you want to. Or like a bitch in heat. But I've got to tell you—if you've got the wrong idea. I won't marry Armistead now. I thought you'd know that when I told you Smitty was yours. I won't lie. If I hated you, I'd still want to sleep with you. But I love you, Tennessee. I love you so much—so much that—that—"

"*You* talk too much," Tennessee growled and stopped her mouth with his own.

Her soft lips opened to his, tremulous with excitement, hungrily responsive, and a storm wind roared in his ears, shaking him with furious, remorseless, irresistible hands. Then, as the gathering storm of desire crashed through his veins, violence had its way with him. He was quickly bereft of all reservation, of all rational judgment, and, finally, he was completely wild. But the woman's slender, supple-limbed body, with the nipples of her magnificent breasts upthrust, was anything but quiescent. She clutched at his back with convulsive hands. She was open and impatient to admit him, her satin-skinned thighs reaching wide, her heels nudging his back. She moaned faintly as she closed on him in the age-old struggle; then she was silent, save for the pulling in and out of her breath, as she pressed and twisted, twining about him, enfolding him, gripping him. She was taking constant punishment, writhing and quivering and jerking like an animal pinned down by the crude shaft of a primitive spear. But she asked no quarter from the grinding maleness she was creature to; furiously, instead, she pressed upward to meet him, straining him ever closer and harder and deeper, until the world stood still for one breathless moment, before mushrooming outward and filling all space with bursting clouds of silver light. . . .

After a time, when they were lying side by side, Stella turned her head. "Oh, my, oh, my," she murmured. "That was dangerous. There was a moment there when I thought—I thought I was actually . . . going to. . . . About three seconds more of that, and . . . and I don't know what. . . ."

Tennessee said nothing, and presently she spoke again. "Poor Armistead! You won't mind if I keep on kissing him when we get to the ranch. For a little while. I'll wait until after we get Smitty back to tell him. He won't be as miserable as you probably think, but he *will* lead the troops with more heart if he doesn't know."

"Like I say, you damned Jezebel!" Tennessee said and pulled her gently back into his arms. "Aw, Stella, there ain't another woman in the whole world like you!"

"You ought to know, damn you! All those sluts!"

"Can you believe that, one way or other, you drove me to every woman I've had since I first saw you?"

She was motionless in his arms. "Maybe I can," she said finally. "You mean that you wanted me so bad you had to make do with lesser sluts?" Despite the gravity of her voice, Tennessee knew that she was smiling.

"Well, that ain't exactly what . . . but maybe. . . ." He fell silent, then drew her closer. "You realize, don't you, that we're explosive as hell together? And that you could be pregnant again right now?"

"I'm counting on it," Stella replied coolly. "The time's right. You'll have to marry me, of course. I can't lay *this* one at Paul's door."

A long while later Tennessee said casually, "No, I won't mind seeing you kiss Armistead. Don't tell him until I come out of that canyon with Smitty. He'd make a better stepfather than I used to think."

He didn't know she was weeping until she whirled her head and buried her wet face against his neck and shoulder. "Shut up!" she said in a muffled voice. She turned her face aside, crying openly. Finally her sobs subsided to ragged breathing. "You'll—you'll come out of there. You know now what—what you'll miss if—if you don't." Then she turned the whole front of her body upon him. "Or do you need another demonstration?"

And the memory of the first day he had seen her, of his shameful desire to take her in her grief as she had told him of the raid on McEveride Plantation, kindled a new flame in his groin. "Tell the truth," he said, with quickening breath, "I learn slow. You got to repeat things for me."

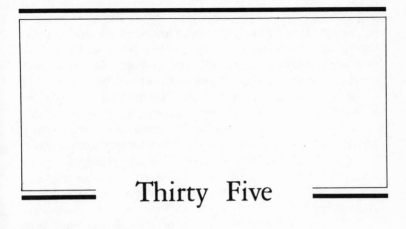

Thirty Five

At a place where the Cap Rock swung around to the south above Yellow House Canyon, a brushy, boulder-strewn ravine cut through the rim and dropped into a gulch which formed a pocket in the shoulder of the slope. Thereafter it made a raw yellowish-brown furrow with slate-gray markings down the greening slope into the valley. By two o'clock in the afternoon, Tennessee was nested up in this ravine at the edge of a thin clump of brush with a hovel-sized boulder at his back. He had walked the last two miles to the drop-off edge of the canyon, having turned his ranch mount loose on the plain to find its way back to Cibolo Blanco Creek.

The walls of the canyon, though several hundred feet high, were not quite so high nor so red as those of the Palo Duro; therefore the Indian village along the stream did not look so small as the larger one along the Prairie Dog Town Fork had looked some three weeks before. But it was larger in number of tepees than Tennessee had expected. The Polka Dot Kid had told him that the main encampment of the Quahadis was beyond the western Cap Rock near Portales Springs. So he reckoned Broken Fang's war party had been joined by some squaws and children and by a good many other warriors as well. There were better than a hundred lodges in the encampment.

Tennessee wished he knew which lodge was Smitty's prison. He had to find out. The Polka Dot Kid had informed him that he did not know where the boy was held, but that Earth Daughter's tepee—or rather Horse Walking's—was the one with the red scarf tied at top beyond the shallow

river. Tennessee would have to go there first, he reckoned, and hope that
the girl had been able to find out where they were holding Smitty. He
hated to risk Earth Daughter's safety more than he had to; nevertheless,
with squinted eyes, he carefully mapped his course. He was stripped to
buckskin shirt, Levis, and moccasins; and he was bareheaded, to avoid
the telltale silhouette of a hat in Comanche country. His only weapons
were two .44 Colts and a heavy bowie knife that was razor-sharp.

After learning all that the Polka Dot Kid had been able to find out
and coaching the white savage at great length on his and Earth Daughter's
parts in the coming rescue, Tennessee had turned the Kid over to Stella,
who had not mentioned the theft of War Drum but had made a deal with
the Kid involving a partnership in a horse-breeding enterprise in Tule
Canyon. When they had arrived at the stockade ranch, they had found
Dick Weatherford, Nueces Riley, John Redwing, and about twenty
additional trail hands awaiting them.

Tennessee had felt Nueces Riley's eyes upon him as he helped Stella
from her saddle. It was the first time Riley had ever seen Tennessee with a
red-haired woman. When Tennessee turned toward him, however, Riley
had managed to present an elaborately expressionless face. Tennessee
knew that the cowboy was thinking of the old Seminole-Negro woman's
hope that the red-haired woman's ass was worth Tennessee's trouble.
Then Riley had watched Stella put a glow into Captain Randolph's
cheeks by kissing his lips—for a long time, too—and then cut her eyes,
with quiet devils sitting in their corners, at Tennessee. Amusement and
pity had struggled for a moment in the young brush hand's eyes before
they had moved from Randolph back to Tennessee and become perfectly
blank.

All the while John Redwing had studied Tennessee somberly, remembering the tawny rider as an instinctive wild one, but he said a
strange thing: He recognized Tennessee's looks and voice, but he was not
sure that he recognized the same old companion he had known before the
war and briefly afterward.

Lying on the ground in the ravine, Tennessee wondered how many
Indians in the village had already thought of using Smitty as bait for
trapping a white-eyes killer they would give a year of their lives to kill and
scalp. More than one, he would bet; but one—that lone-hunting killer
Parruwa—would know beyond any doubt that Tennessee would come
for the boy. So Tennessee tried to determine where *he* would be if he were
Parruwa. A chill touched his spine. Close, he decided; damned close.
First, Parruwa would study the bare, smooth rim of the canyon overlooking the encampment; then he would center on the nearest of the few

rough breaks in the Cap Rock, the only convenient route into the valley that followed a screened trail down the slopes. Tennessee itched to draw himself up the eight-foot height and look over the top of the great boulder at his back. Halfway up the wash a stunted tree stood against the side of the ravine, anchored there by only a few roots on one side. The other roots were exposed and clustered down, partially screening an outcropping of yellow rock. Tennessee's eyes kept returning to that yellow outcropping, trying to see beyond it. There was something about that rock. . . . He turned his head and threw a searching glance below him. A man could be stalked *up* the slope as well as down it. When he looked back at the cluster of hanging roots, strangeness hit him with shock. He stared. The yellow outcropping of "rock" was gone. Before he moved his eyes, a little gray-coated bird in a white vest darted into the ravine, and with quivering wings stood ready to light on a twig—then suddenly whipped away. Almost immediately thereafter the sinister whirring of a diamondback sounded from up the wash. Tennessee had passed that rattler, coiled in the shade of a rock, without disturbing it. The snake's warning sufficed. Parruwa was in the ravine.

When the whirring increased to singing intensity, Tennessee made his move, figuring that the Indian's attention would be on the snake. Standing on tiptoe, he got his fingers over the edge of the boulder and, with an almost simian coordination, went up and over in one almost continuous and soundless motion. Lying flat, he saw at once that fate was going to lend a hand, for at the up-slope edge of the huge boulder was a loose rock that tapered to a height of about two feet. From the tall edge of the rock, he could expose one eye without changing Parruwa's impression of the shape of down-slope features much. Tennessee had his look. Nothing moved in the gully, and the rattler was silent now. For the next thirty minutes there was no movement. If it became a contest of patience, Parruwa would win. The Indian had more time to spare.

Tennessee tossed a pebble fifteen yards down the wash. It struck with a faint rattle. After a long moment he threw another farther—then, after a dozen breaths, another still farther. And Parruwa came off the yellow earth and down the wash with a silent rush, hardly slowing until he was almost even with the boulder on which Tennessee waited. He stopped to listen, standing bent over, holding his breath. Eight feet away from the single eye above the rock, the flat Mongol face, daubed with yellow paint, was as still and intent as that of a stalking cougar, completely predatory. The Indian was tall for a Comanche and massive with brawn; yet he had moved with an almost feline grace and speed. Then he turned his head. . . .

When Tennessee's feet struck Parruwa's back, the Indian plunged to the ground with an explosive outburst of pent-up breath, and the rifle went flying, to clatter among the rocks. Parruwa never quite recovered from the double kick powered by two hundred and thirty pounds of solid might. Though he scrambled around like a maimed cat, a knife blade leaping in his hand and licking the air, he was not moving with his wonted speed. Tennessee, rebounding from the impact, twisted in the air and landed on all fours. Whirling instantly, he flung aside Parruwa's uncertain knife arm and, carrying through with the same motion, struck the Indian's body with his knife. The broad blade went into the Comanche's side, but it turned on a bone to the outside instead of centering into the softer belly part and going upward to end the fight. Parruwa cried out and came up to his feet as if touched by a red-hot iron. Now he had an injured back and a terrible gash in his side; loss of blood would soon weaken him. Eager to finish the struggle quickly, Tennessee came in without feinting and almost got his throat cut. The Indian's blade cooled his jugular area with its wind and sheared off buckskin strings from his shirt. Tennessee leaped back and began using his head. If the Indian had not been slowed and restricted to some extent by his initial injury, the fight would have ended just then.

Tennessee circled, darting in, thrusting, drawing blood, leaping clear. Parruwa kept wheeling and turning, as courageous and deadly as a cornered wolverine. He was losing blood fast and needed to damage the big white-eyes killer quickly—unless he chose, as a last resort, to call for help. Ignoring his back, therefore, he lunged in low, striking for the belly, and Tennessee kicked him in the throat with such fearful impact that he was straightened to a spraddled squat and driven back over his heels. Flat on his back and without his knife, Parruwa clutched at his throat and opened his mouth wide, either to gag or scream an alarm to the encampment below, and Tennessee came down upon him. Ignoring the Indian's enfeebled struggles, Tennessee grabbed a handful of coarse black hair and would have cut the red man's throat save that he thought of persuading Parruwa to tell him where to go for Smitty. He hammered the Indian between the eyes with the butt end of the heavy knife haft, knocking the warrior senseless, then tied the red man's big-boned wrists together with a buckskin thong.

When Parruwa opened his flat black eyes, his arrogant face, with its heavy cheekbones and brutal, wide-slashed mouth, did not even show any surprise that he was still alive. Tennessee squatted beside him, the bowie knife in his hand.

"You son-of-a-bitch," he said softly, "for your sake, I sure hope you can understand English. Where they keeping the little white boy they're holding for Captain Romine? In which tepee?"

Parruwa's copper-colored face remained inscrutable for long moments. Then, very slowly, the long lips lifted over big teeth in a frightful grimace, and Tennessee knew that the Indian understood English. Parruwa's face was a mask of savage pride and contempt for weakness.

"Better tell me," Tennessee said, touching a thumb to the razor edge of the big knife. "You can die clean and be a whole man in the next life. Be honored by the Quahadi back here. But you got to tell me where they're holding the boy. My own *son*, goddamn you! If you don't tell me what tepee, here's exactly what I aim to do. . . ." He reached a hand to Parruwa's breechclout, gave a slash with the knife, and jerked away the loincloth, leaving the great warrior stripped to moccasins and ochre paint. He placed the point of the bowie knife at random against the Indian's genitals and bore down just hard enough to draw a trickle of blood.

"I won't *kill* you, Parruwa. No, sir. I'll just cut off, all at one slash, everything you got hanging between your legs. I'll find your pony and tie you on it and send you into that camp down there like a bloody-cunted squaw. *And you'll be alive, Parruwa!*"

Parruwa braced his thick-boned face with rigid muscles to keep it looking stolid and imperturbable, but he could not stop a film of moisture from forming on his skin. Tennessee understood well enough what he was doing to Parruwa. Probably in his worst years he had never been so nearly merciless to any person. But he had to locate the tepee in which Smitty was being held soon enough to work his way to it before dawn. So to hell with Parruwa! All his life the warrior had made a business and a game out of dealing out death to others. Now let the son-of-a-bitch have a taste of it himself—*after* he told where Smitty was being held.

"You think the squaws won't laugh, Parruwa, when they see where you're bleeding—and why? Know what they'll do? Heist their skirts up and shake their asses at you. They'll spit on you. They'll say, 'The squaw Parruwa is passing blood early this month.' Your own squaws, Parruwa, they'll go ask the heavy-hung warriors to stick 'em and fill their bellies with Quahadi sons. Your squaws will stop bragging at the washing stones about what a stallion of a man Parruwa is. No more. And in the *next* life, no squaws for you—but you won't care, Parruwa. No balls for you, either—no prick."

Though Parruwa was able to keep his face impassive, it was wet with sweat, and shadows were moving in the shallow depths of his black eyes. The lips along his wide-slashed mouth seemed stirred by no more than a breath, but some sound between a sigh and a groan escaped them.

"Hell, I'm through talking!" Tennessee snarled, slicing the air with the bowie knife. "You ready to ride down to that village, you damned squaw? If so, brace yourself, you son—"

Parruwa groaned, "Broken Fang got boy." His voice sounded as if his throat were bleeding on the inside. "Black tepee." He turned his face and stared into the side of a rock and would not look at Tennessee again. Already there was death in his eyes.

Thirty minutes later Parruwa was under a low-hanging cutbank that Tennessee was able to cave in without much commotion. The burial was designed to keep buzzards out of the sky overhead for the rest of the afternoon and keep curious Indians, therefore, from investigating what was drawing the carrion birds together. Tennessee's burly shoulders stirred in uneasy dismissal. "Be honest, man," he told himself. "You'd kill twenty Parruwas to find Smitty—hell, a hundred—and never think twice." Nevertheless, he wished there had been another sure way of finding out where the Indians were holding Smitty. He wished it, not for Parruwa's sake, but for his own.

The black tepee was in the center of the village, and again Tennessee mapped his course. The afternoon wore on. Hunters rode in from down-canyon, leading horses loaded with buffalo meat, which they turned over to the squaws. Soon supper fires were smoking up the valley, and Tennessee, having eaten the lunch he had brought along, had to ignore his hunger pangs. As meat was cooking, a chief with a guard of braves rode down the face of a far cliff and much later crossed a near slope into camp.

Quanah Parker, as Tennessee had learned from the kid, was expected from the main camp to sit in judgment on an old quarrel between Broken Fang and Horse Walking. The latter was claiming now the right by tribal law to kill Broken Fang, who, according to his latest charge, had killed one of his relatives—a wife, the mother of his favorite daughter—Mary Wilson, of course. Tennessee figured that the new arrival was Quanah Parker.

Tennessee did not stir from the ravine until darkness had stilled the camp and the fires had died. Even then he remained where he was for another hour. When the moon had provided him with light and shadows so that he could see where he was going and hide when he had to, he faded down the slope and went to earth beside a boulder at the edge of thin brush. The boulder was about seven feet long and three feet high, and broke his outline in such a way that he would look to the casual eye like a smaller rock lying beside a larger one. The nearest tepee was a silver cone in the moonlight a hundred yards away. Halfway to it stood a small plum thicket. Its sweet fragrance came and went in the moonlit night, making Tennessee think of holding Stella in his arms. He was trying to decide whether to crawl or walk across the moon-washed open to the shadows cast by the thicket when a squat, powerful shape emerged from them and walked toward him. He lay as still as the stone he meant to be taken for.

The warrior came on, a blanket around his shoulders, and took his seat on the boulder almost in reach of Tennessee. Once he chuckled; twice he belched, then broke wind against the rock. Minutes elapsed and the Indian grew restless. He muttered a few phrases and kept squirming, readjusting his breechclout, obviously uncomfortable. Suddenly Tennessee was dismayed by the realization of what sort of business the red man was anticipating. Why, here was a redgut lover waiting for a squaw, probably another buck's wife. No telling how long she would be or how long their business would take. Hellfire, he couldn't wait for the damned squaw! Sometimes he wondered, by God. . . .

Rising silently behind the warrior, Tennessee made his throw with a full-arm swing, and the heavy bowie knife struck with a thud, going in quite easily up to the hilt between the Indian's shoulder blades. The warrior did not get up; he bowed lower and lower and, plunging forward, hit the ground with his face. Tennessee withdrew the knife and wiped the blade on the Indian's hair, then turned the dead lover over with his foot.

"Sorry, brother," he murmured with real regret. "Didn't have no choice." Suddenly he bent low to get a better look. There was no longer any half-grin, nor were the small eyes glinting now; nevertheless, the stilled face was that of the Comanche humorist who had cut the mule's throat in Blanco Canyon and, Tennessee suspected, thought up the obscene and horrible jest of Mary's death.

Why, he'll enjoy hell, Tennessee thought sourly. Get a lot of laughs down there, his sense of humor. He pulled the blanket loose and threw the dead Indian behind the boulder, where he covered the body with old leaves and dead brush. Then, wrapped in the blanket, he stalked boldly across the open space to the plum thicket.

An hour later, from inside the thicket, Tennessee watched a young squaw go by, headed for the trysting place, then return after a while, muttering angrily to herself.

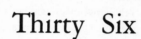

Thirty Six

When the squaw had disappeared among the lodges, Tennessee followed along her path, which she had just proved safe from observers by her passage. The tepees of the war camp were arranged in orderly squares. Selecting a grass-tufted walkway two rows below the row in which stood Broken Fang's black lodge, Tennessee slouched along toward the center of the village, one hand clutching the dead Indian's blanket up close around his face and the other gripping the bowie knife inside the blanket.

Until a voice quavered an interrogation close at hand, Tennessee did not see the old Indian sitting in front of the tepee he was passing. It surprised him to find the grandfather of some brave or squaw in this war camp. Such an old man, unable to sleep and bored with the drag of time, would be interested in anything that stirred, curious about the identity of any stroller in the sleeping camp.

Tennessee had to act quickly. On impulse, he snarled a brutal, unintelligible reply and strode on. His voice was that of an intolerant youth who does not respect old ones who are too weak to hunt or raid and wonders why they are allowed to remain on the earth. The enfeebled ancient sounded no alarm. He knew only too well, Tennessee figured, that whereas a warrior in his prime would be thought vigilant when he challenged a Quahadi strolling late, a weak old man would be regarded as a foolish-minded nuisance ripe for abandonment.

Tennessee kept walking now, moving along in the silent village like a tendril of cloud drifting before a freshening wind. He thought he was damned lucky there were no dogs in this war camp; a bunch of dogs snapping and snarling at his heels was all he would need. What concerned him most was finding a hiding place after he reached Broken Fang's lodge, where he must be at sunup when the stampede was scheduled to start. He thought he had found something he could conceal himself with when he saw an old, ragged buffalo hide lying on the ground beside a tepee. He reached a hand to carry it off, but found it stiff and unwieldy from exposure to the weather. Working carefully and exerting muscular pressure, Tennessee forced the hide into a fold so that he could carry it without great difficulty. Then, when he reached Broken Fang's tepee, he discovered an excess of old hides piled as protection against the wind and rain around the base of the black-stained lodge.

It took an hour of nerve-racking vigilance and patience to select and extract the hides he required, build his cover so that it would appear to be a part of the tepee's weather padding, and get under it—and do it all without making more than the rustling sounds a field mouse might have made. He had designed his cover so that the arch of the stiff, upthrust hide in front of his face gave him good visibility and plenty of air.

Gray light came at last. Squaws began to emerge from the lodges and start the breakfast fires. Through the black wall of the tepee, Tennessee could hear the sounds of rousing movements, murmuring voices. Soon came Broken Fang's snarling voice, ordering his squaws to their work. The timbre of the Indian's voice had been altered radically by the open path of the .44-caliber bullet from Tennessee's gun. When the slurring snarls ceased, a familiar, piping voice confided to the squaws that "old Broke Fang" looked like a dead hog, and a squaw's nervous giggle was cut short by the thud of a blow.

"You old sumbish, you—you better watch out!" shrilled the little boy. "My—my—daddy, he—he's bigger'n you are! And—and he'll whup you when—when he—"

From the sound, Tennessee knew that Smitty had been silenced by another blow. Staying under his hide cover was the hardest task Tennessee's iron will ever forced him to, and remaining still while his son was being abused a few feet away by a brutal, half-crazed savage was a conquest over self that would make all future ordeals easy to bear. That Smitty had settled on Tennessee Smith as his choice when he had greatest need of a father, as Tennessee believed he had, made the big man's heart swell with fierce tenderness. He resolved, among other things, that Broken Fang would not survive the day just breaking.

Three squaws stooped under the entrance flap and straightened to their work, building a fire, going for water, cutting meat. Off to his left

Tennessee saw a stalwart middle-aged warrior emerge from Horse Walking's tepee and walk away from it. This was Tennessee's first sight of Horse Walking. Tennessee could tell that he was a real chief. He leaped the stream like a young buck and strode on toward the lodge where Quanah Parker had taken shelter. Then, as Tennessee watched from his hide cover, old Parson Krull came out of the lodge.

The parson was dressed in buckskin leggings and moccasins and had a rusty black coat draped over his shoulders, the sleeves hanging loose. His black headband offered a stark contrast to his shoulder-length, dead-white hair. The old man started talking as soon as he saw Horse Walking approaching, his voice coming to Tennessee as a faint, high-keyed murmur. When the chief reached the old *comanchero*, they both went through the entrance of the lodge and dropped the flap behind them. By God, things are going to start humming in just minutes! Tennessee thought, his nerves keyed as tight as spinet wires. If only his own life were at stake, but Smitty, Smitty. . . .

Indians were eating in front of their lodges. The squaws carried food into the black lodge, evidently for Broken Fang, as well as for Smitty, since the war chief did not show himself. Perhaps he preferred to thrust food into his ruined face in private. He was still inside when Quanah Parker, Parson Krull, and Horse Walking arrived and entered the black tepee without much ceremony. Even in the smothering confines of his hide cover, Tennessee turned cold. He hadn't planned on risking Smitty by taking him from an armed crowd, and the action was almost ready to break upon the camp. Undoubtedly the stampede, though, would pull some of them out of the lodge.

The voices inside the lodge were loud and angry. As the altercation progressed, they grew steadily more impassioned. Tennessee was chilled by the realization that this quarrel could easily wind up in a free-for-all with Smitty underneath.

All at once Broken Fang's squaws were pointing across the stream and lifting excited voices. High feminine cries ran back and forth in the camp, gathering in volume to a near clamor. Squaws began gathering, and a few bucks followed more slowly. Quanah Parker left the black lodge and stalked back toward the lodge where he was staying. He kept looking at something across the stream. The quarrel inside sounded as if it were rapidly getting out of hand.

Now Tennessee saw the Polka Dot Kid ride up to Horse Walking's lodge with three fine horses on lead—War Drum, El Tigre, and the kid's best Appaloosa mare. Though War Drum was under saddle, the kid was riding a scrubby, flea-bitten gray bareback. That damned pissant! Tennessee swore to himself. Might as well put a sign on that stud that somebody aims to ride him out. Maybe, though, the Comanches will think his mind's on Earth Daughter's ass so close he's liable to do any damned thing. . . . He wondered how the squaws had known almost at first sight that the Kid was on a squaw-seeking mission with the horses. Earth Daughter must have passed the word around, though the Kid was dressed for such an occasion, as far as Tennessee knew, in a new buckskin suit and a bonnet of bright feathers. Tennessee hadn't realized that the Kid was war-bonnet big among the Comanches.

The Kid got off the gray horse and tied War Drum and the two Appaloosas to a pole at the entrance to Horse Walking's lodge. Then he stalked aside, wrapped himself in a blanket he had taken off the back of the gray, and stood waiting like a statue. He was proposing marriage in accordance with Comanche ritual.

A great breath of amazement and wonder swept the squaws. Tennessee guessed what they were saying: These horses were known. What a price to pay for a squaw! What did he see when he looked at her? There were plumper asses and bigger tits to be had cheaper. Suddenly their gabble was shot through with malicious laughter. They were jeering at somebody. Then across Tennessee's range of sight stalked Brownlow Krull, headed toward the stream, his handsome face as black as a thundercloud. One of Broken Fang's squaws shouted some advice at him, and he turned his dark, savage face and cursed her.

What Brownlow was bent on doing, apparently, was almost unheard of among Plains Indians. He meant to challenge the Kid's bid for the squaw. Tennessee's nerves were singing with tension before Earth Daughter came out of the lodge and, in token of acceptance, untied the horses and led them off to pasture. She led them straight past Humping Brother, answering his protest with a contemptuous smile, and came on past Broken Fang's lodge instead of heading up the canyon toward the horse herd. She slowed almost to a stop in front of the black tepee, studying it curiously, her eyes finally pinpointing the very pile of hides under which Tennessee lay. God a'mighty, girl, hurry, hurry! he breathed. He hoped that if knife play did develop across the creek, the kid would remember that at one point Brownlow would become distracted at a disturbance and turn his head. Get across that canyon, girl, because all hell's just about ready to break loose!

Now masculine shouts and laughter were rivaling the shrill gabble of the squaws, and warriors were hurrying past, headed for what was bound to be a fight developing between the kid and Brownlow Krull. "Come on, come on!" Tennessee whispered. "Give me a little help, goddamn it!

What in hell's keeping that damned Redwing, Nueces, and the Tonkawa scouts? Name any promise, and I'll make it, Lord. Just make them slow-assed bastards move!''

The sight of a streak of sunlight filled him with despair. It was sunup in the canyon! By God, he ought to have known he couldn't depend on that damned redgut help!

And then it came—a blood-chilling medley of wild cowboy yells, Tonkawa war cries, and screams of a Southern panther. The stampede was on, as several hundred wild-running horses came thundering down the canyon. Across the stream the clamoring spectators at the fight wheeled about with shouts of alarm. In Tennessee's judgment all hell broke loose none too soon. For simultaneously, inside the black tepee, the sounds of a struggle began. The stomp and scuffle of feet and the surging of strong bodies inside caused Tennessee to explode from his cover and send ragged hides flopping in the air like huge crippled bats. As he came into the open, he heard the struggle end in a great shuddering intake of breath and the roar of a pistol shot.

Desperately aware that he might be too late in getting to Smitty, Tennessee went through the entrance fast, a long-barreled Colt cocked and ready in his big right hand. His blazing eyes grasped the situation in a flash and swept the lodge for Smitty, not finding him. Parson Krull stood with a smoking revolver in his hand above two dead or dying men— Broken Fang struggling feebly on the ground with a knife in his heart and Horse Walking lying across him with a bullet through his back.

"The boy, goddamn you!" Tennessee gritted. "Where is he? Quick, you son-of-a-bitch!"

He saw the parson's eyes flare up with terrible recognition, but the old man's voice, which almost never ceased, was a strident, continuous drone. "I call on Almighty God, uh, to condemn this here rich McEveride, uh, who has done murdered thy poor servant's children, uh, and now has come here, uh, like the goddamned killer he is, uh, to murder the poor man, uh, who was drove out among redgut folks, uh, on his way to hell. . . .''

All the time the parson was talking, he was trying to ease his pistol in line. Suddenly he swung it, and Tennessee tilted his Colt and fired instantly, sending a bullet through the old man's headband and the *S T* under it. Before the parson's body had settled on the ground, Tennessee was desperately moving the tepee furnishings in search of Smitty.

He found the little boy almost completely covered by hides and tied to a tepee stake with a rawhide thong. Tennessee cut the thong and caught Smitty up in his arms. One of the boy's eyes was big with fright and wonder; the other was badly discolored and swollen shut.

"You all right, Smitty?" Tennessee asked anxiously.

The little boy nodded, but his face suddenly wrinkled up and began twisting. Tennessee's arm tightened, and then Smitty was crying against the buckskin shirt. "I—I—told 'em—you—you'd come and get me," he sobbed. "They—they was scared of you."

Tennessee's eyes blazed. "Well, son, we're on our way." His voice was hoarse with feeling. "Hold on tight."

He slid through the entrance, straightened, and started running, one hand and arm holding Smitty, the other hand gripping a cocked .44 Colt. Horses seemed to be everywhere, running through the camp, crashing into tepees, and sending Indians dodging and lunging out of their paths. Tennessee raced along his own back trail, catching glimpses of Nueces Riley and some of the Tonkawa scouts, the latter in breechclouts and war paint, all of them riding like centaurs and firing like demons. And now the Quahadis were rousing from shock and drifting together, returning the fire. A brave with a demoniac face cut in from the left, lifting a Spencer rifle. Carrying Smitty with his left arm as he ran, Tennessee found his position awkward for making an accurate shot. But he had to make do; so he whipped the Colt across his body and Smitty's, and saw the Comanche crumple before he could fire. John Redwing pulled alongside, his black eyes burning, Navy Colt smoking. "A curse on both your damned houses!" the Cherokee snarled, and wheeled his horse away. As he rode back into the battle, Tennessee saw the feathered end of an arrow protruding from high up behind his left shoulder.

Then, just ahead, close to the escarpment, there was Earth Daughter, holding the three horses and jumping up and down with joy as she pointed behind Tennessee. He was in the saddle and whirling War Drum down-canyon, however, before he took a look and saw the Polka Dot Kid running toward Earth Daughter and the Appaloosas. He was damned glad the Kid had come out of the fight alive; he didn't care whether Brownlow Krull still lived. He was no longer interested in Brownlow. . . .

For minutes now Tennessee had been aware of a heavy volume of gunfire from rifles and pistols and knew suddenly, with a feeling of vast relief, that Dick Weatherford and Stella's other men had come down the Yellow House trails in full force and opened the real attack. Less than a mile down the canyon, he passed Captain Randolph's cavalry detail as it came charging up the valley, dust piling high and hoofbeats echoing off canyon walls like sullen thunder. The dust cloud was shot through with flashes of light as the first rays of the sun over the Cap Rock were reflected by tinware, guns, and other metal objects. Randolph was almost on schedule, and Tennessee could predict what would happen when the army men hit the battered and disorganized village. Caught in a nutcracker between soldiers and ex-Rangers, the Indians would scatter and fade like quail, the braves retreating as the few squaws and children who were in the war camp went up-canyon, up the slope, and into the breaks.

In minutes Tennessee and Smitty were far down the canyon, clear of the troopers' dust, and Tennessee pulled War Drum back to a mile-eating canter. He suspected that Stella had tagged behind the cavalry detail with an escort of former Confederates, in spite of Randolph's orders to the contrary, and that she'd be waiting down the canyon for Tennessee to bring their son to her. He held the little boy close in his arms.

"I won't tell Mummy," Smitty said.

"Won't tell her what, Smitty?"

"You cussed in the tent. You said gahdem and sumbish."

"You did, too. You called Broke Fang a sumbish."

"You won't tell on me, will you?"

"Not if you don't tell on me. Smitty, you and me, we got to watch that cussing."

"Aw right," Smitty said, "I'll quit if you will. We don't cuss much, anyhow."

Tennessee squirmed uneasily in the saddle. By God, he meant it! He *was* going to watch that tongue of his. He reckoned he could stop saying goddamn somebody or other; he didn't have to go around calling everybody sons-of-bitches and bastards, either. There were good folks—plenty of them—if he gave them a chance. Look at the soldiers and Stella's men, along with the Polka Dot Kid and Earth Daughter, who had joined forces and risked their lives with little thought of self in the rescue of his son. He owed them more than he could ever pay. But he could pay them something by helping to gentle this raw, savage, and dangerous land. He had the talent for it. He remembered what Stella had said about how much blood it took to mellow a frontier. "You may have to spill a lot of blood on this land—even your own, Tennessee—before it's ready for Smitty." And Smitty had just been snatched from the jaws of death, where wild Indians and evil white men had placed him. Tennessee had had plenty of time to think under those hides, and he'd taken a long, hard look at himself, coming to some unflattering conclusions. He'd made some resolutions, too, that he meant to keep.

He remembered Horse Walking lying across Broken Fang with old Parson Krull's bullet in his back. He remembered the sleepy, sad faces of scalped settlers lying in smoky yards. He remembered seven men buried on a knoll overlooking a ford on the Clear Fork of the Brazos. And, God help him, he remembered Mary Wilson standing on the prairie with bowed head under circling buzzards. As he hugged his little boy closer, he resolved to help give Smitty a better land in which to grow up. He could find the time to "run little errands" for Stella, but she wouldn't need all of his time on her ranches for some years to come. He owed it to the army to scout for them until the Plains Indians were on reservations; then, after Texas was freed of Reconstruction, he would serve awhile with the Rangers and help them prune the population in Texas, cutting out the rotten folk, whether they were the way they had to be, like Jimpson Krull, or whether they were that way by choice, so that the sound folk could have their chance to survive.

Far down the canyon Stella waited, reaching out with her heart and mind for Tennessee and Smitty with a fearful, uneasy longing that trembled on the verge of open despair. Her reason gave Tennessee little chance of coming back and less chance of bringing Smitty out of that Quahadi village, even if the child was still alive, but faith in Tennessee's prowess as a warrior kept some hope alive and helped preserve her sanity. She rode her zebra dun up and down, up and down, a hundred yards up the canyon, then back to the great cottonwood, where her men lounged in their saddles, awaiting the sound of gunfire. She knew she would never dread death as much as she dreaded the outcome of this rescue mission.

When gunfire broke out up-canyon, Stella went numb. She could see Tennessee's dead body, pincushioned with arrows, his arms outspread, and she could hear Smitty crying beneath him. Suddenly she felt so faint and dizzy that she had to hold on hard to the pommel of her saddle. And then she heard, as did her men, the faint drumbeat of a running horse, steadily getting louder, coming down the canyon. Unlike her men, however, Stella found something familiar about that loudening drumroll of hoofbeats. Before the horse burst into view at a bend, recognition came. At first it was a tumult in her heart.

Then she cried aloud, "That's War Drum!" and whirled the zebra dun.

"Wait, ma'am!" shouted one of the men behind her. "May be Injuns taking this way out."

But she saw War Drum now, stretched out, coming fast . . . yellow-haired rider . . . something in his arms . . . a child? She raced to meet horse and rider and what he was holding. Now she saw that War Drum's rider was Tennessee Smith McEveride, and she threw up her hand, crying urgent inquiries that were whipped away by the wind. Was he holding the body of the dead child? She sank lower and hung waiting, not daring to breathe. Then the boy was pushing up in his father's arms and waving.

Stella didn't know how she managed to bring the zebra dun to a halt and dismount; she wasn't conscious of doing so. When she became aware of what was happening, she was crying, and she and Tennessee were on their knees with their arms around each other and around Smitty, who was standing between them in a tight squeeze. . . .

Two weeks later Tennessee and Stella were lying on her bed at headquarters, with Smitty between them. Stella was wearing a night-gown, and the two males were wearing short drawers, since the father would not sleep in a nightshirt and, therefore, the son would no longer do so. Tennessee's reason was that he might trip up in a nightshirt if he was flushed out of his blankets by some bastard trying to get some lead in him. He and Stella had been married earlier in the day by the chaplain at the fort, with Captain Randolph and Nancy Waterton serving as witnesses.

"They'll be married before winter," Tennessee predicted, his amused eyes on his wife's fine-boned, freckled face. "You thought Nancy was coming down to see me. I knew different, but I didn't see no need for *you* to. Maybe she wasn't sure, herself, about Randolph, but she will be now."

"Hmm, so there *was* something—that odd look he gave me—"

"What you talking about?" Tennessee came up on an elbow.

"Not now," Stella said. "I'll tell you someday." Suddenly she came surging to Tennessee's side of the bed and had an arm around Smitty and her head on her husband's shoulder. "Oh, my dearest loves, can such happiness last? Do you know that you're both mine, mine, mine?"

"No, that ain't exactly right." Tennessee moved Smitty farther down his chest and, tilting Stella's face up, kissed her gently. "*I'm* the man. So you're both *mine*. I won't let either one of you get away from me, either."

Smitty's laughter was like the tinkling of crystal chimes. "That ain't right!" he shouted in treble, his seraphic face alight with glee. "You're both mine. And I ain't gonna let you go."

"Smitty, when did you first know I's your daddy?" Tennessee asked curiously. "In Broken Fang's tent?"

Shaking his head furiously, Smitty came up to his knees on Tennessee's hard belly. "When you told me what your pup done."

"Spooky," Tennessee murmured. "Like the old Seminole witch-woman claiming you rubbed off on me, Stella. You reckon all that's happened was in the book and *had* to happen? Could Smitty see *his* mark on me, too, along with yours, maybe?''

"More likely he just adopted you,'' Stella said. "But who knows? . . . Smitty, it's your bedtime. Off with you. I've got some business to take up with your father.''

Smitty stretched out on top of Tennessee and kissed his father's cheek before he slid off to the floor. Stella followed the little boy out, then returned, locking the door behind her.

"Now I'll hate to be away more than ever,'' Tennessee said. "Reckon you can spare me long enough for me to do some scouting for the army? Later I may work some with the Rangers. We ain't got this frontier whipped yet.''

Stella snuggled closer. "I won't mind, if you don't forget where your home is.'' She stroked him lightly from chest to belly with a wandering hand. "And don't forget what's waiting for you at home.''

"We're home now,'' he pointed out. "What's here for me?''

Without a word, she moved over on him and kissed him hard and long. Then, raising her head slightly, she whispered against his lips, "Oh, you sweet sumbish! You want to wrassle?''